GODLY ORACLES

GODLY ORACLES

CHUX ONYENYEONWU

Copyright © 2022 **Ofege Impressions**

All rights reserved. No part of this publication may be reproduced, distributed, or transmitted in any form or by any means, including photocopying, recording, or other electronic or mechanical methods, without the prior written permission of the publisher, except in the case of brief quotations embodied in critical reviews and certain other noncommercial uses permitted by copyright law. For permission requests, write to the publisher, addressed "Attention: Book Rights and Permission," at the address below.

Published in the United States of America

ISBN 978-1-958518-97-7 (SC)

Ofege Impressions
222 West 6th Street
Suite 400, San Pedro, CA, 90731
chuxonyenyeonwu@gmail.com

Order Information and Rights Permission:

Quantity sales. Special discounts might be available on quantity purchases by corporations, associations, and others. For details, contact the publisher at the address above.

For Book Rights Adaptation and other Rights Permission. Call us at toll-free 1-888-945-8513 or send us an email at admin@stellarliterary.com.

GODLY ORACLES

*There Are Oracles; And There Are Oracles
Earthly Beings Imbued With Special Ears And Eyes
That See Beyond Ordinary Time And Space
And Hear The Heartbeats Of The Future
By Quantum Intelligence Beyond Reason
They Hold The Key To The Dark Mysteries of Life
Nothing Happens On Earth Without Their Know...*

*Every Oracle Has Divine Origin
They All Dance To The Rhythms Of Silence
Flawlessly Played By A Divine Orchestra
The Dance Steps May Be Corrupted
But The Godly Song Must Flow Seamlessly
Because Every Oracle Work Together For Good
For They Are All Godly Oracles...*

FRONTISPIECE

"We think this trade must go on. That is the verdict of our oracle and the priests. They say that your country, however great, can never stop a trade ordained by god himself."

King Jaja of Opobo
1821 - 1891

"And he changeth the times and seasons: he removeth kings, and setteth up kings: he giveth wisdom unto the wise, and knowledge to them that know understanding:
He revealeth the deep and secret things: he knoweth what is in the darkness, and the light dwelleth with him."

Prophet Daniel(Belteshazzar)
620 - 538 B.C.

"And at the end of the days I Nebuchadnezzar lifted up mine eyes unto heaven, and mine understanding returned unto me, and I blessed the most High, and I praised and honoured him that liveth for ever, whose dominion is an everlasting dominion, and his kingdom is from generation to generation.
And all the inhabitants of the earth are reputed as nothing: and he doeth according to his will in the army of heaven, and among the inhabitants of the earth: and none can stay his hand, or say unto him, What doest thou?"

King Nebuchadnezzar of Babylon
630 - 561 B.C.

PROLOGUE

London, England
Saturday, November 10, 1990

The sun never came out, because it had drizzled all day. It was a damp and cold typical gloomy London day. Without a timepiece it was difficult to tell what time of day it was.

That was until Big Ben dutifully chimed the noon hour across the city, and to the rest of the world through the radio service of the BBC. The ever-present throng of Asian tourists outside the House of Commons was only mesmerized for a moment; before feverishly reached for their cameras to capture the ultimate moment of their trip. Funny, what people subconsciously do in a moment of sheer excitement.

Though, the rest of London hurry by oblivious to the tourists' exhilaration, Sir Benjamin Towerman was also very fascinated with the bell. He knows it deep down, that the bongs of Big Ben at that instant just did not sound right or tally. And that was a bad omen; *something truly ominous was about to happen.*

Sir Benjamin Towerman, 98 years of age was neither a tourist nor tour guide, but was distantly related to Augustus Pugin who designed the bell tower, but sadly went mad and died, before it was built by Architect Charles Barry. Towerman had dedicated over ninety years of his life to Big Ben. He was knighted for his outstanding service to the Big Ben in 1980. It was the Time Magazine in its cover with his black and white picture that declared; *KNIGHTHOOD FOR THE ORACLE OF BIG BEN.*

Even during the *Blitz* of the World War II, he kept Big Ben in operation. His ominous fear was not just a gut feeling; it was a sacred part of one of the world's most famous landmark that he had come to know. Big Ben had never failed in its over 130-year history. He had climbed the 334 limestone stairs to the top more than any human being alive or dead. He knew Big Ben better than the back of his hand. After over sixty years of working in the bell tower, Sir Benjamin was indeed an oracle. Even in retirement he kept his eyes glued on Big Ben, from his private residence strategically located across the Thames. Towerman was not only an authority; but a living compendium on Big Ben of London.

As he pondered over the puzzle of the bongs from his perch; which was at a precise angle with an extraordinary vista of two of Big Ben's four 25-foot diameter faces, he forgot all about time. Over the years he had come to admit that the eight hands on the four faces were really powerless, they were only perfectly intertwined to perform accurately by the unseen hands behind the facades. He looked down at his gloved right hand, which he tried unsuccessfully to raise up. And he unconsciously mused out aloud;

"More like a hand with five fingers being directed by an unseen finger of God".

"You called Sir?" James Mason, his major-domo of over 25 years rushed over.

"Sorry James, I did not call you, I was only thinking aloud." James quickly tucked in his master's sock-clad dangling foot under the thermal blanket without fuss.

"James, something bad is about to happen today", this caught James off-guard.

"Who told you that, Sir Benjamin?" James retorted with a chuckle trying to relax the old man that he had come to love and treat as his own father.

"Big Ben…yes Big Ben" his eyes pleaded to be taken seriously. "Not even the *blitz* could stop it from chiming reliably".

"Big Ben?" he retorted in an animated voice, so James Mason decided to play along out of tradition. "That is really interesting… tell me more Sir Benjamin".

"James, I have come to know that our lives are really powerless to an unseen hand that effectively creates and weaves time; to give an accurate account of them". Sir Benjamin chose his words to make the right impact on his listener. James Mason was totally speechless; this was totally different from the past. He could not, but listen attentively. He nods to urge the old man along.

"James, take a good look at your five fingers", and James complies by raising his right palm with the fingers spread out before his eyes, "there is an unseen sixth finger directing the affairs of the visible five". He paused to look across the Thames at Big Ben's 14-foot minute hands creeping towards 12, while the 9-foot short hands shying away from 12 towards 1.

"What do you make of what you are seeing, James?" The younger man was perplexed, not really sure, whether the old man was referring to his outspread fingers, or the hands of Big Ben on the opposite bank of the Thames.

"I don't em...em under...understand sir" he stammered. "Something ghastly is about to happen today, it will shake the world...it will become clearer by the next chimes at One...James please increase the heat; I am freezing..."

James did not wait for him to finish, as he dashed towards the thermostat across the hallway, but aborted his assignment as Big Ben began chiming the One O'clock hour. He dashed back immediately to the old man's side who was silent, and totally focused on the 316 foot-16-story-high tower housing the largest clock in the world. When the chimes finally ended there was an overwhelming deadly silence. Sir Benjamin Towerman himself was dead silent, motionless, frozen... because he was dead, stone cold dead. The *oracle* had indeed spoken.

Royal Albert Hall at Kensington Gore is less than two miles as the crow flies from Big Ben. The drizzle of the morning had continued non-stop into the night; but it did not deter the crowd of revelers who had trooped-in in their thousands, to witness the grand finale of the Miss Cosmos contest. Big Ben's 9 O'clock bongs could not penetrate the six million bricks and 80,000 blocks of decorative terracotta, with its glazed dome constructed with wrought iron girders.

It had become the most popular venue for the Miss Cosmos pageant since it took over from the Lyceum Theatre in 1969. Inside the opulent hall were seated over 7,000 distinguished guests; with a pack of television cameras transmitting the proceedings to a staggering world-wide audience of over 1.5 billion. That was why it was the most publicized beauty pageant in the universe. All eyes, both natural and electronic were trained on the massive stage that was showered in different ambience of lights, hues and colors. The spotlight focused on Craig Stephenson.

Craig David Stephenson, CNN Talk Show host *extraordinaire* was in charge of proceedings as the master of ceremony. He had performed professionally so far; despite a sky-high notoriety for the opposite sex. Just 48, but has already been married for a record seven times. It was all over the grapevine, that he was concluding divorce proceedings with wife No. 7. It was on that basis the gambling houses are already placing bets on the probability of the next Mrs. Stephenson coming from amongst these young damsels, that he has been cavorting with. David was not just a prolific talk show host; he is also very prolific and chivalrous with the most beautiful women.

"Distinguished guests, ladies and gentlemen, thank you for your patience" his trademark melodious voice boomed through all the surround speakers "Finally, and finally, we have come to that moment we have all been waiting impatiently for." He sized up his audience. Their rapt attention meant he had them eating from his hand. And as he raised his hands away from him, towards the massive maroon-red velvety curtains that dramatically pulled apart to show a darkened stage with only tiny pin-points of lights on the floor level.

"Put your hands together for the final four finalists that just finished the *question and answer* segment a moment ago" and the spotlights came on, to truly highlight the girls in their shimmering evening gowns specially chosen for the formal crowning. And Royal Albert Hall erupted in an ecstatic volcanic applause.

Maybe it was the klieg lights on the diamonds they were all adorned-with courtesy *Twinkle & Twinkle*, the biggest diamond miners in South Africa, the four girls wearing very confident smiles, were literally twinkling. They could only be identified with the numbers 17; 45; 9; and 23. It must have been a tough job for the honorable panel of judges. Finally, the applause died down.

"I believe the judges have finished their collation" the master of ceremony sashayed towards their table, which was then bathed by some overhead spotlights. The head judge was already on his feet walking towards the stage; and ceremoniously handed over four sealed envelopes. These envelopes contained the final results for the contest.

"Distinguished guests and our viewers on television," and Craig looked and spoke to the camera directly facing him, "now that the judges have concluded their job, we shall now revert to their national identities which were suspended right from the beginning of the entire contest." He paused for the ushers to approach each girl with a gold-colored sash. The lights dimmed, and transformed into an ambience of twilight, as they hung the sashes on the girls.

When the lights brightened again, the dome of the hall literally caved-in with the resounding ovation. The effect was most eclectic; it was like unmasking a masquerade. The numbers transformed into Miss USA; Miss Sweden; Miss Nigeria; and Miss Ecuador respectively. As a realistic moment for patriotic zeal and pride, the master of ceremony joined the compatriots of these countries to savor this modicum of victory; the final four most beautiful girls in the world by nations.

He then introduced the blind magical Stevie Wonder to serenade the four girls with the song; *Isn't She Lovely*. The irony of a blindman serenading these most beautiful women in the world was not lost on the very appreciative audience. An elevated section of the stage with a monstrous grand piano slowly swiveled into view, and as the musician rendered the song he specifically dedicated to his daughter, Aisha. The four finalists could not withhold their tears…it was a floodgate of tears even in the audience.

At that time of the night, Downing Street is totally deserted; but for the 24-Hour security details at their duty posts, it would have passed for any deserted Westminster street. Inside Number 10 is a tranquility that envelopes the place whenever it was not hosting one official event or the other. A massive portrait of Sir George Downing welcomed us into the official residence of the Prime Minister. Though there were over 100 rooms there; you cannot hear the soothing sounds associated with a typical human residence. The few people you get to see move about soundlessly as *phantoms*. Though there is enough warmth inside from the cold outside, it still lacks that human warmth that makes a home, a home.

Inside the library that was started in the later part of the first quarter of the century by a Labour Prime Minister, Ramsay MacDonald; whose huge portrait hung over the marbled fireplace that has a fire burning in it. The rest of the room had dim lights embedded into the ceiling, to give the desk a prominent reading lamp. On the mantelpiece above fireplace were a collection of framed pictures. The giant floor-to-ceiling mahogany, glass-fronted bookshelves were loaded with books that have been traditionally donated by Prime Minister MacDonald and other ministers over the years.

The lone figure sitting behind the desk fills the room with a foreboding presence. Her personality permeated every fabric in that room. She is the first woman ever to occupy that official residence in the capacity of the prime minister. The longest serving Prime Minister in 160 years to have been re-elected for a-record -three times. She is a colossus in every sense of it.

Her mien that evening was a far cry from the callous, confrontational, overbearing, and brusque, media perception of her. She looks vexed, lonely and abandoned. Two files boldly captioned *TOP SECRET* lay unopened on the massive oak desk top. She kept staring at the files; petrified to open them. Each file bore a name handwritten in a red bolt marker pen; the names were *G. HOWE*, and *M. HASELTINE*.

Her very fertile mind was almost running wild; checking out the possibilities and weighing them against the probabilities, permutations, attacks and counter attacks. It was like back to the war cabinet room during the skirmish with Argentina over the Falkland Islands in 1982. Even though Britain lost 255 service men and 3 Falkland Islanders; it was one victory she would relive over and over. She could remember vividly on May 2, 1982 when she gave the order for the *HMS Conqueror* to attack the cruiser *ARA General Belgrano*, who went down with 300 Argentines. It was the turning point in the war; that defining moment of victory and defeat.

Though, this time she is alone; all alone. She did not just adopt the sobriquet of *Iron Lady* as a harmless nickname. She was going to deal with them squarely and decisively…the chicken-hearted-lily- livered lot. You can feel her fury... Shakespeare was right when he said; "…do not underestimate the fury of a woman scorned". She was reliably informed that Howe was scheduled to make his resignation speech in another three days; she could not suppress the nagging ominous feeling that is almost paralyzing. Was Howe going to be her Achilles heel as some people are foolishly speculating?

She had been briefed accordingly of Heseltine's clandestine moves to unseat her already. She was not scared of him; she felt deep down in her that she can deal with him and his cohorts of *Judases*. She will fight them to death if possible.

She was so deep in thought to notice her humming private telephone line. The caller was persistent. It actually took Denis, her husband who sauntered in to ask his wife to take the call. The Prime Minister did not like interruptions in the library, but on the contrary she was gratefully relieved by these interruptions from her nagging feeling of hopelessness. She knew it must be a call from either her *twins* or a very close and trusted friend that have stood the test of time.

"Margaret Hilda Roberts!" it was indeed the familiar and most reassuring voice of Ambassador Daniel Aka, Nigeria's High

Commissioner to the Court of St. James. It was a friendship that dated back to over 42 years.

"Preshent Shar! I mean shar ma." she answered back in an unbelievable timid African accent. And they both burst into a bout of uncontrollable laughter. It was a joke that dated back to their days at Somerville College, Oxford University, as students of the great Dorothy Hodgkin.

"Mr. Ambassador to what do I owe the honor of your call" the prime minister almost restored some degree of officialdom into their discussions.

"I just called to congratulate you!" the man paused dramatically to create the right dose of suspense.

"Daniel, please be serious, I am in the middle of something" she added some modicum of assertiveness to put her old friend on the defensive.

"Maggie, what I am saying is that Margaret Hilda Daniel-Aka is almost carting home the Miss Cosmos crown. I can see that you are not watching the television coverage…"

"What? Daniel please just drop now. I am not going to miss out on my god-daughter's journey to an historical victory. Thanks for calling." She cut him off without much ado, and pressed a switch beneath her desktop. In the din of purring, hisses and hums of hydraulic pumps, a 4 feet by 4 feet section of the loaded bookshelf directly opposite her desk swiveled around to show a 32-inch television set, VCR, and a complete audio set. The prime minister fiddled with a remote control, and the television screen came alive.

Prime Minister Margaret Thatcher with reckless abandon brushed aside the files in front of her; poured herself a liberal portion of her favorite The Famous Grouse Blended Scotch Whiskey, and settled down to watch history in the making. Poised confidently, and stunningly beautiful, and much bigger on screen was her god-daughter, Margaret Hilda starring straight at her. She could not believe that this was the same girl whose black and white christening picture also adorned the mantelpiece in that library. She recalled vividly, how she stood in for the mother, who fell very ill on the morning, a surgery to amputate an extra finger on each hand. Strange then it was; until the surgeon explained the subject of *Polydactyl*, which was a simple genetic error of having extra digits in the hand. Her father Daniel Aka also had it, she was informed later. So very sad when Margaret Hilda's mother died a few days later, from complications of the birth.

There was the sound of protracted drum roll and the hall went dead silent; "Ladies and gentlemen; and the third runner-up is Missssssss Ecuador…" The hall once again exploded in a thunderous applause that reverberated to the four corners of the globe.

Located somewhere between Downing Street and Royal Albert Hall is London Chancery Building, 24 Grosvenor Square, the home of the United States Embassy. Theodore Roszak's massive gilded aluminum–caste *Bald Eagle* with its 35-foot wingspan stood on top of the building and glistened under the drizzle and glare of the search lights. As the extra-massive Stars and Stripes swayed lazily overhead in the cold and damp night air, the American bald eagle kept its steady watch with its stony gaze over the 9-story building, even down to the three floors below ground level.

At this time of the night, the whole square looked deserted but for the occasional vehicle that passed through from time to time. There was a sinister feeling of being watched by unseen eyes; nothing happened outside that building that was not captured and processed by hidden security cameras all around. Inside, in the maze of offices above and below ground was a beehive of activities comparable to inside a *termites' anthill*. The tentacles of the United States of America scattered all over the world were at work, and synchronized round the clock.

Twenty rooms on the Fifth floor were occupied by the United States Drug Enforcement Administration (DEA). The DEA is a United States federal law enforcement agency under the Department of Justice, saddled with combating drug smuggling and use within the United States. It is also the agency with the sole responsibility for coordinating and pursuing US drug investigations abroad. It's headquarters is at 600-700 Army-Navy Drive in the Pentagon City Area of Arlington, Virginia.

Room 537 was the office of the Deputy Director for Europe and Asia. The sparsely furnished office is warm and welcoming. There were no windows for obvious security reasons. A very colorful giant canvas map of the World covered the entire length and breadth of one wall; yellow, green, and red colored pin heads dotted over the capital cities of Europe and Asia, there meaning only to be decoded by the initiates. The other wall painted in brilliant white had several wall-clocks hanging on it showing times in London, Berlin, Rome, Istanbul, Singapore, Dubai, Moscow, Anchorage, Sao Paulo, Washington DC, Houston, New York, Los Angeles; Hong Kong, Lagos, Johannesburg, Sydney, Tokyo, and Beijing. The wall that was supposed to have windows was covered from ceiling to floor with a surreal montage of a serene coastline with a translucent azure sea and coconut filled pristine beaches. It would have been anywhere in the world to be dreamed of. A very long conference table to seat about thirty took the major part of the room that was almost three times the size of the standard office space in the embassy.

Chuck Booker Freeborn IV who is the sole occupant of Room 537 was was not sitting behind his desk today as usual. His solid glass desk top was free of any clutter. There were just two ornamental- framed photographs of his son, Chuck V; and the other of his idol, Booker T. Washington. There were four different colored telephone sets that had permanent places on the desk top. He was at the front of his desk with his visitor. From their friendly banter we can infer that they go way back. An unopened bottle of Remy Martin XO Special, with two crystal globular snifters sat between the two friends. There was something strangely familiar about the two men, though they were definitely not blood-related.

Fabrice Deleon was a Cuban American on his way to the West Coast of Africa on a top-secret special assignment. He had first met Chuck Freeborn back in 1965; when Chuck a then young US Coast Guard rescued him from the clutches of Fidel Castro after the Bay of Pigs fiasco. Though he had made good his escape from Cuba, but Castro's troops were on his watery trail. It was either Castro's troops or the sharks that would have gotten him in the end. It had been a friendship that had thrived over the years. The uncanny resemblance, over the years had become the butt of many a joke and had never been taken seriously.

"So Fabrice my man, what trouble spot are they shipping you to this time" he knew his friend was in the elitist *X-Squad* that was as lethal as they come. There was no way his friend would release any classified information.

"Nothing much my friend; just to keep watch over *Uncle Sam's* basket of eggs" he quickly changed the subject, "Chuck you are looking good; we can't wait to see you step up the ladder in Washington". And the friends burst into laughter again.

"But you know I have reached the end of the ladder for a black man; going beyond this point is just a wistful dream".

"Come on man, we both know things are turning around".

Fabrice slapped his thighs in feigned indignation.

"You can say that again; but not in our own generation".

"I see a dream, that one day in the red hills of Georgia..." Fabrice Deleon tried a very convincing impression of Martin Luther King's legendary speech, with a very faint Cuban-Latino accent.

"Bravo! Bravo!! Great! That is what I am saying…A dream…" Chuck genuinely impresssd applauded, but was interrupted by the ringing red phone. He froze for a moment as his eyes strayed to the Washington clock. "The *witches and wizards* are about to spoil our fun". Chuck said hilariously as he hastily rose and moved behind his desk.

With his pen and notepad ready, he reached for the handset after the third ring, "Hello, good afternoon sir?" He signaled his friend to pour the drinks as he went on talking. "Everything worked out according to plans in Singapore. My report would be ready in a couple of…" it was very obvious that the caller rudely cut him short. "Wow! That is truly nice sir". He answered with genuine enthusiasm after listening for a while. "It escaped me, because of my trip. I will turn on the television immediately. Congratulations in advance sir." He waited a while before replacing the handset. He smiled at his friend, who pretended to be engrossed with his snifter of cognac to avoid the embarrassment of the one-sided conversation with the obvious *Big Boss* in Washington DC.

"Fabrice, an African proverb says; …even with a deluge drenching the leopard, it cannot change his spots". This was expressed with matching melancholy.

"At your level and accomplishments, you deserve some respect man".

"Never! Not with an ordinary die-hard Klansman, but the *all-invincible* Grand Wizard. He is a scion of the first Imperial Wizard of the Ku Klux Klan."

"How can they keep him there? An incorrigible racist bigot... no not even in my Cuba." Fabrice knows when he starts getting angry; an involuntary twitch at the little bumps that were left after the extra fingers were extracted very long time ago. He quickly clasped his two hands together and lowered them inbetween his laps from prying eyes.

"Give me a break, Fabrice. Even in *your* Cuba, the then President Batista, due to his mixed blood, was banned from the Havana Yacht Club, which was the most exclusive of Havana's upper class clubs." Chuck chuckled understandably.

"Come on Chuck, that was long ago; not the Cuba of today." Fabrice did not sound very convincing, even to himself.

"Since you asked why a leader of America's most lethal racist organization is allowed in government. *Politics! Politics.* Fabrice with politics every hand you play must be to win." Chuck declared with so much wisdom, and a note of finality.

Chuck then pressed down a button on the grey phone which buzzed twice, and then a male voice answered. "Hi Sam. Get me the on-going

Miss Cosmos finals on television now." He did not wait for any reply; because the term *excuse* was not in the very proficient Sam Mendoza's vocabulary.

By the time Chuck went back to his former position, and picked up his snifter of cognac and clinked glasses with his bosom friend, a section of the opposite white wall twitched alive. It was transformed into a huge cinema screen with larger-than-life image of the stage at the Royal Albert Hall.

"By Jove! There she is!" Chuck jumped up from his seat almost spilling his drink."

"Who? Who?" Fabrice Deleon asked with equal excitement. "Sophie Fenton-Forest! The Administrator's daughter! The old bugger was not joking..." he was cut short by a strange voice in the room.

"...and for the position of the second runner-up," the booming voice of Craig David Stephenson seeped out from the invisible speakers overhead with a defined clarity. The final three contestants by then, smiled confidently into the cameras without betraying any nervous tension. The MC took the maximum interval professionally allowed to create the right amount of suspense. The suspense got to Chuck Freeborn, because he felt that familiar itchy feeling by the base of his little finger where a sixth finger was removed as he was told. He involuntarily chopped both edges of his hands against the edge of the table to numb the age-long nervous *itch*.

"Shall we put our hands together for the second-runner up; Missssssss Sweden?" This time the whole hall rose in unison in a delirium of applause, including Chuck and Fabrice. The approbation at this point was no doubt for both the victors and the vanquished. Craig David Stephenson, better known as the *Nighthawk* of the Wrecking Crew in the Washington Area Brotherhood was really amazed, and impressed. He recalled his telephone conversation the previous day with the Grand Wizard; "...Nighthawk keep your filthy claws away from my daughter who would be crowned as the new Miss Cosmos". Now he could see that the man is right, with the final two contestants standing... a black girl, and the Grand Wizard's daughter. There is no competition whatsoever...

Outside, though the rain had finally stopped, the chilly winds had increased in intensity. Pedestrians hunched over, hurried home dreaming of warm fires and the comforting warmth of hot liquids and loved ones. The night traffic heading north on Finchley Road was moderate; the squashing macabre music of tires kissing the rain- soaked macadamized thoroughfare enveloped all other sounds. The charcoal black sedan, the latest BMW 325i 1991 Model with its six-cylinder and 24-valve engine purred silently and weaved smoothly at a sedate pace like a ballerina in a swan dance. The dashboard lights silhouetted the chiseled features of the lone occupant's facial profile; a brooding black African male of an indeterminate age. Even with his glinting diamond-encrusted wristwatch and the customized sleek interior of the latest top-of-the-range exquisite luxury on wheels, and a skin color fair enough to pass him as a mulatto; there was so much strange *darkness* about this young man.

This man was believed to be one of the most secretive Africans living in the City of London. In the parlance of the subterranean world; this was the *smoothest fixer & operator*. He has his tentacles from diamonds, arms, gold, to some mega businesses that were only transacted in the cloak of darkness. He was reputed to work hard; and play hard. A man that preferred to tread the fast lanes of life, and their attanedant dangers.

And at that very moment, he was on the final lap of yet one of those dangerous *missions impossible* to mere mortals. And that accounted for his inability to relax and enjoy his first ride on this automotive wonder from BMW. Charlie Stevens, the salesman at *Park Lane BMW* had *particularly promised* him a wonderful experience to drive, the first BMW model to offer a 5-Speed automatic transmission.

His shadowy eyes involuntarily scanned the rear-view mirror for the tell-tale signs of any vehicle on his tail. He was not sure; so much traffic behind him. His mind strayed for the umpteenth time to the two *Louis Vuitton* suitcases in the trunk of the car. The *swap* was made smoothly he recalled; this had been one his most tasking shipments through Singapore. At a point, it looked as if he was going to fail; failure is not in his vocalbulary, and no place in his kind of trade. In this very exacting kind of business you must deliver or you are history… wasted in the prime of life; everything you have acquired, lost in what could pass for a dangerous game of Russian roulette. All of a sudden he felt like a cat with nine lives; that had exhausted the whole nine lives and was now living on a borrowed life. Maybe he should start thinking of retirement and marriage. Yes, marriage. He had never considered marriage, because his kind of business required total focus and no room for sentimental or emotional distractions.

The car handled well, smooth to his deft touch. He was tempted to try out the 5-Speed automatic transmission, but thought against it. It was not the best of times to have the police on his trail for over speeding. He maintained the sedate pace until he connected to Golder's Green Road. Time to shake-off any tail. He turned right into Golder's Green Crescent, and left again into Golder's Way, and drove all the way to the Armitage Road junction, where he turned right into Hoop Lane. He did not notice any lights banking suddenly with him; nobody was following him. So he thought. At that exact moment Sam Mendoza put a call through to Charlie Stevens at the *Park Lane BMW* for a job well done with the pin-point tracking device that was nestled cozily inside the rear view mirror. The monitor in front of him was showing the dot of flashing light going berserk; criss-crossing and zigzagging all over the screen as Oscar Uromi tried to knock out any car following him.

And to make assurance doubly sure Oscar Uromi turned right at Golder's Green Crescent again and drove all the way to Golder's Way and turned right into his own street. There was not a single vehicle moving in sight. Opposite his gate were a BT van and its motley crew working with floodlights over a man-hole in the wintry cold. It must be an emergency he thought to himself; after all he had been away for five days. He did not envy them out in the cold on a Saturday night. Two remotely controlled gates opened one after the other to give him access into his *Smooth Sail Cove*. The lights in his house were on, and even faint music filtered out from within the cottage; it was a clever electronic ploy to deceive any intruder. Oscar smiled at what he considered a perfect air-tight security.

There were four state-of-the-art cars all colored in different shades of black, parked around the drive way. He drove straight into a vault-like garage whose metal doors rose and rolled down again behind him. Nobody came out to welcome him; because there was nobody at home. Oscar lived alone. No wife, no lover, no children, and no relatives of any kind. It was a puzzle for the authorities; *it was as if he was hacked out of a wood.*

A set of very long-standing domestic staff only comes over on specially arranged days. Oscar could make out the muffled sounds of the living room television. He briskly stepped over to a security console attached to a close circuit monitor. He placed his left palm over the screen; it took another five seconds flat to complete a form of complex security clearance. He then punched in a 10-letter and number combination code. A 6foot x 4foot section of the floor at back of the car slide noiselessly apart to reveal a space about 4feet in depth. He hastily took the two Louis Vuitton suitcases and dropped them into the hole. He then punched a blinking red light by the rim of the hole; and the floor slide shut without a trace.

He stood there brooding for a while, his brow covered in cold sweat. He could not feel the usual sweet taste of victory; no victory dance until he gets to hear from his *client;* the lethal Medellin Cartel. *Phew!* So far so good, it's just time to wait very *impatiently* for the very important phone call to end his misery. He nervously rubbed his palms together to relieve the normal *throb* when he got excited.

He went back to the car and retrieved an attach case from the back seat and unhurriedly climbed the flight of stairs straight into his upper level living room. The monstrous fireplace had a warm artificial wood fire burning in it. The sitting room was tastefully done with no expense spared. There was a plush Turkish rug running the entire expanse of the room. He stopped briefly at the oversized television on a special stand showing the grand finale of the Miss Cosmos. He went over to the well-stocked mahogany bar and poured himself a generous portion of cognac from a crystal decanter, which he downed at one fell swoop. He then carried the antique gold phone set over to the giant woolen bean bag seat facing the television, and gratefully dropped into its embracing folds.

He tried to follow the event on the screen, but his mind kept wandering off. If not for the delay back in Singapore he would have been at the Royal Albert Hall; he had been a regular face in the past four Miss Cosmos finals. Oscar Uromi's was not just one of the numerous revelers of the beauty pageant; he was one of its most important sponsors. For he was an executive director at *Twinkle & Twinkle*; and was well-known and welcomed at the Miss Cosmos headquarters at 21 Golden Square. He stared unseeing at the screen, his mind totally engrossed with the call he was expecting from his clients.

There were also other people interested in that call. Inside the BT van parked across the street were feverish activities; the balding senior DEA operative in-charge of the operation nodded understandably at the technician clad in a BT blue overall sitting behind the console. The younger man obviously not happy about a botched weekend furiously typed into the console in front of him. In a micro-second Sam Mendoza at the US Embassy received the message; *the eagle has landed in his nest.* Mendoza in turn buzzed Chuck Freeborn with the dispatch.

Oscar Uromi should not have bothered wasting his time and fuel trying to outrun some imaginary tail on his journey home. The hounds were already hot on his trail; and were waiting for him at home. Then the phone rang suddenly, that Oscar almost jumped out of his skin. It was on the third ring, that he was composed enough to pick up the receiver.

"Hello". There was hidden glee in his voice. *"Amigo?"* The voice on the other end inquired. "Yes?" Oscar answered cautiously.

"You must get it out of town again. It is too hot." It had a thick Latino twang.

"What? That is going to be a tough one, Amigo".

"We have no choice. Name your price. I will call you later". And the line went dead as promptly to fend off intruders or interlopers.

Oscar held the ear-piece away from himself as if it was a venomous snake. His highly intelligent mind was assaulted with a thousand questions without answers. How in the world would he move that shipment safe in his strong room, out of the United Kingdom again, after going through all the troubles to bring it in through Singapore? The more he pondered the puzzle, the more he got excited; and there again was the habitual tell-tale throb at the exact points the extra digits were hastily and crudely extricated after his birth. There is something about danger; that excites the survival instinct. This thrill is only felt by a certain breed of people that are addicted to danger in all its ramifications.

"…finally we have come to the final moments; the climax of the 1990 Miss World contest," Craig Stephenson's voice sliced through his thoughts like a red-hot knife through cold wax, "is it Miss USA or Miss Nigeria?" He paused dramatically as the suspense mounted in the audience.

"That is the million dollar question". The two finalists huddled together holding hands, trying to find solace from each other. It was not only the audience that was caught in the web of the electrifying excitement. It was for a very brief moment, but the very prudent director captured the action. Miss Nigeria quickly released her hand from her fellow competitor to rub her hands together to ease the trembling feeling at the exact points of the surgical amputation back in 1965.

Oscar Uromi could not help but sit forward on the edge of his seat. He could not believe what was unfolding before his eyes. The master of ceremony held up the sealed black envelope to the cameras; you could hear a pin drop. The world waited impatiently with bated breath.

"And the winner is…," he tore open the envelope and pulled out the white slip of paper which he glanced at, and for a tiny brief flitting moment he could not control the grimace that crossed his handsome face as the blood rushed into to his face. Active images in the dark of burning torches, white hoods and cloaks on horsebacks; burning crosses; exploding Molotov cocktails; and cornered frightened blacks running for cover flooded his mind's eye. Impossible! *Him*, a grandson of a

Grand Dragon to announce a black Miss Cosmos? What an irony? What a sacrilege? His entire being repelled what was about to unfold, but years of experience and professional training came to the fore.

"Miss Cosmos 1990… is Miss Nigeria!" it was very obvious that his usual gusto was lacking in his pronouncement.

For a brief micro-second, the universe stood still. Then exploded like a long-extinct volcano; as a billion silver-shiny confetti were showered from overhead upon the stage. The roof literally came down not only in the Royal Albert Hall, but resonated from London to Sydney; from Hiroshima to Vancouver; from Lagos to Siberia; and Santiago to Washington. Oscar Uromi jumped up in excitement, almost upsetting the huge chandelier hanging in the middle of the room, as he went into a celebratory dance for his compatriot's record breaking accomplishments.

When his exhilaration finally died down later. His fertile mind was already doing a somersault with all his permutations. He was seeing all the opportunities and possibilities for business with this new queen. And it was also remotely possible that this could be the moment to finally settle down and retire from his kind of high- risk enterprises. Wonderful! It was unbelievable! This was indeed providence in action. His spirit of the gambler came to fore; time to play his best and biggest hand. He would give the cartel a good run for their money. Maybe…*the ringing phone interrupted his thoughts.*

"Hello" he answered with some degree of confidence.

"Amigo are we in business?" the voice was abrupt and businesslike.

"Yes. This time it is *Fifty-Fifty.*" Oscar replied coldly.

"*Juepula boludo Negrito! Que camello*, this is madness!" The voice swore out.

"Fifty- Fifty; or no deal" Oscar felt as if he was playing a dangerous game of poker with his life.

"Amigo, I will give you thirty percent" the voice wobbled. "Fifty percent or no deal my friend. Not a percent more, not a

percent less." Oscar was not ready to budge.

"*Parcero!*" Oscar could tell that all these Spanish must be some low level unprintable vulgarities, but that did not bother him.

"Ok! Deal my friend," there was no hesitation from the mystery caller, "please bear in mind that no room for half-measures; the deal is signed and sealed in blood. If you fail, kiss your goldfish lifestyle good-bye…" and the line went abruptly dead before it could be traced…*or so he thought.*

The BT van and its motley crew had packed and were already rolling away from the manhole when the call came in. The brief telephone chat between Oscar Uromi and the most wanted *dead* drug lord of the Medellin Cartel had the eavesdropping ears of the DEA. And like blood hounds on a bloody trail; this special shipment worth over a billion pounds sterling was not only in their sights, but in their claws and fangs. A typical case of the hunter, the hunted, and the bait; played out by the mysterious directions of the *Finger of God.*

CHAPTER 1

It all began a very, very long time ago on a very dark night. It was so dark that even the stars were scared to peep out. Neither did the moon venture to put in an appearance; it took a double take, and calmly absconded with its tail between its legs. So the sky was one solid inky-blackness. Down below the tropical forest canopy, the darkness was even darker; the darkness like a blanket enveloping everything in its mysterious folds. The night was so thickly dark that you can even smell it. And the ghoulish painful cries of preys that had ended up in the claws and bellies of the predators added a malevolent ambience to the dark night. The chilly harmattan wind slithered through the bountiful leafy boughs with its scrawny frosty lullabies lulling shadowy villages into deep slumber.

The village of Amaeke-Ohafia was sound asleep. Only a small fire burned in a small clearing to diminish the bullish grip of darkness; and to provide succor against the chilly winds. A lone figure wide awake with anticipation squatted by the burning logs of wood. Since the piece of animal hide could only cover his loin, he was almost pushing himself into the blazing fire to escape the chilly grasp of the harmattan. All around him were shadowy grotesque tangos in the backdrop of the boundary of the fire light.

Onyeobia, *the Stranger*, was deeply in thought. His tired eyes were transfixed on the doorway of his little hut. He pushed the burning cinders together to keep the clay pot of water boiling. His wife, Ihuoma was in labor of their first baby. After almost fifteen rain-years of impatient waiting. He strained his ears to pick up the muffled groans of his wife. He could hear the hard croaky voice of the old village midwife coaxing his wife to *push*. His anticipation was almost exploding; he would not blame the old woman for giving him the marching orders to stay away and look after the boiling pot and the fire. He felt totally helpless; in such a monumental moment in his life. And all he could do now was to watch and pray.

His efforts to say a prayer, was an exercise in futility. He could not coordinate his thoughts and words. His mind was in a riot. Would he choose between his wife and the unborn child if push comes to shove? He berated himself on the extremities of his thoughts. *What is going on?*

Ihuoma actually went into labor before sunset, by the time he had gone and fetched Mgbeke, it was already twilight. From the chill of the night he knew it was gone past midnight. He searched the eastern hilltops for that telltale glint that signifies the dawn of a new day, but it was totally inky-black.

He had waited infinitely for this moment. Chukwu please make it a boy for us; it was a wish not a prayer. The old midwife hobbled over, with a strength that simply bellies her true age. He jumped up with so much excitement to meet her, but the old woman just ignored him, and lifted the boiling pot off the fire. Onyeobia could do nothing but sulk and wait. Now he knows that the darkest part of night is the part before dawn.

"Please God don't let my wife to die" he mumbled aloud this time, "she is all that I have left."

He could recall vividly the circumstances that brought them to Amaeke-Ohafia in the first place. Even after twelve rains of living in their midst, the community had never for once pretended to accept them into their fold entirely. That was why *the stranger* stuck over the years. For them, they had made up their minds that Amaeke would have to remain their adoptive home. Their origin would never welcome them back. In a typical primordial community, the inability to do or achieve the very primal functions of reproduction was looked upon as culpability. So their inability to have children over the rains kept a veil of suspicion over them; and that was why they had been kept at bay. It was not by accident but by design that they were allocated a land outside the core settlement, even with the strong influence of Obidi who brought them to Amaeke.

His real name was Ofobike, he had totally fallen head-over-heels in love with Ihuoma, in their native village of Umuaku, located at the upper course of *Imo Mmiri*. His family had insisted he could not marry her because they were distantly related through his great grandmother,

Ogasi. To him and Ihuoma, this argument did not hold water. So they resolved to force their families to compromise by getting pregnant.

There was no basis for consideration since the whole act was considered as a taboo. It was going to be fire and brimstones from both sides of the family when the news broke; so the lovers decided to elope as far as they can from a land that had given their love no option to blossom. They would prove to them all that true love conquers all. With their secret safely tucked away between them; their feverish preparations went into top gear. Ofobike planned to do enough battering on the next three *Eke Market* days to acquire all they will need for their journey.

Unfortunately, things did not go according to plans; as Ihuoma was caught vomiting one early morning, by her mother who was not fooled by her daughter's flimsy excuse. As a mother many times over, she knew the symptoms. Though, she did not utter a word, Ihuoma could see shock and alarm registered in her eyes. It was the most important Eke Market day, so Ihuoma knew all hell would break loose when they return. She just waited for her mother with her wares to set off on the footpath to the market square; before she sprang like deer through another route to the market square to look for Ofobike. In her confusion she did not take anything.

After consulting with her partner in love and crime; they agreed to set sail that morning. After all, the canoe was all set. There was no time to go home. They surreptitiously made it down the slopes and into the canoe hidden in the brushes and paddled down south on the sedately flowing Imo Mmiri. On that very day, that they commenced their journey of no return, Ihuoma was two moons into her pregnancy. They chose the waterway to the more popular land travel; because their trail would have been obvious to all and sundry. They did not bargain for the troubles of a canoe travel down the Imo Mmiri for a first pregnancy in its first trimester.

By the third day on the river, Ihuoma's health became a cause for serious concern. She developed a serious fever; but urged on her lover to paddle on to distance themselves from their origin. By the time they reached the confluence with *Eme River,* Ofobike had to abort the journey through the river to take care of Ihuoma who was looking worse for it. They sort for help at the little settlement at the confluence. It took almost seven days for Ihuoma to recover fully. There benefactor was a prolific hunter named Obidi Kalu from Ohafia.

It was Obidi who after sympathetically listening to Ofobike's doctored account of their travails that decided to take them with him back to Amaeke-Ohafia at the end of his hunting expedition.

The journey to Ohafia would have been futile without Obidi Kalu; for the Ohafia people and their warlike exploits made peaceful travel impossible. Even with the veteran hunter leading the way through Uzuakoli to Amaeke; the journey took its toll on Ihuoma. And by the time they arrived Amaeke many days later, Ihuoma had had a good battering that led to a miscarriage.

That misfortune later turned out to be a blessing in disguise for the young runaway couple. The sympathies of the womenfolk for a young girl experiencing a miscarriage in no small measure aided their mentor to make a case in their favor, to settle in the community. They had all rallied around to give her all the support. Ofobike could not believe it was almost twelve rains since that fateful day. How time flies? Ogbuisi Obidi, despite their age disparity had remained a true and loyal friend all these rains. Obidi a well-respected member of the community more or less adopted him as the son he never had.

He thought it was his imagination running wild when he heard the thump and jangle at that unholy hour of the night. Until the familiar croaky voice of Agbala; the priestess of Ani and fertility blasted through his thoughts to shake him awake from his reverie.

"Onyeobia!" the voice was not aloud but carried well through the night air from the edge of the clearing. Onyeobia almost jumped out of his skin; but quickly regained his composure with his right hand taking firm grip of his well-sharpened machete.

"*Onye?* Who are you?"

"How dare you question the mouth-piece of the gods? And put away your weapon before thunder dries up your body." She was clad in her ghostly white regalia.

"Agbala, I apologize, it was just that I was not expecting…" he mumbled.

"*Taa! Tufia kwa!*" she cut him short, "If Agbala does not walk by this time of the night, who can?" She thumped and jangled her staff again.

"Agbala, please forgive your impudent child," he paused to remove his hand from the machete "I will use a cock to appease you." "Now you are talking, Onyeobia my son. You have spoken well.

Agbala will accept your appeasement, for you are now the special one." She paused a little before continuing.

"I bring you good tidings Onyeobia. Your days of running are over for *he* has chosen to arrive through your loins. And that means *he* has given you a homestead, in Amaeke. The proof is on him, so glaringly bright, as bright as daylight. And his descendants must bear this burden of proof...*the sixth finger.* He will excel not only in Ohafia's twelve villages; but beyond our lands and across the seas. Be careful, handle him with care, *he* is of God."

Onyeobia stood there befuddled and speechless to the revelations unfolding before him. He felt not only bamboozled but overwhelmed. *Was he just dreaming?*

"Onyeobia, don't dare to ask me any question. I am just the mouthpiece of the gods; Agbala is only their emissary. Now, go and receive your son. Keep this information to yourself alone...not even to his mother." And she turned around and stepped back into the darkness just as she had come.

Onyeobia's eyes strayed to the hilltops in the far east, and there was a glint, a tiny little glint of light... dawn is at hand.

"Onyeobia! Onyeobia!" the voice hit him with the force of a sucker punch, "Are you alright? You look like you have just encountered a ghost?" Mgbeke approached him with a bundle in her hands. His face relaxed into a big smile as he stepped forward to meet the midwife.

"You have a son," the old woman declared with all sense of pride "and your wife is fine, though very tired."

She stopped him before he could run past her, "No! Wait, she is asleep, she needs the rest. It was a long battle for her. First, receive your son." and she handed him the bundle of *Akwa-miri (*cloth of the water). And the first thing that stuck out of the bundle was a tiny and very fair hand with six digits that was enchanting in the smoldering light of the fire.

The midwife met his questioning gaze with a reassuring smile, "It is alright. He is a special one, please keep him warm" she turned around and headed back to the hut; this time her gait telling of the strain of the long night.

Onyeobia properly tucked back the hand into the swaddling cloth and lifted the bundle of joy up into the air towards the rising speck of light in the eastern horizon. "*Chukwu Okike*! God of creation. O behold your gift to me; I commit him back into your hands for safe keeping. I name him *Aka Chukwu*... the finger of God. That he may fulfill your destiny under your divine finger of direction." And the cock crowed to signify the dawn of the new day...*the dawn of a new era.*

CHAPTER 2

After word spread through Amaeke of the birth of a *miracle baby* by Onyeobia's wife, it was only a matter of time, for it to spread like wild fire through all of Ohafia. The story gathered momentum, as it was passed from one mouth to the other; unsolicited interpretations and flavors were added at will to make it more sensational. The fact that Ihuoma's long awaited pregnancy was already a gossip item did not only fuel, but added the right dose of mystery to nosh the whole saga. And the curious and gossips all trooped over to the Onyeobia enclave to see things for themselves.

In no time, those who interpreted the extra digits as a bad omen persuaded Ihuoma to tie tightly a raffia thread around the offending fingers. This was indeed a form of traditional amputation that was practiced at birth for certain defects. Onyeobia bluntly refused all entreaties, and took a passionate stance that the extra fingers must remain to serve the divine purpose for which they were created. This position brought the spouses to the brink of many a quarrel; maybe it was a feminine instinct, for the wife to challenge her husband of some secret he was keeping from her. Onyeobia held his ground stubbornly and did not budge.

So Aka-Chukwu grew up and naturally adapted to the additional digits. Very cool and level headed, stoically absorbed every joke and prank from the other children. His mother who could not be pregnant again after his birth; treated him as a special gift. Ihuoma would cleverly make him believe that his extra digits was because he was created very special by God, more special than all those jokers who were calling him names like; *Maze Nkpisi* …Mr. Finger; or *Isi* …Six".

Ihuoma was so protective of her son, that she even confronted Obiligbo Kamanu, a young bully in his teens, who was the worst of Aka's mental tormentors. That brush with the young Obiligbo remained indelible in the young Akachukwu's mind. For the safety of her only son and child; Ihuoma was ready to take on the whole Kamanu clan, who were reputed to be very cantankerous. His mother's bold confrontation was not taken kindly, and things degenerated into a total verbal warfare that involved the whole family.

The very caustic reply from the Kamanus; was to tell Ihuoma in very mean terms that she and her husband were *osu* outcasts fleeing from justice. That was the meanest form of casting aspersion to say the least. And all hell broke loose. Ihuoma stood alone against them; since his father was away on one of those hunting expeditions. The young Aka was so scared that he thought the Kamanus were going to kill his mother. That was the beginning of a life-long bitter acrimony that festered over the years.

Ogbu-Isi Obidi Kalu playing his chosen role of adoptive grandfather noted everything in his usual calm and dignified persona. And at the precise time, with the covert approval of Onyeobia, he strategically stepped in to nip the mother and son affinity in the bud before it became dysfunctional..

By his fourth rain, Aka as he was fondly called by all and sundry was spending more time with the old man, who was loading the young lad with the adventurous escapades of his hunting expeditions. At seven rains, Aka willingly accompanied the old man on his first hunting expedition.

And the old man gladly honed his *grandson* in hunting techniques and basic survival skills. Before long, the young man could tell scents and decode paw marks and specific call signs, as well as medicinal herbs from poisonous plants. He could imitate fairly most birds and animal calls naturally, to attract them into the different contraptions that were set to entrap them. He had learned to bite into the special blade of grass to avoid uttering a sound during a hunt.

Aka, not only grew in stature but also in all wisdom of the Ohafia primordial society. In farm work which is the main stay of every household, the young man was more than diligent. He was already known for his massive heaps. He never got tired; he enjoyed farm work and treated it as a hobby. He would work from sun up to sun down, only breaking intermittently to gulp huge quantities of water like a camel.

He had also inherited the athletic wrestling skills of Onyeobia his father. In all of Amaeke, nobody ever won a wrestling match against

Aka Chukwu in the junior category. It was then the maxim began that; *azu Aka na so ilu ani*...Aka's back forbids touching the ground. His fame gradually grew by the day and the night across the land.

He was easily recognizable. He had a very fair complexion that barely escaped albinism by the skin of his tooth. Nobody in all of Ohafia had his kind of thick kinky black hair. Another very strange feature he possessed was his almost blue catlike-eyes. It was rumored especially by his opponents that those eyes had hidden powers that could hypnotize them when they stare into them at the start of the fight. The young maidens, who were falling over each other for his attention, would rather defer from their male-counterparts; they felt those eyes were rather romantically alluring.

At twelve rains, Aka and his age graders were led to *Nkpogolo*, in *Ebem*, for the initiation into the masquerade cult. Nkpogolo's forest was totally virgin, just as it had been from creation, because it was forbidden from bush burning, agricultural or hunting activities, though its abundant fruits could be eaten by anybody. Aka, who was already familiar with forest life through the expeditions with Ogbu- Isi Obidi, showed a good prowess and mastery of the jungle. And for the two nights they were there in Nkpogolo, he so excelled in all the activities that their initiators led by Ogbu-Isi Uduma, the greatest wrestler in his time, personally took him under his tutelage. All the initiators overwhelmingly agreed that Aka had surpassed all his peers in this vital elementary education that is potentially related to the *spirit* world.

As his son garnered one laurel after the other, Onyeobia, on the other hand, received them, or their news with a philosophical calmness that justly made his cynical wife to believe her husband was indeed an integral part of a conspiracy of silence with somebody he was keeping close to his chest. Onyeobia was not going to let out how he is privy to all these revelations unfolding before his eyes... *that indeed the sixth finger was in operation.*

It was after his tutelage under Ogbu-Isi Uduma that at 17 rains Aka was crowned as *Eze Mgba*...king of wrestling. He came in as challenger against the then reigning champion, who was eight rains older than him. It was a battle against his nightmare of old. The champion to beat was the most brutal *Back Breaker*, Okoligbo Kamanu. Even with his massive frame and gruesome mien; Akachukwu was able to fall him for the mandatory three times convincingly to all and sundry. And Aka was crowned the wrestling champion, not only of Amaeke, but of all the twelve villages of Ohafia, to break the record of the ever youngest champion of all time.

It was at about the same time, Aka on his last hunting expedition with Ogbu-Isi Obidi, returned home with the skin of a leopard. This most coveted prize was duly presented at the Achichi Square as required by custom and tradition, and the young Aka was catapulted to sit with the elders in governance.

It was only a matter of time, people thought, that Aka was expected to join the most revered *Ogbu-Isi* society. Only those who return to Ohafia with a human head from the annual head-hunting campaigns; would be honoured with the privileged Ogbu-Isi title and wear the *Eagle* plume of true courage. In Ohafia, Ogbu-Isi was the height of social values, because of their almost consuming love and passion for military glory of any kind. They did not have too long to wait for their prophetic thoughts to become a reality.

It was his twentieth rain, after the planting season and midway to the harvest season, Aka was part of the annual head hunting campaign that set out from Ohafia to the interiors for their gruesome goal. Their return was strategically timed to coincide with the superlative harvest celebrations.

It was indeed a moment of exhilaration; as the head-hunters arrived straight from their expedition on a set day, with their *grissly* pots of surprises. Aka had proudly displayed not just a head, but four heads. That day the whole town rose in admiration of a young man that was taking all of Ohafia by storm.

And with that exploit Aka's fame shot up double notch; he rose from a cult-hero status with a mammoth young followership to a legendary prominence beyond all his contemporaries. He became a reference point for all ages and generations; to be eulogized in folklores, even when he was still alive. No moonlight gathering was complete without a song about Aka. A *question and answer puzzle* that was very popular with the very young and innocent children.

> *...They said Aka has done it again*
> *Which Aka is it this time?*
> *So you don't know Aka-Chukwu?*
> *The son of Amaeke's stranger*
> *Aka; whose back forbids the ground*
> *What? What did he do now?*
> *With his hands of God he killed a lion*
> *Please tell me more?*
> *With four heads he became an Ogbu-Isi*
> *Then Aka is better than the best...*

Even his enemies could not but agree, that Aka was an almost perfect sample or specimen of humanoid. And the maidens could not hide their sentiments and emotions; they nimbly amplified their feminine desires in a melodious sonata that had deeper meanings deftly concealed between the lines. It was harmlessly titled *The Udala Song;*

He is ripe, ripe like udala for plucking
He is sweet, sweeter than honey
His sweat at work and play
Cascades like the waters of Ifutiti
Even the twelve special ones
Are not enough to count the victories
O here comes the majestic Eagle;
That eyes that see it must rejoice
Mmphmm! Then what for the eyes that own it?
But To Love, Cherish, and live happily ever after…

CHAPTER 3

Despite Aka's laurels and consequent prominence, he was the most level-headed individual, as could be attested by most elders. He kept no pompous airs about him; he modestly took the accolades and their attentions from home and abroad in his stride. Nwoye, *the witty one,* his closest friend went way back to their childhood days. Nwoye's mother, Adaora was Ihuoma's closest friend because they both shared the fate of waiting relatively long intervals for children that finally came only sparingly. Though Nwoye was almost two rains older than Aka, they were almost indivisible; as the pair was more often seen together than alone. Their *nnu na ose*, salt and pepper friendship was the talk of not only Amaeke, but all of Ohafia; Nwoye's boisterous witty disposition effectively complemented Aka's *less talk but action* critical mien. Over the years, they grew fonder for each other, as they both lacked the solace of natural siblings.

Nwoye had the most dexterous lips and fingers on the *oja* (wooden flute) in Amaeke. His *nwokem (*my man), which was his symbolic pet name for his flute, that was always hanging on his neck on a string like a lucky charm, had many roles for its diverse enchanted audience. *Nwokem's* sonorous voice was a regular feature ushering Aka into the wrestling arena, to vanquish many an opponent. Due to their active vocations, over the years, the friends developed very massive gangly statures that were truly intimidating in their full Ohafia battle regalia. They struck fear in the hearts of those who behold them. That was where their resemblance stopped, because in body complexion they were totally opposites; one was almost white, while the other was as black as charcoal.

After Ogbu-Isi Obidi's health began to fail, and his strength began faltering, the old man chose the better part of valor to go into retirement from active hunting. Aka and Nwoye, who were both under his tutelage became a formidable duo that complimented each other in their hunting skills. Their combined success story was evident in their financial wealth that increased in leaps and bounds. Their hunting expeditions always culminated with their smoked-dried products at the *Eke Ukwu,* Agbagwu Market in Uzuakoli. Agbagwu Market was so popular for its wares like human slaves, live and preserved games, various farm produce, products and implements. The market only convened on the Eke day. It was so popular that some daring traders came from the farthest strange lands that did not even speak Igbo. Some of the unlucky traders never made it home since they were either killed or captured and sold into slavery. Aka, who felt quite awful about the whole idea of slavery kept his distance from that side of the market, though he could not help stealing a cursory glance at the band of cowering naked women with suckling children and the teenage boys and girls. Adult male slaves were a rarity because they would rather die than to be taken into slavery. Slavery in the Ohafia community was not common.

Aka and Nwoye were very popular faces at Eke Ukwu; right from their days of apprenticeship to when they took over totally from their *master*. They were popularly known and identified by their very extreme complexions; *Nwokocha,* and *Nwokoji*. They naturally stepped into the vacuum created by their progenitor's exit. As their reputations grew commercially, so their collection of brass rod-money grew and consolidated to make them quite comparatively wealthy. Though both young men felt fulfilled, they knew it was time they started seriously considering the subject of marriage their mothers had regularly pestered them with respectively.

The footpath was narrow and well-beaten; Aka and Nwoye their rectangle basket filled over the brim and expertly balanced on their heads; walked briskly in a single file back to Ohafia from Eke Ukwu after another very successful enterprise. It was their tradition to be alert and battle-ready; even though they doubt if any mortal in their right frame of mind would dare tackle or confront them. Only when they had transversed and made it through the numerous patches of thick foliage that the footpath wound through, all the danger spots that they would normally relax. It was an unwritten rule that had made the difference between being alive and dead to these young men.

"*Agu!*" Nwoye called out to his friend who was exactly a tactical seven paces ahead. He knew his friend was broody before they set out on the return journey to their homeland that they left almost twenty days back.

"Emmm mmh...*Alusi Oja*, I hear you." Aka answered breaking out of his reverie.

"When are we going to give *them* their grand children?"

"Oh! I see that they have finally gotten you to take the bait," Aka stopped abruptly and turned around to face his bosom friend, "since you and your mothers now believe that children were now venison, you go ahead give them all they want." He burst into a roaring laughter, and turned around to lead the way forward.

"*Agu*, please be serious. I see their arguments. They can't wait to carry our little ones, don't forget that we are not getting any younger." Nwoye spoke with a strange enormity that was totally alien to his witty nature.

"Now that you have become children's advocate, I am changing your title from the Oracle of The Flute to that of children. I bestow upon you Nwoye Kalu; *Alusi Umuaka* from today henceforth." He burst into another fit of laughter.

They walked along for sometime in silence. Nwoye felt good, knowing his friend was giving a serious thought to his proposition. The sun was almost directly over head and was beginning to sting the skin. Their customarily rest point was in sight; a large grassy area with only a huge iroko tree as foliage. It had a good view of all approaches. They helped each other to set their huge baskets down, before gulping down a large chunk of water from their calabashes. They then leaned their backs on the tree to rest out the most lethal period of the tropical sunshine. Even at rest they were alert to any abnormal sounds of the forest.

Nwoye not long after took his *oja* from his neck and started playing a medley of popular folksongs that would have lured any one to sleep except these great Ohafia lions. Aka listened in dignified silence until Nwoye started playing the *Udala* song, which he soulfully accompanied with a deep baritone. When the song finally ended, Aka cupped his hands over his mouth gave the hooting victory call of a giant tropical bird. And what happened next took even Nwoye by surprise.

"*Alusi*! I will name my first son in your honor," as he took up his former position, "you are the only one who calls me *Agu*, the Lion; I will name him *Obele-agu*...the small lion." He chuckled out aloud.

"So when are you going to hunt him down?" Nwoye retorted sarcastically.

"What do you mean? What has hunting to do with fathering a son?" He could not hide his bewilderment.

"Did you not liken children to venison, just a moment ago?" "Come on, *Alusi* my dear brother, I was only joking." He burst into laughter again.

"So? How then do plan to fabricate a son or child Ogbu-isi Akachukwu?" He pushed himself up feigning all seriousness.

"Of course we must first get married."

"When? When our mothers have died or become gnarled with age." Nwoye fired back trying to box his friend into a corner.

"*Alusi*, soon, very soon."

"When is soon? By the next rain? Or two, three, four rains from now? Agu son of Onyeobia answer me." He promised their mothers he must get something definite from his main man.

Aka took his time, and Nwoye waited patiently knowing that he was making headway. He looked away as Aka took a twig and started marking strokes on the dirt. Whatever calculations or permutations he was making was lost on his friend who seemed defiant. They had never had such a confrontation before.

"Why not this season?" it was like his thoughts came alive, "Yes! Why not this season?" Aka looked up, matching his friend's gaze.

"*Agu*, don't play games with me. You know we have only a few moons before the season ends." Even Nwoye was taken aback by the suddenness his friend was adopting into this sensitive issue.

"*Alusi*, who says I am joking?"

"You mean you are prepared to take a wife in the next four moons?"

Aka got up, and stood face to face with his bosom friend. "You tell me why it could not be possible? Between you and me, we have enough brass rods to marry all the willing damsels in all of Ohafia."

"We?" Nwoye tried to clarify.

"Yes, you heard me right. Are you not even older than me? Do you expect me to marry before you?" This time aka was on the offensive; *...the hunter has become the hunted.*

"Alusi my very dear friend, why don't we do something that had never happened before in Ohafia?" This time his voice assumed a conspiratorial whisper.

"Why don't we marry together on the same day, from the same village, and from the same father?" he waited for an answer which did not come, because the man was looking confounded.

"I have it all worked out. Mazi Osita's beautiful daughters in Elu Ohafia will be our ideal choice. I remember that you were head over heels in love with Ifeanyi; I will take Uju." He strutted over to the shrub on his left to ease himself. It was then Nwoye found his voice.

"*Agu*! *Agu* my man. He that the hunters are shooting at but would be eating unflustered. The small smoked dry venison that fills the mouth to the brim. *Agu*; he whose back does not have business with the ground. *Agu*, you are indeed the true son of your father." Nwoye could not help but jump over to embrace his friend from behind who was rounding up his easing business.

By the time, they had taken their lunch of *aki na ukwa*; the sun had lost its biting intensity. They had also examined all other choices; to agree that Aka had chosen well for them. And they then took time to plot their plan perfectly. All this while, only a group of Abam traders in the company of some warriors went by. Aka & Nwoye knew that before dusk they will be home at their usual warrior pace. They loaded up again, and continued the final half of the homeward journey. They travelled in silence, each with his own thoughts.

It was not until they saw the hills of Ohafia basked in the final golden glow of the setting sun, that they relaxed their grips on their weapons, knowing that they were back in home and friendly territory With the end of destination in sight their tired limbs renewed their vigor and vitality, and it was then conversation resumed again.

"*Alusi*, don't you think it is strange that Onyeobia my father had never broached this issue of marriage with me."

"Not so strange, I may say. Some men are not so keen to labor their sons with what they consider as the shackles of marital responsibilities. Until the son involved willingly make their intentions known..."

"But your father from all indications did raise the issue with you." He interrupted.

"*Agu*, not all fathers are the same; they come in different shapes and sizes." Nwoye retorted.

"Sometimes, I am forced to agree with my mother that my father is privy to something we do not know. Now I have to include you with him."

Nwoye burst forth with good natured laughter, "I just think he is just being a man, who is totally independent, and allowing things to fall into place at the right time."

"I will present our proposal to him immediately we arrive. I hope he is better now from the chest pains he was complaining of at the time of our departure."

"I did not tell you, the herbs I rushed off to buy today from the *Igala* woman, are for him."

"Thanks that was very thoughtful of you. No wonder that he told all and sundry that he has two sons."

"And you have forgotten too that I also have two mothers." Nwoye wittily interjected, leading to further laughter.

"I had a dream last night. It was not a good one my friend. I saw Onyeobia from a distance waving at me. He was saying something inaudible to me and was pointing to Ihuoma, my mother who was crying but restrained by some women. I started running after him to hear what he was saying, when I woke up." He did not look back to see his friend's reaction, who remained silent.

They got to the fork in the main trail that led off to Amaeke, while the wider path continued to the other villages and to Aro and beyond. Strangely, they did not meet anybody, especially at this time when the weary villagers would be heading home from their farms. In the distance they could make out few smokes curling skywards from fires preparing evening meals. They had both travelled in silence since the story of the dream ended, their minds trying to find simplified answers to complex puzzle of the dream.

They involuntarily hastened down the trail that led downwards to the stream that served Amaeke as its entire source of water. They could smell and hear Amaeke midway uphill. Even though the shallow waters could be waded across; a massive iroko tree had conveniently fallen crosswise to provide a natural bridge that had been there over the years. The deeply thick foliage around the stream deepened in the twilight of dusk to give the coming darkness of the night no respite. Yet they met no one, especially the final last callers. That was quite strange and ominous.

As they clambered up into the open, in the final moments of dusk just by the junction of the tiny distinct path that plows through the overhanging foliage to the Agbala Shrine, was a ghostly apparition that startled them momentarily. It was the old and now gnarled Agbala herself leaning forward on her equally bald and gnarled staff. "*Nno!* Welcome, fearless lions of Ohafia." Her voice was surprisingly very strong, and indeed reassuring for the duo that

quickly collected themselves.

"Agbala, this is quite a special welcome. We are truly honoured." Nwoye blurted out, while Aka just nodded towards her; deep inside him he knew the worst had happened.

"Akachukwu, son of Onyeobia, won't you greet the mouthpiece of the gods."

"Agbala, I greet you, I was only taken aback." Aka's deep baritone resonated in the still late evening air, followed by Agbala's rustic cackle of laughter.

"Sentimental emotions not the best for a warrior of your caliber," she timely rebuked him, "you must always be prepared for the unexpected my sons."

The two warriors exchanged vacant glances, without betraying any form of eagerness. Agbala took the time to jangle her age-old staff.

"It is getting dark; the night is almost at hand when it will not be safe for mere mortals to be hanging about. The night comes with its own dangers. You men better run off, your wives and children are waiting."

"Agbala, you got it wrong there," Nwoye wittingly enthused and which was met by a raised all-grey eyebrow questioningly, "I mean, we are not married yet."

Yet came another bout of cackling that was supposed to be laughter but elongated with fits of phlegm induced coughing, "They call you the *Witty One*?" she questioned. Nwoye nodded in the affirmative.

"Agbala does not only see today; she has power to see tomorrow. Those Elu twins will make good wives for you. Are they not Uju and Ifeanyi?" She did not require any answer; their astonished faces told the whole story.

"And for you Akachukwu, your father is no more *the stranger*. You have finally given him the honour he *deserved*. Yes, read my lips; I said the honour he *deserved*." She swiftly turned around with a pace that beggar belief and hobbled into the dark foliage behind her that housed her shrine.

The friends did not wait to be prompted, they ran feverishly into Amaeke. It was like some giant hand cleared the familiar paths and square of the usual human presence. A lone wailing voice rang through the hills to usher them to the orchid-covered the Onyeobia enclave. It was as if the entire Amaeke emptied itself into the moderate compound. Onyeobia, Akachukwu's father was dead. He died sometime about noon earlier in the day.

CHAPTER 4

It had been exactly three moons since Onyeobia was buried. The day had started bright, dry and dusty; a thick clayey film covered everything in the open, from rooftops to treetops giving it a strange alien ambience. The few grassy patches that still displayed some form of miserable existence were masterly crafted in deep bronze-brown pastel; a far cry from their natural luxurious vibrant green complexion. Indeed the dry season had overstayed its welcome. Anxiety-ridden faces looked to the heavens for the slightest hint of rain, but no dice; the heavens were not yielding.

As the morning wore on, it became evidently clear that it was going to be yet another stiflingly steamy day. Then, all of a sudden, an unsettling calm enveloped the land. For a very brief moment, it was like all stood still. Even the birds held their breath and went quiet. The wind paused in its gentle stride; and the trees complied by standing still. Dark ominous clouds floated hastily in from opposing directions and converged over Ohafia; and the mid-morning sun disappeared from sight. Within the moment the animals and birds with a keen sixth sense would seek refuge from the brewing storm, the first massive drops of rain started splashing down.

What a relief? The first drops of rain quickly disappeared to placate the dry parched mother earth. It was when the earth was saturated enough the rain collected into little puddles that trickled into little streams that raced into miniature tributaries and rivers that flooded the land. Ohafia's first downpour of the rainy season came down with a fury and lasted all through the morning onto noon. And all of Ohafia safely stayed indoors to wait out the storm. And just as it had suddenly started;

it stopped abruptly. The volatile sun this time shamefacedly kept its distance.

The downpour had effectively cleaned up the dust-laden atmosphere and environment, and also tempered the humid heat. As Aka stepped out from his mother's hut, he could smell the crispy clean air, and savored its refreshing vigor as it filled his lungs. He dragged his father's favorite wooden reclining chair from its usual position under the orange tree into the open air. He swiped the hard wooden stems and twine contraption with the horsetail, whose primary assignment is to deal with flies. He made himself comfortable, and laid back gazing into the ocean-wide clear blue sky.

A flock of *lekeleke* (migratory wild geese), flying in their typical V-formation flew directly overhead. He involuntarily scanned his fingernails to see the white streaks that *magically* come with these mythical birds. His mind wandered to folklores of old that tell of distant lands and the mighty oceans that these mythical migratory birds transverse religiously every year. He envied their freedom and strength; or is it their destiny of daring adventures. If only they could speak; he would want to hear of the mortals that inhabit those distant lands. He closed his eyes to fully relish this singular moment of solace, since the demise of his father. The rains were indeed symbolic, he thought to himself; high time they washed away all the pain and tears for Onyeobia.

He had spent the entire morning, before and during the rain to discuss with his mother, who was scheduled to roundup today the stipulated traditional mourning period for her husband. They had broached many subjects especially that of his marriage, which he had reassured her that something, was in the offing. They did not even notice that the rain had stopped until Adaora came over to help her friend through the minor ritual of *de-mourning*. She must have all hair on her body clean shaven, and then took her first official bath since she started mourning over her husband. The coarse dark mourning regalia she had worn were to be burnt, to signify that she was now free to return to the normal swing of life. Marry again, if she so desire. And thereafter, she was expected to visit friends and family to appreciate them for their support during her time of despair. And it was that customary visitation she had embarked with her bosom friend that afternoon.

The events of the past three moons all flooded back. The news of Onyeobia's demise had spread through Ohafia as a wild fire at the end of the harmattan season. And just as Agbala had foretold; Onyeobia in death received more accolades and respects than in all his lifetime. Ohafia had never given such honour and privilege to any man considered to be a mystery *stranger*. Onyeobia's relationship too to Ogbu-isi accounted for all the attention and acclaim that was showered at Onyeobia's second burial. He was recognized as the adopted son of Ogbusi-isi Obidi Kalu, and the father of Ogbu-isi Akachukwu whose fames were acclaimed all over.

The *Ili Ozu* first burial; was usually an impromptu business due to the difficulties and complexities in preservative embalmment for the corpse. They settled for his father's room to be the final resting place. Early the next day, the male youth of the village expertly dug the grave as their traditional communal duty. By mid-day, the corpse was rolled up in *ute* (straw mat), and interred. After sorting out the corpse with the first burial, then an official date was picked for the celebratory second burial that had all the attendant pomp and pageantry.

As the plans went into top gear for the second burial proper; both Nwoye and Ogbu-isi Obidi Kalu stood solidly committed to give Onyeobia a befitting burial ceremony. Based on reliable information of intents, there were important matters to be met strategically. Nwoye, despite his witty nature was very thorough and meticulous in handling issues. With their combined wealth, money was not a problem; no costs were spared to meet a wonderful burial for Onyeobia. Ogbu-isi Obidi naturally assumed the honorable role of Chief Mourner.

Mazi Okala, the *Eze Ogo* of Amaeke, led his people to throw their doors open to receive the numerous well wishers that thronged their village to pay their final respects to the father of one of Ohafia's greatest sons. Ogbu-isi Obidi's special role of chief mourner was quite apt; since it was by his endorsement and guarantee that provided the then young Onyeobia and Ihuoma a homestead in Ohafia.

The grand finale of the burial became a fan fair of sorts. The *ogo* or town square was jammed with a jubilant crowd that gathered from all of Ohafia. There was indeed excitement in the air as the different contingents of masquerades and dances from about five villages performed to all and sundry. The duo of Mazi Osita's pretty daughters led the dance troupe from Elu Ohafia; and their exhilarating performance of the popular *Udala Song* was electrifying. Aka was convinced beyond doubt that he had made the right choice; he took time to compliment them, and was careful not to betray any emotion. He took time to impress them.

The high point of the day was the much-touted display of the Ohafia warriors. As the distinctive notes of the *Akwatankwa* ensembles supported by the drum and the antelope's horn resonated through the air, people ditched whatever they were doing to converge at the *ogo*, to see the pride and glory of Ohafia.

The nine warriors resplendent in their black, white, and red *okpu-agu* (leopard cap) with an eagle's feather stuck into it, and clad only in a coarsely woven brief dark-blue loin cloths danced in. Their rippling biceps were strapped with a ram's mane, and broad hairy chests heaved and glistened with sweat. The fierce-looking warriors with each eye circled with white chalk, all had a fresh palm shoot clasped in their mouth, and each had a razor-sharp machete strapped to his waist. Balanced expertly on the leader's head was a large blood-blackened pot, and hanging conspicuously from the pot were five human skulls which wore the *okpu-agu*, and the ram's mane.

As the rhythm of the drum rose, so their blood boiled to the sounds of the *Akwatankwa*; galvanizing even the audience into a frenzied tempos of warlike postures. Aka smiled at the all familiar jerky short and abrupt movements of the warriors that culminated to the *ofufu*; which was the skillful art of making the thoracic muscles rebound in a rhythmic dance of its own accord. The cheering crowd all knew the warrior dance that provoked men to do what they must do as Ohafia men who are fearless and courageous as the lion.

Finally, it was time to perform the heart of the *Iri-agha*, which is the zenith of the Ohafia warriors' desire to return home with the heads of their vicious opponents whom they had felled in battle as testimonial trophies. It was the singular dexterity of the Ohafia warrior to be exceptionally skillful with his machete. The breathtaking clinical precision to decapitate a human being with a single clean slash of the machete, the ability to drive the machete through the atlas and C7 vertebrae of the cervical spine or neck, at the right speed and angle to sever the head neatly.

The warriors unsheathed their machetes in a synchronized fluid movement and menacingly approach the giant plantain tree that was transplanted that morning in the centre of the *ogo*. As the drum went into frenzy, the horn called out to an individual warrior to step forward and swiftly slash through the exposed trunk of the plantain tree. Eight machetes at the speed of lightning were almost a blur as they sank through the trunk. At the end, the plantain to the amazement of all stood intact. The drumbeats signaled the eight warriors away from the plantain; and their leader with the balancing act approached the plantain.

The crowd held its breath; because it was the moment of truth. He thrust his right index finger at the plantain trunk and before their eyes; it cascaded down into eight sections with the stump still in place. The mesmerized spectators went into a delirium of applause; and by the time the applause died down the war dancers had withdrawn back to their base.

Then the crowd dispersed expectantly to the various appointed places to an orgy of eating and drinking. At the end of the day, everyone agreed that it was the best burial they had attended in so many years.

CHAPTER 5

Somehow and somewhere along the line, Aka had dozed off in the reclining chair during his reminiscences, and had this vivid dream. He and Nwoye had gone ahead as planned to marry the charming daughters of Mazi Osita in an enchanting wedding that was indeed a first of its kind. And within the first four rains, both wives safely delivered three children each. It was an all-girl ensemble for Nwoye and an all boys with his conspicuous six fingers for himself. It was yet another tale that kept tongues wagging all over Ohafia for a considerable time; as the birth of the six children received every manner of interpretations; sometimes bordering on the crass and mischievous. The bosom friends took every story in their strides, bonding and cementing their families closer; to do most things in unison.

From the time the oldest boy was about four rains, Nwoye took the boys everywhere with him; teaching them from hunting, fishing, to farming. You would hardly see Nwoye, without the three boys in tow. At a point, some people playfully referred to them as the boys with two fathers. At ten rains, the boys had shown exceptional proficiencies in different fields that baffled and amazed all and sundry. They were a joy to behold.

Then came one temperate harmattan evening, when the two friends took the boys out for a stroll in the countryside. They were playing a game of bird calls and cries, when they saw a flock of *lekeleke* approaching overhead. They all, including the adults chorused the *Lekeleke Song* as they flapped their hands in anticipation;

Lekeleke give me white nails
And take away my black ones...
Lekeleke give me white nails

And take away my black ones…

And to their utmost surprise, three of the birds that made the tip of the V-formation of the migratory birds swooped and landed amongst them. The lead bird quickly pulled Nwoye aside, and forced him to perch upon his back. By the time Aka noticed what was happening, the giant bird was already accelerating to take off. He quickly unsheathed his machete and pursued the bird with a mad fury; but alas it was too late as the big bird lumbered into the sky with his human cargo. Aka fell down tired and wailing his throat raw in defeat, as the white bird and his bosom friend melted into the horizon with the golden setting sun.

Tears streaming down his cheeks, he turned towards his sons, but only to find two of them already perched on the back of the second white bird, which was already taxiing to take off. Aka shouted and sprinted with renewed energy to intercept the bird but he was too far to make any impact. Seeing that his attempt to save the two boys was going to be an exercise in futility; he suddenly made a detour for the last boy who was being pushed to climb the third bird. He was screaming like a mad man when he lunged at the trailing left leg of his remaining son as the bird flapped it giant wings to lift into flight. In the din of flailing and slashing talons into his hands and body, coupled with wings beating down on his head, Aka held on steadfastly. His mind was set; he was not going to let go this time; except they kill him.

The combined weight of Aka and his son was beyond the bird's effort to overcome the earth's gravity to lift into the air. The evil bird swiftly chose the better part of valour to surrender; or lose its own life. It carefully swayed and shrugged off the boy and his father from its back. Aka and his son thankfully crumpled into the brush below. Aka with blood oozing from gashes all over his arms quickly checked out his son to assure himself that he was alright. Then he took the young lad into his arms and started weeping, warm tears like a deluge flooded down his face uncontrollably.

"What am I going to tell your mother?" He mused aloud.

"Father where have they gone? Where have they taken my brothers?" The young boy visibly shaken by the experience, innocently inquired.

"My son, I don't know. I have never seen anything like it before." He stood up and looked towards the west hopelessly. And his body shook violently, and he started to cry again.

"Father! Father!! Look." The young lad cried out excitedly. Aka's hand flew straight to unsheathe his machete, as he swung towards the boy. As he looked in the direction of the boy's finger, he saw a figure shrouded in a distinct white mist walking towards them from the twilight that had enveloped the east. Aka quickly pulled the boy behind him and took a protective stance.

"Akachukwu you must take heart", the calm voice floated out of the mist. Aka knew his father's voice. "Just look at you, Aka crying as if you were a baby. Please have a grip on yourself."

"But Father, what do you want me to do?" Aka inquired helplessly.

"You will never see your Nwoye again; but your sons shall return." There was a note of finality in the voice.

"How? Why? When would that be?"

"Questions, questions, questions. My son you always have more questions than answers." The old man reproved him.

"Father, but I need to know. This is not fair."

"Akachukwu, there is nothing you can do about it; life is not always fair. Have you ever wondered why there are preys and predators; the hunted and the hunter; the victor and the vanquished? It is your place to train them on every survival instinct, because they will need it to survive what lays ahead." The voice paused for the facts to sink in philosophically.

"Your boys shall all return home one day. They shall return like chickens that have come home to roost. The sixth finger shall point their way home. Akachukwu bear this message in mind secretly as the events unfold..." And the voice and the mist gradually faded to nothingness; as Aka screamed out in agony and pain like a panic-stricken animal ensnared.

He felt the soft soothing voice of his mother and her firm grip shaking him awake from his reverie. He involuntarily shivered to the cold air that blew across his sweat soaked brow. It was not possible to tell the time since the sun was not still visible, though the daylight was bright enough to show that sunset was still a while away. He was so relieved that it was only a dream. He relaxed to the homely presence of his mother and her friend, who did not betray any emotions.

"It is alright my son; it was only a dream." Ihuoma softly counseled.

"Mother, I am glad that it was only a dream. *Tu fia kwa*...I reject it"

"We return every evil arrow to their senders; they shall fail woefully." Nwoye's mother added for effects. Aka smiled to reassure the very worried women, that there was no cause for alarm.

Somewhere far off he could hear the distinct call of Nwoye's flute approaching the house. Trust Nwoye, their grand plan for the day was already in action. He quickly got up to rinse his face and mouth with water from the clay pot by the corner of the house. Thereafter, he went into his father's *obi* (hut) to prepare *nzu* (Kaolin) and *oji* kola nuts for the advancing visitors. It was agreed that Nwoye would bring along a calabash of fresh palm wine that he had tapped that morning before the rain. They had planned the day to officially unveil their plans to finally marry and settle down, to their parents and mentor.

A moment later Nwoye, his father, Mazi Ekwema, and Ogbuisi Obidi in tow sauntered into the compound. Nwoye had a small calabash of palm wine perched on his head, while his two hands were busy with the flute that serenaded their arrival. Aka jovially received them and led them over to the orange tree with its cane chairs and palm tree trunk benches. He went over to invite the women to join them. After the traditional welcome rituals of the *nzu* and kola nuts. A calabash cup of palm wine was handed over to Ogbu-isi Obidi to pour the libations and prayers.

Ogbu-isi Obidi cleared his throat three times to get their full attention. He lifted up the cup into the air, and brought it down splashing by purpose some palm wine on the ground.

"*Chukwu Okiki* this is for you; *Amadioha* this one is for you too."

"*Ise!*" the others chorused at every pause.

"And to you my people despite the demise of Onyeobia, we shall enjoy sound health." He paused for a resounding chorus.

"We shall be alive to our responsibilities. Let the eagle and the hawk perch together; and may the one that says the other should not perch, lose its wings."

"*Ise!*"

After the libations, the old man took time to pray for them individually. And more cups of the palm wine were poured for everyone. Though the sun was still not in the sky, but it was obvious that night was approaching fast. The old man decided to finally take the bull by the horn. He cleared his voice loudly again.

"I am glad that finally the official mourning time is over; so that the living can carry on with the business of living." The old man in his soft spoken voice chose his words carefully so as not to sound insensitive to his small audience. He carefully examined their faces to observe even the tiniest negative reactions. He found none so he continued.

"You all knew how I took Onyeobia as a son; the son I never had. With his early exit comes a heart-breaking void too difficult to fill." His voice staggered a little almost losing its composure to the emotions that over flooded him. His audience held their ground by tactically looking away from the old man that was obviously filled with grief. He regained his composure quickly and continued.

"Today, I am over seventy rains, and I cannot wait to carry your own children before I am summoned up to join our ancestors." He paused long enough to note their reactions.

"Nwoye and Akachukwu, you must give me a positive and effective response today, or be ready to bury me soon." He stopped abruptly to stifle any emotional eruption.

The silence that followed was indeed electric. The women huddled together relieved that Ogbu-isi Obidi had intervened in this pending very important over-flogged matter. Mazi Ekwema on the other hand avoided meeting their gazes and was furiously flapping his legs. Aka and Nwoye sat and pretended with feigned seriousness, as if they were giving a knotty matter the most desired attention.

Finally, after an interval that seemed like an eternity, Mazi Ekwema cleared his throat. Everyone looked up expectantly.

"Ogbu-isi! I thank and greet you. You will live long. You have truly spoken very well for all of us. Let them tell us their plans to marry this year." The women remained quiet but nodded in support of the flow of spoken thoughts. Up above them the skyline suddenly dimmed with the regular evening ritual of the hundreds of thousands of bats' exodus from their subterranean abode of *Ezie Ofri* Cave. This was a sure signal that the night was just around the corner.

With a knowing nod from Aka, Nwoye got up from his seat wringing his coarse palms together and smiling at the sullen looking adults. He took his time, to take a large gulp from his cup, then took time to examine the remaining contents; and finally decided to finish it with one swift swig. It was a vintage Nwoye, in his typical witty elements. He knew he was creating the right anxiety for the heart gladdening news they had surprisingly for them. They were all ears.

"I have good news for you all," he declared with so much glee which made the women to applaud with excitement. The men did not join in the excitement; there was an obvious air of suspicion. They nodded him to continue; and responded by dramatically clearing his throat loudly.

"Ndi banyi mma mma nu!" Nwoye greeted. "Iya!" They chorused resoundly.

"We had it all set up on during our last hunting expedition, only for the death of Onyeobia to put our plans in check. I and my brother have agreed to marry; and on the same day."

"Now wait a minute my young man; how do you plan to achieve that if we are the ones expected to lead you to the respective places you chose to marry from?" Ogbuisi Obidi inquired sternly while the rest nodded in agreement.

"Thank you sir, we understand the logistic issues, and that is why we are marrying from one family." The young man answered with confidence, now piquing their interests.

"May we know from which household that you have found your wives without our knowledge and approvals?" The old man was dead serious.

"Sir, we have taken time to do some groundwork on our own. We wish to have the daughters of Mazi Osita in Elu Ohafia."

"Nwoye, picking a wife is not as easy as u think. We your parents will search them out and clear them of any form of complications. There is so much work to be done." Mazi Ekwema spoke with so much pride in his voice.

"I don't envisage much work or problems," the puzzled looks of the other adults were directed at him "Mazi Osita is my mother's youngest sibling. My mother is from Elu Ohafia." Ogbuisi Obidi declared authoritatively, sprang sportingly to embrace his prodigies warmly.

"You people just leave everything to me; if it is the last thing I would do on earth, I must finish it." And more cups of the palm wine flowed to celebrate significant victory to all sides.

CHAPTER 6

Relying on Ogbu-isi Obidi's rock-solid filial connections to Mazi Osita of Elu Ohafia, the entire time and energy- consuming process of marriage negotiations was totally accelerated. So many unnecessary demands were tacitly waivered or mellowed down understandably since Ogbu-isi Obidi was immensely involved on both sides. And Ogbu-isi Obidi had a larger-than-life credentials and credibility. Long before they commenced the formal marriage process with the first introductory visit known as *Ibii Ncha*; the old man had consulted widely with his mother's people who by the matrilineal system take him as their own son. And all systems were GO.

Uju and Ifeanyi, when they were tactically intimated of the intentions of *Nnu na Ose*, were naturally ecstatic. The most eligible bachelors in all of Ohafia were asking for their hands in marriage. It was then only a formality when the girls with so much feigned prodding accepted the initial symbolic gifts from their respective grooms at the *Ibii Ncha*. This was the green light to commence the age-long negotiations.

After the *Ibii Ncha*, word got around about the fortunes of Uju and Ifeanyi. As they trooped to the stream in the morning to fetch water in their various groups they were the butt of many envious jokes. Uju at nineteen rains was older than Ifeanyi with two rains, and was able to hold her own in their obvious jokes. They knew that there was nobody who would not want to be in their shoes.

Since Aka and Nwoye were *Ogaranye*, which in the local parlance meant men of means; sponsoring the series of mandatory journeys to Elu was not a problem. Every journey cost money and special products that were presented to the potential in-laws. All hands were on deck to get them married in the shortest possible time, though age-long customs and traditions did not help matters. There were specific seasons and appointed days; that it was a taboo to conduct marriage ceremonies and certain social events; so they were left with a tiny window to work with. They used the long intervals to add new huts into their individual compounds. Communal support was advanced freely from their age grades and the youth.

Even with the enhanced acceleration of the complex procedures, it had taken almost nine moons to get to the *Ila Di* ceremony; it was the traditional wedding proper and the moment to finally escort the brides to their husband's home. Before that day, the girls did a three- month stretch of *Nkpu* or *Nnoba Ulo*; a moment of incubation to groom and fatten the brides as it was expected by custom. It was a stage that the girls were totally excused from household chores and spoilt silly. To round up the *Nnoba Ulo,* Uju and Ifeanyi adorned only with *jigida* beads around their waist were led to the market place on Elu's market day, to do some symbolic shopping. They were robustly fatter and fairer and received so many complimentary gifts from family and well wishers. With their beautiful hairdos and body painting, the grooms cannot wait to have their brides to themselves.

An advance party of close friends of the grooms was dispatched from Amaeke to Elu first thing that morning; their sole responsibility was to be certain that the *Ila Di* was a complete success. They had arrived Elu with a load of gift items that would facilitate their assignment later in the day. Amassed proudly outside Mazi Osita's house were a mountain of various household utensils, appliances, furniture, and foodstuffs. As the evening approached, the mountain of gift items continued to increase in size; it was a simple message to the families their daughters were going that they did not come empty handed.

Finally, the exceptionally large entourage was all set to depart for Amaeke, after the brides were pacified with the first of the gifts by the Amaeke advance party. Amid genuine flowing tears and *crocodile* ones dulled by popular songs and choruses; the party saunters off through the front door; which received loud cheers and ovation. It was symbolic; A back door alternative exit would have meant that the brides were already pregnant. In the walk through Elu, the praises were for the bride's mother, to have brought up model daughters that would be Elu's worthy ambassadors.

No matter the short distance between their house and the destination the journey would be elongated by theatrics of the brides; who must then be spurred on by more gifts. It was already dark when they arrived Amaeke; but Amaeke was keenly waiting to receive their brand new wives. After the brides had been received in their husband houses; the escorts settled down at the central square which had a massive bonfire already burning. Everyone was feted with surplus foods and drinks; then came the entertainment that had a mock wrestling contests, games, songs and dances; that kept everyone engrossed all night.

In the morning the larger part of the escorts returned to Elu, leaving behind only four very close friends to help the new brides settle down properly in their new homes in about three days. Within these three days, the bride and groom would have to wait very *impatiently* to finally sample their new found conjugal rights. Though, how this unusual custom was enforced during these short but definitely long days and nights beggar belief...

Three moons later, when Ogbu-isi Obidi led Mazi Ekwema and other close family members back to Elu to do the *Ikwu Eku Nwami*; the payment of the bride-wealth, both Uju and Ifeanyi were already pregnant. Though this information was not revealed to them; the old man could tell from the very high spirits of his prodigies that something good was in the offing, as they walked them to the stream crossing.

"Eh! Eh!!" Ogbu-isi Obidi yelled alarmingly at one of the young men carrying the kegs of palm wine that is a requirement for the Ikwu Eku Nwami. "All of you be very careful; please no balancing acts. Make sure you have your two hands supporting the calabash."

"Ogbu-isi there is no cause for alarm; we have more than enough in case of any accident." Aka tried to placate the old man.

"My son, I wish it was that easy," the old man lowered his voice to a dramatic whisper, "if any calabash with palm wine fall and break; the marriage must be aborted."

"Why sir?" Nwoye quickly queried. They were now by the tree trunk bridge, so the old man stopped, knowing the grooms were not going beyond that point.

"It simply means the gods are not in support of the union, and they washing their hands clean off the marriages." The old man swiped a stubborn fly off his head.

"Ogbu-isi just one more question before you go. Why did they keep the payment of bride-wealth at the end; I thought it should have been the first thing to settle?" Aka asked quickly holding the old man back, since the rest of the party had all crossed over to the other bank.

The old man smiled mischievously and winked at his boys who had grown swiftly over night, "Now that you have tasted, tried and proven that the products are up to the task; won't you be happy to pay even more for your seeds that are already germinating. We call it the negotiating advantage for your in-laws; now you can pay better." He burst out laughing as he pushed past the dumbfounded men onto the bridge, and sprang athletically across..

CHAPTER 7

From his own reckoning, Aka felt his marital responsibilities did not start with Uju, his wife. He had inherited first through the early demise of his father, Onyeobia's marital responsibilities without the exclusive conjugal rights he enjoyed with Uju. As a bachelor with all his wealth and status he had no responsibility; since his father by all standards was quite privileged and capable to take charge of all his marital responsibilities. It was without any warning then, that he took over the responsibilities of his widowed mother

If Onyeobia were to be alive he would have moved to his own place like Nwoye did; but there was no way he could leave his mother alone to fend for herself. Or even consider remarriage at almost fifty rains, which had the jeopardy of her *mysterious* origin. To him his parents' origin was never an issue; only a misty landmark in the journey of their lives. But, he was wrong, very wrong. It was during his marriage negotiations he knew; the people do not forget, even though they pretended to. In Ohafia, it was only when push came to shove; that the supposed forgotten and buried suddenly bubbled back to life and to be reckoned. Thank God for Ogbu-isi Obidi's involvement, and his masterly handling of the matter that later saved the day.

After over four rains in marriage; he had established that married life was very fascinating. With the added responsibilities, came the increased consciousness to work safe and play safe for the sake of the lives that were intertwined directly to his. He saw a cord that his debility or premature death would throw into discord. He had learnt the lessons from the bitter pills of his father's untimely death. Whether at home, the farm, the forest, or at the market places his mind was focused on his family. He discovered that every new day was like a new leaf, with a life of its own. And just like no two leaves of the same kind were alike; no two days were neither alike. Since each new day came with its bag of surprises; Aka was always looking forward to the dawn of a new day. No wonder that time went by swiftly; the days gradually accumulated into moons; and the moons patiently translated into rains. And the rains, like rain drops in turn crystallized into history and the story of life.

Uju's arrival in the Onyeobia household was truly significant. She quickly filled the vacuum created by Onyeobia's permanent exit; and naturally took the place of the biological daughter Ihuoma never had. To Ihuoma, she was the happiest person; for she gained not only a daughter-in-law; she also got a daughter, and a close confidant. Uju was by nature a very nice person, and would go out of her way to be very helpful. No wonder the women struck it off on a very amiable note from the onset. Their relationship blossomed day-in and day-out to become the subject of envy and discussions. Aka would sometimes feel like a stranger between his wife and his mother. He remembered vividly, how Uju took-in during their honeymoon; it was his mother who got the news before himself. There was no argument he had ever won were his mother was the arbiter.

Recalled how his mother due to the pregnancy news barred Uju from all household chores and even farm work for over three moons. "Aka my son, please we must keep Uju protected for our new baby o." She declared with exhilaration.

"Who told you she is pregnant?" he quizzed comically looking suspiciously at her.

Ihuoma knew that she must have let the cat out of the bag, and quickly resorted to offensive feminine wisdom. "How dare you ask your mother, who carried you in her womb for nine whole moons, such a stupid question?"

Aka quickly beat a tactical retreat, "Ah! Mama I was only pulling your legs, how did you know?"

"Have you forgotten that I am a woman? I can smell a one moon pregnant woman as far away as Ebem or Abia." She burst into a hearty infectious laughter that did not infect her son to say the least. "You are right then; Uju must be protected at all cost. We don't want anything to happen to our first baby." Aka spoke thoughtfully. "That means we must all co-operate with her; to excuse her from any tedious chore. You don't worry; I am capable enough to handle all her chores." Ihuoma reassured her son.

It was this situation that gave Uju all the chance to practice a vocation she naturally inherited from her herbalist-maternal grandmother as a young child. Folk medicine depended solely on the use of home remedies and procedures that had been jealously guided and passed down from generation to generation to the very few chosen ones. The witch doctor appellation and dreaded antics were deviously created to protect a vocation that took care of the community's health. It was due to these unsavory attachments she had secretly withdrawn from the practice. She had always felt over the years, to refine and improve the skills that were faithfully handed over to her.

Despite her passion for herbal medicine; she hated those lonely trips into the damp forest with all possible and probable risks to collect rare herbs. As an ardent lover of aesthetic gardening, her secret dream was to plant a home garden full of these herbs to keep her relatively away from those eerie shadowy forests. Observing the sparse orchard in her husband's compound; she knew that her abandoned romance with folk medicine would resurrect again. All she could see was the picture of her lush herbal garden complementing the scanty orchard. She kept her plans to herself to avoid been branded with the witch doctor appellations and sorts in her new home.

And in no time, she deftly put her plans into action. In the simple aim to beautify the compound she got a very willing and unsuspecting Aka, to map out the compound effectively, with a short wooden stockade and rocks. By the time they finished initial works; the footpaths and free entertainment areas were distinct and cordoned from the greenery. Uju's strategy was to hedge behind the stockade with familiar beautiful flowering herbs and spices without raised eyebrows; because spices had been generally employed for seasoning and flavoring food, and broadly for beverages. Both Aka and Ihuoma were inadvertently actively involved in soliciting from neighbors for the first batches of lemon grass; aloe vera; pencil cactus; bitter leaf; scent leaf; hibiscus flower; goat weed; false thistle; alligator pepper; black berry; and so on.

Soon after, everyone especially the friendly young women in Amaeke were trying to outdo each other with their voluntary fauna donations to get the attention of the most beautiful young wife in their community. Uju would never turn anybody back with one seedling or the other; she would with feigned interest listen to their instructions and qualities in other wider applications in the treatment and management of diseases. With the hedges completed Uju still had more than enough fauna to graduate to well set out patches for the shrubs and trees like;

lime; lemon; cocoa; African bush mango; cam wood; African breadfruit; various palms; various plantain; mustard; bitter cola; etc.

As she was exempted from chores due to her developing pregnancy; she had ample time to gradually stock up her gardens with more rare medicinal fauna she gradually garnered from the footpaths and in the bushes around. By now, none found her uncommon interest strange or related to the dreaded witch doctors. And by the time her first son was about to arrive, her well-manicured blossoming herbal garden was quite impressive to all and sundry; since everyone laid claim to one credit or the other. Uju felt so fulfilled in her husband and her new home. Ifeanyi, her sister was not fooled, but played along keeping her sister's secret.

There was a day she almost let cat out of the bag to Aka. Aka was in good faith condemning a particular plant to be highly toxic and should not be included in the garden. When she got carried away and decided to impress her husband with a lecture.

"My dear, every plant whether it is considered as good or bad has its divine purpose."

"My *Oji-ugo*, this particular plant is evil and deadly." Aka spoke authoritatively with self-acclaimed bravado.

"Nma, please listen to me, you do not understand what you are saying."

"What do you mean, I do not understand what I am saying?" He was no doubt excited from the tone of his voice.

"When the plant is highly toxic, then it is highly preferred to treat diseases."

"Em! Tell me more, my Oji-ugo, I am impressed." Aka looked very somber.

"Yes, the generally nontoxic herbs are used to maintain or effectively manage the body's healing systems." She knew she had over spoken and quickly checked her confident flow.

"That is very interesting. Who told you that?" He was genuinely interested.

"From…well…from some of the people that gave me the plants and lessons." She stuttered and finally managed to wriggle free. She promised herself not to fall easily into an easy trap again.

As the garden of plants matured, she had acquired so many clay vessels and calabashes in different shapes and sizes to contain one dried product or the other of the plants. She got Aka to construct a kind of multi-leveled shelves from tree branches; and her various vessels hanging neatly or sitting neatly on them. She could identify and differentiate the seeds from each other; or the barks; or the roots; or even the leaves. There was no spice she did not have in her kitchen. Aka believed that Uju must have the biggest collections of spice and herbal beverages in all of Ohafia.

Aka could not help but baffle at his wife exceptional dexterity in her passionate handling of the plants. He was happy to find a beautiful wife with so many other skills. His children will be so happy to have their kind of mother.

CHAPTER 8

Uju did not have to wait long before her well kept secret blew up naturally in her face. It was actually a series of related events that happened about three moons after the birth of Obeleagu, her first child. The about mid-day sun was blazing fiercely, unperturbed by the strong breeze blowing across the land. Amaeke was virtually empty, since most adults and the mature children had all gone to the farms. Apart from the nattering colony of busy weaver birds on the three palm trees by the intersection up the footpath, and the occasional cockcrow that resonated uphill; a typical calm pervaded over the land.

Suddenly, a shrill feminine voice in anguish shattered the tranquil environment like red hot knife sizzling through a chunk of wax. It sent chilly shivers down deep into the hearts of all who heard the subsequent wails; somebody was in deep trouble. Uju, who was home alone, and was breast feeding the baby froze in fright. She strained her ears to make out the direction of the wails. It sounded close by, like from the Nwafor's. She quickly backed the baby, and hurried off in the blazing sun to her nearest neighbors' compound.

As she walked briskly past the intersection with the three palm trees, even the boisterous weaver birds were quiet. She could hear clearly excited voices mingled with the wails of death; and a few young men who were building a roof nearby ran into the Nwafor's compound ahead of her.

She met a rowdy scene inside the compound. Nobody noticed her entrance. The two women though struggling to restrain Nwafor's first wife, were wailing loudly with her. She noticed too that the young men who entered ahead of her were surrounding another person sitting on the floor under the shade of a cashew tree. She ignored the wailing women and approached the group of young men; who were actually trying to get some kind of information from Awele Nwafor, who was just about eight rains. Just then another woman came rushing from the back of the main hut with a pot of water that was splashed over the young girl.

Uju quickly assessed the situation, and decided to take charge. It was indeed an emergency situation that needed concise drastic actions to save lives. She had to raise her voice above the din; to ask the young men to clear from the young girl to have air. The young men though taken aback obeyed; while the wailing women were also shocked into silence from their loud business.

She knelt by Awele, and took her hands into her hands. She noted that the hands were warm despite their wetness; fever was setting in. She tried to relax the young girl who was no doubt in a state of shock. She spoke in a calm cool voice and felt her pulse that was beating rapidly. Looking into her eyes, she could tell that the pupils were not dilating yet. Then the young girl retched to vomit, though nothing came out. Nausea and vomiting; the symptoms were graduating towards envenomation. She gently pushed the girl back on the ground until her head was resting comfortably on an upraised root of the cashew tree. And as she made to stretch out her bent knee; she saw the typical two distinct puncture wounds oozing blood, on her left leg calf muscles.

Her brain went into overdrive; to recall the facts that were passed down to her by her grandmother for over twelve rains. There were over 2000 species of snakes that are all carnivores; though only 300 were venomous or inject poison in their bite. And out of these 300 only about five attack or bite without provocation. To administer herbal treatment effectively; it was important to see the snake dead or alive. Early identification timely tackles the varied targets of the particular venomous; some damage the tissues at the site of bite; some end up in dangerous internal hemorrhage; some attack the heart and the blood circulation system; while some destroy the central nervous system.

To cross this hurdle she must get the girl to talk, or get the young men to search for the snake and get it dead or alive. Uju was still considering the options when the girl mumbled something inaudible. She strained her ears to decipher the disjointed words.

"It bit me…I saw it trying to enter the chicken pen…so I stopped; but the fine small snake turned around and chased me, and bit me…it made some funny scratching noise…" the voice did not stop, it just faded out.

Uju knew immediately who the culprit was. She knew that this aggressive profile and character was the call sign of the most dangerous snake in the land. Its most lethal venom was potently disastrous from the points of bite to even the internal organs. It was the carpet viper. And every moment counted; it could mean the difference between life and death. All these happened in a flitting moment.

As she touched the now swollen bite site, the young girl winched in obvious pain. Uju took one final look at the anxious faces around watching her every move. She bent down further and put her lips about the wound and sucked with all her might. She stopped and spat out a dark brown gob. She sucked again' and spat out a now lighter coloured gob. She sucked a third time and spat out pure blood. She then rinsed her mouth with water from the pot that was splashed on the girl earlier.

She then asked for a rope; and firmly tied it a little above the knee to drastically reduce blood flow from the bite site to the heart. She then asked the young men to look carefully around the hen pen for the snake. She warned them to be very careful, even when the snake is killed, because it has the ability to still bite within a short time after its death. She made it clear to them that they were dealing with the most deadly snake in the land.

She walked over to the women who were huddled together looking totally dumbfounded. "Please Nne Awele relax, your daughter would be fine. I am going over to my house to get some herbs for her. Please no more wailing, it would affect her." She spoke calmly and sternly to the women. She then asked the youngest one amongst them to go with her. By now, more people had trooped in. "Please, nobody should be allowed to move Awele, by no means." It was a parting shot to nobody in particular, as they hurried-off.

By the time they got over to her compound she had worked out the portions she would need to prevent infection in form of antiseptic, another to detoxify the blood, and to strengthen the immune system. She handed a basket over to the woman with her. She fetched some garlic, uprooted a curry tree, some scent leaves, a clay pot of palm kernel oil; some dried goose grass, some goldenseal plant, and some dried Echinacea.

As they set off for the return journey, her baby was still sleeping soundly on her back; oblivious to all the events unfolding around his mother. By the time they entered the Nwafor's compound they were met with a loud ovation. The boys had successfully killed the small but beautifully patterned snake. And she was right; it was a carpet viper in its full glory.

She did not waste any time as she set about preparing the herbal remedies. By now more people had arrive to genuinely commiserate, or to satisfy their curiosity. Uju was indeed the cynosure of all eyes, for those who could not believe their eyes. Every one commented on her skill and dexterity with the herbs. They were also surprised that she was not shrouding what she was doing. She even asked some people to help her pound the roots and barks, while another was using the grinder to grind some dried seeds.

Mama Ihuoma was away to the farm; but she would not like it when she finds out that she went on a healing spree with her grandson tied to her back. She kept wondering what would be her husband's reaction to this event; that would spread through Ohafia as a wild fire no doubt.

CHAPTER 9

And indeed the news of the beautiful herbal healer of Amaeke Ohafia spread like wildfire and totally assumed monumental proportion. Awele Nwafor fully recovered, and totally regained her health by the third day, without any side effects. Within those three days, other people with health problems started consulting and receiving herbal portions that truly proved potent. She did not make any official charges; her treatments were totally free, and no hidden charges or sacrifices whatsoever. Neither did she put up with the gimmicks familiar with the witchdoctors. But the fulfilled patients appreciated more than in kind.

Mazi Nwafor in deep appreciation for his daughter's recovery gave a gift of a female goat. Mazi Edozie whose eight moon-old son *died* of convulsion, but was brought back to life with Uju's *Nchanwu* herbal combination; was gratefully rewarded with a cow. Mazi Nkata who had suffered from kidney stones and sexual impotence could not hide his joy when he was healed with a wholesome cocoa plant, cam wood, and milk bush herbal combination. He returned to thank her with a cock and a hen. There were others who could not afford to give her gifts, but they all received their healing.

Aka, who was away on his routine thirty-day hunting expedition, finally returned. Since the whole villages were buzzing with the testimonies of the healed, himself and Nwoye had heard the stories way back at the Abagwu Market session of their expedition. Though he did tell that to his excited young wife; and that they had taken time to study and analyze the developments exhaustively, without finding anything wrong with her taking after her maternal grandmother who was quite famous. He had listened attentively with gusto to her version of the sequence of events; with a bustling Obeleagu in his laps. He observed with keen interest that there were only very faint telltale bumps of where his son's sixth fingers were. The traditional amputation of tying tightly a string around the base of the finger after birth really worked, he thought to himself. She finally rounded up the well-prepared narrative. To Uju's greatest disbelief and utter relief, Aka was quite amused, and took her *new* revelation in his stride. He was quite impressed with his wife's new fame and status.

"*Ojiugo*, remind me tomorrow, to make us a bigger chicken pen."

"*Nma*, but that won't be necessary since the existing one is big enough."

"So you think; but you are wrong, very wrong my dear Ojiugo"

"Why my love?" she inquired naively.

"At the way you have started, you will be more famous than your grandmother." Aka burst out laughing, as Uju opened her mouth to talk, but the words failed to come forth.

"My dear have you forgotten whom you married? We are born to be great, just like this young man we have together. You just relax; we are all in this together." He got up and embraced her with his free hand. She was speechless.

"Not just the chicken pen; I will also include an exclusive enclosed area for the other livestock that will be pouring in soon. I will accompany you to the forest for the very rare herbs you will definitely need." He laughed heartily to truly calm her down, but they were interrupted by some commotion outside.

"That must be Mama Ihuoma; she is back from the farm." She declared off-handedly.

"No, that sounds more like a group of men. You hold the baby; I will go and investigate." He handed over the baby to her, and swiftly reached for his machete and cautiously stepped out of the hut into the shadows..

"*Udo adi kwo?* Is there peace?" Aka's voice reverberated with a masculine ring to the peculiar greeting of a primordial war faring community.

"There is peace, Aka our brother." The voices answered excitedly in unison, as Aka with a machete in his right hand stepped out of the shadows cast by the eaves into the dying glows of the evening sun. Caution, in this warlike society was more than a way of life; and it made the difference between the careless dead hero, and the chary living hero.

They were six men in the party; led by a man Aka recognized very well from the village of Ihenta. The other four were bearing on their shoulders a litter with a grey-haired man lying in it. On close scrutiny he discovered it was Mazi Anyanwu, the Ezeogo of Ihenta. They stood there looking quite a forlorn bunch as they waited to be welcomed into his compound. Aka's mind was engrossed with calculating the risk this kind of situation posed to his young wife and child in his absence. He was shaken awake by the voice of Mazi Anyanwu; who with obvious discomfort inquired.

"*Udo adi kwo?*"

"There is peace my brothers. Please come in, you are welcomed." He called out to his wife, as he sheathed his weapon, and approached them with a reassuring smile. As the litter was carefully laid down; Aka noticed that its human cargo's highly-oiled midsection was abnormally distended. And an unmistaken loud vibrating barrage of explosions emitted from its posteriors; then followed by a malodorous whiff that assaulted his olfactory system. Aka noticed the litter bearers gratefully slipping away from their obvious arduous task to ease themselves. Aka pulled some wooden stools over to where Mazi Anyanwu was writhing in obvious discomfort.

A little moment later Uju came hurrying out with her son safely hitched to her back. She was heading towards the man lying in the litter when she stopped abruptly like she walked into an invisible barrier. It was the putrid smell that was hanging over the sick man like a cloud; Aka thought she was going to vomit. Aka in one fluid movement intercepted his wife, who had recovered her composure in no time. Aka took the baby from her back and headed to a safe distance from the litter.

It took Uju a very short time to complete her examination and declared lightly that Mazi Anyanwu was suffering from an extreme case of flatulence; as against their speculations that Mazi Anyanwu was poisoned at a burial ceremony he attended a few days back. She reassured them that he was going to be fine by the time she finished with him.

She went over to the kitchen and returned with a pot of hot water, some salt, a small calabash containing the gin that was brewed from fermented palm wine, and a swaddle of *akwa-miri*. The local gin was a rarity that was only acquired at Eke Abagwu through the Ijaw traders; because Ohafia and the Ibos in general were alien to any knowledge and method of the distilling process. She added some salt into the hot water, then a sizeable portion of the gin. She swirled the mixture in the pot with the *akwa-miri*, immersed the coarse cloth totally into the mixture. When she was satisfied with the temperature, she applied the soaked cloth over the abdomen; while the sick man responded to her efforts with some lethal salvos from his behind again. Uju quickly hurried off either to escape the now familiar pungent smell or in genuine haste to follow up the next course of treatment.

She returned not long after, with a small basket and went ahead to identity the contents to her gawping spectators as; ginger, lemon, cinnamon, pumpkin seeds, honey, fennel seeds and cardamom. In no time she had a portion ready for Mazi Anyanwa to drink propped up. She politely asked the men to move farther away, because her patient was going to react very soon to her medication with an avalanche of more very uncomfortable discharges. She was still talking when a loud barrage of sounds of escaping gas rented the air. And before their eyes the largely swollen belly gradually deflated in size. And as the sun made to dip over the western horizon, the relieved man was led over to the small back house to offload a mountain-load of putrefied meat and food he had over indulged a few days back.

It was indeed a miracle to see Mazi Anyanwu walking back unaided. Uju handed him a bowl of lukewarm water to drink and to rinse out his digestive tracts. And she declared to the amazement of all; "That is all!"

"How much is the bill." Mazi Anyanwu inquired gratefully.

"Nothing." Uju answered off-handedly

"Nothing?" the old man asked in utter incredulity.

"Nothing, our father." she said with a shy smile.

"You must be joking. You can't be serious." he looked questioningly at Aka.

"Ezeogo, please my wife charged you nothing. We are truly honoured to be of help." Aka spoke with a note of finality as he herded the party of very relieved individuals into the early night as a crescent moon smiled down on them and illuminating their path home..

By the time Obeleagu grew older, and the other babies followed, it was very natural for them to receive both formal and informal training from very tender ages on folk medicine. The *gardening hobby*, as her husband would often say; was passed down to her children; as early as when they could barely walk. As they spent so much time with their mother tending the *garden*, it was natural that they picked up a trait that would be to their advantage. Obelagu, at four rains, even with his limited vocabulary, could identify some of the herbs by their scents and textures blind-folded.

CHAPTER 10

It was the sixth rain of his marriage; and Aka knew that he was yet under thirty rains of age. He could not have asked for more, he reminisced. Uju, his beautiful wife had safely delivered her third child; and they were all males. The first son, he dutifully named *Obelagu* (the little lion), after his bosom friend who gave him the *Agu* appellation. The second son he named *Chukwumaechi* (God knows the future), and the third son he named *Chukwukadibia* (God is greater than the witch doctor). And the once relatively silent compound; was now filled with the cries and laughter of children. Ihuoma his widowed mother; could not but tell any willing audience of how God had favored her and her household.

Uju had become quite popular and famous all over the land through her folk medicine vocation. Even though, they had maintained the "no charge" policy; the fulfilled patients had outdone themselves to reciprocate the kind gestures. The testimony of their success was in the livestock pen that had expanded in leaps and bounds since its first expansion. It was now commercialized in a scale even larger than their own imaginations; their large varieties of livestock now catered to all manner of events and ceremonies. Aka and his wife were by all means and standards, considered a very privileged class in all of Ohafia.

Ifeanyi, Uju's sister and wife of Nwoye, too had over the rains given birth to three children; all were girls. Aka had keenly observed the sequence of unfolding events with a renewed sense of serendipity. The births were bizarrely following a very familiar pattern that was engraved in his memory. Even the past seven rains had refused to obliterate the vivid dream; Aka could not but recall vividly the haunting *lekeleke* dream all over again. He had not mentioned it to anybody, just as he had promised his father's ethereal apparition. He had wished and prayed for the unborn Chukwukadibia to be a girl; to at least contradict the course of the dream, but no dice.

On the other hand; the rest of the puzzle was effortlessly falling into place. Nwoye and the boys were becoming inseparable as they grew older. Whenever Nwoye came around, the boys were all over him like bees and flowers; demanding for one endless folklore or the other. And he noted with some modicum of umbrage, that with Nwoye's witty qualities coming to the fore, the boys were even more relaxed with Nwoye than him. He made so many feeble surreptitious attempts to tear the boys away from Nwoye, but they proved abortive. When his wife and mother raised eyebrows in his stealth moves; he had no choice but to capitulate the entire mission.

He spent many-a-sleepless-night pondering over this particular dream and its realism. His main anguish was walking alone in this quandary, and it was tearing him apart. He had started showing strained signs of trepidation over Nwoye and the boys going out of his sight. So far, the dream had become so realistic to be wished away like so many gray and faded dreams. If the mere thought of the climax of that dream was totally excruciating and unacceptable; its realization was agonizingly unbearable. He must get help from a neutral source before he runs mad.

"Ogbuisi Obidi Kalu; yes it is time to consult with the grand old man with all his wisdom." Aka thought out aloud, as he puts on his *okpu-agu* (cap), and took the horsetail flywhisk, and stepped out of his room into the courtyard. He saw his mother playing with *Chuka* in her laps, while Uju was picking beans in a straw tray under the orange tree.

"*Nna Obele* are you awake? I thought you were taking a nap." Ihuoma his mother called out with obvious display of maternal love as he approached them.

"It is well my mother; sleep did not come as planned."

"I will make you some hot pepper soup with special herbal spice to take care of your sleep disorder. I noticed how you were tossing and turning all through the night." Uju looked up with genuine concern, in the din of bleating goats in the background.

"Where are the other boys?" Aka inquired softly from his wife. "Oh! They went to the town's square with your *Alusi*..." "What? Uju, didn't I make myself clear about my sons not going out of this compound without my knowledge?" Aka cut her short fuming and red in the face.

"You were sleeping, and it was Nwoye's idea..."

"Whose idea?" he interrupted the exasperated woman, "I am their father, and I make the rules. Nobody, nobody else!" Aka walked off, and out of the compound leaving behind a trail of fury in the air. The two women could not understand the unwarranted outburst and anger over a very trivial matter. It took a while for their shock to wear out.

"This is very strange; I have never seen him like this. What is biting him?" the older woman ventured.

"I don't understand too, but why is he taking it out on me." And Uju burst into tears, upsetting the little baby to burst out crying. "It is alright my daughter. It is not about you, it is not even about Nwoye. It is definitely something beyond your husband. I know him very well, it is a frustration that he displays when a problem is beyond his control." She handed over the baby to her daughter-in-law to feed and ambled over to her hut.

Uju, pondered over what the older woman proffered, and tried to make a rational excuse for her husband's rash actions. Never in the past six rains have they ever had any misunderstanding whatsoever. She must get to the bottom of it, she thought.

By the time Aka approached the intersection with the three palm trees, he was so ashamed of his unnecessary outburst. He was so remorseful that he almost went back to mend things with his wife. He knew his mother would do some groundwork for him by the time he came back that would make the peace mission much easier. He walked on, surprised to see that the footpaths were deserted as he approached the town's square.

He heard the cheering crowd before he reached the square, but at the last moment he decided to avoid the square for obvious reasons. He did not want to run into Nwoye and his boys. He took a detour by the massive Iroko tree at the front of Mazi Ubili's house and made a diagonal routing across some small patch of forest that was the shrine of Eke Orie. The path through the shrine was totally deserted, since most people steered clear of it, for eeriness. Ogbu-isi Obidi's compound was only a stone throw away.

As Aka navigated the last bend to Ogbuisi Obidi's massive orchard-filled compound, he saw in the distance beyond the entrance, a receding lone figure with a walking stick. There was no mistaking the very familiar gigantic frame and gait of his mentor and master. He knew the old man was on his customary evening stroll that only a storm had ever stopped him over the past seven rains or so. This outcome was indeed ideal and well-suited for the purpose of his visit. As he went past the familiar entrance into the compound; he stole a furtive glance inside, but did not see anybody outside. There were a couple of grand children staying with Ogbuisi Obidi and his wife of so many rains.

Aka was so anxious that he could have run to intercept the old man before he made a detour not on his usual route; but that would be a story for the familiar faces that had all greeted him with respect; some even stepping out of the way where the footpath was too narrow. He knew the old man was heading to his favorite spot on the hilltop. He had accompanied him there so many times in the past.

Aka slowed to a sedate pace to match the old man's leisurely walk, as he tried to work out the best approach to introduce the subject that was almost tearing him apart. The uphill task here was how to broach the issue without dishonoring his promise to his father's spirit. He had precisely kept the twenty paces he conjectured to be between them. It was strange, Aka wondered to himself, why the old man had not even looked back even once.

The old man paused in his strides to look interestingly up a palm tree after Ezeogo Okala's compound. Aka could not help but also stop in his tracks with nothing to do. The old man then suddenly turned around and faced him. He was not smiling; his face was dead serious. Aka felt like a young boy caught red-handed with his paws in the soup pot. He tried to mumble some form of greeting that did not achieve its objective.

"Yes?" the old man inquired, "Akachukwu, what is it?" That was the old man for you, he never called him by any other way or name but the full AKACHUKWU. The same he did with his father; whom he never called Onyeobia, but his full given name of Ofobike.

"I knew that you have been following me, so I had slowed down for you to catch up, but you too slowed down. What is worrying you my son?"

Aka could not reply. All his well thought out plans of approach were falling apart. The old man with genuine concern continued.

"I hope it is well with your wife? You were suppose to be sleeping; or did she wake you up?" he turned around and headed towards the hillside, with Aka following suit.

Without the penetrating eyes of the old man boring into him; Aka mustered enough courage to retort, "How did you know I was sleeping, sir?"

"Some people have eyes that see beyond the ordinary," the old man burst into good natured laughter just like the days of old, when Aka was just a little boy running to keep pace with him in the forest. "Your brother came calling this afternoon with your boys. I can't believe how fast those children are growing. It is a pity that Ofobike is not alive to enjoy them with Ihuoma…," the old man paused in mid-sentence as the footpath terminated abruptly.

They burst through the dim light under the canopy of trees, into the most breath-taking panoramic view splashed out in the unobtrusive evening sun. The effect had always been the same. It never fails to mesmerize and enchant both the old-time and first- time visitor alike. It was solid dead end.

They were standing on an almost bare rocky-granite ledge that could stand seven warriors side-by-side; on one side was an impregnable grey rocky incline towering overhead, while dropping off on the other side of the ledge in a sheer rocky cliff. Beyond the ledge's edge was a lush green valley spread out like a giant canvas spreading into an horizon of hills. Flowing out at the base of the rocky incline was a spring; that collected into a waist-deep crystal- clear pool in a rocky trough formed at the base of the rock. The over flowing trough cascaded down the cliff-face into the valley below. The fall's cooling effect and its accompanying splashing musical conundrum created a therapeutic harmony that wholly calmed the mind. The evidence of the streams created by the mergence of the fall and other sources of ground water were distinctly highlighted by the deeper and bolder hues of green furrowing through the green valley. The serene blue sky overhead spread into the horizon with different shades of blue that was beyond characterization. White turfs of smokes spiraling into the sky tell of other human settlements in Ohafia and beyond. Strangely, the sky was devoid of birds in flight, though their varied calls filtered melodiously through the air.

They stood still as usual in wordless veneration, drinking-in and savoring a peace and beauty beyond any human comprehension. It was worth the entire journey. They then went over to drink from the very refreshing ice-cold spring, and then settled down on the rocky outcrop by the pool overlooking the valley below.

"So as I was saying," the old man continued as if he never stopped talking, "it is sad that Ofobike is not around to enjoy the children with Ihuoma." Aka remained silent since he did not have anything to say.

"Akachukwu, you know I saw him and my father in a dream some days ago. He was particularly welcoming me into a very big new house. While my father just kept mute and smiled; your father was doing all the talking asking of you and your mother." He paused to see if his protégée would make any input but none came forth.

"My son, I know my time is almost up to leave this world and join them." The old man said calmly, to Aka who looked bemused.

"How did you know that your time is up?" an obviously very shaken Aka finally voiced out.

"The dream. Yes through the dream, my son. It is by dreams we obtain divine revelations. They are indeed the emblematic lingua franca of the future. And all dreams have some elements of admonition of impending events." Ogbuisi Obidi paused to use his fly whisk.

"Does it mean the events in a dream are beyond the control of the dreamer? Aka asked with caution.

"Yes and no." the old man answered candidly.

"What do you mean? I don't understand sir."

"Our people have a saying; *that dreams are indeed the shadows of the future stretching into today.*" The old man declared authoritatively.

"How does this saying happen in dreams?" Aka sounded very obstinate.

"It has been proven that as we sleep, our mind is not just very aware of heat, light, and sound around us; it is also supersensitive to days and rains ahead of the waking mind." The old man looked at Aka who did not show any sign that he understood what he was saying.

"For instance, dead family member emerging in dreams is more often than not to warn of distress or danger in advance. Comprehension of the dream figuratively and literally; would enhance realistic counter measures that might ward off the distress or the danger partly or completely." He noticed Aka nodding intuitively.

"Why then is a dream shrouded in so much complex interpretation or translation?"

"Akachukwu, do not forget that just as thoughts flow from your visible intellect; so dreams in turn proceed from the invisible intellect. Just as our verbal expression of real events fail sometimes; so our interpretation of dreams fail to portray effectively the future events." The old man paused again to scratch his crotch.

"Good. Now, how about the *no* aspect in your answer."

"Yes, some dreams are actually for your information, there is nothing you can do to avert the future event. You can run but you cannot hide from the reality of life; spiritual power is not only superior but will triumph over the physical body. Like my dream that I just told you a moment ago…we will just wait and be prepared for my ultimate demise from this world soon." The old man concluded. "Does it then mean that our over attachment to the visible mind which always comes in contact with the future before it comes to be." Aka was rudely interrupted by the splatter of a small white watery mass by his feet. It was bird droppings; and they both looked up over head to see the culprit. Lo and behold; the distinct v-formation of about thirty migratory wild geese heading on to the setting sun; a grim reminder of the *lekeleke* dream. This was more than a mere coincidence, it was a direct non-complex confirmatory revelation from the gods.

There and then, Aka resolved to himself, to fret no more about his dreams, but to wait and see how the gods would play out the future; with or without his physical involvement. And a sort of peace and calm; a serenity beyond his understanding settled over him. It was indeed time to let go of the dream, and let in a new lease of verve into their lives.

CHAPTER 11

And life indeed returned to uncomplicated normalcy for Aka and his family. He first made peace with himself and then the others. And you would think, that would have been a happy ending to the very sad and disconcerting occurrences; but destiny was just about to commence its own gambit. It all began with Aka's decision to adopt a *sit don* look attitude. Now, it would be unfair to term Aka's new found behavior lethargic; but everyone noted with concern Aka's new attitude to observe events and happenstances with some degree of wisdom without betraying any atom of emotion.

It was like accepting every occurrence in his strides. Never going out of his way to insist to have it his way. If he was hard- pressed to react with any form of utterance, he would say; *its working out accordingly*. Uju, would sometimes mutter out of frustration; *according to what or whom?* It was as if he was an integral part of some form of silent conspiracy. It reminded his mother of his father's attitude after the birth of his son. She would readily tell her daughter in-law; *there is something so familiar about his new attitude; that was how your husband ended up with his twelve digits today*.

Aka's three sons were all bequeathed with their father's very fair skin and the extra digits at birth; but they all had the traditional amputation procedure performed within days of their birth. As they grew older, only a darker skin-telltale-sign remained at the spots where the extra digits were detached.

Time had flown by for the boys so fast, that nobody could believe their very speedy development and progress. Aka had had to work out an ingenious way to keep stock of their ages. A fruit tree within the compound was openly dedicated to each child at birth. And over the years, Aka had religiously cut a notch to represent a rainy season on each tree.. At his last count, Obelagu had notched up 10; Chukwuma 8; while Chuka 6. "How time flies?" Aka thought to himself. He had stoically waited the minimum mandatory two years to process a new baby, without taking in a new wife. He was so happy and in love with Uju. Deep down in his heart he knew he was going to be a one-wife-man, even with all his affluence. Both himself and Nwoye had agreed to tow the same lines with their respective fathers; and provide the best for their offspring. And between the two bosom friends they shared the aspiration to provide the boys with the bests of survival skills and training.

So far, the boys had shown so much promise in their individual developments that they would give their father a good run for his money. He had noted with muted interest how competitive they were amongst themselves despite their age disparities. From every conceivable unbiased comparative analysis, the boys tend to be way ahead of his own development. He tried to console himself with the fact that his own development paled in significance maybe because he was an only child who had only adults for company.

The boys had all naturally mastered their mother's vocation of folk medicine without much ado. The other day when their mother was out on a visit with her sister to Ilu. An emergency asthmatic attack case was brought in; his concerted attempts to convince the highly distraught and despaired party to seek medical attention elsewhere did not yield fruit. |He recalled how his 10 rain-old son, Obelagu surprisingly stepped forward with a panacea that probably saved the life of the patient.

The young man, before him and the adamant party that were not ready to budge about departing; took some *Aku-ilu* (Bitter cola), *Inyinyi-ogwu* (False thistle), *Oroma-nkirisi* (lime), and some other ingredients which he transformed into a concoction that the patient out of desperation readily drank.

And within a very short interval before their unbelieving eyes the patient was totally relieved from the asthma attack. The very relieved people lifted up Obelagu upon on their shoulders and went into a dance of celebration. And when they asked for their bill, before Aka could open his mouth; Obelagu declared authoritatively that; "Nothing. No charge!" And so word of this feat spread out through Ohafia and the other settlements like a deluge.

Before the age of seven rains, they had already acquired also various farming techniques and methods, by accompanying the adults to the farms. Knowledge of the various farm implements and their effective maintenance. They had been taught and perfected the science of how to read the clouds and to smell rain in the air. They could decode the soil from just its look and texture, for the right purpose and optimum utilization. They had also within these first seven rains known every cardinal knowledge of the two most popular farm produce of yam and cassava. Yam was the more respected of the two; and why it was the most celebrated and honoured farm produce in Igbo land. Yam was even worshipped and sometime sacrificed to. Its effective storage in barns to last up to a year; and the production of seedlings by replanting the early harvested stalks, or by cutting up some tubers into angular bits.

Another aspect of their training was to do with what may be considered as the most economic tree, that a man could fight and die for in the land. It was the *Nkwu-enu* (Palm Tree). The boys knew early in life the distinguishing features that stood it out from the multitude of other species; because the palm was counted as part of a man's wealth and inheritance. It was respected as a tree with a thousand uses; from its top to its root no part is wasted. The boys were expected to reel off these practical uses from food to structural parts of building; medicine to the most important aspect of jollity; animal feeds to home and kitchen utensils; cosmetics to erosion controls etc. It was useful in its life of longevity and even more useful at death.

For most species and with age, harvesting the palm tree requires a very complex art and skill of climbing its very straight and branchless trunk. Whether it was the tapping of its sap that is better known as palm wine; or its palm fruits that come in a spiky bunch or its fronds that was also fortified by deadly thorns; it was a job that could easily be life threatening from a fall; or to the bite of venomous bees, wasps or snakes who make abode on the top of the palm tree. No wonder the popular adage the boys were meant to know by heart; *the palmwine tapper may not be a able to tell of all that he saw or sees at the treetop.*

Though people adapted many ways of harvesting the palm tree, but Aka and Nwoye taught the boys what they considered as the safest way to not only scale the height, but do business and to counter any dangerous eventuality up there. They chose the single twisted-creeper rope method; which the boys modified and perfected in no time. Before long, the Aka boys were reputed to be the fastest palm tree climbers amongst their various contemporaries.

Next on their training was the act of palm wine tapping. This was given ultimate attention, since wrong use of the tapping method may spell doom for the tree which would be considered as a premature business loss. Even here the boys performed exceedingly well, and above their mentors' expectation..

As each boy attained the age of seven rains; they graduated to hunting expeditions. As their mentors duly informed them; *Hunting and Fishing were the ultimate survival skills, since they take care of immediate survival that makes the difference between life and death.* They not only provided immediate food, but also cover from the elements. Each hunting expedition was calculated to last over 14 days; as they camped out in the forest, hunting, killing, and preserving. Then the moving over of the preserved products to one of the key exchange markets, which was the climax of every hunting and fishing expedition.

The boys were first taught the melodious and rhythmic Hunter's Chants and Prayers that were spiritual preparation exercises that energize, encourage, excite, and inspire the hunter before or during the *mission to kill or be killed.*

The next paramount part of their coaching was quality physical preparation of implements to supplies, as well as a good knowledge of the prey. Apart from the regular implements of spears, bow and arrows, machetes, traps twines etc; they were also taught the prime sources of neuro-toxic poison from plant saps, snake venoms, larvae and caterpillar of certain insects to lace the arrows and spears. The boys registered with interest how the *Iwelli* leaves and flowers crushed and scattered over a running stream, in a little while produced a bountiful hurl of fishes that succumbed to the anesthetic effect of the poison which does not hurt human.

Their next course of training was the act of tracking game, the traps and baits. The boys received instructions on scat or droppings, rubs and scratches, shelter entrances and exits, tracks and well- travelled trails, calls and signs; food and water sources. Since most animals follow the path of least resistance, to conserve energy, the boys were trained to set their traps accordingly.

Preparing a killed game for the fire and smoking was an important aspect of hunting and fishing that could not be over emphasized. The skinning and dissection needed a sizeable attention and focus, or else the entire expedition could end up in futility, if the products arrived the exchange market in poor conditions. This aspect of their training also exposed them to the various means of exchange, and to other people outside the Igbo land. The most prodigious part of their informal education here was the acquisition of basic arithmetic for use in daily life.

Nwoye had made for each boy; an ornamental necklace out of the claws of a leopard, which he formally presented at the start of each person's first hunting expedition. The years ahead proved that Aka and Nwoye's efforts were not in vain.

CHAPTER 12

And as the years borne on the wings of the rains flew by, like stormy dark and pregnant clouds hurrying to make a rendezvous, the boys developed and matured beyond their rains. It was as if the boys had a premonition of their appointment with destiny; they continued by the day to excel in every feat they had undertaken. It was apparent to all and sundry, that the boys were not contented with just following their *fathers'* footsteps and laurels; they were all set to outdo them. They had never experienced a dull moment in their lives, everyday was a bag full of novel ideas to be acquiesced. Just like the day Obiligbo Kamanu returned from his long forgotten *self-exile*.

It was an Eke market day in Amaeke, a market that held every four days. The square was filled to the brim with the sellers and buyers from Amaeke and its immediate environ. The sellers had started arriving just after dawn to take the best and most strategic positions, the latecomers would make do with whatever was left. The wares which were mostly food and farm produce were spread out on the ground in piles or mounds; some were in wicker baskets or on plantain leaves. Just one or two people were doing farming tools and implements like hoes, machetes, knives, swords, various needles, metal gongs etc. The rest of the sellers were into derivatives from the palm tree like salt, soap, palm wine, brooms, palm oil, palm kernel oil, etc. The market operated by barter only.

As the sun got right overhead you could hear the hum of the market from far away as the day enters its climax. Buyers and sellers haggled over every inch of ground. And since nobody was willing to go home without exchanging their produce for something they desire; there was no quiet moment when the market was in operation. All of a sudden, there was commotion in the market square, as people started running helter skelter. It was the wife of Mazi Ike who came running into the square, screaming her head off;

"I saw him. It is him. He is back" the middle-aged woman collapsed out of breath on to the sandy ground.

"Who?" A hundred voices asked in unison.

"Obiligbo! Yes Obiligbo, the son of Kamanu" the woman managed to answer again. "He is back live; and even looking worse than before!" the right dose of theatrics added for effects.

After the *larger-than-life* Obiligbo lost his crown to the much younger Aka; the shame and embarrassment was more than he could bear. After smarting from that defeat for two *long* days; Obiligbo decided to tow the better part of valour to leave the scene. So, on the third day after his dethronement, just before the break of dawn, Obiligbo quietly slipped out of Amaeke, and Ohafia for good. The story that followed later was that he had gone to study as an apprentice under the tutelage of the most prolific *Okpu-uzu* (Blacksmith) at Abiriba. And that was over 18 rains ago.

After so many rains, the older generation would mention the rapacious Obiligbo in their stories from time-to-time; to them he was history, a sordid part of Amaeke that must be discarded in the dustbins of history.

It was not until about three years ago, that somebody mentioned that Obiligbo was seen live in Arochukwu, and fighting as a mercenary. Initially, the story beggared belief since Abiriba, his original destination was up north, while Arochukwu was down south of Ohafia. On closer analysis, some also believed the story, since Abiriba and Arochukwu were closely related by ancestry *Nwajim*; and Obiligbo could as well followed the original path through the river, Otusu took his group through to find Arochukwu from Usukpam..

The 12-man party looking very disheveled, marched into the market place, closely watched by the crowd. The heavily bearded leader towered over every one in his party in bulk and height. A huge sword hung from his waist. His hair woven into massive chunks that were hanging down upon his shoulders, was complemented with a mat of thick black hair covering his entire body. Obiligbo had not changed much; the nose, the biggest African nose ever was still intact. Something was curiously very wrong with the face; it had a kind of grotesque fixed snarl from afar.

As Obiligbo came closer and turned the other side of his face. *Chei!* A shudder ran through every onlooker; his entire right ear and a chunk of his cheek had been bitten away. The beard had refused to grow back on the scar tissue that ran from the missing ear to his chin. It was as if he had been in a brawl with a lion. From all indications, it seemed as if Obiligbo relished the repulsive effect of the scare; as he matched pound for pound their timid questioning gazes with his intimidating one. The crowd was awestruck.

Shadowing Obiligbo's every move was a short and scrawny fellow with a pronounced goatee, and chalk-white circle painted over his left eye. He had a hyena's hide draped over his shoulders, on his waist was a thick band of amulets and charms fighting for space. He comically supported himself with a sturdy wooden staff with a human skull attached to the top. His head dress of cast iron had two vulture plumes in it. The rest of the party was made up of ten young men laden with huge baskets on their heads. They had only tiny pieces of some animal skin for cover.

Obiligbo carefully scrutinized the crowd for a face that he had longed to see but was not there. The crowd waited patiently for his next move that took them by surprise because of its suddenness.

"Amaeke, go and tell everyone that cared to listen that I am back. Tell them that Obiligbo is back and better." His voice was thunderously arresting. He paused and dared anyone to speak. None uttered a breath, so he continued.

"And let everyone know that I am taking over from where I left off. The man standing behind me is a *Dibia* of note; he is *Ezemuo* (the king of spirits). Try me and see that it will be at your own peril. There is no sickness he cannot cure." He chuckled malevolently to himself.

He scrutinized the market place again, this time his eyes stopped dead on the man with the iron tools and implements. He moved towards him and thundered.

"My friend who are you, and where are you from?"

"Me?" the timid looking fellow tottered, wondering why he was singled out by this overgrown bully for any kind of treatment.

"I hate people asking me questions. And let me take this to be a warning to those who are here, I detest people who answer question with question. Now, you answer me now, before I lose my temper."

"I am from Ihenta, and I am Amadi son of Okoli Ibe." The poor fellow not only looked but was a bundle of nerves.

"Amadi *nwa* Okoli Ibe," there was sarcasm in his voice, "I don't want to see you here on the next market day. This market cannot contain the two of us. And for the rest of you;" he gesticulated with an outward stretch of his hand over the market place and declared with a vigorous roar, "this spot is now permanently mine."

"Why so, sir?" A young voice stealthily filtered through the thundering voice of Obiligbo; and he jerked as if he walked into a solid iroko.

"Did somebody just ask me a question, or was it my imagination?" The entire market was dead quiet, that you can hear a pin drop. Then the silence was suddenly broken by his thunderous laughter, "I thought as much, it was indeed my imagination."

"No sir, it was not your imagination." The young voice shrilled out. This time Obiligbo felt as if he was slapped; as a male teenager stepped out from the crowd confidently.

"With all due respects sir, I believe all of Amaeke would want to know why Mazi Amadi must not appear here in the next Eke day, and why you want a permanent space in the market place?" The young man paused to see if the rest of the crowd was behind him; but they all quickly looked away mortified with fear.

"*Ka laa nwantoo*! (Look at this child)." The jarring voice belonged to the dibia, who spoke in his Abiriba Igbo dialect, was prancing about excitedly. "Somebody better take this child to suck his mother's breast before I dissipate him." The dibia tried putting his hand into the bag hanging on his shoulders.

Either the young man did not realize the danger involved in his confrontation or he did not care a hoot about his safety; because he just observed the reactions around him with open amusement.

"Do you know what you are doing, you small rat? You are playing with fire young man." Ezemuo brought out a red root which he began chewing vigorously, with obvious fire in his eyes. A bemused Obiligbo could not believe what he was seeing; that his first confrontation back in Amaeke was from a teenager.

"Round and Round,
With Our Feet On The Ground
We Walk Around The Pepper Plant
To Harvest It
Nobody Dare Climb It..."

The dibia commenced an incantation to wreck havoc on the young daring interloper who had dared the spirits for challenging his master, the great Obiligbo, but Obiligbo intervened before damage could be done.

"Ezemuo! Biko stop. Our people have a saying that; *if a man should wake in the morning and find a cock chasing him; he should do a rethink and run for cover, whether the cock had grown canines overnight.*" Obiligbo spoke philosophically to the dibia to take solace in his wisdom. The crowd was held spellbound with the unfolding events, while the young boy stood his ground not even winking.

"Pardon my manners young man, I truly apologize, I should have consulted with you first before my actions." Obiligbo's voice softened as he tactically approached the young man with a wicked smile playing on his lips.

"My name is Obiligbo. What is your name?" as he stretched his massive palm forward for a handshake.

"My own name is Obelagu, and that is my little brother Chukwukadibia." The young man spoke with the confidence of a victor, as he pulled his brother from the crowd.

"Obelagu, and Chukwukadibia, I am indeed honoured to meet you." He pronounced the names profoundly to fully absorb their meanings.

"Even though you were not born by the time I left Amaeke, you boys strangely look familiar. Who is your father?"

"Our father is Akachukwu; son of Onyeobia. My father told us that our grandfather died before he even married our mother. My other brother is Chukwuma he is at home helping my mother." The younger boy spoke quickly; Obiligbo's heart almost skipping a beat with all his revelations.

"Oh! That is quite interesting; I think I know your father now. He was em…em my friend." Obiligbo had to muster all his cunning ingenuity to hide the rancor and bitterness in his heart. Time to end this discourse tactically before he implodes.

"Now, you boys run along, we shall continue our discussions later." he had his bearlike paws paternally around their necks, but he rather felt like crushing them together, and brains splattered all over. "Tell your father that you met Obiligbo the *back breaker*, and that I sent my warmest regards." He winched at the sound and taste of those two final words.

"You have not still informed us, why you don't want to see Mazi Amadi in this market again." Obelagu inquired tenaciously.

The little brat, just like his father, Obiligbo thought to himself, then answered impatiently tired of his game of pretence. "Young man here before you is the best *okpu-uzu* in the land, and *your Mazi Amadi* and his business will die of hunger because his prices won't be able to match mine as a producer. I am only helping your friend." He resumed his mocking thunderous laughter to prove that the game is over.

But the young man was indeed relentless like a bulldog; he was not finished yet with this big bully. "You be very careful, today's Amaeke is different from the old one; I will advise that you find wisdom in the adage that says; *let the hawk perch, and let the eagle perch; may the wings of any that deny the other to perch suffer irreparable damage.*" And the boys walked away without another word.

Obiligbo was stupefied; he was at loss to what action to take. He just watched the backs of the two boys walking away from him. And he felt so humiliated and angry with himself. It was as if the elements were on his side as the sky overhead darkened with pregnant clouds suddenly. He looked up with apprehension into the sky, he could tell that a storm was brewing, just like the storm brewing inside his heart.

"Amaeke will never be the same again; because I, Obiligbo is back for good, whether you like it or not." A dusty whirlwind furiously cut him short, and sent everyone running for cover in different directions to signify the end of the market day. As Obiligbo and his gang also beat a hasty retreat.

The old man quietly watching the unfolding events from the safety of his nearby hut could not but mutter aloud; *this is twilight at noontime*; and it does does not portend well for our Amaeke. *Tufia kwa...the goat in labour cannot die during child birth when there is an adult at home.* The old man was not thinking about the rain, when he stepped into it, to commence his journey to Eze-ogo Okala's house.

Later that night when Amaeke had settled-in for the night; just before they fell into deep sleeps that accompany market days, the *ikoro* (the giant wooden gong) sounded loud and clear through the still dark African night air. It is believed that its message could travel even as far as other surrounding villages People sat up on their beds and mats to listen attentively to decode the message of the ikoro; *koi- koi; koi-koi...ghoom ghoom ghoom doom; ghoom ghoom doom; ghoom doooom; ghoom doon-doon-doom; ghoom doon-doon-doom; do-doom do-doom do-doom...do-do-do-dooom...*

It was Amaeke's signature tune. A matter of emergency for its citizens; death was not involved. It was a matter of urgency; and that all should gather at the square before the dews of the night dried up in the morning sun. The peace of Amake was under threat from within, not without. No cause for alarm for its neighbors. The deep-throated drone of the ikoro repeated its message until it lulled the people into fitful sleep…what could be of clear and present danger to their relatively calm coexistence.

CHAPTER 13

The sun did not fail to rise from the east that morning, and as its rays lapped the night dews from the treetops, the *ogo* began to fill up. Nobody dared disregard the call of the ikoro in that primitive community; it could mean the difference between life and death. The inquisitive with itchy ears, were the first to arrive; on their wake were the curious buoyed by their speculative tendencies. The indifferent were the next group to arrive; you can decipher that from their unhurried steps. Finally, those in the know sauntered in with some air of importance.

The ikoro was housed in a low thatched hut without walls at one end of the square, and was at that time calling out; *kedum-kedum- kedum; gegerege-gegerege; kedum-kedum-kedum; gegerege-gegerege... those who were in transit or still at home to hasten up.* An old man stood hunched over the gigantic hollowed wooden stem instrument that was suspended between two sturdy knee-high forked stems. As he struck out the notes with the freshly cut bamboo stems, he angled his head assiduously to pick up the amplified output. Two young apprentices sat in the front of the old man totally absorbed and enchanted with the old man's gusto and dexterity on the ikoro. Their primary assignment was to translate verbally what they heard. How the player connects with his target audience was a mystery.

The old man hunched over the ikoro was Mazi Osita Agwu; he had been playing the ikoro even before Akachukwu was born. He was known through the length and breadth of Ohafia and beyond as Eze-ikoro. Mazi Agwu was technically an institution or an oracle in the highly skilled fabrication and handling of the ikoro. A very secretive skill that was passed down to him from his grandfather a very longtime ago..

The village assembly was the ultimate forum to tackle public issues in the open. Leadership was vested in the people; where all accomplished genders contribute to the organ of governance. The status of the Eze-ogo was indeed a leadership with no hierarchical rights in every particular village. Even though the village was the principal component of government, the village in turn was socially sub-divided into various kindred. The kindred, was simply a cluster of families that could trace their descent to a common ancestral denominator. Governance in the village setting had direct democracy applications, which counted on all male adults to be pro-active. The village assembly was a forum for all and sundry to be part and parcel of a far-reaching decision in the general interest of the village..

The elders and the very accomplished sat under the thatched stand facing the grand audience that had formed into a semi-circle. The very old and aged had come equipped with their lounge chairs from home, and were positioned next to the thatched stand under the shade of the colossal bread fruit tree. The very young children sat on the floor in front of their grandparents whom they had led to the square. The young adults and other adults made themselves comfortable standing around.

When the ikoro finally went silent; to cue the assembly to commence business. The crowd went silent with anticipation. Ogbuisi Uduma got up and cleared his throat loudly three times.

"Cha! Cha!! Cha!!! Amaeke kwenu!" Ogbuisi Uduma's voice was loud and intimidating, and complemented by his boisterous masquerade movements.

"Eeee ya!" the crowd resonated loudly.

"Cha! Cha!! Cha!!! Amaeke kwenu!" he repeated his former body language.

"Eee ya!" the crowd once again answered in unison.

"Kwe zu enu o!" He rounded up the traditional greetings perfectly with the crowd reciprocating infectiously. Then an uneasy calm enveloped the square.

"Our people have a saying that; *no matter the pressure you put on a man with elephantiasis of the scrotum to adjust his sitting; he would never make the mistake to sit upon his scrotum.*" He paused momentarily with a dignified air to assess his audience.

"Yes! The man can never make any mistake to sit on his scrotum; because he knows that it is a very delicate and sensitive part of his anatomy that he should guard jealously. It is with such gravity we also treat our internal peace and security. Amaeke Ohafia does not toy with her peace and security" Ogbuisi Uduma noted with pleasure the vast sea of nodding heads.

"Never in the history of our land, had the eke market ever closed at mid-day. No, no, no, not because of the rain my people. Obiligbo, the son of Kamanu appeared from nowhere and shut the market down." A wave of murmuring rose amongst the crowd to temporary interrupt Mazi Uduma's speech. There was a late entrance into the square that caused the ripples.

It was the larger-than-life Obiligbo in a very strange ferocious battle gear. And right behind him were a retinue of his kindred and staff; they walked in as a people with a purpose to be dispensed with expediously. The women and the children took one good look at Obiligbo's mien and regalia, and hurriedly took to their heels. While their men, who pride themselves as the lions of the jungle, and the proud and gallant descendants of Uduma Ezema stood their ground.

Mazi Uduma was a huge man by all standards, but the *man-mountain* Obiligbo towered over him in size; "How dare you accuse me falsely?" he thundered, his deep voice resonating beyond the square. "How dare you *shave my head in my absence*?" as he spoke and gesticulated the massive sword swung to and fro on his waist.

The older man did not show any sign of intimidation; rather he looked brazenly at Obiligbo and calmly whispered loudly to him to go and find himself a seat. Obiligbo felt insulted, and was red- hot furious; it was obvious that he was a clear and present danger to his older compatriot. And as if cued by an unseen finger, Mazi Uduma was promptly surrounded and shielded by Aka and his age- grade members, who looked up to Mazi Uduma as their mentor who initiated them into *mmuo* (masquerade), many years ago.

When the heat finally died down, Aka with the eagle plumes impressively decorating his head gear took over from Mazi Uduma. Obiligbo noted with some modicum of green envy the obvious rise and rise of his arch-enemy during his self-exile. When he started his speech, Obiligbo confirmed where the young man that challenged him the previous day got his boldness from. He cannot deny that Aka was quite an orator with panache and stately diplomacy.

"It was our fathers that said; *no matter how dirty the baby is, nor how daft the bather is, she cannot throw away the baby with the dirty bathwater*. Today should be a day of joy and merriment in Amaeke; for our son that we thought was lost is back. Not just back, but hale and hearty." He paused for the applause that greeted his opening remarks to die down. He was very happy that the tactical angle that he deftly employed to diffuse the existing tension worked out to the letter.

"We cannot but wish our brother Obiligbo well; just like he also wishes us well. From all indications Obiligbo had travelled and conquered far flung places; which Amaeke cannot but learn from him. Amaeke, can you see where I am going?

"Eeyaa!" the audience replied with a resounding affirmative monosyllable. Obiligbo was more than bemused with what he was hearing. He came with the plan to be offensive to every form of confrontation that he had anticipated like when he arrived the square. He was indeed at loss of how to tackle the angle at which this smart ass, Akachukwu was setting him up. He knew deep down in his heart that his age-long rival was digging a grave for him to walk in on his own volition.

"We learnt from our Nri homestead; of the equality of human beings, that indeed all people small or big, rich or poor, are equal before *Olisaebuluwa* (God), and these truths we hold to be self evident over the ages." The very attentive audience applauded in total agreement again. Aka knew it was time to put in the final nail into the coffin. He tactically put on his charming smile to soften his serious mien.

Obiligbo sat uncomfortably on his seat under the covered stand fuming, gob smacked that the crowd was lapping up the idiot, Akachukwu's tomfoolery. He could not wait for his turn to speak; so that he would cut him to his miserable size.

"Obiligbo, my brother welcome home…" Aka turned sharply around from the centre of the square with arms dramatically outstretched for a massive bear-hug with Obiligbo who sat passively without betraying the fire burning inside him. It was total confusion for Obiligbo who did not know how to react to this offer of right hand of friendship from a character that he had blamed for all his misfortunes.

Aka was just three paces from him, when the diminutive dibia swiftly stepped in between them; taking everyone by surprise including Obiligbo, who was so relieved with the timely interception. "Stranger! How dare you stand between brothers? You have no rights in Amaeke. Give way; before I prematurely send you forth to the land of the dead!" Aka's right hand slipped deftly to the butt of the machete hanging on his waist. Obiligbo quickly saw his chance to make gobbledygook of all of Aka's antics and overconfidence. He knew Aka had just committed one simple blunder.

"Akachukwu, son of *Onyeobia*! Did you hear your name? Did you take note of your father's name?" His voice thundered through the square, as he pushed aside the diminutive comic figure of the dibia between them. Aka and the entire audience were totally taken aback; so there was an uneasy solid wall of calm that echoed the questions over and over again.

"Aka, how dare you talk about *a stranger with no rights*? How did Onyeobia, your own father come to have rights in Amaeke? What differentiates him from my Ezemuo? Or was it because he was smuggled into Amaeke by the great and *legendary* Ogbu-isi Obidi Kalu?" The questions came cascading down with a bitter vehemence, begging for the answers that were not forthcoming.

Aka could not utter a word he felt so ashamed of himself. He searched through the crowd for his boys. They were huddled together around Nwoye. They consciously avoided his eyes. He breathed a sigh of relief that Uju, their mother was not there.

"Somebody more than Ogbu-isi Obidi is standing before you. I have fought everywhere…I have even fought with the devil and live to tell the story. You can see my face. So Amaeke, whether you like it or not; Obiligbo is here for good, and I demand to be respected. And for any of you that think otherwise; the battle line is drawn." Time to leave before they recover. "*Una o!*" he shouted out and briskly led his party out of the square, to return to their base.

Before the Eze-ogo could talk; Ogbu-isi Obidi Kalu now looking frail and grey all over got up to talk. The chattering that rose with Obiligbo's dramatic departure now died down to a murmur.

"Cha-Cha-Cha Ama…Ama…Ama e eke kwe…kwe…kwe…" the old man first stammered, then stuttered, staggered and went into a fit of wheezing and coughing; and then collapsed into the willing hands of Aka who was standing by. Before they could get him water to drink the old man was dead, just like that.

CHAPTER 14

And the old man died. Ogbuisi Obidiali Kalu died in the arms of his adopted grandsons Aka and Nwoye, in the raucous presence of the whole village. It was pandemonium at the square as the crowd that started off on a mere panicky note, dispersed with a dead body and a funeral on their hands and minds. So many people voiced out their impression immediately that Obiligbo was to be held liable for the old man's unlikely demise. Nwoye had in a furious display of bravado called for Obiligbo's hut to be burnt down. The voracious youthful age grades tasting blood; ably supported Nwoye's drastic call in its entirety, and began mobilizing for a mob action.

The Ezeogo knew that he needed to call his subjects to order before somebody got hurt in the resultant overwhelming conflagration. He was a forlorn figure, with grief and sadness written all over him, when he got up to address the square. The excited crowd after so much prodding and respect for the old man went silent to hear him out. He took the traditional salutation without the usual vive, and the crowd also responded with a lack luster roar.

"My people, I know that our hearts are on fire. What we need now is how to put out the fire before it consumes us from within. Our people say, *no wise man, leaves his hut that is on fire and burning, to chase after the rats for dinner*. That is why we must restrain ourselves immediately. Do not forget also the proverb that says; *you cannot chase after the madman and act like him, and claim that you are sane and better than him.*" He noted with relief that the audience was listening attentively.

"I totally concur with you that we should hold somebody, somehow accountable for the anguish that we are suffering today. But we must out of respect for the dead, first take up the *Ili ozu* (first burial). And that we must set out to get done today by sunset. I beg you all to hold your peace like *Mother Bedbug* advised her young; ... *to be very patient for that which is very hot, will definitely become cold later*." And he gratefully sent them off on various errands, as the body of the dead was conveyed over to the Ogbuisi Obidi's compound by the direction of the duo of Aka and Nwoye.

And everything went smoothly, and the body of Ogbuisi Obidi was guided home into the bosom of mother earth, just as the sunset took its final bow for the day. The befitting Igbasu *Mmadu* (second burial) was fixed for another three moons.

That night Aka could not sleep, he wept like a baby, in the privacy of his hut. He was inconsolable; both his mother and wife tried unsuccessfully to raise his spirits to no avail. His thoughts were fixated on how to avenge the death of his mentor. Tried as he might he could not get Obiligbo out of his mind. He had finally fallen into a fitful sleep as the cock crowed just before dawn.

Even in his sleep, there was no respite for Akachukwu. It was as if he had murdered sleep. It was from one vivid nightmare to the other. And it was always Obiligbo and his cohorts trying to either strangulate or skin him alive. The other members of his family were not left out either in the dreams.

There was also the nightmare about Nwoye that was so vivid and real. Aka from a long distance could see Obiligbo sitting precariously on the top of a giant bird cage, and playing Nwoye's oja alluringly. Nwoye attracted by the familiar tunes of his *nwokem* stepped out from the back of a small bush dancing with gusto towards the cage whose trap door was held open by a giant albino hiding inside. Aka was screaming with all his strength to warn his friend of the danger lurking inside the cage, but Nwoye was deaf to all other sounds around him. It was then he noticed Obiligbo's *dibia* in full regalia was busy fanning away; clasped in his hands was a gargantuan cowhide fan towering over his diminutive frame. Aka tried to move from his perch but also discovered that he was tightly bound down with fetters of blacksmith's iron. By the time he looked up again, Nwoye was dancing a tango inside the locked cage with the albino to the thunderous mocking laughter of Obiligbo.

"Agu! Agu!! Agu!!!" It was the voice of Nwoye calling out his name. He jerked awake, still disoriented in the dimness of his sleeping quarters. He was covered in sweltering sweat. "Agu; the only man that roars and quakes the coward to soil himself." It was the sing-song voice of Nwoye his bosom friend. *Phew*! He was so relieved that it was only a dream.

The friends sat just outside the hut on the elevated clay bed under the eaves and did a postmortem of the entire events of the previous day. They cannot but agree that they just had to hold Obiligbo responsible for the death of their progenitor. They came up with different permutations of how to level up with Obiligbo, without raising any suspicion. What totally annexed their hearts was the burning desire for vengeance at all cost. Aka was still smarting from shame and disgrace he felt in the hands of Obiligbo; he had no choice but to broach the subject with his bosom friend.

"Alusi Oja, please tell me the truth as your friend. Did Obiligbo make a fool of me yesterday?" his eyes were truly pleading.

"What do you mean, *make a fool of you*?" Nwoye tried to sound off-handedly.

"Come on Alusi, you know that he made those disparaging remarks about Onyeobia, to discredit me." Aka retorted thoughtfully.

"*Biko*, please disregard that big good for nothing bully; even his clique took it with only a pinch of salt. Who did not see that you turned him inside out with all the philosophy of *our equality before our creator*," he laughed out cheerfully to unwind his friend, "you could feel him shrinking into his chair, as his bulging eyes searched for an escape route."

"Are you saying that; that people truly felt that it was only diversionary tactic, to say my parents were smuggled into Amaeke through the back door?" there was a hint of bitterness in Aka's voice.

Nwoye was not comfortable with his friend's frame of mind, so he made up his mind to change the topic. "How could you think like that, my friend? Your father was proudly identified and called Onyeobia until his death. Does that sound like a man who was hiding? Please just disregard all that he said, they were the ranting of a mad man." He paused as Uju brought in a wicker basket of fried bean balls and pap for the friends. They sat in silence as she deftly set the breakfast clay utensils between them and left the scene without uttering a word.

They ate in silence, each totally engrossed in his own thoughts. He could see Obele in the herbal garden picking out ripe berries and seeds for processing, while Chuma and Chuka came into the compound with bales of freshly cut elephant grass to feed the livestock.

"How are Ifeanyi and the girls? I have not seen them since the last eke market day?" Aka inquired as he licked his hands to round up his breakfast.

"They are fine. You can see that her stomach is slanting already; she is almost ready. I have told the mothers and Uju to prepare for the D-day."

"I am sure she will come up with a replacement for Ogbuisi Obidi, an *Onochie*." Aka chuckled thumping his friend on the shoulder.

For an answer, Nwoye took the flute hanging on his neck, and began playing a very soulful tune. It was like all stood still when Nwoye was playing his flute. His slim fingers were a blur as they swiftly ran across the holes on the sides of the flute as his lower lip sat nimbly on the lips of the flute. There was mysterious perfect relationship between the man and his instrument...no wonder Aka aptly calls him *Alusi Oja*, the flute oracle. Aka knew everyone would have stopped in their tracks, arrested by the melody flowing from the lips of the duo of humanoid and implement. Suddenly, he stopped in mid-tone; examined the time smoothened wooden equipment affectionately, and declared sadly that the instrument was in the throes of death.

"Come on Alusi, don't be a kill joy. It sounds as good as ever to me."

"Agu, I know my *nwokem* inside out. You don't have to see some things before they exist. Why do you look puzzled my friend? Do you see the wind? But it exists. It has worn out from inside" he continued to examine the flute until he found what he was looking for.

"Here, here, see here; see this tiny black line running the entire side of the flute. It is a deadly crack" Nwoye gave his friend the flute to see.

He was right. Aka could see a very faint almost invisible line running down one side of the flute. "So what next?"

"I must get a new one made before Ogbuisi Obidi's second burial. I will go and get the wood today."

"No! No!! Alusi not alone. We must accompany you." The outburst took Nwoye unaware.

"Agu, why all the fuss? What has come over you?"

"My brother nothing has come over me. Our people say; *you dare not use what you use to play with the ear; to play with the eye.*"

"What is that supposed to mean, if I may ask?"

Aka felt ashamed of himself, an Ohafia decorated hunter and warrior, was behaving like an alarmed teenage girl over a mere dream. So he tried to soft pedal.

"I mean, maybe em...its too early for us to go out because of our master's death that just occurred yesterday." Aka mumbled incoherently.

"Aka, you know that I am not going hunting or farming; after all the flute is even for the purpose of the burial. I must find a properly seasoned Blackwood early enough to get my flute ready. You know that even under normal conditions it takes the very high density wood almost three years to cure and season properly, before the actual carving process that will gulp almost two moons."

"Maybe you should wait for me to go with you."

"Akachukwu nwa Onyeobia! Akachukwu!! Akachukwu!!! How many times did I call?"

"Three times." Aka answered soberly.

"Mind yourself o, since when did I become a baby, that you want to babysit me? Aka, I know you very well…your worry and headache is Obiligbo." Nwoye burst out laughing as Aka could not hide his genuine concern.

"Alusi that bully does not portend well for any of us. We have already started counting our loses with Ogbuisi Obidi."

"Agu, you just relax; we can take that man out any day. Have you forgotten that, you did it before? For Ogbuisi Obidi his time was up, it was just unfortunate that it occurred on that day. Too bad, that we have to make him a scapegoat."

Aka was not comfortable with his friend's infectious display of over confidence. At the back of his mind was the nagging adage; *that pride goes before a massive fall*. He decided to steer the discussion towards the immediate issue of concern.

"So how are you going to find a three-year old seasoned Blackwood, and get a flute made in the next 3 moons? That is the question begging for answers."

"All I need is to find a tree that was felled by nature that had gradually seasoned naturally over the years. Somewhere in the bush, there is a tree just lying there and waiting for me to just come and pick it up."

"Just like that?" Aka asked.

"Yes, just like that." Nwoye burst into his loud laughter that tended to smoothen out all his listener's apprehensions.

"Nwoye, please you just be careful." As Nwoye was busy shouting out compliments to Uju and the boys who were all engaged with their various chores.

As Nwoye approached the entrance to the compound, he raised his beloved flute on to his lips, and serenaded all ears around with a soulful melody that sipped into the bottom of their hearts. Even though Aka had heard Nwoye play a million times; there was something strange and phenomenal emanating from that *dying flute* that enthralled his soul as never before. Long after he had gone Aka was still hearing vividly the haunting notes of Nwoye's *oja*.

By nightfall later that day, the alarm had been raised. Nwoye was nowhere to be found in Amaeke. All the men that answered to the summons of the ikoro were broken into various search parties. They had been sent off in different directions deep into the night to search and rescue him in the event that he was injured or ill. The last persons that saw him Nwoye alive that day were Obi Nwarapu and his son, who met him at the stream crossing. They had stopped to condole with him on the demise of his mentor. He had told them he was only going to get a wood for his new flute. He had a short axe hanging on his shoulder.

The search parties had searched all through the night with nothing to show for it. One of the search party leaders had said something that sent a cold chill down Aka's backbone. The man had excitedly said, *It was as if he was neatly picked up and lifted by a giant bird into the sky without leaving any trace.*

CHAPTER 15

Nothing had the eyes ever seen to make it flow blood instead of tears. It had been thirty very long days since Nwoye Ekwema disappeared. Life had gradually returned to some form of normalcy in Amaeke. But for Akachukwu and his household life would never be the same again. He had waited expectantly every new day anticipating some news of his beloved friend, but deep in his heart something told him the *Lekeleke* dream had been fulfilled... *that he would never see his bosom friend ever again.*

If a part of the dream had been fulfilled then what would happen to the rest of the dream? It was a bitter concoction to swallow. But did he have a choice? There is nothing he could do now, he would just wait and watch events unfold...*how his two sons would follow suit in the disappearance saga.* He sat up on his bed, as even the mere thought of this possibility was almost driving him insane. There was some commotion outside his hut; he swiftly grabbed the sheathed machete leaning against his bedside, and sprang out in one fluid practiced motion.

Outside his wife's hut were about twelve young people all talking excitedly at the same time. He waited a while for his eyes to absorb the full glare of the rising sun, before sedately walking towards the gathering. They were so engrossed with the subject at hand that none of them noticed him until his booming voice cut through their excited voices.

"What is all the noise about? Can't a man have some quiet moment to himself without your disturbance?" He kept the excitement out of his voice; though he was quite curious and excited too.

"Father, see Alusi Oja's *nwokem*." Obeleagu raised up the wooden musical instrument above their heads. The string was cut, and a part of it was missing. "Obinna found it near the *Ajo Ofia* (the evil forest), when they were hunting."

"Give it to me!" This time he could not hide his excitement, "Oh God! They got him. Eh! Alusi Oja, so they got the better of you…" He could not stop the tears that cascaded down his cheeks like a deluge. He quickly headed towards his hut, with nobody following suit. They knew the man needed his privacy to mourn his friend finally with this new evidence.

He was still weeping like a baby, when Uju called out to him; that she was rushing off to Nwoye's house that her sister Ifeanyi was in labour. He could not but agree that Nwoye was on his way back to life through this baby. He came out to see the back of his wife and her youngest son hurrying out of the compound. He got some water from the big pot of water to wash his face. He noticed that his two older sons with their friends were seated under the orange tree. He knew it was going to be a very long day ahead.

"Obele, please get me some breakfast," he called out as he rushed back into his hut, "better to start the day with a full stomach..

By the time he got to Nwoye's house, he met a celebratory dance by the women. Ifeanyi had been delivered of a healthy baby boy. Mazi Ekwema and his closest neighbor, Mazi Okwe were seated under the huge mango tree with a calabash of palm wine between them. The older man jumped up to embrace his son's bosom friend; who was equally like a son to him. As Aka finally settled down to join the men after seeing Ifeanyi and her son, the grandfather totally shook him with his demand.

"Aka, my son what would you name your new son?" The old man was in very high spirits, not by anyway under the influence of the palm wine. Mazi Okwe just watched the two men with much admiration.

Aka smiled and pretended to be thinking up a name. He could feel the eyes of the two men reading his every body language. After what seemed a lifetime, he heaved a sigh of relief, then cleared his throat, and began to talk.

"My father, we have a son who is indeed *special*, my brother told me he would be named *Onochie* (Replacer)." Their questioning gazes with mouths agape did not faze him, because he was prepared for them. Aka did not wait for them to ask the burning questions in their minds bordering around mystery.

"Please, don't get me wrong my father. Nwoye did not mean a replacement for himself. This young man whom he wished and prayed for, was born to replace a very special person to both of us." Aka purposely paused to make the right impact with the final part of his information.

"Onochie was born to replace our mentor and teacher, Ogbuisi Obidi." You could hear an ant's whisper with the pervading loud silence that welcomed this piece of information.

CHAPTER 16

Onochie's official naming had come and gone; all in attendance believed the young man was named to be a replacement for his missing father, whom many considered to be strange, since Nwoye was not presumed dead. Nobody, dared ask the burning question that begged for answer; and neither Aka nor Ekwema made any clarification either. All that was important was that, the new born definitely diverted full attention from his biological father's mysterious disappearance, since everyone in the family was occupied and involved in his well-being.

Aka, simply watched things from the sidelines; waiting for the ultimate part of the lekeleke dream, that he was convinced must come to past. He did not still share his secrets with any human being. And the days wore on.

It was finally the eve of Ogbuisi Obidi's second burial. Aka had led his sons and other youths to the village square to put it ready. It was on the footpath they ran smack head-on into Obiligbo's medicine man and his entire crew coming from the opposite direction. Nobody could recall how it degenerated from the usual name calling into an almighty altercation. It was the timely intervention of Aka that saved the day; as Obiligbo's medicine man was already on the ground mobbed by the youth that was unofficially led by Obeleagu. As he was finally pulled away from the crushed but alive body of the medicine, he screamed out loud and clear;

"You and your master will all pay for it; nobody will tell you to leave Amaeke!" that threat re-echoed in the ears of everyone present. It was going to be a very grave mistake later..

Knowing Obiligbo's antecedents, it was indeed a surprise to all that were at the square that, the unsavory incident ended without any further development. They had all expected to see him bounding into the square to retaliate the shame and disgrace meted out to his accomplice. As they headed home after completion of their assignment, Aka could not but register his astonishment.

"That *old fox* must be up to something. I know him very well; there is no way he would not ask for his pound of flesh for what you did, Obele. We better keep our eyes open so that he will not take us by surprise..." Before Aka could finish his last sentence Obiligbo's bulky frame, like a ghost stepped stealthily out from the bushes onto the footpath. Aka suddenly stopped in his tracks, signaling his boys to steady for battle, as his own right hand unsheathed his razor-sharp machete glinting in the dying rays of the sun.

It was quite a sight to behold; a sight that would have sent icy cold chills down the spineless. Obiligbo's man-mountain frame silhouetted against the rays of the setting sun. His grotesque face, shrouded in a massive dark mask. His outspread legs almost covering the entire width of the footpath. And behind him were his rag-tag army entirely dwarfed by their mentor.

"*Mazi Nkpisi!*" his booming voice was contemptuous and disparaging, just like their childhood days, "or shall we say *Ogbuisi Akachukwu Onyeobia*; please forgive my rudeness." He burst into laughter, as he played to his gallery of lackeys who joined him in his laughter. Aka watched him silently without betraying any emotion.

"You are a fool. I thought you should know better as an accomplished *Ogbuagu* (a lion killer), *that nobody toys with a tiger's tail that is asleep, or presumed dead.* Have you forgotten that *the foolish child that says his mother will not sleep; should not prepare for sleep either?*" Aka kept mute, so Obiligbo continued his monologue.

"I am not a fool like you, my friend; because I know our tradition very well. I know that the gods of our land will come down on me if I shed a drop of your miserable blood. I just want you and these brats that you call sons to know that the battle line is drawn. You have put yourselves in danger by picking on me; from this moment my dear friend you will do yourself a great disservice to sleep with your two eyes closed." He stopped suddenly and with the lithe sleek movements of a big cat stepped back into the bushes with his team.

Aka and those with him waited quietly for awhile to make doubly sure; that Obiligbo would not pull a fast one on them. Even though he professed a tradition that was self-evident in Ohafia; but that would not hold water with his followers who were not indigenes of Ohafia. So they could kill or be killed.

It was already twilight by the time they finally got home, because they trod the relative short distance with caution, anticipating some form of martial confrontation from Obiligbo's mercenary ranks. At the entrance to their compound, Aka called his boys together, and in a conspiratorial whisper, warned them not to say even a word of the events of the day regarding Obiligbo, to either their grandmother or mother.

That night, the *ikoro* reverberated through the still darkness of the tropical night, to announce the second and final burial of one of Amaeke Ohafia's most decorated sons coming on next day. It called on all and sundry to join Amaeke to give and honor Ogbuisi Obidi with a most befitting burial. It was the *ikoro* that finally lulled Aka to sleep with its repetitive message.

The burial ceremony for his mentor was at its climax. The *ogo* was packed to the brim with Amaeke people and representatives from the other twelve villages that made up Ohafia. And all agreed that Ogbuisi deserved all the pomp and pageantry to bid him farewell from this earth. Then came the moment everyone was waiting; the outing of the majestic *Ijele* masquerade. From the special quarters that were built on the eastern side of the ogo, to house the massive masquerade, came the distinct rhythmic beats to signal the greatest display of the day. One side of the *Ijele's* special quarters was pulled down to reveal the most colourful masquerade on earth. Since a door would not contain it, an entire side is taken out. And there stood the *Ijele* in its full glory; an entire village on a head.

The exhilarated crowd applauded with glee. The accompanying musicians went into a slow march beat to cue the *Ijele* forward. The magnificent masquerade took one-two-three regal steps and crashed to the ground and lay deadly still…and the music died. Aka suspecting that the masquerade was in danger run forward to unmask the great masquerade. And behold it was Obiligbo that laid there dead, not dying. As he tried to resuscitate the dead man behind the masquerade, he felt strong hands grabbing him from behind and holding him down, as others gagged and tied him securely with twines.

He was accused of a sacrilege; unmasking a masquerade, not just any masquerade but the awesome *Ijele*. He struggled to profess his innocence but nobody was willing to hear him. He was shamed-faced as he was lifted up in his bonds and ridiculed by all and sundry… the loudest of the laughter was emitting from the dead man behind the masquerade. And he startled awake sweating from all pores in his body. Aka could not sleep anymore; he lay wide awake until the cock crowed.

CHAPTER 17

If Onyeobia's second burial ceremony was rated as a funfair; then Ogbuisi Obidi's own was indeed a fiesta. Unlike Onyeobia's; all strata of Ohafia were present with their peculiar masquerades or dance troupes. No community was left out. This was a raw testimonial of Ogbuisi Obidi's popularity and importance in all of Ohafia. The Ikoro had started playing out its message from sunrise, the square was filling up gradually. Those who had started the journey at dawn, would arrive find some shade to rest their feet and catch a nap before the show proper would begin.

Meanwhile, there were dancing, games, and wrestling competitions among the children and teenagers. There were so many prizes ranging from food stuffs to pots that were won. There were points for food and refreshments and guests were led to be served. Aka had on his own had sponsored the slaughter of two cows, three goats, and five chickens for the day. He was the chief mourner, as the only surviving adult male relative. There were also points for palm wine that was inexhaustible. Some drinkers were already showing the toll of commencing early; as they were increasingly finding it hard to find their balance and focus. There was so much excitement in the air to celebrate the lifetime of a worthy son of Ohafia; the *ijele* outing was to be the climax of the day.

When the sun finally got overhead, the show began in earnest. As usual the men of achievement were given the grandstand. To the surprise of Amaeke people, Obiligbo appeared with his entourage; and insisted that he must seat in the front row. He finally had his way, as Mazi Ukachi was moved to the back row to accommodate him. As he took his seat with so much narcissism; he waved at the Ezeogo, who was four seats away.

The very popular Emeka Ichoku Ogazi; the man who was best known as a human parrot coordinated the program. *Ichoku* was indeed a veteran of many high profile burial ceremonies. He was very conversant with the profile of each performing group; and he sang and eulogized them, as they paid their homage and last respects to the dead.

The entourage from *Isi-ugwu* had an ensemble that did the monkey dance; they emulated a band of banana-eating monkeys. It was a comedy of sorts that had people wailing with laughter. By the time they exited the centre stage, the whole place was a sea of yellow banana peels and people still reeling on the floor with laughter.

Then came the archery contest that had seven villages contending for the coveted price of a female baby Billy goat. Since Ogbuisi Obidi was an accomplished hunter; this contest was sponsored by the elite hunters' cult to honour their departed comrade at arms. Amaeke was represented by Obeleagu Akachukwu and his brother, Chukwuma, who were the best young archers in Amaeke. Each village team was represented by two contestants who were allowed a total of five arrows between them. They were expected to hit as many of the available targets as possible.

Since safety was a matter of importance in this sport for both the contestants and spectators. The targets were secured high up on the udala tree for everyone in the square to see, though the immediate vicinity of the udala tree is cleared of spectators. The spectators were left in a kind of horseshoe-formation. A green watermelon was left dangling from the end of a tender woven raffia rope. There were seven of these watermelon targets swaying gently in the wind, at a height of about twenty masculine paces.

The contestants score just a point to sink an arrow into a watermelon; but they get the maximum ten points to cut the melon down, by aiming at the rope. Arrows that miss the targets fall harmlessly back to the ground, without endangering anybody. Each set of village contestants were allowed to work out their own strategies to achieve their set targets. The two judges were keenly assisted by the eagle-eyed spectators who excitedly counted out the dispensed arrows for every individual team.

Amaeke's team, as the host was given the home advantage to begin the contest. The Akachukwu boys stepped out with an uncanny resemblance that was baffling; they would pass as twins to any stranger. They waved to the applauding crowd to acknowledge their support. They then, conferred briefly putting their heads together on factors like wind speed and deflection, the home crowd was roaring with excitement. The younger of the two boys went over to a pile of bows; and tried a couple of them, before settling for one.

While his older brother took his time to pick out five ramrod-straight arrows with barbed iron heads; these were then duly handed over to the second judge for inspection. The boys then keenly inspected the seven targets, and finally settled for the central one. The judge with the arrows stepped over to them and handed over their five arrows.

Chukwuma first took the brace position, then placed the arrow between the cured-hide string and the bow, and pulled looking straight at the stem of the tree. Obeleagu then stepped forward to steady and align his brother's elbows at an angle best known to them; and in one swift fluid movement maneuvered the bow and arrow to point upward at their chosen watermelon. The crowd could not contain itself any more at the amazing display of precision, and burst into a thunderous applause. The first judge with a stern unsmiling face raised his two hands up to signal the applause to stop. The crowd obeyed instantly.

The younger boy with the bow and arrow stood transfixed to the spot, like stone statue. It looked like he held his breath just like the crowd that waited with baited breath. The brother carefully stepped away from him, and screamed; *"Gbamm!"*

In one swishing bolt of lightning speed the first arrow found its mark and the central watermelon came crashing down and exploded into a very colourful mush of colours as it thudded on to the sandy ground. The crowd this time exploded into a din of deafening ovation. After the ovation had finally died down to few inconsequential whispers.

The younger man took the second arrow, and proceeded into what they did before, this time targeting the last watermelon to his right. As the older brother gingerly stepped away from his brother's side he landed right on a banana peel. He lost his balance and thudded back into his brother, who also lost his balance to hit the dirt floor, as the arrow went off flying across the open space to find a mark. It was a most unlikely target. Obiligbo's mouth opened in a soundless cry, as a third eye opened right between his two eyes. The barbed iron arrowhead disappeared deep into his skull.

And for a tiny, very brief moment, it felt like time stood still, as Obiligbo's body sat upright as if nothing happened. Then he slumped backward into the man seated right behind him. The shocked and shaken man bravely and carefully lowered the massive bulk of Obiligbo to the ground. He noticed the first thread of blood trickling down by the bridge of his nose and collecting into the left eye. Ukachi knew immediately that Obiligbo was dead; though he was still warm in his hand, but the man was stone-cold dead.

CHAPTER 18

And the man died... Yes! Obiligbo of the Ndiagha kindred just died like that. It had been thirty days since that incident.

It was pandemonium at the square that day, when it was confirmed that Obiligbo was dead; death was caused by an arrow fitted into a bow in the hands of the children of his arch enemy. For the lily-hearted the first reaction was to distance themselves from the scene as far as possible. For the curious, their desire to get a firsthand account put them in the way of those who had a genuine motive to help. At a point, from the cacophony of voices nobody had an inkling of what action to take.

Some youthful members of the Ndiagha kindred had rushed over to hold down the supposed murderers for traditional justice to be meted out appropriately. Their minority voice to have immediate vengeance dispensed on the culprits there and then; did not overwhelm the voice of the majority that stood their ground that it was an obvious freak accident, and that the boys should not be held liable.

For some, that were not as vocal as the first two groups; it was that *Chukwu* was not asleep, and he would always right the wronged. That what comes around, also goes around. It was not a coincidence that; right on the final burial day of Ogbuisi Obidi, God had deemed it fit to sort out publicly, the direct or indirect cause of his death. *What an irony?*

It looked like things were totally out of control, until the Ezeogo timely resorted to his repository of sound wisdom to douse the consuming conflagration of bitter vengeance. He called for all warring parties to sheath their swords, and to give peace a chance to reign supreme.

"My people! My people! Please, please and please! I beg you to hear me out." He clapped and called out for their attention until they finally calmed down.

"Today, my heart bleeds for all of Amaeke. As we once again, experience another monumental death. It seems as if we have just moved from one calamity to the other. First and foremost, we must first bury our brother as a matter of importance. This will make for a smooth passage to meet his maker." He paused to catch his breath, and to register their reactions. A few people nodded in agreement.

It was finally resolved for another meeting to be convened within thirty days of Obiligbo's first burial. This interval would be a kind of healing process and moment for people to cool down their overheated minds to carefully look and study the plethora of possibilities staring them in the face. And the people had left with long faces each to their home, to prepare for the dead man's burial..

And Amaeke had waited patiently for the town crier and his gong. Last night as they were preparing to settle in for the night; the unmistaken raw shrill sound of the metal gong resounded through the early night air, complimented by the screeching loud voice of the evergreen Mazi Agbai. He had served Amaeke as her official town crier for the past seventeen years meritoriously.

"*Ndi Amaeke!* The Ezeogo had asked me to inform all men to gather by noon tomorrow at the town square. A very crucial matter is to be discussed. Men that do not attend would be fined accordingly".

And as the sun traveled through the day, to finally settle directly overhead; the Ezeogo arrived in company of some elders into the square. An uneasy calm pervaded over the entire square. As the other elders took their seats the Ezeogo went straight ahead to address the meeting.

"*Amaeke kwe nu!*" he greeted exuberantly
"*E ya!*" the men's chorus was resounding.
"*Amaeke kwe nu!!*"
"*E ya!!*" they chorused again
"*Kwe zue nu!!!*"
"*E ya!!!*" they answered with a sense of expectation.

"We have stayed too long here; we must have to move on. Within the past four moons, Amaeke had witnessed so much pain and tears, than any other time in our lives. They must stop. And that is why we are here." He whisked the horse tail at a stubborn house-fly.

"Let us speak with open minds, please. Make your contributions concisely and to the point. Let me once again sympathize with all our bereaved brethren, God will console you all. Let me once again appeal to all of you to leave the dead, as dead; so that the living can go on living in peace. *Dalu nu*... thanks to you all." He took his seat expecting anxious speakers to rush in, but no one was willing to start the fray. A thick silence encased the audience.

The Ndiagha kindred who sat apart put their heads together for a brief moment before their leader stepped forward. His name was Mazi Ose Ndiagha, his complexion was soot black, and his bulky frame was a smaller version of Obiligbo's. He looked very tired; the strain of the events of the past few days written all over him. With his all grey head, you can tell that he was above sixty rains, but he displayed the nimbleness of a man in his thirties.

"Cha-Cha-Cha Amaeke kwe nu!" his deep voice resounding. Deep voice.

"E ya!" the other men chorused in response.

"I totally agree with our Ezeogo that we have stayed too long on this matter. Yes! I also agree with him totally that the living can go on living. Yes!" From his comportment you could tell that he had an exaggerated opinion of himself.

"But I tend to differ with his idea that the living will live in peace, if the dead do not rest in peace. Yes! All we are asking for is justice. Yes! The laws of our land abhor and condemn the spilling of our brothers' blood; and to bring to book all that are found guilty. Yes! *A witch cried in the night; and in the morning a healthy baby is dead; must we suffer the witch to live*? No! The murderers of our brother, Obiligbo must taste the wrath of justice. And do not forget that *justice delayed is justice denied*. Yes!" He took time to look around matching stare for stare eyes that dared meet his own, before sitting down.

It was Ogbuisi Uduma that spoke next. He hailed out his greetings with so much celebration before commencing his address.

"My people before we begin a presumptuous journey, why don't we first examine the facts before us. The fact that the tortoise's grandmother said; *if there is a stampede, I will trample upon the elephant's mother; would that statement make the tortoise's grandmother liable in the event that elephant's mother dies in a bizarre accident*? This simply meant reason and not mere speculation that must prevail in such situations. Though justice might be *blind*, but she is not *deaf and dumb*. And Justice insists, if our brother Mazi Osi Ndiagha must know, since he admitted it in his address; only those proven guilty beyond all reasonable doubts must be made to face its wrath." He paused to sternly acknowledge a wave of murmuring from the angle of the Ndiagha contingents.

"The events surrounding the demise of Obiligbo did not happen under the cloak of darkness; nor in the isolated depths of the evil forest far from preying eyes. It all happened before our very own eyes. And the judges who are natives of Asaga and Ezi Afor respectively, who are renowned champions of the bow and arrow, have reliably informed us that, it was near impossible for what happened to have been premeditated. My people it will not only amount to a travesty of justice, but indeed a tragedy of sorts to punish the innocent to please the dead, and fulfill the inordinate wish of the living. *Amaeke kwe nu!*" He sat down without much ado.

Mazi Osi Ndiagha jumped up from his seat, as if he was stung by a bed bug in the seat of his buttocks. He loved the fact that he was the cynosure of all eyes. "May I ask our big *ope ikpe* (lawyer) to clarify to people like me who are stupid; whether the so called *experts in the business of bow and arrow* actually said; it was near impossible, or totally impossible for the boys to have killed their father's foe? Yes!"

The silence was stifling. Ogbuisi Uduma was conscious of all the eyes focused on him; their gazes felt like sharp darts pricking into his skin. He sat there immobile like stone stature afraid to even exhale.

"Ogbuisi, you heard Mazi Ndiagha, can you please answer the question?" it was the calming voice of the Ezeogo that shook him from his reflections. Ogbuisi Uduma needed time to squeeze out of the corner he had been boxed into; he needed to put up some form of diversionary tactic to take off the heat.

"They said near impossible," and before anyone could react, he quickly added, "If the boys are guilty as charged, it will be only a matter of time before the gods would avenge for the victim, just like the gods avenged for Ogbuisi Obidi..." He was rudely interrupted by Mazi Ndiagha who was shaken by this allegation.

"*Alu!* Shut up your foul mouth. What do you mean that the gods avenged for Ogbuisi Obidi? We all knew that the old man had a foot already in his grave." Mazi Ndiagha was furious; he was barely able to check himself from hitting his opposite number. Uduma was satisfied that his tactic worked perfectly.

"All I am saying here, my very dear friend; is that the gods of our land are very capable to dispense their justice and wrath without recourse to any of us raising a finger to help. And that is indeed the situation at hand." Ogbuisi Uduma knew he had thrown bait that the opposition would not refuse.

Mazi Ndiagha quickly consulted with his kindred including the Ezemuo who was actively involved in briefing Mazi Ndiagha. The rest of the people sat in silence and watched the unfolding events. Mazi Ndiagha left his group smiling, as he went back to the centre stage.

"You are very right, Ogbuisi my very good friend, I agree with you. Yes! The gods do not need our help to dispense justice to the guilty. Yes! There is nothing more to say then, than to allow the gods to have their way. Yes!" Mazi Ndiagha spoke with a wry smile pasted on his face as he headed back to his seat. The majority of the crowd could not help but to applaud with excitement, what they considered as a victory for Ogbuisi Uduma and those that he represented.

This development took everyone by surprise, though the Ezeogo was not taken in by the sudden capitulation of Obiligbo's kindred. He knew deep down in his heart that they had an ace up their sleeves. He knew the Ndiagha folks to be very cunning. At that point it was as if the man could read his mind; he swiftly turned right back to the centre stage. The resounding applause stopped abruptly.

"Yes! Lest we forget Ezeogo, since we all agree too that *justice delayed is justice denied;* we would need the gods to act expediently and speedily. I just want it to be on record that my friend concurred formally to handover the case to the gods.'

"Ogbuisi Uduma do you have any objection to leave the matter in the hands of the gods? The Ezeogo asked warily, hoping to get him to object and stall whatever evil plan they had in mind.

Ogbuisi Uduma threw caution to the wind, and answered with some degree of over confidence. "Yes, let us hand the case over to the gods to deal with the guilty as charged." He kept a straight face.

"We need a god that would do it in record time; without much ado, if you don't mind. Our gods of our land are too familiar. Yes! Ogbuisi Uduma, what do you think?"

"The faster the gods act the better for us all. Just like the Ezeogo said earlier; we want to get the living to get on with their lives."

"Do you have any god in mind with a reputation that could dispense justice quickly and speedily?" Mazi Ndiagha asked off-handedly without arousing any suspicion.

"Who cares; any god would do." Ogbuisi said recklessly without thinking.

"Ezeogo, and my dear people of Amaeke; I recommend we take the matter to the one and only *Ibini Ukpabi.*"

"Ibini Ukpabi?" Ogbuisi Uduma almost shrieked.

"Yes! Ibini Ukpabi of Arochukwu. Yes! Or are you scared that your innocent boys; may have soiled their dainty little hands with blood after all. Let them escape the wrath of Ibini Ukpabi, to prove that their hands are indeed clean. *Amaeke kwe nu!*" There was no more applause; for the tide had changed. But in who's favor?

CHAPTER 19

It had taken another seven days to prepare the entire entourage for the journey to Arochukwu. The Ezeogo had personally delegated Nwokoro, a middle-age accomplished warrior to lead the delegation; that also included an intimidating detachment of warriors to provide security against any eventuality. It would take the better part of a full day to complete the journey to Arochukwu.

The Ezeogo, who was so concerned about the group's personal safety, personally made all the arrangements. He had after due consultations with Aka and Nwokoro; given his blessings for the journey to commence before the first cockcrow of dawn. This was to avoid unnecessary attention of sympathizers in Amaeke, and the other villages that they would go through.

Aka, who had stoically received the news of the verdict to take the matter to the Ibini Ukpabi shrine, remained philosophical declaring that his sons were innocent, and would come out unscathed. Deep down inside, he had a nagging feeling that this incident was not unconnected to the dreams. There was nothing he could do to change the events as he had come to know and understand now. He had maintained a very calm dignity of somebody who was privy to a secret that was about to happen.

On the eve of their departure, he was tempted to break his secrecy pact with his father's apparition. He had at some stage, called in Obele and Chukwuma into his private quarters for some private moments. The boys were so exuberant, and so confident of their safe return, that he had truly felt ashamed of his fears and anxiety. The boys were genuinely embarrassed when he tried to embrace them, with tears pouring down his cheeks. He knew that this was the last time he was going to see his boys alive.

"Father, what is all these? Please stop embarrassing us. You are behaving as if we are guilty, and that Ibini Ukpabi will have us for dinner. I bet you, that we would be quite a mouthful." Obele burst out laughing with his brother; and Aka could not but join in the laughter.

"Chukwukadibia had asked to go with us, to experience the adventure..." Obele was cut short with a voice that indicated a shrouded fear.

"Chuka is not going anywhere with you!" when Aka realized that he had over reacted he tried to make amends, "Who would be at home to help your mother and grandmother during your journey?" He quickly dispatched them to be by himself.

Not long after, Uju, his wife, knocked at his door, and came in. She looked quite apprehensive as she went ahead to register her concerns too about the developing events; "...if every one is saying my sons are innocent, why would they be allowed to go to Ibini Ukpabi? To prove what; and to satisfy whom?" she waited for her husband to answer, but he seemed not be interested.

"Please, my husband do not consent to this journey to Arochukwu. I am starting to have somber sensations about the whole journey. Did you hear that, that Obiligbo's sinister *dibia* was seen sneaking out of Amaeke today, with his boys? They said, it looked like they were leaving Amaeke for good."

"Give me a break woman! All you have are questions, and more questions, begging for answers. Let the boys go and prove their innocence. You and I know that they are totally innocent."

"I know my children are innocent. Just think of it; what if something goes wrong? She started to sniff and rub away the tears that were welling over her eyes.

"What will go wrong? Eh! I am asking you? Please just let me be, I have more than enough to worry about. Why not go and make us all some special supper, so that we can celebrate in advance, our victory over Obiligbo even in death." Aka signaled that the meeting was over.

That night, Aka could not sleep. He kept tossing around. He had been exempted from the Arochukwu journey, due to ill health. He had not recovered fully, since his friend went missing. And there was no way he was going to allow his third son to be part of the trip. *Tu fia kwa!* God forbid! Now come to think of it. Why would Ezemuo depart Amaeke on the eve of a journey that he had influenced? Was his sneaking out connected to this journey? What could go wrong on this journey to endanger his two sons? Was this going to be part of the dream that is yet to be fulfilled? Questions! Questions!! Questions!!! It seemed as if he even had more questions than his wife.

A series of perfect yowling pierced through the night; they did not sound out of place; but these were indeed artificial ululation. By their count and spacing, were identifiable to the Ohafia warrior, as a call sign or wake up call. Aka counted and waited for the equally perfect yowling that were responses. When he heard three distinct yawls within his compound, he stepped outside to find his boys all set to hit the road. Nwokoro was in the midst of about twenty-five warriors all set for action; he could see the razor-sharp blades of their machetes glinting in the moonlight.

"Proud and valiant sons of *Uduma Ezema* I salute you; the lions of the jungle, I greet you" Aka dramatically whispered, and they nodded in unison.

Aka counted five others who were not in the warriors' gear, whom he knew to come from the Ndiagha kindred. He went over to embrace his sons quickly, and whispered softly;

"Don't forget who you are. That you are the sons of *Akachukwu;* the one and only child of *Onyeobia*. Go in peace." He bade them, as they marched off into the night. He watched them until they disappeared; blended totally into the moonlit darkness.

As Aka turned around to walk back to his room, he was startled to see Chuka standing in front of his hut crying. Aka walked over to him clasped him on the shoulder.

"Father, when are my brothers going to come back?" The forlorn young man inquired calmly.

"Soon, very soon. Yes, soon, my dear son." Aka answered thoughtfully without betraying any emotion. They held hands and walked over to sit under Onyeobia's orange tree. The night air was chilly, but not uncomfortable. This was the darkest part of the night; the part just before the dawn of the new day. And Aka chose this moment to tell his youngest son some facts of life.

"My son there are things we may not understand because they are beyond our understanding. Though our human understanding is limited; it is not restricted to just this world that we see. For those who have developed their minds; they have superseded the factors that restrict us to the visible and the physical, into the invisible spiritual. There is something about us; you and I that is a mystery." Aka spoke authoritatively without any interruption.

"Just look around us; you will find different forms, colors, signs, symbols, wood, and stones representing the intermediaries of *Chukwu*.

The *Amadiohas*, the *Njokus*, the *Nkamalus*, the *Ibini Ukpabis*, the *Nja Ikwus*, the *Agba-alas* are just a few of these our man-made spiritual intermediaries." Aka paused to swipe at a mosquito droning by his right ear.

"Chuka, it is remarkable to note that *Chineke* or *Obasi di nelu* is never represented by any form of carving or some natural features moon, sun, rivers, mountains, trees, or caves. He is totally invisible; never seen with ordinary eyes, as we are meant to believe. That is why it is the invisible that controls the physical. All affairs of men under the sun are controlled by Chineke, Chukwu, or Obasi, as we may choose to call him. We, and everything created are testimonies to the invisible God. That was why you were named *Chukwu Ka Dibia*; God is greater than the witchdoctor. I was named *Aka Chukwu*; the hand or finger of God. Your brother *Chukwu Ma Echi*; God knows tomorrow. Our people believed in this almighty God from time immemorial..." Aka continued into the mysteries of life, that he had come to know and experienced firsthand.

At that very moment, when the night was at its darkest hue, about a full day's journey away from Ohafia, another clandestine party was convening under the cloak of darkness. Even though, it was unimaginable to have anyone eaves dropping in this sacred enclave; for the consequences would be fatal, the five shadowy figures sat huddled together, and discussed in very low conspiratorial voices. The log fire that burned behind them kept them in perpetual shadows, just like the vocation they perfectly operated shrouded them in the deepest darkness.

"...so they killed him to avenge the old man's death; or they even suspected him for the man that went missing?" the voice was deep and unsympathetic.

"It happened before my very eyes, and over 200 other people in broad daylight. I can assure you there was no foul play..." this faceless voice sounded very familiar; though was rudely interrupted by a superior and more authoritative voice.

"If it was not foul play, then why him?"

"That is what I am saying; it must be an act of God; the mysterious act of Chineke; *Chukwu*; *Obasi di nelu*." The familiar voice was begging to be taken seriously. "That is why I am thinking we should give a verdict of innocent and set them free immediately. So that we should get them out of our hair as soon as possible. They are a bunch of trouble makers; they will be accompanied by their fearless warriors too.

"Just shut up your mouth; if you don't have any sensible thing to say. What do you know about the true god? Listen we have an order to deliver, and time is not on our side. We will definitely take the two and any other we can grab by fire or by force." The *non-sympathetic* voice ordered.

"Now let us go over the details again, before you go underground for good. You said they are siblings; the name of grandfather is Onyeobia; their father is Akachukwu; their mother is Uju, *nwa* Mazi Osita *na* Elu Ohafia; the senior is Obeleagu..." *Superior Authority* displayed so much intelligence reeling out these facts he had just been equipped with a moment ago. No wonder that he had managed one of the biggest ruses in black Africa successfully during his reign. He droned on and on over these very important details that was part of their modus operandi.

Aka spoke and his son listened attentively. They continued until the cock crowed. They were still talking and listening, when the sun sneaked out over the eastern hilltops in a glorious radiance. Uju had woken later than usual. She had had her own fair share of the sleepless night; crying and tossing. She was surprised to see father and son totally engrossed in their discussions.

She had with a very long face sauntered over to greet her husband; and like an automaton inquired of his health as expected by tradition. Aka knew she was still angry and smarting from his outright refusal to stop the journey to the Ibini Ukpabi shrine. She did not know, he thought to himself, that there was very little we human could do to sway the flow of the *Finger of God.*

She took the brush-branch broom and started sweeping the compound; this was supposed to be Chukwuma's morning chore. As she swept, she started singing in a mellifluous voice, a very soulful melody; Aka noted with some modicum of sadness that there was a stinging melancholy in her tone, that the hearer could not ignore.

"*Nne-nne udum ala putam o, udu...*" Uju's voice rang through the morning air of Amaeke Ohafia, waking up to the challenges packaged in the new day.

CHAPTER 20

The team from Amaeke had finally arrived Arochukwu a little before dusk a little tired, but not too worse for tear, due to their training. Arochukwu was larger and more populated than their Amaeke, and they spoke a distinctly different dialect of Igbo. By the mere mention of Ibini Ukpabi; they were duly directed from a safe distance to the outer fringes of what was considered as the sacred grove.

The sacred grove was located a little distance outside the town on a narrow valley surrounded by undulating hills. The footpath was narrow and winding, bordered by very thick elephant grass and vines, and a dense vegetation further outwards. Its width could only take an individual at a time. The soil beneath their feet was firm and hard; to prove that the path was frequently well-used, but by a few people. They set off evenly spread in a single file; a tactical formation to foil any attack from all directions. The footpath abruptly terminated into a grove of gigantic trees with huge boughs that looked menacingly sinister in the dusk. They did not notice the eyes watching them from the safety of the clusters of overhanging vines on branches.

Even though beyond the first row of trees was dim, nobody could ignore the array of sun and rain-bleached white human skulls hanging from the branches above to form a festooned curtain wall. It was a cavalcade that sent cold shivers down the spine of the bravest of them. If this spectacle was calculated to scare any innocent intruder, the initiator succeeded. They were oblivious to the ghostly character that was enjoying every minute of their discomfort and consequent reactions. He could not but agree that they lived up to their esteemed reputation as very brave warriors. He would not cross paths with them for anything; as Ezemuo rightly briefed and warned them. He must dispatch message immediately to their leader, to sort them out immediately, and get them out of Arochukwu as soon as possible.

And as they overcame their initial shock, they were then confronted by the ghostly bulk of an albino dressed in white from his shoulders down to his knees. His left eye was circled in a prominent black color. This albino was some sort of priest; who acted as the oracle's receptionist. He was heavily-bearded, but with a contrastingly clean-shaven head, was of an indeterminate age from the failing light. He stood protectively blocking the only defined entrance into the grove. His white toga was tied on to his left shoulder, and flowed loosely over his knees. The group stopped abruptly with a signal from their leader who was in the front. The man smiled to show that he had a couple of teeth missing. He spoke with a strange permanent husky-whisper, like somebody who had had his larynx torn out in a mishap. He introduced himself to Nwokoro, as *Udene* (the vulture).

Despite his weird look and nomenclature; Udene was adept at his job. He fluently spoke their Ohafia dialect of Igbo; and displayed a good knowledge of Ohafia, where he claimed to have lived in Ihenta and Ezi Afor for some years. Before long, they had warmed to his well-practiced diplomacy. He ushered them through the fringes of the grove to a clearing with a massive open hut, that was enclosed on three sides, and that could sit over fifty people. This was going to be their official lodgings for the night, and the entire duration of their consultations with Ibini Ukpabi, they were raucously informed by their official host, Udene.

Through the peaking twilight, they could see frenzied activities by an all-male team of workers or servants; whom Udene had called the *osu* Ibini Ukpabi. They were slaves dedicated to serving the oracle for life. The *osus* with their completely shaven heads walked about like zombies, totally engrossed in their immediate tasks. It was as if they did not possess a mind of their own. They were tending to different huge clay pots on equally massive stone tripods with burning fires.

In the course of the evening, Nwokoro had also intimated their official host, Udene, of their intentions to consult with the dreaded oracle of Arochukwu. It was then; Udene had informed them that the main shrine of Ibini Ukpabi; where the god dwells in the bowel of the earth, was yet some distance further off. All entreaties to intimate Udene of the object of their mission was brushed aside by him; with the assurance that Ibini Ukpabi who sees beyond yesterday, would sort that out at the appropriate time. His primary assignment was to see to their welfare and upkeep, as well as their fulfilling to the letter all the sacrificial rites expected for their consultations. He promised Nwokoro of accelerated hearing of their case because of the peculiarity of their delegation. They were to freshen up and take a well-deserved rest from their journey. Nwokoro, as leader of the delegation, was to prepare for an initial audience later in the night with the oracle's Chief Priest.

Back in Arochukwu, it did not take long for the news to make the rounds that a platoon of the most dreaded Ohafia warriors were in Arochukwu to consult with Ibini Ukpabi; but nobody dared approach the sacred grove to authenticate the news, for they were all aware of the dire consequences. The few curious citizens that had tried such a journey were neither seen, nor heard of again; it was like they just disappeared from the face of the earth. These mysteries by all means added to the reputation of Ibini Ukpabi as a fiery no-nonsense, all-consuming god that dastardly dealt with any being that crosses its path.

Ibini Ukpabi was just one or two other gods who was accredited with supernatural powers of divination in all of Igbo land. This reputation was consciously oiled by a group of clandestine agents and recruits that were dispatched to other lands to increase its shrine's reputation and subsequent patronage from far-away lands. It was generally accepted as the final court of appeal, and whose verdict was final, and would not be contested.

After Udene had left them to freshen up, Nwokoro had worked out a sentry duty roster for his team. The contents of the huge boiling pots finally turned out to be boiled yam and goat meat sauce; which they gratefully consumed. He had barely dozed off on the mat, when he was frantically woken up by one of his sentry-warriors on duty. It was the arrival of the Chief Priest's forerunner entourage, for the pre-arranged meeting. He had asked everyone in his entourage to be woken up accordingly.

He had strapped on his machete, and gingerly stepped outside the hut, to be confronted by the bright glaring light of the huge bonfire that was burning in the middle of the clearing. The place was as busy as if it were day. Not long after he had gathered his team together, and were duly directed to be seated on huge logs of wood neatly arranged for that purpose, on one side of the square, a loud wailing horn sounded through the night. The Ohafia warriors looked around cautiously but kept their composure; while the osu Ibini Ukpabi went about their tasks as if they were deaf and dumb. Another loud blast of the horn serenaded the chief priest, accompanied by Udene and a retinue of staff carrying a wooden throne behind them.

The throne was set directly over a small burning wood fire facing the log seats. The Chief Priest, surprisingly a portly and demure midget dressed in a white toga similar to Udene's waddled over. With a practiced dexterity, he swiftly clambered nimbly upon the throne that towered over him. Worn squarely upon his disproportionately-oversized head was a headdress of eagle plumes, and in his right hand was a double-headed sword. He made himself comfortable, without taking his eyes off the audience. He had massive bulging eyeballs with an uncannily cold stare that penetrated right through into your soul; and made your skin to crawl. And when he spoke, the voice was dismembered from the almost comical figure sitting in front of them. It was incredibly authoritative and commanding; it exuded power, as of one who must be obeyed. One who held sway in the matter of life and death over mere mortals.

"You are welcome to Aro-Okigbo great sons and lions Ohafia Uduma Ezema of twelve villages." The magical voice addressed them in their Ohafia dialect, "Ibini Ukpabi, the only one that can accord you the charming treatment of filling your basket with the waters of kindness and raw justice. Ibini Ukpabi, the creator of all and sundry; he that can decode the hearts of men; he that can kill a man on his happiest day; he that is the ultimate judge of the jailed and the jailor; the perfect revealer under whose eyes the wizard and the witch have no hiding place." Nobody else uttered a word. The night became deadly silent, that the crackling ambers in the bonfire exploded loudly like thunder.

"You have come to the right place to get justice. Ibini Ukpabi will dispense justice with lightning speed." His big bulging eyeballs rolled around like a mudskipper's not missing anything worth knowing.

"The night is no more young. Udene! You may commence proceedings!" It was a command not a request. Udene sprang forward as if his life depended on his strict adherence to obey the command to the letter.

"Will the defendants please rise and step out here." Udene pointed the Akachukwu's boys to left side of the throne and continued, "How do you plead your case? Guilty or not guilty?" he made the right tonal stress to emphasize the final question.

"Not guilty!" the two boys answered confidently smiling. The chief priest noticing there overconfidence decided to whip away their silly grins.

"Not guilty of what, young men?" the voice had the effect of a cat of nine tails streaking and slashing across a naked back, and drawing blood.

The boys were taken aback not very sure of how to respond to this unanticipated line of questioning. Help was not coming from anywhere; they suddenly realized that it was not as easy as they thought all along. All of a sudden their confident smirks were erased like rain falling over a drawing on sand. It was like time stood still as everyone waited for their answer.

"Not guilty of killing Mazi Obiligbo. I mean em..." Obeleagu stuttered, before finding his tongue again, "em...that we did not kill Obiligbo intentionally, it was a pure accident that happened in broad daylight..." the young man was abruptly stopped by a caustic cackling that proceeded forth from the chief priest.

"What you are saying is that you killed the person, but it was an accident not intentional. Correct?" His gaze was fully focused on the boys who felt very uncomfortable to respond in the affirmative.

"Obelagu and Chukwuma?" mentioning their names almost knocked them over, "I take it that, 'Yes', is your answer. You will leave Ibini Ukpabi to unveil and ravel your intentions and motives in due time. Udene please proceed with the plaintiffs."

The two boys could not but huddled closer to find warmth and strength from each other. The chill of the night bit into their naked torsos as never before. Nwokoro sat upright like a stone statue, surrounded by grim familiar hopeless faces.

"Will the plaintiffs rise and stand over here." Nobody stepped forward. Prompting Udene to loudly repeat himself again and again. Nwokoro noticed the chief priest and Udene sharing very furtive uncomfortable glances; something was not going according to a very good laid out plan, he thought to himself.

"These young killers, did not certainly on their own bring themselves before Ibini Ukpabi; somebody or people wanted justice for their brother who was murdered defenseless and in cold blood." The chief priest by all means was secretly cajoling somebody to step forward to save the situation.

After some embarrassing hesitation, a lone, tall, dark, and balding figure from the Ohafia delegation stepped out into position. Everyone breathed a sigh of relief. The chief priest immediately recognized the balding man based on Ezemuo's briefing.

"It is your accusation that they wantonly and willfully killed Obiligbo?" Udene's voice was a bit shaky, not fully recovered from the narrow escape just a moment ago.

"Yes, without any fear of contradiction, I believe that these two brothers did the heinous crime."

"*Uchechi Ndiagha, brother of Obiligbo,* are you sure?" it was the chief priest interrupting with an obvious revelation that shocked his audience to unfolding powers of this oracle..

"Yes," Uchechi answered with some restrain, and pointing to the boys, "they killed my brother to avenge the death of Ogbuisi Obidi."

"It is alright Mazi Uchechi Ndiagha; now that you have brought your case before the great Ibini Ukpabi; you must leave it to him for justice to be done properly." The chief priest's declared authoritatively.

"Udene, so let the trial begin by first light tomorrow. The gods have spoken. Lest I forget, Nwokoro need I remind you that you are in the presence of Ibini Ukpabi; and your weapons will not be allowed beyond this point. Do I make myself clear?" Nwokoro was visibly taken aback with this new development that he only nodded in the affirmative.

"I believe Udene is making your stay comfortable, please cooperate with him accordingly. Thank you." The loud wailing horn sounded from behind to startle all of them. By the time they looked back again, the entire throne vicinity was engulfed in a thick smoky darkness.

When the haze or smoke cleared in a little while, the chief priest had gone. Yes, gone with the smoke… he had disappeared right before their eyes. As the throne was carted away, Udene took Nwokoro aside to finalize the arrangements towards the trial at the shrine proper.

That night the boys could not sleep, they kept tossing and turning. Nwokoro could not sleep either. He knew deep down that something was very wrong with this entire Ibini Ukpabi thing, but tried as he might, he could not really finger it. Now this plan of disarming them; what were the deeper implications? What were they afraid of? Why did they panic when Uchechi Ndiagha suddenly developed cold in his pedal extremities? He was not going to allow all his warriors to be disarmed. He would find a way around it. It was then it started to rain.

CHAPTER 21

By first light that morning it was still raining heavily, it had even developed into a thunderstorm. The inclement weather did not in any way deter them from the rituals that must be performed before the litigants even approach or enter the shrine and sanctuary of Ibini Ukpabi. Mid-way between the sacred grove and the cave the religious rites must be completed before the deity would be woken up from its slumber. The male goats that would be slaughtered and their blood smeared all over the litigants as a form of purification were all ready when Udene showed up with five of his staff.

Nwokoro had also chosen just four of his warriors and himself to be disarmed, to follow the litigants all the way to the cave. A mild drama ensued that morning as Uchechi could not get any of his kindred to pair him as official litigants to go through the cave. It took the intervention of Udene to convince them to come along, though only Uchechi would officially stand for them.

They had finally left in a single file with Udene leading the way. They had progressed through the grove in semi-darkness, and puddles that had formed with the torrential rain. As they finally burst through the trees on the edge of the hill that gently sloped down to the valley below; their progress was slow because of the wet slippery floor. All along the footpath in the gloomy morning light one could make several animal skulls, there were discernable human skulls like in the front of the grove. The rain suddenly stopped and the sun peeped out from the hilltops in the East.

By the base of a massive Iroko with a festoon of fresh palm fronds tied around it as a girdle Udene stopped the party. Looking back the way they had come; you can see the sacred grove visibly highlighted against the morning light. It was not a long distance only that it was treacherous uphill task. The base of the tree had several animal heads scattered all over in various shapes and sizes of clay pots. Several white egg shells strewn all around almost turned the floor white. Udene made a sign to the entire party that nobody was allowed to utter a word from that point. Blades of green grass were distributed to everyone, to be clasped between their lips, to avoid talking of any kind.

They pulled over to Udene, who briskly rubbed down the goats with a pile of lemon grass. He then cracked twelve chicken eggs on each goat before they were slaughtered by his assistant, their blood were carefully collected in the clay pots. The three litigants were asked to strip bare, and were bathed with the goats' blood, the piles of lemon grass were used as sponge. Another set of eggs were cracked on everyone's forehead accordingly. Udene thereafter picked up his staff and led the team to a large pond that was fed by a stream flowing from the direction of the cave. The pond was teeming with life; grayish catfish of various sizes filled the pond to the brim. By the rim of the pond was a mountain of broken clay pots; the mound of broken pots went higher as all the pots that were used a moment ago were also broken there.

After the ritual of breaking pots the entourage was led to the point where the little stream entered the pond. Udene signaled everyone but the litigants to sit down and make themselves comfortable, as the staff skillfully started a fire to roast the carcasses of the sacrificial goats. The three litigants were stark naked with blood gradually caking over their hair and bodies. The very fair complexioned Akachukwu's boys were now looking totally different as if they had been skinned alive. Nwokoro noticed with deep interest that the fish milling in the overcrowded pond did not make any effort to stray or move into the very clear stream that was feeding the pond. It was indeed very strange that the stream had no life in it.

As the sun finally rose over the eastern hills, the first part of the roasted beef was brought over and handed over to the litigants to eat. They did not hesitate to consume the portions hungrily. Udene then poured out from a calabash what looked like palm wine which he first sipped and gave a cup full to each litigants. They were then blind folded and led away towards the cave mouth that had a mud wall shielding it from view. Only three of the staff and Udene had proceeded beyond that point. Nwokoro had been informed the previous night that, at this point, they either come out alive or the stream flowing out from the cave would turn bloody to signify that Ibini Ukpabi had dispensed justice by making a meal of the guilty party.

Udene and his three assistant had shortly returned to join them in the feast of the roasted beef and kegs of palm wine that freely flowed. Under the ample shade provided by the palm trees they had waited patiently dozing off and waking up intermittently. Nwokoro finally fell asleep out of tiredness, when the sun was directly overhead. Maybe it was the effect of the palm wine; for he slept soundly as if he was in his own hut.

When he finally woke he noticed that the sun had travelled halfway towards the western horizon. He jerked up with his eyes focused at the crystal-clear water of the stream for any bloody tell-tale signs. The water was even clearer than it was before. He noticed too that Udene was snoring loudly a little distance away from him. He looked to his immediate right to see the reassured glances of his warriors huddled together. He stretched and went over to the cover of a nearby shrub to empty his bladder that had been stretched to its limits. He wondered if he was breaking some law; so he strained and strained to rush it through, but the bladder refused to be rushed. Finally, he felt empty and dry, totally relieved. He was walking back to his former place when he noticed that the streamed had changed color, to a deep red. He signaled his warriors, and pointed to the stream.

The more they looked, the more the water in the pond began to pick up a cloud of the blood red color. They did not even know what to do. He noticed that the other two Ndiagha kindred were coiled up sleeping. *Whose blood is this?* Deep down something told him this quantity of blood was more than from one person; that means the Akachukwu's boys had been proven guilty. What if the blood is from three people? Does it mean both parties of litigants could be guilty? What if the verdict says both parties were guilty? What would be his own reaction?

Just then the snoring Udene stirred and woke up. He lifted his upper body braced on his elbows. He immediately jumped up and ran over to the stream. Just then a deep rumbling sound emitted from the cave and thick black smoke spiraled into the sky. And the chief priest emerged with a lone naked bedraggled figure staggering behind him. When they got to the waiting team, he handed over Uchechi to Udene to give him the mandatory cleansing bath in the pool. He turned around and without a word waddled back to the shielded mouth of the cave, where Ibini Ukpabi dwells.

For Nwokoro, it was time to go home, the grim gloomy journey back to Ohafia. It was going to be one long journey never to be forgotten. *Different strokes for different folks;* some will be celebrating, while some will be mourning…

CHAPTER 22

The mind must be allowed to wake long before the body; not the body before the mind as it is commonly observed. These words of his father kept re-echoing loud and clear in his mind. So he kept his eyes shut in feigned sleep. His breathing and pulse, sustained its sleeping tempo. He could feel his body rubbing against hard coarse wood. The sliding forward motion of whatever was transporting him, he could feel in his stomach and back. He could smell water and the putrid stench of vegetation and mud. He could hear distinctly the voices talking in low tones above him; the dialect was not familiar. He strained to decode the voices; none of them was female, and there were at least five people. What could be these swishing, splashing, and sometimes sloshing sounds? He noticed a rhythm between the forward motion and the splashing sounds. Yes, the water and the mud smell…it was a canoe been paddled. He could feel the ropes biting into his ankles and elbow. He could smell dried blood on his own body. What was happening? He tried to open his eyes, which only met solid darkness. And the young man panicked.

What was he doing here? How did he get here? Where were they taking him? His mind was almost running riot. *Calm down, relax Chukwuma, you must not lose control of your mind.* From time to time he could feel the sunshine in his face; though he could feel more shadows than the sunlight; to indicate that they were following a trail more under the canopies of trees. What time of the day he could not tell, though it was not certainly in morning; this he could tell by the warmth he could feel from the touch of the sun. He could feel a persistent numbing pain at the back of his head. *His head!* Yes his head, something heavy had hit him on the back of his head, and he had fallen endlessly into a deep bottomless chasm that was dank and damp, before he had blacked out totally.

Now he remembered. Arochukwu…the Trial. The events at the Ibini Ukpabi shrine. The diminutive chief priest with the commanding voice. What he had feared most had happened… somebody was fooling everybody and profitably taking them for a ride.

After the blood bath and the blindfolds, they had led them to some distance before separating them from each other. He had then suddenly felt dizzy and light headed; it must have been the contents of the clay cup that they drank. It must have been spiked. It was then they had bound his hands tightly behind his back, which he tried to resist feebly, but they overpowered him. He remembered vividly the authoritative voice of the chief priest urging them to "be quick, time is not on our side". He tried to shout but he could not even hear himself. It must have been the effect of the coca leaf extract in the palm wine he had suspected..

Thereafter, he was led into the cave, that was dank and damp, and had an overpowering stale smell of bats and their feces. It was at that point something heavy thudded on to the back of his head and he blacked out. Between then and now he could not remember anything.. Yes! *Where was Obele?* Was he killed, or were they all passengers in this canoe? No rushing, he must first work out a game plan. There was no harm in still sleeping to keep them focused on other things, while he fully assessed the situation he was in. Then he heard totally new sets of voices coming from the bank or shore of the body of water.

"Ezemuo! The king of ghosts!" A voice called out loudly from the shore.

Eh-eh! I am the one. Who has visited the land of the dead, and return to tell the story?" A voice that had strangely remained silent all along rang out from the canoe.

Ezemuo, the only nonentity you can only underestimate at your own peril. You are welcome." The voice from the shore concluded in what sounded like a coded message.

"Tell them, I am the fire that razes the green grass in the storm." Ezemuo retorted, before directing the canoe to turn and head for the shore.

As the canoe moored alongside another canoe, Chukwuma could make out other voices on the shore that came to receive them. They had made a big deal of helping to secure the canoe fast.

"Well done Ezemuo. I can see that you have got two there. Well done, we are not doing badly." The first voice from the shore, now spoke with a conspiratorial tone.

"*Agwo!* Snake, you are the true son of your father. I was a bit disturbed that there was no reception at the other two checkpoints." Ezemuo replied excitedly in a voice that now sounded very familiar to Chukwuma.

"Come on let us do some re-arrangement to see how we can contain my cargo of five." Agwo spoke with a modicum of accomplishment.

Five? *Agwo*, the viper! *The only one that bites, that tomorrow will be too far to get an antidote*. You have done very well. Five in a row?" Ezemuo exclaimed with equal enthusiasm.

"It was an entire household that stayed too late at the farm. They won't be missed though; for we got the entire family." The voice on the shore burst into a heartless laughter.

"You have a point there; they won't be missed. After all, there is the adage that posits that, *the family that stays together cannot go missing*." Ezemuo's irony was bitterly cold and stinging.

"Ezemuo you and your mouth. Please let us get you on your way. I am sure with the stock to be acquired tomorrow at the slave market at *Ahia Nwaebule*; you will have a full cargo load for Calabar." "Agwo, you have done so well." That was all Ezemuo could mutter.

"Please give this parcel to *Otiji* for me; he is waiting for you and your cargo at *Azumini*. I believe you are all going to Calabar together. I envy you." Agwo spoke with a tint of envy.

"Otiji, the grand commander going to Calabar with cargo? That is strange, very strange." Ezemuo uttered thoughtfully.

"What is wrong with the cargo? I hope they are not dead." Agwo effectively changed the topic to steer away from trouble; one cannot be too careful discussing openly affairs of the dreaded *Ekpe Secret Society*.

"They are alright. It was like Udene over spiked their drinks in preparation for *the tunnel of disappearance*. I am sure they will be fine." Ezemuo reassured him.

It did not take long to rearrange the boat's former seating, and expertly load the family of five who were also blindfolded. While the man maintained a dignified silence, the woman was just crying until the canoe made to cast off, and she began to wail loudly. It was a soul-rending wail that could have moved any man with a heart to tears, yet the slavers ignored her as if she were not even a living thing. As they waved their goodbyes, and then set sail downstream for Azumini, which was the final Igbo settlement on the river before what was considered as Ibibio country. The plan was to spend the night there, and be part of the big slave market day, the next day..

CHAPTER 23

They had disembarked that night accordingly at Azumini. Mazi Ibeji Otiji, a loudly ebullient and amiable fellow in his sixty-fifth rain, was on hand to meet the boat with a retinue of his staff. The captives who were now identified as slaves, under heavy guard were led over to a defined slave quarters where they were sparsely billeted for the night. With their blindfolds taken off, the slaves looked curiously and suspiciously around their new environment. They knew without being told that they were a long way from home. Chukwuma was so relieved to see Obelagu alive and well; they had exchanged knowing glances without words. The slavers had replaced their bonds with iron chains and shackles that were sturdily buried into the walls.

Chukwuma was so famished, that he thought he was going to die. Just when he was going to scream out to ease the pangs that beset his stomach, some staff appeared with a pot of boiled cassava to be served with red palm oil. The slaves silently wolfed down the food in no time; and it tasted better than the most delicious meal that they had ever had. Drinking water was in ample supple, and they drank to their fill. It was after the meal, they were led out individually by guards to relieve themselves in the nearby bush. Thereafter, they all fell into a deep fitful sleep, a natural panacea by the body to fully recover from the trauma of the events of the last few days.

Ezemuo and his crew had been led to Otiji's private quarters, where they were feted to a big lavish meal of pounded yam and bitter leaf soup. The ebullient Otiji was in his characteristic element as he feted his men with the best palm wine. They drank late into the night. It was either too much that he drank that loosened his tongue, or pride.

"Ezemuo, I have not told you yet, that I would be going with you to Calabar this time. I am sick and tired of those so-called Efik middlemen or overlords or whatever they call themselves. They just sit there and make us do all the work, while they grab the lion share of the proceeds." He paused to pour himself yet another cup of palm wine. Ezemuo decided to tread with caution, as he nodded in agreement.

"It was agreed in *Obinkita*, that I should go and renegotiate with them in Calabar a new deal, or else we will boycott them and take all our subsequent cargo to Bonny." Otiji paused once again to belch loudly; Ezemuo continued to nod his head like an agama lizard.

"Is it not because they speak the white man's language, and write like him that we have been relegated to the background? All that will be over soon. That is why I am taking along my two sons with me to acquire the white man's knowledge and wisdom." He burst into a full-throated laughter.

"How do you intend to pull that great fit Mazi Otiji, if I may ask? Ezemuo asked with a feigned puzzled look.

"You can't get it Ezemuo. You will be a genius to understand it. Some years ago the white man started a place of learning there in Calabar, up on the hilltop. My sons will be quartered with my sister Nwamaka whom you all remember; I gave to the *Obong* (king) of Calabar in marriage. In another year or two my boys will be able to communicate directly like the Efik with the white slavers. In that scenario the Efik overlords will become out underdogs and can hang themselves for all that I care." He slammed down the clay cup that shattered into a thousand pieces. Ezemuo jumped up and started a celebratory dance that everyone in the room joined in.

When morning came, Ezemuo and his crewmen were fast asleep with a hangover that came with a splitting headache. Mazi Otiji was up and early at the market. It was indeed a big slave market day in Ahia Nwaebule; and all roads led to Azumini as they played host to communities from far away than the nearby communities. Most had arrived by the Aro Blue River.

As the sun gradually rose from the east, the market gradually filled, and picked up its tempo. The traditional hum of a market in action could be heard in nearby villages. Even though it was a specialist market for slaves, there were also other products like farm implements and farm produce for sale.

The market was located around the big and massive *Achi* tree. Nobody could guess the age of this legendary tree. Everyone came to meet it there. Apart from its gigantic shade, it also had exposed massive surface or exposed roots that were put into a good use. The captives or slaves for sale were secured tightly to these exposed roots. Mazi Otiji's early call had given him a very good bargain for seven more slaves between fifteen and twenty-four rains. They were good to go. He had gone home to grab a well-deserved sleep and rest, before they depart for Calabar, through the famous Itu slave market.

CHAPTER 24

From Azumini, the convoy of now three canoes to accommodate the additional seven slaves, Otiji and his two teenage sons, and his personal army and staff, had set a southward course for Itu. Itu was situated in Ibibio land at the confluence of the Eyong Creek and the Cross River, and was frequented by Aro traders. Its slave market that held every four days was very popular with the Inokun slave dealers who raided all villages to gather slaves either by peaceful means or forcefully. Since it was the tradition of slave dealers to market slaves, in markets far from their communities of origin, Otiji was hopeful to buy so many Ibo slaves from Itu; there was high demand for slaves of Ibo origin by the Efik middlemen.

Otiji had assumed authority and command of the voyage by sitting in the first canoe, he divided his sons into the other two boats for reasons best known to him. Ezemuo was relegated to the background to be in the third and last canoe. Otiji was a very cautious man, that accounted for the relative success he had garnered as a sourcing arm for African slaves for the trans-Atlantic Slave Trade.

Their plan was to travel through the night and arrive Itu by first light, and be the first buyers in the market. Otiji's ploy was to grab all the Ibo young slaves on sale. After all, the Ibo slaves earned better prices in their resale. He smiled confidently to himself as he assessed his convoy, he felt like a king who was invincible. The slaves were made once again to wear their blindfolds, the tradition is only to remove them when they arrive in the strange Ibibio country, where escape is near impossible because of distance. His army numbered about fifteen, and were armed and dangerous.

The journey from Azumini to Itu was uneventful and they had arrived Itu by first light as projected. Otiji and ten of his soldiers had clambered up the steep bank of the river to the central market that was situated only a short distance from the river.

By mid-day Otiji had successfully sealed the deal for another eight young Ibo slaves. The pathetic fellows three females and five men claimed to be from very far away, in Onitsha Ado of nine villages, located at the eastern bank of the great Niger River; were totally disconsolate. From a little crafty prodding from Otiji, whom they mistook his concern for sympathy; they told how a trusted uncle of their's; a giant of man from their native village of Ogbeoza had tricked them out from the safety of homes to be sold off to Awka slave dealers. They had relayed their experiences as the Awka slave dealers had in turn sold them to the Inokuns who brought them to Itu. They had naively promised to settle Otiji three times what he paid for them if only he could lead them safely back to their native Onitsha Ado ni Idu. It was then Otiji had barred his claws; he had laughed them silly, before asking his staff to bind them accordingly.

"Alright. Nwa Onitsha! So you want me to take you back to Onitsha?" He mimicked flawlessly their Onitsha dialect and accent; and burst into a fitful bout of laughter that ended with a choking bout of coughing. The slaves could only look, wish and pray that he would choke and die right before their own eyes.

After stocking up on supplies and foodstuffs for the journey; they had swiftly set sail for Calabar. Otiji was well-known as a powerful figure of the Akunakuna and Aro combined, and was respectfully recognized and duly accorded his respects by the Umon and the Enyong; who under normal circumstances would not have allowed him direct access to the Efiks in Calabar. Most of the supplies were actually gifts to massage long-standing diplomatic relations on the route. Otiji in turn was lavishly feted by all the royalties all the way to Henshaw Town, Calabar.

By noon of the next day, Otiji arrived Calabar and was personally received by the Obong, his brother-in-law. After the slaves were sorted out and led away to the barracoons. Otiji, his sons, and the personal staff were led up the hill to be given a lavish welcome. Queen Amaka his sister, who was unfortunately childless was as beautiful as a *mammy water*, was obviously thrilled to see her nephews. Otiji had cleverly officially informed the Obong of his intention to leave his sons in the palace to give their aunt some succor because of her understandable situation. It was even the Obong, who had suggested that the boys would be enrolled at the Hope Waddel Institute to make it worthwhile; which to Otiji worked out perfectly to the ultimate fulfillment of his plans.

The queen who was annoyingly proud, rude, and insensitive to others feeling was so excited with the whole idea. She was known to crassly acted or spoken to challenge and embarrass the king in the presence of his chiefs and Etuboms. The king in the privacy of their bedroom had always cautioned her to be careful with her tongue. The other queens had also not been spared the vitriolic end of her tongue more often than not. It was in the heat of the royal reception for Otiji, she had loudly expressed her pleasure to the hearing of some Etuboms, that by the time her nephews finished from the white man's learning place, her brother would even be more powerful than the Obong, her husband; since Otiji would have direct access to the *mbakaras..*

Later than night, as Otiji and his entourage mercifully surrendered their battered bodies to sleep in the official guest quarters. Not very far away in the very secret hallowed chambers in the palace, the Obong who was also the *Cymba* (the most supreme Ekpe title) listened attentively, to what the council of Etuboms and highest ranking cadre of the Ekpe Society considered as a subtle ploy by some foreigners who had infiltrated the palace to wrest their monopoly of trade with the white man. After very exhaustive deliberations that lasted to the early hours of the morning, the tired council rose from their meeting, with the overwhelming verdict of *GUILTY*.

What was initially presumed to be a subtle threat was now categorized to be very serious threat of clear and present danger to the whole Efik kingdom and its most protected commercial and economic interests. The group had also unanimously settled on the DEATH penalty by any means to exterminate all that were remotely and immediately involved in the ploy. The Obong was numbed with all the overwhelming evidence of the characters impersonated, and obviously found culpable by the most powerful group of people in the land. It was a decision that must be effected without appeal and optimum confidentiality.

He was left all alone, with a numbing headache behind his eyes. He thought about the far-reaching implications of sentencing his queen, her brother, and her two nephews and his retinue of staff to death. There was nothing even he, the Obong could do; the council had spoken. Nobody was more than the land and the people; the culprits must pay the ultimate prize to safeguard the sanctity of the land. Two Etuboms saddled with the responsibility to advise the king on the best way to carry out the executions without undue repercussions, were to advice him accordingly by mid-day later.

He knew that it was only a matter of time before something very terrible happened. Now, the bubble has burst in their faces. He was even tired of warning and warning. Had warned his wife times without number to check her tongue; that it would land her in trouble one day. He tried his best, nobody would say that he did not try. He yawned and stretched himself, tired to the marrow of his bones. He was still troubled deep down inside, he finally dozed off on his throne.

CHAPTER 25

Queen Nwamaka had woken quite early that morning, which was a rarity; because she seldom wakes before noon. She had had her servants to prepare a big impressive breakfast for her brother and his people. Immediately after breakfast, she had in her usual rambunctious over zealousness marched off her two nephews over to the school set up by Reverend Hope Waddel of the Free Church of Scotland on the other side of the hill. She had noticed furtive glances on her and her party, that she had consciously ignored. For somebody who courts controversy, she always enjoyed these attentions from the so-called nosy busy-bodies, who would never mind their business.

The first person the king asked for that morning was Queen Amaka; he was told that she went with her nephews to the school. He had quickly taken his bath and gotten ready to hear from the Etuboms with the grim assignment before him. With the heaviness in his heart he could not even get himself to take breakfast. He was just brooding, he could hardly get himself to focus on any state matter. Before long, the Etuboms were announced. The Obong could not wait for them to report.

"Gentlemen, I hope we can quickly get this matter quickly sorted out." He spoke with a heavy heart.

"Your Highness it is not as easy as we thought. There are over thirty-eight lives involved." The older of the two Etuboms answered gravely.

"Listen, Etekamba, I am not interested with the statistic. Have you gotten or settled on a particular method to carry out the penalty?" A servant came in to announce that it was a matter of urgency; that Etubom Bassey and a Captain Brian Luckbone was outside to see the king. The king asked them to be ushered in.

Captain Luckbone was well-known and familiar with the Obong's court. His vessel, the *Sea Fairy* had berthed in Calabar thirty days back with its cargo of bags of salt; varied iron implements; bales of tobacco; thousands of bottled spirit; bales of calicoes; handkerchiefs; mirrors of different sizes; jewelry; glass and earthen jugs and jars; umbrellas of different colors; shapes and sizes; and arms and ammunition from Liverpool. Its cargo would be exchanged majorly for its illicit cargo of African slaves, and some palm produce for camouflage.

The heavily bearded Captain Luckbone wearing a menacingly-looking dark patch over his left eye, that gave him that daring look of a potential pirate, was born as Brian Ferguson in Liverpool, England in 1805. To fulfil his burning desire for adventure, he had become a sailor at eighteen at Bristol and migrated to the West Indies, and joined the team of the legendary Don Pedro Blanco, who was firmly established on both sides of the Atlantic. For the twenty-two years Brian Ferguson worked under Mongo Blanco, he was part of over twenty-eight voyages to the West coast of Africa to boost the trans- Atlantic slave trade.

Within the period of his tutelage, the young Brian became a walking compendium of the triangular geographical formation that was structurally formed by the routing of the trans-Atlantic slave trade. He could navigate blind around every sneaky creek from the Senegal to the Congo. By 1845, when Pedro Blanco stepped aside, and he went on his own, his specialty became the Bight of Biafra and the innumerable murky waterways of the Niger Delta serving the slave ports of Brass, Bonny and Calabar. Like his mentor Mongo Blanco who befriended King Siaka; he had also befriended both the King of Bonny as well as the Obong of Calabar for better business relations. Within twenty years he became the most daring and successful captain of the illegal slave trade era that thrived around Cuba. It was then he had adopted the name referring to the shark tooth talisman that seldom left his neck to disguise his English origin, and the vessels that he sailed with multiple identities and flags for varied purposes.

Etubom Bassey, who was also at the council meeting, was one of the most versatile of the trade captains in the Efik kingdom. He had like the king, his uncle been sent to Liverpool for a brief spell with this same Captain Luckbone, when his own father was the Obong. He came in with a worried frown, with an imposing big log book clasped under his left armpit, with a brown leather satchel bag in his right hand. They breezed in as if they were desperately out of time.

"Captain Brian Luckbone I thought we have settled you for good?" The Obong spoke very fluent impeccable English, which he picked in Bristol and Liverpool during his five-year long sojourn.

"Your Highness, we have just received message from the out lookers that the coast is clear; the cruiser *HMS Maeander* is headed for Fernando Po for minor repairs and supplies. That means we must cast off tomorrow night." He paused for Etubom Bassey to explain their difficulty.

"So far with the Otiji's stock, we are still about fifty short of the two hundred target. So far we have received any news of intent from Umon that their consignment of forty slaves from Ikom will be here in three days." Etubom addressed the king in Efik.

"Captain must you leave tomorrow?" the Obong asked his friend.

"Your majesty, I don't want to mess with Captain Barnard with his 44 pounder carronades and 60 marines under his command. I have not come this far, to be taken to the cleaners by the West African Squadron. I better sneak out when the cat is taking his well-deserved nap." Luckbone answered gravely, and burst into laughter.

"So what do we do?" the king asked in Efik and repeated in English. There was uncomfortable silence as they all tried to think up something. Somebody cleared his throat twice; it was the younger of the first two Etuboms.

"Yes, Effiom?" the king gave him the nod to speak.

"Your majesty, I believe we have a solution to all the log jams." He hesitated looking concernedly towards the captain who was engrossed in his own thoughts.

"Effiom, get on with what you want to say; do you think he has learnt to speak or understand Efik in the last thirty days that his ship berthed." The king prompted him to continue.

"Since you have been concerned about shedding the queen's blood, why don't we convert the thirty-eight people we have placed on death sentence into the much needed cargo for our *mbakara*, and make us good money, and avoid spilling blood?" Effiom felt so elated as he saw their faces light up with excitement.

The Obong rose promptly from the throne to embrace him; while the others all patted him on the back in a raw display of bonhomie. Captain Brian Luckbone looked up puzzled and quizzically at the uproarious salutations.

"By Jove! Captain Brian Luckbone you old sea dog, go and get your sailors ready to sail; I have thirty-eight very lucky slaves to make up your cargo for your *Sea Fairy*." The Obong this time mimicked the cultured blue-blooded accent of British royalty.

"Your majesty, like I told you earlier, this is my final trip to finally wrap up my dangerous career of piracy; I don't want to end up as my mentor and teacher, Captain Pedro Blanco that lost everything. You have been a true friend Richard." And the two men embraced.

"Brian, you don't forget that you have a second home here in Calabar. Break a leg or may your road be rough, my good friend. Run along, I will see you tomorrow."

The Obong waited for Etubom Bassey and Luckbone to depart before he commenced talking. He adopted a conspiratorial tone to perfect the biggest offset in Efik and Aro diplomatic relations. The Obong needed to cross-check every plan, until there was nothing more to add or subtract. It was unanimously agreed for the banquet to honour the queen and her visiting brother to hold by lunch time the next day.

By bedtime that night the news was already agog all over Calabar, that the Obong had given his blessings for the queen to return home with her visiting brother to visit her Aro homeland. The guards at the barracoons were discussing it in low tones as they packed and transferred the huge mounds of yams, beans, cooking palm oil, pepper, plantains, limes and lemons to the cargo ship that had been refitted by local craftsmen to suit its illicit cargo of human beings. In the dark poorly ventilated rooms were over 150 naked men, women and children were jam-packed, the mosquitoes descended with a vehemence to suck out all their poor miserable blood. By now the guards were so used to their unearthly groans and cries that they now hear them no more. At that particular moment the sickly elderly man shackled next to Obeleagu finally expires in a deep sigh of breath. The smell of death was over powering in the stuffy bland air.

CHAPTER 26

Etubom Effiom took one final look around to make sure all were in place as planned for the state banquet. The Obong had insisted that nothing should go wrong; or else that would be calamitous for the Efiks from the more enterprising and skillfully troublesome Aros. The sun was already overhead, any moment now the Obong, his queen and the other honored guest would come streaming in with all their attendees. So sad that his good friend, the most flamboyant Etubom Reginald Bassey, Esq. would not attend because of pressing state matters; he was busy supervising the final loading of the *Sea Fairy*. He had noticed as he passed by the beach front in the morning, that the canoes to go alongside the ship were been loaded with the slaves. Though he had consciously taken his eyes away from the sights, but he could not block his ears from the horrified and heartbreaking cries that echoed through the morning air.

It was a slow painstaking exercise as slaves seeing that they were cornered, and faced with no hope of return would momentarily go berserk. Some, especially the Ibo slaves even opted for suicide by jumping overboard. Jumping overboard at the moment of embarkation was always a painful total loss to the slaver factions. It was on this premise that each canoe and cargo was well guided and guarded to reduce the anticipated loss through total despair. It was now traditional to commence the loading by first light, when most of the captives were still in a disoriented state, and not actually sure of the intentions of their captors. To say the least, it was a most harrowing experience to stand-by and watch the hopeless soul-rending cries in different languages and their desperate reactions of futility. Some would glue themselves to any immovable object that it would need stronger multiple hands to pry them loose. For some, who would be unnaturally calm and detached, and in a state of psychological disassociation; they would have zombie-like glares that could thaw an Egyptian mummy.

Though Effiom had kept it to himself, it had never ceased to weaken his resolve not to do that slave business, no matter its profits. His friend Reginald had told him of renewed efforts by some white men in their lands, fighting tooth and nail to totally abolish this inhuman commercial venture. That was why he had shamefacedly admitted with so much glee this assignment to give the heartless Otiji and his accomplices a dose of their own medicine. He could not wait to see their faces, when it dons on them that it was pay-back time, and that indeed a Daniel had come to judgment. This feast was one feast they would not forget in the rest of their miserable lives if only, they would be allowed to remain alive by their strangely very familiar new colleagues in those cargo holds. He suddenly felt so elated as he heard the sound of clanging bells and distant drums.

From the commotion outside, he could tell that the dignitaries had arrived. He gave a thumb up sign to his supervising staff before stepping out to receive the Obong and his guests.

It had indeed been a very elaborate feast with all the rich delicacies of the Efik country. There was the choicest of the raffia palm wine variety that was common in Calabar and its riverine areas. And courtesy of Captain Luckbone some jugs of pure Jamaican rum, a rarity that was wolfishly downed by Otiji and his people. Etubom Effiom and his team had done the jobs very well, by strategically spiking food and drinks served Otiji and his team. It was during the calculated very boring Obong's long speech that they started falling asleep. Before long, they were all soundly asleep. Effiom and his band of trusted staff swiftly went to work securing them in bondage.

As the sun finally dipped over the horizon and twilight shrouded the land of Calabar; the thirty-eight very angry persons, too angry with themselves for letting down their guards were loaded on board the *Sea Fairy*. This time the usual cacophony of cries and lamentations that usually accompanied loading was missing. They were loaded on to the deck, stripped naked, and duly shackled and headed into the grated hatch at the bow. The children who were on deck were too befuddled to recognize the new comers.

Captain Brian Luckbone, in the new design of his ship, had fallen back on all his experience to refit it to only take 200 manageable human cargo. With improved ventilation, better spacing, improved health and nutrition, basic comfort, and improved vessel speed that was independent of the wind, his fatality target was just 3% as against the common average of 15% fatality. For the benefit of doubt, some drums of palm oil had been loaded on the deck as a decoy. Down below, in the cargo holds the very frightened band of naked men craned their necks to see the darkness beyond the multitude port holes.

At exactly 2200 hours that night, the *Sea Fairy* with its fires fully stoked that fueled steam engines that in-turn drove the rolling paddle-wheels, raised anchor. Without hoisting a flag, it swiftly sailed down the *Rio Real* on its projected five-week journey to Cuba. For all the shackled passengers there were no excited good-byes from the shores; yet it was the last they would ever see again of their native land. Not a captive eye was dry, and they cried themselves to sleep..

CHAPTER 27

There was nothing like the surreal feeling of waking up in the middle of the ocean where there was no land in sight. The monotonous swishing and sloshing music of the paddle-wheels that finally lulled them to sleep was still there. The sky was bluer and even closer overhead, and as the early morning fog cleared, they were confronted with the gigantic magnitude of the waters that was as far as the eyes could go. For most of them who were procured from the hinterlands, the largest body of water they had ever seen or encountered were rivers and streams. Encountering the wide blue gently undulating waters of the Atlantic Ocean was indeed a sobering experience for all. Sea sickness was the very first of the numerous sicknesses that they were to encounter, it was a good thing that Captain Luckbone had strictly recommended empty stomachs to commence the voyage to strategically minimize the side effects of vomiting.

Captain Luckbone had brought all his veteran experience to the fore as a prodigy of the ambidextrous prince of slavers, Don Pedro Blanco, and as a partner of the most versatile Theodore Canot, to safeguard his precious cargo. Luckbone had staked his life savings to sponsor about eighty percent of the entire voyage and venture. To him, it was one voyage that must succeed. He shuddered reflecting on his mentor's business empire collapse in 1848, and consequent dismal death in 1854. Come to think of it; there was something truly bizarre and jinxed about this slave trade business.

Captain Luckbone was on the bridge alone with the night officer. The ocean was calm and almost still, like a mirror reflecting the rays of the sun behind them. He trained his binoculars on the horizon for telltale signs of trouble, while he continued to mull over the great debate on the trans-Atlantic Slave Trade. If the abolitionists were condemning him and his ilk; how about the African leaders that captured and traded their own flesh and blood? Whether it was the very refined Obong of Calabar, or the crude King Siaka of Sierra Leone, or even the devil's incarnate and the monster of West Africa, King Ghezo of Dahomey, they were all the same kettle of fish. It was so ironic that Ghezo's thousands of slaves were guarded by powerful band of women-warriors who were fiercer than even their male counterparts.

He had always felt that Wilberforce and his spoilt brood of slave-lovers had been allowed too far with their campaign. They had finally gotten all colonial powers to come together against the transatlantic slave trade, which automatically transformed him into a pirate, if he was caught. Just imagine the absurdity of trade that the African king of Bonny posited; *We think this trade must go...that your country however great, can never stop a trade ordained by God.* It was very unfortunate that nobody was seeing the good side, of transporting these primitive things away from diseases and ultimate tortuous death in rituals, or to satisfy the palates of blood thirsty natives to civilization. Just consider the fate of the queen on board; she would have been just wasted back in Calabar, just like that.

He could smell the breakfast they were preparing in the galley. He stopped suddenly, paused and took the binoculars away from his eyes, and squinted his eyes; for the eye patch was surprisingly gone. It was a faint plume of smoke far away on portside. From the tilting angle of the plume, he could tell that it was a ship headed for Africa on a more Southerly direction, which must be the Kongo River slave ports of Cabinda to Benguela. It was possibly another *Baltimore Clipper* that would bluff their way through the Royal Navy warships effectively with manufactured products, and be refitted in the African ports for slave cargo on their outbound voyage, just like his *Sea Fairy*. He smiled to himself; it was time to groom his valuable commodity.

He had agreed with his 40-man crew for extra bonuses to achieve his goals and objectives. To counter all the common contagions like smallpox, dysentery, measles etc., it was agreed that the holds and the slaves must be hosed down daily. All slaves down below-deck must be taken up to the deck for their feeding and some exercise. Wickedness or any form, or excessive torture to any slave would not be condoned. The safety nets to prevent suicidal acts of jumping overboard must always be in position. All mature slaves must remain in *twin-shackling* all through the journey, it was targeted to encumber and also discourage sexual activities by the crew. Captain Luckbone's experience from a couple of slave insurrections onboard was that, *total prevention was cheaper than cure, and could make the difference between life and death.*

So far so good, they had cleared the immediate coverage of the West Africa Squadron, who was the cat in this *cat and mouse* illegal trade game. It would be like a pin in haystack to encounter any cruisers between there and Cuba. Since they had left Calabar in a hurry, the customary shaving of every body hair, and the heated silver wire branding of every slave was scheduled before breakfast. Even Captain Luckbone was looking forward to that moment of truth when the former captors would come face-to-face with their former victims. He could only imagine the outcome, though he had resolved to keep them apart as much as possible so that he would not end up with the ultimate loss.

Brian Luckbone were not much of a spiritual person, though he could not but agree that some form of divine destiny was at work that pulled these animals together. *Animals?* Yes animals, over the years he had never regarded them as human beings, but as *ebony* or *sacks of coal* as they were referred to in their trade parlance.

Below deck, was a direct opposite of the serenity of the ocean. Even with the fresh sea breeze blowing steadily through the holds, the stench was thick and unbearable. It was a nauseating pot pourri of stinking unwashed bodies mixed with stale rotten breaths blended into smeared fresh human feces, ammonium-rich urine and vomit. The pungent odor did not only assault the nostrils but the entire being.

The clanging sounds of iron shackles, heavy chains, leg irons and manacles were so depressive that they subdued both the body and soul of their very hopeless and helpless wearers. Chukwuma felt so ashamed and humiliated when not long ago, he could not hold it any longer, as he defecated all over himself. Even though it was a relief to finally let go, he felt as if the endless mass slipping and pushing through his buttocks was going to go on forever. Finally, it thankfully stopped, and he felt totally drained and empty. He could do nothing but to lie squarely still in the mound of sticky offending waste that he had expelled. And for the very first time since their capture he wept and cried like a baby, over his pathetic situation. Where was Obele, his brother in this mass of writhing black bodies in chains?

It was just then the armed guards opened the grates and climbed down into the holds. The guards were physically assaulted by the filth that confronted them, just after one night. Two of the guards reeled back and uncontrollably spewed their own vomit to add to what was already there. It took them some time to regain their composure, before they began shouting;

"Up! Up! Up all of you." They continued shouting and banging on the iron pillars. The slaves who could not comprehend, but all sat up, it was all the headroom they could manage. Even though they had whips in their hands they were not using them. They held to their noses as they quickly slid open apertures on the floor level that the gutters terminated, before powerful jets of salt water hit the captives and the floors. The jets that were trained on each captive washed away every debris in its path. Chukwuma who felt so scared at first was really relieved by the turn of events. In a very short while the holds and their occupants were relatively clean to some extent. Close inspections were made, and subsequently hosed down accordingly. Thereafter, they were led up in their shackled pairs.

On the deck and in the open, there were more armed guards strategically positioned to repel any insurgency. They were horded together under the watchful eyes of the guards; but their interest was on the open waters that differed any idea of escape. All you could hear amidst the shouting of the guards was a backdrop of clanging fetters, not one African cry or voice. The captain stood safely away on the bridge from the madness below, but observing every single slave. He could not spot any trouble-maker.

It took seven crew members to descend expertly on the slaves with shaving knives. When each slave had completed his cut, he was rewarded with a whole boiled plantain with an orange as breakfast. They were so famished and drained that not a soul rejected what he was given. Captain Luckbone was happy with their reaction, it showed that his cargo was ready to live, and not a suicide-bound set that would rather choose to end it all. It was time to brand them, Dr. Morgan the quack, was ready with his coal stove, tongs and soothing salves. He would spare himself the agony of watching and hearing their animal squeals, by retiring to his cabin for a well-deserved rest. After all it was time to sample the queen that he had secured up in his cabin for himself. There was nothing like a hot-blooded sturdy African lioness…he smiled to himself.

CHAPTER 28

Just like the featureless wide ocean, the days at sea too were monotonously featureless. It was the same routine daily; the rowdy pungent wake up and refreshing salty-water hosing down, then the clambering up onto the deck for breakfast. If the weather was good they were kept on deck until towards sunset when they were served some sort of gruel or mush for dinner before they were sent down back into the holds. They had come to look forward to the meals, even though not much but calculated to sustain. They had gradually lost count of the days. There had not been any incident that occurred beyond the ordinary; and the slaves had gradually accepted their joint fates and destinies impotently.

Chukwuma had not one day sighted his brother since they embarked on this voyage and were separated; he had feared for the worse. It was not until the previous day when he stood next to Ngozika, the fairest of the three Onitsha Ado girls that were purchased in Itu, that she told him that she saw his brother and her people the day before. It was indeed cheery news for Chukwuma. When he was eating the piece of boiled yam and coconut that was his breakfast, he was humming to himself. Another puzzling news from Ngozika, was that Otiji, the slave factor was also on board as a slave, including all his crew. His immediate reaction was to know if she was certain that Ezemuo was also on board. She did not know Ezemuo personally, so she could not confirm his presence on board.

All of a sudden Chukwuma felt light-headed, he felt a serenity that he had never experienced since he was captured back at the Ibini Ukpabi shrine at Arochukwu. How on earth did Otiji and his people end up on board? Now he knew that God was totally in control, and that the long road to vengeance had divinely commenced for him. He was going to do everything to stay alive, and finally return to his homeland to expose the fraud that was the Ibini Ukpabi oracle. He resolved to himself that Otiji and Ezemuo must be summarily dealt with for their atrocities against humanity.

The more he thought about the total reversal of fortunes for Otiji and his accomplices; he could not but respect the white man cunning wisdom. If they could pull off this major coup on the so called invincible Otiji, then he, Chukwuma must not ever underestimate his multiple skills that were more than wizardry..

Captain Brian Luckbone sat on the sturdy oak desk in his cabin, his left hand unconsciously fiddled with the ever-present lucky charm hanging on his neck. He examined his records, then paused to set his spectacles on the table. His calculative mind was active, and went into overdrive. He could not believe his luck that halfway through the voyage he had not recorded any death in his crew or human cargo. There had been some isolated cases of measles and smallpox that was effectively contained by the quack. *Quack or no quack*, Dr. Morgan had fully justified his inclusion on this voyage. Even the nutritive ration plan for both the crew and the human cargo was designed by this brilliant medical personnel who fell foul of the ethics of organized medical practice in Baltimore. He had recruited him only as a favor, since his license to practice had been withdrawn for life. Luckbone was in on his little secret through a privileged source.

The captain had also made giant progress in his amoral relationship with the queen. She had noticed the sheer appalling conditions of her fellow female captives to really appreciate her privileges. Her innate urge for survival had come to the fore, and she had reciprocated the kindest gestures of the captain. She had actively participated with some gusto to thrill her benefactor to no end, in their amorous escapades. The captain, though quite impressed with her excellent performances, had yet kept her in shackles; he was not taking anything for granted. No captain in his right mind would forget the lessons of the tragedy of *The Amistad* whose human cargo rebelled and successfully took over the ship to the USA, and subsequently gained their freedom.

"One cannot be too careful with these ferocious animals..." He muttered aloud, startling the queen who was alluringly lying naked in bed, to look towards his direction.

"You say me?" the queen called out softly in her little smattering English.

"No not you. You go to sleep, Queen Amaka." He reassured her before stepping out to the bridge for the night watch.

Even though she was shackled to the bedpost, she could freely move about within the cabin because of the allowance of the long chain. Could she have withstood the shame and disgrace on the deck with all those commoners? She could imagine what her brother, Otiji was passing through. That was if they had not killed him out of vengeance by now. She had grown up in a prominent household that thrived on the slave trade. Her grandfather would turn in his grave to see his grand and only great grand children in a slave ship as slaves. She heaved a deep sigh of grief.

She had known Captain Brian way back in Calabar as a very close friend of the Obong, her husband. In that year alone, that was his third voyage. She had first resisted the advances of the captain initially, whom had not pressed further but had understandably left her alone to sort out her choices. She had noted with anger that she was a fool, what and whom was she protecting or safeguarding with her chastity? Did the Obong after all these years, blink or hesitate to sell her into slavery? The only option was the deck with about 200 miserable naked strangers; she would rather stick with the captain. She had always been a secret admirer of the danger-courting white man. She would make the best out of her situation; who knows whether something good would come out of it. Something good like beautiful half-cast babies…the captain may even make her his queen. And she drifted off to sleep smiling...

CHAPTER 29

It was the fourth week into the voyage from the captain's records. And the strangest things began to happen. Queen Amaka had woken up with a very severe headache and vomiting that morning. The concerned captain, suspecting some bug or something had promptly sent up for Dr. Victor Morgan to examine her. He had left them to see what was happening at the galley.

On the other hand Chukwuma and Ngozika's affinity had gradually grown beyond the elbow as the popular adage would say. She too never hid her childlike excitement whenever they showed up. Chukwuma, all the while was shackled to a very strange fellow of about his father's age with a stranger facial scarification. He had initially suspected that the fellow was not an Igbo, since he was strangely uncommunicative. Then over time he had come to believe that the man was deaf and dumb, since he was totally taciturn. Just as he had never uttered a word, neither had he betrayed any form of emotion, nor displayed any negative reaction since they were paired. Even his eyes had a kind of mysterious unfathomable depth. In dignified silence, he would willingly follow Chukwuma as he steered them to where ever Ngozika would be positioned to startle her.

"Ha-ah! Chuma it is you. Good, you have started looking brighter." She keenly examined him from head to toe, though consciously averting her eyes from his extra large circumcised genitalia.

"Ngozika, *nwanyi* Onitsha! It is you; you are the brightness in this boat. You even get more beautiful by the day." Chukuma would answer in a croaky whisper, and his own inspection with emphatic nods at her proudly upright twin mammary mounds.

"Chuma, what are you staring at? You should be ashamed of yourself." She playfully berated him and folded her arms around her upper torso.

"Nwanyi Onitsha *biko rapum*! Please leave me alone to appreciate God's handiwork." Then he would quickly change the topic to quickly suppress the throbbing urge down in his loins. "So what is new, my fair lady?"

"Have you heard that the queen of Calabar is also onboard?" she inquired in a whisper that could only be heard by the four people who made up their shackled pairings..

"It is a lie. Don't tell me now that she is also one of us." "What do you mean by *one of us*, Chuma?"

"Is she also a prisoner onboard?" Chuma retorted gravely.

"Yes. They said she is a younger sister to our monster friend, Otiji." She whispered.

Chukwuma could not hide his mien at the mention of that foul name. His entire face contorted into a wicked snarl that frightened Ngozika.

"Chuma, what is the matter with you? You terrify me with that look." The young lady said earnestly.

"We must not allow them to leave this boat alive. They must be killed, all of them who had put us through all these troubles." Chuma whispered menacingly.

"Chuma please stop that line of thought, it is not safe." She glanced furtively around them.

"Ngozika, we can't just seat here. We must get this boat back to our land…"

"Chukwuma please I don't want trouble. If you go on this way, then never talk to me again. You are a mad man. You are insane." She quickly pulled her shackled partner to her and they hobbled away with the chain between them.

Chukwuma could not stop her; he wanted to but did not know what to say or do. It was then he noticed that his partner was tugging at the shackle between them for the very first time ever. Out of custom that he was always the one leading, he did not budge. When he finally peeled his eyes away from the retreating backs of Ngozika and her partner. He was shaken to the marrow of his bones not by what he heard, but by the speaker.

"Chuma! Chukwuma my son, the young lady is right, you are a mad man and a big fool." It was coming loud and clear from his partner whom he thought was deaf and dumb. This time he was the one that was really gob smacked.

"Come Chuma, let us find somewhere to seat down. I want to talk to you, like a father to a son." The voice was genial and yet authoritative. Chuma mechanically followed the man to where they could find a seating space from the maddening crowd.

"Now you relax, let me reassure you that your girl shall return to you, in the fullness of time. I know that she is a sound wife material for you."

"How do you know, sir? And who are you?" Chukwuma reeled off cautiously.

"My name is *Udochi*, peace of God, I am a prince and priest from Nri. You can see my indelible *mgburu ichi* marks. These *ichi* marks were performed on me when I was only 14 days old." He parted the incisions running from one side of his forehead to the jaw.

"As an *Ndi Nri*, I am supposed to be sacred and untouchable as I do my migratory works as an agent of the Eze Nri to expand the kingdom by only peaceful means." He stopped to handle the next question.

"Why by only peaceful means?" Chuma asked.

"Because the Nri Kingdom and sovereignty were established on the ideology of cultural tranquility. We believe in the concept of fundamental human rights. We respect human life and condemn and abhor any form of inhuman treatment. That is why Nri does not accept slavery or the local Osu caste system." The man paused to lean properly on the wall.

"I was in Arochukwu to warn them that the slave trade was abominable, when Otiji and his cabal threw caution to the wind to capture me at the oracle of Ibini Ukpabi. Now you can see why and how; I understand what you are passing through, please don't let it to consume you. I can feel your burning passion since that day you first heard that Otiji and his people were on board." The man tried to look into his eyes; but there was something odd and fixating about them.

"I cannot understand you sir. Are you saying we should allow these vermin to live after all their atrocities? Chuma asked incredulously.

"Yes! Unfortunately yes. They are already under a corporate anathema. When they laid their filthy hands on me, I told them their cup was full… they have gone beyond redemption, that is why they are riding in this boat with us. Leave vengeance to Chukwu Okike, the creator of everything. They have faulted the natural laws of justice, my son. It is payback time for them all. So you better stay out of it, young man." The man spoke philosophically, carefully choosing his words.

"What laws of God did they fault?" Chuma asked grudgingly.

"It had been passed down over the ages at Nri where any slave that sets feet on the land is freed that; *all men were created equal by their creator*. And my son we hold these truths to be self evident that The Creator endowed us all with certain *sacred rights to be free, to be happy, and to live life to the fullest*... and any man who denies another these rights is cursed." The man declared as if reading from a tome. Chukwuma was speechless, but was really impressed. He knew that he had so much to learn from this very unassuming sage.

Captain Brian Luckbone was just stepping out of the galley when he ran into Dr. Morgan waiting out by the rails and enjoying the benevolent morning rays. Luckbone was wondering why the quack was beaming with naughty smiles when started towards him.

"Yes Victor, I hope it is not any serious bug?"

"Well, nothing to cause any alarm. She caught the bug alright; but one that is making the woman screeching and dancing to high heavens." The doctor could not hide his amusement with the captain's puzzled expression.

"Damn you Morgan, could you please erase that silly grin on your face and tell me what kind of bug makes people screeching and dancing". The captain was dead serious.

"I am sorry captain. Forgive my insensitivity sir. The woman is about four weeks pregnant, but is so excited with the news." The doctor knew when to be serious.

"Em...pregnant. Now, that is what I consider a very interesting commercial development, Dr. Morgan. Thanks for your professional support. May your day be rough." Captain Brian Luckbone turned gingerly and marched off to the bridge, whistling a melodious tune.

CHAPTER 30

It was indeed a most glorious dawn over the Atlantic Ocean. The magnificent dazzling sunrays dancing over the undulating mirrored face of the ocean never cease to captivate the veteran mariner. Though there was yet no land in sight, there was the prevalence of gulls following their wake, to signify that land was somehow nearby. Captain Luckbone standing on the bridge and scouring the horizon with his binoculars knew they would make harbor in Cuba by nightfall.

Cuba was the most popular destination for slave ships during this era of illegal slave trade, because it was yet to abolish the trade. Though Havana, Santiago, and Cienfuegos were the three key markets for the fresh slaves from Africa; Santiago de Cuba had a reputation for its large slave-contraband. The Sea Fairy was actually destined for Havana, but after off-loading its human cargo under the shroud of darkness at one of the hidden coves that dot the island. It would then officially berth at Havana and to be transformed into a blockade runner to be loaded with munitions and very essential war merchandise and posts; that would fetch it the Letter of Marque from corrupt government officials, that would provide them with a delicate mask of validity in the event of capture.

They had hoisted the American flag the previous day as planned, and by mid-day today they would swap it with the Spanish flag. The application of different flags was calculated to overcome the complex intricacies of the legal and technical procedures of the illegal slave-trade era. One little oversight, and Captain Brian Luckbone would kiss his beloved *Sea Fairy* and all his life-time savings investment good-bye. The tradition to auction captured slavers and their non- human cargo, and the proceeds shared amongst the sailors of the particular blockade vessel that effected the capture. It had wrecked many a slaver. The South Atlantic Blockading Squadron operated out of Key West, so Captain Brian Luckbone had an uphill task before him if he was to operate around the United States.

It was going to be a very busy day ahead, with all the final cargo refining to make before they disembark. They had the previous day, tactically done the traditional head shaving before disembarkation. Every slave on-board, had their head shaven, except the queen who was still lying low in the captain's cabin. Talking about the queen, the captain could not but heaved a sigh of relief for what he considered as a brilliant verdict.

After so many sleepless nights, he had finally jettisoned the choice to sell the queen with her unborn baby, which would have fetched him a tidy princely sum. He had earnestly considered his two failed marriages that all floundered without offspring back in his adopted city of Baltimore, with this development he could finally prove that he could father a child. He was not going to sell the queen. He would keep her for himself to make more children. He knew deep inside that this is one arrangement that would not go awry like the previous marriages to his kind. The queen would not be considered as his wife, but a property, his property dedicated to bearing children alone. Neither the law nor anybody would fault him, and he would eat his cake and have it.

He felt so happy with himself it seemed like all were going well for him. Not a single fatality in a cargo of about 200; it was unbelievable. He knew with the new design for his Sea Fairy it was achievable; though not this good. He surpassed his every projection. Thank God for the pumps powered by the steam engine to pump the high velocity water jets to flush both the cargo and the decks and holds. He also knew that taking Dr. Morgan along also did well.

For a change the captain, had asked the galley to serve a triple helping of both breakfast and dinner today. A change from the routine of minimal feeding to just sustain them. With the feverish pitch of preparations for the port, everyone was in high spirits. The crew were looking forward to spend their hard earned bonuses on the usual sailor-frivolities. The captives cannot wait to discover what lay ahead at the end of the voyage and dislodged destinies.

CHAPTER 31

As the Havana waterfront gradually faded and blended into the bluish-green waters of the Atlantic Ocean, so the weeping gradually subsided for the twenty slaves that were reloaded on board before the *Sea Fairy* set sail as the rays of the sun lapped the Eastern horizon. The 15 males and 5 female slaves who had been given some form of coarse clothing were cramped into three cabins, since the holds had been refitted into new and appropriate uses. If everything worked out in their favour the *Sea Fairy* would be in port again within 48 hours.

Captain Luckbone was on the bridge with his first officer busy calculating and plotting out their co-ordinates for the benefit of subordinate. They had to make time allowance to steer totally clear of the Key West area, and it would take only an old sea dog in the caliber of Luckbone to navigate successfully through an area of the Atlantic that was so treacherous to be named the *Graveyard of the Atlantic*. As a blockade runner allowance was also made for moonless nighttime when they could run past the Union Navy.

Captain Luckbone was confident that his steamship with its low profile, high speed, and shallow draft would outrun any of his adversaries in the blockade squadron. He was an admirer of Edward C. Anderson a native of Savannah who owned and captained the *Fingal*; the most successful blockade runner for the Confederates to the Savannah port. It was the gambler in him, coupled with the prospects of finally settling down, that had made him to take up this dangerous and somehow obscene contract. He just wanted to make Captain Anderson and his Fingal pale in significance compared to him and his *Sea Fairy*. *The Gambler*; that nomenclature would sound apt for his next vessel…and he began to hum to himself a country song that eulogized *the gambler* as his mind played back all the events that had happened since he arrived in Havana..

They had been unduly delayed in Havana; he had surpassed the interval to refit, and restock the vessle by a whole two weeks. After the slave cargo had been marched off to the barracoons where they would be imprisoned until they were collected by their owners, or directly sold off to prospective buyers that would first prod, poke, pinch, and fondle them in the guise of inspection for all imaginable forms of defect. Even though the slaves were fed better in the baracoons, their living conditions were still very appalling and deaths to sickness and diseases still claimed these lucky survivors of the middle passage. There was no way to hide the horrified blood-cuddling wails and cries of the inmates to the prospective buyers and passers-by.

It was always the tradition that during the interval of refurbishment, he was sure to get his next contract. It was within that interval, Dr. Victor Morgan procured some sort of formal documents for a brand new identity, had jumped ship to fully settle down in Cuba, and begin a new life and practice.

He was just three days in port when this tailor-made contract arrived. It was tailor-made for the insane voyager. It was a typical Luckbone kind of deal; an undertaking that was not for the lily- livered. It was not surprising then when most of his sailors decided to jump ship. They were unwilling to stake their fortunes with an America that was already under a civil war. That setback did not worry Luckbone one bit, he knew where he was going. He was set to be a very rich man at the end of that voyage. Even though under great pressure from his people, Thomas 'Hunter' Lamar, some sort of Confederate agent in Cuba, had waited patiently for Captain Brian Luckbone for three months to return to port. All the blockade runners he had approached had turned down the offer to deliver his special cargo to Savannah, for the obvious reason that it was just too risky. Though they had all unanimously recommended Luckbone. So Lamar had no choice but to wait, for the man whose name obviously sounded like his lucky talisman.

They had met, and true to type, Lamar was impressed with Brian Luckbone who was a man of few words. Lamar, had observed within a short time that Luckbone with his varied experiences exuded so much confidence that was infectious to a degree. They had taken to each other as bread and butter from the moment they first shook hands. That was how Luckbone had confided in his plans to finally retire to a beautiful city like Savannah that was the proposed destination. Lamar was not called *Hunter* because it sounded musical; he was the hunter in every connotation of the word. *The hunter then had played a hand that the gambler could not resist.* A thick brown envelope duly addressed to his younger brother, Gazaway Bugg Lamar, had all the necessary documents to effect and claim ownership of the plantation and the balance of the fees. There were two other sealed envelopes addressed to Mayor Richard Arnold, and General Hardee of the Confederate Army.

It was after the deal had been sealed, that Luckbone had specifically handpicked twenty premium Ibo slaves from the barracoons, for his new plantation. He might as well start searching for a new name for it. It was during the selection process for the ideal Ibo slaves, who were reputed to be very clever and resourceful, that he had broken apart two brothers whom he recalled had a very emotional reunion when the slaves were discharged in Cuba. With his experience in the trade, he knew that unusual affinity spelt real trouble if they were allowed to stay together in the long run. It was in the same vein he had also split another batch of five males and three females whom he later learnt originated from Onitsha on the Niger River. It was so heart-rending to witness their disillusionment and melancholy at their final separation; that even a hard-hearted old sea dog of his pedigree had to swallow hard to hide his emotion.

In replenishing his stock, he had also taken delivery on board some kegs of turpentine and bales of cotton back in Havana, the uninitiated would not understand why anyone would take cotton to Savannah, the home of cotton. Just like carrying coal to Newcastle, as the saying goes. For at the most critical moment of this journey, he was going to resort to cotton saturated in turpentine as fuel to power the steam engines; though more expensive but was very efficient since it produced less smoke and more heat for optimum speed. That critical moment would be a straight Westerly course off the path to Bermuda, that would take them to the mouth of the Savannah River. He had been to the Savannah port for over ten times in his career as a captain.

The Savannah city and port was just about 19 miles from the entrance of the Savannah River into the Atlantic Ocean. The city was so prosperous to be considered as the sixth most populous city in the confederate states. The munitions and the other critical warfare materials safely packed in the cargo holds were badly needed there by the Confederates to frustrate General William T. Sherman's claimed march to the sea. After much contemplations, he had finally resolved that Savannah held the perfect blend to his prospects to finally retire from this dangerous vocation.

While it had taken Captain Brian Luckbone additional days in delay time to replace his very depleted crew, Lamar had almost driven him almost mad with anxiety to depart Havana immediately. It was after he (Luckbone) had threatened to back out, that he was informed of the pressing urgency for the delivery. With the Union's successful capture of Atlanta, it was speculated that Savannah maybe the next target. General William Tecumseh Sherman and his 62,000 troops were plundering everything in their way. It was on this note Luckbone was offered twice what he got initially as fees to set sail immediately to give the city of Savannah a fighting chance. The deal was to be settled in part with the 500-acre Hunter's Plantation with the only five old slaves left in it. The thriving Hunters Plantation was doing well until the Emancipation Proclamation of 1863 finally put it in the doldrums. The Hunter's cotton and sugarcane plantation was situated just outside Savannah at the Little Ogeechee River.

He had promised 'Hunter', that even if it would need his blood, he would get the precious cargo to Savannah intact. 'Hunter' had also concluded all clandestine procedures to ease them out, and into port. The captain understood what that meant; certain strategic authorities had been *persuaded* to look the other way to facilitate their timely passage. It was either that Hunter Lamar did not know, or that he pretended not to know that Fort Mc-Allister had been defeated by Brigadier General William B. Hazen of the Union Army on December 13, 1864. That much, Captain Brian Luckbone did not know as he set out on that voyage of make or mar..

He had been informed as they raised anchor that morning, that one of the slaves was vomiting with a very high fever. He had asked them to isolate him from the others on the deck to avoid infection. The woman in his cabin he had not counted as a slave unconsciously, because he had considered the prospects ahead beyond this voyage. He was convinced that Savannah was it. He had fallen in love with the city of Savannah, since he first visited it in 1836 with Don Pedro Blanco. How could he forget that journey? He had never seen a more serene and beautiful city.

Another unforgettable visit was that of March, 1859, when he had left his vessel undergoing exhaustive repairs to really tour the city as never before. A friend had promised him the biggest sale ever in US history. The venue was the Ten Broeck Race Course in Savannah. The event later came to be known as "The Weeping Time"; a whooping 436 enslaved persons from a single owner, Pierce Mease Butler of the Butler plantations, were presented for sale. *The Weeping Time* expression was to capture the harrowing experience of pain and anguish of the slaves that were forcefully separated from lifelong families and associations. To learn later that the whole sale was to recover from gambling debts and stock market loses; made him truly curious. It was one event that would remain vivid in his lifetime, just as the beautiful Savannah stuck.

"Captain sir! Capain sir!!" He was shaken from his reverie.

"I am sorry to disturb you sir, but the slave boy is getting worse." His oldest and trusted crew was standing by the door to the bridge.

"What do you mean by he is getting worse?" the captain quickly gathered himself.

"He is totally unconscious sir." The crew answered grimly.

"Just like that?"

"Yes sir, just like that sir."

He tapped the first officer on the back, and quickly slid down the pole to the deck, with the crew man right behind him.

He saw two crew members just hanging around without touching the body lying immobile on the deck. He bent down and felt for his pulse, but suddenly pulled back his hand as if he was burnt by some red hot iron. Examining the boy without touching him, he noticed the right ankle of the sick slave was disproportionately swollen, with a nasty looking old wound oozing creamy puss. That must be it; an old festered wound that accounted for the fever. He had felt the pulse before the body heat scorched him. The body naturally switches off as a form of defensive mechanism to absorb trauma and pain. The boy was alive alright; but something must be done urgently to salvage the leg. The greenish tint of the face of the wound was a sure sign of gangrene setting in. Then he noticed ruefully that it was the boy… The very fair-skinned young man he had separated from his older brother back in Cuba.

CHAPTER 32

It had been a little choppy all day but nothing really serious to warrant concern. Captain Luckbone had displayed all the cunning and experience that he had garnered over the years, for many in his trade to swear that Luckbone was indeed a cat with nine lives. All through the daylight hours, he had consistently announced *loudly* his presence and direction with bellowing thick black smoke from burning the cheap coal. He had set a steady course for Bermuda to mislead obvious covert interests in Nassau and the Florida coasts. It had been totally uneventful except for the very sick slave boy that he had handed over to the queen and two slave girls to look after. They had bathed him with cold water to bring down his temperature. They had also bathed and dressed the wound that was caused by the rusted heavy leg iron shackles. When he had last checked on him, he looked like somebody in coma. He had left without saying anything; he wanted to just concentrate and get the *Sea Fairy* safely to Savannah.

He had noticed other vessels too far to see even with the binoculars, their tell-tale trail of smoke snaking lazily behind in the clear blue skies. Sunset finally came in a blazing harmless golden glow, that transformed everything in its trail to a solid golden tint. The sun, at its very final moments, in a golden-orange hue boldly stood still like it was reluctant to say its final good-bye for the day. Then suddenly, it sank into the horizon as if it was pulled down by giant invisible fingers. This phenomenon had never ceased to amaze Captain Luckbone who openly professed to doubt the presence of God, nor any form of supreme being that was involved with creation.

With the onset of darkness, because it was a moonless night, the captain had directed that they now switch to burning the special anthracite coal that was smokeless. The directive that no one should put on any kind of light went into force immediately. The bales of cotton and the turpentine were made ready for later use in the night. As they approached 32° 05'N 75° 34'W, Captain Luckbone started a gradual shift to portside to hit 32° 18'N 81° 01'W. He then gave directive for them to switch to the cotton and turpentine combination from the anthracite coal. All of a sudden, there was a total calm upon the sea; the kind of calm that heralded a storm.

Through his binoculars, the captain could make out the lights of at least four vessels, from their sizes he could tell that they were the Union Naval cruisers at anchor. Beyond them he could pick out Tybee Island Lighthouse. It was going to be an outright suicide to think he could sneak through this solid blockade. He cut the engines to slow down the vessel. Was this a dead end; a dead end to all his proposed plans? Not even the Letter of Marque in his possession could bluff him past half a dozen cruisers, with his cargo of arms and ammunitions, with fresh slaves from Africa. His British citizenship which he could flaunt as a last resort, would come crashing down like a pack of cards in this logjam. The only thing for him now was to retrace his steps, with his tail between his legs? After all, every gambler knows when to bow out…then he heard the loud booming voice of his first officer muttering loud, as if he could decode his own thoughts.

"It will take only the hand of God to squeeze us through this cruiser-barricade."

"That is if there is a god, who is capable to do it. My friend shut up, I am thinking." The captain retorted.

"Oh my God, please give us a miracle, I beg you." The first officer said this prayer under his breath, but dramatically loud enough for the captain to hear. And as if on cue, the heavens opened up with a fierce blinding rain storm. The amazed captain peeped out into dark night at the murderous rain lashing furiously at the re-enforced glass panes of the bridge. He did not know exactly what to make of it at first, but it was raining cats and dogs outside; just what they needed now. It was more than a coincidence; his first officer called it a miracle, he thought to himself.

"Hallelujah! Hallelujah!! Thank you my Lord. You are God indeed." The excited First Officer burst into excited chants of praise to his God. The captain was speechless, totally speechless and overwhelmed. He could hear the animated singing of the man, whom as far as he was concerned had just wrath a magical wonder for him to witness.

It was a brief moment, but it seemed like a lifetime as the captain finally cranked the engine and the *Sea Fairy* surged into life totally noiseless in the face of the tropical storm. The captain knew deep down that there was no way any human being would be standing or keeping watch at that point in time.

Before long the *Sea Fairy* was surging past the rain dimmed lights of the Naval might of the Union Army. He positioned the Lighthouse light to his portside as slipped into the yearning mouth of the Savannah River, and in a flitting moment Cockspur Island was zooming past on his portside. How glad was he to see the familiar features of the storm drenched Fort Jackson? And as branched to the left at the fork in the river, the storm just stopped as if a giant hand just switched it off from above. The first officer just crumpled on to his knees, and started weeping with tears of joy like a baby. Looming ahead in their path was the bulk of the *CSS Georgia*. The captain quickly ordered the first officer to unfurl the Confederate flag as he cut off the engine and dropped anchor. They were three miles from the city of Savannah.

Captain Brian Luckbone in all his life had neither seen, nor heard, or experienced anything of this nature. His knuckles were white and sweating, gripping the wheel as if his life depended on it. He was totally drenched in sweat. He knew the sweet-sour numbing taste of victory as an addictive gambler that courted with and thrived in danger. In this instance, there was no such taste in his mouth, because this victory was not his making at all. Now he was more than convinced that a divine and supreme being truly fingered and handled the affairs of men.

The CSS Georgia swiftly dispatched a rowboat with five armed naval officers to row across to the *Sea Fairy*. As they clambered on board expertly at the stern, Captain Luckbone armed with the various letters from Hunter Lamar was there to meet them. The naval team was led by a young Lieutenant Francis Gulliver who smartly saluted and introduced himself and his team courteously, before asking for documents confirming the Sea Fairy's official business in Savannah. Luckbone spoke confidently with his reserved English accent. He introduced himself formally, before he handed over the envelopes to be dispatched immediately, as demanded by a Thomas Lamar in Cuba. *Thomas Hunter Lamar,* the name had a positive effect on the young Lieutenant who did not forget to salute before they scrambled off the boat back into their rowboat.

At that particular moment, in the hallowed chambers of the Savannah City Hall on Bay Street, a very critical meeting that had started at about 9 p.m., was still in session. It had dragged on all through the night without making any head way. The 56-year-old Mayor Richard Arnold, a medical doctor by training was treading a not-very-familiar ground. He was chairing the meeting of very prominent stakeholders of the city, and Lieutenant-General William J. Hardee, 49, who was Commanding Confederate Forces in the Savannah Field and the greater Missisippi Division. Amongst the stake holders seated in that room were former mayor Charles C. Jones, Jr., who became mayor at 29, and was both an attorney and author, and a die-hard supporter of the Confederates; the accomplished English cotton merchant Charles Green, whose grand Madison Square home was purported to be the most expensive in all of Savannah; Reverend Garrison Frazier, the former slave from Glenville, South Carolina who bought his own freedom; the very wealthy Gazaway Lamar, the multifaceted entrepreneur with his paws into anything that yielded money, was a close relation to Hunter Lamar in Havana, Cuba.

The bone of contention had been first, the General Hardee's adamant reply of no retreat, no surrender to General Sherman's letter requesting an unconditional surrender to spare Savannah the fate that befell Atlanta. While majority of the stakeholders were for total peaceful surrender to spare them and their beloved Savannah the attendant pain and destruction of defeat. There had also been a total condemnation and vituperations for Lamar, their agent in Cuba who had not brought in the much needed munitions as agreed. There was also the argument that General Hardee's 10,000 troops could beat or not stand General Sherman's 62,000 troops even though fatigued from marching all the way down from Atlanta.

It was this totally tired, sleepy and yearning band of disenchanted people that Lieutenant Francis Gulliver delivered the impossible breakthrough information of the *Sea Fairy* to. The letters were delivered to the owners who with renewed vigor sprang into collective and individual actions.

CHAPTER 33

Everyone in the city of Savannah that was not bedridden trooped out to the serene River Street waterfront to catch a glimpse of the so called "nick of time liberators" of their beloved city. A very boisterous Mayor Richard Arnold led everyone that mattered in Savannah to give Captain Luckbone and his motley crew a most wonderful and rousing reception. To be able to outwit Admiral John A. Dahlgren, the United States Commander of the South Atlantic Blockading Squadron; Captain Brian Luckbone was already a living legend to the people. If only they knew the truth, Captain Luckbone thought to himself.

It was exactly 8 O'clock by the hands of the clock on the dome of the City Hall, and it was the 19th day of December, 1864. As the early morning rays of the sun cast its valiant brilliance to chase away every shade of the night, to usher in a new day, the *Sea Fairy* with the Confederate flag flapping confidently overhead sailed proudly between the ironclad *CSS Savannah* and the *CSS Georgia* into the city of Savannah. The familiar riverside walks were filled with cheering and waving civilians and soldiers. The first officer was now kneeling in some form of adulation to the God that had proven beyond doubt that he is in existence and in total control.

Yes! It took the *hand of God* to see them through that blockade. Luckbone could taste salt not the one in the air. The salty taste of tears that were freely cascading down his cheeks. And something struck him like a thunderbolt…the apt and symbolic name for his new plantation. No! Not after *the Hunter*. No! Not even after *the Gambler*. It would be called the protective and providential hand of God… *Hand Of God Plantation*.

After the *Sea Fairy* moored and was secured, Captain Brian Luckbone resplendent in a navy blue embroidered bluecoat with white facings, worn unbuttoned over brilliant white breeches and equally brilliant white stockings, with shiny black gold buckled shoes. His Captain's hat had a majestic colorful red plume stock into it. He stepped confidently down the gangway into the embrace of Mayor Arnold and a very relieved Savannah citizens. In a very brief but emotional ceremony Captain Luckbone and his entire crew were made honorary citizens of Savannah. Thereafter, the mayor announced to the admiration of all that his council members had unanimously voted Captain Brian Luckbone to be honored with the exalted position of an alderman to the city of Savannah.

A very sober and totally humbled Luckbone, thanked the mayor and the people of Savannah for the honor done to him and his crew. Words, he emphatically declared would not be enough to express their gratitude and honor. He concluded by declaring that all the credits and commendations actually belonged to the Almighty God that was instrumental to a feat that was beyond any human comprehension and capability. It was on that basis he was rechristening the *Hunters Plantation,* as its new owner, *The Hand Of God Plantation.* The whole audience was silent, and under the grip of a known and confessed atheist, until the Reverend Garrison Gazier exploded with an earth quaking thunderous *Praise the Lord!* Which the crowd equally replied in a vibrating *Halelujah!*

The army had waited very impatiently for the brief ceremony to close, then had quickly directed the inquisitive crowds away from the waterfront. The soldiers had effectively cordoned off the immediate area of the *Sea Fairy* from prying eyes. As chain gangs were skillfully positioned between the *Sea Fairy* and Warehouse 3, 4, and 5.

The crew members were the first to come down with their bags, and were ferried over in horse drawn wagons to official guest houses where they would be quartered as guests of Mayor Arnold and his council. Thereafter, some horse-drawn military wagons were provided to ferry Captain Luckbone and his slaves over to his plantation. The sick slave boy lying prone on a stretcher was carried down obviously still in bad shape. Ngozika looking very pensive was dabbing a wet rag over his sweating face as the stretcher was carried over to a smiling Reverend Frazier and a group of black church members. A black man with an unsmiling face readily took the wet rag from Ngozika, who was then gently led over to the wagon carrying the rest of the female slaves, she just burst into tears as she took her seat. The queen looking dignified in her flowing black gown, pulled the young girl onto her bosom, while she kept a straight face.

As the Captain made to climb on to the last wagon, Reverend Frazier moved over with outstretched hands and a deep booming and reassuring voice; "Brother Captain Brian its sure well with you"

"Reverend, thank you for everything. I hope he pulls through." The captain answered solemnly.

"You not to worry about nothin', the young man will pull through like a bull. Before you go sur, may I know the young man's name?"

"Oh, the young man, em…yes, come to think of it. Yes, I did not tell you yet." The captain felt like a little child caught with his hand in the soup pot. The wagon started rolling away when he seemed to get his thoughts together.

"His name is *Freeborn*…Freeborn. Did you hear me?", he called out looking backwards, before adding to the amazement of all the people, "Freeborn, because he was *born free*.

CHAPTER 34

It was another three days before Chukwuma recovered his mind fully from the land of the dead. He had woken up on that day, in his usual manner of waking the mind before the body. Everything felt so strange. He had listened to the muted voices that were never raised above a whisper. Though, the voices spoke in the white man's language, they sounded very different from the ones in the slave ship. The harsh biting sting in voices was absolutely absent.

The scents he perceived were so nice, clean, and refreshing, for him to actually believe he was not on earth anymore after the reeking stench of the barracoons and the ship holds. His skin felt so good to whatever was wrapped around it. His body strangely felt weightless, there was not restrictive added weight of the chains and shackles. His spirit was wholly relaxed; the body and the soul were in perfect harmony. The signs were clear that he was in a friendly environment surrounded by true love, yet it was very strange. Strange, due to the muted voices to maintain some modicum of secrecy. Somebody on his side was afraid of somebody who was not on his side. So there was a dangerous enemy to be avoided.

He had lost every sense of time. His effort to recall the sequence of events up to that moment, kept getting muddled up. What he could recall distinctly was the forceful separation from his brother, Obele, after their reunion on land at the end of the sea voyage. His joy and happiness was cut short so soon. Even the consolation of being herded together with his beloved Ngozi, did not ease the sense of searing pain of loss in his heart, that he would not see his brother again. That was how he lost it; he went berserk.

He had swung out in fury like a caged animal at the closest guard, but did not connect. He screamed and swore in frustration. Until he had no strength left in him. It was then he knew, he must have aggravated his ankle wound. With the energy and focus he had mustered to fight the perpetrators, he had let his natural defenses down, for his body to succumb to the toxins that had been plaguing his body. He also recollected the admonishing looks from Udochi, the Nri priest, to check and control his negative emotions, but he, Chukwuma was past caring.

He remembered vividly, the twenty of them were led away from the barracoons. After, what felt like an eternity they were finally loaded back on board some days later, and as the ship pulled out of the harbor, he was overpowered by the feeling of nausea. He had vomited the little food inside him, before being overwhelmed with a dizziness that swirled his head out of its socket, before the deck came swishing swiftly to smack him like a boxer's sucker punch. That was when everything blacked out.

So much had happened since Captain Luckbone and his slaves departed for *The Hand of God Plantation.* Chukwuma, who was now identified as Freeborn was rushed to the small decent private quarters attached to the First African Baptist Church at Franklin Square. It was from there he was fretted over to a very secret address later in the day. It was secret underground hospital facility operated by some white abolitionists. After thorough checks, the doctor had promised Reverend Frazier, that they would do everything to save the leg that was in pretty bad shape. It was later, Pastor William J. Campbell, who was the pastor of the church, had joined them in the plans for the young man's rehabilitation.

At the Savannah wharves, the soldiers whom they left behind were just concluding the offloading and stacking into the appropriate warehouses of the ammunition cargo from Cuba, when messengers arrived with a message from General Pierre Toutant Beauregard for Lieutenant-General Hardee.

General P.T. Beauregard was the Confederate Commander of the South at that particular time. He had approved for his general to begin an immediate evacuation of his troops from Savannah into the neighboring State of South Carolina. It was his opinion and judgment to save the soldiers, than to fight and defend Savannah. He knew that his 10,000 troops were outnumbered by General Sherman's 62,000 troops. Allowing Hardee to confront Sherman would be a sheer suicidal mission, and that was why the commander had chosen the better part of valor to step out of the way, or be shamefully crushed.

General Hardee had thereafter summoned his commanders to work out a way of escape. They agreed to construct two pontoon bridges across two branches of the Savannah River, through Hutchinson Island straight across into South Carolina. As the army engineers went to work; the evacuation was fixed to be done under the cover of darkness on the night of Tuesday, 20th December 1864.

Mayor Arnold had also summoned his council members together with the solemn news, and called for ways to work out their peaceful surrender. Their ultimate desire was to avoid mayhem, destruction, and casualty of any sort. It was resolved that the mayor and some aldermen would very early on Wednesday morning rush to meet the Union Army General to negotiate an unconditional surrender. And the man to meet was the very charismatic 45 year- old, six foot six, 260 pounds, well-decorated veteran of many battles and wars, General John W. Geary.

By the morning of Tuesday, 20th December, 1864, the citizens woke to feverish army engineers coordinating the first section of the pontoon bridge from the waterfront on to the long stretch of island separating the two branches of the Savannah River. Another set of engineers were placing the pontoons from the other side of the island to the South Carolina side of the river. By sunset, the curious observers noticed that the Confederates had scuttled both the ironclad *CSS Savannah* and the *CSS Georgia*. The move to destroy their entire fleet on the Savannah was very curious and bizarre to those who poised to confront Sherman's plundering army.

As darkness fell over the land, the evacuations commenced smoothly with military precision. The pontoon bridges were designed to carry the men, animals, and all their equipment and ammunition. Just a little before dawn, the final couple of soldiers left set about their grim assignment to obliterate the pontoon bridges with fire. It was this floating fires that spread all over the river that inadvertently burnt to cinders the sleeping *Sea Fairy*. To this day, people had wrongly thought the demise of the *Sea Fairy* was a willful act by the evacuating Confederate Army..

As agreed, at the break of dawn on Wednesday December 21st, 1864, Mayor Arnold and his team of aldermen headed out to intercept General J.W. Geary with the news that General Hardee had evacuated from Savannah with his 10,000 troops. General Geary personally came into Savannah to assess the situation, before marching in jubilantly with his Union army, later in the day.

It was early the next day, General Sherman arrived and set up his Headquarters at Charles Green's Madison Square home. He thereafter, proceeded to send a telegram to President Abraham Lincoln offering him the city of Savannah as a Christmas gift. It was after that, that General J.W. Geary was made the Military Governor of Savannah, to tackle situational issues and restore normalcy.

It was at the reception of General Sherman, that Campbell and Frazier had been informed that Freeborn had regained consciousness. They had stolen away as soon as it was convenient to find their way to Freeborn's bedside. They met the doctor and a black nurse examining him.

Freeborn had looked their way, his eyes acknowledging them silently. They all noticed that there was no fear in his eyes. This was a very brave and confident young man, not the least timid as they come straight from Africa. Reverend Frazier liked him immediately.

"We won't be amputating, though he would limp slightly for the rest of his life." The doctor looked up at them with a big wide smile, his voice in a dramatic whisper.

"Praise God! Hallelujah!" The ministers chorused together.

"Wow! That is sure good news for the whole congregation." Pastor Campbell declared satisfactorily.

"This young man is directed by the *finger of God.*" Reverend Frazier added.

"He would have totally made it through, except that he lost some muscles and nerves. We must start making him feel at home, so that he could recover fully. His rehabilitation commences from here. Good day gentlemen, there is some urgent business to take care." The doctor rushed off, with his nurse following him as if she was glued to his tailcoat.

"Thank you, Doctor Albert." They chorused together again before reverting their attention to the young man watching his benefactors with keen interest.

"Him is Pastor Campbell" pointing to Pastor Campbell and repeating over and over, then thumping his own chest, "Me is Reverend Frazier". He noticed the young man mouthing the words after him, which was very impressive.

"You, what?" Frazier pointed to him and smiled.

The young man did not smile back. He looked despondent and thoughtful as if searching for the right words in futility.

"You what?" Frazier repeated slowly, but the young man stopped him angrily shaking his head in obvious disagreement.

"What mba! What mba!!" touching his chest declared slowly emphasizing on the syllables, *"Chu-kwu-ma, Chu-Kwu- Ma"*. And smiled satisfactorily at them.

"Chuckooma! Chuckma! Chuck! Yes, Chuck will do." They both repeated, tasting the strange word on their tongues again and again.

"Me is Reverend Frazier; Him is Pastor Campbell; and you *Chuck*." Frazier emphatically pointing to each of them accordingly with a big broad smile. And the young man also smiled and nodded as he mouthed the names accordingly.

There was a gentle knock on the door, and the nurse came in with a covered tray of food. They nodded at her, and proceeded to leave the room. As they got to the door, the young man cleared his throat loud enough to stop them in their tracks. The voice was a little faltering but distinctly clear.

"Revend Fa-chia; Pasto Campu-bel...Thak yo. Thak yo. Dalu nu!" Chuck Freeborn spoke out his first words in English and burst into a hearty laughter as they could not hide their shock and surprise.

"Thank you Brother Chuck Freeborn, and welcome home to Savannah." Reverend Frazier called back heartily and hastily left the room to hide the hot tears that were streaming down his cheeks like a flood gate bursting under pressure.

CHAPTER 35

It was definitely the gloomiest Christmas ever in Savannah's history. With most households having one or more members willingly recruited or conscripted into the Confederate Armed Forces, it was neither a joking matter nor a time for families to layback and enjoy carols. Some die-hard Confederates had even had the effrontery to brand Mayor Richard Arnold and his aldermen traitors to their face, for negotiating a peaceful surrender for Savannah. Folks like Gazaway Lamar had also not help matters by rushing to take the oat of allegiance to the Union, to protect their varied interests and investments from confiscation. General Sherman's the *Green-Meldrim House* headquarters was a beehive of activities.

Even though it was an exceptionally cold winter, it was not the reason the black population was even colder to the Union Army in Savannah. They were still smarting from the senseless loss of 600 newly emancipated slaves at Ebenezer Creek, on December 9th, 1864, indirectly through the callous directives of General Jefferson C. Davis. This Union General Jefferson Davis was not a relation of President Jefferson Davis, the Confederate Commander-In-Chief. The entire black community was under some kind of mourning, and not in the mood for the usual Christmas jollity.

For Chuck Freeborn it was his ever first and best Christmas. Even with the wound getting a very fierce scrubbing and dressing that Christmas morning, he could not but agree that life outside his native Amaeke had some pecks, He could not believe that one could get that much choice to eat and drink at one seating. It was the biggest meal ever in his life. The Church had sent over a whole Christmas turkey over to the hospital, for him and the two staff that turned up for work. Chuck had gorged himself to the point of nausea. He had with youthful exuberance tried every food and drink on that banquet table.

In the spirit of Christmas, General William Tecumseh Sherman also took time out to fete his officers to a massive Christmas dinner at the *Green Mansion*. Since the General was known to work hard; and play hard; the local grapevine could not wait to serenade Savannah citizens and beyond with mouth-watering snippets of the dinner. There was already a rumor making the rounds in the grapevine that there was already a very beautiful mistress there in Savannah. Some were even swearing on their mother's grave that, it was for her sake a shot was not fired in Savannah's takeover..

Chuck had indeed responded very well to treatment, and was on New Year's Day duly discharged. He had started walking with the aid of a very sturdy iron cane to support and take the stress away from his ailing left foot. That night, Reverend Frazier had ridden a wagon drawn by a horse through a maze of back streets to pick him up. He had taken him over to his own house, were adequate provision had been made to accommodate him in an outhouse.

The young man was a quick learner, Frazier observed. Within the first three days he had mastered the use of different utensils that were supposedly strange to an African first-timer in America in 1864. On his first morning in the Frazier household, he had foraged through the woods behind the house for a better part of the morning. Even though the vegetation was green, it was somehow different from those of Amaeke. He had recalled and resorted to all the principles his mother had emphasized to identify species accordingly when picking herbs for herbal medicine.

He had finally appeared with a variety of leaves, roots, and berries. These he had studiously crushed and mixed together expertly to make a salve from. He had then carefully removed the hospital dressing with very hot steaming water that he had boiled with some of the leaves. Frazier had watched with horror the extent of the exposed raw face of the wound even after about ten days in the underground facility. Chuck had then applied the salve amply over the wound, and covered it with the boiled leaves. He had then taken the old bandage which he had heated over the fire to finally wrap up the ankle. Sweating from all his effort, he gave his benefactor the big wide smile that had gradually become his trademark, muttered something in his language.

When the nurse came calling two days later to dress the wound, as pre-arranged. She ran screaming over to the reverend in horror. The good man had painstakingly reassured her to wait and see the result in another two days; the wonders of African folk medicine could only be experienced to be appreciated. He told her he was equally expectant of the outcome.

Two days later the nurse came accompanied by the doctor. Chuck had gotten his paraphernalia ready awaiting their arrival. The salve had been stored in a glass jar that the reverend gave him. He had picked fresh leaves to be boiled as antiseptic earlier that morning. When finally the wound was opened it was unbelievable. The wound face was now a very healthy pink, and had sealed up totally. The doctor was very impressed with the progress.

On Sunday, the 8th of January, 1865, when Reverend Frazier had taken him to attend Church, he was already limping along unaided with his cane. He was the cynosure of all eyes, as he was announced to be the *last brother* out of Africa, that had just arrived Savannah. Though he had sat through the service silently, there was nothing that happened during service that he missed. Reverend Frazier observed that Chuck was a very keen observer, which is the secret of every quick learner.

At the end of the service, most of the older folks came by to greet and cheer him up, some even attempted to utter some semblance of an African language for the young man to identify with, but no dice. An old woman of his grandmother's age almost bent double from weeding and picking the cotton fields, was weeping as she embraced him emotionally. It was a very touching moment for both the white and black folks who witnessed the emotional display of the 82 year- old Grandma Lois, who also arrived in America straight from Africa over sixty years ago. None could withhold the tears from flowing as the old woman displayed so much emotion.

Chuck was indeed a natural with the horses, he had groomed, fed and watered them like he had known for ages. Reverend Frazier had made it a tradition to carry the young man along to anywhere he went. By the next Sunday, Chuck was already communicating in his spattering English that setting everyone on edge. Reverend Frazier knew deep down inside him, that this was one African that would not be a push over with the White man. There was something very uncanny about Chuck Freeborn from any other Black man he had ever encountered. He was convinced that it would be only a matter of time before he would manifest.

CHAPTER 36

It was just one of those days that you wake with an expectant feeling that is not of expectations, but of something positive that was ready to happen. That uncanny feeling that is so reassuring that it is already settled from above; that is the difference between expectation and expectancy.

It was finally January 12, 1865, the day the representatives of the Black community were scheduled to meet with General Sherman, and Edward Staton, the Secretary of War. The Blacks had lobbied with everything in their purview, including the inglorious Ebenezer Creek disaster of which Sherman had absolved his officer Jefferson Davis from blame. Since the previous day, when the group of 20 men had overwhelmingly nominated Reverend Garrison Frazier to be their key spokesman, he had had butterflies in his stomach.

As a minister of God with over 35 years in the ministry, Frazier knows the impact and importance of prayer. He had prayed and prayed, before turning his attention to detail, presentation and comportment. He could hardly sleep a wink the whole night, worrying about the right words to use that would succinctly present their case in the best way to garner their support, so that freed black men could enjoy some respite. He was well informed of *The Negro Problem,* as the Whites tend to define, the uncertain faith of the millions of the soon-to-be-freed Black men. He was going to raise the danger of doing nothing and falling into the callous hands of the likes of the Union officer who was preparing to export a group of African Americans to Cuba for sale, before he was caught.

On the pro-active aspects, Frazier planned to submit for consideration the theory of the Economist Edward Atkinson that,

"...free labor would be more productive than slave labor...". He also planned to argue that it would be a travesty of justice not to reward the generality of Blacks who had totally remained loyal to Union either under slavery or not. It was high time we got rewarded as against those who have turned their backs against the Union. *Who says we cannot make do with their abandoned properties?*

He looked at the image staring back at him in the mirror. He was not looking badly, for a 67 year-old former slave. As he fitted in his dog collar, he smiled at the handsome black man resplendent in a tail suit. He could not help but to address him accordingly; *"Garrison Frazier you have indeed come a long way from Granville County, North Carolina. That $1000 in gold and silver to buy our freedom was not in vain."* His deep baritone resounded with authority in that empty room.

As he stooped to pick up his attach case, he winched at the biting nagging pain in his groin, as well as the corresponding numbing fingers of pain at the base of his ribs cage. The ailment the doctors had failed to find a permanent cure; and it had gradually sidelined him from very active duty in his divine calling. Who knows, maybe that was what Chuck Freeborn had been sent to do for him with his proven expertise in African folk medicine?

He went ahead to pack the neat pile of notes in his very artistic hand writing into the attach case and stepped out of his room to head to the dining table for his breakfast and cocktail of daily prescribed drugs. He stopped abruptly and hurried back to the room as if he forgot something, he looked into the mirror again, and consciously patted the pronounced fringes of grey on his thick black hair and said; *"Today, one bold moment for Garrison; a bounding leap for the Black Race in exile."*.

When Reverend Garrison Frazier finally stepped out of the house that morning with his black bowler hat firmly in place, even Chuck could not help but to bow to greet the all-important looking man.

"Good mornin' sha!" he greeted confidently.

"Good morning Chuck. Good morning s-i-r." Frazier replied, made to correct him as it was now their tradition.

"How are you, Chuck?" As he put the attach case on the wooden seat and made to climb up.

"I amu very wellu s-i-r." Chuck taking correction immediately.

"I am very well sir." Frazier took time to repeat patiently before taking the reins. "We are going to the Green House at the Madison Square."

"Yes o, good-good, Green Hose goody-goody." The young man replied excitedly. He pulled his slightly oversize coat to shield him properly from the wintry cold biting in the wonderfully bright sunny day. As his fertile mind took conscious notes of the names his benefactor was pointing and reeling out as they rolled along at a sedate pace.

Outside the Green-Meldrin House, there was the parade of guards in process when they arrived. There were over two hundred soldiers involved. As they joined his other colleagues who arrived earlier, Frazier noticed the thrill in the eyes of Chuck as he drank in this regimented spectacle with his eyes. He did not forget to point to them and whispered to him loudly; "Soldiers! Soldiers! Soldiers!".

Finally, the morning parade came to an end. As the soldiers marched out to the band playing the *Battle Hymn of the Republic*, while the soldiers in one solid voice sang with gusto *John Brown's Body* to their beat; there was not an onlooker in that square who was not moved by the choreographed men in uniform swinging orderly to this very catchy tune…

John Brown's Body Lies Smoldering In His Grave
John Brown's Body Lies Smoldering In His Grave
John Brown's Body Lies Smoldering In His Grave
But His Soul Goes Marching On…
Glory, Glory Hallelujah
Glory, Glory Hallelujah
Glory, Glory Hallelujah
For His Soul Goes Marching On

Not long after, Reverend Frazier and his other 19 colleagues were ushered in for the meeting no one could tell how long it was going to last. Chuck made himself very comfortable in the back of the wagon on a burlap and fell asleep…*as he was thinking about Amaeke Ohafia, his father – Aka the great wrestler, his mother – Uju, his younger brother – Chukadibia, his grandmother Adaora…no wait a minute, not Adaora but Ihuoma. Adaora was Uncle Nwoye's mother. Uncle Nwoye just disappeared just like that. Very strange happening, just like his predicament with Obele. Where would Obele be now? How about Ngozi? The last he saw her was when they were reloaded into the slave ship before he passed out. Does it mean he would never see them again?*

CHAPTER 37

There was no mistaking the soulful tone of the flutist. It was obvious that it was a true master's lips and fingers romancing the wind instrument as if it was a living part of his body. *John Brown's Body* flowed forth smoothly as a funeral hymn. The song enveloped his entire being and escalated him to a surreal splendor found only in the land of dreams. What a melodious dream? Then the song expired, just when he thought it would never end. A moment later, the flute started again with yet another dirge- like tune. This time, it was the *Udala* song that he knew the lyrics by heart, after all, it was in honor of his father, Akachukwu.

He is ripe, ripe like udala for plucking
He is sweet, sweeter than honey
His sweat at work and play
Cascades like the waters of Ifutiti
Even the twelve special ones
Are not enough to count the victories
O here comes the majestic Eagle...

The flapping wings of the bird overhead was loud and clear. He knew it that it was not a dream bird. It was real. No it cannot be, because Chuck Freeborn was wide awake. It was not a dream. Somebody in that Madison Square in Savannah was playing the *Udala Song*. He quickly clambered down from the back of the wagon. His heart pounding against his chest with excitement, he strained his ears to pinpoint the direction of the flutist. Like an enchanted man he went in search of the flute that was still playing the *Udala Song* with gusto. As he turned the corner of the building, he saw the sprawling bulk of a man in the Union Army uniform. The soldier backing him was seating on the edge of a military wagon.

Chuck stopped in his track, scared to move forward. This huge back was no doubt Uncle Nwoye's that went missing, or was it a ghost? The soldier sensing somebody was watching him stopped his music and looked back. The eyes were really sad and penetrating, as they just went through past Chuck without any iota of recognition. It was Nwoye, his father's closest friend clad in the White man's strange apparels. There was no way he could recognize him in that slightly oversized winter coat and the hat. The flutist resumed his playing, and Chuck took off his hat and started singing along;

He is ripe, ripe like udala for plucking
He is sweet, sweeter than honey
His sweat at work and play
Cascades like the waters of Ifutiti...

That did the trick. The flutist quickly dropped his flute, removed his hat, and turned towards the singer. They both started towards each other and clashed into one another screaming and crying with excitement. The noise commotion brought out other alarmed soldiers, as well as the important people holding their meeting inside.

They were still crying and talking animatedly with each when General Sherman and Secretary of War Edwin Stanton expecting the worst rushed out with the leading twenty black leaders right behind them. By the time they were briefed of the situation by one of the senior officers, it was a beaming General Sherman assisted by Reverend Frazier that finally pried them apart. It was right there the General ordered for one of his bravest soldiers to be formally relieved from duty to be fully united with his family from home. The ebullient General showed his raw human side by declaring that; "… this not an accidental meeting, neither is it a mere co-incidence, it is the *finger of God* at work.".

Four days later, on January 16th, General Sherman's Special Field Order No. 15, which was birthed through his rapport with the 20 leading Black men of Savannah, received the explicit approval of Abraham Lincoln, the President of the United States of America. The order provided 400,000 acres of confiscated properties of the core Confederate losers and coastal land running from Charleston, in South Carolina to the lands bordering the St. John's River, North Florida. It covered over 1,600 sq kilometers; to be redistributed 40 acres per freed slave. Blacks all over on face value celebrated what then was considered to be the best reparation for the sweat, tears and blood of generations of the Black race that was forced into slavery in America.

On the morning of the 21st day of January, before General Sherman finally embarked on the steamer headed for Beaufort, South Carolina with his entire Headquarters retinue of staff, he conducted a very brief but very significant ceremony. Corporal Boye Africana *(Nwoye)* was duly decorated for his bravery and formally retired from the Union Army. And thereafter, Boye Africana and Chuck Freeborn became the very first set of Freedmen to be allocated the *"40 acres and a mule"* by Brigadier General Rufus Saxton, who was responsible for the implementation of the Special Field Order No. 15.

General Saxton in his brief speech said; "…the very rarest of breeds of the human race like Boye Africana, gladden the hearts of all abolitionists. We are all familiar of the saga of Boye Africana who rebelled and fought his captors right from the sea, and into the courtrooms in New York. And right before our eyes he won a very symbolic victory against the perpetrators of this ignoble vocation. He proved that he was the noblest of all men, by stepping forward to fight on the side of the Union Army, against the Confederates rebels that would not allow him to be free. And to his adopted son, Chuck Freeborn who grew up under his tutelage back in their native Africa… and their reunion here in Savannah under our noses, is to inform us that God neither sleeps nor slumber. Chuck Freeborn, I am reliably informed that, at this very spot, he got the name FREEBORN; because his owner truly believed he was born free. He stands officially today as the last African import to arrive in Savannah…"

CHAPTER 38

So much had happened in very quick succession since that day. Exactly, on the last day of January, the 13th Amendment was approved into law by the House of Representatives. Though it outlawed slavery and involuntary servitude all over the United States, people received the news with a pinch of salt, because of numerous antecedents of policies with all bark and no bite attitude. The abolitionists with President Lincoln in the forefront decided to follow up with some form of affirmative action. General Rufus Saxton, who right from his days as military governor of Port Royal back in 1862, had advocated Black permanent control over land championed the cause. In his address to a large meeting with Blacks at the Second African Baptist, Savannah meeting, very early in February 1865, painstakingly outlined the entire process of settlement of freedmen in the so called confiscated lands.

For the much publicized land allocation to the duo of the brave Boye Africana and Chuck Freeborn, and 18 other fearless black soldiers also retired on that same day was supposed to serve as a pilot program, by General Saxton and his abolitionist-colleagues. It was all a well-calculated plan to make them self-sufficient in defense, in the face of threats from the die-hard Confederates. They were duly allocated the abandoned 1000-acre plantation isolated up the Savannah River on the watery border between Georgia and South Carolina. It was owned by a Confederate General that was killed in the Chattanooga Campaign of 1863. At his death he was a childless widower.

There were people who were not happy with what their President was doing. The president and his supporters did know the length they would go to achieve their objectives. Until John Wilkes Booth on April 14, 1865, secured for himself a dastardly notch in history, as he had

President Abraham cold-bloodedly assassinated at the Ford's Theatre in Washington DC. It was indeed a gloomy season for the free voices of freedom call.

The *voiceless* Vice President Andrew Johnson, had hardly warmed his new seat behind the most important desk in the Executive Mansion (before it became White House)', when he began to bare his fangs. He exhibited a raw display of bravado, as he immediately dismantled key government policies and personalities in various spheres. It did not take long for people like General Saxton to be barking up the wrong tree in freedmen settlement efforts or progress.

All was not going well too with the Confederate Eldorado. Like a pack of cards the Confederate Army in an avalanche of surrenders started by General Lee's April 9 surrender at the Appomattox Court House, Virginia, signaled the point of no return to all and sundry. With General Johnston's military capitulation in North Carolina to General W.T. Sherman on the 26th of April, all signs were go for the Union Army. Then with President Jefferson Davis' capture two weeks later, on the 10th of May, even the toughest die-hard confederates admitted *that things had fallen apart, and the centre could no longer hold*. The final battle to be fought in the Civil War was the Battle of Palmito Ranch in Texas from May 21 and 23, 1865, which sounded the death knell for the Confederacy, and slammed home the final nail into the Confederate coffin.

Meanwhile, President Andrew Johnson was raising a cloud of dust in his wake. It was on May 29, when the Blacks who were still sorting out themselves on the *"40 Acres and a Mule"* Settlement were confronted with President Johnson's Amnesty Proclamation to ordinary Confederates who swore to loyalty oaths…to get political immunity and claim back their confiscated lands and property. For the Blacks, Andrew Johnson would have had the medal for the most hated man of the century by his revocation of the Special Field Order No. 15. It was then people started asking the questions; *Who is Andrew Johnson? Is he a dangerous green snake in green grass.? Is he a Confederate wearing Union colors.*

It was not until August 20, before President Andrew Johnson finally declared the end of the war, and made a clarion call for America to earnestly commence Reconstruction. For President Johnson, who was an embodiment of the American Dream, that you can aspire to be anything you so desire; for he rose from his tailoring background, and private tutelage from his wife to become the President of the United States of America. And also died as Senator for a record two times. His political climate was a total disaster for the majority of the Freedmen.

The very reliable pro-black officials had been replaced with non-sympathizers of Black reparation. The beneficiaries of the *"40 Acres and Mule"*, like Boye Africana and Chuck Freeborn had pooled themselves into rock-solid solidarity fronts to dispel any attempt to reclaim what they had inherited as compensation for 200 years of forced slavery. They would not hesitate to take up arms to defend their rightful property with their blood if need be.

On March 1, 1865, rag-tag team of Boye Africana, Chuck Freeborn, and the other twenty-four families finally arrived their 1000-acre *Devil's Bank* Plantation on the Georgia bank of the Savannah River, after all official paperwork had been concluded and certified. First they had to change the name of the plantation from *Devils Bank* to Saxtonville in honor of their benefactor Rufus Saxton. With 25 families, made up 146 individuals on ground it was like building a new town that some had unofficially christened *Little Savannah.*

Before setting off from Savannah, they had all agreed to work together without sharing the plantation into bits and pieces. The leadership had been unanimously vested on Boye Africana. They had all agreed to live and work together, or if need be die together. Pastor Campbell of the First African Baptist had also committed the church's assistance and promised to start a branch there within the first year. The Mayor Richard Arnold had also asked them to consider themselves as a *Little Savannah.*

Later in the year, the likes of Robert K. Scott and Daniel Sickles who succeeded people like Saxton, resorted to legal and foul means to evict or deny the presumed black settlers. Some covertly resorted to intimidation, blackmail, outright fraud, intimidation and arson lynching to forcefully take back the land. These callous acts brazenly carried out without fear or concern for the long arms of the law, gradually transformed into the hydra-head monster that came to be known as the *Ku Klux Klan.* The Klan or KKK was birthed on December 24, 1865, in Pulaski, Tennessee, by former Confederate General Nathan Bedford Forrest with five other Confederate veterans. General Nathan Bedford Forrest was the Grand Imperial Wizard, who was the overall leader. With their white robes and hoods, the Klan went to town, armed with guns, burning flames and Molotov cocktails dispensing mayhem and death to those who dare challenge White supremacy. Terror was their official trademark to thwart the hopes and aspiration of their upward mobile small black communities. And they were going to find more than their match in Saxtonville alias Little Savannah.

CHAPTER 39

It was another June 13th, and as it had become a private ritual for Chuck Freeborn for the past four years, as the golden sun sets over the marshes to pay homage at the graveside of his *uncle* and mentor, Boye 'Nwoye' Africana. The *Shagbark Hickory* seedling that he had planted on June 13th, 1866, on the head of the grave during the interment was already providing shade over the grave. And as he stood there under the shade of the Hickory tree he could feel Nwoye's spirit all over him.

That was why he had chosen the Shagbark Hickory, whose deep roots would eat up the remains of Nwoye and be part of it. With an average longevity of 300 years and maximum height of between 80 and 100 feet, it would serve as a lasting memorial. The gorgeous Shagbark Hickory also represented the qualities of Nwoye; who was totally dependable, independent, and immeasurable in his provisions. It was so sad to lose him so early into their saga in this strange land. He looked up into the sky to see a flock of white migratory birds flying in the usual v-formation; he could not but reminiscent on those days when he would be riding on Nwoye's shoulder and chanting loudly the *Lekeleke Song*, with arms flapping like the birds. This must be their origin. Suddenly, he felt the tears rolling down his cheeks uncontrollably, as he felt all alone and so far from home. If only he could send a message home through the *Lekelekes* to his mother and aunt. He must find a way to get message home that, that oracle that was most revered was a colossal ruse. An unfathomable fury started welling up in his heart.

He recalled how Nwoye said he was captured by Obiligbo and his cronies that day in the bush and was handed over to Mazi Otiji, who also facilitated his transit to Calabar, and into the hold of the slaver *Pilgrim's Haven*. He related how himself and his colleagues at 40 days into the voyage had unshackled themselves and taken the crew by surprise and killed them all. Only to find out that none of them knew next to nothing about ship sailing. Their ship floundered to and fro by the wind and currents for over a month until they were found, and towed to shore by a US cruiser. That shore turned out to be New York. With the help of the Abolitionists, they were set free after a protracted court battle. With his Ohafia warfare background, he then chose to join the Union Army who was recruiting. It was during the brief stint he had proven himself to be recognized by General Sherman who took special interest in him. And that was how he arrived in Savannah.

June 13, 1866, would remain indelible for Chuck Freeborn as long as he lived. They had just sorted out a new influx of blacks that just wanted to distant themselves from Memphis as far as possible, after the Memphis Massacre that killed about 46 blacks and over hundred injured with over 100 homes, churches and schools burnt to cinders. It was sometime before sunset when Saxtonville received the news of Congress' approval of the Fourteenth Amendment to the Constitution. This law was to guarantee due process and equal security within the country to all and sundry. What was really worth celebrating was that it granted to all African Americans citizenship, due process and equal protection under the law. Though it was difficult for most of them to fully understand the full implications, they had joined in the general celebrations.

They had celebrated long into the night, just like a majority of the black communities that could give some kind favorable interpretation of the amendment to the best of their limited understanding. They were filled with hopes for a brighter and better future for every black man in America. As the lights went off one by one, as they succumbed into deep tired sleep, a band of armed strangers on horseback stayed back in the shadows of the wood bidding their time.

At exactly 12 midnight, the fifty horsemen in white cloaks and hoods, and now with flaming burning torches galloped into Saxtonville. As they shouted, and shot into houses and released motley of Molotov cocktails upon some houses, it was utter confusion for everyone. For Boye who had slept off on his hammock on his veranda, he was woken by the sudden noise and commotion. He boldly challenged and confronted the Ku Klux Klan raiders for a brief moment to give his people the needed time to regroup and to counter the attack. He screamed in a very loud voice that must have awaken anybody who was still sound asleep. As he made for his gun, he did not stand a monkey chance against the hail of bullets that thudded into his massive bulk. By this time Chuck, had grabbed his bow and quiver of poisoned arrows and melted into the woods behind the house. At a vantage point he had effectively taken pot shots at the flaming torches darting about the settlement and torching roofs. His quiver could only take twenty-five arrows, before he ran out of arrows he could hear counter shots from his colleagues who were still alive.

When the smoke of battle finally cleared, after the depleted Klan force beat a quick retreat; Boye Africana lay almost dead with more than twenty bullet wounds. He finally breathed his final breath in Chuck's laps as the new day dawned. When they took stock later in the morning, the settlement had lost four men, five women and three innocent children. Over nine buildings had been torched. Dead from gunshot and arrow wounds were twenty-two white-robed stone-cold dead Ku Klux Klan attackers. Message was dispatched to the Mayor of Savannah and the First African Baptist.

Later in the day official teams had arrived from Savannah to take stock and document the unfortunate event and resultant carnage. Pacifications and promises were made to find the living perpetrators of this heinous crime and punish them accordingly. The whole settlement went into mourning. Chuck had sworn to avenge the death of his mentor and the other colleagues, with the imperial blood of the ghostly Ku Klux Klan.

And over the past four years Chuck Freeborn as a one-man crusader had made good the threat. He had personally struck deep into Ku Klux Klan strongholds in their nighttime gatherings. He had struck clinically with his lethal machete or his most deadly arrows and simply disappeared into the cloak of darkness. It had become a tradition for these meetings to count huge losses in leaders without apprehending the culprits. The Grand Imperial Wizard, had in his numerous trips to Atlanta in 1868, had indirectly called for a truce, by declaring that they made a blunder to have attacked certain communities. He muted that it was his belief that the subsequent fatal depletions in his officer-ranks were not unconnected with the attack on Saxtonville. It was so obvious that the modus operandi was a recurring decimal in all the killings. He recommended that they would rather encourage Black Codes or Jim Crow Laws to enforce black segregation or restricted movements and freedom of expression. That was back in 1869.

After that attack, Chuck had taken it up to train all men in Saxtonville in the clinical machete and archery warfare. They made their defenses so impregnable that all other subsequent reprisal attacks were abysmally thwarted to the chagrin of the Klansmen. When

Bennettsville, South Carolina was to design their own defense, they had to learn a lot from their brothers in Saxtonville.

Before long, Saxtonville had become the success story everybody clamored to be part of. The plantation had grown into all facets of agriculture ranging from cash crops, to aquaculture and even birds and animal husbandry. Chuck had also developed an angle of folk medicine to some extent that was gaining ground. Savannah, on the hand counted on Little Savannah to tackle it food demands to some extent too. Chuck had without any controversy stepped into the leadership vacuum at the demise of Boye Africano.

The branch of the First African Baptist, known as Little Savannah African Baptist was doing very well. They had provided facilities for basic primary education for both the young and the old. He, Chuck had also availed himself of the opportunity to read and write. By the time President Andrew Johnson was impeached on March 4, 1869, and the great Ulysses Grant stepping in as the 18th President of the United States, Chuck was reading the newspapers by himself, to get all the juicy details. He held in his hands a sheet of paper showing the census figures for 1870, of a total population of 39,818,449, Blacks accounted for 4,880,009, of which Saxtonville was 349 persons. He shook his head in disbelief; they had come a long way, from under 150 to 349 persons in Little Savannah. He placed the sheet of paper on the mound of slightly upraised earth that was the grave, bowed his head for a moment and retraced his steps back to his lonely home. He must start to do something to fill it up with children; after all the whole of Little Savannah was growing..

He had been duly baptized into the First African Baptist Church by immersion in 1865. With his African background it would not have been easy to imbibe the new religion, but with his raw and rare experiences he had wholly embraced God. And since then he had taken his Christian life seriously and looked forward to the General Convention that would be hosted by the First African Baptist, Savannah, in July. He had remained a very active member of both the church in Savannah and the Little Savannah. He had remained grateful to them for their love and care since he arrived in Savannah. It was time he paid heed to the call for him to find a good strong Christian lass to settle down with. Grandma Lois had promised to carry his son before she goes to join their ancestors. He was playfully referred to as the Mayor of Little Savannah by the members of the Savannah church.

The advent of President Grant, whose father was a renowned abolitionist was a massive blessing for all African-Americans. His antecedents of recruiting blacks into the Union Army and his confrontations of President Andrew Johnson regarding protection of Black citizenship was known to all and sundry. It was another moment for blacks to celebrate as the Captain of the *Black Marines,* as he was disparagingly called by the reprehensive Democrats. Something told Chuck that President Grant tenure would be of good omen to his people. After all, his predecessor's greatest undoing was to veto the Civil Rights Acts of 1866. Yes, it was President Andrew Johnson's most grievous mistake… or was it truly a blunder?

CHAPTER 40

It had been raining cats and dogs all morning. It was not until about noon when the rain finally stopped, and the sun stepped forth shining brightly. Chuck had lifted up Ivy, his four year-old daughter on to his shoulder and set out for the hillside to perform his annual ritual at Nwoye's graveside. It was June 13, 1875.

As they stepped out of the house, he called out to his two- month pregnant wife Zika, who was picking vegetables in the garden. He would never understand the American way of life, always kind of carefree. Especially the reckless abandon with which they panel beat people's names to suit their tongues and convenience. He had named his daughter Iffy after his mother's sister, Ifeanyi; the Americans changed it to Ivy. He told them his name was Chukwuma they turned it to Chuck. Nwoye told them his, they turned it into Boye. The name Ngozika was still intact until they parted company; only to discover that the Americans had tinkered it into just Zika.

Names in Africa are rich in meanings and connotations. That is why they come lengthy, because they are not just a word, but sometimes a sentence or sentences. Embedded in every African name are the dreams, hopes, fears, consolations, felicitations, and aspirations of the immediate parents and the extended family and friends. Names and the naming ceremony itself are never toyed with, except in America.

It was very obvious that Chuck was very popular within Saxton, from the way people called out their greetings or waved animatedly to father and daughter. Most of them Chuck recalled were all present at his wedding that took place in October, 1870. How time flies?

It was at that Baptist Convention that took place in July, 1870 that he had ran into Ngozika, whom he thought he would never see again.

She was part of the choir and delegation of Ogeechee Baptist Church. He had not noticed her in the crowd of uniformed singers. It was after the service, when he was talking with Reverend Garrison Frazier, a familiar face beckoned to him with excitement from behind the reverend. He waved back without paying much attention. It was after the reverend departed he went over to the familiar face. As he got closer, Chuck almost had a fit; the familiar face was Ngozika, though she was now known as Zika.

Three months later they were married by Pastor Campbell at the First African Baptist Church. In attendance were some of the freed slaves of the *Hand of God Plantation,* the captain had slumped and died way back in 1865, when he received the news of the unfortunate end of the *Sea Fairy.* And on June 17, 1871, Iffy was born quietly at home in Little Savannah. Over the years he had finally accepted Ivy for her too.

As they approached the green grassy stretch of gradient to higher ground were a herd of three hundred cattle and horses were grazing freely, he set down Ivy, who took off running towards the hickory tree in the distance. The tree was now the tallest tree around. He could not help, but to run after her. They finally reached the grave together, with Chuck bending over to catch his breath as he held on to his daughter's right hand securely. Within a moment that feeling of serenity rapidly overwhelmed his entire being. It was a very special, mystical feeling that had never failed over the years.

As if on cue not a wind passed through the treetop, as Chuck and his daughter stood together in solidarity to an important link to their roots. Then his mind went on an overdrive to update Nwoye of the important events that interestingly occurred so far.

With the establishment of Birmingham by a real estate firm on June 1, 1871, he had tactically procured some lots. The promoters had painted it to be the city of the future with its strategic location at the crossing of the North and South railroads, as well as the Chattanooga and the Alabama lines. He had even opened a major store marketing all their products from Saxtonville last year. With the promise of its achieving an industrial center status in another few years, he had already concluded plans to invest in a residential scheme.

The Ku Klux Klan was having a field day dispensing their kind of warped *justice,* everywhere in the South. The so called *Redeemers* had resorted to pure terrorism to obliterate especially the black population in the corridors of power. The other day, a mob had totally humiliated Abraham Coby in front of his family by flogging him 100 lashes. While Abram Turner another expelled African-American legislator did not count himself lucky as his colleague, who at least lived to tell his tale of shame. They had with aplomb dismantled opposing political meetings with multiple killings to drive home the message that they were above the law. *It was a moment the blacks were left between the devil and the deep black-blue sea.* Chuck had tried in his own little lone-crusader mode taken out his anger on the KKK, through what they themselves had come to admit were *impossible killings* amongst its blue blooded champions.

President Ulysses Grant had lived up to his top billing of the appellation of *"nigger loving jackass"* given to him by the white supremacist crowd. He had found a most wonderful and willing partners in Amos T. Akerman as Attorney General, and, Benjamin Bristow, the first Solicitor General of the USA. It was the combined concerted efforts of these duo that brought thousands of indictments against the KKK under the 1866 Civil Rights Acts. In fact the 1870 and 71 Force Acts we were told, was specifically calculated to tackle the excesses of the KKK. And we believed that they were effective; so far there had been relative calm from them.

How well the recent celebrated Supreme Court expected judgment in the case of *United States versus Cruikshank* in the battle against the the Ku Klux Klan was still unfolding. Over 105 black lives were at stake if the judgment favored the whites against the black. The Colfax Massacre happened on Easter Sunday on April 13, 1873, in the State of Louisiana. The case had been dragging on since.

"Away from all these KKK dreadful news to some news to cheer you up Uncle Nwoye; you have another grandchild in the making again. My wife, Ngozika is heavily pregnant with our second baby. I pray and hope that it's a boy." Chuck did not know that his thoughts came out in words.

Chuck looked down at his daughter tugging at his hand; it was time to go home. The dark clouds were gathering again, preparing for another showdown beyond the one that happened earlier in the morning hours. He took one last look up into the expanding boughs of the Hickory tree, heaved a deep sigh of relief and said aloud;

"So long, Nwoye, Alusi Oja. The one and only oracle of the flute! I will see you soon. Please do keep an eye over your son and all that is his own, in this very strange land and stranger people. Sleep well." Though it sounded very strange, but he had spoken out in Igbo.

"Daddy, what is that? What are you saying?" The little girl asked innocently.

CHAPTER 41

Letters and words had always fascinated him right from the beginning. It was for that burning desire to decode and decipher words, to read and to write, that he had willingly without any persuasion or incentives enlisted for the Adult Literacy program. Chuck made himself every teacher's delight because of his insatiable zeal and childlike enthusiasm towards learning. He was always asking questions; always asking, he was never tired of asking questions. His colleagues never hid the fact from him that he was a nuisance, and a pain in the neck with his unending chains of questions. He found solace in the fact that his teachers thought otherwise and continued to encourage him.

Right from the moment he acquired the *magical prowess*, as he termed it, to create uncountable meaningful words from just the 26 letters of the English alphabets, he was hooked and addicted. He began with reading anything that was readable; *devoured,* yes devoured. That was what he did; he devoured anything in writing. He read road signs, adverts, newspapers, magazines, and books. He discovered quite early and appreciated that books were the repository of information and wisdom. So he made books his closest friends; and to later know too that writing actually originated from Egypt, in Africa, was exhilarating.

Reading what others had written he felt was to decode and decipher their thoughts, while the act of writing was a different ball game entirely. To Chuck, writing was even more laborious than reading. The man with the writing prowess must have at his disposal words of all dimensions in meaning. He would then choose the right words to make individual sentence. Thereafter he sews the different sentences together sequentially to complete the story, that emanated from his thought process. Chuck's objective was to acquire both writing and reading prowess.

The Harper's Weekly was his favorite reading of the day. He made it a point of duty to collect and read every copy he could find. It was from this popular newspaper he kept abreast with all the happenings in America from his out of the way Little Savannah. What was the trending news was the *United States versus Cruikshank* Supreme Court judgment. It was believed to be the most important ruling in constitutional diktat. The ruling when it finally came in 1876, shook the whole nation from the North to the South. It took three years to arrive at the judgment after the Colfax Massacre.

The Colfax Massacre, Louisiana occurred when over 105 African-Americans and 3 white men were killed on Easter Sunday, April 13, 1873. It all happened in the Grant Parish Courthouse where an armed militia of Democrats attacked Republican freedmen. It really got out of hand that President Grant had to send in Federal troops to reinforce the election of Governor William Kellogg. Under the Enforcement Act of 1870, some fraction of the white mob were indicted and charged accordingly under a 16-count charge.

Until the final minutes, the eight associate justices were at par; 4 on either side. It was not until, Chief Justice Morrison who authored the majority opinion not just swayed but swung the pendulum against the dissenting and concurring opinions. That singular ruling pulled the carpet from under their feet, to give impetus for unhindered violence against the blacks. All the human rights laws achieved during the Reconstruction Era went with the wind; the blacks were left hanging high and dry. Neither was their federal protection against any violence against the blacks, nor were they allowed to bear arms to defend themselves against the violators of Civil Rights.

The Cruikshank ruling did not only kill the spirit of the black man in the journey towards his total emancipation into America, but took away the fight from the Northern white who stood relentlessly for the oppressed black minority.

Chuck also noted with interest a distraction that the ruling class could not ignore. It was the economic depression that was knocking at doors. By September, 1873, there was noticeable economic turmoil as certain corporate entities began to collapse. What later came to be known as the Long Depression, started off as the 5-Year Industrial Depression. Some people who actually thought some others were crying wolf; could not help but agree when 87 out of the United States railroads companies kissed the dust, and waved goodbye to their investments. At

Little Savannah, things could not be better, as their food crops did not lack demand because people must eat.

President Rutherford B. Hayes had entered White House as Grant's successor with a deal to without delay remove all federal troops from the South. With this parody, the Confederates who were still looking for their pound of flesh, stepped comfortably back into their slave-master relationships. Some blacks started peddling rumors that there was a North-South Compromise, to sacrifice black's civil rights and racial justice on the altar of American Unionism.

Blacks of every social stratum felt abandoned and betrayed by their Union benefactors. The similarity to the 1864 General Jefferson C. Davies 600 Blacks abandonment at the Ebenezer Creek for the Confederates to make mince meat of came to the fore of conversations again. It was difficult to believe that there was no conspiracy. Blacks who were still celebrating the demise of the Ku Klux Klan, when a new brand of white vigilantes that did not hide under hoods and cloaks began ruthless and oppressive operations in broad daylights. They were called the White League or the Red Shirts.

Chuck had put his people on alert, and in war mode. It was as if they were told, The Red Shirts or *black shirts* kept their distance from Little Savannah. They were instrumental to blacks being kept away from the polling booths and almost total black absence from the hallowed chambers of legislation. As they maimed and killed defenseless blacks in the South, the state government officials and law enforcement authorities turned a blind eye.

With the emergence of the equally very ruthless Red Shirts, Chuck had tactically relocated his family from Savannah; his wife and two children were now close to him and under his close scrutiny within the conducive serenity of Little Savannah.

CHAPTER 42

Chuck Freeborn after so much persuasion, had over the years finally come to adopt January 1, as his official birthday. He had picked the first day of the year for no sentimental reason, after all there was no pros and cons attached to any particular day he had observed. Since the day was January 1, 1900, which was not just the first day of the new year, but also the first day of a new century, he could not but take the day more seriously. In reminiscence, the last century to him was indeed a mixed grill of fortunes; with the unhappy moments far more than the cheery ones. He was all alone. It has been five years since he sent off his son to school at Tuskegee, Alabama

As he stood in front of the mirror with a large towel around his waist, he examined closely the man in front of him. The image in the mirror was also examining him closely with deep penetrating eyes with a hint of sorrowful lips. So much sorrow that had eaten up his youth. Though the circumstance of being deceived into slavery was painful and sorrowful, but it paled in comparison to the deaths of Ngozika and the baby during the birth. He would never get over it, even after twenty years, it still felt fresh. Chukwuma Akachukwu, alias Chuck Freeborn a widower at his age. Who would believe it?

The man in the mirror was very fair in complexion, tall and handsome, with a crop of thick black hair that had distinct grey splashes at about the forehead. His beard was totally grey given him a much older look. The exposed part of his torso showed rippling biceps, but his midsection was thickening and showing signs of love handles. Aged about 51 years. What? Just 51 years? Yes, he was about 15 rains when they arrived Savannah, a few days to 1864 Christmas. Why won't he look older than 60?

In 1878, Ngozika was delivered safely of a male child with a sixth finger just like the sister, Ivy. Just like the case of Ivy, the experienced black midwife without even consulting with him, had tied a string tightly at its base. A few days later, the finger had desiccated and fallen off with just a little trace. He chuckled to himself at both instances, and muttered; *Even in this strange land, with stranger people Akachukwu is standing with his children.*

He would never forget that day, it was the day President Garfield's was elected in 1880. Ngozika had gone into labor with their third child at about 8 pm that evening. Compared to the other two earlier childbirths, it was relatively a very protracted labor. Chuck had stood by his wife all through the night, encouraging and supporting, as the midwife and her assistance did their bits. The groans and moans had dragged on all through the night. Just as the sunrays of the new dawn caressed the eastern horizon to melt away the darkness of the night, Ngozika frail and exhausted, face smeared with tears and sweat, and as the equally exhausted midwife urged her to push one more time, she passed out. Then tragedy struck. Before anyone realized what was happening, Ngozi had slipped over to the land where there was no pain. Zika Freeborn died in her husband's arms without even a word of farewell.

After mourning his wife for a brief while, Chuck had to return to reality. His interest for life and living began to wane. He had to abandon work at the home, that they were building at Savannah. What was the need to continue if, there was no Ngozika to share with? He was so depressed. He had to remind himself that the two other children needed his attention too; at least he owed his wife that responsibility. His hobby for reading became his solace and comfort; he buried his head in books and other periodicals.

President James A. Garfield had started his presidency on a very promising note with the several appointments of blacks in federal government positions in 1881. The blacks were yet celebrating their new Messiah's first 100 days in office, when he was shot by a disgruntled Charles J. Guiteau on July 2. Even with the media hype on President Garfield's attempted assassination, the news of a 25year-old African-American, Booker T. Washington starting a sort of vocational school in Tuskegee, Alabama, on July 4, 1881, would not miss his attention. Chuck felt really proud of the *brother's* rare feat. He promised himself to keep a tag on his progress.

Sadly, President Garfield after struggling for another 80 days, succumbed to the fangs of death on September, 19th. While Vice

President Chester A. Arthur smoothly took over the reins accordingly; Charles Guiteau was found guilty and put to death in 1882.

It was very obvious that Chuck and his colleagues were doing very well at Saxtonville. Saxtonville had become the most successful rock-solid reference point for the Federal Government policy of Freedmen settlement. It was on this premise he had been recognized and duly invited to many high profile programs not just in the state of Georgia, but all over the South.

His personal investments in Birmingham, Alabama, were yielding good dividends. He had gone into real estate which was effectively catered to the housing needs of trooping migrants that were attracted to the *Pittsburg of the South*. Chuck Freeborn was gradually becoming a man of means, and was also consolidating his financial empire. After much persuasion, Pastor Emmanuel King Love of the African Baptist Church Savannah, had finally convinced Freeborn to resume work again on the abandoned private resident project in Savannah.

With all these developments, racism still thrived especially in the south. Chuck could not but agree that America remained a *strange land with a stranger people*. In July 23, 1890, the New Orleans Riot occured that lasted for a whole 4 days. When the smoke had cleared and the warring parties had sheathed their swords, 19 peoples laid dead. There was no stopping the bad ones, as the Southern States brazenly enacted laws that were systematically targeted to disenfranchise the black population.

Sometime in 1893, Chuck Freeborn was invited to the International meeting of Christian Workers that took place in Atlanta, Georgia. And low and behold a Booker T. Washington was scheduled to give a lecture. Chuck could not contain himself; so finally he was going to meet his young idol. Surprisingly, he spoke for only five minutes. Chuck was more than impressed with what he heard and saw. The over 2000 audience was indeed overwhelmed with a spectacular vintage Booker T. Washington presentation.

Chuck Freeborn had approached Washington at an ideal time to make his acquaintance.

"Good day Mr. Washington, that was the best speech that I have ever heard."

"Thank you, sir. I am truly flattered." Washington seeing a potential benefactor for Tuskegee put on his charming nature.

"My name is Chuck Freeborn; I am a fan of yours even though from a distance. I am very glad your school is coming through."

"Mr. Freeborn, I am equally excited to make your acquaintance. We just wish we could do more sir. With people like you supporting us whole-heartedly the sky would not contain us." Washington chuckled showing a good glimpse of very white dentition.

"That is why I am here, Mr. Washington. Please find here a check for $300. I am truly honored to support your work for all of us."

"We are very grateful for your very generous donation, Mr. Freeborn. May I know where you are from." He quickly brought out a notebook and pen to write.

"I am an African. A freeborn African....

When it looked like he was back to winning ways calamity was lurking once again in the shadows ready to strike. The private residence project was making very good progress; Chuck had taken the children to Savannah to assess things when the hurricane struck. The 1893 Sea Island hurricane left 2,000 people dead in its wake. Though Chuck and his son, Junior survived without a scratch, Ivy was not that lucky, she was counted amongst the dead. Freeborn was totally inconsolable...

It had to take Booker T. Washington, who had suffered losing more than a spouse to personally come to Little Savannah to condole his new and budding friend. That really helped to heal the wound faster. Chuck Freeborn by then, had developed and progressed in his relationships with both Booker T. Washington as a person, as well as the Tuskegee Normal and Industrial Institute.

After the death of Ivy, Chuck could not bear to allow his son to leave his presence. He had to also rearrange his plans for Chuck Junior to attend school at Tuskegee. The whole project had to be delayed for him to mend fully from losing another loved one. After all *Number II* as he was called at home, was only 17 years old. Chuck was torn between sending his son to the relatively new Georgia State Industrial College for Colored Youth, in Thunderbolt, Savannah, founded in 1890, or Tuskegee. Just like Washington, Georgia Institute's president, Major Richard R. Wright Snr. was also well-known to him.

CHAPTER 43

The Atlanta Exposition that opened on September 18, 1895, was the biggest news for the period. It was on everybody's lip. It was believed to be the grandest event to be hosted by the South. As usual Chuck Freeborn had garnered every vestige of relevant information on the event. He had been officially invited and looked forward to the opening with so much anticipation. Saxtonville was also given the honor to be one of the numerous exhibitors like Hampton Institute and Tuskegee Normal and Industrial Institute.

It was something they all looked forward to; even *Taliaferro* informed him that he was billed to speak at the special opening. Taliaferro, he loved the sound of the name. It sounded like a true African name. So Taliaferro he preferred and insisted that he would call Booker T. Washington. After hearing his full story, Washington ready to learn from the original source became very fond of the Freeborn. Washington was convinced that their generation of African-Americans had so much wisdom and knowledge to receive from the unadulterated black blood. So their friendship blossomed right from the onset.

Chuck Freeborn I and Chuck Freeborn II had arrived Atlanta on 15th September, three days ahead of the opening to put Saxtonville's exhibition in the right perspective. They were exhibiting every business in Little Savannah, from food and cash crops to poultry, venison, aquaculture. The special display was on traditional preservation and the folk medicine. The younger Freebone, who had acquired the traditional skills of his father from hunting, to fishing; and from farming to the folk medicine administration, would be playing a major role in the exhibition.

Chuck I, had arranged with Taliaferro who was also arriving Atlanta with his entire family a day earlier, to have dinner together on that eve of the exposition. Atlanta was filled to the brim, every guesthouse and boarding quarters were taken. That evening, Chuck armed with his quarterly check for Tuskegee, had led his son to dine with the Booker T. Washington household of five. The parents were already acquainted, so it was more an event to get children acquainted for the very first time. Even though Chuck II was older than the other children they had taken to each other swiftly, leaving the parents to wonder in amazement. After dinner, Chuck had presented the check.

"Mr. and Mrs Washington, we can never thank you enough for your efforts. Please keep it up, we are all solidly behind you. That is why you are being celebrated today."

"*Chief*, my dear, you are indeed the one to be celebrated. Like they say in my native Mississippi, he that pays the drummer, owns the music." Margaret replied with gratitude.

"Mr. Freeborn I have said it again and again, that as long as your kind remain in the Negro race, we shall overcome." Mr. Washington spoke with all sincerity.

"Now, Chief," for this appellation Margaret had steadily called him since she knew of his authentic saga, "how long do you wish to keep Number II from school? Is it when he is due to marry?" They all burst into laughter.

"There is a time and season for everything under the heavens…a time to plant and time to harvest." Taliaferro enthused with his popular lecturer mannerism.

"I am waiting for the right time my friends." Chuck II spoke with a hint of sadness that he tried unsuccessfully to conceal. The children were busy in their own worlds, listening attentively to Number II, telling them some African folklore that he had passed down.

"My dear friend, there is no tragedy under heaven as; doing the right thing at the wrong time." Washington gushed with laughter, as he bent sideways to whisper into his third wife's ear.

"For crying out loud, Chief, I am taking Number II back with us to Tuskegee next tomorrow. The young child needs some mother's loving care." She declared authoritatively, as they all waited anxiously for Chuck to make his response.

"Well, em…em…you know em...em... Margaret…em." Chuck Freeborn knew when he was cornered. Trust the master schemer Taliaferro, to come up with a water-tight scheme to beat him hands down. He knew the impact of getting Margaret involved.

"Ok, ok, you win. I give up. Margaret, he is all yours, you can have him, but slow down on the mother's love thing. Taliaferro, I want him to be hard as stone, please the entire fireworks to give him a breathing chance in any situation that he would find himself in this your strange people and a stranger world. I would stay out of the picture as long as it would take. Five, six, or seven years." He quickly dabbed the tears away.

Booker T. Washington had to take charge, for his wife Margaret was also crying, "Come on Mr. Freeborn, you are in safe hands, you can count on me. I will go beyond the call of duty to churn out a young man that one day will go back to the native land and expose the charlatans and pretenders in that cave that sold you out. Seven years would do. Yes, seven years would be more than ample..

The next day, September 18, 1895, was the D-Day for the Atlanta Exposition, you could feel it in the air, that history was about to be made. The sun rose quite early, and hot and bright. The whole place was filled with people who came from all over. Chuck Freeborn I, had reached the audience room very early to find a vantage point to watch his good friend make history. One or two familiar faces had called out to him as he finally sat. The hall was exceptionally huge, but there was no way it could contain that milling crowd outside. Except for the reserved seats that was meant for the official procession, almost half of the chairs were occupied already. It took two and half hours for the formal procession to reach the Exposition grounds that was only minutes away.

Chuck recalled how the other items on the program before Washington's address went by flittingly. He noted the exact words of Ex-Governor R. Bullock to introduce him; *...a representative of Negro enterprise and Negro civilization.* Chuck could not help but smile with pride at the words Negro civilization. Chuck did not know when he joined the furor of applauding band of colored people. The black shiny star stepped over to the podium, his mien and carriage not betraying any emotion. Booker T. Washington was composed, not a hair out of place. His voice was audible, strong and confident. He dramatically surveyed the audience without paying any particular attention to anybody. His salutation was brief and concise, to show that he meant business. Though Chuck did not miss a word of the speech but these words stuck in his memory.

One-third of the population of the south is of the Negro race... cast...cast down...cast down your bucket...cast down your bucket where you are. Cast it down in agriculture, mechanics, in commerce ...we can be separate as the fingers, yet one as the hand in all things essential to mutual progress...

Booker T. Washington was not done yet; *...there is no escape through law of God from the inevitable; The laws of changeless justice bind oppressor with oppressed...this coupled with our material prosperity, will bring into our beloved South a new heaven and a new earth.*

Finally, and finally, the Booker T. Washington's Atlanta Exposition address finally came to an end. The auditorium literally came crashing down, as Ex-Governor Bullock threw decorum out of the windows and ran over to take Washington by the hand to congratulate him in front of both the Northern and Southern whites. That was how Booker T. Washington became not just the biggest sell of the Atlanta Exposition, but the biggest sell from the Negro race in the century.

His profile shot like a meteorite all over America as the newspapers went to town and qualified him as an instant hit. Everybody wanted a piece of the poor colored Hampton graduate. He had fulfilled his own prophetic words; *that there is something in human nature which always makes an individual recognize and reward merit, no matter under what color of skin merit is found..*

Chuck Freeborn I, had taken all night to prepare his son for his seven year-tutelage under one of the brightest icons that the Negro race was about to offer the world. They had arrived long at the train station before the Washingtons, who arrived with barely enough time to catch the train. After they had all boarded, the two men stood facing each other;

"Taliaferro, I cast down my bucket where you are, to fill him with all the fresh wisdom and knowledge. Destiny has brought us together for an uncommon purpose. May your road be rough, my brother."

As they embraced the final whistle went off for Booker T. Washington to clamber onboard. As the train slowly rolled off and gradually picked speed, and disappeared into the distance, something reassured Chuck Freeborn I, that he had taken the best decision for his son..

CHAPTER 44

Thirty-six years…from 1864 to 1900. It was 36 long years already, since he set foot in America as a captive, but never practiced as a slave. *Freeborn*…it sounded incredulous to learn that the slaver and captain of *the Sea Fairy* gave him that name. *Wow! Who would believe it.* He continued to stare at himself in the mirror, before picking up the wooden comb, to comb through his still thick and bushy hair. Thirty-six years is indeed a very long time; no wonder, that he had lost track of names and even the Igbo language. The brain, more often than not, has a tendency to erase an original tongue in a bid to learn another tongue, if the original tongue is not used frequently. He tried to smile; but it came out more like a snarl.

At least, he thought to himself, that there was still something to smile about, in the din of all these pain and sorrow that he had suffered. Indeed, the last five years had been the most rewarding and hopeful since he arrived in Savannah, Georgia. Dispatching Chuck to Tuskegee, to study under the mentorship of one of America's most gifted and charismatic black men, was the ace.

From all indications, Chuck II was blazing a trail that was intimidating everybody in his wake, as Taliaferro himself had told him, when they accidently met some months back in Atlanta. The plan for the older Freeborn to stay out of the picture for the expected seven years duration had also paid off. He had remained even more persistent with his increased donations to the Tuskegee Institute in the past five years, since Chuck II, moved into Booker T. Washington's household.

The past five years had also been his *loneliest;* for he had truly missed the company of his son. In the years immediately following his wife's death, he had trained and retrained his son with every aspect of training he had received back in Africa. They had taken good time out to go hunting and fishing in the swamps and woods around Little Savannah in the true African ways and methods. He had taught the young man everything about herbs, barks, roots, and seeds that he learned from his own mother. How to start a fire, and other basic survival techniques he had faithfully passed down to Chuck II. And what gladdened his heart was his discovery that the boy was a natural learner with an insatiable desire to learn.

Yes, the past five years had also been his loneliest. With his level of economic success and fame there had remained a string of ready and willing ladies at his beck and call that he had disappointed, *for not letting the handshake to go beyond the elbow.* He had made up his mind not to marry again, so as to keep the memory of Ngozika, his wife sacred. On the other hand, it was also for the sake of the children. He knew it was the little price tag he must pay to provide the best he could provide as a father. At the end of the day, it would better the lots of his son, and his children's children in this very strange land, and of stranger people.

So far Chuck Freeborn I, is very impressed with the extent his son's exposure under the shadow of Booker T. Washington. He was part of the team that gave President William McKinley a most impressive welcome in 1898, when Tuskegee became the first colored institute to host the President of the United States and his cabinet. Chuck Freeborn II went along with his mentor to Harvard University in 1896 to receive the first-ever honorary award given to a black man. When the great George Washington Carver, arrived Tuskegee in 1896, to head the Agriculture Department; it was the young Freeborn who was seconded to work and learn from him in close quarters.

Booker T. Washington had also reliably informed his friend, that the University was initiating a brand new inter-disciplinary study, that would be the first of its kind in all of America around Chuck Freeborn II at graduation. The study would be called Negro Civilization…it was to cover everything about Africa that he had successfully passed down to his son. A chunk of virgin land would be set aside as a reserve to effectively serve that program from 25,000 acres of land donated by the Congress to the institute.

Chuck was really gob smacked with all that he was hearing. *Negro Civilization…*he now remembered where he had first heard the term before. Yes, it was at the Atlanta Exposition, when Booker T.

Washington was introduced by that former Governor. *Negro Civilization* that would cover the whole gamut of African lifestyles.

He was also informed that Chuck Freeborn II would be part of the Tuskegee team that would be at the Buffalo, New York, Pan- American Exposition to be officially opened by President William McKinley on September 6, 1901.

All Chuck Freeborn I could do was to hold his friend's hands together in gratitude, and prayed fervently for him. All Booker Washington said in return was;

"*Any man regardless of color, will be recognized and rewarded just in proportion as he learns to do something well – learn to do it better than someone else – however humble the thing may be..*

Chuck Freeborn dropped the wooden comb in his hand on the dressing table, smiled at his image in the mirror, before pulling on his underwear. Something told him the brand new century had so much in stock for him. He heaved a sigh; could it ever be worse than the previous century. He could only wish himself the best of the new year.

CHAPTER 45

Maybe Chuck Freeborn I was right, when he described America as *a strange land, with a stranger people*. The celebrations for the brand new century were still re-echoing, before they were rudely marred by the first high profile senseless killing in the corridors of power.

With a soaring popularity garnered through the victory in the Spanish-American War, it was no problem for President McKinley to get re-elected for his second term. On March 4, 1901, his second inauguration went uneventfully. As the president and his vice, Theodore Roosevelt who replaced the first vice president, Garret Hobart who died in 1899, settled down to state business, little did they know that death was crouching at the door.

As Chuck Freeborn II and his colleagues were putting finishing touches to the their exhibition items, for the long-awaited New York Pan-American Exposition September 6th, 1901 official openning, 28 year-old Leon Czolgosz, a self-acclaimed anarchist fatally shot down President William McKinley in the venue of the exposition. The president finally died eight days later, to gangrene and infection. America sadly mourned and buried their President, and went after Czolgosz to collect their pound of flesh accordingly.

Czolgosz's trial commenced on September 23; and a guilty verdict was swiftly returned the next day. The judgment was that Leon Czolgosz was to be executed. On October 29, the prisoner was moved to Auburn Prison New York, where Thomas Edison had designed an electric chair for execution purposes.

It was after this assassination, the Congress passed a legislation to effectively give the secret service the responsibility to protect the president. Vice-President Theodore Roosevelt who stepped in, like

William McKinley remained a friend to Booker T. Washington and the Negro race. And to prove the point, Booker T. Washington was invited to dinner at the White House with Roosevelt. He was the first Negro ever to achieve that feat 1901.

June, 1902, was Tuskegee Annual Graduation ceremony, and father and son finally met after seven years of intentionally staying apart. Chuck could not recognize his son, he was so grown and mature. He was a carbon copy of his grandfather Aka, the way he smiled reminded him so much of his father. He arrived Tuskegee the previous day to a hero's welcome. He was one of the official guests of the Institute. At dinner with Mr Washington, and his faculty staff, he had been warmly introduced as one of the very consistent benefactors of Tuskegee. Nothing was said about his relationship with Chuck II who was also at the dinner. He did not know that Taliaferro was keeping the best part for the graduation ceremony proper.

It was much after dinner, that the two men, as father and son had time in private to sit and compare notes dating back to that fateful morning at the Atlanta train station almost seven years back. After they had covered every lost ground, the younger of the Freeborns quickly stepped out of the room and returned with an ebony-black pretty girl in tow.

"Dad, I want you to meet, Martina. Martina Leonceto. She was originally from Cuba." The young man spoke lightly.

"Good… eh…eh Mar…tina, I am truly honored to meet you." The older Freeborn was completely taken aback for a very brief moment… there was a striking resemblance that he could not immediately place.

"Dad, I am the one that is honored. I have heard so much about you from *Number 2*." The young lady though was shy, sounded confident, displaying snow-white perfect dentition. "My father Maximo, insisted on us to bear his father's name, for sentimental reasons best known to him", she added pointedly.

"I sincerely hope… eh…eh your friend spoke well of me." He burst into a good natured hearty laughter to hide his obvious distraction caused by his roving mind to place that face in his past. "Your grandfather must have been a hero, for your father to insist on bearing his name", he quickly added to hide

"You can bet on that sir, not a single negative word was said." She laughed, obviously infected by the older man's laughter.

"Good. So, to what do I owe this honor of meeting you?" He looked from one person to the other, and quickly added, "Or am I meeting my daughter-inlaw?"

"Dad! Nobody said anything like that to you yet." The son said with a fake plaintiveness that was so obvious.

"Alright, I am sorry, please forgive me. Then you must have found me a wife to replace your mother then." He burst into his infectious laughter again, as the young lady looked away in a feigned embarrassment.

"Dad, please! You will have a long day tomorrow, so we can leave you to rest."

"That is nice, then we are on the same page. If you really want me to rest well-well. Then tell me that Martina, is the one for us, both of us." Chuck Freeborn could not hide his glee for his son's obvious choice for a wife.

"Alright, you won, Dad. Yes, Martina has agreed to marry me. I mean us." He added playfully as an after thought.

Chuck Freeborn I embraced both his son and daughter-inlaw together, as tears of joy flowed down his cheeks. At least there was hope that he would continue through the seed of his loins, Akachukwu's name in this strange land with a stranger people.

Later that night, Chuck Freeborn I, could not sleep tried as he could. Martina Leonceto's facial features remained transfixed in his mind. That striking resemblance was close yet too far back to place in his memory. *Martina Leonceto...* he spoke out the name couple of times, yet it did not get him closer to solving the puzzle. He finally drifted off to sleep in the early hours of the morning, dreaming about his father and mother back in Ohafia; it was the eve of their fatal journey to Arochukwu.

The next day, as Freeborn I joined the other very important dignitaries on the grandstand, he did not feel out of place. His graduating son had proven that he was the true son of his father, he thought to himself. Chuck Freeborn II had carted home almost every prize in his class. The older Freeborn was full of pride for his son's outstanding excellent academic laurels.

Then came the climax of the ceremony; the address by Booker T. Washington. The President of the Tuskegee Institute proudly and candidly spoke of the challenges of the early years, that they did not allow to weigh them down. The price they all paid to achieve success and the heavier task to sustain it.

"Does it surprise you that the mammoth crowd present here today, only started with thirty ragtag-team of pioneer students, in what you may consider a ramshackle shanty-house in the most miserable condition. It was a classical case of the rejected boulder ending up with the most honorable status as the top cornerstone of the building." Washington paused for the rousing applause to die down before his next thrust.

"...all we had then, and even now, that brought us to this point was our faith; our undying faith in God. Though the Negro race had been totally short-changed by humanity; dehumanized by our neighbors; disenfranchised by the powers that be; beaten, bruised and battered by the brothers with a different color of skin. Whether it was in the dark swampy expanse of Louisiana, to the snowy ocean cotton fields of Georgia; or the endless fertile black soil of Mississippi that nurtured the best of America, to the lush green fields of Texas that grazed our thoroughbreds, we had kept our black waning hopes alive." This time half of the sea of heads were crying and shedding tears.

"Negro Hope and his Dignity had remained a tough, hard, rough sod to surmount. And that, we have made our responsibility at Tuskegee. Our message was clear from the origin; that come what may, we must hold our heads up, finding strength and consolation in our collective dignity and prowess." The audience once again roared in animatedly.

"That was why we went in search of the great George Washington Carver to perform the miracles with our food baskets and Negro enterprise. Today, we can thump our hearts and say we are better for it. For Negro Enterprise is not a question of possibility; no, because it is already a part of our lives. I have always insisted that no matter how much we are browbeaten or brainwashed to believe the lies; we must not forget that Negro Civilization, is the cradle of civilization." He paused once again for the ovation to simmer down.

"That is why you must know the truth, the truth that will set you free. You must know where you are coming from, to know where you are going. That is why, we have insisted that Negro Civilization must be studied to restore our broken racial psyche. Another uphill task we are not afraid to climb. And the search for the right human tool began. We did not only find one but two, a father and son combination, the real McCoy. Born, bred, and tampered in Africa, then shipped over to the New World without the adulteration of back-breaking weighty burden of slavery. It had taken the most delusional of us to confirm with our mouths that it is purely a divine arrangement. My brothers and sisters, it is my pride and pleasure to announce, and present to you the

Department of Negro Civilization." It was a very resounding ovation that reverberated through the Tuskegee air.

After the noise had finally died down, Booker T. Washington, now proceeded to present the duo of the father and son combination with these words.

"It is our firm belief that Tuskegee, would take the study of Negro Civilization to every nook and cranny of America. Every colored school must be reached. Distinguished guests, ladies and gentlemen, I present to you Chuck Freeborn II, who is a faculty member and to be advised by his father. Their story alone is a key chapter of study in Negro Civilization." The gathering at this point erupted like a volcano.

CHAPTER 46

Teaching Negro Civilization both at Tuskegee and as a visiting professor at other schools was very tedious, indeed more tedious than ever projected. The theories in the classrooms and the overnight field trips into very deep swamps and woods for the practical aspects. The consolation for Chuck Freeborn II, was that he made acquaintances in almost every colored school in the South. His best teaching experience was at A & T College, in Greensboro, North Carolina where he bonded so well with staff and students.

It was under his very tight schedule in 1904, he married Martina Leoncето after she completed her studies in Tuskegee. And the boys to their grandfather's delight came in quick succession. Chuck III was born in 1905; Booker, who was named after Mr. Washington, by his protégée, arrived in 1908; and Gossamer, who his grandfather named after his benefactor, was born in 1910. Thereafter, the children just stopped coming. Martina, who had arrived America alone from Cuba, and had lost all touch from her folks, actually had her mind on at least six children.

With both Chuck II and his wife fully engaged in their specialties, they were more on the road together empowering colored folks. Chuck Freeborn I was more than glad to be of service, baby sitting and having fresh minds and keen ears to pass down every knowledge of Africa. And they learnt so fast that by the time they went to Tuskegee in 1915 for the interment of the great Booker T. Washington, the two older boys presented a mock wrestling contest to honor an *iroko* of a man. With the new additions to the family, Chuck Freeborn II now got the catalyst, he craved to totally transform the old man with so much misfortunes bottled inside. Everyone that came across the old man commented of his youthfulness and vibrant nature. He would say there was nothing better than the ready willing love of one's family.

For the old man it seemed as if life had indeed changed for the better, and that true love had indeed conquered all. Little did he know that it was only a very brief respite that would soon fizzle out to more senseless violence, butchery, destruction and deaths. While the political events in Europe looked and sounded so far away, yet they were congregating like dark cumulus clouds that would culminate into the storm, with the swirling vortex of a tornado that would suck in the whole world, in what came to be known as the World War I from 1914 to 1918.

The year 1915 had its own fair share of bad news. Between 1915 to 1920, cotton production in the South suffered a deadly blow from The Boll Weevil attack on cotton. While the plantations that were mostly involved in cash crops like cotton had no choice but to go under. Most blacks on contract or share cropping arrangements had to pack and seek for greener pastures up North. As these immigrants blacks appeared in relatively new communities; there began new consciousness to protect their own raised anti-immigrant feelings.

Other interest groups who were anti-Catholic, prohibitionists, and those with anti-semitic agenda joined forces to have a common front to mete out their jungle justice under mob actions targeted at blacks and their sympathizers. The Ku Klux Klan was then still comatose. It was the lynching of Jewish businessman Leo Frank in 1915, who went on trial for the murder of Mary Phagan, that awakened the comatose KKK into action.

The Knights of Mary Phagan actually came into being during the 1913 trial of Leo Frank, and naturally metamorphosed into the Klan, it readily became the platform that they had been waiting for. It was William J. Simmons, from the State of Alabama, who formally launched the new KKK from the top of Stone Mountain on the outskirts of the city of Atlanta.

The new Klan's tradition of burning the Latin cross was targeted to terrorize their potential victims. While their religious tradition to pray and sing hymns was totally to mislead the gullible. The white uniform of cloaks and hoods was also calculated to scare the average blacks who believed in ghosts, spirits, and the para normal. The KKK was better organized in this era, and believed to have over five million members. And they wreaked havoc on their mostly defenseless victims with impunity as their members were people in high places. As they killed and maimed with reckless abandon there were relatively very few convictions.

The World War I was raging on, while the US had maintained neutrality until March, 1917, when German submarines accidently or by design sank some US merchant vessels. President Woodrow Wilson had no choice but to declare war on Germany on April 6, 1917. Chuck Freeborn II was with the Seniors of A&T College, Greensboro, North Carolina, on a field trip, when they all agreed to enlist in the US Army that was recruiting.

Chuck Freeborn II recalled how they had arrived at that mass decision. He was explaining the uses of the Polkweed. They were to note the delicate balance between its edible uses and it potent poison qualities. He had mentioned that its potent poison on arrowheads was an effective weapon of African warfare. Somebody had playfully asked if it could work against the *Germans*. And another had suggested boldly, why they should now all enlist and try out all they have learnt. Nobody backed out, and so they all enlisted.

Chuck II had rushed home with just time enough to put his house in order. His father was really elated with the news; *war was in* their blood. He had given him his blessings. While Martina, on the other hand was almost weeping her eyes out. He reassured her that he was going to come back.

"People who die in the hands of the Klan, were they safer than those who went to war and returned." Chuck II quipped.

Tuskegee, the President, Major Robert R. Moton was very physical about the whole mission.

"Go and defend your nation, and don't forget we want you back immediately for there is work to be done. And be very careful with the Germans, they are known to be very meticulous; a kind craze for precision…"

CHAPTER 47

Camp Wadsworth was their first port of call for their formal combat training. It was located in Spartanburg, South Carolina, which was a typical rural community, whose respect for the colored people was nothing to write home about. The trainings were combined for both white and colored Divisions. Chuck Freeborn II and his pack of enthusiastic students were going to learn certain bitter lessons of life.

Within a few days in the camp, the soldiers acclimatized and accepted each other; their skin colors not considered just like the color of their eyes. Even some of the colored could not get used to it. Chuck noted it to them as Lesson 1; *when men were ready to fight and die together, they realize that the red blood flowing in their veins is the common denominator behind their skin colors.*

Little did they know that the hopes and aspirations of General John 'Black Jack' Pershing, General Officer Commanding, World War I American Expeditionary Force in Europe, was not shared by some of the white folks either in the immediate environment of Spartanburg, or the greater community of the United States. When the news filtered back to camp that some white shop owners were refusing or ignoring to serve colored soldiers, it was first shock and disbelief for even their white colleagues. Lesson No. 2; *to the racist your military uniform, whether fatigues or camouflages does not cover, or make any difference to your offending skin color.*

It took the joint intervention of the soldiers in the other Divisions to threaten the racist shop owners with total boycott, before they grudgingly succumbed to serve the *black boys*. Lesson No. 3; *esprit de corpe in the Army, simply means in dead or life we stand together as comrades.*

They were in Wadsworth for six months training; sweating from one obstacle to the other in combats, endurance, intelligence gathering, survival techniques. In this six months they ate, drank, slept and dreamed together. They learned to trust and support one another. They chanted it over and over again; All for One, and One for All. Lesson No. 4; *the only visible difference between two soldiers, is dead or alive.*

During the passing out parade, which was attended by the Military high brass. The very dashing General J. J. Pershing, addressed the men and officers.

"Even though we have in the past few months transformed you into a *mean fighting machine,* also remember that you must be an officer and a gentleman…be benevolent in victory, and be graceful in defeat, because the bones of both enemies and colleagues that fall in battle are all white. Always get the mission accomplished as the consummate professionals that you are…I wish you God's speed."

Chuck Freeborn II noted to his boys later, Lesson No. 5; *no human being, black, white, brown, yellow or red is neither inferior or superior to another, they are all structurally white beneath their skin..*

The Black regiment had spent Christmas in New York, and promptly on December 27, 1917, joined the rest of the US Expeditionary Force, that set sail for Europe via France. During their voyage from New York, Chuck had started taking a special interest in a Simon Alexander from his hometown Savannah. It was until they disembarked in France that he knew their Savannahs were miles apart as they joked about it. He was actually from Savannah, Tennessee, not Georgia. There and then began a friendship that was to last more than their lifetimes.

The black regiment under the 185th Infantry Brigade was segregated against like any other colored regiment, because the generally held opinion in the US Army was that the black soldiers were not capable to hold positions of responsibilities. It was on this premise that from January to April 1918, they did not see or smell any combat. They were relegated to do only labor duties. And those duties, Chuck advised them to do with relish, so as to gradually win the approval and better ratings of their superiors and officers. Lesson No. 6; *do small assignments paying attention to detail, they definitely lead to bigger assignments and responsibilities.*

Little did they know that General Black Jack Pershing was paying attention. It was not until April 8, 1918, when they were formally transferred to the direct command of the French Army. Here the regiment was accorded more respect and subsequently treated equally with Francophone colleagues. Lesson No. 7; *do not be distracted, remain focused in whatever you were assigned to do, for your gifts will find you out.*

Under the leadership of Staff Sgt. Chuck Freeborn II, the regiment went from one victory to another; gradually becoming the toast of the French Army. They fought with a fierceness and boldness that was modeled by their leader. His colleagues could not but address him as *Lion-heart*. Staff Sgt. Chuck *Lion-heart* Freeborn, that name naturally stuck over time. There was a tour of duty, that they spent over five months without re-enforcement. It was like they were totally forgotten. They had to resort to bows and arrows and other methods of warfare of Negro Civilization, when they totally ran out of munitions. When they also ran out of their rations Chuck once again came to the rescue with knowledge of African traps and snares to feed the entire regiment. Against injuries his mastery of figs, herbs, barks and roots saved many a life. It was to his credit that not a single soldier was lost in his regiment, during the campaign.

There was an incident when they took a unit of German soldiers as prisoners of war. They did not know that they were specialists in German Propaganda; until they started effective moves to turn the black soldiers against their America. When Staff Sgt. Freeborn had confirmed the hidden agenda of the Germans, he taught his students Lesson No. 8; *be a honorable black man that people can count on; for there is honor even amongst thieves.*

That incident happened before September 1918, when the war-front moved to Meuse-Argonne. It was a tough battle but the regiment at the end of the day captured the strategic village of Sechault. By November 26, 1918, the black regiment became the first unit of the allied forces to land at the Rhine River. They had achieved what no other detachment could do. And true to type the regiment was loaded with accolades and medals of honor by the unbiased French Army and public.

Finally, the regiment headed back home to New York. They were finally demobilized at Camp Upton on February 28, 1919, without any fanfair. So they had all looked forward with all their medals of honor, to the 1919 Victory Parade. That parade too they were sadly not allowed to be part of. Staff Sgt. Chuck *Lion-heart* Freeborn II felt truly very disappointed, that he considered it, the lowest ebb of the whole war for him. All he could say to soldiers was Lesson No. 9; *a prophet more often-than-not is not honored in his own country.*

Thereafter, contacts were exchanged, as men who had sworn to live and die together, put their relationships on hold, as they began the long journey home to loved ones, for the lucky ones. For some the Army had become their only family, for these were the ones that found the Army as a lucky escape from agonizing backgrounds.

It was on the train heading South from New York, they learnt from the newspaper that a colored World War I veteran, in full uniform was killed by the Ku Klux Klan as he arrived in Atlanta, Georgia. As they read further with interest, to discover that it was Pvt. B. T. Longleaf, one of their youngest colleagues. All of a sudden, the atmosphere inside that *Colored Only* cabin became colder than the freezing cold outside. Some of the men could not hold back the tears. Chuck Lion-heart knew he must say something to calm the frayed nerves and hurting hearts.

Pvt. Benjamin Tomlasson Longleaf survived all the German war machines and the mirage of diseases that depleted the expeditionary force; to only crumble miserably to his own people in cloaks, hoods, and burning crosses. So very unfortunate. Lesson No. 10; *the black man must rise above his immediate environment that is riddled with hatred and racial bigotry; you must disabuse your minds, don't ever let them pull you down to their level of derangement.*

CHAPTER 48

Friendships that developed out of military service stand the test of time more than any other kind of friendship. When men stand to fight back-to-back, they learn to entrust their safety and lives to one another. No matter their race, color or creed, they truly remain brothers-in-arms, that is way beyond friendship, more binding even than blood relations. That is why they never forget those close calls to death, and heroic deeds of colleagues dead or alive that led to spine-tingling daring escapes. Though, Chuck *Lion-heart* Freeborn II, had returned to his work at Tuskegee, still in charge of the Department of Negro Civilization, he remained more of a cult hero to his boys that he fought side-by-side with in the WWI.

They were all in steady contact with him through the mail, or by physical visits. There were so many social engagements that they all wanted the wonderful Staff Sgt. *Lion-heart* to grace. Some involved very long and complicated train rides to attend. He tried his ultimate best to honor the most important ones with emotional and sentimental values.

One of the numerous invitations came from his good friend from Savannah, Tennessee, Simon Alexander. It was to his wedding to a Belinda Brady in the summer of 1920, in Hennings, Tennessee. Chuck made up his mind that this was one invitation he must honor. And he did to the exhilaration of Simon Alexander, who proudly introduced him to all and sundry as his teacher, and superior officer. Chuck noted with a smile that Simon was indeed a smooth operator, he married into a very wealthy family from all indications. He never mentioned that to his man.

As the marriage was blessed with children, Simon Alexander made it a tradition to intimate Staff Sgt *Lion-heart* accordingly. Amos the first child came in 1922; Randy, the second boy arrived in 1925, and the last boy, Matthew landed in 1929. As Simon progressed in life he kept his friend informed.

When he became a professor of agriculture, and started teaching at A&M College, at Normal, Alabama; there was a day the great Staff Sgt *Lion-heart*, after so much persuasion finally breezed into the campus with his first son to visit them. It was a very exciting experience for the Alexander boys, who had heard so much about the great *Lion-heart*. That at some point, the boys had started thinking whether the *Lion-heart* adventures was just a myth, and the figment of their father's fertile imagination. It was also a great pleasure for Belinda who was also seeing him since the wedding.

After a very long and protracted lunch, because the World War I stories of escapades were retold again and again, for the friends to once again relive their evergreen memories. It was then Chuck III had led the boys outdoor to try out some hunting skills. Since he was much older than the Alexander boys, they animatedly trooped and milled around him to get all that he could teach them.

When the boys later got home in the evening, the adults who were all academicians were seated out in the garden with a half empty jug of lemonade between them. The boys were so proud to show off the two succulent looking rabbits that they had ensnared in their first practical lesson in hunting. After showing them to the appreciative adults, Chuck III had taken the rabbits with the figs, wild herbs and spices that he had picked to prepare spicy roasted rabbit as he was taught by his grandfather. It was a special African recipe that is winner any day.

"Just like that. Is rabbit hunting that easy?" Belinda Alexander asked innocently.

"Well, it is kind of easy when you have mastered Negro Civilization." Her husband answered.

"And do not forget that their tutor is the real McCoy, that taught me too." Chuck II quipped. "Wait until you taste the end result. There is nothing that tastes better."

"Maybe we should recommend it for the KKK; it may cure their anger." Belinda tried to return them to their discussion prior to the boys arrival.

"Do they look hungry to you? At least we saw them march proudly down Pennsylvania Avenue, in Washington DC." Her husband readily took the bait.

"By that single step they had proven that they are not a secret society. If you can parade people like Governor Bibb Graves, Supreme Court justice Hugo Black, Senator Thomas Heflin, and Alabama's Attorney General, Charles McCall amongst their ranks; you underestimate them to your own peril." Staff Sgt. *Lion-heart* expounded.

"BeeGee, I think I know the perfect place you should go for that nagging toothace, when you arrive Texas for the forthcoming Conference for Women Professionals."

"Oh, that is very nice of you, Simon darling. Better tell me now so that we won't forget." Belinda spoke without any iota of suspicion. "Hiram Evans is one of the best dentists in Texas." Professor Simon Alexander, quipped with a mischievous grin.

His wife suspecting a foul play in the offing, playfully directed her question specifically at the man her husband respects and treats as an elder brother. "Sir, is this your officer truly a gentleman? I can tell when he wants to pull the rug from under a lady's feet." She burst into an infectious laughter, that carried the men along.

"Professor Belinda Alexander, you can bet my last dime on him; your darling husband is indeed an officer and a gentleman. If he proves otherwise, you trust me to court marshal him and hand him over to General Black Jack Pershing for some good hiding. I can see that he wants to not just remove the aching tooth but damage the rest of your perfect dentition." He paused, trying unsuccessfully very hard not to burst into laughter.

"Em…I don't understand. Not just remove…but damage the rest of my dentition." A frown crossed her beautiful face in the golden glows of the setting sun, as she tried to read her husband's face, who quickly looked away to avoid her probing eyes. Finding no hints there she returned her gaze to Professor Chuck Freeborn II, who was waiting to twist the *knife*.

"You don't understand. We are actually looking for some form of damage control my dear Belinda." Chuck suspended her in midair as her dear husband finally pulled the proverbial rug.

"BeeGee, what Staff Sgt. Lion-heart is saying is that your new dentist, the great Dr. Hiram Evans," he paused dramatically to wear his shoes and cleared his path for quick takeoff, "is the Imperial Wizard of the Ku Klux Klan…"

"What! God forbid." She screamed picking up the baseball bat on the grass and went for her husband who was already three steps ahead of her and squealing with laughter. While Chuck tumbled on to the grass with rib-cracking laughter.

Later that evening, after dinner that the special roasted rabbit was the main dish. The rabbit with the wild spice and herbs combination was winner and lived up to its billing. Just after dessert, the husband and wife performed together for their honored guests, and the boys. Performing old Negro spirituals like *When the Saints Go Marching On*, and the *John Brown's Body* amongst other songs, as Belinda played the piano, while Simon accompanied her with his deep melodious voice. It was very obvious to everyone that there was so much love and connection between the two. The boys also took turns to play the piano, before they finally retired for the night.

Early the next morning, as the Freeborns waved their good-byes and commenced the long drive home to Tuskegee in the Ford Model A pickup. Chuck loved driving the car than taking the train, for the obvious reasons of discrimination. Most of the long drive home, Chuck III noticed that his father was quiet, and in deep thoughts. He knew that something was bothering his father.

The young man was right. Chuck Freeborn II could not erase the golden image of Belinda Alexander with the baseball bat raised over her head chasing after her husband into the setting sun. That golden image was frozen. Then, the other image that just refused to go was the image of Belinda and Simon sharing very deep loving looks, as they performed those songs together under the blazing crystal chandelier over their heads. It was like something telling to engrave those happy images on your heart, because you would *never see them again.* It really bothered him, though he would not drag his 25-year-old son into such a complex spiritual matter. Chuck II could feel it deep in his soul that something ominous was about to happen to this wonderful young family that he had come to be part of.

CHAPTER 49

By 1931, the Great Depression was already taking its toll on America, and other key world economies. The actual Wall Street crash of October 29, 1929, that drastically translated to the downturn in the economies, were now history, yet the consequences were bringing upon the people untold hardships. On that Black Friday, it took only a few hours to turn millionaires into paupers as the value of their investments in stocks and shares were so pummeled, that they cost less than the papers they were printed on.

The cataclysmic effect was the untimely death of major banks and blue-chip companies involved in stocks speculation. The sudden unexpected change in the tide of business became too much for some of these chief executives to bear. To the point that Wall Street's concrete itself was splattered with blood and brain matters of those who tried to defy gravity by stepping out through the windows of their skyscraper gilded offices.

There was no place to hide for even the poor, as unemployment was rising everyday, due to failing business. The agricultural industry also took a battering due to failing prices. By this time, unemployment figure stood at over a staggering 12 million, the highest ever recorded.

The administration of President Herbert Clark Hoover, was not let off the hook, as it was blamed for government economic policies that resulted in domestic overproduction, without a corresponding international trade activities. The government tried so hard to restore confidence into businesses by balancing the budget. It even set up The Reconstruction Finance Corporation to loan out monies to businesses to survive the crunch. Every panacea recommended to normalize the economy, did not provide succor as projected. The economic depression was adamantly stubborn; it was like a sickness that was resistant to every doctor's prescription. There was no relief in sight as the government ran out of ideas, this impasse gradually eroded the popularity of President Hoover.

At the 16th Street Baptist Church, Birmingham, Alabama, a host of friends and close family members were celebrating with the grand old man Chuck Freeborn I, who was celebrating his 82nd year. Due to the spring in his steps and sound health, it was difficult to believe that he was an Octogenarian. Chuck Freeborn II had taken time to summarize how they arrived at 82 to the august gathering.

"My father had arrived Savannah, Georgia, on the eve of its surrender during the Civil War in 1864. That automatically translate to 67 long years he had spent in America so far. If he was a 15 year- old, when he left the shores of Africa; then you must agree that he is indeed 82 years old." He paused to acknowledge the resounding applause from the audience.

"It is my pleasure on behalf of the Chuck Freeborn's family to welcome all of you for coming to honor our father. We will now give you a brief moment to say a thing or two about *the birthday boy*." Another round of applause saw him off the podium, and welcomed a well-dressed man that took over from him.

"My name is Major Robert Moton, President of the Tuskegee Institute." A resounding applause greeted his introduction.

"Chief Freeborn, as I learnt from Mrs Booker T. Washington to address him, is part and parcel of Tuskegee, long before even Professor Chuck Freeborn II joined us as a student. Over the years, Chief Freeborn had remained consistent in his unquestionable support for Tuskegee, even in these days of the Great Depression. All I can say to you Chief, we wish you the best from Tuskegee that you have given true life. I cannot leave here without telling you how your good friend Taliaferro Washington described you to me; *that man Chuck Freeborn I is a living museum of Africa, and Negro Civilization, so Tuskegee must do everything to honor him.* Many happy returns from all of Tuskegee, Alabama." It was a resounding ovation again.

After another three speakers from Little Savannah; Birmingham; and Savannah, Georgia, who all respectively eulogized the octogenarian. The microphone was finally taken to the patriarch to respond on his seat.

The old man now all grey on the head, stooping slightly forward, to the amazement of everyone, gingerly mounted the steps to the podium.

His voice sounded strong, as if from a younger person. His dentition was complete and white.

"I greet you all, my children and people. I am glad too, like you. Thank you and thank God for me. God is good. I landed America alone, but see me today. With a son and daughter, I have increased." The audience laughed and cheered the old man.

"Please in closing my speech. May I use this opportunity to invite you all to my 90th birthday, that is coming very soon. Thank you all very much." The old man with a big wide smile, waved and cheered at the audience.

Chuck III was on his way to MIT, Boston, Massachusetts. He had told everyone that he wanted to pursue a career in Agricultural Engineering. His grandfather had encouraged him to go all the way, and like George Washington Carver; to change the face of agriculture through technology. It was his belief that future of agriculture is in enhanced technology.

His younger brothers, Booker, and Gossamer, after their stint at Tuskegee were back in Little Savannah, taking charge of affairs as their grandfather went into a well-deserved semi-retirement in Birmingham. Birmingham just like Little Savannah, was built from the scratch, and totally free from traditional ties and encumbrances. It was gradually becoming the hotbed of civil rights. Characters like Chuck Freeborn I were gradually becoming the catalyst to spur African Americans into positive action, with their financial backing and influence. The 16th Street Baptist Church was already in the spotlight, for firebrand preachers that could talk people into wars.

Chuck II had noticed that his two younger sons were not academically inclined like their elder brother. From his discussions with them, he was convinced that the two boys were passionate about their desire to join the military force. They were not interested in anything else.

The other Sunday, after Church service, Chuck III had invited a beautiful Cuban girl, Olivia Baptiste over to the house for lunch. Chuck II noticed how smitten his wife, Martina was with her fellow compatriot. They were giggling like love-struck teenage girls; slipping into Spanish from time to time. Chuck II wondered aloud, why another Cuban? One was enough already for the Freeborn household. He knew that the largest number of foreign students in Tuskegee were Cubans. Now, come to think of it, this Cuban fixation was not ordinary, he thought to himself. He suspected his wife of this Cuban conspiracy, though was oblivious to any deeper attachment, like in his wife's stricking resemblance that later became household discuss.

Chuck II had patiently waited for his wife or son to broach the topic of the Cuban girl but no dice. He had seen her around the house couple of times, like during birthdays helping Martina with the cooking and serving. He recalled the day, a neighbor refered to Olivia as Martina's younger sister, it did not mean anything significant to him. All his son had said all this while was; "Dad meet my friend, Olivia Baptiste... she is from Cuba. Olivia had also migrated to America, like mum did way back". Chuck II knew his oldest son, to be man of very few word.

Sometime, later in the year, he was in the office of Dr. George Washington Carver, when a messenger tracked him there, with a telegram. The telegram was from Normal, Alabama, for him. His heart skipped a beat. He signed for it, and then opened it; *BELINDA DIED YESTERDAY AFTER BRIEF ILLNESS BURIAL IN 7 DAYS REGARDS SIMON* All of a sudden Chuck II felt his blood rushing into his head; then he felt the whole room swirling and spinning all around him, until he slumped back into his seat. He could not hold himself and wept for his very good friend and brother. He wept for the boys Amos, Randy, and Matthew. He vividly recalled the golden images of Belinda and Simon, their chase and singing duet.

The burial was in seven days; he made up his mind to endeavor to attend, come rain come shine. First, he must reply the telegram before anything....

CHAPTER 50

It was 1940; and 1932 seemed and felt like a dim star in the past. It was the 1932 Presidential election when African Americans overwhelmingly supported and voted in Franklin Delano Roosevelt against the incumbent President Herbert Hoover. FDR as he was fondly called was a friend to the major minority groups like the Jews, the Catholics and the African Americans, he came into office with so much sympathy. For a man that overcame the debilitating fangs of polio that he suffered in earlier years, all eyes were on him to overcome the bitter pills of the Great Depression. With 2 million people homeless; unemployment at its worst level in America; and agricultural products prices that had fallen by 60%, it truly looked gloomy on March 4, 1933, as the 51-year-old President Franklin Delano Roosevelt came into office.

Without mincing words President Roosevelt had taken the Great Depression head on, when he revealed in his inaugural address that, *...the money changers have fled from their high seats in the temple of our civilization. We may now restore that temple to the ancient truths.* Seven years later, with two successful terms already in his kitty, even his detractors and enemies would agree that indeed, *The Happy Days Are Here Again* song rang true. The Great Depression was now only a painful part of history many would rather forget, and not even talk about.

Life in the Freeborn household had once again experienced some misfortune, that resulted in death. It came at a time when everything was going well for them; they had continued to blossom in every sphere, even in the din of the Great Depression. Chuck III had successfully completed the Master's Degree program, and topped it off with a first class Doctorate Degree. He had just married Olivia Baptiste, in a massive high society wedding in Birmingham, when the callous dastardly killing happened The family was yet to get over the shock of losing one of the least violent amongst them. The murder that was perpetrated in the hands of the Ku Klux Klan in a small Alabama town, in 1938, had remained a mystery. The Klan had targeted and stalked the victim for a while. They had finally waylaid him on a solitary county road. What they had thought was going to be an easy kill… was totally underestimated. For Chuck Freeborn II, aka Staff Sergeant Lionheart was not a lionheart for nothing.

On that fateful day, the evening sun was yet to dip over the horizon, when a forest-green Ford Junior Tudor sedan carrying a pair of clandestine lovers, who were both respectively married, and on a secret tryst, pulled off the major road just before the wooden bridge, on to a gravel path running parallel to the river. The lovers had cast furtive glances all around them before backing into the covering safety of a Weeping Willow with very thick lower branches. It was not their first time there, because they were familiar with the surroundings. They had hastily slipped out of the car into an intense amorous embrace, oblivious to the slowly flowing river next to them. Little did they know that they were about to witness murder and killings most foul.

With an intense hunger for each other, they had feverishly torn off every shred of apparel on themselves to be consumed in the chasm of their illicit burning passion of their bodies. Such passionate fire, that could only be doused by the nectar and sweat of the volcanic climax of their intertwined anatomies.

When the act was done, and the saturated secret lovers relaxed in the cozy comfort of each other's arms on the soft leafy-carpet under the Weeping Willow, that was the only silent partaker of their secret. They first heard the car, before it appeared in the distance from the direction of Williamsville. The Ford Model 48 boldly marked *Sheriff Williamsville* had slowed down and finally parked, blocking the entrance of the narrow wooden bridge. They had first involuntarily ducked down out of sight for a brief moment before realizing that they were secure in the thick foliage of the willow.

When they looked up again, they saw the amoebic bulk of Sheriff Tommy Wilburpoint opening the hood of the engine. Engine trouble no doubt, they nodded at each other. The desire for self-preservation overwhelming their already spent passion, communicating with only their eyes, the partners in sin agreed to get dressed. It was then they heard the distinct sound of an approaching vehicle from Williamsville. Well, it seemed like the notorious sheriff was in luck; help was on his way. The lovers sensing there was no cause for alarm, found solace in a somber embrace obviously lacking fire and passion of the earlier one.

The vehicle, a charcoal-black 1936 Ford 5 Window coupe, and its owner were well-known to the African American lovers. It was the visiting professor from Tuskegee; who was their Negro Civilization teacher. The car stopped a safe distance from the broken down police car. The driver's door swung open, but before the professor could step out of his vehicle, a truck came hurtling down from the opposite direction of Tuskegee. The battered red 1934 Ford truck, was loaded with about seven white men. It thundered right on to the bridge and stopped short of the police vehicle. The armed men consulted briefly with Sheriff Wilburpoint, by then Chuck with a gun, had slipped out of his car and quickly ducked under the vehicle.

The group of newcomers had paused to take directions from a bulky fellow, before advancing towards the professor's vehicle. About twenty feet from the car, the bulky fellow stopped them and called out in a deep threatening voice.

"Come on boy, get your black nigger ass over here."

Chuck II smelling real trouble had his fully loaded *M1 Garand* trained at their knee level, as a wicked grin crossed his face. That tingling excitement that wells up, when you know you were two steps ahead of the adversary. He had expected this to happen one day, that he made that special storage for a gun and ammunition. He counted fourteen knees cautiously, but foolishly advancing towards him. The eight bullets in the clip was more than enough to tackle them.

"Boy! Come on boy. Didn't you hear me? Or are you deaf? Just step down from your fancy ride, with your hands above your head." The leader bellowed again.

The hollow voice echoed back in the silence that surrounded them. The now shivering secret lovers held their breaths, watching the event as it unfolded before their eyes.

"Alright boy, you won't say, I didn't give you a chance. I will blow up your bleeding black ass to high heavens."

"Common Mr. Fletcher, we haven't got all day. Let's get it over with this fancy black ass racoon." The sheriff called out as he made to close the hood of his car.

Without much ado Mr. Fletcher let off a shot from his rifle that shattered the windscreen into a million shards. And to their utmost amazement a blaze of bullets from beneath the car thudded into their legs, shattering flesh and bones. With the trained skill of the professional, he slipped in a new clip and completed the job. By the time Chuck Freeborn II rolled out from beneath the car, not a man was standing. He tactically inspected the mass of bodies lying dead on the macadamized thoroughfare. One or two were still in the throes of death.

Professor Chuck Freeborn II, better known as Staff Sgt. *Lion- heart*, in the Army stood tall, confident, and victorious over his attackers. *Maybe little more than over confident...* it was then a single shot rang out resonating in the final ambience of daylight. It was like everything stood still for a brief, but a very long moment as Chuck *Lion-heart* Freeborn II went down on his knees, a distinct third eye appearing on his forehead, then crashed face-down dead. His warm African blood seeping out as a libation to appease once again the land of America. That single fatal shot emanated from the barrel of a gun in the hands of Sheriff Tommy Wilburpoint, an Imperial Kleagle (Recruiter) of the Ku Klux Klan.

Sheriff Wilburpoint did not wait to assess the carnage spread out on that solitary county road, he hastily turned his car around and headed back to town, like a bat out of hell. His mind working out how an emergency meeting of the Klan must hold tonight to clean and clear up this shambolic outing. One of the massive crosses must burn tonight at the scene of that carnage. He warned Night Hawk Fletcher to be careful with Professor Chuck Freeborn II, but the official in charge of security had under-estimated his warning call to his own peril.

A moment later, the forest-green Ford sedan, with two very rattled passengers shivering in their seats, pulled out from under the foliage and sped with tyres squealing towards Williamsville. Their individual minds were pre-occupied with how to safeguard their secret escapades and obviously threatened marriages. Not a single word was exchanged between them until the lady dropped off at the *usual spot*.

Early the next day in Williamsville, seven households surreptitiously received letters on the official letterhead of the KKK, and duly signed by the Imperial Wizard respectively, that their spouse and father was on an emergency assignment out of state. Therefore, there was no cause for alarm, as a sum of $100 was enclosed for any pressing expenses.

At about noon, a forest-green sedan drove at a sedate pace from Williamsville to the wooden bridge on the solitary road to Tuskegee. The lone occupant of the car did not notice anything out of place. If not for his secret lover to corroborate his story, he would have thought that it was only his imagination. There were no bodies, no bloodstains, no wrecked vehicle, no bullet casings, not even shards of glass, and not even people alive or any news of the event of the previous evening.

He drove back to the police department at the town's center, where he noticed the Sheriff's marked car in the parking lot. He parked by it, and stepped out confidently, walked toward the sheriff's office. Some female cop on the desk, informed him that the sheriff called in sick that morning. He had mumbled something about coming back later, and walked out to his car by the sheriff's car, he noticed two fresh bullet holes on the back fender. Who would believe his story without a faceless collaborator? Like he had agreed with his lover; this story would die with them a secret.

The Puzzle of the Missing Professor story was carried by every newspaper in the nation. Tuskegee Institute was not going to stop at anything to find their staff, or what became of him. A reward of $1,000 was declared in 1938; it was raised to $3,000 in 1939; and in 1940 was increased to $5,000, for any information that will lead to solve this mystery. His myriad of students over the years had on their own dedicated so much resources and time to no avail. It was like the man disappeared without a trace. Both whites and colored worked together, yet nothing came up. All police department finally said, was that they would keep the file open under unsolved mysteries.

CHAPTER 51

Dr. Chuck Freeborn III had inherited his father's academic works in Negro Civilization, and naturally stepped into his father's big shoes. By the time he wedded Olivia Baptiste, he was already a faculty staff at Tuskegee. His wife was also a staff in the Accounts department. His residence was only a stone throw away from his parent's. Immediately after the disappearance of his father he had gotten Olivia to move in with his mother, to keep a close eye on her. He would go over there to have supper and spend the night with them.

At the end of 1938, Mrs. Martina Chuck Freeborn II had made up her mind to resign and head home to the family house in Birmingham. She had always insisted she does not want to end up a burden for her son and new daughter-in-law. They had their own lives to live. At least she could take care of her father-in-law who was now approaching 91. Tuskegee Institute community had sent her forth with so many tributes.

One Sunday afternoon, in the early part of 1939, a brand new Ford Model A Deluxe Roadster had parked in front of his quarters. *Surprise, surprise!* It was his father's colleague back in the Army… Professor Simon Alexander, stepped out with his three sons. The boys had grown into young men since he took them hunting before their mother's demise. The visit was a kind of solidarity visit, because Professor Alexander said with so much certainty that Staff Sgt. *Lion-heart* will definitely resurface soon. Chuck III recalled how the man had spoken these words with tears in his eyes, to encourage him. He had also emotionally embraced Olivia as if she was his own daughter. He had then predicted a baby boy for the couple for obvious spiritual reasons, that was purely an African thing.

They had lunched together, as one big family. The older man had told how he had remarried in 1933, and had a daughter, Gloria to soften up the all-boy ensemble. Chuck III had also learnt from Amos, that he was going to join the US Coast Guard later in the year. The teenage Randy, had confidently declared that he wanted to be both a lawyer and a senator; which the adults had laughed off. While Matthew, who was turning ten, had declared that, he would like to be a soldier that fly planes. Chuck had then promised to take Matthew to the people in Tuskegee who were training already for what he would want to be.

For Olivia, who was meeting them for the very first time, had truly enjoyed their company, especially their father who kept teasing her. He had asked the boys to remind him to come for the baby boy that was coming very soon. Surprisingly, Professor Alexander did not mention the WWI action, it was like he did not want to go to an area that his tough man posture would not contain.

They had finally departed Tuskegee after paying a brief visit to the residence of Professor George Washington Carver. They met Professor Carver who was almost 80 still busy in his workshop/ laboratory. The shelves were lined with innumerable products that were inventions and discoveries of this great black man in different fields. For instance, there were 300 samples of products derived from peanuts. Dr. Chuck Freeborn III told the boys that, George Washington Carver was a jack of all trades and a master of all. He had declared to the agreement of their father that Professor Carver was indeed one of the greatest human beings alive.

The hallway was filled with considerable awards, certificates and pictures with various United States Presidents to Governors, Senators to various classes of students. There was even a framed picture of Chuck II with Professor Carver, it was even Amos who pointed it out to Matthew. The boys all received small token plastic animals as gifts from the great man. Plastics was the old man's latest inventions..

It was when he got home much later that evening, he met his brothers who came in from Birmingham. Olivia had told him animatedly at the door, that they were quite excited; that maybe there was a new angle or development to *No 2's* disappearance. Booker had waited patiently for his older brother to seat down, after all the pleasantries and inquiries, before broaching the issue of an envelope that arrived in the mail exactly two days back. Their grandfather had specifically asked them to bring it to him for *action*, like they do back home in Africa. Chuck III could read between the lines, that means a total warfare as the old man personally instructed them all from birth.

His brother just handed over a postage stamped brown manila envelope to him. It was addressed to Chuck Freeborn, #12 Christopher Columbus Drive, Greenfair, Birmingham, Alabama. He took time thoughtfully to scrutinize the front, and even the back of the envelope that was obviously blank. The brothers watched him patiently, knowing their brother was truly bothered, not certain, and feared what it was all about. Just then Olivia came in with some more refreshments, and her husband swiftly concealed the envelope and changed the topic of the discussion.

"So you guys want to join the Army, just like that?" He queried.

"Yes sir. We just want to serve our great country." It was Gossamer that answered playing along with his oldest brother. They could see their sister-in-law slowing down, almost dragging to pick up as much story as possible.

"Is mum aware of this move?" The brothers knew their brother was now referring to the envelope.

"No! Grandpa said you are now the head of the family; that he is only living on borrowed time, and just waiting to name your son." Booker answered with enthusiasm noticing that his sister-in-law was rearranging the refreshments for the second time.

"Very well," their senior brother concurred, "men will be men, and boys will be boys. You will have your way then." He concluded, knowing his wife was saturated with these bits of controlled information. And she sauntered out knowing that her husband would complement the rest of the story later. At least she had the satisfaction of knowing why they called. If only, she knew the truth; that back in Ohafia, the women folk were left out in warfare matters. When she had gone from them, her husband now opened the envelope containing a foolscap-sized typewritten sheet of paper.

There was no address of the sender, just the city and state, and dated seven days back;

Williamsville, Al.

18th February, 1939.

Dear Sir.

I feel so ashamed, that I have waited this long to write you. And because of my impudence more people have not only suffered but have been killed by the Klan to avenge the seven that your son killed, when they attacked him, when he was going about his own business. I was an unwilling witness to the carnage last year, that also claimed your son, who was my teacher.

Please forgive my rudeness for not introducing myself, my reasons are obvious; I am a respectably married man who is in an affair with a supposedly happily married woman. It was our selfish fear, that had kept us from acting for justice to take its course. The fear of exposing our closely guided secret that had made me a Judas. My lover and I, were at our usual rendezvous by the wooden bridge on the old road out of town. The KKK people led by Sheriff Tommy Wilburpoint laid a disastrous ambush for your son who valiantly defended himself, as a true African warrior.

I must admit sir, that he died gallantly. The single bullet that killed him was fired by Sheriff Wilburpoint of Williamsville. The KKK members that got killed; to their families respectively, had been sent on special assignments out of state to keep them mute. The Klan members who fell to your son's blazing gun were led by Bunny Fletcher, the others are Gerald Gibbs, Danny Black, Sammy Fields, Frank Olson, Vinny Dampner, and Harry Tooting, to corroborate my story, these people have not been seen since the day they attacked your son. Their families are even too scared to even go to the authorities.

From my own findings, the KKK cleared and swept the crime scene clean of every evidence, on the night of the killings. It is my considered opinion that your son's vehicle and his body must have been buried in the depths of the river that flows through where he was killed. There was no way they could have gone further.

Please sir, accept our sincerest condolences to you and your family for this great loss through the senseless bloodbath of the KKK. I sincerely hope at least with my revelations, you can all lay him to rest, in peace. I still beg to remain faceless for the sake of the innocent parties, my lover and I, have cheated upon. May God forgive us.

Best regards sir.

Yours sincerely

When Chuck III finished reading, he quickly tucked the letter away in his pocket. Though he was speechless, but his mind was busy adding up what he had just read. He searched his brothers' faces, for some hint of information, but they did not betray any emotion. He took a sip from the glass of juice that his wife placed before him, a moment ago. All of a sudden he felt a sense of relief, since his father just disappeared into thin air. He breathed a sigh of relief. Now we know the truth; the puzzle is solved.

"What do you guys make of this?" he inquired grimly.

"I think it adds up. It shows that God is alive." Booker answered enthusiastically.

"To me, it just shows that good must triumph over evil no matter how long." Garrison added with philosophical wisdom.

"Now, we must sit down and fashion out a line of action that will move smoothly without hiccups, we cannot afford to lose any more of our own. We must make it look like the Klan was fighting its self; a question of bad blood within the imperial bloodline." Chuck III spoke for a very long time weighing every option available. His brothers also made very valuable inputs to the final plans. At the end of the day, the battle line was drawn, and the die was cast.

Williamsville, Alabama: Two days later, at about 5 pm, a much younger looking version of Garrison, bare-footed and aptly dressed in the trendy style of Southern poverty, called in to see Sheriff Tommy Wilburpoint in his office. At that particular time the sheriff was all alone. The young man had knocked slightly at the door.

"Yes?" The sheriff bellowed, but the young man out of fear waited, with no intention to go inside by himself. After a moment the young man tapped slightly again.

"Yes? You can come in." The sheriff looked up from the newspaper he was reading. When the door did not open again, the sheriff angrily put his newspaper aside approached the door. When he pulled back the door, to find a whimpering colored boy, you could see the disdain in his eyes.

"Damn you nigger, what do you want?" He spoke with enough venom and chill, to kill and freeze a rabbit.

"Good evening, Massa Sheriff, I is very sorry to disturbance you." He paused to add the right effect to his timidity and ignorance.

"Come on boy, stop wasting my time before I throw you in the banger for disturbing my duty." From his body language and tone, there was no love lost between the sheriff and the black race.

"Am sorry Massa Sheriff. Me thought it sure interest you to hear what I sawn at the old bridge deep in them river bottom."

"What the hell were you doing by the river?" The shocked sheriff shouted down the young man.

"Am sorry again, Massa em…em Massa Sheriff, I is goned fishing for fishes." The young man nervously twisting his fingers was so convincing.

The sheriff lowered his voice as he quickly asked the young man to come into his office, while he stepped forward to inspect the outer office and outside. Garrison noticed that the sheriff was slightly fidgeting when he came back to his seat.

"So whom were you with, when you went fishing, boy?" His voice had dropped to almost a whisper.

"Me is… was only me, Massa Sheriff."

"Good," the sheriff seemed to brighten up with that piece of news. "Are you sure nobody knew you were coming to see me?" He asked lightly.

"No, Massa, I come up straight to your office sa." "So tell me, what did you see in the river?"

"Massa Sheriff, me saws motor car, with bones floating under water."

"Come on boy, how did you see it that? Are you sure what you are saying?"

"Massa I sure what I saws down in them river." The young man was convinced beyond doubt. The only way out Wilburpoint thought, was to shut him up for good.

"Come boy, you come and show me to be sure. What is your name?" The sheriff took his hat and car keys and led the boy out to the police car.

"Me name is John, but me momma calleds me Johnny Boy, 'cos me daddy who is died, is his name Johnny." Garrison could not believe his luck.

In the car, the sheriff had put Garrison in the back seat, as a suspect for anybody who was interested. Even from the back seat Garrison had continued chattering about his momma and daddy. He first drove into town to confuse any bystander, it was when he had satisfied himself that no person was paying him any attention, that he then headed out of town to the old wooden bridge. Even though they had not passed any other motorist, the sheriff was careful enough to park off on the dirt track.

As they got out of the car, the sheriff had taken his pistol out of its holster ordinarily. The sheriff had stolen furtive glances to ascertain their privacy. The younger man had led them to underneath the bridge, and pointed into the water.

"See, see, there. Right over there." Garrison pointed into the deep waters. Pretended not to hear the distinct sound of the release of the safety catch.

"It alright, boy. You just stand still. It is time to kiss your black nigger ass good-bye. Just turn around slowly with your hands in the air." Gossamer obeyed the instructions obediently. Even as he saw his people stepping into position, he pretended to show fear.

"Young man you should have minded your own business, your meddlesomeness is now your greatest undoing." Tommy Wilburpoint's now sounded chilly and deadly.

"Please don't kill me. I have not offended you, even though you killed my father." Garrison feigned a very frightened voice.

"That is it. Yes. You sure resembled your father. I thought of it, that you looked familiar. Too bad, boy must die just like him. You filth of the earth…" It was a momentary pause in response to the tiny glint of the razor sharp machete in the final rays of the setting sun, coupled with the swishing sound of the machete slicing through the air, and hitting the fat neck at the right point as they were tutored by their grandfather. The machete came through clean, and completed the swing perfectly.

The body stood frozen for some time. It was the pistol that dropped first, before the head tumbled off, then the massive headless body crashed thunderously backward. They quickly lifted the cross into place and set it on fire, and quickly left the scene, driving into Williamsville that they saw a massive burning cross by the old bridge. By sunset the old wooden bridge was a beehive of activities as the curious and sightseers had converged to see things for themselves.

The next day, the newspapers tabloids were all carrying the photograph of the flaming cross, with the grotesque headless body of Sheriff Tommy Wilburpoint, with the bold headlines; *Battle Within The Kingdom; Taste of their Own Medicine; Empire Divided Against Itself*…was fighting for attention with *FDR Cancelled Trade Agreement With Japan.* For the boys it was mission accomplished. Period.

CHAPTER 52

Come what may, life must go on for the living. 1940 was without doubt a watershed for the Freeborns. The WWII was already raging in Europe, though America had remained neutral so to speak, the handwriting was clearly on the wall that it was only a matter of time before they declare for the Allies. President Franklin Roosevelt had this time around imposed a trade embargo on Japan; halting all exports of iron and steel scrap, gas, and petroleum products. The Japanese who were still smarting from the trade agreement cancellation of the previous year, made concerted efforts to resolve the conflicts. A peace talks was arranged for Washington DC, sometime later in the next year, for their respective envoys to seek ways forward.

Both Booker and Garrison Freeborn had successfully enlisted in the US Navy and after the completion of the rigorous training, were home on a two week-break before their permanent postings. Since the death of Chuck II, the family had closed ranks and to stay closer together to console and safeguard themselves. They were all at the sprawling Greenfair, Birmingham family home. Olivia had some months after the Williamsville saga, to the joy of the whole family, finally taken in and gave birth to a bouncing baby boy, a few days back, there in Birmingham. The baby's great grandfather, who was beside himself with joy, had traditionally named the 12- fingered baby, Chuck IV. He had told all the curious that cared to listen; *that the sixth finger was their burden of proof of where they originated from.* Little did they all know, that all that would change in the twinkling of an eye.

In those intimate gatherings Chuck I would not allow anybody to carry his great grandson, and he would say; *because my days with you people are numbered, allow me to enjoy my son*. Whenever Olivia and Chuck III with his great grandson returned to Tuskegee, were his worst moments, it was like a torment to him, that he would be counting the days before they come again. He had suggested they leave him with them. This would not be until Olivia took in for her second baby a year later.

By July 1941, President Roosevelt took another swipe at Japan again, when he ordered all Japanese assets in the United States to be frozen, thereby terminating every existing bilateral trade and economic interests. This time Japan as an Ally of Germany and Italy, was ready to bare her fangs as an Empire that was worth her weight in gold. If FDR purposely underestimated the Japanese, he was about to discover his folly that; *those who live in glass houses should not throw stones anyhow*. One of the greatest three American presidents was made to pay for his crass judgments, with many American lives coupled with a colossal and collateral damage to his air and sea fleet in one single day.

This very coordinated attack on America by Japan, that FDR himself declared as; *a date which will live in infamy* was on December 7, 1941 launched from Aircraft Carriers in the Pacific Ocean. As early as 7.55am when the attacks commenced and ended at about 1pm when the victorious strike force headed home; there were over 2,200 dead soldiers, 159 damaged and 169 lost vessels and aircrafts. The Japanese had lost only 29 fighter vessels.

It was certain misfortunes for both the *US SS Arizona,* and *US SS Oklahoma* that took direct hits and sunk with all its men. It was one of the gloomiest days in American history. The Freeborns had two of their own in the irreparable losses in lives. When the official confirmation got to Greenfair, there was nobody to console the other, as it was indeed everyman to himself and God for us all as they mourned. The patriarch took everything in his strides as brave as they come, but he was never the same again. Their mother never recovered fully until she died on April 24, 1942, of a broken heart of losing a husband and two sons within a space of four years.

By December 8, 1941, America declared war on Japan, and indirectly Germany and Italy in tow. America declaration of war was to turn the course of the entire World War II. America and President Roosevelt was not to be appeased until it took her pound of flesh from Japan by dropping the atomic bombs in Hiroshima and Nagasaki on

August 6th, and 9th 1945 respectively. The harvests of hundreds of thousands of deaths in one fell swoop, was enough for the Japanese to *fall on their swords.*

Japan finally surrendered on August 14, 1945, and the World War II officially ended with the signing of the peace treaty with Japan on September 2, 1945.

CHAPTER 53

By the end of World War II in 1945, Olivia had had two more babies, Jane and Joyce. Both births were a cause for celebrations for the great patriarch and the grandson. As usual, both girls also had the *sixth fingers* that were traditionally taken out few days after birth. Even with the arrival of the girls, the grand old man continued to show his obsession over his great grandson. Since the great grandfather was too old for the active outdoor life, the young boy missed out on all the traditional survival trainings that his forebears got during their time

By always hanging around his great grandfather, what the young man did not gain in the outdoors, he got in wisdom through myriad of the first hand stories of his African roots, through the kindly old man. It was only natural to see that Chuck IV had developed a passion to avenge the injustice meted out to his ancestors by their fellow human beings. With the old man's active involvement and sponsorship of civil rights activities, there were very few meetings the young man did not accompany the old man to attend. By the time he was 10, he knew and identified with the major players that idolized his great grandfather, and grandfather.

In the 1950s, African American Civil Rights assumed a totally new tempo and a dimension. The actual gains of the WWII and the subsequent Cold War that came after started manifesting. The success and acclaim of the Tuskegee Airmen over the German Air Force could not be relegated to the background. People started to appreciate the Eleonor Roosevelts of America for their unwavering support for this brave and responsible group of African American men.

The veterans of these wars had returned with experiences of social acceptance in the different European communities that had hosted them.

They had eaten and drank together, or even driven in buses or trains without any form of segregations. If they had a kind of an unconditional social acceptance over there, then should it be different in their home country that they fought and died for.

The National Defence Act of 1947, which desegregated and integrated the armed forces under President Harry Truman also sent the right signals to civil rights movements. If desegregation was good for the military, then it should be applied to other facets of the American society.

It was under this consciousness the young Chuck IV grew up. Living in the Tuskegee environment had also sharpened his black awareness. His idol after his great grandfather, was Booker T. Washington. At age 10, the young man baffled all and sundry with his knowledge and profile of the great African American. An interesting event happened in a civic class one day, when the young man was asked for his middlename. He thought for a while and wrote down the letters in capital *BTW*. And from that day he made it a tradition to write his name so; Chuck B.T.W. Freeborn. These initials stock with him for life.

His most impressionable visit to Little Savannah, was in 1950, when his father drove his sisters and him to meet with Great grandfather there. It was like all the old folks wanted to touch him and his sisters; Chuck BTW Freeborn actually felt like a star. The early next day, before they departed Saxtonville for Savannah, the old man led all of them laboriously up the hill to the old Hickory tree, and introduced them to *Boye Africano* as if he was alive. The old man had passionately insisted to be buried beside the old grave of his mentor, and some kind of uncle. On the drive home, the young Chuck BTW had thought about the symbolic significance of the old man's final desire at death.

It was after that trip, the old man became very sickly, that he stopped going out. The African American civil rights people would rather come to the house to consult with the old man who kept up his financial backing for their activities like civil disobedience, community education, civil resistance and resultant court cases.

When television sets appeared in the scene in 1950, the Freeborns were not part of the first 1.5 million to acquire one; but a year later they got one of the 15 million television sets that graced privileged American homes. The grand old man would sit and monitor the happening events in the front of the television set all day.

The *Brown v. Board of Education* case had dragged on for a while, and had consumed so much resources. Though the case was originally instituted by Oliver Brown and his daughter, Linda, who would not be allowed to attend a school close to her Topeka home, in Kansas, because of segregation laws in place. Since the outcome of the case would either make or mar all cumulative efforts of the African American civil rights movement, one of the groups had indirectly financed and taken over the case. For a case that had generated so much interest, all eyes and ears were on judgment day, the 17th of May, 1954.

That 17th day, Chuck BTW would remember as the happiest day for his great grandfather, and his own saddest came the day after. When the news finally came, that the Chief Justice Earl Warner of the U.S. Supreme Court, had declared in his verdict to not just the overcrowded courtroom, but to the rest of America and beyond that, the United States constitution was *color blind,* you could hear the celebrations exploding across the continent. And that by this singular verdict, the Topeka Board of Education was ordered to end segregation in all its schools. The old man was beside himself with excitement.

The day after, Greensboro, North Carolina, became the first city to issue a public announcement in the South, to abide whole-heartedly with the Supreme Court's verdict. This ripple effect was the green light that the *doubting Thomas's* needed to let their hair down to celebrate a victory that had taken too long to arrive. That evening the whole lot of the civil rights big wigs had come to celebrate the victory with the frail old man who had remained a financial livewire in the case. The old man was all smiles, he looked so fulfilled and happy.

Everyone present in that victory outing complimented the old man for his strength and health. All Chuck IV would remember was that his great grandfather was all smiles, not a single word tumbled out of his mouth. The old man neither ate nor drank anything that evening. There was so many bear hugs and embraces, and a lot of back slapping. There were no official speeches. He had stood by his great grandfather who nodded slightly as they bid their goodnights at about 8 pm. Reverend Ralph Abernathy and Rev. Martin Luther King were the last guests to leave. The old man still had the fulfilled smile pasted on his face, and for the very first time that evening he said something;

"Young man how old are you now?" The voice was faint and tired.

"Baba, don't tell me you have forgotten my age." The young boy burst into laughter.

"Alright, I have forgotten. Please tell me."

"I am fourteen years old. So what about it?"

"Good. Now you listen very well. I was exactly your age, when my journey to America began. Don't you ever take anything for granted. Be very careful, America is a dangerous place. Life may not be fair at all times; don't you ever forget that you are led by an unseen finger. You can call it the sixth finger; you will understand when you are old enough. Always remember where you come from. Resist and expose evil as long as you live. Remember all that I have told you about Africa. I am tired. Be a good boy and get me Virgil." He sounded tired but tried to maintain a dignified façade smiling

"Yes Baba, you can trust me to tread carefully. Let me get Virgil to get you set for bed."

Chuck IV was only away for less than a minute. He returned with Virgil, the old man's very trusted handy man in tow, who would bath him, and put him to bed. The old man was still in the position he left him just a moment ago; but something was deadly amiss. He looked around the large parlor, it was coldly silent. He walked over to the window to draw the curtains, as a cold chill ran its frosty fingers down his skin. This was totally a strange feeling.

Then he heard Virgil's startled cry. He ran over to see that his great grandfather was dead. His closest relative was *stone cold dead...* yet with that fulfilled smile on his kindly face. The fourteen-year-old boy just did not know what came over him; he just went berserk. He screamed and cried, but was inconsolable...nobody could console him.

CHAPTER 54

It had been two years since then. Despite the loving and caring efforts of his mother and sisters, he could not refill the vacuum created by his great grandfather's death. Everything since then had happened in a blur. The eventual announcement of the death of the man considered as an oracle of Negro Civilization and an unshakable supporter of the African American Civil Rights Movements, was received by the colored community with genuine outpouring of grief from the North and South. The National Association for the Advancement of Colored People (NAACP) undertook to take up the burial as a state burial.

The lying-in-state was at the 4-acre Kelly Ingram Park, right in front of the 16th Street Baptist Church, where a brief church service under the ministration of Reverend Fred Shuttlesworth took place earlier in the morning. By noon, the park was jammed with people from all around, and the other surrounding states. The entire gamut of the African American Civil Rights Movement led by Rev. Martin Luther King, and his close friend and colleague Rev. Ralph Abernathy, Philip Randolph, Jo Ann Robinson, Rosa Parks, Oliver Brown, and others.

From the Tuskegee Institute was a high powered delegation led by the new President, Luther H. Hosler who came in after Patterson. Even the community of Saxtonville were well represented. Even Savannah, Georgia's mayor attended with another very powerful delegation.

As the mid-day sun shone with an exceptional brilliance that afternoon, though its intensity tempered down by a divine intervention, the speeches and honors cascaded from the mouths of the people who had gathered to pay their last respects to a great man out of Africa. As the citations flowed, so the tears flowed unhindered. It was as if everyone that came across the old man was impacted positively.

President Luther Hosler of the Tuskegee Institute informed the gathering how Chuck Freeborn I had not only supported Tuskegee with financial resources since the days of Booker T. Washington, but had secretly provided a scholarship scheme for forty indigent students per annum since 1915, when his friend died. This he totaled to over a thousand colored young men and women whom the old man had lifted the *veil of ignorance from*. Tuskegee couldn't but honor him; the largest central park, was now named the Chuck Freeborn Park.

Finally, it was the turn of Rev. Martin Luther King to speak. As his name was called the whole park went silent, as if water had been poured over a raging fire. All eyes were on the young pastor who heads a church in Montgomery, but was gradually becoming the most recognizable face in the African American Civil Rights Movement.

"My brothers and sisters... so much had already been said about Chuck Freeborn I. That I wonder, if what I could say would sway the flow of thoughts that had been overwhelmingly postulated. Chuck Freeborn I was a giant amongst us that are mere mortals. When they forcefully took him away from the shores of Africa; they did not get any inkling that they had bitten more than they could chew. That was why, the filth and stench of the cargo holds could not cage him, nor the chains and fetters of iron hold him down. He survived the deadly voyage because he was made of sterner stuff. He was too hot to put in chains, that the slaver that bought and brought him into Savannah, Georgia, could not but testify that he was a FREEBORN!

America could not change him, because he was unchangeable; he was a catalyst. A catalyst has power to change all around him, but remains unchanged. That was why Chuck Freeborn touched lives, changed lives, transformed lives, added value to lives, and solidly enforced their God given inalienable rights. In the course of fulfilling his assignment, he also paid the price... I don't know how many of us lost an uncle, that was like a father; then a son; and then two grandsons to a cause. Chuck Freeborn did... and lived to tell the story in his lifetime.

So people of Little Savannah weep no more, Birmingham, I beg you to dry your tears, and you American Colored cry no more. For Chuck Freeborn has conquered death. Today, he lies here not dead; but alive... because he will live forever in our hearts. My friend told me back there, that Chuck Freeborn I lived for 105 years. Chuck Freeborn I lived for just 105 years? That is a lie, because Chuck Freeborn will never die; he will live forever. He will live beyond a thousand years, because in us all there is a monumental Freeborn spirit...God bless Chuck Freeborn, and may God bless America.

The attentive crowd rose in unison, applauding loudly and cheering a gradual rising star, that turned out finally to be one of America's greatest orators. From Birmingham, the huge burial party set off for Savannah, and finally ended up in Saxtonville for the internment.

Before the final rays of the sun sank into the horizon, to usher in twilight, on the first day of June, 1954, Chuck Freeborn I was laid to rest under the Hickory tree by the grave of '*Boye Africano*, in a pact that was made way back in some quaint little settlement in the thick tropical jungles of Africa.

Chuck IV had gone ahead to complete high school at Tuskegee living with his parents and sisters in 1956. Everybody noticed that the young lively boy was never the same again; moody and distrustful of people. It was like he never recovered from the death of his great grandfather. Chuck III had mentioned his son's strange behavior to friends and relatives for some kind of advice. They all tend to feel, it was a matter of time. That time would heal his trauma.

He mentioned it to his father's good friend Professor Simon Alexanda, on the phone, the other day. Professor Alexanda had laughed his good natured laughter, and promised to do something about it. He had said his son Amos had had such psychological trauma with the death of his maternal grandfather when he was a young boy.

A lot of people had ignorantly believed that the 1954 verdict in *Brown v. Board of Education* actually overturned the *1896 Plessy v. Ferguson* verdict of *separate but equal*. They were ignorantly wrong. The 1954 verdict specifically upturned segregation in schools; while 1896 verdict was supporting segregation in buses. It took the famous 1955 Rosa Parks Rebellion and consequent organized bus boycotts in Montgomery that lasted almost a year to achieve a supreme court verdict to upturn the 1896 *Plessy v. Ferguson* ruling.

It was not until 13th November, 1956, that the United States Supreme Court ruled that segregation on buses was illegal. It was on that fateful day that a letter arrived in the mail for Chuck BTW Freeborn. It was from an Amos Alexander, in United States Coast Guard. The father had watched his son with keen interest as he received the strange letter without any excitement. He had pretended to look away as a glossy black photograph fall to the ground as his son opened the envelope. That must be Professor Alexander's hand at work as per their discussion and promise couple of weeks back. He made a mental note to call and appreciate the older man later.

8thNovember, 1956

Dear Chuck IV,

I hope you would not mind if I call you BTW; because I am also a huge follower of Booker T. Washington. He was unarguably one of the best brains that walked this earth. My name is Alex, and I also share a first name with my father; the professor that you are very familiar with. Our families go way back to your grandfather who was my own father's teacher, then my father mentored your father, and your father also mentored me, and my two other brothers. He taught me so many survival skills that I still use today. It was your father that taught us how to catch a rabbit, and roast it into a most sumptuous finger-licking good meal. A winner any day. I hope I will get to teach you too the recipe one of these days.

Your father told me, we (you and I) share so many things in common. I heard that you also love writing like I do. He told me that composition and comprehension are your best scores. I also love travelling a lot, and this I do a lot in my job. I literally live on and by the sea. I have by virtue of my career in the Coast Guard visited many exotic lands. That is why I have not been able to meet you, though I met your mum before you were born. Wow! BTW that is quite a long time to have been away from home; that was since you were born.

I can't wait to show you around when you visit me in my office very soon. The enclosed photograph was taken on the day of my promotion to the post of Chief Petty officer, it is a record for an African American. It is my dream that one day people like you would get to the highest hierarchy without any hindrance. Those were the things that Booker T. Washington emphasized.

It is time to go. Remember that he that cannot forget the past cannot move forward to conquer new frontiers. We must let go of the past, not forget the past. Please extend my warmest regards to your mum, dad, and sisters. Lest I forget, congratulations on your graduation from high school.

I can't wait to hear from you very soon. Let me know what you plan to do. I know you want to do something very exciting. Bye for now.

Yours sincerely,
AmosAlexander

CHAPTER 55

The mail from the Coast Guard Headquarters had arrived that morning to a tumultuous welcome in the Tuskegee residence of Chuck Freeborn III. His son had passed the enlistment interview, and he was expected at the Manhattan Beach Training Station in New York, for the 4-Week Basic Course. This was the culmination of the faltering relationship that had in the past three years gradually blossomed through the tender care of Amos Alexander. Chuck IV had totally recovered from his trauma, and grown into a very confident young man keen on following his mentor's career footsteps in the U. S. Coast Guard. The older man had painstakingly pulled the younger man out of his shell like a true professional, and groomed him to go out and conquer the world to make his *Baba* really proud.

After his high school, Chuck IV had registered in a 2-Year Education Course in Chemistry and Biology at Tuskegee. This he had completed in flying colors, and had earned him a two-week vacation with his mentor in Washington DC. They had gone fishing and hunting together, and bonded together. It was during that vacation he had taken up the challenge to enlist in the US Coast Guard. Alex had easily arranged for the enlistment interview, without going beyond its timely facilitation. The boy he knew was very intelligent, and would on his own please his recruiters, and pass successfully.

It was April 1959, and the stretch of vegetation bordering the rail tracks were in full greenish-bloom, and as the train gradually lumbered and snaked towards New York, Chuck IV sat back in his seat and heaved a sigh of relief. He stretched out his long legs and began to read the newspaper he bought, before boarding the train in Atlanta that morning.

The entire front page was dedicated to the visit to the United States of Prime Minister Fidel Castro of Cuba, who arrived the US the previous day. It was the first state visit, the die-hard heavily-bearded revolutionarist was undertaking since he successfully deposed Fulgencio Batista, in January 1959.

DISASTER! The headline screamed in bold black capital letters. There was a photograph the previous day of President Dwight Eisenhower swinging a golf club in a golf tournament; while another captioned photograph showed Vice President Richard Nixon receiving the Cuban leader. This was going to make for an interesting read, the young man thought to himself. Why would a hale and healthy president rather choose to play golf, and delegate his vice president to receive another visiting head of state? It was a puzzle the paper tried to get the reader updated.

The paper went on to state in full details, the deteriorating state of diplomatic relationship between Cuba and the United States. Cuba, the island nation that was colonized by Spain till the beginning of the century, was so synonymous to revolutions, that some historians refer to it, as *the nation of a thousand revolutions*. It was difficult to outline an interval in the life of this island-nation when it was free of one revolution or the other. Chuck IV sat upright remembering that his great grandfather's brother, as well as his great grandmother's sisters where dropped there on their voyage to America. Cuba was more than a passing interest even his mother and his father's mother were also Cubans. This finding also piqued his interest.

The man, that Fidel Castro and his band of revolutionaries overthrew just four months back, was Fulgencio Batista. Fulgencio Batista with his checkered civilian and military background, had a very interesting character and profile. He was indeed the first ever colored person to lead a Cuba that was very racially discriminatory. It was the *1933 Revolt of the Sergeants*, that first put Sergeant Batista in the political spotlight of Cuba. In the eventual success of the putsch, he transformed into a Colonel, and self-appointed himself as the chief of the armed forces. And in that position, the man effectively used various puppet presidents at will to administer Cuba until he was formally elected as President in 1940.

He interestingly served out his term in 1944, and departed for the United States for reasons best known to him with a mass of ill-gotten wealth. The addiction to absolute power, pulled him back to Cuba again to try out his hand for the 1952 election. When he saw the handwriting on the wall of sure defeat; the desperate man resorted to a military coup to successfully topple the government of Carlos Prior Socarras. And from all indications he did as if he was going to be there forever, as he suspended the Cuban constitution that he re-instated back in 1940.

As he revoked most laws to suit his whims and caprices, government policies tended to favor the rich at expense of the poor. The American Mafia complete with their traditional vices appeared in Havana. His secret police haunted down any form of opposition within those seven years, over twenty-five thousand lives were decimated. At this point, Batista was a willing ally of the United States who supported him with all kinds of aids.

Fidel Castro of privileged parentage was a rising star, popular as the people's lawyer, who represented them *pro bono*. The dictatorial government of Batista actually survived two different attempts by Castro to overthrow it. Fidel Castro's July 26 Movement was unrelenting in the fight to overthrow Batista, even from exile they kept the fight alive. Their features of unshaven beards and berets, as well as their urban and guerrilla tactics became the mantra of other revolutionaries the world over. Somewhere along the line the Argentine-born Dr. Ernesto Che' Guevara was recruited amongst them.

Finally, after so many struggles the Batista government capitulated on New Year's Day of 1959. Batista gathered his family and close associates and fled to the Dominican Republic. When he noticed it was too close for comfort he finally departed for Portugal. Batista was believed to have made Cuba poorer with a loot of over $280 million. The paper also stated that it seemed the United States face-off with their former ally in no small measure contributed to his final fall from grace to grass.

The paper declared that Fidel Castro and his alter ego Che' Guevara were communist apologists who idolize both Marx and Lenin. It was this communist posture that had broken the rank and file of the Castro Revolutionaries, and that had now led to another faction starting War Against the Bandits. They were groups who felt short-changed and betrayed by the totally new ideals propagated by the duo of Castro and Guevara that leaned towards communists tendencies. The paper wondered whether the snubbing by President Eisenhower would not spell doom for US-Cuban Relations.

The paper concluded on a cautious note; that it would be only foolhardy to rebuff and chase away a next-door neighbor into the warm communist embrace of the USSR. The implications were monstrous and far reaching because of the Cold War in process. It hoped that the United States would be able to sleep with her two eyes closed.

Chuck IV looked up from the newspaper, to see the other passengers either busy sleeping, reading, and looking out of the window and enjoying the rich panoramic sceneries. His mind was engrossed with why his family right from their origin in Africa were at home with warfare. What fate had dispersed them to only trouble spots? *Baba* said something about being directed by a *Sixth Finger*, which he had said he would understand as he got older. He examined his palm rubbing unconsciously at the slight bump that was the remnant of his own sixth finger. He felt the drowsy hands of sleep weighing down his eyelids, the newspaper slipped out of his hand in a slow motion ended up on the carpeted floor in a pile. As the sound of the train in motion rocked and lulled him to sleep, he began to dream.

It was a bright and beautiful day, and the blue waters of the waterfront even looked bluer as they mirrored the clear blue beautiful sky. Blue waters lapped the metal embankments giving off a slightly muffled clapping sounds. Neat columns of young Coast Guard officers outfitted in brilliant white colors stood ramrod, unfaltering in the shimmering heat. Chuck IV felt drops of sweat trickled down his neck to soak his under garments, he remained at attention without twitching a muscle. It was the passing out parade of his boot camp set of Coast Guard trainees. The special guest of honor was surprisingly his mentor and friend, Amos Alexander in full ceremonial gear.

The special guest of honor went on to inspect the parade, but as the bespectacled chief petty officer got to the front of his protégée, the band that was playing stopped, and every person suddenly disappeared, leaving just the two of them alone. Chuck IV standing about 6feet 3inches towered over his mentor's 5feet 10inches; and without uttering any word, they marched towards the gangway of the 120-Foot Multi-mission USCGC *Destiny* which was moored at the wharf. As they boarded, Chuck noticed that there were no other crew on board. Just then he got his official orders from his mentor in the capacity of the supposed captain.

"Sailor!" Amos Alexander called out crisply.

"Yes sir!" Chuck IV responded at attention.

"We set course for Havana, Cuba to trace your people who are there. They are expecting you." The voice suddenly changed, and only for Chuck IV to discover that Amos Alexander had transformed into his great grandfather.

"Oh! *Baba* it is you!" The young man could not hide the excitement in his voice, by then the ship was already maneuvering itself out of port.

"Young man it is time to go and pick them up; that is what you have been trained and prepared for." The old man's smile was reassuring to his great grandson.

"*Baba*, there is little problem there. How would I know them after all these years." Chuck IV asked incredulously.

"That is very easy young man. By the finger you shall know them, Have you forgotten that they are the children of *The Finger of God* (Akachukwu)?" The old man's gaze this time was fierily quizzical.

"Yes sir!" The younger man shouted out with excitement, knowing he had fumbled after all the years of acquiring instructions from the old man.

Just then he felt a feathery touch on his shoulder, as he shook awake staring into the kind gentle face of an elderly Negro ticket collector, who bent down to pick up the disheveled pile of newspaper, and handed it to him. He smiled back at the old man who reminded him of a younger version of his *Baba*. He noticed that the train was still lumbering towards it destination, as his fellow passengers were all looking at him with strange embarrassed looks. No! He must have shouted out in his dream. No wonder, it was so very vivid.

CHAPTER 56

President John Fitzgerald Kennedy, with Lyndon B. Johnson as running mate, had narrowly beaten Richard Nixon in the presidential election of 1960, to take over the presidential mantle of leadership from Dwight Eisenhower in 1961. Everyone saw the power of television, as the first ever presidential debate took place between Nixon and Kennedy. Kennedy was duly credited as the obvious victor of that debate, and he went on to win the election proper. It was one moment in the United States history that so many first timers were attained.

"JFK" as he was fondly known and called, was of Irish descent and a catholic; it was the first time a catholic would occupy the White House. At 43, during the November 1960 elections, he became the youngest person ever to become president of the United States. For the very first time the youths were ready to identify and work with the White House; an angle that his inaugural speech had vividly expounded. Right from the start people were willing to give credence to, *ask not what your country can do for you; ask what you can do for your country.*

Kennedy had inherited from his predecessor the on-going civil rights battles in the South, where every inch of victory was countered by the KKK with more viciousness. The birth of the Freedom Riders was borne out of youthful exuberance of both colored and white volunteers to test the 1960 verdict in *Boynton v. Virginia* where segregation on interstate routes was outlawed. As the Freedom Riders progressed through the Southern cities, they met with a wrath of outstanding proportions that were upheld by the Jim Crow laws, that were brazenly applied by state officials and the KKK or anti-black groups. It was conspiracy that was displayed in broad daylight.

The Peace Corps was also established to respond to the call of the young ones to; *ask not what your country can do for you...* The American youths stepped out in their thousands to develop communities in the Third World countries. It was indeed an era of young and enthusiastic young Americans to see and experience beyond their immediate environment that they had come to take for granted. It was a project that involved hundreds of thousands young Americans to everywhere in the world.

The Cold War was at its zenith with the USSR. The Cuban relationship was totally out of order, and hastily moved towards a precipice. Kennedy had also inherited from Eisenhower plans at advanced stages to overthrow the government of Castro with disgruntled Cuban exiles. Over $13 million had been dispensed to the CIA to achieve a change in government in Havana without hitches, Kennedy had willingly consented to it at the inception of his administration.

Unfortunately, the grand plan to train, equip and support about 1,400 Cuban paramilitaries who would be dropped into Cuba through the Bay of Pigs in April 1961 to effect an invasion failed woefully. The invasion fell flat on its face right from the planning stage that was keenly countered by Castro whose Intelligence apparatus monitored them closely. Almost the entire La Brigade were injured, killed, or captured. It was America's biggest shame and disgrace.

On 29 December, 1962, after the US had negotiated and paid over $50million in drugs and food to Cuba, President Kennedy went with his wife to the Orange Bowl in Miami to welcome back the lucky returnees. It was where JFK made this statement to sum the whole fiasco that tainted America's invincibility. *...the old saying that victory has a hundred fathers and defeat is an orphan... are not to conceal responsibility because I'm the responsible officer of the Government...*

Within this period Chuck Freeborn IV was posted to different US Coast Guard vessels. It was like the US Coast Guard and not the Navy was indeed in the thick of things. He came across so many Cuban Americans that were rescued directly or indirectly by him, that he lost count of them. Of all the rescue missions, there was one that remain very vivid to him; *the banana tree man as they finally came to call the Cuban African lone survivor.*

It was the keen sight, coupled with the obstinacy of Chuck Freeborn that made the rescue possible. To the rest of his Coast Guard colleagues, what they saw that day floating harmlessly and aimlessly in the shark infested waters of Atlantic Ocean, was a clump of banana tree. What made the difference to Chuck was the positioning. It was familiar to a system his *Baba* had explained to him years back. It was a complex but simple and effective African survival strategy of tying two banana stems into a make-shift raft. The banana leave would be set in a way to act as disguise or cover. He knew beyond all doubts that somebody was lying dead or alive beneath those leaves.

It had taken a bet that he had covered against the rest of his seven colleagues, before he was lowered alone in a skiff to go and verify. To their greatest surprise he had won the bets and gained his monthly wages. He had returned with a Cuban African who was so dehydrated and almost dead. He turned out to be the only Cuban American exile of La Brigada that had made good his escape from Castro's people.

The man's name was Frabrice Leoncito, he was brave and bold as they come. It became an harmless banter as people quipped on the canny resemblance between the rescued and his rescuer. They had immediately become very close right on board; but had lost touch after evacuation on shore.

Another major crisis that the Kennedy administration was to tackle drastically since it was to threaten America's safety, and indirectly the entire world's wellbeing was the Cuban Missile Crisis. The USSR knew they were way behind in the nuclear arms race with the USA. In as much as they were threatened with America's powerful arsenal, they needed to annex Cuba as a missile base to keep the United States within range of their nuclear capability.

When the United States discovered the plans unfolding in Cuba through their spy satellites; America took bold steps to terminate the works. Out of many options America had to quarantine vessels headed for Cuba to cut off the much needed supplies. Even with the clear and present danger of USSR, the US just called their bluff. Both Kennedy and Krushchev his Soviet counterpart finally worked out solid arrangements that averted a war that would have been World War III.

At the homefront, the civil rights movement would not have had a better opportunity to finally deal with the vexing issue of segregation. JFK as a catholic had tasted segregation firsthand. The KKK had also vilified the catholics, and included them as a target in their demonic agenda of segregation with the Jews and African Americans. President Kennedy did not hide the fact that he empathize with the steady victims of the southern segregational laws. Consequently, he had effected the Justice Department to get the affected states not to interfere negatively with, but to provide travelers unrestricted access to integrated public facilities.

The Freedom Riders had paid the price, some even the ultimate price to have covered so much grounds to expose without ambiguity the southern racist in his true colors. It was like they knew that time was not on their side, as if it was running out with somebody like JFK in the White House. They had every reason to believe it was then or never with these words from the mouth of President Kennedy himself; ... *We preach freedom around the world, and we mean it, and we cherish our freedom here at home, but are we to say to the world, and much more importantly, to each other that this is the land of the free except for the Negroes; that we have no second-class citizens except Negroes; that we have no class or caste system, no ghettoes, no master race except with respect to Negroes? Now the time has come for this Nation to fulfill its promise. The events in Birmingham and elsewhere have so increased the cries for equality that no city or State or legislative body can prudently choose to ignore them.*

For the stage was set for the mother of all civil rights battles; what might be termed as the battle for the last frontier of American segregation. The Kennedy administration was not ready like most of his predecesors to bury their heads in the sand, or simply adopt the agelong, *hear no evil see no evil* modus operandi. For everything there is always a price tag; were they willing to pay the price? *Only the future could tell.*

CHAPTER 57

What he was seeing on the television screen, could not be real. It must be some kind of Hollywood movie set. He stood mouth agape watching vivid images of bombed and burning residences and motel. Children ranging from about 10 to 18 years of age being threatened and savaged by police dogs. Chuck IV shivered at the horror of the images of these children pounded by powerful jets of water from Fire Brigade hoses, transforming them into rag dolls that are tossed about by gale force winds. The camera zoomed in on the men holding and directing the hoses, the bold insignia on the raincoats B.F.D.; stood for Birmingham Fire Department. It was just unbelievable, but it was true, it was May 2, 1963, in Birmingham, Alabama.

Chuck IV was overwhelmed with a fury he had never felt before, as he saw very familiar faces of whites and blacks he grew up with in Savannah. He saw these young children who had lost their innocence as they were arrested and loaded into vans and school buses and taken over to jail until there was no more space. Over a thousand school children were arrested in a space of time.

Yet, the demonstrations continued with an unwavering tempo, as new sets of children replaced the arrested ones. All of a sudden all his fury dissipated as he remembered what his great grandfather told him; *it can only be a tragedy when good and powerful men just sit and look when the innocent are being oppressed and suffering... you must carry on until something gives way once and for all.*

Bull Connor, the same man that dealt severely with the Freedom Riders in Birmingham, was having a ball as he seemed to counter every attempt of Civil Rights Movement leaders with an imaginative mind that was nurtured in hell. It was him that called out the fire brigade with their hoses. He was adamant as he is supported by Confederate flag-waving white folks insisting that they want their Jim Crow laws. The KKK had bombed homes and businesses of prominent blacks or their sympatisers, until somebody had coined the word *Bombingham* for Birmingham.

Reverends Fred Shuttlesworth, Martin Luther King Jr., and Ralph Abernathy had spearheaded others to map out strategic options that gave the authorities sleepless nights as they tend to pull down all machineries of segregation in America. The organized sit-ins were staged at lunch counters across Birmingham and were targeted to cripple businesses. The sit-ins took off at Britt's Lunch Counter, Pizitz Lunch Counter, H.L. Green Lunch Counter, Atlantic Mills, Lane Drugstore, Tutwiler Drugstore amongst others.

Even as their leaders were arrested and clamped into solitary confinement, the battle continued for the others. It was then only a matter of time for the prominent Birmingham business community to capitulate, and give in to their demands. The business community in a meeting with the Africa Americans willingly integrated lunch counters and recognition of blacks in employment. Bull Conors and his city officials were not in support of the peace moves by the business community, and thereby registered their objections accordingly.

It was not until July 23, 1963, when the new Birmingham City Council, unconditionally repealed all the segregation laws. It was too early to shout eureka, for the big masquerades (the *Ijeles*) of American segregation were yet to play the ace up their sleeve.

On August 28, 1963, the biggest gathering ever in favor of a cause in American history held in Washington DC, with the consent of President Kennedy, who feted the black leaders after the event, in the White House. It was called the March On Washington for Jobs and Freedom. Prior to the 28th of August morning, all roads in the air, land, or water led to Washington DC. Even Chuck Freeborn III, his wife and two daughters had joined the bandwagon, they actually departed Tuskegee on the 26th of August to spend sometime with Chuck IV. The aims of the over 800,000 people of different races that converged at the foot of the Lincoln Memorial, and extended to engulf the whole entire National Mall. The numerous placards cut across one of these subjects;

Broad based federal works program!
Equitable employment for all citizens!
Develop more decent housing!
Effective Civil rights legislation and statutes!
The right to vote and be voted for.
To put in place a more integrated education!

It was a day of speeches. That at the end of the day, Rev. Martin Luther King Jr., just shone like a million stars with his melodramatic delivery of his *I Have A Dream*. Even the hardest critics of the civil rights movement knew that the days of American segregation were numbered. It was time to marshal out the *Ijeles*.

Governor George Wallace of Alabama was a desperate drowning man; he knew it was time to cut out the proxies and mercenaries, and dirty his fingers to get the right (or better still the wrong) results. He was so desperate to cage the African American that he came out of cover; he allowed his passion to not only override his fair judgment, but becloud his moral obligations to his subjects as a leader. He personally took it upon himself to bar blacks from five Alabama State-owned schools with state officers. As America and the rest of the world watched in further shock and disbelief on the 9th day of September, 1963, President John F. Kennedy was ready to step forward and save the names and reputation of good men who stay passive when a few evil men go passionate on the weak and defenseless.

The next day, President Kennedy became the black man's best friend and defender by unequivocally ordering his Defense Secretary to pick and utilize any of the nation's Armed Forces to fight against any attempt to return segregation in Alabama schools.

Now, it was time to shout *uhuru;* for finally a Daniel had come to judgment. Yes, indeed a Kennedy had come to judgment; but at what price? It was to open the floodgates of assassinations as we are wont to see. Conspiracy Theories or not; somewhere, somebody, somehow, and somewhat believed that the only option left to frustrate and derail the flow of goodwill towards the African American Civil Rights Movement was in a harvest of death.

CHAPTER 58

Between 1963 and 1968 it was indeed a harvest of deaths. The first one that shook the nation and the entire world to the marrow of the bone was the assassination of President John Fitzgerald Kennedy in Dallas, on November 22, 1963. A young and vibrant life cut short in the prime of life. African Americans came out to mourn one president that came all out for the American blacks to have total freedom and equality.

And like the true martyr that he was, his blood was not shed in vain. Instead of scuttling the civil rights gains, that had led to President Kennedy to submit his Civil Rights Bill to congress on June 19, 1963. His untimely death had rather fuelled his successor Lyndon B. Johnson and other well-meaning members of the congress to fast-track the signing of the Civil Right Act on July 2, 1964.

That very night, the day when the Civil Right Act was signed, Chuck Freeborn IV, had received a phone call from his mentor Amos Alexander, from Chicago where he had gone with Malcolm X to an Awards. Amos had since his retirement back in 1959 from the US Coast Guard finally gotten a significant book job. He was working closely with the fiery civil rights campaigner on his autobiography, which actually started in 1963. Amos had also confided to his protégé that he had just collected a large sum of advance from the publishers. "Mr. Alex, why Malcolm X of all people?" Chuck could not hide his shock.

"What do you mean, BTW? Don't you know Malcolm X?" The older man chuckled, amused at the younger man's astonishment.

"Who does not know him? Is he not direct opposite of Martin Luther King?"

"Now that you have revealed where you stand, Chuck. It may interest you to know that the writer and the readers are more interested in the abnormal than the normal. The normal is dull and boring. We all pant for some form of controversy or the other." Amos Alexander started to lecture.

"Sir," the younger man interrupted respectfully, "for somebody who is propounding *The Ballot or The Bullet* for African American civil rights is certainly on a suicidal mission for himself and his supporters. We have come this far, there is no way we will throw everything away just like that."

"That is it young man, you even have the answer. The *death wish* you might say, is the big selling point or factor the publishers are zeroing in at. People are interested in people who tread where even devils fear to tread. They would want to know whether it is the same red blood they too have in their veins. Do they sleep with their two eyes closed? Do they eat and make love too? For their extra-ordinary traits that the ilks of Malcolm X become mystified; and the readers would not only feed their curiosities, and then demystify them."

"That is really interesting, very interesting. Tell me more Mr. Alex."

"Good. And that my boy is where I come in as a writer. My job is to profile the personality and character, if possible with a microscope. With my pen I dissect him to reveal that he has a heart like any other human being born of a woman. My book would not be complete until he looks like a goldfish in a bowl with no hiding place." Amos Alexander burst into deep throated trademark laughter, the younger man had come to really admire.

They had as usual discussed other issues from work to the families, and as they were about to round up, Amos Alexander suddenly recalled something important that Chuck must get done immediately.

"BTW, lest I forget, make sure you pick up the forms for the post-graduate program on Forensic Science immediately. It is very important that you get that done within the shortest possible time".

"Why the hurry sir? I thought I would take a break or indeed deserve a break after the rigorous first degree program." Chuck Freeborn IV asked.

"Yes, you deserve a break after topping your class, and don't you think you deserve even a bigger break after completion of the post-graduate program." The older man chuckled to encourage the younger man.

"Alright, you win, but why the hurry if I may ask, Mr Alex." Chuck IV asked thoughtfully.

"Chuck you must be prepared for the opportunities that would soon open up for Black America. With the legendary Civil Rights Act that was signed today, there will be a lot of affirmative action and policies that would favor only the blacks that are prepared in advance. That is now. There would be top positions that blacks would be expected to fill. You see why you must consolidate academic attainments now." Amos Alexander laughed one of those his reassuring laughter again, knowing beyond any iota of doubt that Chuck BTW Freeborn IV, was going to rise all the way to the top of his chosen career. He knew he had his protégée eating from his hand now, and he quickly added;

"Chuck, please hold, somebody wants to say hello to you." Chuck could hear muffled voices talking in the background. Somebody cleared his voice in his ears.

"How are you doing, Chuck? My name is Malcolm. I have heard so much about you. I can't wait to meet you very soon." The voice had a razor-sharp edge to it.

Chuck was shocked beyond words. "The honor is mine sir. I can't wait to meet you too very soon." The next words almost knocked off Chuck from where he was standing.

"Chuck?" The voice called out.

"Yes sir!" Chuck answered military-style.

"I perceived that you don't like my style of returning violence for violence; neither do I like your non-violence for violence posture. We have suffered too long in silence, it is high time we showed we can bark and bite. We can all work together to achieve the ultimate result that we all desire. You go on with your non-violence, while

those of us who are not handcuffed by the disarming philosophy of non-violence will protect your backsides. After all it is the end that they say justifies the means; or is it the means that justify the end?" And he finally paused for Chuck to slip in his thoughts.

"Mr. X that is very noble of you to watch out for brothers. My concern for people like you is that, the enemy would rather handcuff you with death. How long would they allow you to live." As Chuck paused, the voice that claimed to be of Malcolm X cut in.

"Young man no man lives forever, we shall all die one day, whether we are white or black, brown or yellow, small or big, violent or non-violent. Good night young man." And the line went dead. Chuck looked at the dead phone in his hand, and banged it back on its stand. He felt really furious at his fake sense of safety that a voice had just mockingly exposed.

By December 10, 1964, Rev. Martin Luther King Jr., at 35, had gone on to be the youngest person ever to be awarded the Nobel Peace Prize.

Even that monstrous recognition did not slow him down from his focus of the Voting Rights Act that was going through a grilling process at the congress. President Lyndon B. Johnson had gone on in the footsteps of his predecessor to give the African American civil rights movements the presidency's solid support. The president had granted Dr. Martin Luther King and his colleagues numerous audience.

Malcolm X had on his own taken the African American fight to every civilized point on the globe and was receiving rave audiences. On his visit to Nigeria, he was given a Yoruba name Omowale; meaning *the child had returned home*. Malcolm X had spoken so emotionally of how much he cherished that honor. He had parted ways with the Nation of Islam that actually put him in the spotlight. In fact there was no love lost between the two.

Great orators from down the ages must be complemented by an all-attentive audience. Malcolm X was one of the best that captivated his numerous audience. And the man enjoyed giving speeches. That was exactly what he was doing on February 21, 1965, when the voice of a man shouting distracted the audience and the speaker for just a moment for the assassins to strike down Malcolm X in a hail of bullets.

Out of the multitude of wreaths and tributes that the widow of Malcolm X received were two distinct messages. The one from Dr. Martin Luther King who admitted that even though they had their differences in principles, yet they had planned to work together. The other that was attributed to the Supreme leader of the Nation of Islam; he had declared that Malcolm X had it coming. This statement was later quoted totally out of context and later needed so many rebuttal to calm frayed nerves.

Sometime later that year, The Autobiography of Malcolm X was published by another publisher who stepped in when the initial publishers that made the advance fee earlier backed out of the deal. The book later went on to be an international best seller, selling in the millions. Apart from the juicy royalties, the book went on to place Amos Alexander on sound footing as a great writer.

Later that year, on August 6, the President Lyndon B. Johnson signed the Voting Rights Acts 1965 into law. For all the African American it was a glorious day, for this was more like the last frontier to overcome. And indeed it was, for blacks now had the power to influence and sway those who ruled and governed them. The words of the old Negro spiritual that Dr. Martin Luther King Jr., talked about indeed came to live...*free at last...free at last...thank Good we are free at last.*

Chuck BTW Freeborn IV finally completed his academic program in flying colors to exhilaration of both family and friends. Amos Alexander was already considered as family for Chuck IV. All the while the words of Malcolm X of how death was a must for us all, especially the part about both *the violent and the non-violent.* It made him to shudder whenever he sees Reverend Martin Luther King Jr., always full of life and in that trademark sing-song tradition pounding away in what had finally stood him out of the crowd, as outstanding.

The stage was Memphis, Tennessee, the sermon that was so moving was titled *I've Been to the Mountaintop,* and the date was April 3, 1968. Chuck IV who was watching it on television could not help but shudder at what he was hearing and seeing. He did not realize when he joined the audience that was applauding and cheering on the speaker. All he could mutter at the end of the speech was; *Prophet Martin Luther King Jr., you are just too much, Malcolm X was wrong about you. You shall live long to shame your enemies.*

The next day, April 4th, Rev. Martin Luther King Jr., was assassinated. The news was too much to bear and contain. The fury of this assassination welled into a simultaneous conflagration that enveloped black neighborhoods in over one hundred cities in the United States. The wanton damage and destruction that accompanied these riots was to say the least very violent. The display of violent dispositions and temperaments to mourn a legendary figure whose middle name could have been *Non-Violent* was to say the least a most bitter irony, but the deeper connotations we could trace back to the spirit of Malcolm X, who was living up to his promise.

For others who openly supported the so-called *King Riots* like Stokely Carmichael, the Black Power supremo, it was like juxtaposing William Shakespeare's; *...Macbeth has murdered sleep so he shall sleep no more. They have killed Martin Luther King, Peace himself; peace they shall have no more.*

CHAPTER 59

It was the year 1970. President Richard Milhous Nixon was occupying the White House as the United States 37th president. It was the same Nixon who had lost to the dashing John F. Kennedy; then gone on to lose the California Governoship in 1962; who had returned confidently to beat Hubert Humphries who was Lyndon Johnson's vice in 1968. Apart from the War in Vietnam, everything was going well for both the United States and the very intelligent lawyer president. He had made giant strides in both Chinese, USSR, Egypt, and Israel relationships.

In the home front, it was not the same story of giant strides, Nixon had consistently not consolidated on the gains of his predecessors in the African American civil rights breakthroughs of the 1960s. He had not taken up policies to really improve the African American lot economically, educationally and socially. On the statistics of higher crime rates Nixon had asked for strident enforcement of laws to counter and check crime.

On February 16, 1970, Joe Frazier was declared as the World Heavyweight Boxing Champion after Muhammed Ali was deposed for reasons that were not unconnected to the Vietnam War draft. It was on that day Chuck Freeborn V was born in Tuskegee. It was on the 8th month in her pregnancy, he had packaged his wife home to his parents who were still working at Tuskegee. From the excited telephone conversation with his parents his son came complete with the now recurring sixth finger as usual.

He had against all odds married Patsy Franklin who was a native of Tuskegee, on the Easter Monday of the previous year. His mother had tried every trick in the book to get her son to settle for one of the bevy of her Cuban compatriot-descendants. Chuck had adamantly refused to even consider them as friends, he told his mum without mincing words that he was not going to tow the line of his father and father's father who all fell for Cuban women.

He had met the 23-year-old Patsy on one of his visits home to Tuskegee about three years back, when she was an assistant secretary in the office of the president. She had kept the affair at arm's length, rebuffing all his attempts to get more intimate. Her excuse was that she way below his social class, and does not want to be taken for a ride and be dumped later. Apart from her intelligence and natural beauty, Chuck IV had been captivated by her sincerity and down-to-earth nature. Chuck teasingly called her in Spanish; *mi senora chocolate celestial*. Chuck had honed his Spanish over the years in the DEA.

Patsy could not believe her luck, that a scion of the famous Freeborn family would want her for a wife. *Who did not know the Freeborns either in Tuskegee, Birmingham, and Savannah?* They were known and respected by all and sundry. His mother who had ran out of antics to favor her own candidates, just could not wait for him to finally settle down, and just give her the grandchildren.

For his father, Chuck Freeborn III he could only pretend not to notice the *cat and mouse* game of mother and son, and the roles of the very keen and willing human baits. He wondered why the mother would not just let the young man find himself a wife without interference. Who even said it must be a Cuban or nothing? He neither encouraged or discouraged both mother and son.

Patsy was indeed black and beautiful as they come. She had that gleaming ebony black complex that had never been mixed before; pure as it was when her ancestors arrived the shores of America from Africa. She was the 4th of six children. Her father had died when she was just 10. Over the years, Patsy had come to really know what it meant to be privileged, because she was born into abject poverty. Her mother had worked all through her life to give her children some form of education which she had confessed was the best legacy. Mrs Eudora Franklin was truly over the moon with her daughter's luck in finding a suitor from such a pedigree. They may not have money, but they have dignity. Mrs Franklin had asked the daughter to *stall a little* to get the best out of the heir apparent to the massive Freeborn empire. It was a bluff that paid off well much later.

It was after his promotion to the rank of Petty Officer 2nd Class, that he had intentionally attended his younger sister, Jossy's wedding in 1968, in full ceremonial uniform. He had personally invited Patsy to the wedding. Even though everyone complimented him in his new officer's uniform, he knew too that he looked quite impressive. When Patsy finally showed up at wedding reception, Chuck could see in her eyes that she was equally impressed, as he strode over to welcome her, he noticed how stunningly beautiful she was. As he bent over and kissed her on the cheek, he had whispered; *have you finally agreed to marry me, mi senora chocolate celestial?* She had pretended not to hear him, but he saw the answer loud and clear in her eyes. He had led her over to greet his mum and dad, who were very warm with her.

Chuck IV was slated to take the *Vote of Thanks;* and he had his plans all worked out. He briskly stepped up to the podium to deliver his brief speech, he searched and patted his pockets for the speech that was *not there*. He had waved at Patsy to bring up to him the sheets that were on the table before her. She had smartly gathered the sheets together and hurriedly stepped up to the podium, by then all eyes were on the podium.

"May I have your attention ladies and gentlemen." His voice boomed out from the speakers. "Thank you very much Miss Franklin." As he took the sheaf of papers from her. "Miss Franklin, please just a moment." It was like everything stood still, there was dead silence. As he ruffled the sheaf of papers as if looking for something, as Miss Franklin all of a sudden looked nervous.

"Miss Patsy Franklin! Will you marry me?" he went on to repeat the query as he went on his knees, as hushed silence enveloped the hall. Miss Franklin looked as if she had seen a ghost, she opened her mouth to speak but nothing came out. "Please marry me Miss Franklin."

She tried again to speak but the words failed her again. All she did was to kneel by her suitor and pulled him into a warm embrace as the hall exploded in a tectonic applause. When the applause finally died down, Chuck pushed the microphone into her hands. And she lifted it towards her mouth.

"Yes! Yes!! Yes, Chuck I will marry you." Her excited sonorous voice squealed out of the loudspeakers, Chuck already pulled out a little silver-colored box from his breast pocket. Snapped it open to reveal a modest engagement ring which he slipped on her finger, as the whole hall resounded in a most thunderous applause.

Feverish plans started immediately for the big wedding scheduled to take place within 1968. It was the totally unexpected death of Mrs. Franklin that year, that scuttled their plans for the wedding. It was for that sensitive reason that the wedding was postponed to 1969. When it came, it was the biggest private social event that happened in Tuskegee that year. The US Coast Guard friends and colleagues of Chuck IV had stormed Tuskegee to add true color to the wedding with their special guard of honor. Chuck BTW was also so thrilled to have Mr. Amos Alexander and his younger brother, Randy honor his invitation. He had formally and proudly appreciated them in his own speech.

During the toast for the couple, which Amos Alexander in his own right as a celebrity author, with the best-selling Autobiography of Malcolm X, was a cynosure of all eyes, as he freely referred to the groom as his *baby-brother*. He had also added to the puzzlement of all around that there was some kind of spiritual umbilical cord binding the Alexanders from Savannah, Tennessee; and the Freeborns from Savannah, Georgia. He categorically said that, he was convinced that the answer to the puzzle lies somewhere in the tropical jungles of Africa. *How true were his hunches?* Only time shall reveal in its sacred traditions down the ages.

Chuck IV had after the conversation with his parents, quickly relayed the good news of the birth of his son over to his mentor. Amos Alexander, who was beside himself with joy. He had just returned from yet another research trip on the current project he was working on. It was both a pet and dream project; searching for his

She tried again to speak but the words failed her again. All she did was to kneel by her suitor and pulled him into a warm embrace as the hall exploded in a tectonic applause. When the applause finally died down, Chuck pushed the microphone into her hands. And she lifted it towards her mouth.

"Yes! Yes!! Yes, Chuck I will marry you." Her excited sonorous voice squealed out of the loudspeakers, Chuck already pulled out a little silver-colored box from his breast pocket. Snapped it open to reveal a modest engagement ring which he slipped on her finger, as the whole hall resounded in a most thunderous applause.

Feverish plans started immediately for the big wedding scheduled to take place within 1968. It was the totally unexpected death of Mrs. Franklin that year, that scuttled their plans for the wedding. It was for that sensitive reason that the wedding was postponed to 1969. When it came, it was the biggest private social event that happened in Tuskegee that year. The US Coast Guard friends and colleagues of Chuck IV had stormed Tuskegee to add true color to the wedding with their special guard of honor. Chuck BTW was also so thrilled to have Mr. Amos Alexander and his younger brother, Randy honor his invitation. He had formally and proudly appreciated them in his own speech.

During the toast for the couple, which Amos Alexander in his own right as a celebrity author, with the best-selling Autobiography of

Malcolm X, was a cynosure of all eyes, as he freely referred to the groom as his *baby-brother*. He had also added to the puzzlement of all around that there was some kind of spiritual umbilical cord binding the Alexanders from Savannah, Tennessee; and the Freeborns from Savannah, Georgia. He categorically said that, he was convinced that the answer to the puzzle lies somewhere in the tropical jungles of Africa. *How true were his hunches?* Only time shall reveal in its sacred traditions down the ages.

Chuck IV had after the conversation with his parents, quickly relayed the good news of the birth of his son over to his mentor. Amos Alexander, who was beside himself with joy. He had just returned from yet another research trip on the current project he was working on. It was both a pet and dream project; searching for his own African roots through bits and pieces of stories that had been handed down, from mouth to mouth over a space of two centuries. He had spent over ten years and a sizeable lump of money on the project, and the story was yet to have credible flesh.

Since Chuck's arrival in Washington DC, in the past three years, he had hosted his mentor couple of times when he came over to Washington to do his back-breaking researches. He was so familiar with the staff, that they were already on first names basis at the Library of Congress, National Archives, and in the Daughters of the American Revolution Library. Mr. Alex, who then lived in New York City had personally told him that, he had sifted through mounds and mountains of records on papers and micro-films in over 100-odd archives, libraries, scholars and griots, custodians of records in the maritime and other establishments in three continents.

Even Chuck IV had been made to sit over and over, again and again to listen to snippets of the gradually unfolding saga, that he knew so much of the names and characters by heart. They had also tried, many a time to compare and contrast his great-grandfathers experience to find any conceivable co-relation. No matter how much they tried the stories remained steadily and consistently different as the North and South Poles. Though Chuck was very glad to hear that day, that the book was finally ready to roll. *Ready-to roll* means the actual penning of the book proper, which might take about a year or so to complete before the editorial commenced.

CHAPTER 60

When the DEA was formed in July 1, 1973, Chuck BTW Freeborn IV armed with his excellent academic qualifications in the very relevant disciplines, coupled with his cognate military experience in the US Coast Guard and proficiency in Spanish was amongst the key pioneer staff of the DEA. The policy of affirmative action; just as predicted by his mentor way back had not only eased smoothly the transition from one federal agency to another, but had given him a better chance to get the post of Assistant Chief of Operations. That made him the highest ranking African American in the outfit.

Chuck BTW had commenced work right at the 1405 I Street NW, Washington DC, headquarters of the DEA. He was later moved to the DEA Academy, at the US Marine Corps base, Quantico, Virginia. He spent only a year there teaching Forensic Science, and Chemical Constituents. Then he took up position as area chief of operations in *notorious* Field Divisions like El Paso, New York, and Miami. Though he had stayed barely a year in each of the cities; he had always made his mark. The need to establish a Foreign Office in Colombia, became necessity and not just a desire for the DEA, as the drug trade exploded in leaps and bounds. Colombia was credited with a major chunk, over 80% of the world's entire cocaine production, and over 90% of the cocaine delivered into the United States.

All intelligence reports had fingered the Medellin cartel in Medellin, to be responsible for the bulk of the delivery into the United States. This cartel which was believed to have started in 1978 was operated by very ruthless men, who from all indications had become tin-gods and obviously above the law in Colombia. The Medellin cartel had with his massive resources in a few years, specialized in flying into the United States utilizing small aircrafts, rather than the cumbersome and riskier *suitcase and traveler method,* tons and tons of cocaine worth hundreds of billions of dollars.

The reports had also confirmed that the Medellin cartel with its unlimited resources had the best equipped hi-tech laboratories; communication gadgets and centers; scores of helicopters and other effectively small air and water crafts; a well-trained security personnel that used the best mercenaries from even the USA, Israel, UK and other European nations.

It had also become a cause for concern for Presidents like Gerald Ford, Jimmy Carter, and the current Ronald Regan to smoke out not just the stakeholders in Bogota and Medellin; but also in the US and other European city-destinations.

The Drugs Enforcement Administration (DEA) over the years had recommended counter measures; to infiltrate the stakeholder- groups in Colombia and outside, to return their assassinations with well-organized counter assassinations, enact and tighten laws on money laundering and related offences, to protect and shield the DEA agents home and abroad, and to workout an extradition treaties in various related countries. It was also on this line of action, it was suggested for the DEA to set up a Foreign Office in Bogota, Colombia, for effective monitoring and implementation purposes.

Setting up openly a DEA office in Colombia's 4-6 million people capital of Bogota, or the 1.4 million people second largest city of Medellin, would have been pure suicidal. The beautiful Medellin, which was also called, *Ciudad de la Eterna Primuvera,* (the city of eternal spring) was ironically reputed to be the most violent city in the world. It was on this premise the DEA top brass had chosen to operate incognito in Colombia for the safety of its agents. The choice of the area chief of operations for the Colombian Foreign Office, was indeed a very difficult task. It took the top brass many a sleepless night to arrive at a choice; at a stage the administrator had confessed that it was like condemning such a fellow to certain death in the hands of the very venomous cocaine cartels.

The job must be done; so finally the lot fell on one of the chief of operations in the field offices. The top brass guiltily agreed to promote the person to Deputy Director to operate in that capacity. To this day no one had been a able to ascertain the basis for picking the new deputy director; if it was on excellent service, pedigree, or racial extraction. To echo the declaration of one of the presidents... *nothing, nobody, no mountain nor ocean was going to stand between us and the war against the drugs lords who had sworn to make our streets, cities and minds unsafe.*

CHAPTER 61

Cristobal DaCosta had arrived El Dorado Airport, Bogota on the 11.45 Air Panama from Tocumen Airport, Panama City, that Sunday morning. All 135 passengers had hurriedly headed towards Immigration to encounter the backlog of the 11.35 Avianca flight from Madrid that arrived a moment earlier. The queue had gradually snaked toward the rows of counters until he got to the head of the line. The supervising official, an old woman with very obvious Indian features, looked like she was ten years overdue for retirement, quietly pointed him towards the available Counter 4 manned by a pretty Afro-Colombian woman.

He had stepped forward, holding out a little dented, and obviously a very used Republic of Panama passport. He tried to insipidly look the facts that were contained in the passport. His date of birth was 5th August, 1942, and was born in the banana port of Almirante. He practiced Rastafarianism; about a million black people who believed and adored Emperor Haile Selassie of Ethiopia as a direct descendant of King Solomon, the son of King David, and accepted him as a divine Messiah. He wore very neatly kept dreadlocks, that was evidence of his religious claim.

The immigration official took one long look to confirm that they were both of the same negro race. With the lightweight grey suit with a white shirt without a tie, he looked alright for a business executive that he also claimed. No need to harass the brother man she thought to herself; she just stamped the passport and returned it to him smiling, displaying a perfect dentition that would sell any brand of toothpaste.

"Bienvenidos…Welcome to Colombia Senor DaCosta." The pretty immigration official flirtingly greeted cheerfully. It was part of the test, as she observed his response and body language closely. She was fully convinced that there was no cause for alarm with his response.

"Gracias a mi querida hermana linda." (Thank you my dear pretty sister) He answered in fluent Spanish and matching her smile.

He proceeded unhurriedly toward the baggage reclaim area filled with the usual excited passengers at the end of their journey. Luck was on his side, he spotted his orange suitcase immediately. Dragging behind him the large suitcase on rollers he approached Customs. The three custom officials looked away disinterestedly as he approached them. *He had nothing to declare and they believed him.* They did not even bother to open his luggage. So he confidently strode through the short corridor towards the arrival hall.

He stepped out into the cavernous arrival hall, to be welcomed by a crowd of anxious noisy welcome parties. It was his ever first trip to Bogota, and the South American continent. It was exactly 12.45pm, by the wide-faced ornamental wall clock. He had spent just one hour to clear both immigration and customs, not as bad as they claimed. He still had over an hour to wait for his own reception party, whom he had telephoned back in Panama City before boarding the flight. The man who was coming in from Medellin had projected to arrive El Dorado too at about 1.30pm. Give or take about ninety minutes to relax and do some deep thinking. The airport did not seem to fascinate him, he had more serious matters on his mind. He looked for the Bacata Bar that he was instructed to wait at.

The glitzy *Bacata*, was not difficult to find, it had the largest number of patrons. He stepped over to the long bar ably-manned by three barmen to order a very stiff drink. He could not recognize himself from the image he saw in the huge mirror behind the barman. The image in the mirror looked more like a Rudd Gullit. He smiled, and the image smiled back at him. It was him no doubt, that meant his new façade and identity could fool even his own dead mother too. He paid for the drink, and took his drink and single luggage over to a corner that he could sit alone undisturbed. He took the first sip and savored the burning feeling and taste down his gullet right into his stomach. With the second sip he stretched out comfortably and closed his eyes to the exhilarating feeling of the spirit warming through his entire body..

The last ten years, that stretched into the early 1980s, had been very rewarding and at the same time heart-rending for him. His sudden break from the turbulent tides and oceans of the United States Coast Guard, where the mighty power of God was self-evident; to playing hide and seek with ruthless dramatis personae in the high-risk deadly game of drugs. He recalled how his second son, Booker was born on August 9, 1974, the day President Nixon resigned due to the overwhelming implicating revelations of the Watergate Scandal. Vice President Gerald Ford took over from Nixon, and went on not long after to pardon his former boss of any wrong doing.

In 1975 alone, President Ford went on to survive two assassination attempts just within an interval of 17 days. Maybe a signal that some vicious citizens did not share his view of pardoning his former boss. The discontentment was further manifested in the next year's election when Gerald Ford lost to Jimmy Carter, of their Southern state of Georgia.

As America celebrated 200 years of independence in 1976, *Roots* by Alex Haley Jr., exploded worldwide with record acclaim, selling in the millions. And just overnight the author's profile and star ranking shot through the roof. And then also came the unpalatable distractions and unsavory appurtenances of stardom. 1977 Pulitzer Award to Alex Haley Jr. was indeed a silver lining for, then followed the *Roots* Television mini-series that was aired with record massive audience the world over. Over 150 million viewers saw it worldwide.

The death of Elvis Presley, the legendary *King* of Rock and Roll indeed dampened the tempo of things again. As powerful entertainment star and icon was harvested by the gnarled fangs of hard drugs. It was recorded that over a hundred thousand fans lined the streets of Memphis, Tennessee to bid him farewell at his funeral.

He was just 42 years of age; he was cut down by the hard drugs that he could afford as a star. In those final days he was a shadow of himself.

The final years of the 1970s were taken over by events in the middle East, especially the Iran Hostage-Crisis, as well as the Israel and Arab Conflicts. These were the days when non-violent civil rights movement took a backseat for The Black Power activists. People like Muhammed Ali had returned again to reclaim and lose again and again the World's Heavyweight Boxing crown that he was stripped of back in 1967.

The new decade took off with more bad news of assassination as another legendary figure in music, John Lennon of the Beatles fame was shot dead in New York. Another harvest of drugs, as the perpetrators must have been under the influence of some hard drugs to carryout the dastardly acts. And then came the Hollywood star, who went to be governor of California, and went further to defeat President Carter in the 1980 elections. President Ronald Reagan was inaugurated in 1981; the very same day Iran whether in good fate or goodwill released all hostages held captive since 1979.

It was also in 1980 the *Miami Vice Massacre* occurred. Three generations of a close-knit African American family were wasted one evening by a drug gang related to the notorious Medellin cartel in a retaliatory senseless killing spree. The victims of 1980 Miami Massacre were all related to him. As the DEA chief in Miami, he was aware that the cartel had a contract out for him; the cartel had sworn to take him out because of the damage he was doing to their massive operations. Not in his wildest imagination could he believe that they would go that far.

Jossy, his younger sister and her family were based in Miami before his posting there. It was the event of the birth of her third child, that had brought his elderly parents and his other sister to visit from Birmingham, Alabama. The drug gang had trailed him there earlier in the evening, and returned with their arsenal to perforate everything in that house with bullets. He had returned only a moment later with his brother-in-law's power motorbike that he had taken for a brief spin to discover that his life would never be the same again. They killed his 75-year-old father, his mother, his two younger sisters, his brother-in-law, and his three nephews. He believed that he was only left alive to avenge their deaths. He knew that he was *indeed a dead man that was walking*.

The world was just warming to the ebullient President Ronald Reagan when a certain John Hinckley, pointed, and fired his gun to kill the president. The bullets found their target but did not achieve their deadly errand. Ronald Reagan survived to make a *joke* out of his own assassination.

And the Medellin cartel in Colombia became richer feeding fat on the blood and lives of Americans that found succor and solace in their deadly cocktails of cocaine, while the innocent bystanders were made victims. The more bloated with their ill-gotten billions they become, they also become larger than the laws of their own lands. And the United States, and the *presumed dead* Chuck Freeborn IV, had declared total war; and nobody whether president or common thief who have had his fingers soiled by drugs, that was safe. They must be brought to book whether by civil or jungle justice.

Cristobal DaCosta opened his eyes to see that he was still at the El Dorado International Airport in Bogota. Bogota was a gargantuan mega-city of over 6million people; comparable to only New York City and Mexico City in North America. He was in Bogota on a covert mission, a mission some in the know had dismissed as just suicidal. It was simply a mission impossible, a mission that only the living dead would undertake. *Living dead...Cristobal DaCosta* was indeed dead to the world, at least dead to those that desperately wanted him dead in Miami.

He was part of the battle to dislodge the drug lords from their almost invincible positions. Deep inside him he felt like a pawn in this deadly war that could crush him without any acknowledgement. He finished his drink and checked his wristwatch that showed that it was already 2 pm. No time for another leisurely drink, so he decided against it. All around him was the increased air and excitement of travelers and various reception parties.

Just at that moment, a sudden abnormal lull fell upon the crowd in that arrival hall. DaCosta looked up wondering what created the sudden silence. It took just a flitting moment to find out. Standing by the furthest entrance point to the Bacata Bar area was a man-mountan. It was a Caucasian male, of about 60 years of age, with a thick mound of grey or blond hair. He stood over seven feet tall, with the massive bulk of a Russian tank weighing over 220 kilograms in muscles and very little fat. Though all eyes were on him, Juan Nunez looked unruffled, his eyes slowly and painstakingly searching across the bar for somebody. He recognized Juan Sebastian de Nunez immediately from the photographs that he had seen and memorized to heart. DaCosta smiled at the thought that it would be an abnormality not to stare at this massive specimen of creation. Coupled with the facts of his most recent kidnap ordeal, that had had that strikingly chiseled face plastered over all the papers and television screens in Colombia.

Nunez was like royalty in Bogota, being a direct descendant of one of the very prominent Spanish conquistadors that founded Bogota. It was therefore, not only unthinkable, but sheer sacrilege to kidnap a *Sebastian de Nunez* that was almost an institution that was over four centuries old. The Sebastian de Nunez hacienda and colossal estate is a good chunk of the entire La Candelaria; yet one of the notorious drug cartels kidnapped one of them, to send a message to all and sundry that nobody could stand in the part of their illicit desire and business. Not even a personality of the caliber of a *Sebastian de Nunez*. Juan Nunez was reputed to be the only drug cartel kidnap victim in Colombia to ever regain his freedom and live to tell of the bitter ordeal.

Before the kidnap ordeal, Juan Nunez was the chairman and chief operating officer of Nunez Haulage & Exports, a frontline indigenous company operating in Bogota and Medellin. Six months after his kidnap saga the business was offered up for sale for very obvious reasons. Nobody in Colombia was interested in a business that the notorious drug cartel had left their inglorious calling card with. It was not until a month ago, some Panamanian investors had shown vague interest and finally ended up grabbing the deal. The entire deal of the sale or *disposal* of Nunez Haulage & Exports was played out in the pages of the Colombian newspapers and television, for a special reason by a special interest group.

Cristobal DaCosta, was supposedly an integral part of the new owners who was in Colombia to assume control and the management of NH&E. Even though he was there in the interest of the United States of America, he had his own personal agenda...*a vendetta he had promised his dying father he must sort out himself.*

DaCosta stood on his feet and waved excitedly at Nunez until he caught his eye. Juan Sebastian de Nunez, also known as *De Destroyer* in his hey-days of professional wrestling was still very nimble on his feet, he smartly cut a b-line toward him. They were meeting for the very first time ever. This was the man who would put him solidly on the ground in the war against the drug lords in their own backyard. No concise plan had been laid out, DaCosta was to use his own discretion to get to the point that he could always call for special expeditionary force backup. His preoccupation would be to infiltrate the cartels and collate detailed vital information that would be used against the drug lords at the appropriate time, to inflict collateral damage.

The first step was to let the drug cartels to know that a new man was in Bogota to run Nunz Haulage & Exports. This was undertaken immediately. Nunez had gregariously ordered drinks for both passengers and airport staff to toast to the arrival of DaCosta in their midst. It was deemed the fastest and most effective means to achieve their desire since the drug cartels must have reliable informants amongst the airport staff, and luck might also be on their side with some passengers who might be from the right people that they were targeting.

After their drinks, they had left for the NH&E office that was about five kilometers away on Avenida El Dorado or Calle 26. They were picked up in a big black limousine that sedately eased its way on to the main highway leading back to town. Traffic was light, so in very little time they turned off the highway into a service lane that led right on to the headquarters of Nunez Haulage & Exports. The gatehouse carried on its roof the black bold letters that spelt out the full name of the company. A thick hedge of thorny overgrown rose securely kept the activities behind and beyond the hedge from preying eyes and fingers. There were four armed uniformed security guards visible inside the glass encased gatehouse. One of the guards with an AK 47 riffle approached and cleared the chauffeur-driven car, before they could gain access through the massive metal gate on rollers. As the gate rolled back into place, there was yet another impregnable gate about 25 yards ahead of them.

"*Si!*" Nunez answered his questioning gaze, "Water-tight security is not a luxury here in Bogota, it is a necessity."

"I see with the cartels playing god with people's lives." Chuck retorted.

"The security was not this tight, until after my abduction. We needed to reassure the trouble makers Nunez Haulage & Exports was going to be a hard nut to crack."

They drove past a row of warehouses bordering the paved private drive way lined with exotic palms. One or two male workers in orange-colored overall were seen lolling about. The drive-way went uninterrupted for over 300 yards before they saw the story Administration building with about ten black limousines similar to the one they were riding in. Cristobal thought to himself, that he was to personally fit each of those vehicles with snooping devices in the shortest space of time, to keep tabs on the clients who were mostly the cartel members and their families. *Where were the fleet of articulated haulage trucks?*

A five-man team, in white short sleeves over black trousers were waiting to meet their new boss. Amidst very jocular pumping of hands, Cristobal was received and taken around to the other offices. He also discovered that a very cordial relationship existed between Nunez and his band of *rolos*, as they, the natives proudly called themselves in Bogota.

Two hours later, after being shown around the whole complex, Cristobal was driven over to the town office in some address in Chapinero, just a stone's throw from the Theatron de Pelicula. The town office equally had another fleet of limousines and other choice brands of luxury on wheels. It also had a showroom for very exclusive brand of vehicles for sale.

It was finally at about 6p.m., tired and fatigued, that he was finally dropped off at Ciudad Salitre, in El Salitre, what would be his official residence in Bogota.

CHAPTER 62

So much had happened since that Sunday morning that Cristobal DaCosta landed at the El Dorado International Airport. The DEA plan to use the genuine business activities of Nunez Haulage & Exports to effectively infiltrate the rank and file of the cartels had paid-off handsomely. The legendary drug lord, Carlos Lehder who acquired a part of a Bahamian island, where he built his own airstrip and conveniently operated his fleet of special cocaine- laden aircrafts into the USA had since been extradited to the US, convicted and condemned to spend 135 years of his violent life in jail. The 135 year-sentence was part of a negotiated deal, as Lehder's cooperation enhanced the capture and extradition of Cristobal's Panamanian leader, Manuel Noriega. The United States was making giant strides in its resolve that *...nothing, nobody, no mountain nor ocean was going to stand between us and the war against the drug lords who had sworn to make our streets, cities and minds unsafe...*

The journey to that point had been slow, thorough, and painstakingly dangerous. It was a methodical affair; DaCosta was forced to resort to good old-fashioned clinical investigative legwork. It commenced with the most mundane nitty-gritty of manning those massive limousines sometimes. First, he perfected his knowledge of Bogota's very complicated house numbering system. He had to memorize effectively the numerous *Carreras, Calles, Transversales, Diagonals,* and *Avenidas*. He then not only learnt by heart, but actually drove and covered hundreds of thousands of miles of Colombian highways and deadly off-tracks with the articulated trucks under the cover of NH&E's business in coffee export, to get firsthand evidence for his people to follow up with appropriate actions.

The cartels operating in mostly cities like Medellin and Cali, were a highly organized networks of cultivators of coca fields located in the relative safety of deep and remote jungles; processors of the harvested coca leaves first into paste; transporters of the paste to high-tech laboratories and scientists; who then churn out the cocaine hydrochloride; then followed the very high risk transportation, smuggling and distribution to major cities all over the world, with the US having the lion's share. These activities of the cartels were backed by bankers, assassins, lawyers, politicians, corrupt government agents etc.

The price differential of a kilogram of processed cocaine at source in Colombia of about $1,450 to over $50,000 in the streets of Miami or Los Angeles, made it the big business for not the lilly-livered but the devil's incarnates. That was why the Colombian drug lords were made of sterner stuff; they were the most affluent, powerful, and the most lethally dangerous in the whole world. Nobody dare stand in their paths of business in Colombia and even in their destinations. Characters like Jose Santacruz-Londono, who was top-shot in one of the cartels, and was behind the largest clandestine cocaine laboratory right in New York City in 1985, silenced and sent so many people to the grave to keep his operations safe.

With Colombia's unique geographical location, as the only South American enclave possessing coastlines in both the Atlantic and the Pacific; other major producers of coca like Bolivia and Peru would rather pass their produce through Colombia with ease. DaCosta had painstakingly filed over details of his surveillance to his people, in conjunction with the National Police of Colombia, who had systematically eliminated these coca paste processing plants and the humongous coca plantations, and effected thousands of arrests.

All the while, the man who was now known as Cristobal DaCosta did not forget his main objective to Colombia. The subject of his vengeance was Ramirez Castro Bacata, the supreme drug lord who ordered his whole family in Miami to be killed to send a message to all DEA officials who had remained adamant in the face of very tempting bribes, and had lethally caused massive blows and losses on the drug trade. DaCosta literally lived and relished the moment he would come face-to-face with the supposed King of the drug trade, how he would first reveal his true identity, before killing the man with his bare hands. He pursued his desire with a kind of maniac death wish; *no mission was dangerous or impossible.*

So far the impact of DaCosta's relentless efforts were paying off, as the Colombian National Police was dismantling very key and strategic personnel and operations of the drug trade in both Colombia and the surrounding coca producing nations. Also in the destination-nations of the United States and Canada, there had been superlative bursting of lethal drug gangs in the major cities. And the drug cartels were fighting back with their series of unconventional arsenal of violence and death that became their trademark. It was on this basis the key cities of Colombia ended up with the sobriquet of the *most dangerous place on earth*. DaCosta had had his own fair share of very close calls, as he had seen and witnessed hundreds of deaths, of his willing and unwilling corroborators in the hands of the vicious cartels. There was a massive hunt for a mole within Colombia; the cartels had put out contracts on him *dead or alive*. It was his very first closest call, they almost got him.

He won't forget easily that April 30, 1984, when the Minister of Justice, a very staunch supporter of the war against the drug trade was brazenly killed on a Bogotá highway by two gunmen on a motorcycle. The vehicle he was driving was just two vehicles behind the minister's car, he saw the assassins approach the vehicle in the traffic and opened fire at point-blank range. They were actually heading to a rendezvous, when that dastardly act took place.

The following year, sometime in July, another very high profile violent death was that of Superior Judge Tulio Castro Gil, who had then just indicted one of the most powerful drug lords in Colombia. Cristobal DaCosta was surreptitiously following the judge to inform him that the cartel was on to him, when gunmen on a motorcycle killed him right in front of DaCosta. Within exactly a year of Superior Judge Gil's murder, a Supreme Court Justice, Hernando B. Borda, was also gunned down in Bogota, within very close proximity of DaCosta. Over two thousand police officers and other government officials were decimated by the drug lords in Colombia within that period.

Only two people in all of Colombia knew of the very close- guided secret of DaCosta's true identity and covert mission. One of the two was Colonel Jaime Ramirez, who headed the anti-narcotics arm of the Colombia National Police; it was him that provided Dacosta with most of his official logistic support. The other person remained a close guided secret. In November of 1986, a pre-arranged meeting on a Medellin thoroughfare was scuttled by a gang of gunmen, who killed Colonel Ramirez, and only luckily wounded the wife and two boys who were with him in the vehicle. DaCosta's articulated NH&E truck had arrived only moments later to meet the bloody carnage. Even Washington was concerned for his safety; the cartel's hit men were getting too close for comfort.

Another very high profile vengeance of drug cartels was the December 1986 killing of Guillermo Cano Isaza, the heavyweight of *El Espectador,* by another band of killers on a motorcycle in Colombia's major city of Bogota. Isaza was to pick up some critical information left somewhere by DaCosta when he was killed. DaCosta knew it was time to ask his people to send in the Special Squad to counter effectively the killings through the source that was almost on to him. It was not fear, but self-preservation that Cristobal DaCosta reacted to, so as to enhance the fulfillment of his personal vendetta.

By early January, 1987, twelve members of the elite X-Squad with very sound Spanish backgrounds clandestinely filtered into Colombia to provide adequate cover for Cristobal DaCosta to operate. Within ten days of their arrival, they had tactically taken care of every clear and present danger to DaCosta and his informants and corroborators. Amongst the elite X-Squad that arrived and worked closely with DaCosta in Colombia, was a certain Fabrice DeLeon, who was formerly known as Fabrice Leonceto, a Cuban that was rescued out of the Caribbean Sea as Fabrice Leonceto back in 1963 by the US Coast Guard. DaCosta recognized him immediately, but kept his cool for obvious reasons.

The twelve members of the X Squad were severally absorbed into NH&E in various capacities. Their main mission was to counter the killing machines of the cartels, through tactical assassination of the cartels' field and operation commanders. The X-Squad, who were hand-picked and specially trained was the best in their deadly trade. Within a relatively short interval of their arrival in Colombia, they had effectively turned the table around in Bogota and Medellin; as gradually *the hunter became the hunted.*

That year, even though there were more killings, they balanced out, as the enemy was made to taste his own unpalatable medicine. Those who were not luckily killed were extradited to the United States to face jail terms. Some drug lords, when the heat on them became so hot and unbearable, eloped into Honduras, Bolivia and Peru.

The Cali cartel, which also went by the name of *Cali's Gentlemen,* was based in Cali, in the southern part of Colombia, effectively sided with the Colombia National Police and United States DEA to strategically eliminate their opponent-cartels, so as to leave them to monopolize the trade. DaCosta was made to understand that after the

Medellin cartel had been caged, the Cali's Gentlemen were totally expendable at the fullness of time.

Meanwhile, Ramirez Castro Bacata, the object of his whole-being and desire was more elusive than the proverbial *Bigfoot*. His person, as well as his immediate whereabouts were a closely guided secret in the subterranean world of the drug trade. DaCosta had told his superiors that he was not leaving Colombia without finding Bacata.

CHAPTER 63

It was almost looking like the whole idea of a lord of all the drug lords was a fallacy; that Ramirez Castro Bacata was a ghostly myth that he, Cristobal DaCosta had naively bought hook, line, and sinker. Tried as he could, he ended up on a dead end. Every lead to establish the existence of his quarry in Colombia, ran out cold. Some were even so scared to even mention the name, they pronounced it in whisper, as if afraid that the wind would tell on them. Whenever he inquired off-handedly of Ramirez Castro Bacata, the person would customarily take a furtive glance around before quickly answering in the negative. It was a situation that he found very despondent and discouraging. He kept telling himself that he was going to find Bacata, even if he resides at the end of the earth.

Then came January 1988, when Carlos Mauro Hoyos, Attorney General, the only surviving government official in Colombia who was in on the covert mission of DaCosta, was also killed by gunmen in the city of Medellín. After the assassination of Jamie Raminez back in 1986, the Attorney General would always reassure him that he was safe. Hoyos killing, even with the X-Squad on ground, really shook DaCosta's confidence.

Hoyos was in Medellin to investigate why a certain drug lord was released from jail mid-way into his sentence. An eyewitness had told how Hoyos official Mercedes Benz car was ambushed by three Jeeps with about a dozen men, who had sprayed the Mercedes Benz with machine gun fire. Hoyos driver and bodyguard were killed immediately. Carlos Hoyos was kidnapped, with *The Extraditable* secluded estate far from preying eyes off the I-24, at about where it meets the elongated Calle 3 on the outskirts of Popayan.

In the cover of darkness, DaCosta and Espindola had taken the two mountain bikes secured at the back of the truck and headed for their target. They had hidden the bikes and clambered through the wooded hillside on to the laboratory. They had observed the pristine facility through their binoculars for a while. There were about ten armed guards who all looked lax; people who were used to uneventful duty periods. It had taken Espindola ten minutes flat to place the timed to detonate Semtex (plastic explosive) at the most strategic points to escalate their collateral damage.

They had returned to their bikes, and ridden off without any notice of the two bikers leisurely enjoying an evening ride. They had enjoyed a sound peaceful sleep in the well-equipped cabin, and left at the first light of dawn on the I-25 headed North to Cali, the base of the Cali mafia. The Cali Gentlemen had with some sound modicum of evil wisdom joined forces with the Colombian National Police to fight their competitors in the inglorious cocaine trade. DaCosta did not see any problems, though he would not mind to take a swipe at the devil in disguise.

They had just got on the bridge on the Rio Cauca when they heard the first muffled sound of the explosives, and the sky over Popayan glowed orange bright in the sober light of dawn. The three men rode in silence as more thundering explosions travelled to them in the still morning air. That was one less evil of destruction to the civilized world, DaCosta thought to himself with relish.

CHAPTER 64

They had entered Cali through the Jamundi route. The plan was to stay over two nights in Cali. Cali with a population of about two million was much larger than any of the cities they had passed through. They had followed the Simon Bolivar or Calle 36 to a truck park, where their truck was given a safe berth and well-deserved rest. DaCosta knew the men also deserved a good rest, so they distributed themselves into various 4-Star hotels. They were to keep their ears to the ground and gather important information.

Back in their hotel rooms that evening, was the news of the fire incident in a medical equipment laboratory in Popayan. As the TV Cameras panned into show the grim magnitude of devastation, DaCosta noted grimly that Espindola was a true professional. The newsreader had added that the police did not suspect any foul play; while a representative of an insurance company had promised prompt claim settlement on the basis of the police report and findings. The drug cartels were very smart, they had pulled all the rights strings to clean up their mess. He had used the phone to call some emerald dealers for standard effect to hidden ears.

It was not his first time in Cali, he had visited Cali over ten times since his arrival in Colombia. He had taken a good long bath, rested then hit the town with an hotel car hire. The driver was more than friendly, and tried as much as he could to get information out of DaCosta. DaCosta tried to play dumb and bored to get the talkative driver to lose his initial interest. He had by 4a.m. called in at three different nightclubs; it was time to return to his hotel and hit the sack.

They had all tried unsuccessfully at the local bars to get snippets of information on Ramirez Bacata, but no dice, nobody was ready to offer any iota of information. The next day, DaCosta had met with a couple of *emerald dealers* in the hotel lobby. After exhaustive negotiations he had settled for a handsome quantity to be packaged for exports. They had early the next day set course for the Coffee Trail of Colombia; Armenia, Pereira, and Manizales to load up 2,000 bags of best Colombian coffee through established longstanding contacts. With the full load of coffee, DaCosta and his team had driven through Medellin up North on the I-25 that ended at Barranquilla. After Sincelejo, they had continued up North until Villa Silvia, after which they had veered left on to the Road 90 route which was relatively secluded to the port city of Cartagena. Cartagena, with a population of about 600,000 inhabitants was the third busiest port in the Carribean, and also the capital of the department of Bolivar. Columbia fifth largest city was replete with rich and engaging history dating back over 500 years. With DaCosta's fear of heights; Cartagena at just seven feet above sea level was DaCosta's favorite Colombian city.

Just before Road 90 transformed to Calle 31, DaCosta had taken over the steering from Deleon to give them a guided tour of Cartagena that was founded in 1533, and was named after the Cartagena in Spain. As they progressed through the city, DaCosta excitedly pointed out the important historical landmarks with the enthusiasm of a professional tour guide. He even packed at the famous Cartagena's colonial walled city and almost impregnable fortress teeming with tourists to tell its history, and how it was designated as a protected UNESCO World Heritage Site, only a couple of years back in 1984. Espindola who was also a keen history enthusiast was really enthralled. Calle 31 first transformed into Avenida Pedro de Heredia, then into Avenida Venezuela, this was just beginning of the longest road in Cartagena.

It was at the point the road transformed to Avenida Blas de Lezo that Espindola directed their attention to an engaging darkened bronze statue of a man with a leg, an eye, and a hand. "Wow! What tragic history cost this poor fellow to have shared some of his paired anatomies with Colombia?"

"That," DaCosta paused to engage gear, "...that fellow is a living legend in Colombian history. General Blas de Lezo, was a proud mariner of Spanish descent who fought bravely in 1741 to protect Cartagena from a combined British and American attack."

"Damn!" Deleon could not help but exclaim, "No wonder he looked really battered."

"Every Colombian child is taught proudly how General Blas de Lezo in the Battle of Cartagena with less than 3,000 men with just 6 ships was able to take on the 186 armada and over 23,000 men of Admiral Edward Vernon who was commanding the combined British and American colonial forces." DaCosta had told the story with relish, even to how Lawrence Washington, a brother of the famous George, had named the plantation Mount Vernon after Admiral Vernon.

Deleon and Espindola had listened intently to their superior, with obvious respect for his intelligence in Colombian and Spanish history. Deleon could not but disabuse his mind about some nagging feeling that DaCosta was an American he came across over twenty years back. This man, Deleon thought to himself, who spoke so proudly of the General Lezo's successful repel of the combined colonial troops of British and American could not be the American that went out of his way to save his life, that he had lost touch with since.

They drove in absolute silence through the El Centro neighborhood, absorbing the blazing techni-colors of the majestic colonial architectures and the luxuriant exotic landscape as they came alive in the glow of the afternoon sun. As they aproached the massive Satander roundabout both Espindola and Deleon could not hold back their exclamations regarding the astonishing scenic landscape.

They had gone right on the Avenida Santander, and drove at a sedate pace along the very imposing shoreline and its numerous breakers as DaCosta resumed his concise commentaries. They finally arrived at the front of Aeropuerto Rafael Nunez, and took the first exit to turn back to retrace their steps.

Back at the Satander Roundabout, they had turned left back on to the Blas de Lezo, and this time seen the Parque de la Marina in its full glory. Just before the Clock Tower Gate they took right onto Calle 24, and drove through the Getsemani neighborhood. DaCosta chose the more scenic Calle 24 waterfront route for the sheer scenic beauty which was very therapeutic. They had at its end merged on to Calle 25 to cross the bridge to Cartagena.

At the Parque Henrique Roman end of the bridge, DaCosta had briefly slowed to crawl as he searched for somebody or something only known to him. His attention was focused more at the area the Transversal 17 came from under the bridge to merge on to Calle 25. What he was looking for actually packed across the road by the petrol station. It was a blue and red bullion van with its bonnet open. DaCosta blared his horn twice to catch their attention. The two occupants quickly closed the bonnet and jumped into their armor- plated bullion van and began to trail the NH&E truck. Espindola and Deleon exchanged incongruous glances that said so much about what they thought was an innocent drive-about in their favor. They turned right onto Carrera 17 and then connected on to Calle 24 which also ran along the Bahia de la Animas waterfront. Their little journey finally ended up on Carrera 26 which was bordered on one side by the solid impregnable fence of the Container Terminal,

The rest of the journey was in total silence, every man absorbed in his own thoughts. DaCosta thinking about the consignment of cocaine in that bullion van that would be allowed into the United States to maintain the relationship with the Cali cartel. The people in Washington called it *controlled entry*; meaning every grain of cocaine dust was traceable to an end user and recovered without raising any suspicion. How they get to do that task successfully was better imagined than practiced? Some orders in the field were beyond his competence to question, just obey or follow the flow of command. He bluntly refused to believe that some top brass in the Pentagon may be smiling to the bank in this covert assignment.

With the bullion van following them as if towed by them; they finally arrived at the huge black gates of the high-walled NH&E, Cartagena. As they approached the address on Carrera 26; the gate parted to let the two vehicles in smoothly. The name of the company was engraved on a 3ft by 1ft polished solid brass plate embedded on to the gate.

As the huge gate swung back into place behind them, the truck and the bullion van parted ways. The truck headed straight into the open cavernous doors of the massive warehouse occupying the whole right hand side of the compound. Inside the warehouse were about twenty workers adorned in the bright orange NH&E overall, all busy with various activities like in the labyrinth of a termite hill. DaCosta parked in the middle of the warehouse with stacks of coffee bags on pallets towering towards the roof. He swung gingerly down from the cab, and in one fluid practiced move threw the truck keys over to a grinning supervisor, who was on hand to commence off-loading. The spare driver and the motor-boy stayed back to assist the off-loading of their cargo.

DaCosta exited the warehouse through a side door that led straight to the front of the tidy one-story office block. The bullion van was nowhere in sight, because it was already parked inside the lockup garage meant specifically for that purpose. He was met at the door of the reception by Fabio Falcao, his manager in Cartagena. They shook hands and briskly walked over to his(DaCosta's) office which was adjacent to the garage. As he pushed open the connecting door, he noticed three ordinarily looking coffee sacks stacked neatly on a weighing scale. The two smart suited men that came with the van were talking in low tunes, and leaning against the back of the van with its rear door ajar. As the door closed behind them, the three coffee bags gradually glowed into a deep fiery red.

DaCosta went over to the scale confirmed the reading, then quickly signed a sheaf of documents placed on top of the bags. Fabio Falcao stepped over with a shiny small briefcase, which he snapped open to reveal a neat stacks of mint-fresh crisp US Dollars. The bulkier of the dark-suited men took his sunshade off to inspect each pile of the bills to his satisfaction. He snapped back the briefcase and nodded at his colleague to get moving. No handshakes, no pleasantries; that was the typical *Cali Gentlemen* for you. The entire transaction was in total silence, as if they were all under some form of a conspiracy of silence. That was the typical conclusion of the deal with the Cali *emerald dealers*.

As the bullion van reversed out of the garage, a solid iron curtain rolled down from the ceiling to cut out the vehicle from view, before the outer door opened. By then DaCosta and his man had already commenced paper work to cover the shipment and logistics to Houston, New Orleans, and New York City.

CHAPTER 65

It was two days later, after the departure of *MV Radiant Glory* with its NH&E cargo of the best of Colombian coffee beans, and the three special sacks of first grade cocaine, that DaCosta and his team commenced their journey back to Bogota. His colleagues noticed that he was abnormally quiet, absorbed very much in whatever was occupying his mind. It was the communication that he had received from Panama City that morning before their departure.

Dear Senor DaCosta,

Thanks for your detailed update and report on our activities with NH&E. The Board had asked me to express our appreciation for your outstanding responsibility and unequalled call to duty. It is on this premise the board had nominated and approved you to the elevated position of Director of International Affairs with immediate effect.

Luis Gustavo Escobar, whom is well known to you, will be taking over from you accordingly. He would be in Bogota by Sunday, we sincerely hope you will have a very smooth transition.

We look forward to seeing you back at the headquarters in your official brand new capacity. Please once again accept our very hearty congratulations.

Yours faithfully.

Enrique Raul Estefan
(Director Human Resources).

DaCosta was not happy with the new development of events. He was yet to find Ramirez Bacata, the man that had caused him so much pain and sorrow. He is being recalled home by his superiors without recourse to his own consideration. Should he turn down the elevation, resign or retire, and stay back in Colombia until he gets his man? But how far could he last without the almighty backing of the organization? Would he stand a chance alone against the deadly onslaught of the cartels? Since the kidnap and killing of the Attorney General, his superiors were a bit jittery about his continued stay in Colombia. He could understand their concerns; but he was also a very troubled man.

Would his beloved grandfather, parents and siblings ever forgive him, if he leaves Colombia without avenging their most dastardly killings? Would he ever find peace? Just more questions, upon questions. He didn't even know what to do, or even where to start from. He could feel that he was very tense; he could feel the dampness in his palm, and that accompanying itchy feeling. He leaned back and eased down his passenger seat to relax his aching mind and frame. He shut his eyes to relieve the aches hammering away inside his forehead. He took a very deep breath and fell asleep almost immediately.

"Come on *Number IV!* You are almost there. Don't give up, for you do not walk alone. Have you forgotten who you are? You are blood and flesh of the great *Akachukwu*." It was his great-grandfather urging him on.

"Look here son, we are not resting in peace, until you nail that Bacata, the good for nothing devil's incarnate true and proper." This time it was his own father reaching out to him.

Then he saw the ladies with tears in their eyes. There were six of them. He could recognize his mother and his two sisters; and they were singing a very glorious voice; "It is just a matter of time, Number IV. He is all yours for the taking." They chorused and pointed at giant vulture flying just overhead with a man with a cape on its back. He took aim with the traditional bow and arrow in his hands,

and fired off. It was a bulls eye, as the arrow pierced the vulture and it went crashing down into a foliage. He ran over to the point the bird came down, but found only the immediately rotting carcass of the vulture without Bacata anywhere in sight. He fell down on his knees and was sobbing and screaming; "No! No!! No!!!". It was then he felt the hand of his father hugging and consoling him…then he woke up to the firm but gentle shaking of Deleon..

They had later stopped to eat at Sincelejo. When Espindola had taken time out to ease himself, DaCosta received another shock that morning.

"Chuck Freeborn IV! My very own rescuer." It was whispered in English, "How did you ever think, I would not recognize you?" Deleon said it not as a question but a statement of fact.

"Even after over twenty-some years, Fabrice I thought my cover was perfect."

"My dear friend, there is no perfect cover that lasts forever, as we were taught back in the spy academy; every perfect cover has a life span." Deleon retorted with a wicked grin on his face, as he noticed Espindola making his way back to their table.

"Si, Senor DaCosta we shall make good time." He reverted to their usual Spanish.

"Just drive carefully, I am not feeling well." DaCosta answered equally in Spanish with a straight face, as Espindola fell gratefully into his seat.

Since their target was to spend the night at Medellin, they had gone at a very sedate pace, stopping at every averagely major town to make subtle inquiries about Bacata without raising eyebrows. They had put some guns in the cabin, in the event of any eventuality. The person seated by the driver was saddled with scurrying the distance with a very high definition military binoculars. It was smooth sail all the way, not a moment of anxiety at all.

After the dream, DaCosta was convinced that something big was about to happen. It was a steady nagging feeling that refused to go away. On the other hand he was consoled that it was Deleon that was in on his well-protected secret, at least that was somebody he could count on his alloyed loyalty. Though, it was totally disconcerting to know that his cover was not totally foolproof. It means that he was not truly safe anymore. Maybe his people in Washington were right.

They had just passed the intersection to Monteria, and there were long stretches of the road without human habitation. The binoculars picked out the major curve ahead with prominent multiple directional signs, and a dirt road veering off to the right into grassy fields with an unhindered view into the distance. Bordering both sides of the road were uniform low trees. Immediately after the border of the trees on the left was a small river running parallel to the highway. Deleon noted with interest three vehicle parked at a very awkward handle. He had handed over the binoculars to DaCosta, and deftly reached for his assault rifle. DaCosta confirmed that it was a kidnap in action from what he could see through the binoculars. He asked Espindola to step down on the pedal as he too reached for the automatic machine gun. They were going to foil it.

Their truck came through the bend at some reckless speed and purposely rammed the last vehicle to set the four kidnappers scampering for their lives, as both Deleon and DaCosta fired from their windows gunning down all four of them. Deleon went over to the balaclava clad bodies to confirm that they were all dead. By then, DaCosta had forced open the trunk of the first car to reveal a sweating very frightened white middle-aged male. It had taken less than thirty-five seconds. No vehicle had come along from either directions.

The freed kidnap victim was too shaken to drive, that Deleon had to drive his brand new Mercedes car behind the truck, while the man rode in the truck. And they sped off towards the next town which was Caucasia.

By the time they arrived in Caucasia, the man had already dissuaded DaCosta from going to report the incident at the local police station. His argument was quite a revelation that almost gave DaCosta a heart attack. The man whose name was Juan Miguel Fernando, was from Yarumal, a small town with a population of about 30,000 people, and only about 83 kilometers from Medellin, in the department of Antioquia. And Yarumal, the man had revealed was where Ramirez Carlos Bacata originated from. It was his considered opinion that the kidnap was by Bacata's henchmen based on what they had said when they intercepted and captured him.

They had said the *big boss* was coming to town later in the day, to personally deal with his case. The *big boss* was no doubt Bacata, Fernando declared with all certainty. He had told his baffled listeners how Bacata had asked for his own land that was adjacent to his parents home, because it was ideal to use as a heliport just next door. DaCosta was not only shocked, he was dumbfounded to hear that both of Bacata's parents suffering from Alzheimer's disease live up there in Yarumal, and Ramirez popped in irregularly to visit them. Bacata, whom he knew from childhood, had first made very juicy offers which he rejected, then resorted to subtle threats. Fernando knew that disposing the property would negatively affect his own mother's health who lives there with him, she was also stricken down with Alzheimer's.

DaCosta had quizzed Fernando further on the Alzheimer's angle, which the man revealed was very common in Yarumal. There was ample scientific evidence that due to some kind of genetic mutation prevalent in Yarumal, many of its inhabitants suffer from an early-onset of the disease. DaCosta was excited beyond control. Now he believes beyond doubt that the legend of his family's *sixth finger* was for real, and not a myth. Ramirez Carlos Bacata, the lord of all drug lords, whom had remained elusive all these years to him, was now presented to him just like that on a platter of gold in his final days in Colombia.

CHAPTER 66

It was Juan Miguel Fernando who had insisted for DaCosta and his men to stay over the night in Yarumal as his guests. It was the least he could do to show his appreciation for their timely intervention to save him from the kidnappers. It did not take him long to convince them. DaCosta after hearing his stories was already working out his own game plan. They had worked out a perfect plan to arrive Yarumal differently so as not to arouse suspicions.

Little after the San Andres intersection, and few miles to Yarumal, when the road was relatively quiet, they had stopped and Juan Miguel Fernando had quickly taken over his car. He had driven off, leaving the truckers to put their truck in readiness to enter Yarumal with enough racket for people to remember. Espindola who was an automobile mechanic back in Mexico, tinkered about with the engine, until he was satisfied with the result. When Deleon turned on the ignition, they were greeted with a strange deep thunderous roar, and inky black cloud of smoke oozing out of the engine. When he tried to engage the gear to move on, the massive truck heaved and groaned like a heavily pregnant woman, and slowly moved forward.

Yarumal was directly on the I-25, 384 kilometers from Cartagena, and about 84 kilometers from Medellin. Bacata's numerous foot soldiers and informants had noted with interest when Fernando had driven alone into Yarumal, he had taken Carrera 19 into town. And since then, they had noted the identity of over twelve vehicles that had entered Yarumal after him.

It was about 5.30pm, almost a full one hour after Fernando was timed in, that an obviously troubled massive NH&E truck had lumbered into the first petrol station in a cloud of smoke. Some of them had strolled over to pick up any information that might be useful to Senor Vasco de Zappata that pays them monthly. They noted with disinterest the two blacks and a Latino who had totally ignored them and set about trying to find professional help to resurrect their temporarily grounded vehicle. The curious informants did not share their optimism to depart for Medellin that same evening.

The mechanic that was summoned, after inspecting the engine had passed the grim verdict that work could be completed at about noon the next day. They were still standing around the open bonnet when they head the unmistakable sound of an approaching helicopter. They all looked up to see the helicopter with blinking lights actually heading towards them from the setting sun. The mechanic and the other curious locals dispersed from them immediately. The helicopter banked to the South and completed a full circle, hovered overhead to land. DaCosta who was an ardent fan of *Igor Sikorsky* could tell that it was a Sikorsky S-62A that had been refurbished. It was not a small helicopter, because it could accommodate up to eleven passengers.

It was then DaCosta noticed that an open area about 250 feet away, adjourning their petrol station was cordoned off by fierce looking men wielding AK47s. The piece of land free of any structure sloped and settled out in a tableland that was skirted by rocky boulders and tall grasses before dropping steeply downhill. There was an area about the size of half a lawn tennis court that was cast in grey concrete marked with a bold white circle in the center. DaCosta noted that the space was more than ample to contain the Sikorsky S-62A with its wingspan. He was so elated about the scenario that was playing out before his eyes, that he almost forgot the camera.

As the pilot steadied his aim for the center of the white circle, a convoy of two limousines and two other cars with darkened windows pulled into the area, staying clear safe distance from the marked spot. And as the dust thickened with the helicopters descent, DaCosta quickly slipped into the cabin and picked up the very reliable Canon EOS 650 SLR with its fitted long range lens and taking very strategic shots. The locals continued to go about their businesses without showing any visible interest on the helicopter and its occupants. The first persons to step down from the helicopter was Mrs Bacata and her three teenage sons. Then followed two aides who all filed into the vehicles.

Where was Bacata? Just when DaCosta made to lower his camera, he came bounding down from the aircraft, and quickly dashed into the second limosine. He was wearing a flowery Bermuda beach wear with a brown fedora perched stylishly on his red mane of hair. He was a very huge man; nearly six feet six inches, and weighed over 200 kilograms, just like his DEA dossier stated. DaCosta squeezed in as many shots as possible, before the convoy of vehicles headed across the road into town.

Much later, before the sun finally settled in for the night, DaCosta used the binoculars from the safety of his cabin to survey the vicinity of the helicopter and its guards. There were exactly six of the armed guards left behind to watch over the aircraft. It was obvious from their postures that they had never experienced any mishap in the past, so to them it was one easy duty to relax and enjoy themselves. Before the shops closed, one of them rode off on a motor-bike and returned shortly with some packs of Pilsner.

While Espindola and Deleon were busy tinkering with the engine outside, DaCosta continued to monitor the helicopter and the guards from within the cabin. They had descended on the beer, and consumed the 24 cans in record time. The same guard on motor-bike left again and returned with packs of food and more Pilsner. After their dinner, they now settled down to more Pilsner and some game of cards under the floodlights.

DaCosta and his colleagues also cleaned up later, strolled over to Carrera 20 to meet Fernando at his own little restaurant. He had feted them to some special Colombian delicacy and ample Spanish wines and rum. Unlike the guards with the helicopter, DaCosta and his boys did not over indulge because they had work that would need all their senses to be in peak condition, later that night. They had left Fernando's at about 11pm back to their truck, they had civilly turned down all of Fernando's entreats to spend the night at his lodgings or a decent guest house.

On their way back to the truck, they had perfected their plot. Two of them would continue to work on the engine through the night to distract attention from the one that would proceed to rig up the helicopter with C4 plastic explosives. Since they could not project Bacata's time of departure, DaCosta had swapped the detonator timers to altitude sensitive. DaCosta had chosen C4 as against the Semtex that they used back in Cali, because C4's composition of RDX and TNT and aluminium was deadlier.

As DaCosta and Deleon kept themselves busy with the engine for the benefit of any interested party, Espindola slipped into the cabin and changed into an all black sleeping gear, with rubber soled footwear. By then, Espindola gathered through the binoculars that all the six guards were crumpled out on the floor in different alcohol induced sleeping positions. With his equally black canvass hold- all slung over his shoulders he slipped out of the cabin and melted into the shadows towards the boulders and the tall grass behind the helicopters.

In exactly, fifteen minutes flat, he had completed planting the plastic explosives, and slipped back into the cab without even his colleagues knowing. That was how good Espindola was in his job. He was indeed an *Oracle* in the cloak and dagger business. It was not until he tapped three times on the windscreen, that they knew he was back, his mission done and dusted. They noisily and promptly gathered their gears together, and gratefully retired for the night tired and worn out. It has been a very long day, DaCosta yawned.

CHAPTER 67

The men slept soundly late into the morning. It was the soft tapping on the driver's door that had woken them. As they pulled apart the blinds, the bright morning sunlight flooded in, DaCosta's eyes first roved over to the helicopter that was reassuredly standing where it was the previous day. He looked out of the driver's window to find a young delivery man who had tapped at the door. He had brought them a basket of hefty breakfast from Miguel Fernando. DaCosta had gratefully collected the basket with his warm and sincere compliments to their host.

The combined scent of the finest grade Colombian coffee and scrambled eggs, within the cab had woken everyone up. And they could not resist the temptation to tackle the contents of the breakfast basket. By the time they finished their breakfast it was already 7am. It was bright and beautiful Thursday that promised to be sunny. Activities were warming around the petrol station, as some trucks were pulling out, a new set was taking their place. By the time the mechanic appeared a moment later, they were all down from the cabin.

It was exactly 7.45am, when a mini-van drove by the helicopter to discharge the pilot and his mate clad in white overalls. They were still discussing with the guards when Vasco de Zapata pulled in hurriedly with a squeal of tires. From his gesticulations, it could be inferred that there was need for urgency. The pilot and his mate had quickly belted themselves into their seats, earphones in place, and in a brief moment the GE CT58-110-1 turboshaft engine burst into life. The massive rotors with a wingspan of almost sixty-foot diameter, had just started rotating when the first of the convoy appeared by the side of the helicopter. DaCosta without raising any suspicion, quickly climbed back into the cabin, drew the blinds and took up his camera and began to snap.

Zapata recalled how all hell had broken loose this morning, when the big boss asked for Toni Alvadi, that led the mission to kidnap Miguel Fernando was told, that the 4-man team had not returned, though Fernando was back in town, and going about his business. The Big Boss had made just one call, that set the alarm bells ringing. People who were still in bed were pulled out and put on the run as if the house was on fire.

The two aides of the previous day had boarded the helicopter first with the three young boys who were in their pyjamas. Then from the first limousine had emerge Mrs. Bacata with hair in rollers, followed by her parents-in-law who were hand lifted by two hefty goons into the aircraft. The second limousine delayed a little to make sure all was set before the occupant stepped out unhurriedly, with an Havana cigar clamped in his mouth. It was as if he was not part of the mad urgency he had put everyone through. Ramirez Castro Bacata was surprisingly still in the Bermuda beach wear that he had on the previous day. He paused to drop his half-smoked Havana cigar on the concrete, which he also crushed with his right foot. DaCosta zoomed in and caught Bacata's every move on camera. He zoomed in on the left hand middle finger with the trademark massive raw diamond ring.

From a nod from Bacata, Zapata who had stood by personally closed the doors from the outside, and quickly moved away, consciously bent over from the swirling helicopter blades that were raising so much dust. Vasco de Zapata was a very worried man, because his neck was on the line. The music of the engine to a trained ear changed to signify that the blades have been angled to achieve lift and propulsion. The Igor Sikorsky invention indeed rose to the occasion, as it heaved and rose a few feet, then paused, suspended skillfully in mid-air, before rising in one fell swoop into the crisp morning air. *Nothing happened...*

All heads down below, curiously strained their necks to follow the progression of the Sikorsky S-62A as it banked to the North, and gained altitude to clear the immediate mountain range. DaCosta kept the lens of the camera trained on the rising aircraft and silently counting. Then he lost count; and alarm suddenly replaced his elation. Something must have gone wrong; maybe be Espindola did not get it right? Maybe the plastic explosives had expired? Maybe it was... then there was a bright blinding flash from the helicopter, followed by a loud deafening massive explosion that drowned for a split brief moment every noise down below. The helicopter and its eleven occupants became one gargantuan pyrotechnic display. The resultant fireball shredded into a million tiny bits of fire and smoke spewed gratefully over the uninhabited mountainside. It was like time and everything froze and stood still, for the tragic spectacle of carnage that had just happened before their very eyes.

DaCosta was not excited. He was all of sudden totally drained and empty. He had sort vengeance with all his heart and might for a very long time, but now that it has been fulfilled, it was not sweet. It left a sour taste in his mouth. What made him different from Bacata and the rest of them? Would the children of the innocent bystanders like the pilot, his mate, and the two aides, also go in search of him to destroy him to avenge them? It was all a mad cycle of a world that was blinded by rage to settle scores; eye for an eye, and a pound of flesh for a pound. And he was not just an innocent bystander, he was also part of the madness. He could feel his emotions running wild, clashing, and counter clashing. It was the moment of truth for those who live by killing or be killed…

He could not help or stop the tears that flowed uncontrollably down his cheeks. The tears flowed for all the innocent bystanders. Those young children, that would never taste parenthood, the older generations who were not given the choice to die peacefully in their sleep at a ripe old age. He wept and wept with an aching heart. He was still weeping when his colleagues found him. It was time to go home. Time to go home to what was left of a once happy larger family full of love and kindness. Yes, it was time to return home. His mission had been accomplished.

CHAPTER 68

It was Christmas of 1988. *Bogota, Colombia, and Cristobal DaCosta* did not just sound thousands of kilometers away; but was exactly 3,800 kilometers away, as Chuck Freeborn IV sat at dinner with Amos Alexander, his mentor and friend, in Washington DC, the capital of the United States of America that evening. They had chosen the very reserved and secluded *Top Notches*, a highbrow restaurant on Wisconsin Avenue, Georgetown, that was preferred by the diplomats and the eggheads at the capitol. Mr. Alex had specifically flown in from Seattle, which was now his base, to be part of this special dinner, their first since his return from Colombia.

With the right ambiance created by digitalized soft and dim lights with a therapeutic theme, coupled with the classical music filtering overhead from hidden speakers, even the tamed sound of solid silver cutlery clashing against the very finest of crockery was in harmony with the almost whispered muffled voices of the patrons. It was behind this din and the backdrop of the healing properties of the almost silent splashing waters of an indoor rocky waterfall; Mr. Alex sat attentively to hear out the adventures of his protégée after the superb dinner that would cost an arm and a leg.

Chuck and his team had returned to Bogota later that very fateful day, to find the tragic news of the Bacata Helicopter Crash on every television channel. There was a video shot of all that was left of the Sikorsky S-62A; a pathetic still smoldering distinguishable GE engine with its boldly engraved engine number. There were various file shots of Ramirez Castro Bacata, and shots of the small town of Yarumal where the accident had happened. The video clip shown on the various television channels were all similar. This Chuck had found very unsettling; it was as if it was a sponsored news item. And knowing the Medellin cartel, it could be their handiwork for various obvious reasons to drum up sympathies against the *puppet* Colombian Government and the *big bully* United States in the purported war against Colombians and their *legal* businesses.

The White House had waited to confirm from him before its poignant press release. A junior White House spokesperson was saddled with the responsibility to a smidgen of White House correspondents; *...the White House has confirmed today, the sad and tragic death of Ramirez Castro Bacata with his entire family in an air mishap. As sad as it is, we cannot but believe that his tragic death is a significant progress in the war against the most dreaded and deadly Colombian drug lords. The United States government had been trying to extradite him to the US to answer to many drug related killings, like the 1980 Miami Vice Massacre that decimated three generations of a single family. The United States will not relent in its resolve to bring every drug lord to book for crimes against America, and the rest of the world...*

Though, the United States did not claim direct or indirect responsibility for the accident for obvious negative connotations, but the handwriting was clear on the wall. For those who were in the know, and could put *2 and 2 together,* they know the score. It was also a coded message to Pablo Escobar who had naturally stepped into the vacuum created by the exit of Bacata, that he was now in their sight.

Later that night, Washington had not just insisted, but made sure he was on the first available flight to Panama City the next morning. Pentagon had sent people to handle his debriefing over there in Panama City, and commenced the shedding of his **Cristobal DaCosta skin,** and molding back into Chuck Freeborn IV. He had finally arrived back to a hero's welcome in Washington. The post of Deputy Director was specifically created to reward him, then a dinner at the White House with the president, who took the opportunity to decorate him with the Union Star of Bravery. The president was profuse in his praises and appreciation on behalf of the citizens of the United States of America, for the ultimate prize paid by his family.

The DEA on its own, had taken possession of the three rolls of film that recorded the last 24 hours of the inglorious life of Bacata. He was granted the accumulated leave for the entire period he was in Colombia. He was expected to resume work on January 24, 1989, in London, England, as the Deputy Director in-charge of Europe and Asia. He was also given the choice to take his family along on the new posting, which was considered as part of the little perks in his new capacity.

It was during the debriefing he had learnt of the mystery of Fabrice Deleon and Fabrice Leonceto. He was reliably informed that Leonceto was replaced with Deleon to preserve and protect the subject in his new department at the Pentagon. The whole idea was to sever the *Cuban factor*. He was informed too that Deleon was actually now a kind of ambassador plenipotentiary, or ambassador- at-large for the United States in his very special field work.

For his bespectacled mentor and friend, Chuck could not but compliment that he was really aging gracefully. Despite the success of the world acclaimed book, and its attendant distractions from various litigants, he had spiritedly kept his head above the waters.

"Chuck BTW, my man, I have learnt to just take things one step at a time." He answered in his very confident voice as he adjusted his very thick spectacles.

"So what is in the pipeline now, Mr. Alex?"

"Couple of books on the line, and a Scholarship Fund that I hold dear to my heart."

"Is it for the promotion of the black community?"

"No, not particularly for race, gender, or creed. It was designed on the basis of economic inadequacies. To support eight indigent candidates financially through freshman year to graduate school every year." The older man paused to sip from his goblet of wine.

"Wow! That is something, every black man must be proud to associate with. It is a way you are keeping Martin Luther King's Dream alive. Well done sir."

"You are right, BTW. I felt very bad that Dukakis did not pick Reverend Jesse Jackson as his vice. It was not fair."

"You were not alone, I felt the same way too. Who knows, maybe that was why the cookies crumbled." They all burst into laughter, as one or two patrons stepped by to greet one of the world's greatest black men alive.

"I think Vice President Bush will deliver on age-long American values, he had promised to continue from where President Reagan stopped." The older man resumed their conversation.

"Yes, I believe him. I met him during our dinner at the White House. He sounded very sincere to me. He had confided in me that the war on drugs must continue, or else our tomorrow would be ruined. He was down to earth. He actually said to me, that America need *Oracles* like me. I was really touched by his down to earth nature."

"Down to earth? He is a true officer and a gentleman. Didn't you hear what he said when the November 8th Election results came through?"

"No, sir, I did not." Chuck was all ears.

"He said, *The people have spoken.*" They both burst into good natured laughter again. It was very clear to anyone watching that the two men had so much in common, and respect for each other, something mysteriously deeper than chemistry and color.

"So you are off to London, immediately after the presidential inauguration?"

"Yes, sir." Chuck answered with military precision.

"Good. Now you listen to me very well." The older man pushed aside the empty glass of wine in front of him.

Now you listen to me very well …those words sounded very familiar. His brain went into overdrive to process the deepest recesses of his memory. Yes, The same words… the same words his great-grandfather used when he commenced his final speech to him as a teenager. He was shocked and baffled; he did not know what to say, so he just nodded as the older man clasped his hands in his very warm hands.

"Chuck Freeborn IV, you are destined for greater things. That, I am convinced beyond doubt. And do not forget that you have a special pedigree, that nobody can deny you of. Always remember as you deal with people that somebody infinitely supreme and divine is guiding you. You do not walk alone. Do not fear man more than God. I am convinced beyond any doubt that the best is yet to come. Go and serve your country my boy, but always remember that you are citizen of this world, so fight evil in any guise, creed, race, or color. Be bold to speak out in the face of tyranny or oppression. Do not forget that there is a part of BTW inside you. May your road be truly rough and tumble my boy. Go…go…go my boy all your folks are routing and watching out for you." Mr. Alex finally stopped his monologue.

Chuck could see that the older man truly looked relieved for pouring out his mind. For Chuck, he was so thankful to God for bringing this genteel great man into his life. He had so much to say, but could not say them. With his owlish spectacles and splashes of grey hair, he really looked as if he carried the world's entire wisdom. No wonder that his tomes were a testimonial to his wanton prowess. He took a sip from his snifter of brandy, looked around the room that had just three other patrons left.

"Mr. Alex you are all that I have left from my past. I want to just thank you for always being there for me. I don't want anything to happen to you. You are now my father and mother, and my sisters. I promise you I shall not let you down. Never!"

CHAPTER 69

Chuck Freeborn IV and his family arrived London, on a very cold and damp January wintry morning. His DEA people were at Gatwick to pick them up, and settle them down. They were to lodge at the Park Lane Hilton for a week before they could move into his official residence at Regent's Park. It was his first visit to London, England, so it was not just the boys that were excited. They had taken the first two days to acclimatize. Arrangements for the teenage boys' education had all been sorted out.

On his first day at work, at the US Embassy at Grosvenor Square, he had convened a general meeting of his entire staff in London. After the customary pleasantries, he had set them in motion reviewing their goals and targets.

"We must not just chase the drugs, we must be resolved to apprehend those who are responsible for importing them and distributing them." He paused to open a red folder in front of him. "I must emphasize the administration's desire to have all of us safely protected from danger. Do not forget that as we make it our business to put the drug people out of business, it is also their burning desire to do away with us ruthlessly for good. *A dead agent is of no good to anybody*; so be alert to always stay alive." The group chuckled nervously.

"We must distance ourselves from any guise to compromise your position and the DEA's. Anyone directly or indirectly involved in hard drug trafficking, is trafficking more than dangerous drugs, they are agents of pain, sorrow, and even death. So do not soil your hands no matter the prize. We know that the drugs from South American enter Europe indirectly; they must pass them through the Caribbean nations not to arouse suspicion. The same thing with the heroin from

Afghanistan or Vietnam, that is better brought through the land route. For that reason we must increase our surveillance on legal truck cargos of vegetables and fruits into England from the continental shelf. We must not only counter but stay two steps ahead of them." He smiled at the figurative language that he had used.

"With every operation we must measure our level of success by finding out how much we have impacted negatively the supply of the drug into the UK or the continent. The quality or purity of the cocaine on the street is related to whether demand is meeting up with supply. If supply is short, the gangs that distribute would resort to cutting the drug with some other material to give it quantity mileage." He took a brief moment to study the folder again.

"We can improve on the report before me. Ninety percent of arrests and convictions here," he emphatically slapped the folder, "are just minions and small frees in the business. We must pull in a big one very soon or heads will roll. Maybe some of us maybe on the flight home very soon; if we don't kick asses soon, and not just any ass, but some god forsaken almighty drug lord ass." He frowned to drive home his subtle threat. His listeners, who were all aware of his antecedents, knew that the Deputy Director meant every word that came out of his mouth.

"The big fishes in the business are not ghosts, but flesh and blood that lives within our communities. The huge blood money profits are cursed so they cannot hide for long. Yes! They are bound to expose themselves by their lavish lifestyles with posh suburban mansions complemented by an array of classic luxury *toys*. They leave big. They party big. They spend big. In fact they are too big to hide. When you leave here, I want results. Sniff around like the blood hounds that you are, we must get on their trails. Can we do it?" It was the ideal climax for his inaugural meeting.

"Yes, we can" they all roared in unison.

"Then let's go guys. Just remember that there is *no retreat, no surrender in this war against drugs.* Come on guys, let's get ready to roll." Chuck himself started the clapping, and before long everybody in that room was clapping and high-fiving. Every war general from Winston Churchill to Adolf Hitler, from Eisenhower to Chaka the Zulu, all had their exclusive styles to psyche their armies into battle to kill or to be killed. Chuck Freeborn IV, the great grandson of Chukwuma, son of Akachukwu Onyeobia of Amaeke Ohaofia, had the unique black blood of time-tested warriors flowing in his veins.

That same day the Deputy Director had made courtesy calls at the various headquarters of the three police forces that police Greater

London. He had commenced first with the Metropolitan Police, then to the City of London Police, before ending the day at the British Transport Police. He had both acquainted and asked for their support in various magnitudes to apprehend the drug lords and their couriers. The heads had promised their unconditional supports and resolve to clear their city of every vermin of drugs.

The next day, he had converged all DEA agents stationed in every major city in Europe and Asia in his office, for a 5-hour brainstorming session that was very fulfilling to the convener as well as the convened. It was like utilizing a massive dragnet to clear their territories of every visible iota of drugs and its dealers.

In the rest of the days of January, Chuck Freeborn IV, would go the extra lengths on his own to know London and its 33 boroughs. He communed like any one of the over ten million human beings that live in London. He had like made a pilgrimage to the Roman Wall that was still standing as a legacy to its Roman founders. He had on his own, without his family, taken guided tours of almost every tourist attraction. He had tried to build some form of spiritual connections with the most visited city in the whole world.

He was very fascinated with the famous London Underground, which is the oldest railway network in the world. His uncountable rides underground was like feeling the pulse of the heart of London, and discovering and familiarizing with all its innards. It was like a physician and patient confidential relationship, very intimate and yet not too close. He had taken pains to study and identify the numerous graffitis as the distinct primordial instinct of mammals that mark and map out their sacred territories with feces or urine. Chuck could tell with clarity, bordering on some form of inhumane prowess, the various gangs and their sacred territories from over ground and underground. He went so far to consciously identify and document their trademark tattoos. He was able to systematically classify the gangs in their main divisions of; religion, racial, commercial, and criminal. And that was how he was able to zero into those that were drug gangs with a modicum of forensic expertise.

It was after he was satisfied with knowledge and prowess of London that he finally scheduled a courtesy visit to the mayor of London. He remembered very well the day, it was March 7, 1989, the day Iran broke off diplomatic ties with the United Kingdom over Salmon Rushdie's explosive tome, *The Satanic Verses*. It was in the middle of their discussions that the mayor was hurriedly summoned over to Number 10

Downing Street, to be part of a meeting that was to fashion out some form of diplomatic counter measures to balance events and their reactions, as they unfold in the diplomatic circle.

It was not until May 24, 1989, Freeborn IV met the ebullient mayor again, but in very unsavory circumstances. The DEA had in conjunction with the London Metropolitan Police had after reasonable surveillance, stormed a place in Heath Town on suspected drugs business. To the police's greatest surprise they were surrounded by riotous mob of over 500, welding missiles and Molotov cocktails demanding for their heads and blood in broad daylight.

The matter had gotten out of hand and had required the timely intervention of the elite swat team. The DEA deputy director, and other very top ranking brass of the police force were immediately as a matter of urgency summoned over to the trouble spot. The mayor of London also came over to Heath Town, to see things for himself. It was not until the situation was brought under control, that Chuck stepped forward to greet the mayor who was already on his way.

"Mr. Freeborn, I presume." The honorable mayor uttered to him rhetorically.

"Yes, Mr Mayor, you have a most wonderful sharp memory." Freeborn answered, stretching forth his hand for a very firm handshake.

"Thank you Mr. Freeborn, now I am convinced that with your cooperation, we will put every drug trader under lock and key."

"Mr. Mayor sir, it will be just a matter of time." Chuck retorted with a burst of laughter.

"Thank you Mr. Deputy Director, the City of London truly appreciate you and your men." And he added as a parting shot, "You are welcome to London." as he gratefully dropped into the back seat of the black chauffeured Rover, that hastily drove away from the crime scene.

CHAPTER 70

Within seven months of his arrival in London, England, Chuck Freeborn was convinced that he was latched on to a truly big fish. *All the signs were clear.* The overwhelming excitement from within that tend to bubble and overflow, to make the heart feel lighter. The thrill of the fisherman when the line draws taut and vibrates in his hands to indicate that something had taken the bite. That thrill and feeling deep within the guts when the hunter sights the game in his crossbow, before letting go of the arrow. He knew that he must resort to the clinical precision of his African ancestral roots to reel him in this big catch.

He had sat with Duncan Bronco, his chief of operations, to personally filter and analyze every information and report from his agents. There were couple of wild geese chases, and a couple that were too speculative, yet their trails had run cold in the preliminary investigations. There was a niggling report that hinted of a steady downward trend in the street price for the top quality of cocaine over the past ten months all over England. The DEA analysts had overwhelmingly agreed that there was definitely a new source that was flooding the market with high grade cocaine, from all indications..

There had been a couple of very successful raids, since the Heath Town botched operations. The joint DEA and the police counter operations in both Liverpool and Glasgow was a huge success. There were arrests that had led to conviction in the court of law. The DEA had confiscated a large cache of information from the three operations. The phone logs of the key characters was astounding; while their filofaxes contained a long lists of coded names and numbers. It did not take long for both the DEA analysts and Scotland Yard to break the amateurish codes. The names and numbers belonged to their patrons and key suppliers.

One particular mystery telephone number was like a recurring decimal point in London, Liverpool, and Glasgow. In no time it was traced to an address in a highbrow London neighborhood. The telephone number was registered under the name of Oscar Uromi, a shady businessman with a record of brushes with the law.

Twenty-four hours later, the DEA had gotten all the official approvals with the help of Scotland Yard and the MI5. The deputy director had officially contacted the CIA to roll in any iota of information on Oscar Uromi, 28, a Nigerian-born British citizen. It was on August 31, 1989, the day Buckingham Palace officially confirmed the separation of The Princess Royal and her husband of sixteen years, that the DEA officially placed Oscar Uromi under surveillance and covert investigation.

On that very day, Oscar Uromi, a director of the South African diamond company, *Twinkle & Twinkle*, was seated in the boardroom of the corporate headquarters of the Miss Cosmos Pageant, on 21 Golden Square, London. The massive boardroom was filled to the brim with pressmen; the flood of klieg lights of different television channels was already causing some form of distraction and discomfort. The claim, that the Miss Cosmos was the most publicized contest in the world was self-evident to all and sundry.

Though, Twinkle & Twinkle had for the past two editions, sponsored the Miss Cosmos Contest, signing of the Memorandum of Understanding was just a formality to publicize the year's forthcoming events. Uromi, resplendent in a complete-white-ensemble handmade suit from the famous Saville Row, was leading the *Twinkle & Twinkle* delegation to formally sign the contract for the sponsorship of the 1990 Miss Cosmos. He sat there mesmerized by the array of microphones sitting in front of him to pick every word that would proceed forth from his mouth. He had been duly informed that the cameras would start to roll in another three minutes. The whole world would be listening to him, him Oscar Uromi. He was sitting between the current Miss Cosmos, and the president of the Miss Cosmos Pageant. He had come a long way from the back streets of Lagos, Nigeria. He would need to pinch himself to be sure if it was not just a dream, he thought to himself.

He never had or knew the taste and feel of a father. He was born on Nigeria's Independence Day in 1960, his mother had told him, and added to good measure that his birth was *purely an accident of her foolish teenage infatuation and not love*. His father whom she knew only by his first name *Uzo*, an Ibo of the Eastern region of Nigeria, had disappeared into thin air, the day after he was informed that she was pregnant. When the pregnancy could not be hidden anymore, and the news broke; she was out rightly ostracized and disowned by her father, Deacon Matthew Uromi, a very strict Christian from the Mid-West region, to save face from his wayward daughter.

She was later accepted by the Apostolic Sisters of Saint Paul's Catholic Church, Lagos, who took care of her until she gave birth to a bouncing baby boy with an odd sixth finger on each hand, that was *stringed off* at birth. This *sixth finger*, his mother had told him, was all that he bequeathed from his *devil* of a father. Not even the name of his father did he possess; for the Apostolic Sisters proudly named him Onesimus Casmir Uromi. Right from the moment he could utter his first words, the young man vehemently protested those names. *Oscar* was a skillful coinage of his first and middle names which he wholly adopted in the high school. The young Oscar grew up aware of his mother's bitterness towards his father, to really understand the term; *the fury of a woman scorned*.

He had from an early age learnt to fend for himself, growing up in the city of Lagos with a single mother and no relatives. It was the January 15, 1966 military coup by mostly young Ibo officers that ushered Chief Tajudeen Adeyemi Osogbo into their drab lives. Chief Osogbo, a Yoruba from Nigeria's Western region was a very successful textile merchant, who was involved in an accident in the heat of the coup, and would have died if not for Helen Uromi's angelic intervention and nursing skills.

Chief Osogbo out of gratitude had gradually warmed his way into Helen Uromi's heart, and made her at first a concubine. By July 1966, when the retaliatory coup of mostly military officers of Northern extraction took place Helen Uromi was already pregnant for Chief Osogbo, who predictably elevated her to become wife number five. Chief Osogbo, a Muslim with strict disciplinarian upbringing had over twenty children, which was typical of a polygamous home. The man ruled over his household of wives, children, and extended family with high handedness; he did not spare the rod for any erring member of the household.

Transforming from his simple and uncomplicated lifestyle of living with a single mother to the hustle and bustle of a polygamous household, was better imagined, than experienced. Just as the wives fought for the love and attention of one husband, the army of children harried and fought over everything from meals, sleeping space, bathrooms and household chores. It was a case of survival of the fittest; every activity was done under pressure and rush. This was because the whole family was housed under one roof; and it was the apt atmosphere for wrangling and petty jealousies.

Oscar Uromi, was never welcomed fully into that household, he was daily reminded that he was a total stranger in that house. He hated every moment that he spent in that household, and wanted to escape from its stifling shackles as soon as possible. After series of pogroms in Northern Nigeria, the Eastern Region had no choice but to secede to become the Republic of Biafra. It was on July 6, 1967, when war was declared to Keep Nigeria One, that Helen Uromi lost the baby under very mysterious circumstances. All efforts to get pregnant again did not yield fruit, for Helen Uromi

As the Nigerian Civil War raged on in the East, the Ibos in Lagos were either arrested or killed. Oscar was strongly advised not to ever mention that he was a descendant of an Ibo. Though, that was not necessary since the other wives and their children on the slightest provocation would taunt Oscar by calling him *Omo Ibo*; which was totally disparaging to say the least, even though it simply means Ibo boy in Yoruba. Throughout the period of the Nigerian Civil War that finally ended on January 10, 1970, mother and son lived in constant fear and threat of exposure.

There were two features Oscar inherited from his father, his mother would not openly admit for obvious reason. Oscar's outstanding intelligence and handsomeness were also traits that he inherited from his *fugitive* father. At least these were consolation and hope for his mother. Due to the double promotion that he won couple of times, Oscar only spent four years in elementary school before proceeding to the elite King's College, Lagos with a government scholarship at just 11years, to keep him ahead of all his peers.

Everything went smoothly for Oscar, in all the years that he spent at King's College. Since his mother, Helen had remained Chief Osogbo's favorite wife, he never lacked for anything. His mother had always confided in him that, her biggest regret was that she did not have a surviving child for Chief Osogbo. As it was destined to be, tragedy struck at the end of his final year. After his final examination, he had returned home to hear that his mother whom had visited him the Sunday before the examination started just slumped and died. She was buried later in the evening according to Muslim rights. His heart-broken stepfather had told him that, since he was in the heat of his final examination, not to inform him.

He was dumbfounded and frozen stiff with fear. He just could not believe what he was hearing. His mother dead…it was the end of the world for him. There would be nobody to turn to. Without his mother, he had no place in Chief Osogbo's household. He was just alone, with nobody to turn to in the whole wide world. The world had dealt him a callous painful blow. He was not too young to understand, he was sixteen years old. He did not cry. Neither did he weep. He just knew that the whole world had just let him down, and learnt to be cold and calculative. He was totally drained of every atom of emotion. Oscar Uromi started his journey of survival. A journey to become one of the world's coldest and most heartless smooth operators.

"Distinguished guests, ladies and gentlemen. May I have your attention please?" The amplified voice of the president of the Miss Cosmos Pageant emanating from monstrous speakers shook him awake from his reverie. "Welcome to the 1990 Miss Cosmos Contest signing of Memorandum of Understanding with our key and major sponsor and partner, Twinkle & Twinkle. Our friends are reliably represented here today by the always dashing, Mr. Oscar Uromi." As he began to clap cheerfully to cue the whole hall to a resounding applause.

Oscar smiled and rose to his full intimidating height of 6feet and 8inches, bowed and waved to the cheering crowd, knowing the effect of his electric persona on the opposite sex who were carried away in the frenzy. He tried to look uncomfortable and embarrassed by the unusual attention, though he was enjoying every moment of it. He enjoyed to be the cynosure of all eyes in any event.

When finally, it got to his turn to address the world press, his dramatic skills and eloquence came to the fore. He had learnt over the years to develop a façade of enigma, by being extra temporary explosive without allusions; and to make his audience always yearn for more of him. His richly deep and rare voice was music to his audience; and he knew when to stop just before the climax to make them hanker and pander to his every whim and caprice.

"Your Majesty…our Miss Cosmos, ladies and gentlemen, once again Twinkle & Twinkle is committed to make the world's most beautiful women to glitter, because they deserve the best diamonds. Twinkle & Twinkle cannot but remain committed to see that they travel the world in comfort and in class. I know that this is not a speech making occasion, so let the show begin. Thank you Miss Cosmos Pageant for considering us to be a worthy partner. Thank you." That was vintage Oscar Uromi, articulate but always very brief and concise. The audience rose in unison and applauded for more, but that, they would not get from Oscar. For Oscar Uromi had returned to his shell timely.

CHAPTER 71

At that very moment that Thursday, when Oscar Uromi was addressing the World Press at 21, Golden Square, London another very special event was unfolding at the Court of St. James's, less than a mile away as the crow flies. The newly appointed Nigeria's High Commissioner to the Court *of* St. James' was about to present to her Majesty Queen Elizabeth II his Letter of Credence. This brief but very important formal ceremony was to give the new envoy and suite a formal reception and audience with The Queen in her official courts.

The day had began from the Nigeria High Commission at 9, Northumberland Avenue, just a breath away from Trafalgar Square, when two traditional red colored State landaus, all impressively dating back before 1872, and each pulled by two well-groomed thoroughbreds from the Royal Mews, had picked up Ambassador Daniel Onochie Aka and his suite, for the traditional ride to Buckingham Palace via The Mall. The official escort for the event was the Marshall of the Diplomatic Corps who had donned a traditional full regalia with a hat and plumes to match. The Marshall of the Diplomatic Corps who acts as the link between the British monarch and foreign diplomatic missions who was permanently based at St. James' rode in the first carriage with the High Commissioner and his only child and daughter.

There was still summer in the air, as the sun shone brightly from a cloudless light blue skies over London that morning, as they rolled along the royal stretch of The mall. It was a most memorable day for father and daughter who were proudly attired in a richly- finished Yoruba *aso-oke* in Nigeria's solid colors of green and white. The usual crowd of multifaceted brood of tourists who had just finished watching the daily traditional parade waved excitedly and took pictures of the State landaus and their occupants as they rolled into Buckingham Palace.

Ambassador Daniel Aka was a man that paid attention to detail; and could not miss the delicate balance of almost *German* precision and English orderliness at Buckingham Palace that morning as compared to their earlier visit. Earlier to the set date for the presentation of credentials at St. James' Palace, they had been invited over to the palace to receive practical instructions and the expected protocols to be observed. The Marshall of the Diplomatic Corps had led his charges through gilded golden corridors with the most beautiful plush carpets, with walls that were adorned with massive priceless masterpieces, to wait in an ante-chamber. The High Commissioner from Singapore was scheduled ahead of them in the presentation of credentials.

They were all speechless, totally intimidated and mesmerized by the surrounding opulence of the British Monarchy. The silkiest lace blinds with very elaborate embroidery combining with the most exotic velvety curtains cascading down from high up alcoves to shimmering floors with glazed tiles. The glitzy ornate ceilings where giant artworks in sheer splendor with a hint of gold or polished brass with exquisite quality. Hanging down overhead in the middle of the chamber was the largest magnificent crystal chandelier Margret Hilda had ever seen in her 24 years of life. The very impressive furniture were the top of the range of British heritage dating and cutting across various eras. Living here would be like living in a treasure trove as witnessed only in an *Arabian Nights* tale.

As Ambassador Daniel Onochie Aka grateful sank into his delightful neoclassical chair, he could not but reflect on how far he had come from his little tidy village smack in the thick of the tropical African jungle. His Amaeke Ohafia even with the arrival of modern civilization was a far cry from this paradise on earth. They had about 20 minutes to wait and *catch their breath*. He closed his eyes, took a deep breath, and went into reminiscence.

He was born a day after the death of his great-grandfather Chukwukadibia, the direct and only surviving son of the legendary Akachukwu with twelve solid digits. That was why he was aptly named *Onochie*, he has been replaced. It was believed and accepted in their primordial tradition that he was indeed the reincarnation of the dead great-grandfather, who had returned back to his homestead. And true to type from very rare surviving photographs of the patriarch; Onochie had the most uncanny resemblance to the grainy images. The other resemblance was of course the recurring sixth finger syndrome in all *Akachukwu* descendants, which had over time officially become the burden of proof for his numerous offspring.

His naming ceremony was delayed, and fixed twenty days after the elaborate traditional burial rites and customs of his famous progenitor. It was then, he was given the name Onochie. The avalanche of the wishes and prayers on that day, were that Onochie should attain and surpass the achievements of his forefathers. The naming of an African child is an arduous task on its own, for the chosen name was not only history, it also reflects the hopes and aspirations of the child's immediate environment. For Onochie, right from that day a standard was set for him to maintain or beat.

For his own father Obidi, and his sibling Ikechukwu, were the only sons of Chima who was one of Chukwukadibia's two sons. Chima's only sibling was Onyekachukwu, who had two sons Kalu and Nwoye. Nwoye fell to an illness as a teenager, while his brother Kalu, a very adventurous character died fighting as one of the native troops of the West African Frontier Force that fought beside the French troops to beat the German garrison in the Cameroons.

His father, Obidi was literate as he had attended the first mission school in Amaeke. It was him, that had provided his official birthday as 4th of July, 1925, when he Obidi was 25 years old. His only sibling, Azubuike arrived five years later. It was during baptism at the local church he was christened Daniel, while his brother was christened Adam. It was until he was about six years old that he was permitted to start school with the encouragement of his grandfather Chima. His brother, Azubuike who was not keen about school even started at eight, the year their cousin Uzoka, uncle Ikechukwu's only child was born.

With the advent of the World War II, Obidi and his brother had proudly left Amaeke, after leaving their wives and children in the care of their father Chima. They were part of the over 500,000 Africans that became the Royal West African Frontier Force, a military formation of British colonies of Sierra Leone, Nigeria, Gambia, and the Gold Coast. They saw real battle as men of the 81st and 82nd West African Divisions who displayed their war prowess in Burma, against the dreaded Japanese.

The Akachukwu Brothers were bold, fearless, and outstanding in every battle, and became very popular with their commanders and colleagues. It was as if fighting was in their blood. The British tactically spread the rumors that the African *troops were cannibals that make mince meat of their enemies and eat them*, to set real fear in the Japanese camps who were very ingenious in utilizing natural vegetation as camouflage.

By the end of their World War II campaigns, the dead and wounded numbered over ten thousand. Unfortunately, Sergeant Ikechukwu Akachukwu was also among the dead, he was not among the returnees who became the Burma boys, and went about with a swagger and war stories that got better and more daring by the day. Like the vampire-like blood sucking tiger leeches that are abound in the Burma jungles, that from a miserable pin size could suck human blood and expand to the size of a sausage. By the next time you hear the same story from the same Burma Boy, the leech would have been a match-size that expanded into a fist size with human blood. Then you would hear how he, the Burma Boy waded through a pool swarming with the blood-sucking leeches after a band of the dreaded Japanese and riddled them with hot bullets. Sometimes it was discovered that *certain* Burma Boys were mere odd jobbers like load carriers, cooks, messengers, and handy men.

Sergeant Major Obidi Akachukwu with a splendid meritorious service had returned from the World War II, and chosen to pursue a career in the colonial army and was stationed in Zaria. *Samanja*, within a short interval of time, the adulterated version of his rank had taken over his real name. He had visited Amaeke, as a hero, and taken Azubuike Adam, his second son, Uzoka, his late brother's son, and his wife back to his station in the Northern part of Nigeria. By then his son, Daniel Onochie who was so brilliant and outstanding at the famous and prestigious Christ the King College (CKC), Onitsha, had already gained admission into the most revered Oxford University, through a British Colonial Government scholarship. Daniel was already making waves in his studies and getting acquainted with the likes of Margret Hilda Roberts, in far away England.

At graduation, Daniel had officially shortened *Akachukwu* for *Aka* (which means finger or hand), and he was then easily and conveniently known as Daniel Aka. He not only lived up to the expectations of his benefactors, he carved his name into the annals of the world's most revered citadel of learning. Daniel Aka, carted home the most outstanding student award since the inception of the institution in the 12th century. Though there were various mouthwatering teaching offers from other universities, he decided to settle for the offer from Oxford University to teach, and study for a Doctorate degree.

He had gotten through with his doctorate degree in another round of flying colors, and fully settled down with his teaching career at Oxford University for good. His colleagues always teased him that all that was left to complete the picture was a fine lass to give his bachelor pad some warmth. It was sometime in 1964, that he met and fell in love with the pretty 22 year-old Halima Khalifa. Halima was the only child of Egypt's ambassador to the United Kingdom. She was a final year student in Political Science. Their relationship gradually developed into very intimate affair over a period of time, though he had visited with Halima at her parents Belgravia palatial home, neither him nor his host and hostess ever broached the topic of his interest in their daughter. Ambassador Khalifa who was also an erudite scholar, was always excited to have him visit for those exciting power-packed academic arguments and analysis late into the night.

It was on June 5th, 1965, Halima's birthday, when she had broken the news to him that she was pregnant. Daniel was overjoyed with the news, though he could see the obstacles ahead; they were from different cultural backgrounds, their basic religious backgrounds were as different as day and night. He had toyed with the idea of marriage to Halima, but it was inconclusive because of these factors amongst others. He had taken the matter up with the ambassador and his wife, who did not take kindly to the turnout of events. The ambassador not only lambasted him but called him a cradle thief for taking advantage of his young and innocent 22-year-old baby. They finally calmed down after much pleadings to give them their consents to them to marry.

Halima's bulging stomach, and other changing features did not go unnoticed for long. Before the tongues started wagging. They took the leap. They hurriedly arranged a very simple and private wedding at a little chapel on Magdalen Street. It was a select crowd of close friends and Halima's family in attendance. To the couple's greatest surprise, the news of the quiet wedding was carried in the tabloids in London. After the wedding the Daniel-Akas moved into a much larger and befitting accommodation there in Oxford, and Professor and Mrs Daniel-Aka gradually fitted into the social life of the academic community.

It was the week before Christmas and the Daniel-Akas were visiting with the Ambassador and his wife in London. About noon on that very chilly wintry day, the Khalifas were chauffeured over to the Egyptian Embassy for a function. It was about three hours later, the phone rang, and was answered by Halima. Things happened so fast that it was difficult to put the sequence of the events together again. Daniel just recalled how his then heavily pregnant wife just screamed and slumped, the ceramic handset crashed and shattered into a thousand pieces on the marble floor..

Daniel had dialed 999 with shaking hands, the next he remembered was the race across London in an ambulance. Then she was wheeled into one of the emergency labor rooms of St. Mary's Hospital, at Greycoat Place, London. She was accompanied by an anxious and nervous husband, and Margaret Hilda Thatcher, who rushed over to join them at the hospital. An hour later, a healthy premature baby girl was delivered through a cesarean section. The pretty little baby inside the incubator had a very fair complexion, that Daniel Aka for a moment panicked, his heartbeat rising in tempo. The baby did not look like she was fathered by a black man... not a trace of blackness was evident. Nobody, he thought was going to be fooled. He was going to be the laughing stock of his social communities.

"Impossible, this is unacceptable." Daniel Aka muttered under his breath, feeling like a drowning man.

He stole a quick furtive look around the Intensive Care Unit that was totally empty, with no tiny occupants in the four other idle incubators. His mind was in a whirlpool turmoil A frown crossed his face as he could not come to terms with reality that *his* Halima had another man in her life, that bordered on infidelity. He could feel the fury of betrayal welling up inside him like a rumbling extinct volcano about to erupt. He had murder in his mind; and that he was going to do. Just then, at the nick of time, the sleeping tiny tot inside the glass incubator opened her eyes and yawned. Daniel Aka who was about to lift up the glass incubator cover, froze as if he had been electrocuted. A tiny hand with a blue name tag stuffed her tiny fingers into her mouth and started to suck hungrily. And there in the soft full glare of the fluorescent bulbs, were five normal fingers, and a limp boneless *sixth finger* complete with a pink nail by the base of the small finger. Daniel Aka fell on his knees on the disinfectant coated tiled floor and wept his heart out. This little girl, whom he was about to murder, just a moment ago was a true descendant of Akachukwu Onyeobia, with the age-long indelible and irrefutable burden of proof. He was so ashamed of himself.

The amiable Ambassador Khalifa and his peaceful wife would never see or carry their first and only grandchild. For it was the news of their death that landed Halima in hospital. Their official embassy vehicle which had a bomb planted on it exploded in a big massive ball of fire, which decimated all the occupants in the car. It was a cold blooded murder, the world condemned in its entirety.

The toddler named Jane Margaret Hilda Daniel-Aka, was discharged only two days later, while Halima, her mother remained in the hospital for another one week. The doctors had told Daniel Aka that her pregnancy induced high blood pressure had refused to normalize. And had tried all means to counter it, but it had stubbornly refused to go down. The doctors' fear was that she might end up with resultant seizures that might be fatal. And Halima never fully recovered.

Exactly ten days after her discharge from the hospital, after almost three weeks in the hospital, Daniel Aka arrived home one afternoon to find his wife having multiple seizures. An ambulance arrived to convey Halima to hospital within a few minutes. She died on arrival at the hospital.

"His Excellency, Professor Daniel Aka, the High Commissioner of the Federal Republic of Nigeria…" he was shaken awake from his thoughts and ushered into the presence of Queen Elizabeth II, to present his credence.

CHAPTER 72

Later that evening, Oscar had one of those rare companies in his gilded quarters at the *Smooth Sail Cove*. He was hosting a former Miss Cosmos that was in London on a private trip. He had arranged a *full treatment* to really impress his guest. The full treatment which was calculated to really impress was a private dining ordered from the Mandarin Kitchen, one of London's finest Chinese cuisines, to serve him and his guest at home, complete with a team of waiters. Down in his basement which had been converted into a wine cellar, Oscar had a rare collection of vintage wines from all over the world.

Talking about rare collections Oscar Uromi, had gradually developed a keen interest for vintage things ranging from pretty women to cars; wines and watches to rare art collections. Collecting these rare items had gradually become an addiction and a weakness. Since money was not his problem he could go out of his way to possess a masterpiece or a very rare and exotic art forms at prices that most of his peers would consider as outrageous. He knew what he was doing, he may not have a fat and juicy bank account, but he on his own designed a perfect way to launder drugs and other illicit incomes. His total collections were in excess of over $200million. Oscar Uromi, worth over $200 million? Incredible! It also sounded surreal to him, considering his background and origin from the back streets of Lagos. He looked to be engrossed with his food but his mind wandered to his past to retrace his journey to the present.

After the news of his mother's demise, he had resolved to walk away from Chief Osogbo's household, without even a backward glance. There was no way that household would be home to him without his mother. So, it was more like good riddance to bad rubbish; after all he never liked that kind of family setting. He was able to hang around with friends who were more than willing to provide him with accommodation. He hung around with these friends for awhile until he was able to get a one-room apartment in Surulere, a medium-scale residential suburb of Lagos.

Oscar Uromi's handsome features and likeable persona stood him in good stead with the older womenfolk, especially the mischievous. He quickly learnt that with a flattering tongue he could effortlessly parasite on the rich middle-aged widows and divorcees looking for a good time. These ladies were usually tagged *High Society Ladies,* they flaunted openly their toy-boys to arouse the anger of their ex-husbands. For some of these women in their 60's, it was a psychological victory to be seen romping around with virile young boys who were sometimes younger than their own sons. As many of them were wont to recklessly declare, *that a virile young blood is bound to make the old lady happier and younger.*

Oscar did not really experience any difficulty eking out a decent living out of the gullible morally bankrupt dregs of the society. Within a year of his mother's death, Oscar got his first break into the big league. He had looked forward to the day he would meet a *sugar mummy* to take him abroad. With this expectation he acquired for himself a Nigerian passport under a false name, and safely tucked it away, hoping and waiting for a breakthrough.

It was through one of these high society ladies, popularly called *Cash madam,* that he met *Auntie Brixton,* at the 50th birthday party of *Madam Gold,* a known dealer in jewelry and prominent Lagos socialite. *Auntie Brixton,* who was said to be a top flight business woman in London, had all the trimmings of the jet-sets. They were all seated on the same table which had over 16 guests, Oscar noticed that she could not take her eyes off him. He could decipher the fire in her eyes. Over time he had come to decode the signs of ordinary platonic interest from the raw animal sensual desire. With a kind of basic animal instinct he could feel and smell a female admirer in heat. The more Cash Madam flirted openly with him, to deter her, the more she came stronger. An opportunity opened when 'cash madam' was at the bandstand to acknowledge their praise singing.

Auntie Brixton had her complimentary card ready, with her hotel room number at the Lagos Sheraton and Towers scribbled on the back. Before the possessive Cash madam could rush back, they had an appointment fixed for the next day. Thereafter Auntie Brixton left the party with an older man, who was a renowned millionaire.

The next day, Oscar had the courtesy of calling Auntie Brixton before he showed up at hotel room. She was so impressed with him. Oscar himself took extra care to treat her specially. He was at his best, always teasing and pampering. She just could not have enough of him.

Before the end of the day she was persuading him to depart for London with her. *What?* Maybe he did not hear her well. He could not believe his luck. Yet he pretended as if he was not interested. He stayed over the night at her hotel room. And was indeed a very long night. Oscar was becoming a consummate professional, for he took the long night to really worm his way into the lonely woman's heart and her story.

Her real name was Gina Obembe-Samba; and was married for ten years with no issues, to Dele Tunde Samba, the heir apparent to the Chief Ademola Samba's industrial empire. Though, her divorce proceeding was messy, she made a kill from the alimony a British court had mercifully granted her. It was with her divorce settlement, she had commenced the buying and selling business in various continents. And this she had totally made a success of. She had craftily glossed over and evaded all his questions on what were her stocks in trade. She had quickly added that he would see when they get to England. It was a promise she told him, and that he would not regret going over to England with her.So *he had grudgingly* agreed to go with her.

Ten days later, Oscar with his travel expenses fully paid for by his new found friend had arrived in London Heathrow, on a Nigeria Airway flight alone. Gina Obembe-Samba had come up at the very last minute to abort the trip, because of a call that she received from business contact. Oscar could not hide his total disappointment. To appease him, Gina had suggested the alternative that, maybe he could go ahead with their baggage, and wait for her at the Heathrow Sheraton. Oscar Uromi already packed and ready to commence his odyssey in Queen's land was exhilarated with the new plans without any suspicion. He was willing to arrive London without her.

And that was how Oscar Uromi had arrived London that bright and beautiful summer morning, with a perfectly innocent story that the Her Majesty's Immigration Officers had swallowed hook, line, and sinker. He had sailed confidently through customs without baiting an eyelid, as he pushed the trolley laden with his and Gina's suitcase through the green *Nothing To Declare* channel. To the custom officers behind the mirrored glass he looked quite normal, and not betraying any guilty traits, to warrant any interests.

Outside Arrivals, just as planned there was a white man with a white cardboard with OSCAR UROMI boldly written in black. The unsmiling and ruthless looking man had introduced himself as Jack, in a soft spoken voice that Oscar could not but strained to hear. Jack had courteously taken over pushing the trolley to the Taxi Stand and dutifully loaded them into a black cab that took them to Sheraton Heathrow.

Oscar had innocently tried to make conversation with the unfriendly Jack, who had kept a straight face all through the brief ride to the hotel. At the hotel Jack had pulled out a brown envelope containing $1,000 in crisp $50 bills. All Jack said in his loud whisper was.

"All right mate. You will stop here, there is reservation for you already. I will deliver the *baggage* myself. Take…you take your bag." Jack did not wait for any response as gingerly picked the correct suitcase and handed it over to him.

Oscar Uromi was not just surprised but perplexed. How did Jack know his own baggage? He was still contemplating his next cause of action, as the cab sped off in a slightly smoky wake. He looked at the brown envelope in his hands, he had nothing to lose, he thought to himself. He was passed caring or bothering over what he could not explain. He surveyed his bearing and headed towards the reception, dragging his suitcase containing all his earthly possessions behind him. He just knew something was not just *adding up* with this new development, but that was none of his business. He was finally here in London, and whether *Gina or no Gina*; he was set to make it in England, or conquer the world, through England. He paused a little at the revolving glass door to survey the massive foyer, before heading towards the mammoth reception counter smiling, but smiling to no one in particular.

It was then somebody cleared his throat loudly, he looked up to find the amiable lead waiter, a remarkably very tall Chinese from the Forbidden City smiling down at him with a chilled bottle of Champagne Montaudon. Oscar noticed that his beautiful guest had a porcelain pot of minty green tea in front of her already, he beamed his disarming smile at her, before addressing the waiter.

"Yes, Chang my good friend, how rude of me, please go ahead and pour. Thank you." He had come to know and like Chang, whom he had always insisted on.

He noticed that his very beautifully enchanting guest was engrossed at the massive television screen, with its volume turned down. It was the

ITV 9 O'clock News showing a clip of Nigeria High Commissioner presenting his Letter of Credence to Her Majesty, Queen Elizabeth II.

"Wow!" Oscar exclaimed involuntarily, and startling the waiter to slightly spill the very expensive vintage wine. "That must be a Nigerian, I can bet with my life." He quickly reached for the remote control to increase the volume, as the clip changed to The Queen with her customized smile posing between the envoy and his beautiful daughter before fading out.

CHAPTER 73

The morning after the presentation of credence, Ambassador Daniel Aka had arrived at his office earlier than usual, because of the phone call that he had received late into the night. It was the High Commission's military attaché, who had informed him of a red priority meeting with a high-powered joint delegation of the MI5 and a team from United States Embassy, at 9a.m. Red Priority was the Foreign Service code or parlance for, an urgent matter of international security. No embassy or high commission toyed with matters of international security which has far-reaching connotations as emphasized by the Geneva Convention.

The top most floor of the Nigeria High Commission on Northumberland Avenue was totally dedicated to the High Commissioner's immediate office and his very senior key staff. The usual traffic bedlam of Northumberland Avenue at that time of the morning, did not pervade the luxurious ambience and serenity of this revered quarters. The High Commissioner sat behind the gargantuan ornate oak desk facing the window with a commanding view of London's Embarkment and the Thames, and beyond. It promises to be another very sunny beautiful day, just like the previous day.

The military attaché, Lt. Colonel Victor Obahon, in full military gear sat facing the ambassador as he briefed him regarding the agenda for the proposed 9a.m. meeting. Colonel Obahon reminded him of *Adam*, his younger brother who was privileged to be one of the thirty pioneer intakes into the Nigeria Military School, Zaria, on May 20, 1954 that came to be known as the *First Platoon*.

Adam in their characteristic tradition excelled in both academics and sports, and later rose to be the House Captain of Fairbanks. Daniel Aka had no doubts that his brother would make a good soldier, and based on their steady exchange of mails, Daniel was kept up to date, with Adam's progress. Sadly, it was indeed at the funeral of Sergeant Major Obidi Akachukwu, on the eve of the opening of the school, that his son was offered a place in the new school, to honor him for his loyal services to The Queen and his motherland. Sergeant Obidi's widow and nephew later relocated back to Amaeke, Ohafia, leaving Adam at the military school, with several guardians from the horde of family friends.

Adam, after graduation, was later posted and stationed in Lagos, where their cousin Uzoka moved in to live with him, at the Yaba Army Barracks. That was where they were until a few months before Nigeria's Independence, when Adams discovered his cousin had disappeared without any warning and trace. It was the police that had counseled Adam to relax, since Uzoka disappeared with his portmanteau and small belongings. That was the last they saw or heard from Uzoka until the coups and the pogroms that subsequently led to the Nigeria-Biafra civil war that lasted almost three years.

Adam Akachukwu, regrettably did not survive the Nigeria Civil War; and his brother recalled the uncanny circumstances surrounding his death, that became a legend of sorts, and was told on to that day..

Colonel Adam Akachukwu, who became a full colonel in the Biafran Army, was before then known in the Nigerian Army as Major Adamu Samanja. The incident about the name was an unintentional oversight by one of his father's illiterate colleagues who thought Adam was for *Adamu*, while *Samanja* was his father's name. Over the years the necessary changes were not effected timely, and became too late when all his official documents bore the inoffensive nomenclature. And since Adams was very fluent in the Hausa language as the natives, Adamu Samanja was playfully regarded as Hausa until most people actually forgot that he was an Ibo.

This complicating backdrop to his dual identities, later turned out to be a blessing in disguise, and to work out in his favor. That was how he escaped been killed when some of his Ibo officers were targeted and killed in the second retaliatory coup masterminded by army officers of Northern extraction in Lagos. Major Adamu Samanja went about unchallenged as his fellow native Ibo officers escaped, went into hiding, jailed, or were killed. It was almost a year later that he made his way into Biafra, and against all doubts was warmly welcomed to Biafra by the rebel leader himself, with the rank of a full colonel.

The official story of his brother's death by his colleagues, was corroborated by Colonel Chukwuemeka Odumegwu Ojukwu, the Biafran warlord himself, whom he had met after his national pardon and return from exile. Colonel Adam Akachukwu, who was *brave and bold as a lion,* died gallantly thorough *friendly fire,* when he was trying to protect an *enemy* that spared and saved his own life. The Biafran warlord told how the supposed enemy, a mercenary jet-fighter pilot on the Nigerian side finally ended up with him, as an honor to Colonel Akachukwu. Unfortunately, he could not take him along when he left Biafra to the Ivory Coast on exile.

"The major factor on the agenda is the concerted war against drugs, and international drugs smuggling…" the attaché raised his voice intentionally to courteously wake his boss from his reverie.

"I hope some of our countrymen have not again rubbished all our efforts to keep a clean sheet on drugs?" The ambassador inquired with some modicum of genuine concern.

"Not exactly sir." The attaché answered uncomfortably.

"What do you mean by not exactly, my friend?" The ambassador retorted.

"The United States DEA officially would want us to provide them with every information about a Nigerian called *Oscar Uromi.*" "Oscar… Oscar… Oscar Who?" Ambassador Daniel Aka countered incredulously.

"This is a file photo of Oscar Uromi, your Excellency." The Military Attaché pushed a 10 x 12 inch black and white glossy photograph across to his boss.

The ambassador momentarily froze as he examined the photograph closely. The more he looked, the more the furrows of his brow deepened, the military attaché observed with interest. A total stranger to him, but with an uncanny familiar resemblance, the ambassador thought to himself. He returned the picture to his subordinate without uttering a word, his mind busy calculating and considering every probable and possible permutations without uttering any words.

Oscar Uromi himself, was just steering awake at just that point in time. He had purposely ignored the alarm that first woke him two hours earlier. He had not slept well, because of his date that ended most abruptly and tragically. After Mr. Chang and his waiter cleared their stuffs and left. Oscar knew it was going to be a very exciting night ahead. It was not the first time Lima Gonzales was staying the night at his *cove*. She was a very passionately agile woman, and was well informed about how her mother's native Indian tribe women in Yarumal, Colombia, sensually handle their men affectionately. She was an amateur contortionist, and could get very imaginative in bed. He had popped another bottle of Champagne Montaudon and filled their flutes before stretching beside her on the twin lounge chair on the upstairs patio. The starry night sky was filled with the luminance of the full moon.

"So Lima my dear, what brought you to London from Bogota this time?"

"Job. I need a job. I need a real job, Oscar. *Not all these goldfish-in-bowl kind of jobs."* She teasingly flicked an imaginary speck off his well-groomed mustache.

"Oh, come on Lima. You don't need a job. All you need is a nice wealthy husband to take care of you and your children, as many as you would want." He burst into laughter, and almost choked on his drink.

"Oh, stop fooling Oscar my darling. I am serious." Oscar noticed that she was truly serious.

"So what high profile job are you searching for, Lima baby." He continued in the humor that he started with.

"Oscar dear, please be serious for a moment." She sat up and carefully put her drink aside on the marbled floor. "Oscar, I want to work with you. Please." She knelt down and put her head on his tummy.

"What?" Oscar pushed her away as if she was a rattlesnake. He jumped up looking really livid. "Lima, what did you just say?" It was obvious that he was hyper-ventilating.

Lima was totally flabbergasted. What did she say or do wrong? She opened her mouth to answer, but no word came forth. Oscar in his rage, just flung the champagne flute over the balcony onto the well-manicured lawn, and stepped briskly back into the sitting room. He stepped into the toilet, and locked the door behind him. He sat on the toilet seat fuming and angry at himself to have let his guards down. Then he understood the popular saying; *what goes around comes around.* As he sat there on the covered toilet, the past and his most guided secret life just flooded back.

Just when he felt all alone, and lost in the whole wide-world Gina Obembe-Samba appeared in that hotel room at the Heathrow Sheraton. It was the day after he checked in. Just when he was so confused about what to do, he needed somebody to lead him through one of the world's most populous capitals. He was so happy, and it was so obvious that Gina mistook it for sexual passion. Which of course Oscar Uromi was so happily relieved to oblige her to her fullest satisfaction. They had spent the whole day and night in bed.

They had checked out from the hotel and moved over to her detached home at St. John's Wood that she got as a part of her divorce settlement. Oscar was really impressed with what he saw on ground. She was really doing well in her business across the continents. He never bothered to ask again, he knew that it was just a matter of time, he would be wiser. All he wanted to do then was to know the city of London first. It was the true mark of survival of a man to have a good knowledge of his new environment. He was so enchanted with the London Underground, that within his first month, he had used and visited every tube station on the Central, Circle, and District lines. The human mole, Gina had playfully called him.

Within the first year, Oscar had visited over twenty-five countries with Gina, without being told she was into big time international drugs smuggling. Until the day like Lima, he had insisted to Gina that he wanted a job working with her. She had insisted that he did not need a job, for he was a kept man, like a goldfish in a bowl. She had finally capitulated and opened up a little pending when he could be trusted beyond doubt.

Before he joined Gina Obembe-Samba, she smuggled her cocaine on her person. The substance was stuffed into extra strong condoms which were anchored with a string, and were then inserted into the dark innermost recesses of her womanhood. When he joined Gina, they became a perfect team. They changed the old procedure; this time Gina would be clean as whistle, getting to immigration or custom she would then create a false alarm on herself, thereby drawing attention to herself, and creating a distraction on him, who was loaded, and was about two or three persons behind her. He would normally work through customs unmolested. *Lady luck smiled on them.*

Though he was well-cared for, Gina kept all other information about their operations from him. She failed to see that Oscar was overly ambitious. She also failed to see, that with his new found prosperity, he needed his freedom from her lording over him. She underestimated his intelligence, thinking he was stuck with her. And that was her *greatest undoing.*

Oscar was only in his second year with her, when he put his plans together. There was no way he could be a free man if Gina was alive. After the little while he had spent with Gina, he observed that she was not very smart. He had come up with the good ideas and strategies most of the time. He wanted a bigger piece of the action, than the pittance, that he was getting. He wanted more than the good dressing, that made him feel more or less like a stuffed teddy bear at her beck and call to play with. He resolved to opt out of the existing arrangements.

It took him, little less than a year of meticulous planning to get his act together. He needed to know their business contacts in the various continents, before he could put Gina out of circulation, so he would take over the business. Gina had a little black address book that she kept with her at all time of the day. Oscar knew that it was all that he needed to do effective business without Gina.

It was all part of his plans to enroll in a private college within London to study computer programming and communication, and artistic make-up. He had told Gina he just wanted to keep himself busy, instead of staying idle between trips. He completed the tuition in flying colors. Armed with his newly acquired knowledge, he got down to work, as he cleverly procured all her contacts' telephone numbers. It was kid's play procuring both the telephone numbers and the entire conversations, by simply using his computer and the telephone modem. He had everything in place but *chickened out* when it was time to go into action.

One beautiful summer day, Gina caught him chatting up a beautiful Jamaican girl not very far from the house, and she went berserk. She threw tantrums and raved and threatened him with fire and brimstone. She had threatened that, "he was going to be homeless and penniless, the next time he throws a glance at anything in skirts".

Oscar Uromi was scared to the marrow of his bones. That was it. He was not going to wait for Gina to blackmail him all his life. That galvanized him into action; to get the next phase of his plans in execution mode. He had waited till they came back from a trip to South America, which was one of their biggest shipment ever. With his computer he monitored Gina and her wholesale distributors. They had various rendezvous set out over a period of time.

The night of the very first rendezvous, Gina came home to meet a strange white man relaxed in her living room. A puzzled Gina nearly collapsed from fright. She heaved a sigh of relief when it turned out to be Oscar trying out a proposed new strategy for their subsequent trips. Gina agreed that since it fooled her it would fool anybody. They went out immediately without Oscar taking off his make-up. Since the Jamaican girl incidence, Gina had shown frosty signs that she was already fed up with Oscar, he had also smartly gone the extra mile to really please her.

Carrying Gina's oversized heavy handbag was one of those antics to curry her favor. As had waited for the best chance to put the climax of his plan into action. They were at tube station they turned out to be the only commuters. He took his time to clearly show his made up features to the close circuit cameras and monitors. When the train came speeding by, he cleverly shoved Gina Obembe-Samba onto the tracks. When the train finally stopped what used to be Gina was a squashed messy mass of flesh, blood, and crushed bones.

In the din of the consequent confusion Oscar left the scene. The police with the aid of the cameras and witnesses in the train, started a manhunt for a male Caucasian suspect. Unfortunately, the badly mangled body of the obviously black woman, of a possible African descent because of her colorful attire, was not carrying any form of identity.

Neither did anybody report her missing. The London Rail Police recorded it as death by misadventure. The London papers, who were in the thick of a Margaret Thatcher cabinet resignations and reshuffle, did not bother themselves to be distracted by a little freak accident.

That night Oscar showed up at the rendezvous, with what was expected, and he was given the agreed cash. Oscar had never seen such amount of money ever. From that day he started showing up at the various rendezvous with what was arranged, with the story that his aunt was indisposed. They got what they wanted or ordered, and they settled accordingly. And gradually over time, he naturally eased into the flow of things. That was how he settled down into the dangerous world international drugs smuggling. Now it seemed as if his past is about to catch up with him, with Lima's desire.

He resolved within himself that he would never allow himself to do anything with Lima Gonzales ever again. He would even just go and drop her off for good. He was not going to keep her in his house one minute longer. He was not going to allow what he did to Gina, to happen to him, with Lima or any other person. He was going to remain *a lone shark, or a lone ranger.*

CHAPTER 74

There was a kind of an unwritten code of agreement existing between Ambassador Daniel Aka and his daughter, Jane Margaret Hilda, whenever they were separated to at least speak to each other on telephone every other day. She had flown back to Kaduna via Lagos, where she was stationed as a member of the National Youth Service Corp, the day after his presentation of credence. The bond between father and daughter was developed over the years that they had consistently remained together, without a wife or a mother. At every opportunity of free time or vacations the duo must spend quality time together, bonding more and more as they found solace in one another. And their close family friends would swear that the professor loved his child to death.

After the death of his wife, Daniel had sworn to himself not to remarry, so as to preserve the memory of his wife, Halima. He had gotten a Ghanaian childless widow in her 60's to work as a permanent nanny to his daughter. Madam Aggrey had moved into his residence and cared and nurtured Jane Margaret Hilda into a very courteous and confident lovable girl. When Jane Margaret Hilda was six years old, and the civil war had ended, Professor Daniel Aka had headed back home to Nigeria.

They were received at the Ikeja Airport, Lagos by an enthusiastic reception party. The Lagos Branch of the Ohafia Development Association had organized their famous Ohafia War Dance troupe to welcome their illustrious son, who had beaten the white man in children in the civil war. The woman had lived in England with her husband for over ten years, before returning home to Nigeria just before the civil war crisis, was well versed, and a trained opera singer. During her interview, her story had truly touched the professor who took genuine liking to her, and gave her the job. It was the very dedicated Mama Caro, that taught her the Igbo language and other traditional behaviors. It was like Mama Caro transferred all her accumulated love and attention to *the poor motherless girl*.

The amiable Jane Margaret Hilda, was placed in the University of Lagos Staff School to continue her primary education. Though Jane Margaret Hilda was a very keen player of the piano, it was also Mama Caro that sharpened her skills and turned her into a child prodigy. Her blossoming child beauty was commented about by many people who encountered her, as she progressed through all the grades of the University Staff School.

On the other hand Professor Aka's intelligence was well-appreciated by the Ministry, and Federal Government; his reward was a kind of rapid upward acceleration to the top. Since his acclaimed fame and recognition was acting like magic negotiations, within five years of his return to Nigeria, he became an ambassador designate. He was in this capacity for a period of two years before he was posted to the United States of America as Nigeria's Ambassador. After four years as Nigeria's ambassador to the United States, he was moved again to the United Nations as Nigeria's ambassador for another four years. It was after his stinct at the United Nations that he was recalled to Nigeria to run the Federal Ministry of External Affairs as its Permanent Secretary. He did that function successfully, before his recent posting as High Commissioner to the Court of St. James.

All the while Professor Daniel Aka was traversing the globe with his blossoming ambassadorial career, his daughter stayed put in Lagos, with Mama Caro always hovering close-by. Jane Margaret Hilda, approaching twenty years of age, had developed over the years to a very desirable goddess of womanhood. Her versatility on the piano had also brought her fame and popularity, even as a child prodigy. Her face was well-known on the local television channel. And like moth to a flame, there was a steady string of male admirers at her beck and call. She finally rounded up her studies at the University of Lagos, with a first class Master's Degree in Architecture, at the age of 23 and half years..

Every Nigerian fresh graduate of any higher institution was expected to serve a period of twelve calendar months in a programme that was named the National Youth Service Corps (NYSC). It was mandatory, exemption could only be allowed on the grounds of age, marital status, and poor health. Jane Margaret Hilda was posted to

Kaduna State, in Northern Nigeria. It was preceeded by a compulsory one month of toughening up in an orientation camp, where the *corpers* were put through a rigorous para-military training by army drill sergeants hewn out of *stone*. The *corpers* were also given an opportunity to learn a basic local language and customs and traditions of their immediate environment.

Nigeria, a nation with more than 250 tribes and twice as many languages, it was a big task. The *corpers* were then posted to a place of primary assignment in the host state for remainder of the service year. The primary objective, was for the *corpers* to serve the immediate community, and contribute to its socio-economic development, and thereby promote the Nigeria's diverse unity, as a whole. So after the traditional passing out parade in a military fashion, attended by the governor of the state, Jane Margaret Hilda was posted to Kaduna, the capital city of Kaduna State.

Kaduna was a thriving modern industrial town, which was once the colonial political capital of Northern Nigeria, before the amalgamation of the north and south by Lord Fredrick Lugard. In the modern day Nigeria, Kaduna was considered to be the *Lagos of the North*. It was centrally located and believed to be the abode of the political ruling class and power brokers of the North.

Jane Margaret Hilda was happy with her posting, for she dreaded the general idea of serving in the rural communities, which mostly lacked basic infrastructures and amenities. Jane Margaret Hilda was conveniently posted to serve with the state owned Kaduna Urban Town Planning Authority. She had secured a one-room self- contained accommodation in the exclusive *Tudun Wada* suburb of Kaduna, a walking distance to her office.

It was only a matter of days, before like moths to flame, the admirers and suitors started showing up. They came in different shapes and sizes, arriving to impress in various top-of-the-range vintage automobiles. She was moderately firm and kept them at bay without being offensive.

Jane Margaret Hilda Aka was an amiable person, that did not in any way disturb her being also a very private person. Throughout the entire period she spent in Kaduna, she made only one close friend. That friend was Rakiya Danbaba, who was about her age. They became the best of friends, even closer than blood sisters. The more confident and strong willed Rakiya instantly became a strong influence in Margaret Hilda's life.

Jane Margaret Hilda was about half way through her service year, when the two girls met under the queerest and strangest of circumstances, that undoubtably cemented firmly their friendship.

It was at the wedding of Fatima Baba, Jane's supervisor at her place of work. It took place at a church in Kaduna South. Fatima, a scion of Aliko Baba, the multi-millionaire sugar and flour merchant. The venue was packed with the *who is who* in the society. A huge crowd of gaily dressed guest were all seated, and the service had already started when Jane Margaret Hilda arrived.

Both Jane Margaret Hilda and Rakiya, who had never met before were dressed in the same *aso-ebi*. The *aso-ebi*, was a mode of uniformed group dressing at ceremonial events common with the *Yorubas*. It became the vogue at weddings, funerals and other social engagements in any part of Nigeria. The quality and quantity was an effective parameter to categorize a particular social event. Due to the African concept of extended family system, social events like weddings were sometimes a funfare of guests who through one way or the other were related to the bride or bridegroom or both.

The *aso-ebi* in this instance acts as an identifier of a guest and to whom, or what group he belonged. The aso-ebi gives credence to the adage that said, *birds of the same feather flock together*. And true to type, guests of identical *aso-ebi* seat, eat, drink and party together.

The aso-ebi Fatima Baba's family and friends had chosen was a two-piece wine-colored *aso-oke* with a lacy cream voile for the blouse. *Aso-oke* was a Yoruba word for *high society wear,* it was a quality traditionally woven material only common in Yoruba land. Fatima Baba's *aso-ebi* ensemble was indeed top of the range.

Margaret Hilda had arrived late to the church, and quickly slipped into the first available empty seat at the back row. Though, she could see her aso-ebi colors well-displayed towards the front rows, she could not summon the courage to walk up the aisle to seat with them. It was during this solemn religious service that the *weird events* of that day started.

It began with a tiny excited wave from a strange man across the aisle from her. She politely acknowledged with an harmless smile, and resumed witnessing the ongoing activities at the altar. She did not even give it a thought, because she was now wiser with the antics of the numerous opposite sex that admire her. Then there was another excited wave, and another and yet another; but this time they were all women, yet she could not fathom those excited faces from the deep recesses of her heart. That was strange, and nagged at her heart.It later grew into a puzzle that gave Jane grave concern, when a strange lady, patted her and whispered an affectionate greetings, and went along to find a seat further upfront. She barely held herself from screaming when the next strange face waved and smiled exuberantly at her. *"Oh no! Not again."* She muttered under her breath.

Three rows away was another frantic wave meant to catch her attention. She ignored it. There was definitely a mistake somewhere. Then a flitting thought crossed her mind. *Amnesia?* Yes, that was the term; Amnesia. Her troubled mind skipped a beat. It was running helter-skelter. Was she a victim of amnesia? The temporary total loss of one's memory, that might even become permanent. Margaret recalled all the strange stories that abound of people who woke up one morning and could not even remember their own names. *Just like that.*

Their memory erased totally clean, like deleting stored information from a computer data bank. Jane Margaret Hilda to say the least was disturbed and distracted. She waited impatiently for the church proceedings to end, so she could put her troubled mind to rest for good. Then, they would be at freedom to mingle and talk.

After the church service, Jane hastily disentangled herself from the exodus of relations, friends, and well-wishers, through a side entrance. She was frantic to find a face she could recognize, that would definitely confirm her sanity. She wanted to stay ahead of the crowd, where she would take a vantage position to inspect and search the crowd. It was even difficult to identify individuals because of the aso-ebi dressing.The scene outside was rowdy, as many guests who were not interested in the church proceedings waited for the customary photo session. It was a typical African greetings galore; a classical exhibition of genuine concerns and emotions, uttered in loud uninhibited excited voices, celebrating the euphoria of long lost but found acquaintances. The volcanic bear hugs, and back-slapping chicanery of sworn social and political rivalries to hoodwink the ordinary onlookers.

Considerable time was given to photographs, this was also attributed to the extended family factor. A long list of all imaginable group-combination was given to somebody to supervise the photographed and the photographers. Every guest was expected to appear in at least one group-combination. A photograph was an incontestable evidence against any accusation of non-attendance which was normally taken very seriously.

Jane was standing alone from the crowd, still weighed down with her immediate dilemma. She turned round to find a tall dark and handsome young man with equally pretty young lady coming towards her. The next thing she realised was that the young lady was smiling broadly, then broke out and engulfed her in a stifling embrace. "Amina! Amina!! I am very happy to see you after all these years." The lady had tears of joy in her eyes, as she held onto her presumed long lost friend. Jane Margaret Hilda was almost mortified She could neither extricate herself from the embrace or utter a word. She was just speechless. The young lady's consort looked approvingly at the friendly gesture of his mate.

"Friday, this is Amina Danbaba my bosom childhood friend you have heard so much about. Amina, meet my fiance, Friday Odey." The total stranger said excitedly to Jane Margaret Hilda who was smiling shyly.

Jane was getting even more confused. She was torn between admitting the friendly stranger was not known to her or that she was indeed a victim of amnesia. How would she cope with the resultant embarrassments either way? She chose to play along perhaps she might find a clue to the entire riddle. She was still thinking of what to do, when these words broke into her thoughts.

"Ekaete, there is something wrong here. It seems your Amina childhood friend does not share your convictions." The man said to his female companion who was ready to burst into tears; but it was the lifeline Jane was looking for to start a new personality of somebody known as Amina Danbaba.

"Please Ekaete my darling friend, pardon my rudeness," Jane quickly said nervously with a splash of wide smile that could have woken the dead, "I am indeed very excited and surprised to see you after all these years. Ekaete, just look at you, you have changed so much." Though Jane Margaret Hilda was a superlative actress, she did not convince Ekaete who had a distressful mien.

"Amina, please tell me what is the problem? I know something is definitely wrong. Where is Rakiya?" Ekaete said with a note of finality.

"Who? Which Rakiya?" a very confused Jane Margaret Hilda asked without thinking.

"Which other Rakiya?" Ekaete retorted with deep hurt in her voice. Her greatest apprehension was that her bosom friend had gone mad. "I am talking of your sister."

"Oh! Ekaete, please once again accept my apologies, Rakiya is somewhere around." Jane Margaret Hilda then knew there was no way she could get through the day without getting in to trouble. She was getting out of that place as fast as possible, or else she was going to go crazy.

"You guys run along, I will join you in a jiffy. Friday, its nice to meet you." She then whispered into Ekaete's ears, "I am pressed, I have to find the toilet or I am in trouble. I have a feeling it is the *monthly visitor*." She lied. She was amazed at the ease at which it flowed.

A relieved Ekaete nodded understandably. "I see, you will find us with Rakiya then. I hope you have enough tissues on you." The supposed childhood friend asked with genuine concern. Margaret Hilda nodded in the affirmative and hurried towards the back of the church that was deserted. She could feel their eyes like searing arrows boring into her back before she turned the corner.

A flitting thought suddenly crossed her mind. Check your handbag there must be some form of identity. She was certain her identity card was not there, but there should be her little NYSC pocket diary. In that bag there must be something to help solve her identity predicament. Why didn't she think of it since? She quickly emptied the entire contents of her bag on an elevated marble slab without looking. There were the usual appurtenances always present in a girl's handbag. There was the green NYSC little dairy. She picked it up sat down on the stone-cold marble slab, and oddly felt its coldness seep through to her buttocks. In her state of mind, she did not even realize she was seating on the grave of the founding pastor of the church. Lined neatly behind her were rows of gravestones, it was the church graveyard, no wonder it enjoyed its relative serenity.

Most people have an uncomfortable phobia for graves and the dead, and they steer clear of graveyards. Jane Margaret Hilda was one of them. Her mind was far from reality. She would love to wake up from this nightmare. As turned the plastic cover to the front page that she had filled her personal profile, she heard the excited voices of girls approaching. She looked up immediately to see three girls in their early twenties turn the corner towards her.

They did not notice her immediately, as they were engrossed in their animated discussion. They were dressed in her kind of *aso-ebi*, her heart soared, but nose-dived immediately. She did not recognize any of them. That was when their eyes met. And they stopped like they worked into a brickwall. Thier eyes and mouth went agape. They looked very terrified beyond words. Jane Margaret Hilda just stood there looking at them as they responded with morbid fear. Then she saw the girl in the middle feebly muttered *Amina*, her eyes rolled over, and she slumped to the ground lifeless. The other two girls threw down their handbags and took to their heels screaming; *"Ghost! Ghost!!"*

They left behind in their wake shoes, handbags and headgears. She stood frozen to the spot, then she noticed the gravestones and the graveyard. She was petrified. She could not tell whether she was more terrified of the graveyard environment or the weird reactions of the girls to her identity. A few paces from her was the inert body of the fallen girl. She was confused. She did not even know what to do. To run or to wait? Things were getting out of hand. Her thoughts had lost all semblance of objective reasoning.

Jane Margaret Hilda just stood there shivering with fright and shock. She was not even suffering from amnesia, she was now convinced that she was a ghost. *Was she really a ghost?* In an environment where almost every natural mystery was attributed with supernatural powers, spine-chilling stories of ghosts mingling with the living abound. Though these stories have a questionable credibility, their sources most times go unchallenged since they claim the hearsay immunity. Despite their horrifying flavour, most children and even most adults not only enjoy these stories, but swallow them both hook, line and sinker.

The reaction of the crowd in the middle of the photo-session, to the evidently frightened and hysteric fleeing girls was something else. It was not only that of surprise but was also filled with exhilarating curiosity. For once, those present were going to tell this ghost story authoritatively, without recourse to the usual hearsay credibility. The rowdy, but orderly proceedings of the photo-session was of course disrupted. The initial reaction was that of flight, but their curiosity had the better of them, as the strong hearted and die-hards headed back to catch the rare glimpse of the abominable dead who was still wondering in the world of the living, instead to rest in peace.

In a rare display of courage, the parish pastor armed with the silver crucifix strung on his neck, and a small bottle of holy water that mysteriously appeared from within his cassock ventured forward. As he cautiously moved towards the back of the church, a handful of men including the bridegroom followed suit. The rest of the crowd kept a safe distance as they monitored events as they on fold. Jane Margaret Hilda heard their commotion before they turned the corner. The harsh croaky voice vehemently reciting a supposedly spiritual incantations in a strange language, with a handful of people trailing him cautiously.

The pastor's fiery eyes roamed around the graveyard ignoring the two figures dressed in aso-oke. Though he registered in a glance the forlone figure of Jane Margaret Hilda propping up the slumped figure on the ground. He was more interested in locating the possible target of his exorcism. His eyes roamed the deserted parish cemetery. She noticed his look of disappointment mixed with relief. The band of people following behind, observing there was no cause for alarm, quickly rushed over to Jane Margaret Hilda and the immobile figure on the ground. As they tried to resuscitate the girl, the pastor approached Jane Margaret Hilda who had a distant look in her eyes.

"What happened, my daughter?" The pastor asked in a confessorial tone.

Jane Margaret Hilda opened her mouth to speak, but no words came forth. She felt her throat parched and dry. What could she say. To confess that she was the ghost that was causing all the havoc and disruption. Her next bid to speak again, still came out with nothing.

It was at exactly that point the girl that fainted came to. Her name was Rakiya Danbaba, a first cousin to the bride. She sat up and looked vacantly around her. She was yet to realize what really happened. She looked up, to find the Pastor and Jane Margaret Hilda in an animated discussion. She just pointed at Jane Margaret Hilda, and with evident fear relapsed into another fainting spell. again. That was the cue the mob needed to pounce on the harmless *culprit*. As a battery of questions were fired at her, the young girl just began to cry.

The pastor with dexterity, splashed the contents of holy water bottle on her. His croaky voice went up to a crescendo. All Jane Margaret Hilda did was to cry.

"J.M.H.! J.M.H.!! What happened?" It was the bridegroom, Aliko, with the two hysterical runaway girls in tow. He could recognize Jane Margaret Hilda; he had met her many times in his wife's office. He then stepped between the pastor and her protectively. She was so relieved that at least she could be recognized by Fatima and her husband. She was overwhelmed with joy. Her heart was almost bursting with joy. The sheer realization of the confirmation that she was not a ghost, or suffering from amnesia. The excitement was too much for the heart to take. And she allowed and surrendered herself to nature's soothing elixir over emotional moments like this. She passed out cold.

Moments later, Rakiya and Jane Margaret Hilda got fully revived, and both were confirmed healthy by one of the many medical doctors present. The wedding guests who had now regrouped discounted the entire incident as a joke, and were making fun of each other's reactions and antics. The pastor discovering his mistake and over-reaction, had quickly taken to his heels to avoid further embarrassments. The photo-session was successfully concluded, and the wedding party proceeded to the adjoining cavernous reception hall for the official wedding reception.

Jane Margaret Hilda and Rakiya took to each other immediately. All through the reception that took the better part of two hours, the two girls were inseparable. On closer scrutiny, it was very clear that they displayed very uncanny resemblance. It was very clear that Margaret Hilda was much fairer in complexion, with a more pronounced facial features inclined towards the North Africans.

It was then the bizarre occurrences of the morning were explained to her. It was purely a multiple case of mistaken identity that was overtly over-exaggerated. *J.M.H.* as was now called by all, thought to herself. It was a big puzzle everyone agreed. How could individuals who were not in any way blood relations have that kind of uncanny resemblance? *If everyone was taken in, not the Danbabas, the parents of the late Amina, and Rakiya who were twins.*

Amina was sadly killed in a road accident about six months back, on the Kaduna–Zaria Road. Amina until her death was an undergraduate student of architecture at the Ahmadu Bello University in the ancient walled city of Zaria. She met her death on the eve of her twenty-third birthday. She was on her way to celebrate with her family. The Danbabas were yet to get over the death of their child.It was not until much later that evening, through the consistent insistence of Rakiya that J.M.H. had paid a visit to the opulent residence of the Danbabas.

The Danbabas were very accommodating, they had met Jane at the reception and were indeed puzzled by the degree of resemblance.J.M.H. could not wait to see a picture of the late Amina, and Rakiya readily presented her with a calf-bound picture album.

"I created this album in memory of Amina." There were tears in her eyes as she handed the album to Jane Margaret Hilda.

"Rakiya you have cried enough for one day. Please accept Amina's fate as the destiny of God." She said with concern as she turned over the leather-bound cover of the album.

Her heart actually skipped a double beat. It was like she was looking into a mirror. She actually felt like she was seeing her own image. For the 10 by 12inch portrait of the late Amina, at a first cursory glance was a very close resemblance.Rakiya, who also left the Ahmadu Bello University, Zaria with Bachelor's Degree in Mass Communications works in her fathers communication firm right there in Zaria. Before the end of the day, Rakiya did not waste time to inform M.H., that she was not only going to be a friend, that she was also going to adopt her as her one and only sister. They became so close that a lot of people thought that they were blood sisters. It was on this premise the Danbaba's brought in M.H. to live with them, all through the service year in Kaduna..

Ambassador Aka was still in Lagos when that incident had happened and was briefed accordingly by his daughter. Though he was yet to meet the Danbabas physically, he had seen and met Rakiya twice when she visited Lagos with Jane Margaret Hilda. He had also noticed the features that were very obviously similar, though there was no way they could be related except through Adam and Eve, he had joked.

Talking about uncanny resemblances, that Oscar Uromi fellow, strangely looked very familiar in a very odd way. Unfortunately, there was nobody alive on his side and generation to corroborate his suspicions…those eyes and forehead reminded him so much of Uzoka Akachukwu, his cousin that disappeared almost thirty years back..

The big black embassy Mercedes Benz, chauffeured by an embassy security staff, briefly paused at the traffic lights by Trafalgar Square, before turning left to join the late evening light traffic on White Chapel Street. Ambassador Daniel Aka was actually on his way to the Number 10 Downing Street, private quarters of Prime Minister Margaret Hilda Thatcher for a very private dinner, when his daughter called to inform him that she had arrived safely in Kaduna. The Danbabas had also used the opportunity to congratulate him on his new posting that they all witnessed on television. The ambassador just smiled to himself, grateful to God, that had led him this far. It was another wonderful opportunity to catch up with his very good old friend, and her husband, Denis. The chauffeur noticed the satisfied smirk on his boss' face and wondered what the man was thinking about.

CHAPTER 75

It was like Oscar Uromi was an impenetrable fortress. It was like nobody knew him on any form of informal or personal basis. The few women who claimed to know, could not go beyond his bedroom in their knowledge of him. The DEA was not making much progress either, as they rose from another meeting that did not bring them closer to cracking the puzzle that was Oscar Uromi. Chuck Freeborn IV had admitted to his team that, *it was like the man was hewn out of a rock by nobody.*

The much the Nigerian High Commission provided was that though Uromi was a bona-fide Nigerian, he had not entered Britain with a passport bearing that name. A trace on him back in Nigeria ran cold after his spell at King's College. The problem was that Oscar Uromi was not a team player, he operated better as a Lone Ranger… never any loose end to tie up or messy angles to clean and clear up.

"We are not going to give up gentlemen," the DEA chief declared with resolve, "we must keep him in our sights until he fumbles, which he is bound to.."

At that particular point in time, Oscar Uromi was not in the DEA sights; because Chuck Freeborn IV was actually underestimating his adversary. Uromi was always two steps ahead of his hunters by matter of a principle that had kept him alive so far, and to be referred to as an *Oracle* by his present Colombian principal client. The client who calls himself *Amigo*, had wondered aloud, if he, *Oscar ever failed in a project?*

"If that had happened I won't be alive to run around to please you. In my kind of business there is no room for failure or bungling up.

Would you Amigo place your bet on a failed horse?" He paused for his answer that took time to come.

"No way, amigo. You are damned too smart for a *mayate*."

"Why?" Oscar Uromi retorted.

"Why? Because you are an Oracle; and mayate cannot be oracles." Burst into a good natured laughter to diffuse the tension in his assertions.

"Be careful man, you don't have to be insulting. I feel insulted already." Oscar sounded serious. "Please let us just do business. I don't need a friend in you. I am busy." And he cut off the telephone discussions. The man knew where and when to draw the line; which was the secret of his *success*.

Unknown to the DEA *blood hounds* it was indeed Oscar Uromi's busiest day in the year. The 1989 Beauty Contest was concluded the previous day, and the victors and the losers had emerged. And this day, the losers were homeward bound as was the tradition, while the victorious queen, and her first runner-up would stay a while before their official departure back to their home countries. The queen would be based in London officially during the duration of her reign.

Uromi, was far away in his cozy warm study safely monitoring his special protocol staff from London's *Twinkle & Twinkle* office with the help of a little rent-a-crowd that had been boosted by curious onlookers and travelers at both Gatwick and Heathrow Airports. The brief ceremony at the airports was to issue each contestant a cuddly Teddy bear and a boxed Twinkle & Twinkle trinkets, they would take as carryon hand luggage as they were ushered as worthy ambassadors of their various countries through the fast track beyond security.

Oscar Uromi still in his super silky Japanese kimono, poured himself another flute of Champagne Montaudon to celebrate yet another very successful outing under the noses of the DEA and their British cohorts. He could not help but laugh out aloud in a monologue; *Oscar Uromi you damned bastard, you will still outwit them in hell, when that time comes to be...*

At that very moment in Kaduna, Nigeria, Jane Margaret Hilda and Rakiya were seated under hairdryers in a very highbrow beauty salon on Ahmadu Bello Way. *Queens' Grooming & Spa* owned by the present Military Governor's wife, was the place to be for the patrons who could afford to pay a little extra. It had all the comfort of the latest high-tech grooming equipment imported in from France, and was compatible to like places in Los Angeles. It was Jane Margaret Hilda's birthday, and Rakiya was giving them a special treat, having their hair and full manicure and pedicure. The bill would cost Rakiya an arm and leg, but she felt JMH deserved it.

The previous night's Miss Cosmos grand finale was showing on the Satellite television, and everyone was engrossed with the pageant. When Miss Nigeria did not survive the preliminaries, though the audience in that room were disappointed as true patriots, some felt that Nigeria's representative was not the best that Nigeria could offer, while some felt it was all stage-managed. A very vociferous lady was of the opinion that *a black girl will never smell the world's most coveted beauty crown*. Others were of the opinion that how would a black girl smell the beauty crown if the beautiful girls do not get to participate in the first place. And the arguments almost got out of hand if not for the timely intervention of the owner to calm them down, to see the contest progress to the end.

As the new Caucasian beauty queen was crowned to the consternation of the whole world, somebody in that room just declared; *it is not fair, that queen is not even as beautiful as this lady right here under the dryer*. As if on cue all eyes turned to Rakiya and Jane Margaret Hilda. Margaret Hilda who was not even paying attention to the discussions since she was wearing ear protectors, did not understand what all the fuss was about. It was Rakiya that spoke on her friend's behalf with the proprietress of *Queen's Grooming & Spa*, who promised to groom and sponsor MH in the next year's Miss Nigeria in the Kaduna Zonal Contest. It was also agreed that Rakiya would serve as her chaperon.

When Jane Margaret Hilda was informed later of the proposal, she just laughed it off as a huge joke. At the end of the day, Rakiya was able to convince her bosom friend to accept for the fun of it, and the almost one year of free grooming from *Queen's*, as they fondly called the salon. It was a deal, the highly unassuming MH could not refuse.

The Governor's wife took her proposal very seriously, and proposed some professional crash programs during the Christmas and New Year long holidays. Within the three weeks she was in London with her father, she took courses in carriage modeling and updated her skills on the piano. She did not tell her father about the proposal, as had been agreed between the friends. The deal was between the friends and governor's wife.

CHAPTER 76

By the time Miss Nigeria adverts started, the proprietress was impressed with how she had transformed the beautiful girls. She was really hopeful of the end result, that she had craftily struck a deal with them to be the faces of *Queen's*, which was now a household name all over the Northern part of Nigeria. That her patrons come from even far flung places like Abuja, Jos, Minna, and even Lagos. That was why it became really explosive when the official face of Queen's stepped out to be part of Kaduna Zone preliminaries.

Before the forms could be obtained, Jane Margaret Hilda developed cold feet, and confided in her friend that she was pulling out. Rakiya knew that her friend was lacking confidence to continue. Rakiya would not hear anything of sorts. She gave her a good hiding, before building up her confidence.So with Rakiya playing the dual roles of chaperon and consultant, JMH entered for the Northern Zone preliminaries of the Miss Nigeria Beauty contest.

JMH and her supporters were surprised at the outcome. She beat all the twelve contestants to emerge Miss Kaduna Zone. It was all she needed to psyche her to the next round of the competion. As Miss Kaduna Zone she was automatically qualified for the grand finale to hold in Lagos. The grand finale would comprise the various winners of all the zonal preliminaries. The eventual winner would emerge as Miss Nigeria.

JMH and Rakiya arrived by air into Lagos. Mama Caro still going strong was at the airport with a driver to meet them. They chattered all the way excitedly to the house. Ambassador Daniel Aka also received the news with enthusiasm. The ambassador also found it really amusing to think of his daughter as a beauty queen.

"Mine, my darling daughter for the Miss Nigeria crown, that is going to steer your mother awake in her grave." He chuckled "How did you get there?"

"Daddy, please be serious. I want your blessing and permission to go ahead." JMH knew he did not take her serious.

"My dear, you do not need my permission, you have already started the battle." Cutting out his laughter completely, "Though you have my express blessing to snatch home the crown for me." He burst into laughter again.

JMH almost went hysterical with joy "Daddy, I love you for that and many more." She screamed into the receiver to the delight and relief of her carer, and friend. They had all been apprehensive, thinking the ambassador would not give his approval for the whole venture.

"Jane Margaret Hilda do me a favor give them a good fight. Show them that you are an *Akachukwu*." He once more burst into his loud laughter. "Please do not come home without the crown." This time even Jane joined in the laughter.

The grand finale of the Miss Nigeria pageant took place five days later on the eve of Nigeria's independence anniversary. The venue was the main hall of the National Theatre, the country's foremost venue at Iganmu. It was one Miss Nigeria contest to be remembered for a long time to come. Unlike the contests before, it was crisis-free. Everything went right. The capacity audience went wild applauding the eventual winner and ultimate choice of the judges. Not a single voice disagreed with the decision of the panel of judges. So it came to pass in an exceptionally keenly contested edition of the Miss Nigeria Beauty Pageant, that the coveted crown was carted home by the beautiful, talented and well-spoken only child of Ambassador Daniel Aka. The new queen carted home a brand new saloon car, including an avalanche of prizes. Included in the package was a one-week all expenses paid trip to London with her chaperon, to participate in the Miss Cosmos Beauty Pageant in the month of December, 1990.

Jane Margaret Hilda and Rakiya were over the moon with their victory in the Miss Nigeria Contest. In the midst of the celebrations, they did not lose sight of the forth coming London trip which they referred to as the 'Big One'. Ambassador Aka and the Danbabas were all elated with the conquest. They all agreed there was work to be done, if they have to make any impact in London. The organizers had worked out a form of crash program to prepare the Miss Nigeria for the Miss Cosmos Contest. The crash program covered aspects of civil ethics, basic modeling, English Language grammar and diction, and World History and Contemporary Affairs.

When the crash program started in earnest, Jane Margaret Hilda found it all flattering. "Are all these actually necessary? It is even tighter than normal school." She said earnestly to her friend and chaperon.

"JMH you are now the most beautiful woman in all of Nigeria." She paused to let it sink in. "In London you will be meeting your colleagues from the rest of the world, but not on equal terms."

"Why? Why not on equal terms?"Jane Margaret Hilda interrupted.

"Because it is the honest truth." Rakiya taking her time to allow her friend to digest properly the logic. "When people from diverse cultural and ideological backgrounds converge, there are bound to be advantages and disadvantages for some people. Then you will find out the field of play will not be level for everybody participating." She once again paused to examine her friend.

"Yes, I agree with you, there are bound to be differences, which are irreconcilable." The beauty queen interjected.

"That's right sweetheart, you are right with me. Though I will beg to differ slightly somewhere." Rakiya smiled at her friend.

"Where?" Margaret Hilda's interest was piqued.

"The differences are not irreconcilable. We create allowances and buffers for them. That is what the entire program is all about, because you are going to beat the bests in the whole wide world." Rakiya paused to smile reassuringly.

Margaret Hilda nodded in concurrence. Rakiya knew when to fire on.

"Miss Anny Zibbo, who is supervising your crash program, was at the Miss World some years back, and also made her name as an international model. We should trust her judgment. She could tell exactly where our playing field is not level, and how to level up. MH, if only we could turn our disadvantages into advantages, there is no girl who is going to stand you. You, Margaret Hilda Aka will not only go to London to participate, but will conquer the whole world. JMH, we are going to blaze the trail for others to follow." Rakiya was breathless her eyes radiating confidence and hope.

Rakiya got through to her friend. She could feel the stirring inside her. Her eyes lighting up to rare potentials and opportunities that would come with victory.

And Jane Margaret Hilda for the very first time saw herself actually wearing the crown. A barrage of camera lights almost blinding her, but she was composed and smiling, knowing she was becoming history for generations yet unborn. Yes, she was going to do it. Though the whole idea was flattering, but it was achievable.

Anny Zibbo was a consummate professional, with an eye for minute details; sometimes cajoling, persuading and haranguing at times. The idea was to have both girls in all classes, though the emphasis was on the Miss Nigeria. After a full month of serious hard work, the instructors did a form of assessment and evaluation of their ward. They were all pleased with the outcome. Anny Zibbo was not only pleased, she declared it called for a celebration.

Miss Zibbo personally hosted the Miss Nigeria and her chaperon to a sumptuous dinner at the Lagoon Restaurant in Victoria Island. She commended their dedication to the program, and confided to them that she was confident that Jane was definitely going to make an impact in London.

With their confidence fortified, the girls had a swell time enjoying the 3-week break before their departure to London for the 'Big One'. There were social engagements for them to attend in their official capacity. In all the outings the new Miss Nigeria was always the centre of attention, and she was able to put to test all the training of the crash program.

CHAPTER 77

Chuck 'BTW' Freeborn IV, was not a happy man. From his reckoning, he had been in Europe for over twenty-two months. He had just finished a report from the Director's office, which made him despondent. He was very sad about the deteriorating situation in Colombia. And he was mad with himself for choosing to depart Colombia when it mattered most. He *chickened* out under very little pressure from his bosses. Now look at what *Bacata's alter ego* had turned into. Pablo Escobar was running *mad and loose like a bull in a china shop.*

Pablo Escobar who stepped into the shoes of Ramirez Castro Bacata was having a field day back in Colombia, killing as if he manufactured life. He had surpassed all of Bacata's killing records. In 1989 alone Escobar had masterminded the bombing of an Avianca Airliner with 110 lives on board. His targets were two passengers suspected to be government informants. The DEA records had confirmed that over 2,000 law enforcement officers, various government officials and civilians have been killed by the direct or indirect complicity of Pablo Escobar.

The same Pablo Escobar, in the same 1989 had been fingered in the car bomb killing of the governor of the department of Antioquia, Anthonio Roldan Betancur. Gunmen believe to be from Medellin also murdered Waldemar Franklin Quintero, the commander of Antioquia police. On that same day of the brazen killing of Police Commander Quintero, Luis Carlos Galan, was killed by gunmen in his presidential rally going on in Soacha. In that same month of August, 1989, Superior Judge Ernesto Valencia, who indicted Pablo Escobar in the killing of Guillermo Cano, was killed by suspected cartel gunmen. Before 1989 ended in Bogota, Enrique Pulido, of the Jorge Enrique Pulido TV, was murdered in cold blood by a group of gunmen.

Pablo Escobar had succeeded in making Colombia, the most violent country in the whole world. If only he had remained back in Colombia, he was convinced that he would have gotten Escobar too by now. Was it possible to work his way back to the danger zone? As far as he was concerned the war with the Medellin cartel that murdered his parents and sisters and his nephews and their father was not over, *until deaths do them apart too.*

The DEA had recorded a major blow in 1989 against Escobar's Medellin cartel, with the massive capture in Sylmar, California, of 47,554 pounds of cocaine worth over $3.2 billion. This was a huge loss that could make many a man to run crazy; maybe it was why Pablo Escobar was behaving like *a Turk looking for a windmill to tilt.* It was a record seizure in the life of the 15 year-old DEA as it moved into their new offices at 600-700 Army-Navy Drive, Pentagon City Area of Arlington, Virginia. Even at that, he could see that they were not winning the drug war.

Talking about winning the war, he had made his impact felt in Europe. He had checked the excesses of the Dutch drug lord, Klaas Bruinsma, and the likes of Johannes van Damme, who was married to a Nigerian, who was unbelievably clean as a whistle. He had once trailed Oscar Uromi all the way to Singapore, where the drug people had a clandestine meeting at an hotel at the Changi Airport. He had put tabs on all of them and it was only a matter of time, he was going to pull them in. He was only waiting for the Colombian conduit to expose himself. Chuck was certain that there was a very big fish in London. Jorge Enrique Pulido before his killing had told him somebody bigger than Escobar was lying low in London.

Chuck did not believe him. He even had goose bumps for even trying to consider that hypothesis. The only person bigger than Escobar was dead, blown to pieces right before his own eyes. *Ramirez Castro Bacata was dead and scattered. Period.* And now Pulido was dead. Killed by somebody who was doing everything to keep his Judge Ernesto Valencia, who indicted Pablo Escobar in the killing of Guillermo Cano, was killed by suspected cartel gunmen. Before 1989 ended in Bogota, Enrique Pulido, of the Jorge Enrique Pulido TV, was murdered in cold blood by a group of gunmen.

Pablo Escobar had succeeded in making Colombia, the most violent country in the whole world. If only he had remained back in Colombia, he was convinced that he would have gotten Escobar too by now. Was it possible to work his way back to the danger zone? As far as he was concerned the war with the Medellin cartel that murdered his parents and sisters and his nephews and their father was not over, *until deaths do them apart too.*

The DEA had recorded a major blow in 1989 against Escobar's Medellin cartel, with the massive capture in Sylmar, California, of 47,554 pounds of cocaine worth over $3.2 billion. This was a huge loss that could make many a man to run crazy; maybe it was why Pablo Escobar was behaving like *a Turk looking for a windmill to tilt.* It was a record seizure in the life of the 15 year-old DEA as it moved into their new offices at 600-700 Army-Navy Drive, Pentagon City Area of Arlington, Virginia. Even at that, he could see that they were not winning the drug war.

Talking about winning the war, he had made his impact felt in Europe. He had checked the excesses of the Dutch drug lord, Klaas Bruinsma, and the likes of Johannes van Damme, who was married to a Nigerian, who was unbelievably clean as a whistle. He had once trailed Oscar Uromi all the way to Singapore, where the drug people had a clandestine meeting at an hotel at the Changi Airport. He had put tabs on all of them and it was only a matter of time, he was going to pull them in. He was only waiting for the Colombian conduit to expose himself. Chuck was certain that there was a very big fish in London. Jorge Enrique Pulido before his killing had told him somebody bigger than Escobar was lying low in London.

Chuck did not believe him. He even had goose bumps for even trying to consider that hypothesis. The only person bigger than Escobar was dead, blown to pieces right before his own eyes. *Ramirez Castro Bacata was dead and scattered. Period.* And now Pulido was dead. Killed by somebody who was doing everything to keep his secret. Who else could be greater that Escobar; if not Bacata? But Bacata was dead, and could never be alive again. *Or was it that Bacata did not die in that helicopter?* That was one question that was almost driving him nuts.

He sat there mulling over the question. Why did God bring him to London, if he was needed in Colombia? He picked up the phone to call his boss at Arlington, then something just stopped him in his tracks. His eyes strayed over to the picture of Booker T. Washington in front of him. What would his model leader do, if he had found himself in this situation? He would declare loudly to all and sundry to *cast down your bucket right where you are.*

All of a sudden, the office felt stifling. Chuck knew he just must get out of that office immediately. He put on his top coat and a flat cap that cast a shadow over his face. He did not take the lift, he took the flights of steps down to the lobby, cleared security and was out in the crisp cold November air in 180 seconds flat.

It was a very bright mid-morning, that was chilly without the traditional wetness of London. He walked briskly along Grosvenor Square bordered by the Grosvenor Square Garden that had lost most of its foliage. He entered the garden, and walked up the concrete walkway to the base of the Roosevelt Memorial. At that time of the day, only a handful of people were around with the usual multitude of pigeons. An elderly roguish man was walking his two dogs, another much younger couple were jogging around, while the only other occupant of the park was an elderly woman with her cat, who was seated on a cold concrete bench, she had first draped with a small woolen blanket. The black stone-cold massive statue of one of America's best presidents grimly stared back at him without the answers he was desperate to find. Rather, he felt the cold stony eyes of President Roosevelt challenging him to go ahead and solve the puzzle.

Though Chuck felt a lot relieved from the outdoor air, he was still far from the issue that was troubling him. *Is Ramirez Castro Bacata still alive?* He briskly walked through a smaller path leading to the Duke Street exit. There were no oncoming vehicles on Grosvenor Square, he continued at his brisk pace across the pedestrian crossing on to Duke Street heading North, without taking note of anybody, his mind running riot with the remote possibility and the direct and indirect implications of Bacata being still alive on this earth.

He paused by the intersection of Weighhouse Street to take his bearing, deep inside he knew he had no particular destination in mind. He just felt the urge to just move on, he was oblivious to the activities all round him. Right across on the other side of the street was the Ukrainian Catholic Cathedral of the Holy Family in Exile. His mind consciously ruminated on this very oddly long name for a place of worship. The exotic brick-building was designed by Alfred Waterhouse in 1891, and was sold to the Ukrainian Catholics in 1967. There was no human activity happening there as he surveyed the structure that was in very good shape. He continued forward on to Oxford Street which he could see clearly in the distance.

As he reached the point at which Oxford Street intersected with Duke Street, he could not ignore the imposing and very impressive façade of Selfridges. All around him were tourists from all over the world; though Oxford Street, was a Mecca of sort to the teeming tourists, the Londoners, naturally give it a wide berth for very obvious reasons. He turned to his right on Oxford Street headed towards the Bond Street Tube-station, as if tele-guided by an unseen finger. He swiftly showed his pass and joined the crowd using the escalators down to the train levels. He took the maze of corridors leading to the Jubilee Line platforms. The squealing sounds of trains arriving and departing were very audible. Some people obviously running against time brushed pass him running to catch up with the train that was about to depart. He took his time, just engrossed in his thoughts, after all he had no appointment, or even a destination. *Little did he know that he had an appointment to keep with destiny.*

Just at the final moments, a bulky fellow in a dark woolen suit, with his top coat draped over his left arm clutching a silver-colored metallic attaché case, almost knocked him over as he ran for the train doors that were beginning to slide shut. He barely made it, as the fibre-glass doors slide shut behind him. As he took hold of an overhead safety strap, the passenger turned to face him apologetically smiling and mumbling something that was not English. The facial features remained unchanged, and very familiar. Chuck Freeborn froze in his tracks, shocked to the marrow of his bones, as the train pulled away in relative silence. *Stanmore*…the illuminated letters at the back of the train remained visible even as the trained burrowed deep into the dark tunnel. It was the north-bound Jubilee Line terminating at Stanmore.

The last time Chuck Freeborn IV saw him and caught him on camera, the swirling blades of the helicopter had his mane of hair standing on an end, and giving him a comical cartoon look. It was Vasco de Zapata, Bacata's henchman who saw his boss off at that makeshift helipad in Yarumal. It was Zapata that actually shut the helicopter doors after his boss. If Zapata was in London, then it was possible then that Bacata was alive and right there in London. He suddenly felt weak in his knees, and looked for a near-by vacant bench to settle into. Then a sudden whiff of ice-cold air enveloped him, and felt his teeth chatter against the cold. Something must be done as a matter of urgency, the platform had started filling with prospective passengers for the next train expected in the next 5 minutes.

He took time hastily to assess the present situation. A colorful route map on the wall directly in front of him; showed Stanmore Tube Station was exactly 13 stations away. He factored in the fact too that Zapata could terminate his trip in any one of them or even make possible connections at Baker Street, Finchley Road, West Hampstead, or Neasden Tube Stations. He would call an emergency meeting at his office with all the collaborator-agencies immediately. It would not be a problem to track down Zapata since he knew the train he was riding on and time. The London Transport Police would be the catalyst to get this done effortlessly with the numerous cameras in position.

By the time the rail lines rumbled to announce the imminent arrival of the 11.45am Northbound Jubilee Line, Chuck Freeborn IV was bounding up the escalators and flights of steps back to the surface, like a diver reaching for the surface from the depths of the sea. He quickly hailed a black cab on Oxford Street that took North Audley Street to Grosvenor Square. Chuck paid his fare with a very generous tip and smartly bounded up the distance to his office to commence the actual search for Vasco de Zapata, and his *dead* boss.

CHAPTER 78

At the cold dawn of a very foggy Sunday, in the first week of December, British Airways flight 095 from Lagos touched down smoothly on autopilot, guided by the highly precise instrument landing system (ILS) at the Gatwick Airport. Amongst the 228 passengers onboard were the current Miss Nigeria, Miss Ghana, Miss Liberia, Miss Gambia, Miss Ivory Coast, and Miss Senegal and their chaperons. They were in London for the Miss Cosmos Beauty Contest. By the time they had cleared immigration, and Her Majesty's Customs Service at the North Terminal, 18 other international flights all touched down safely.

They had all flown across various time zones in the night to arrive London. Onboard each flight was at least one contestant or more. When Margaret Hilda and her chaperon stepped into the arrival hall, there was a flurry of activities. First there was a crowd of spectators, then a solid wall of journalist and cameras. Rakiya, pulling behind her a hold all hand luggage approached an official displaying a placard boldly written Miss Cosmos Beauty Pageant for assistance.

They were received warmly by a group of officials amidst a flood of camera lights. Margaret Hilda was presented with a sweet smelling bouquet of flowers by a little pretty Japanese girl, before they were ushered into a lounge. As they were made to wait for some later flights, which were ferrying into London more queens. By 8am, they were ushered over to the lobby of the Forte Crest Hotel within the airport for breakfast. There, they met a number of other competitors and their chaperons who had arrived earlier that morning. They were seated comfortably all around and quietly sizing up each other. They all looked radiant and fresh, the long distances they had travelled not evident in any way.

Rakiya and her queen were in a very cheerful mood. They attacked the buffet breakfast to satisfy their craving. By the time they finished breakfast they had made friends with Miss Australia and her chaperon. They answered the naive but innocent questions about Africa without bitterness, because the questions were absurd and condescending.

"What is it like to live in the forest? How do you people cope with the other wild things?" The Miss Australia who looked about 17 years old went on with her questions.

"In Africa it is not all bushes, there are towns and cities that are equal, if not bigger than your Sydney, Brisbane, or Melbourne." Rakiya was patiently tutoring the ignorant girl.

"Alice, on the question about the other wild animals, in the town where I live, I too visit the zoo to see them, like you do in Perth." Rakiya laughed cheerfully at the girl who looked surprised.

Margaret Hilda on the other was also patiently answering even more absurd questions from Gill, who was Alice's mother and chaperon.

"Gill, we do not sleep on the tree tops, we cut them down to build houses of steel and concrete in the towns and cities. For the elephants, they would not be enough to go round as our means of transportation; so we use cars, trains, aeroplane and other means of modern transports."Margaret Hilda could tell that the older woman was even more surprised than her daughter.

The Gatwick Reception party, complemented the other group who were stationed at Heathrow too to officially receive a part of the 90 contestants and their chaperons arriving through London's most popular airport. The contest for the most prestigious beauty crown in the world was scheduled to take place on Saturday. All arrangements were in place to convey the bevy of beautiful girls and their chaperons in a police escorted convoy of limousines and luxury buses into the heart of London.The stately convoys from both airports were arranged to arrive the 300-room 5-star London Hilton on Park Lane, in the heart of Mayfair to discharge their dainty fragile passengers. Outside the hotel, in the wintry chilly winds was a crowd who were expecting to catch a glimpse of the contestants as they arrived.

The London Hilton on Park Lane was the official accommodation for all the contestants and their chaperons. The choice of the hotel was applauded for it had magnificent views over Hyde Park and the city of London. It was walking distance from popular tourists haunts like the Oxford Street, the Piccadilly Circus, Buckingham Palace, and the London West End.

Each contestant was allotted a room to be shared with her chaperon. Margaret Hilda got a room on the seventeenth floor overlooking Hyde Park Corner. After they settled in, Rakiya left to attend a meeting of all chaperons holding at the banquet hall. MH was left alone to unpack their two suitcases. She looked at the contents of the suitcases and smiled to herself. They really came prepared. They had everything they would need ranging from cosmetics to hair styling materials, and to clothing including traditional African wear. She neatly hung up the clothes in the wardrobe, and meticulously arranged all their cosmetics on the dressing table with the huge mirror.

When she looked out beyond the patio door again, it was already dark. How time flies, she thought out aloud. She looked at her wrist watch to see it was only 3.38 p.m. She put the watch to her ears, thinking something was wrong. It was only then she remembered it was winter in London, when the days were shorter, and nights fall early. She chuckled to herself and moved toward the patio glass door. She could see far beyond the lights of Belgravia Square, past Knightsbridge area. She could make out the distinctive lights of Harrods, the apex of exclusive departmentalized stores. She could see the streams of light belonging to vehicular traffic plying through Park Lane to Victoria Station, and Piccadilly Circus through Hyde Park Corner to Knightsbridge. She could also see tiny little figures of people at the foot of the well-lit Wellington Arch.

Somewhere among all those bright lights of scenic London was her father, she thought to herself. She thought of calling him later, she knew he would be at the Embassy. Ambassador Daniel Aka was a natural workaholic. She was heading towards the bedside telephone to call her father, when it rang startling her. She sat on the bed and let it ring twice more to regain her composure, before lifting up the receiver. "Hello, this is Room 1724, Margaret Hilda speaking." She answered in a very polite cheerful tone.

She heard the strange voice on the other end chuckle before replying in a deep-throated cockney accent."May I speak to the next Miss Cosmos please?" Margaret Hilda could not tell whether he was serious, or Rakiya was pulling a practical joke on her.

All the same, she responded earnestly and courteously. "My wish and aspiration is to be the next Miss Cosmos, but that won't be until Saturday sir. How may I be of help sir?" Margaret Hilda heard herself say without any trace of presumptive airs, as she was tutored back in Lagos.

There was intimidating silence from the other end. Then to her greatest surprise and relief, the voice burst out with a now familiar laughter. *"Daddy!* Oh, my goodness. I should have known better. You really got me. I am going to kill you." She screamed in excitement.

Ambassador Aka was choking with laughter. He was fond of pulling pranks like this on his unsuspecting daughter."How did you find me? She asked. I was just about to call you."

"Nigeria's High Commissioner to Britain will not encounter any problem trying to locate any of his citizens. Especially, when that subject happened to be his one and only child." He burst into his trademark laughter again.

"Daddy, what a pleasant surprise..." she was cut short by her father's booming voice in a voice reserved for bureaucratic moments. He cleared his throat theatrically. "Miss Daniel-Aka, by the powers conferred on me as the representative of the head of state of the Federal Republic of Nigeria in Britain, I welcome you to London. It is on behalf of the Head of State and Commander-In-chief of the Armed Forces, and the entire law abiding citizens, I welcome you. The whole country is solidly behind you, in your bid to bring glory to your fatherland. I wish you had a very successful and fruitful journey. The entire embassy is at your service, feel free to call us if you need any form of assistance". He said with a note of finality.

Margaret Hilda did not really know what her response should be. She quickly composed a reply. "Thank you, your Excellency. I and my entourage are greatly honoured to have your esteemed presence at our service. Please confer to the Head of State, and the good people of our great country, that we shall bring nothing short of glory home. Thank you Mr. High Commisioner once again, and long live the Federal Republic of Nigeria." Margaret Hilda said crisply.

Margaret Hilda's short response was impressive, and the father applauded her cheerfully. *"Bravo...Bravo,* dear Margaret Hilda my daughter, you have certainly come of age, and I am very proud of you." Ambassador Aka spoke with all sincerity. "How was your flight?"

"Fine. It was fine. We travelled First Class...We?" He feigned surprise. "That is Rakiya and I, you have forgotten that she is my chaperon."

"Please forgive me your Excellency, it slipped my mind, the queen travels with her lady-in-waiting." The ambassador said sarcastically. "By the way, how is Rakiya your friend and sister?"

"She is ok, she went to a meeting of all chaperons."

Their entire conversation had lasted about seven minutes, dabbling into all issues, but flavored with good natured father-and- daughter banter. He promised to call her every day, and they said their goodbyes.

Oblivious to the father and daughter, their entire conversation was monitored by a special section of the British Intelligence. After she had replaced the handset, she fell back on the bed and laughed out loud, "I hope I am not dreaming." She was still admiring the intricate design of squares and circles on the wallpaper when she fell asleep. A sleep borne out of exhaustion, through all the preparations and the flight from Lagos.

Then she dreamed. It looked so vividly real. In the dream, she was wearing a shiny pair of golden shoes and running through the streets of a big African city, in hot pursuit was a riotous mob. The mob was armed and looked dangerous and threatening. It was broad daylight, not a pedestrian was ready to heed her cries for help. She ran, and ran, and no matter how fast she ran, the mob was right on her tail. She could even feel that her feet were not making contact with the ground. Yet, the blood-thirsty mob was almost breathing down her neck. She was breathless and panting, fit to drop, but she kept running for her dear life. She thought she saw a refuge, when she saw a group of passengers in a slow moving open-back truck beckoning to her feverishly. She ran up to the truck, and clambered up, as eager hands pulled her up over the tail board. As she fell over to the cold steel floor, she felt the truck surge forward, leaving behind her pursuers in a dusty wake.

After catching her breath, she sat up to thank her rescuers, but met only stone-cold hostile gazes. She was still wondering what to do, when the truck pulled up abruptly. Margaret Hilda saw herself a captive, pinned down helpless by vice-like hands. First, they forcefully took off her highly prized shiny golden shoes. She screamed in sheer terror of the deprivation, as they in turn passed them over to her pursuers who were clamoring down below. She went on screaming and throwing tantrums like a toddler who had her ice-cream forcefully taken from her.

It was when, her captors were trying to decide her fate, when one of the same captors surprisingly snatched the golden shoes from the leader, and handed them back to her. The mob then descended on the man for his unsolicited heroics, with a pent-up rage and fury. She could see that they were lynching him, but there was nothing she could do. She watched helplessly in horror as her savior went down in a pool of his own blood. She could see that he was at the throes of death, when she heard first the distant clap of thunder. The lynching continued, the sound of thunder continued too. Nothing could deter the mob from their dastardly act, though the man's brow was bloody but he did not bow out. There was the persistent disturbing clap of thunder again, though this time nearer. Then she woke up from her nightmare, to the loud persistent knocks on the door.

Margaret Hilda was sweating profusely, and her heart was thumping. Her dress was drenched, and she could feel the wetness of tears on her cheeks. She was thankful it was only a dream. There was the persistent knocking on the door. Where was she? Then, she came to realization.

"Yes! I am coming" she called out, and ran thankfully to open the door. Standing by the door was a distraught Rakiya, and a black-uniformed security personnel. MH happily fell into the open embrace of her friend. A relieved Rakiya who was worried sick, held tightly to her friend, knowing the worst was over.

"It is ok, baby." Rakiya said soothingly. "You have been crying, what is the problem? Is anything wrong? Rakiya asked anxiously.

"Rakiya it was a terrible dream. Thank God, it was only a dream."

"It is ok then, that it was only a dream" Rakiya tried waving it aside.

"I have a premonition something terrible is going to happen. Rakiya you know, I seldom dream. It is a warning, a sign of something bad about to happen." Margaret Hilda started crying all over again.

"Shut your mouth, naughty girl!" Rakiya scolded her harshly "God forbid it, nothing bad is going to happen to any of us." She patted her friend on the back.

All the while they were still standing out on the corridor. The battled and somehow embarrassed security man observed all the display of emotions with interest. He cleared his throat to draw their attention. "Excuse me ladies, It seems to me all is well, and there is no cause for alarm. Except you have any other need for me, I would like to get back to my desk." He sounded very polite.

"Oh! I am sorry Duncan, please pardon me. That will be all for now, thank you very much." Rakiya quickly dismissed the hotel employee.

They went into their room, and shut the door behind them. Rakiya then quickly placed her handbag and a green paper folder on the bed, and hurriedly ran in to the toilet. She called out to her to study the contents of the folder, that she was coming to explain later after sorting out the very pressing matter of the moment with her almost bursting bladder.

The documents in the folder were two sets of accreditation and identity cards, a pictorial guide and map of central London, rules and regulations for all contestants and their chaperons, a detailed itinerary of all the program of events leading to the Saturday grand finale.

Jane was still examining the documents when she heard the toilet flush. And a moment later, Rakiya came out clad only in her white underwear. She went over to the wardrobe for her nightgown. As she was slipping into the nightgown, Margaret told her of her father's telephone call. Then she told her in full details the dream. Rakiya listened attentively. As the details progressed she became apprehensive, but she did not show it. Somebody must be in control, and she–Rakiya was that somebody.

Before the end of Margaret Hilda's story, Rakiya was already looking for ideas to water down the dream. She knew this particular dream was absolutely serious or should be taken seriously. For Bailey said; *dreams are rudiments of the great state to come. We dream what is about to happen.* Rakiya was very knowledgeable about dreams, she took an elective that exhaustively handled dreams way back in the university. According to Gustavus Hindman Miller; *all dreams possess an element of warning or prescience; some more than others.*

Dreams that leave a vivid impression on the awake or conscious mind were defined as spiritual. And these class of dreams Miller said; *...are brought about by the higher self-penetrating the soul realm, and reflecting upon the waking mind approaching events.* There was no way she was going to reveal her fears to her friend, it would kill her fighting spirit.

Rakiya, thankfully resorted to Miller's comment on dreams classified as physical. She off-handedly but tactfully told Margaret Hilda, the dream was more or less unimportant, because it was super-induced by the anxious waking mind, and so possessed no visible connotation or significance.

Rakiya, then carefully changed the subject from dreams to the chaperons' meeting with the pageant organizers. She started her story with all gusto, to catch and occupy her friend's troubled mind. You know these chaperons are something else. Some came with the most ridiculous requests and demands. I saw all sorts today." She clapped her hands in the typical gossip fashion.

"Eh! What did you see?" Margaret asked with unabashed curiosity.

"Could you imagine requests for extended wake up time, special toilet seats, special bedcovers and what have you." Rakiya burst out laughing.

"Tell me something." Margaret sat up properly, and was all ears. Rakiya smiled to herself and fired on. The prospects of a good story and gossip, instantly dissipating Jane's melancholic disposition. The burden of her dream giving way to curiosity. Rakiya's immediate task was to give her friend a clear head and mind to put in her ultimate best for the entire competition.

"There was this particular chaperon who demanded for a water-bed, that her ward was not used to sleeping in a normal bed."

"So, how was that resolved?" Margaret Hilda asked with enthusiam.

"Of course, the pageant official, to the satisfaction of the rest of us, politely told her off. Just like the other chaperon who requested for a life-size teddy bear" Rakiya went on without pausing. She also got engrossed in her real and fabricated stories. She finally burst into a full blast of cheerful laughter, that Margaret Hilda also joined in.

Margaret Hilda was bent over with laughter, with tears streaming down her cheeks. Rakiya was happy with this picture of her ward and friend.

Then Rakiya, launched into the serious issues and deliberations at the meeting proper. "At 11 a.m. tomorrow, there will be rehearsals with ... guess who?" Rakiya paused for an answer from Margaret Hilda.

"Okay, I give up. I concede defeat" Margaret Hilda said with feigned frustration.

"Jane you would not believe, but who is in London life and direct. The one and only Stevie Wonder!"

"*O-KO-KO-BI-OKO A BA MI EDA!*" Margaret Hilda exclaimed in a typical Nigerian parlance..

She threw herself on the bed, spread-eagled. "I am suddenly very hungry."

"Me too," cried Rakiya "let's order some room service." Rakiya picked up the telephone receiver to make the order. "What would you like dear?"

"Anything, anything my chaperon deems fit for us." Margaret Hilda answered with her good natured laugh. Rakiya placed order for vegetable salad with plain dressing, roasted chicken sandwich, and orange juice for two. Then she turned round and continued with the report of the meeting, as Jane was examining the accreditation and identity tags. "We were asked to carry those on our persons at all times. The pageant organizers were very concerned about safety, because of the IRA and other terrorists' threats."

"The IRA? That I do not find funny." Margaret Hilda chipped in.

"Likewise the pageant organizers, it is indeed their biggest nightmare." Rakiya saw her friend shudder at the mention of the word, and inwardly berated herself for the blunder. "We are going to be involved in a very busy week, they warned us." Rakiya quickly added hoping to get Margaret Hilda back in the line. The queen was studying the various programs with concentration and interest. "You can see there is no room for personal escapades, the organizers purposely designed it that way."

"Why?" Margaret Hilda asked.

"It is the only way, they could maintain and monitor an effective security. Being able to account for each contestant and her chaperon at each point in time." Rakiya paused to look through her bag for the notes she took during the meeting.

"Did they accept the request for the grand piano?" Margaret Hilda inquired anxiously.

"Oh, yes they did. You are going to be using the same grand piano with your Stevie Wonder."

"That alone has made my day." The queen grinned from ear to ear.

"I also receive the exceptional approval to be back stage to handle your hair, makeup and dressing, if you scale through to the ten finalists. That indeed is the least of our problems because we are there already." Rakiya declared with all the confidence in the world.

"Rakiya, you are a darling. I wonder, if I could ever do anything without you." Margaret Hilda said cheerfully as she moved over to give her bosom friend a hug. But what came next stopped Margaret Hilda in her stride.

"MH! Stop it forthwith. What is the problem with you? Are you crazy?" Rakiya was spitting fire. Margaret Hilda was shocked beyond any doubt. She was shivering. And just as suddenly as the outburst came, it fizzled out like a bolt of lightning. The two friends were both crying. Rakiya stood up and took the confused and shivering Margaret Hilda in a warm embrace. There were no words to be said. They just stood and cried for a while.

Rakiya felt bad, but she knew it had to be done for their own good. It is now or never, to psyche up her friend. She had to be independent, and fight her own battles. Dreams, color, race and all other negative influences must be thrown to the wind. The road to the crown was not an easy one, but was not impossible. It could be attained by sheer determination, hard work, flavored with a modicum of confidence.

"I am sorry for the outburst, MH. Please pardon me." Rakiya said soothingly as she ran her hands through her friends back. Her friend was still sobbing. "I think we are all feeling the pressures of the contest. MH please I want you to understand that, there are things we could work together to achieve, there will definitely be a stage you must accomplish on your own." Rakiya spoke slowly and distinctly, making sure her friend was ready for the next very important words that will make or mar.

"Like when you step out on the various stages of the competition in front of the judges and audience. You will be alone, but doing what you know best. The ultimate reward is the crown. I will be in the wings, only a whisper away, waiting on you to bring glory to all our people." Rakiya turned Margaret Hilda's face to look right into her clear beautiful and enchanting eyes.

"You saw almost all the other girls earlier today, there was nothing special about them. On a level ground you will give them a good fight; *pound for pound.* And I your sister will be right behind you." Rakiya could see the close resemblance to her dead sister vividly. She saw the immediate twinkle in Margaret Hilda's eyes. She observed with relish, the fighting spirit touched by mere words; a spirit spurred into action.

Margaret Hilda started nodding, and she wiped away her tears as if they were a taboo. Then she smiled. Rakiya was shocked, but pleased to hear. "Rakiya, what are we waiting for, let's get the show on the road. Let's go and kick asses; as the Americans would say." There was fire in her voice as she chuckled cheerfully.

Four hours later, after an hour of aerobics and massage supervised by Rakiya, as she was instructed back in their crash program. They had a leisure warm bath, and their dinner and retired to bed early. There strategy was to keep the local Nigerian Time, which was an hour ahead of London time. Long after they had retired to bed, Rakiya could not succumb to the bosom of sleep. She could hear Jane's relaxed breathing, and the soft features of her face above the cozy warm covers. Jane was fast asleep. She was busy thinking about the events of the day. The most distracting and unsettling factor was the vivid dream Jane had. She tried for the umpteenth time to find an interpretation. She was positive it was a warning, and it must be heeded. Her positive oriented mind refused to accept all the probable meanings her mind proffered. She gave up later.

She knelt down quietly by her side of the bed and said a silent prayer. She prayed for about ten minutes, it was a fervent prayer to God to intervene on their behalf. It felt strange, for she had not prayed for a very long time. The prayer actually unburdened her heavy heart. For she knew that the sleeping mind is not only supersensitive as to prevalent external sounds and light, but it often sees hours and days in advance of the waking mind. This seeing into the future is manifested through dreams.

Rakiya later stealthily climbed back into the bed without rousing her sleeping friend. As the nibbling incisors of sweet sleep gradually gnawed at her consciousness, a poem by the American, Langston Hughes lingered on her mind; *what happens to a dream deferred; does it dry up like a raisin in the sun? or fester like a sore–and then run.*

At that very moment at the Blue Room restaurant on the ground floor of the Park Lane Hilton, Oscar Uromi with the top management of the Miss Cosmos Pageant, were having drinks prior to their scheduled dinner meeting. It was Oscar that had convened the dinner meeting, since he was going out of the country to attend to a very urgent business. He had arranged the London Manager of Twinkle & Twinkle to see to every arrangement accordingly. He was not very sure yet, but he promised to be part of the grand finale on Saturday.

Seated just two tables away on a non-descript table were an odd couple that were two DEA agents, who with hidden ear pieces were part of the ongoing discussions at Uromi's table. Thanks to the highly sensitive microphones that were cleverly concealed in the glass flower vase. At least they know that he was going out of London for an urgent business.

That confirmed the information that filtered out of Oscar Uromi's meeting with Vasco de Zapata at the Claridge's earlier on in the day. There was a big shipment of drugs about to be delivered into London. The DEA like blood hounds were on to the scent, were not letting go until they draw blood.

For Oscar he had let his guards down at the most crucial moment, and like for a boxer its to his own chagrin and doom.

CHAPTER 79

The next morning, Jane Margaret Hilda and her chaperon woke at 6 o'clock, while the other contestants were all sound asleep. They had two hours of combined aerobic and yoga exercises, directed to condition the body, and to relax and focus the mind. Rakiya as usual was in control following all the instructions to the letter. Then they had their bath, and ordered up a continental breakfast. They still had about an hour to kill before the scheduled rehearsal time, so for want of something to do Rakiya went downstairs to purchase the daily newspapers.

She stepped out of the lift into the lobby, to be confronted by an expectant crowd of photographers. She found it amusing and flattering when a couple of flash bulbs bathed her. Under the curious gazes of the photographers and celebrity watchers, she walked gracefully to the Hotel Shop that also doubled as a newsagent. She quickly picked and paid for four London dailies, and retraced her steps back to the lift. She shared the lift up with four other passengers; three hotel guests and the hotel security personnel.

Rakiya recognized the security personnel immediately. He was Duncan, the man who assisted her the previous day when she could not get into the room. She smiled at him gratefully and mumbled a greeting. Duncan responded cheerfully with a very crisp and professional greetings, and thereafter maintained a dignified silence until the three other guest disembarked on the tenth floor. Rakiya who had always had phobia for lifts, and would never feel secure in a lift leaned back on the burnished handrails with eyes closed. She could feel the dizzying effect of the exceptionally fast lift in the depth of her guts. Rakiya was startled when she heard the voice in a conspiratorial whisper. She opened her eyes to see Duncan bending low to be audible above the swish of the lift.

"Madam, I will advise you to be very punctual for today's first schedule, because the organizers have a surprise for..."

Duncan stopped abruptly as the lift pulled up on the 17th floor. The lift doors opened to show three guests waiting by the doors, that put paid to Duncan's privileged information. Rakiya was barely able to restrain her curiosity. She was surprised to hear herself say; "Thank you Duncan for the ride." She accompanied it with a bright smile and alighted gingerly from the lift.

While Duncan once again the polite hotel employee responded with a standard "Have a nice day madam."

As she approached their room, she tried to figure out what *surprise* Duncan was talking about the organizers had. For whom? That they would find out soon. She glanced at her Cartier gold wrist watch, a birthday present from her father. The time was about twenty minutes past the hour. There was enough time to heed the kind and considerate advise of Duncan.

Inside, Rakiya and Margaret Hilda shared the papers amongst themselves and got engrossed in their reading. All the papers at least rated the arrival of the 87 beauty queens in London, a front page issue. *The Eye,* had it an headline, *Race For Beauty Crown Heats Up!* The paper did a full four-page supplement on the forth coming beauty contest. It was Rakiya who was reading the The Eye. She could not believe what she was reading. The more she read, the angrier she became. She stole a casual glance at Margaret Hilda, who was engrossed with The Sun. Then she resumed her own reading once again.

Rakiya allowed her anger and passions to have the better of her, she lost all sense of time. Rakiya forgot all about the Scotish man and his warning. She even forgot the morning schedule. Rakiya also forgot she was suppose to be in charge. She indeed forgot she was on duty.

Then the telephone rang. It seemed a deafening ring. Their initial response was that of disdain for the offending equipment. Then the second ring, that was when all hell broke loose for Rakiya. She was indeed in a state. Margaret Hilda thought, her friend was about to have a seizure. It was indeed alarming for her friend, to see her in that state.

"What is it? Rakiya! What is it?" She asked with grave concern. But no answer was forth coming from the bewildered Rakiya. On the third ring, Margaret Hilda picked up the receiver, and she heard a surreptitious whisper "You have very little time to catch the bus". Then the line went dead. Margaret Hilda looked lost.

"I suppose it was a wrong number, somebody said something about catching a bus..." Rakiya did not wait for her to finish, she pulled her out of the room running towards the lift. An alarmed and frightened Margaret Hilda who was almost dragged at first, suspecting real danger ran along. As they approached the lifts, a lift door opened magically. Standing there was the hotel employee wearing a name tag, with the legend– *'Duncan'*. He had a fixed smile on his face. The grateful Rakiya collapsed gratefully into the lift speechless. Duncan sent the lift hurtling down in the express mode. "Oh, my God, Duncan how could I have forgotten." Rakiya kept repeating.

Margaret Hilda was wondering what secret pact was between these two, when the lift doors burst open. They ran out like bats out of hell. Rakiya held on to Jane, as a barrage of flashlight bulbs captured them on film. She did not slow down and Jane went along. They ran past a puzzled crowd of spectators who were at a loss. They ran into the cold chilly winds of winter. They saw the first of the convoy of four buses carefully pulling into the Park Lane morning traffic.

Margaret Hilda found a seat quickly in the scantily filled bus, and as they pulled into the traffic heading down the Hyde Park Corner, she waved excitedly at a relieved Rakiya who was standing at the sidewalk and waving back happily. As the relieved Rakiya turned around to move back to the hotel, she saw a band of excited contestants and their chaperons who missed the bus. They were a few minutes late. It was amusing and pathetic the same time, when Rakiya discovered they were only excited because they thought they came out too early. Rakiya could not help but notice the look on their faces when they were informed of the true situation. They all tried talking at same time and ended up saying nothing. It was in this *tower of Babel,* that an official appeared to take care of things. But it was too late the journalists and photographers were already having a field day with the unsuspecting girls Rakiya stood by and watched events unfold with keen interest. Gradually the number of latecomers swelled. The look of indignation as they were told they had missed the rehearsal was indeed amusing. First the relaxed happy look, transpiring first to doubt, then the shock of the reality.

It was a cacophonous scene as they set on each other. Chaperons against contestants, contestants against chaperons. Accusations and counter-accusations. An obviously amused pageant official, clapped his hands to call them to order. The unfortunate contestants and their chaperons could not see why, the man was amused with their predicament. He smiled and then addressed them. The official was actually happy because he was the progenitor of this strategy. And it worked perfectly again. This strategy was adopted by the organisers as that of a natural selection to curtail and regulate the number of contestants to participate in the choreographed opening act for the actual contest night. It was a case of the fewer the better for effective rehearsals. The officials called it the *early bird strategy*. They also observed it puts the contestants and their chaperons on their toes, since thereafter they become punctual in all subsequent engagements and schedules.

The official instructed them to return to their rooms and await further instructions as the day progresses. The man reiterated the importance for them to remain indoors, due to the security measures already in place. "No person is to leave the confines of the hotel for any reasons." The man said with a note of finality. The instructions were received with evident disdain and contempt, it was more than the official could manage since the complains were made in various languages. Though the official was not one bit bothered about their opinions. When the heat became too much the veteran pageant official brought a copy of the Rules and Regulations for all contestants. He pointed out page 17 to them, it stipulates that the pageant reserves the right to disqualify any contestant, based on her misconduct or her chaperon's. That put paid to all the wrangling.

The grumbling subsided drastically, and the crowd reluctantly picked their way back to the lifts. The security personnel efficiently blocked off the curious pack of reporters who wanted to follow them back to the lobby, at least for snippets to make a story. Rakiya went along with the crowd into the lobby her eyes roamed the length and breadth of the lobby silently searching for her *genie*, Duncan. She did not find him. Unfortunately, he was also not in the lift she rode up. As she disembarked later on her floor she made a mental note to give him a big tip later.

Rakiya pushed opened their room door to be confronted with the scattered pages of the newspapers, that almost marred her duties of a chaperon if not for Duncan. She gathered the scattered pages together, made herself comfortable on the bed, and proceeded to read the offending article all over again from the beginning.

In the centre-spread was the lead *All Hail The New Queen* and spread across the lower half were color passport-size facial photographs of 48 contestants. Embedded strategically amidst the smaller photographs were postcard-size portraits of Miss United Kingdom, Miss Germany, Miss U.S.A., Miss France, and Miss Canada. The story categorically said that the fifty-three photographs were; ...those of the contestants whose beauty was worthy of mention. And the writers did not only write-off those whose photographs were not shown as the no-competition contestants, who were in London just to boost the number of participating contestants. The paper also opined that in future contests, not every *Tom, Dick and Harry* should be invited to run for the Miss Cosmos, because they happen to be a beauty queen of one rag-tag banana republic.

In a final display of very unprofessional journalistic conduct, and utter disregard of civility, the writer or writers insinuated that; the organizers erred in lodging all the contestants in the Park Lane Hilton; for some category of the contestants would have been more comfortable, camping out in the nearby Hyde Park. Rakiya felt sick deep down to her innards. She was shocked and disgusted. These were definitely the views of an incorrigible racist bigot. She felt weak thinking about freedom of speech and its demerits.

She pushed herself to finish the concluding part of the article. There was a wager for interested readers to call some listed numbers to place bets that one of the contestants in the larger photographs would emerge as the eventual Miss Cosmos come Saturday at the Royal Albert Hall. 99 pence per minute was the cost of the expected call.

Rakiya all of a sudden found her fury and anger decimate into understandable amusement. She saw through the commercial purpose of the newspaper article. That not withstanding, something told her she was going to use this story to their benefit. It might even slope the playing field in their favor. She concentrated her thoughts. She went into deep thoughts. Her fertile mind tried all possible permutations. Then it came as a bolt of lightning. She knew she had it all wrapped up. Yes! She had the various angles of the entire newspaper supplement figured out. She had a perfect bargaining chip in her hands. This was her thinking, the entire write-up was bias and full of vitriolic vituperations, which was a calculated attempt to adulterate and sway public opinion and its fair sense of judgment. It was also calculated to demoralize a large proportion of the innocent contestants. Somebody somewhere tried a cheap shot and she was going to use it against the whole system to the advantage of the underdogs.

She proceeded to examine the photographs with a more appraising eye. It was not very long before everything fitted together like an Indian puzzle. Then Margaret Hilda's dream all of a sudden came to her mind. Was this to confirm the warning or sign of the dream. She was not going to allow JMH to see the paper. Now to her next course of action.

For the better part of an hour she fine-tuned it mentally. She was convinced it was proper and right, she was only turning an obvious disadvantage into an advantage. The important point was to get it done meticulously. She took a tiny scissors from her toilet bag and neatly clipped out the entire article. And she seated herself behind the table with the huge mirror and began to write. For two solid hours she went on. The absence of a dictionary made the writing difficult but that did not deter her. She wrote, cancelled, wrote cancelled until she ran out of paper. She called for more hotel stationery.Finally, she was done. She proof read it again and again. She felt good. There was no harm in trying she thought. She looked around her, and noticed the floor littered with crumpled papers. She smiled to herself as she bent over to tidy the place up, before leaving the room to put the letter in a presentable state.

She was humming under her breath, Ain't No Stoppin Us Now, a song by Luther Vandross, and written by McFadden, Whitehead, and Cohen, when she entered the lift going down to the lobby. The sole occupant of the lift, a conservatively looking Englishman complete with an umbrella and bowler hat, observed her with undisguised disdain. Rakiya pretended he was not even there and made her song even very audible to the man's obvious discomfort;

"...*Ain't no stoppin us now*
We've got the groove
There's been so many things that have held us down
But now it looks like things are finally commin' around
I know we've got a long, long way to go
And where we will end up, I don't know..."

Rakiya was still humming her song when she walked in the hotel's business centre. She typed the various letters herself, which was a relief to the staff who was indeed busy with other guest. She was still humming the same song when she sauntered over the vacant concierge desk and deposited the various addressed envelopes for delivery.

Rakiya was still unconsciously humming the song when she strolled into the restaurant for her lunch. She had a good meal. After the lunch, she went back to the room and fell into a deep fit-free sleep. It was a deep sleep of contentment. It was like a big burden was lifted from her shoulders. Rakiya slept through the rest of the cold wintry day. It was a tired looking Margaret Hilda that shook her awake at about 8 p.m. later, when they returned from the rehearsal. Margaret Hilda herself was even too weary to talk as she fell asleep immediately.

The story was that, on the previous day, the about 40 contestants who missed the rehearsal were left in a state of suspense as they waited anxiously for the phone to ring in their rooms. The anxious moment was spent watching the television. For some it was a sullen moment. For some it was too much to bear, the fact that they would not perform with the legendary Stevie Wonder on Saturday. For those who made it to the rehearsals it was a tedious experience. It was definitely not an easy task trying to organize a pack of excited girls, some very childish and spoilt, into a meaningful group of professional performers in a day. But the organizers were used to it. They had their modus operandi fashioned out.

Within two hours, the wheat was separated from the chaffs, only forty girls who were keen and had a natural aptitude for the choreographed steps were left on stage. The rest became audience, maybe they would have been better off watching television in their rooms back in the hotel. The rehearsal was a time consuming exercise. The choreographer was faced with the challenge to train forty girls to master a complex dance routine that took professionals many hours of dedicated practice.

As the final forty girls got engrossed in the rehearsal proper, time just flew by. Lunch was snacks and soft drinks, that was in abundance. It was almost 7 p.m., and the girls were barely able to stand on their feet, when the famed choreographer summed up their effort.

"Okay! Okay!" He clapped his hands beckoning on the weary girls to close ranks.

"Okay ladies, it is now time for the scores. I have to tell you the truth..." he paused dramatically, as all the forty pairs of eyes pleaded with him. He alone has the verdict to move them to the next stage of the rehearsals. "I think you would do!" The man said casually. It did not register, as the girls looked for reassurances from each other. He laughed and applauded cheerfully, as the girls went berserk in a wild dance of celebration.

It was worth all the victory dance and self-congratulations. The girls had worked hard, they had survived the relentless cajoling voice of their instructor, who mentally tormented them to work harder. It was indeed a great consolation. When their bodies felt weak and tired, it was the constant thought of performing with a living legend, that kept them going till this climax. The instructor who was getting a bonus for his initial success smiled and called them to order once again.

"You ladies did well and I am proud of you, but I must remind you this is just the beginning. The dress rehearsal is on Friday morning. He paused as the girls gave him a puzzled look.

"Does it mean, we are not even certain of performing on Saturday night? The boisterous contestant from Greece asked.

"I am afraid that is the honest truth." The instructor said with evident sincerity, though he was lying through his teeth. That bit of information was not very consoling, though the girls were now resolved to be on that stage on Saturday night, performing side by side with one of history's greatest performers.

By the time they made it back to the hotel to meet the anxious dreary eyed girls who missed the rehearsals, they were too tired to tell their stories. Their weary bodies were crying out for the comfort of their beds. Every request to tell of the events at rehearsal was postponed to the next day.

CHAPTER 80

It was 8.50 a.m. Wednesday, at the corporate headquarters of the Miss Cosmos Beauty Pageant at 21, Golden Square. Official business would not commence until 9 a.m., but Don Baldwin, 44, President of the Pageant was already seated behind his huge ornate desk. He was looking worried. The desk top was bare of anything but for the devastating 3-page type-written letter addressed to him. Don Baldwin threw a wary glance at the letter for the umpteenth time as he chewed on his ulcer medication, he could feel the burning sensations deep down in his stomach, it all started after he read that letter last night.

Baldwin, at 37, became the youngest person to ever run the Miss Cosmos Beauty Pageant. He joined the services of the Pageant at the age of 34, after vacating a top flight executive position with the highbrow advertising firm of Goldstein & Weiners at Dover Street, a stone's throw away. He came into the Pageant as Vice-President in-charge of Logistics and Planning. For watchers of the industry, it was not surprising that he got the plum job. Goldstein & Weiners had over the years handled the world-wide advertising for the Miss Cosmos Pageant, it was Baldwin who had handled the account.

The youthful Baldwin, who was blessed with an awesome intellectual capability, came with new and refreshing ideas that could not be ignored by even the die-hard conservatives in the pageant. His ideas and suggestions in no-small-measure revolutionized the world-wide beauty pageant industry. So by the time, the 68-year- old Lord Steven Hardaway went into semi-retirement due to failing health, Baldwin got into the thick of affairs of the Pageant. Not long thereafter, Lord Hardaway went into full retirement, by then Baldwin had passed the acid test, and cut his teeth, he was the natural choice to take over the helm of affairs.

The resultant hue and cry went from London to New York. It did not in the least deter the meticulous and ambitious Baldwin who had his eyes set on his goal, to change the beauty pageant scenario. Within a period of 3 years, even Baldwin's biggest critics conceded defeat, for Don Baldwin had transformed The Miss Cosmos Pageant from a charitable entity into a multi-million dollar going concern. Baldwin owed it all to his aggressive marketing strategies founded on meticulous planning. Baldwin had an obsession for planning, every step must be planned.

To Baldwin, there must be a plan either on paper or mentally for any project to be undertaken. His father, the Late Canon Isaac Quittine Baldwin harped on it endlessly; "...*Men Fail, Not Because They Planned To Fail But Because They Failed To Plan.*" Donald Baldwin was meticulous to a fault, in his private life it cost him his marriage. His wife of two years, a former Miss Cosmos cited it as a ground for divorce. In the divorce proceeding that was widely reported, she declared that, *"He was so meticulous that he drives me almost to the point of insanity. Everything must be in place. Every minute detail is put into consideration. It has become a psychological torture to co-habit with him."*

Baldwin did not contest her claim. Divorce was granted without much ado. Baldwin made double sure that settlements were meticulously sorted out. That was vintage Don Baldwin.

This morning Don Baldwin was infuriated with himself because he had erred in his usual routine of planning against all foreseeable possibilities. It was not an erring wife, far from it, because he had resolved against anymore wives at least not for now. His concern was the strong worded letter in impeccable English from a faceless writer. The contents were serious enough for him to summon an emergency meeting of his Organizing Committee. He could see into the adjoining conference room on his desk monitor. He could see they were all seated, nobody was absent. It was a minute to 9 a.m., when he gathered up his folder and the letter and passed through his secretary's office to start the emergency meeting.

With ten seconds to the hour, Don Baldwin walked smartly over to his appointed place at the head of the oblong table. The conference room was quiet and tense. Each member of the committee was indeed apprehensive, for their president only calls an emergency meeting if a crisis situation was imminent. Over the years, as veteran staff, they had imbibed certain idiosyncrasies of their boss. The agenda for the meeting was usually unknown, that was the reason for the prevalent state of apprehension. And knowing Baldwin, he would be smarting all over like a bear with a sore head. The fate of a latecomer to an emergency meeting was better imagined than experienced. Baldwin was known to hate emergency meetings, and at the very rare emergency meetings, he had always said, ...*that an emergency meeting was a sure sign of a panic situation, that resulted out of oversight or omission in ones plans. This raises very serious questions and doubts about ones managerial capability. Plans and planning are the road map of a good organizational manager"*.

There were no pleasantries or formalities, the writing was on the wall; *nothing but business!* The 44-year-old president took a flitting moment to roam his eyes around the table; to obviously ascertain that no one was missing. Too bad no latecomer to absorb the bulk of the salvo that would go round, for no one in the planning would be spared. They poised for the barrage of words. Surprisingly nothing came out. They were disarmed. Don Baldwin gave his traditional nod to the vice-president for planning and logistics to set the audio recorders rolling. The meeting was officially in progress.

"Good morning ladies and gentlemen" Baldwin said crisply, while an incoherent mumble of responses came from the eight ladies and six gentlemen sharing the conference table with him. "An hydra- headed problem that we did not put into consideration had just reared its heads", he paused slightly to open the black ostrich leather- bound folder in front of him, to avoid the embarrassed gazes of his dedicated staff.

"Time is not on our side this time, so I have gone ahead to examine it. The problem has far reaching potentials to make or mar the Saturday event." Baldwin spoke as if delivering a sermon. His audience was breathless as they waited for him to land. No one shifted in his seat. "If handled properly, it might jolt our tactics and strategies over the years but in our overall interests, but if not tactfully handled we are doomed and would become history."

Twenty-eight eyes exchanged glances for a flitting moment, and met his gaze pound for pound, they confirmed he was dead serious. "I am confident, I have the best brains around me," Baldwin paused and smiled reassuringly, as he glanced at his gold Rolex Explorer II. "We must find immediate and counter solutions or else consider the Miss Cosmos Beauty Pageant history. Ladies and Gentlemen this is our challenge." Baldwin concluded with a note of finality.

Don Baldwin slowly looked around the attentive faces of his audience, he took his assessments, he was satisfied that his message got home. In a single fluid movement he punched a button on the white telephone in front of him. He spoke quietly to his secretary in the next room, as the members of the Organising Committee remained immobile. Ten seconds later, Christine Kline, the president's beautiful secretary pushed through the heavy soundproofed glass doors into the conference room laden with bundles of documents. She quickly and efficiently placed a set of documents in front of everybody, and left silently without any fuss. Everyone except Baldwin descended voraciously on the documents placed in front of them. They had waited impatiently for this moment. They were about to find out the mystery behind this emergency meeting, and the threat to their livelihood. The document was letter addressed to the President, and dated Monday.

Dear Mr. President,

We appreciate your breaking away from your absolutely busy schedule to dedicate some time to our letter, we assure you it would not be time wasted. With all respect, we implore you at this juncture to first peruse objectively the attached clippings from the *The Eye* of today. This would enhance a better understanding of the near and remote motives of this missive.

Now that you are done with your perusal of the clippings, please hear us out before any criticism, and subsequent judgment is given. From the four corners of the globe, we had willingly converged with youthful exuberance and the famed spirit of sportsmanship under your auspices, to compete in the Olympics of beauty pageants,,–The Miss Cosmos Contest. We left our various sovereign climes, believing it was a great honor and privilege to be part of an epic event, that promotes cordial and peaceful coexistence of the world's peoples. An epic event bat-blind to race, color, creed, or religion.

It was on this premise, that we totally surrendered to the ideals of the pageant, that the contestant as an individual, who is to be fairly and justly judged on her beauty, talent, and intelligence, independent of her country or background. It was our sincere desire to commence the contest as equals, no underdogs whatsoever, so our eventual victor will be honoured and respected universally as primus interperes, the first among equals.

It would be prudent to keep our faces behind veils not because the The Eye has declared us too ugly to be part of the competition, but because we now have genuine doubts and fears over our continued safety. We, like any right thinking civilized person see the publication in very bad taste in all its entirety. It's obvious racial undertones, coupled with its vitriolic and vituperative comments are not only an affront on our persons and the sovereign nationalities we represent, they are also a calculated attempt to demoralize and marginalize some of us. The publication's obvious prejudice will definitely sway and bias its numerous minds of readers. Who are the readers? The Public of course, who will be the target audience and the judges.

It would be a waste of your precious time and space to go ahead to analyze further why this piece of profane literature is disadvantageous and detrimental to the chances of 48 innocent contestants who have put their trust in you. A thorough perusal shows that the basic factors and grounds of the marginalization are rooted in geographical location and color. Though we would not want to cast stones, *because he who seeks equity must come with clean hands*, but we would fail in our duties if we do not intimate you, that your pageant is indicted, since its all part of your sponsored publicity. It is incontrovertible that the entire photographs used in the supplement were contestants' file photos with you.

Knowing your brilliant testimonials and antecedents, we are convinced, you cannot destroy what you have labored so much to build, we believe it is definitely the handiwork of a callous staff. Howbeit, it would be practically impossible to absolve your office from blame, because like the Americans aptly put it ...*you cannot pass the buck, it ends on your table*.

Mr. President, without fear or favor, we consider you an embodiment of all that is good and godly. It is our fervent belief that you will rise up to the occasion, to right the wrongs, and appease the wronged timely, for the credibility and the continued corporate existence of your noble organization. It is in ultimate good faith that we proffer these possible solutions, if you deem them fit;

1. To immediately disabuse the minds of the public, your dissociation and total condemnation of the write-up.
2. To jettison all current judging methods, that inadvertently places a contestant and her country for judgment. We suggest the use of numerics in place of countries.
3. To reassure all contestants of your trust and fair play and impartiality before the actual contest.

We wish you God's speed and wisdom in all that you plan to do regarding this matter. Please do not consider our letter and demands as any form of subtle threat by any means. We are also committed to making you better, which has been your ultimate desire. We thank you sincerely for hearing us out.

Yours faithfully,

MARGINALIZED CONTESTANTS

Don Baldwin allowed them fifteen minutes to read, peruse and digest the documents. You can hardly hear them breath as they did their reading. He knew they were already individually working out possible solutions. He counted himself lucky to have such dedicated staff, what could he do without their support. He knew they would stand by him through rain or shine. Later each person was allowed a limited time to address the issue, and then proffer their own solutions. Notes were taken, then more observations were made. Within a space of two hours the meeting had reached a far-reaching resolutions. The president then addressed the forum.

"Ladies and gentlemen, we have reached a conclusion, and that means we have found a solution. We must not fail to commend the brilliant writer or writers of this letter, who in no small measure performed our paid job for us", he paused to examine his notes. "At this moment, we shall conveniently ignore the subtle threats hidden in the body of the letter, and use the substance to our ultimate advantage. I presume we all agree to adopt the solutions suggested by the so-called marginalized contestants. May God help us all."

That was it, and the meeting was over as each member stood up armed with a part of the agreed plans to implement. Don Baldwin stayed back in the room and watched them file out, he was wondering who was the traitor amongst them. That was his business to deal with.

That Wednesday morning, as the members of the 1990 Miss Cosmos Contest organizing committee brainstormed over steps to be adopted to right the wronged, most of the contestants and their chaperons were still in bed, worn out from the fully-loaded excursion of the previous day.

The excursion party in a convoy of buses and police escorts had taken the M40 from London, and exited at Junction 8 to the most historic British city of Oxford. They had spent all morning visiting all 39 Colleges and structures that made up the oldest English speaking university in the universe that was founded in 1249. The party was quite impressed that twenty-two British Prime Ministers, including Margaret Hilda Thatcher, were educated in the various colleges. The party was broken into five groups to be able to cover only about 8 colleges per group within the available time.

From Oxford, the convoy of buses had headed 8 miles North on the A44 for Blenheim Palace, Woodstock, which was considered to be England's largest private home, with its over 300 rooms. Blenheim Palace, was built for John Churchill, 1st Duke of Marlborough, and became the principal abode of all the dukes of Marlborough. It was designed and set by Sir John Vanbrugh on 2,100 acres of country land. It was the only residence in all of England, that was referred to as a palace without the presence or connection to the monarchy. The breathtaking magnificent splendor of the birthplace and ancestral home of the great British Statesman, Sir Winston Churchhill, had the girls all impressed. The girls had enjoyed the exquisite landscaping of the Marlborough Maze by *Capability* Brown; and had lunch served to them at the restaurant overlooking the Water Terraces.

After lunch they had left Woodstock and headed North through the back country roads to Stratford-upon-Avon, Warwickshire, William Shakespear's birthplace. The serene beauty of the English countryside was quite refreshing and therapeutic. Even though, the Henley Street residence of the young William Shakespear, could not stand the grandiose splendor of the Blenheim Palace, it had exuded a very humbling effect that one of the world's greatest literary personalities started life there, just like the great Sir Winston did at the Blenheim Palace. This was a Mecca of sort for all lovers of literature. They had finished within and began the journey back to London on the M40.

They had finally arrived London at about 6pm and headed straight for their final itinerary of the day at Tooley Street, in London South-East. The climax of the day promised to be an electrifying experience of an orgy of grisly entertainment, it was one nightmare the whole entourage could not wait to partake in. Under special group arrangement The London Dungeon, was kept open to entertain them.

Experiencing the thrills and bone-chilling screams that accompany the various tours of the ominous catacombs that came alive in the true sense of the word, had advised against, including it in future excursions. Ironically, even the girls' scary reactions almost scared the hell out of the dungeon managers themselves. By the time, the entourage with cold sweats and goose pimples settled down to dinner that was set out at the banquet hall, most of them were still pale and shivering with fear. The London Dungeon that was developed with over $30million, and opened to the public in 1974, lived to its billing that it was London's most haunting attraction.

They did not get into their beds until about 11pm. The organizers had with wisdom given them to noon to recover fully from the entire excursion day. As they sleep and laze about they were oblivious of what was going on to change their destinies..

Their first program, the preliminary contest for TALENTS AND PRIVATE INTERVIEWS was slated for 1 p.m. The program was indeed the beginning of the actual contest, though it was to be performed just for the 30 preliminary judges, who were specifically trained to spot and evaluate technicalities. It was their verdicts for today, and the verdict for the preliminary Evening Gown Competition scheduled for tomorrow, that would be the backbone for the scores for the Saturday grand finale.

The preliminary Bathing Suit Competition was scheduled for the grand finale introduction, thereafter the panel of 20 celebrity judges would take over from the 30 technical judges to choose the eventual queen from the 10 finalists. The 10 finalists for the contest- proper emerge based on the total scores of the Panel of Technical Judges for all the preliminary competitions. The 10 finalists are picked in no particular order, it was on these basis that they start on a clean slate with the panel of celebrity judges. This arrangement augurs well with the length of time available to come up with the eventual winner.

In Room 1724, Margaret Hilda and Rakiya were already up. They were following their pre-arranged training routines religiously. They had taken their baths and gone down for breakfast. They were among the very few that showed up for breakfast. If Rakiya had an inkling of what was giving Don Baldwin and his cronies a problem she did not betray any obvious sign, neither did she tell her friend anything.

Much later after breakfast, Margaret Hilda was busy with her recommended reading for contemporary issues, she was reading aloud from James Aldrid Doyle's *Unequalled Contemporary Speeches of Great Statesmen*. She was on the inaugural speech in 1961, of the 35th President of the United States of America, John F. Kennedy, while Rakiya was listening and from time to time correcting her diction, was also busy straightening Margaret Hilda's emerald green-white- green sash, with *Miss Nigeria* emblazoned on it in reflective gold. Rakiya's thought strayed to the letter she had written to the pageant's president on Monday. It seemed, her gamble had not convinced the man into adopting any changes. She almost burst into laughter about her little secret, that Margaret Hilda was totally unaware of the whole episode. She felt relieved that, that would keep the queen in the clear, in the event of any eventuality.

The ringing telephone interrupted her fluid thoughts, as well as Margaret's Hilda's reading exercise. "Hello! Good morning, Room One-seven-two-four." Rakiya answered cheerfully.

"Good morning, Room One-seven-two-four," the friendly voice chuckled, "my name is Lloyd, Charles Lloyd from the Organising Committee." The voice paused as it heard the sharp intake of breath by Rakiya. Charles Lloyd nodded to Don Baldwin who was watching him, and listening in on the conversation.

Rakiya's heart actually skipped a beat, "H...ow...How... may I help you sir, em ...Mr. Lloyd?" she stammered through, her thoughts running madly wild.

"It is okay, just to inform you of certain statutory changes the pageant is adopting forthwith. All contestants are directed to discontinue the usage of their official sashes in private or public throughout the duration of the contest. The pageant would make available new identities which contestants would be known and addressed with. A circular to that effect is on its way to you." The purported voice of Charles Lloyd paused.

Rakiya did not know whether to shout or scream for joy, though she was overwhelmed, she tactically put her emotions in check. Margaret Hilda was watching her with interest, and was dying to hear the entire conversation. Jane knew when her friend was in an excited state.

"Please, may I know whom I am speaking with?" the voice inquired suddenly, knocking Rakiya off guard.

"Oh! My name is Rakiya, I am the chaperon to Miss Nigeria."

"Pardon?"

"R-A-K-I-Y-A; and D-A-N-B-A-B-A!" She patiently spelt out her full name.

"Thank you Rakiya, that would be all for now." The voice concluded, and then added as an after thought; "The pageant appreciates your very kind co-operation and support. Have a nice day." It was said pleasantly, but in a conspiratorial tone.

Rakiya was indeed tongue-tied and failed to say anything, then she heard the chuckle at the other end and the line went dead. Rakiya then dropped the receiver and screamed with excitement at a puzzled Margaret Hilda. "Yes! Yes!!" she thumped the air with knotted fists.

Margaret Hilda could only smile and wait patiently, as the exhilarated Rakiya went on in a frenzied victory dance. A moment later, she picked up the official sash of Miss Nigeria, rolled it into a ball and flung it into the open door of their bathroom. Then she told Jane the whole story, starting from the Monday morning newspapers. At the executive penthouse office of the President of the Miss Cosmos Beauty Pageant, Charles Lloyd, the executive assistant to the president was reporting to his boss.

"The lady was no doubt the writer of the letter, my call scared the hell out of her. She was jittery at the begining. And at the end she was dumbfounded, I believe she thought I was pulling her legs." Lloyd smiled his boyish smile, as he paused for his boss to say something.

"How did you so quickly zeroed in on her? And secondly, how are sure she is alone in this business?""It was an open and close case sir, though I must say luck was also on myside. Knowing the letter was written, and typed on Monday within the confines of the hotel. My first port of call was the hotel's business centre. With the co-operation of the hotel's security manager, I examined the video reel of the security monitor covering the business centre. Bang!" Lloyd banged his right fist into the palm of his left hand, "there she was banging away on the typewriter. Further inquiries confirmed she was the only customer who indeed typed her own letter on that particular machine. We took out the Canon CR-100 ribbon cassette, and there was the letter word for word."

Lloyd paused to bring out the ribbon which he dropped on the table. "That confirmed we inspected tapes of the security camera covering the front desk. And there she was dropping two white envelopes at the concierge desk. That closed it. As regards being alone, a congregation had not been possible amongst contestants to discuss any issues, with the conditions on the ground." Lloyd once again smiled as he saw Baldwin nodding in agreement.

"Charles that was neat and smart, you did well. Very impressive, I am impressed, Charles."

"Thank you sir." Lloyd said, feeling like a Sherlock Holmes.

"The radical changes would go ahead as planned, it is still in our own corporate interest and existence. There is another matter you are to look into. I want you fish out the mole or moles in this organization." Baldwin said with all seriousness, as if his life depended on it.

Rakiya was still on her book on speeches, when they left to the hotel's banquet hall, the venue of the first preliminary competition. They were officially issued sashes bearing bold numbers written in words and figures, in place of their individual country identifications.

Except for Rakiya and Margaret Hilda, not one contestant knew the reason for the drastic changes. Rakiya inwardly counted it as their first victory. With each contestant with a number for identification, they got down to the business of the day. The race to the Miss Cosmos Crown had began in earnest. Rakiya remembered the words of the great war general; ...*everyman to himself and God for us all.*

In the thick of the preliminary competitions, the days went by so quickly, Wednesday and Thursday were now history. The girls who were engrossed in the anxiety and rigors of impressing the thirty eagled-eyed judges with their individual performances; that they hardly realized the passage of time. Before they realized it, it was Friday which was free from any of the preliminary competitions. It was totally dedicated to charities and all dress rehearsals. The girls were commencing the day at 11 a.m., after recovering from the hassles of Thursday..

At that hour in London; it was exactly 5p.m. in Singapore City, also known as one of the Asian Tigers. Sir Stamford Thomas Raffles sailed into Singapore in 1819, to make it a British trading post, and over the years had transformed into one of the most organized and orderly city states in the world, with a Cinderella-like story of from grass to grace. Under Prime Minister Lee Kuan Yew's direction and leadership Singapore with its deep natural harbor had developed rapidly into South-East Asia's foremost international trade centre, as a Freeport. Singapore's citizens enjoy the highest standard of living in Asia only next to Japan and Brunei.

With the international shipping success story had also appeared drugs from South America via the Colombian ports in the Pacific Ocean. It was on this basis Oscar Uromi was visiting Singapore on very short notice. From all intents and purpose it was a very successful trip. And like he had promised the Miss Cosmos people he was already on his way to Changi Airport to head back to London, on a British Airways flight. He looked out of the taxi, they were already on Mountbatten Road, give or take the airport would be just about 12-15 minutes away. He gave a sigh of relief, satisfied that with his deft touch everything went according to plans. He would be in London with enough time to be part of the grand finale of the Miss World contest.

Little did Oscar in his wildest dream ever suspect that Chuck Freeborn IV and his Asian DEA agents had been on his tail since he arrived in Singapore a couple of days back. Five vehicles behind the Oscar Uromi's fare were Chuck and his agents in different vehicles. Chuck Freeborn also yawned satisfied that it was indeed a very fruitful trip for the DEA, and his desire to close in on Zapata and his boss. He smiled and closed his eyes relishing that very final moment of victory once again.

They had trailed Oscar from the airport to check-in at one of the beach resorts at the popular Sentosa Island. They were aware of his rental of wet suits and other equipment to enhance underwater survival and activity. With the co-operation of their Singapore counterparts they had bugged Oscar's room, and were silent partners in the conversations, when Captain Alfonso Santos Manizales of the *Ocean Warlord* visited his hotel room.

All binoculars from a safe distance were focused at the Ocean Warlord, when they jettisoned a water-proofed cargo overboard just at the time Oscar was riding by. They had captured Oscar's every move as he hooked-in the floating package and headed by to shore, and the safety of his room.

They had later that night listened in on the telephone conversation from Oscar Uromi to confirm to Captain Manizales that; *the consignment had arrived in perfect condition.* Chuck Freeborn IV in his room directly a floor above Oscar's had also listened to the conversations with two low Singaporian criminals to act as decoys for him to beat attention and scrutiny at the Heathrow Airport. Chuck felt good that his snare was closing in gradually.

Just as his body relaxed and surrounded to enticing embrace of sleep, they were already pulling to a stop at Changi Airport.

CHAPTER 81

Friday morning was dull, chilly, and windy, the London winter was gradually picking up its sting. A heavy shower was forecasted by the weatherman for the mid-morning hours. The contestants were programmed to visit three charity homes and three major hospitals within London. For the purpose of the scheduled visits, the contestants were divided into 6 equal groups. Each group was assigned to cover a particular charity. This was in a bid to provide quality time for the place of visit. The arrangement was for each group to have lunch with the inmates of their various places of visitation, and converge back at the hotel by latest 4p.m. This they believed would give everybody ample and adequate time to prepare for the special program slated for 6.30 p.m.

Margaret Hilda was in Group 5, who were scheduled to visit the St.Mary's Children Hospital at Greycoat Place, London SW1, there was something familiar about the name, though she could not place it at the time. There was indeed a surprise awaiting her. Bus No.5 and its police escorts arrived the hospital shortly before noon, the passengers were discharged right on the other side of the road by the roundabout. Margaret Hilda came down and looked around at the various ancient and modern architectures. Right beside the hospital was a brick 3-Story apartment building with a bold sign saying Greycoat Gardens, and from a first floor window was a gap-toothed smile that undoubtedly belonged to a male face that was Nigerian. She returned his friendly wave, and walked across the street to the hospital with the other girls. Margaret Hilda did not know that she was waving at *the man that later became the author of her story and others*.

They walked into the warm embrace of the inmates of the hospital who had flowers for each contestant. The girls had a great time playing with the children, those who were too weak had a real beauty queen read a story to them in bed. Presents and gift items that were thoughtfully provided by the pageant were shared amidst so much excitement to the children. They then all had lunch together. In the din of all the excitement, time went by quickly, before they realized it, it was time to go.

Parting time was tears for everybody, both the inmates and their visitors. It was then Margaret Hilda got her surprise. She was truly surprised when she was singled out from all the other girls, and presented with a big Teddy Bear wearing an apron marked, *WELCOME HOME, MH!* A placard size of her birth certificate was then presented to her. Margaret Hilda was really taken aback to learn, to the amusement of the staff and children of the hospital, that this was her birth place many years ago. She was really moved emotionally to tears, and wept as she hugged every child.

Her response was short and simple; "I shall return someday."

On the drive back to the hotel, a 1-page document was circulated to all contestants in the bus. It was a press release from the pageant to the print and electronic media houses. It read;

PRESS RELEASE

THE MISS COSMOS BEAUTY PAGEANT NOTICES WITH DISMAY AND UTMOST CONCERN, A CERTAIN PUBLICATION TITLED *ALL HAIL THE NEW QUEEN?* IN THE MONDAY EDITION OF *THE EYE*. WE CONSIDER THE SAID PUBLICATION TO BE IN PURE BAD TASTE, AND CONTRARY TO THE IDEALS OF THE MISS COSMOS BEAUTY PAGEANT. ON THIS PREMISE, WE DISSOCIATE OURSELVES FROM THE SAID PUBLICATION, AND CONSEQUENTLY CONDEMN IT IN ITS ENTIRETY, TO ALL AND SUNDRY. WE ONCE AGAIN REITERATE OUR UNWAVERING COMMITMENT TO UNITE THE WORLD ACROSS ALL NATURAL OR ARTIFICIAL BARRIERS.

THANK YOU. MANAGEMENT

As the convoy, wound its way through Victoria Street, an official announced that, the President would be addressing all contestants at the hotel banquet hall, on their arrival. At the hotel, as they stepped down from their various buses they were herded in the general direction of the banquet hall. When the last bus had arrived the hotel and they were all seated, Don Baldwin accompanied by a retinue of aides breezed into the hall. He did not waste time with frivolities, went straight to the point. It was the sign of a very busy man.

"Good afternoon to you ladies, appreciate your kind appreciation to honour my invitation, despite your very busy and tight schedules." He paused in his crisp manner of talking. Some of the girls already found him attractive.

"I just want to reassure you that all is well, and that we are on course. The pageant is doing everything in its power to see that you enjoy the honor of being part of the Miss Cosmos pageant." He paused again to study their faces.

"I understand that some of you are not very happy, please be rest assured that we are at your service 24 hours of the day, please do not hesitate to call on us for anything. Your interest comes first and foremost, and takes pride of place in our hearts. He paused as the girls applauded.

"I wish you all the best of luck tomorrow and may the best of you win. Thank you." Baldwin crisply concluded and waved cheerfully to the applauding girls.

He stood up and made his way out of the hall followed by his aides. The girls made small talk, as they filed out of the hall and moved toward the bank of lifts. They were still trying to piece events together. A very excited Margaret Hilda, took the latest victory to Rakiya, who was over the moon with happiness. They analyzed the situation that it was not in anyway disadvantageous to them. They were convinced that *all systems were Go.* As Rakiya started getting her charge ready for the evening event, she started humming *There Aint Stoppin Us Now We Got Grove...* before you know they were singing and jamming together in very high spirits until the phone rang to stop them. It was Ambassador Aka calling to wish them both the best of luck, "...whatever the outcome you have made us all very proud of you..

At 6p.m. prompt, the convoy of vehicles laden with contestants and their chaperons had promptly departed the hotel for the Royal Albert Hall. Not one person was missing, as they all looked forward to the dress rehearsals with so much enthusiasm. Every contestant must have her moment of glory in the first march in of the night. They were given numbers in no particular order. They were between 01 to 100 There were final checks on lights, sound, audio, decorations, seating arrangements, television stands to be completed within a stated time limit.

The Royal Albert Hall, the venue of the epic event was a beehive of frenzied activities in the din of workmen putting finishing touches to everything. There was a form of organized running around by various staff ranging from stage designers, various television crews, audio, lighting and computer personnel, musical directors, and security personnel. Every person to a purpose working feverishly towards the successful culmination of the day, like in an ants' community. The stage was already transformed into something else, a far cry from what they used and saw on Monday's first rehearsal.

A huge, and heavily bearded fellow, with a megaphone called everyone to order. He more like addressed both the contestants and the technicians together for about two minutes, before cueing the show to start. He formally introduced the Master of Ceremony, Craig David Stephenson, who waved with equal excitement at the contestants. After the procession march involving every contestant, as directed by the stage director; The curtains came down.

When the curtains parted a moment later only the 40 lucky contestants for the dance routine were in position. The rest of the contestants and all the chaperons were seated orderly in the stands watched the proceedings with keen interest.

For two good hours, the girls on stage went through a grueling time, but they worked hard with unconcealed gusto, having the gumption to know their ultimate reward. The dance director almost shouted himself raw; pushing, persuading, cajoling, and at times threatening and intimidating. Deep down the director knew the girls were really trying, but there was room for improvement. Finally, at about 10pm, the directors were convinced that they were good to go, and decided to call it a day, to the relief of everybody, as they all applauded loudly.

CHAPTER 82

Saturday, dawn took longer than usual in coming, even longer for the anxiety laden passengers of BA 345 from Changi Airport to London Heathrow after, a 4-hour nerve-racking technical delay. While Chuck Freeborn IV had had a most restful and fit-less sleep in his Club World Cabin; Oscar Uromi flying First Class had in the contrary tossed and turned without a wink. He was not at peace with himself. Things were not naturally fitting into place; he had noted with trepidation three moments he actually thought it was over for him and his deadly consignment, but only to see the officials looking the other way at the very last moment for him to slip through. He had not even touched his dinner. For once Oscar felt really threatened, which was totally unheard of.

Finally, the cold grey day dawned as usual with the sun rising sluggishly from the east, and giving the huge mechanical bird a race to the west. Oscar Uromi, was sure that with delay back in Singapore, there was no way he was going to be part of this year's Miss Cosmos's grand finale. That was if he could slip through Heathrow with his illicit cargo. It was going to be a very long day ahead. He suddenly felt old and tired. It was time to settle down and leave this rat race for younger and more adventurous hearts. With this realistic admission sleep just thankfully overwhelmed his anxiety ridden mind and body.

The time was five minutes to the hour of 7 p.m., the London nightline was ablaze with a kaleidoscopic array of lights, which highlighted the starless dark sky above. The chilly wintry wind of December, with a loud hissy whisper, ran its chilling fingers on those unfortunate to be outside and unprotected. The flood-lit gigantic dome of the circular concrete-burnt brick edifice of the famous Royal Albert Hall, Knightsbridge, was distinct against the London skyline. In its grounds were hundreds of milling disappointed guests,

who tried as they could, but could not gain entry into the venue of the Miss Cosmos Contest. The doors were opened about two hours ago, and the colossal hall was now filled to capacity. The richly and intricately designed sitting arrangements of the hall had every available seat occupied by a daintily dressed guest. Its customized age-hold labyrinths resonated with a melodious medley being played by the irresistible Royal Philharmonic Concert Orchestra.

Behind the huge mass of oxblood-red velvet stage curtains were frenzied last-minute spot checks by various engineers to make doubly certain, there were no last-minute hitches. Television cameras were all in place, ready to roll. Pageant officials scanned the contestants to confirm for the umpteenth time that all was in place as was rehearsed. The contestants could not take their eyes off the solid mass of velvet separating them from the crowd, their cultured smiles was perfect cover for their pounding hearts.

As the distant muffled sound of Big Ben got to the dejected crowd outside the hall for the hour; inside, as if by a single remote control the music of the orchestra and all the lights fizzled out. The expectant audience waited expectantly knowing the hour was at hand. Then came the drum-roll, slowly at first then got to its crescendo, as the electronically controlled huge stage curtains parted regally to show a lonely figure spotlighted on the stage. The audience held its breath, as the familiar crispy voice of Don Baldwin came over the loudspeakers presenting the master of ceremonies.

With a clash of electronic thunder accompanied with a colorful display of fireworks the rest of the stage was lit up to show, the smiling resplendent figure of a man clad in tuxedo, waving animatedly at the cheering audience. It was Craig David Stephenson, he was reputed to be the highest paid television talk-show host in the world. At that very moment, a group of communication satellites positioned 600 miles in orbit round the Earth was relaying the proceedings captured by specific cameras in that hall to more than 1.7 billion viewers glued to their television sets, across the various time zones.

As the fireworks petered out, the applause continued, the amiable MC illuminated under a bright spotlight that left the rest of the stage in ink-black darkness, knew what to do. He was a professional, trained and skilled to take charge, and control the emotions of the audience from start to finish. He assumed control immediately, he did not wait for the ovation to die down as he launched into a classic inaudible speech. The applause died down immediately, and he effortlessly and smoothly in his customary booming voice read his opening lines from the teleprompter cleverly concealed into the glass podium.

"WEL-CO-ME! WELCOME!! Welcome to the greatest event happening in the universe right now." His mellifluous voice boomed through the ossified cavernous interiors of one of England's classiest hall. The excited crowd applauded these lines, but Craig David Stephenson lived up to his professional billing by taking control by going onto his next lines. The audience got the message; they calmed down immediately.

"Good morning, or Good afternoon, or Good evening where ever you are. This is London, England, the venue of this year's Miss Cosmos Contest. We have brought from around the world 90 of our world's most beautiful and intelligent women." The entire stage was now illuminated in brilliant floodlights to show the 90 smiling contestants standing in a two-tier formation clad in various array of swimsuits. The audience went berserk in frenzied applause. "Only the Miss Cosmos Pageant could do it; to bring the world's most glamorous and beautiful women under one roof. And by the time we leave here today, we must have the answer to the billion dollar- question of *who wears the crown?* Looking at this bevy of beauties, ladies and gentlemen I am glad I am not part of the panel of judges, for it will be a tough nut to crack." The audience burst with laughter at the harmless banter.

"As the night progresses you would notice changes to certain age-long procedures that the pageant considered prejudicial to its equality and fair play stance. For instance for the best of intentions the contestants for the first time in history, would be identified with numbers instead of their individual countries. Let us please welcome our 90 beautiful contestants for tonight starting from number one."

The amazed crowd applauded in unison as the backdrop behind the parade of contestants was transformed into a colorful sandy beachfront complete with green palms and a blue smooth sea reflecting the golden glow of a setting sun. It was so realistic. As the orchestra went onto a classical rendition of *How Deep Is The Ocean* by I. Berlin, each contestant took turn to walk across the stage cued by the MC. "Contestant No.1, is 19 years old ...", there was no mention of countries or names of the contestants, but the spectators were either too engrossed with the voluptuous swimsuit-clad bodies, or they did not mind the new changes.

The preliminary judges got down to the final phase of their onerous assignment, as the excited spectators cheered each contestant equally. By the time Contestant No. 90 walked or glided literarily across the stage, the audience cheered gleefully not because she was from Venezuela or Bermuda or Zimbabwe; but they cheered because they enjoyed what they saw. As the judges were busy collating the marks to arrive at the overall preliminary scores. It was this final total score that would decide the ten finalists. The spectators still excited from the effect of the swimsuit competition settled down for the next act of the evening. "Distinguished ladies and gentlemen, only the best is good enough for you, so we present to you not just one of the best, but the *most magical wonder of them all... Stevie Wonder"*

The hall erupted with an ear-rending ovation, as the familiar up tempo pulsating beat and rhythm of *I Just Called To Say I Love You* filled the air, the stage lights gradually faded and dimmed to semi-darkness. When the bright lights returned, on the deserted stage was giant egg-like object. Before the spectators could make out what it was, it blew up with loud bang and a puff of smoke. In the middle of the explosion appeared an all white clad Stevie Wonder, seated and playing on a gleaming white grand piano, as if he was floating amongst the clouds.

As the *clouds* gradually cleared, what looked like white swans decorating the whole length and breadth of the stage transformed into living human beings, …the forty beautiful contestants magnificent in their costumes sprang into life flowing fluidly to form delicate dreamlike formations and lifelike shapes with a rhythmic dances flowing to the song. The crowd sat in a trancelike state drinking in the euphoria of the resultant combo of various creative geniuses. Just when it looked like they had run out of ideas, the girls crumpled into eight shapely heaps one-by-one, on top of each other. And as Stevie Wonder hit the crescendo of his song, the human heaps transformed into a giant rose flower with petals opening and closing in an array of colors masterminded by a superb lighting effects.

Then as if pushed by unseen hands, the hall erupted like a dormant volcano in a delirium of applause. The thunderous ovation continued as dancers and the star acknowledged the applause. An evidently elated Stevie Wonder clapped and pointed to the girls who waved excitedly at the crowd as the huge velvet curtains came together.

"Thank you! Thank you!! Thank you!!!" The master of ceremony's voice boomed through the hall moments later as the ovation of the rumbustious crowd continued unabated. It indeed took a while for the crowd to sober from the hypnotizing and magical effect of the performance. It was indeed a perfect presentation, the girls all deserved the resounding applause.

"As the contestants get ready for the next stage of the competition, may I use this opportunity to present to you, the main man behind everything that you are witnessing tonight. Ladies and gentlemen, the President of the Miss Cosmos Beauty Pageant, Mr. Don Baldwin."

The crowd rose in unison to give a rousing standing ovation to a no-doubt very proud Baldwin decked in an all-white tuxedo with black tie. He walked gingerly out from the left wing to shake hands with Craig David Stephenson at the centre of the stage. The men took a friendly high five before Stephenson conveniently faded into the shadows as the spotlight remained on Baldwin. The applause continued, then receded.

Don Baldwin smiled appreciatively at the full house, then went on professionally to read his address from the teleprompter. He read in his crisp clear voice for a little over eight minutes, all targeted to give the final ten contestants enough time to prepare. He touched on all challenges of organizing the contest, and the commitment to the United Nations in fostering world peace, and providing succor to the unfortunate victims of wars and conflicts. He spoke of *"positive radical changes adopted to go with the times, to erase all vestiges of bias, marginalization, discrimination due to a contestant's country"*. He called it, *"the new world order"*.

Baldwin finally concluded by thanking all the numerous sponsors, as well as the audience, and the viewers worldwide who were the life-wire of the pageant. The audience once again gave the dynamic leader a resounding ovation.

As the master of ceremony resumed duty once again; he started off by introducing the panel of celebrity judges who would commence the semi-final phase of the contest on a clean slate. The Semi-finalists Stage would be adjudged on the basis of Talents and Skills of the ten lucky qualifiers, from whom the four finalists would emerge.

"Ladies and gentlemen, for the very first time in the history of beauty pageants, it is my pleasure to introduce to you, *Mr. Linguist*. Mr. Linguist, is a translator in 18 major international languages, who has the capability to translate verbatim within five micro-seconds. It was one of the latest innovations into the Miss Cosmos Contest to check human errors and bias in translations. Mr. Linguist is not human; it is the latest in Japanese Electro-Computer technology with a capability that could only be imagined. The user simply talks into it in one of the major languages and it translates automatically in a matter of micro-seconds in a voice almost similar to the input." The crowd were totally lost here. Just then the red light on the teleprompter blinked and glowed green, to signify all was set back stage for commencement of the semi-finals.

The huge curtains once again parted to reveal the 90 contestants. It was a parade of elegance all clad in a motley of delicately sequined silks, lace, chiffons, and velvets. The reflective green and yellow silk sashes with boldly emblazoned numbers also made a statement of their own. They had fixed broad smiles, not even a tiny twitch to belay their riotous heart beats. The crowd acknowledged their pleasure with a resounding ovation. They were strategically positioned that no girl covered the other. It was a magnificent sight to behold, complemented with the simulated huge fountains and colorful lights in the background. A resounding ovation greeted the parade of ever- smiling girls.

The head of the preliminary judges went up stage and presented a sealed envelope to Stephenson without much ado. "Thank you, Mr. Lucas." The MC waved the envelope over his head for everyone to see.

He then went on to open the envelope with feigned nervousness, as the hall suddenly went quiet in anticipation, the long pause heightening existing anxiety. Both contestants and spectators restrained themselves from screaming at the affable master of ceremony, for the inordinate amount of time at opening the envelope. Just before the crowd's breaking point in their patience, his voice boomed through the cavernous hall.

"I have to remind you that the 10 semi-finalist are not called in any particular order. "Ladies and gentlemen, here according to the thirty preliminary judges are the 10 lucky semi-finalists; Contestant *Nos. 74; 32; 9; 83; 23; 45; 38; 17; 64;* and… " The crowd just cheered and cheered as each qualifier stepped forward to be highlighted by a very bright spotlight. The master of ceremony tactically paused to cross-check his list with contestants that had stepped out, knowing there was just one more contestant to complete the ten semi-finalists. You could hear the heart beats of those 81 contestants pounding furiously, Stephenson's loud and clear voice repeat the numbers without any particular emotion; the crowd remained dead silent.

"The last but not the least of the ten semi-finalists is Contestant No. 50." Then the MC took everybody by surprise when he called the final number without further ado. Contestant No. 50; the girl wearing the sash did not move, and the crowd roared with applause, as the MC repeated the number before the lucky girl realized what was happening and broke into tears as she stepped forward into the spotlight. Leaving the remaining 80 girls in a comforting sudden darkness as they wept their eyes out, for crashed dreams and ambitions. The orchestra went on to play *Tell Me Who Is the Fairest* by Wilcox Langley.

"As the judges collate the results for the evening gown competition, let me quickly brief you about the next competition which is the Talents and Skills competition. Each contestant would get a maximum of 2 minutes to perform or exhibit her talent on stage." The green light signal glowed for the MC to clear the stage.

"Please ladies and gentlemen put your hands together for the ladies as they step aside for the competition to begin." The lucky girls filed out with a resounding ovation. The next 40 minutes was quite entertaining as the spectators were treated to very spectacular performances by the semi-finalists.

Clinically orchestrated performances ranging from an amazing quick draw artist that did a very convincing portrait of the MC; *a vocal/dance act that did a Tina Turner act; an orchestra conductor that took the orchestra through a classic; a lovely tap dancer; an amazing ventriloquist; a classical piano recital, a captivating ballerina, a powerful poem recital; to a superb classical vocal.*

The most amazing of all the acts was Contestant No. 9 who dexterously played Stevie Wonder's *I Just Called To Say I Love You* on the piano blind folded. At the end of her performance, the impressed audience gave her a thunderous standing ovation.

Announcing the four finalists was equally nerve racking for both contestants and their friends and relatives who were seated in the seventh to tenth rows. Each contestant was given two complimentary invites. They had experienced and shared in the joys and agonies of their contestants onstage. They sat and fidgeted anxiously as the master of ceremony pushed their patience to the limit as he resorted to every delay tactics in the book to announce the final four. The final four contestants in no particular order were; *Contestants 23; 45; 9; and 17.*

The six not very lucky semi-finalists departed the stage politely waving to the enthusiastic crowd who cheered and cheered. Contestant No. 50 who was emotionally distraught for not making it into the final burst out crying before she could make it to the safety of the wings.

"This is the final stage of the contest ladies and gentlemen. The pageant could not ask for a more appreciative audience, and we thank you profusely." Craig David Stephenson carrying a glass bowl loaded with twenty envelopes announced that it was the Questions and Answers time.

"This is where our Mr. Linguist comes in handy for those who could not speak or understand English language." He motioned to an aide who wheeled out Mr. Linguist next to him. "The goldfish bowl here contains twenty envelopes with twenty questions composed by ten different professors in International Affairs worldwide with a singular theme."

The audience took this information with a pinch of salt by their reaction, which Stephenson did not lose any sleep about, because he continued nonplused. "A contestant's question must be answered within the limit of two minutes, you and the judges would assess the individual finalist's confidence, vocabulary, intelligence, aura, candor, personality, opinion, and perception of global affairs and events." He looked around him and took his cue to proceed.

The four finalists spread out in a single file like lambs for the slaughter as they listened attentively to the Master of Ceremony, as a somnolent calm settled over the entire expectant audience. "Will Contestant No. 17 step forward please" the beautiful girl glided over to to him, with her heart in her mouth, but she did not show it, "thank you No. 17, please fish for your question".

The contestant rummaged through the glass fish bowl, picked an envelope and handed it over to him, who then read it aloud; "As a citizen of the world, what is your greatest concern for this world, and if you were to be crowned Miss World today, what would you do about it?"

The contestant rolled her eyes upwards as she composed her thoughts, "My greatest concern today about our world is global peace. If I were to become the next queen I would make it a priority during my reign. I would assume a major role in brokering peace amongst warring or hostile nations." She answered in good English without any trace of an accent. The crowd seemed pleased with her short answer because it cheered happily. The judges on their own sat impassively through the applause like stone figures.

She walked across to the other side of the stage, while Contestant No.45 was summoned to take her place by the master of ceremony. "Contestant No. 45, if you were God and is faced with the task of remaking the world, what would be your priority, and why? "If I have to remake the world, I would start by creating all human beings to have one colour, race, and creed. They would be created equal with equal advantages or adversities. When I take this course of action I would then be hitting at the root cause of the world's major problems." She spoke well in communicable English with a heavy accent. The crowd acknowledged with a resounding ovation.

Contestant No. 9 dipped her long pretty fingers straight into the glass bowl and picked out the topmost envelope. Her effortless smile expanded as she handed the envelope over to the celebrated master of ceremony. There was an air or aura of confidence exuding from her like a strong perfume. "No 9 if you were to be made the political leader of the whole world today, how will you go about making yourself the ideal leader to be universally accepted?" A hush fell over the whole hall as each listener mentally tried the question. The smile was wiped off the face of Contestant No. 9, as she marshaled out her thoughts, it was a serious question to be handled seriously. Then she homed-in on her answer.

"A political leader to be universally accepted," she paused and cocked her head to one side, she had the obvious accent of those who probably adopted English language as their lingua franca in an environment of diverse languages "first and foremost I will congregate the best brains in the world to rub minds together with me. We will analyze properly the good and bad qualities of great and renowned world opinion and political leaders. At the end of the day we will sieve through our findings to come up with a unique political ideology that will at each point in time benefit the majority of the people in their daily life." The hall was dead silent, nobody made a move, it was like they were transfixed. The contestant saw in the eyes of the master of ceremony a new respect, and encouragement to carry on. So she continued.

"Personally, I would refer from ancient times;" she indicated by counting her beautifully manicured fingers;

1. Biblical King Solomon; his unfathomable wisdom.
2. General Julius Gaius Caeser; his uncanny stratagems.
3. The Chinese Confucius; his ethical moral codes.
4. President Abraham Lincoln; his patience, fortitude, and patriotic devotion.
5. King Shaka the Zulu; unalloyed determination even in the face of a stronger enemy and adversities.
6. Geronimo, the Apache Indian chief; his resilience in the face of a stronger power.
7. Mohanda Karamchand 'Mahatma' Ghandi, and Reverend Martin Luther King, Jr.; their persistent non-violent attitude even in the face of provocation.
8. Sir Winston Churchill; his principles that made him the greatest ever war leader.
9. Adolph Hitler; the highly controvertible factors that made him a political genius.

10. President John F. Kennedy; his obstinacy coupled with his youthful exuberance.

These, I am convinced would do in any situation, sir."

The crowd was fascinated beyond words, they could not compromise the beautiful unassuming girl with the authority and intelligence that she convincingly exhibited. It was incredible, as both the crowd and the judges, remain captivated on the edges of their seats without any form of applause.

For once all evening, Craig David Stephenson felt threatened as he could not find his voice. He incoherently mumbled something under his breath that was not very complimentary.

Stephenson finally found his voice. "Miss ... Contestant No. 23." He paused and smiled at young lady as he offered her the contents of the goldfish bow. Even the judges felt for her, they knew the last contestant had impressed everybody, with a standard that was unbeatable. It was going to be an uphill task.

The head phone inserted into Mr. Linguist was placed over her head by a stage assistant, and the noise died down once again in the hall.. "No. 23, if you were to address a group of school children on the topic, Making the World a Better Place, what would you say? The emcee handed over the special microphone to the contestant, as the stage assistant manipulated buttons on the computer. It took just a microsecond for the versatile language computer to analyze the input, and come up with its output. As the contestant spoke into the microphone the closest tone to her voice was reproduced loud in the closest English translation or vice versa in the headphones.

"For the children to grasp the import of what I would be saying, I would go down to their level by simplifying the topic. Our world, I would make them understand, had been in existence long, long before we were born, many uncountable years ago. And some day we would die and go, and the world would still remain. That is why, it is extremely important to make the world a better place not only for ourselves but for even those yet unborn, our children, and their children's children." The young lady paused briefly to assess her attentive audience.

"My main theme would be love. Love for ourselves, as well as our neighbors. Our neighbor, I would inform them extends beyond the next door neighbor, that means even people from other countries, people with different creed and religion, people with a different color of skin from ours. And I would advice that we should all be honest and be sincere with ourselves in our dealings with other people. And if we follow truly this message we would definitely make the world, and later leave it a better place for everybody." Audience applauded the speaker well.

The ovation continued as the four finalists filed out to freshen up as the judges began the final audit and tabulation of the final results. The master of ceremony announced the next program which was the final walk and speech by the reigning Miss Cosmos, then the finalists shall return to be crowned by the reigning queen.

CHAPTER 83

It was about noon on Sunday, the day after the coronation, as the final batch of the other contestants checked out from the hotel for their onward journey home, Margaret Hilda was sound asleep in her new official suite as a Miss Cosmos. Rakiya who was already up was busy browsing through a bunch of London dailies in the sitting room. They had moved straight into the suite when they came back victorious from the Royal Albert Hall. All the papers made the Miss Cosmos Beauty Contest, a front page story. A full portrait of Jane in her crowning moment of glory accompanied all the stories. Rakiya turned on the television set with the remote control, not forgetting to turn down the volume as not to disturb the sleeping Jane.

Rakiya was so happy that they made it not only to London but actually captured the whole world. She flicked through the four television channels, three of them were on the new Miss Cosmos, and the contest of the night before. The hotel was indeed bombarded with a deluge of telephone calls from all over the world from all sorts to congratulate the new queen, who could not be reached. Rakiya felt like she was the happiest person alive. She had specifically won the battles in all fronts. She was able to influence a change in beauty pageant history. She was able to change long established procedures that were prejudicial. She was now not bothered any more of how they unveiled her identity, there was nothing to be scared off.

Leaving the Royal Albert Hall, the night before was an herculean task, the brood of photographers and journalists were more than a nuisance as they clamor for every snippets of information about the new queen. When they finally made it to the hotel, they were surprisingly ushered straight to the suite on the 12th floor instead of their former room, by pageant officials. They observed with relief that all their personal belongings were there already. There were fresh flowers every where. They hugged each other tightly, it was the first opportunity they were having to themselves since the victory. They screamed and danced wildly, then threw themselves on the bed with bizarre excitement.

It was bizarre, yet it was all they could do in the circumstances, all systems was go for them, and the world was at their feet with their victory.It was who Jane noticed it first. A white envelope strategically placed on the mantle-piece. It was addressed to Miss Rakiya Danbaba. Inside were a note and an 18-carat gold pendant and necklace. The beautiful pendant had the insignia of the Miss Cosmos Pageant engraved on it. The accompanying note was type written on official pageant stationery.

>Dear Rakiya,
>
>This is in appreciation of your support and contributions to the growth and development of the Miss Cosmos Pageant. Please accept this little present as a token of our gratitude and appreciation of your invaluable services. Be free to contact us if you need our humble assistance, we would be honoured to give you any assistance.
>
>We respect and and share your views in various issues. It was indeed an honor and privilege for us to have made your acquaintance. Congratulations too.
>
>With very affectionate regards,
>
>DON BALDWIN

Rakiya quickly explained it off as a custom accorded the chaperon of every new queen. The excited girls were still admiring the necklace when the doorbell rang.Rakiya opened the door to admit a waiter with a bottle of vintage Champagne Montaudon in an ice bucket, and a tray of glasses. Behind the waiter was Perry Wilson, the hotel's General Manager with a grin from ear to ear, with a giant bouquet of flowers clutched in his hands. The big American stepped into the room bending to peck the chaperon, and moved respectfully towards the newly crowned Miss Cosmos.

"Your Excellency, our hearty congratulations," he spoke with a Texan drawl as he handed her the bouquet, "the entire group of the Hilton family wish you a successful tenure. You'll get to meet us gradually as you start your duties hopping round the world, then you'll confirm that traditional hospitality is our second nature." His cheerful laughter boomed around the room.

"Thank you Mr. Wilson I feel really privileged and honoured" as she extended her dainty right-hand for a handshake, then smelt the flowers, and handed them over to her chaperon who placed them in a flower vase in the sitting room.

"It was a well-deserved victory ma'am, you are worth your weight in solid gold. I was right there at the Royal Albert Hall." The man from Brownsville, Texas, burst into his resonant laughter again. "The champagne is on the house to toast to your victory. We at Hilton, are at your command and service always, please help us make your stay all round excellent. Welcome to the throne Queen Jane Margaret Hilda Daniel-Aka." The huge amiable American finally concluded.

"It is indeed very considerate of you sir, your tradition is well-known, we are grateful." She extended her pretty hand to him which he grabbed and kissed theatrically, before saying goodnight.

The girls quickly undressed, and clad only in their pink underwears descended on the bottle of bubbly vintage. The duo in giggling fits sipped the classy vintage as they celebrated their victory dancing late into the night. They talked excitedly on their fortunes in the year ahead and thereafter. It was not until the hours before dawn that they finally fell asleep out of weariness.

All scheduled programs for the new queen were shifted to the evening, this was to grant her some respite and the much needed rest she spoke of at the interview after her crowning. The new queen would be meeting with pageant officials who would be arranging her entire schedules in her official capacity as the reigning Miss Cosmos for the next twelve months. As a goodwill ambassador to the United Nations, she would be expected to broker peace amongst warring nations, and caring for the victims of any form of conflicts. There would be appearances at various social and political events and functions respectively.

Much later in the evening, at the hotel's conference centre, the queen was billed to meet with the international press. The press would get to know her better, and be informed of her chosen pet commitments, official projects and her stance on international issues. From the press conference, they will attend a sumptuous dinner with the various sponsors also scheduled to hold at the hotel's banquet hall.

There, the new queen would familiarize herself with their various corporate interests, during her tenure. Over the dinner the corporate sponsors in the same vein would be expected to read her the riot act, regarding where to tread or not to throughout the duration of her tenure. A sort of working relationship must be established for all the parties involved to protect their various interests. This is the moment the queen who might have any reservations would table them to be agreed upon.

Apart from the United Nations assignments, the Miss Cosmos' tenure would be filled with appearances ranging from commercial and sponsor bookings to civic and charity events which will involve more than 45,000 miles in air travels. The queen and her travelling companion, travel only first class, and all other expenses would be settled by the booking party.

A small team of staff were dedicated to work with her at the London Miss Cosmos Pageant office. The pre-planned schedules would involve various fund-raisers, other pageants and parades, political conventions, visits to hospitals, product endorsements all over the world. Rakiya and her friend had resolved before they fell asleep to honor all activities as long as their safety would be guaranteed.

At that very moment, Oscar Uromi could not sleep too. He had been engrossed with the new turn of events with the consignment from Singapore. Even though he had succeeded in striking the biggest deal in his career, there was a deep ominous feeling in his heart, that something may go terribly wrong. Nobody fails to deliver to the world's most deadly cartel, and survive to tell the story, except he would beat them at their own game. Oscar Uromi had come too far after paying his dues to just fail and end up as food for the fishes.

He was a born survivor, with an uncanny attitude to always beat the odds that were stacked against him. He took a look at the invites to the Miss Cosmos' Stakeholders' Dinner scheduled for Sunday evening. Time to start getting his plan to use the new queen together. He heaved a sigh of relief, knowing there was a vacuum in his life, that he just can't fill easily.

Harry Fenton-Forest sat gloomily at his very posh townhouse, only a couple of houses away from 3307 N Street, Georgetown, Washington DC, where President John F. Kennedy lived until his inauguration in January, 1961. The DEA Director, was a very bitter and angry man about the outcome of the 1990 Miss Cosmos contest. He was still smarting from what he felt, was a humiliating defeat his daughter suffered in the hands of that *black thing*. What an insult? How could an imperial wizard, and a direct descendant of the Grand Imperial Wizard of the dreaded Ku Klux Klan succumb to such an anomaly?

He was not just going to suffer the indignities that his progenitor suffered in the hands of the so called legendary African slave, *Freeborn*, back in the day in Georgia. That was why, he could not stand that cheek, Chuck Freeborn IV, but the man had the stubborn blood of his cantankerous ancestors flowing in his veins. No matter the distance or connection, *black was black*. He was going to visit the evils of Freeborn upon his great grandfather on any black person that venture to cross his part; *whether they were related or not*.

"He was going to do something about it. *How?* We shall see how it pans out". He spoke aloud to himself.

Sophie, his only child, was his heartbeat; so her defeat was also his defeat. The bid to influence the judges through the press was timely nipped in the bud by those *nigger loving creeps* at the Miss Cosmos pageant. He could not believe how age-long customs and traditions were overturned overnight, to finally dispossess his own daughter, in favor of a bloody nigger. He was not just going to seat down here and leak his wounds; he was going to do something very drastic about it.

That was why he had asked his wife and daughter to relax a little in London on a well-deserved vacation. He was going to join them before for Christmas. He was going to get his people in London to move them over to a suite at The Ritz London on nearby Piccadilly. That would be more befitting.

Between then and Christmas he would have perfected a water-tight plan to disgrace *that thing* out of office, so that Sophie Harry Fenton-Forest would rightfully take and occupy her rightful birthright in the annals of world's most beautiful women. He poured himself yet another generous portion of the cognac from the crystal decanter, to drown his sorrows in and placate his mean miserable spirits. He decided against another call to them in London, because it was well past their bedtime then. It was too late for a social call.

He picked up the telephone handset and made two quick calls, one to the Imperial Khaliff, and the other to the Kligrapp in the Washington DC, KKK. After the calls, he quickly unzipped the black duffel bag on top of his desk to ascertain that his full regalia and all the other accessories were in place. Tonight, he was going to sort out things at the meeting coming up at the Oak Hill Cemetry, where *Willie*, Abraham Lincoln's son was buried long ago.

CHAPTER 84

Queen Jane Margaret Hilda Daniel-Aka had commenced her reign on an uneventful note. She had worked out her first month of reign to be active in London, then head home back to Nigeria, a week before Christmas. The Miss Cosmos office had put that into consideration as they plotted her itinerary up to 17th of December, and for her to depart for Lagos the next day. There were invitations from various Black and African communities in London, that she had chosen to honor. The Nigerian High Commission was amongst the numerous organizations that hosted dinner parties in honor of the new Miss Cosmos.

She had made it a priority to pay a courtesy visit to her *godmother* just two days after her coronation. It was a very high profile visit the key management of the Miss Cosmos Pageant all came to accompany her; visiting 10 Downing Street was not an everyday occurrence. Despite the political bickering and wrangling within her fold, the *Iron Lady* was a perfect picture of contentment, and never betrayed any form of weakness throughout the duration of the two-hour lunch. The prime minister had told all present that she was very proud of her goddaughter. She had given everyone a special souvenir at the end of the day.

The Miss Cosmos was so sad and also cried her eyes out on the 14th of November, when Prime Minister Margaret Hilda Thatcher left Downing Street in tears, before the official resignation two weeks later.

Another very prominent individual invitation the Miss Cosmos received, was from Oscar Uromi, a jet-set Nigerian millionaire businessman and director of Twinkle & Twinkle that sponsored the Miss Cosmos contest. The handsome Oscar Uromi, at 30, was one of the most eligible bachelors in London. He was voted as the most desirable male by the female readers of one of the very prominent tabloids. Oscar's patriotic invitation to honor the Miss Cosmos, for the London grapevine had all the ingredients for a blossoming romance between the handsome, rich and youthful businessman, and the woman adjudged most beautiful in the whole world. The tabloids went to town with the juicy story of a union that was made in heaven, even hinting of marital bells for the two week-old queen.

The forthcoming Oscar Dinner to honor a compatriot, received rave reviews in all London tabloids. Some even printed a specimen of the very impressive invitation card which was dispatched only to the crème de la crème in the society. The dinner was billed to take place at the exclusive Claridge's, on the eve of the queen's departure to Nigeria, her home country exactly a week to Christmas, since winning the crown.

Chuck *BTW* Freeborn IV, was in his office at the United States Embassy, and was in a bad mood. He was furious, not for the newspapers and their gossips or anything directly contained in them, for he had not even touched the newspapers on his table, which was his habit every morning. The Deputy Director was mad over the Administrator who was visiting London and had insisted he pulled in Oscar despite the fact that he was yet to lead them to the *Colombian Big Boss*. Chuck could feel that he was under pressure; his stomach ulcer was at it again. He had chewed three of the soothing sodium bicarbonate tablets already, but there was no soothing relief in his gastrointestinal tracts.

His thoughts shifted to the endoscopy the Embassy doctor recommended some months back, if the ulcer degenerated to the bleeding stage. Endoscopy, Dr. Weinstein said was a process of repairing the damages of the ulcer without an operation; a flexible fibre-optic tube is passed into the abdomen and under a direct vision on a monitor, a remote-controlled stitching machine sews up the ulcer. It gave him the jitters to even think of it, but he might consider it sometime. He picked up a newspaper, at least it would take his mind off the issue that had sparked off his ulcer. He sat down stretched out, his feet on top of the table, as he scanned the front page. A lead caught his eye; OSCAR FETES MISS COSMOS

A bell; an alarm went off somewhere in his brain. That name Oscar Uromi was like a recurring decimal now with the DEA. He quickly scanned the other papers the Oscar's Dinner also received good coverage. Somebody was doing a good publicity campaign. Something big was in the offing, he could swear on his father's grave.

Chuck Freeborn was galvanized into action. He threw a glance at the wall clock as he pulled the telephone toward him. He feverishly put a call through to Calvin Quootin his most senior field officer to rally the *war cabinet* for an emergency meeting immediately.

He then put a call through to his boss at the Ritz London. His wife had to wake him since his body clock was yet to acclimatize to the new time zone. He briefed him accordingly, and after conferring for another seven minutes Harry Fenton-Forest gave him his express consent to go on with his plans. Chuck could not believe his luck. Getting his way with Harry in seven minutes was a record. The old fox must be up to something. There was no love lost between the two of them, he was well aware..

He then quickly gathered the newspapers and the reports, and then retrieved two files from his confidential cabinet, and rushed over to preside over the meeting of his war cabinet. True to type Chuck Freeborn boldly engraved and displayed these words of Booker T. Washington as his maxim; *The Individual Who Can Do Something That The World Wants Done Will In The End Make His Way Regardless Of His Race.* Chuck was a passionate lover of the Booker T. Washington'sthought provoking wisdom. This harmless obsession of Chuck did not go down well with some official quarters. For somewhere in the depths of bureaucratic records in Washington DC, he was branded with excessive traits of black consciousness.

Another wisdom of BTW he had built his life around was; *There Is Something In Human Nature, Which We Cannot Blot Out, Which Makes One Man In The End, Recognize And Reward Merit In Another Regardless Of Color Or Race.* The emergency meeting of his war cabinet had consumed all of two hours, and it was a huge success, because even the nagging pain in his abdomen had receded. They had agreed at the meeting to upgrade Oscar Uromi and his state-of-the-art *Smooth Sail Cove* abode under a 24-hour surveillance. The war cabinet also agreed to have its agents to wait on tables at the dinner at Claridge's on Brook Street, which was a walking distance from the U.S Embassy.

Exactly two and half hours after the emergency meeting ended, a greyish blue British Telecom truck lumbered up Millionaires' Row in Golders Green. It packed right across *Smooth Sail Cove* and set up shop. The five rugged workmen men dressed in blue overalls with bold BT logo got busy immediately in the stinging cold winds of December. They set about their job of marking and cutting up a portion of the macadamized street lugubriously. They had about them that easygoing unhurried look of workmen who were paid on time basis. They even allotted more time to a steaming kettle of coffee that was passed around.

The first shift of DEA field agents to keep watch on Oscar Uromi had their hi-tech equipment rigged up within a couple of minutes. The actual act was inside the vehicle, the outside group was to present a facade to any curious eye. The well-equiped all purpose van they would intercept and monitor not all incoming and outgoing telephone calls, but even human and vehicular traffic in and out of the residence. All information collated was immediately transcribed and forwarded straight to Room 3127 at the U.S. Embassy for evaluation and assessment by a standby squad. When the DEA was on to something, they moved like a blood hound on the scent of raw blood. Even when it was a gamble, just a hunch, it was an expensive business..

The well publicized *Kingly Reception for a Queen*, went on as scheduled at the Ballroom Reception of the Claridge's, unarguably one of London's finest tradition. The entire 250 seating capacity was filled. The charming host, Oscar Uromi, was on hand to receive the honoured guests. He was decked out in a complete flowing black richly embroided agbada, with hand-made footwear of the same material. The formal native attire gave him the regal and enchanted look of an African prince and royalty. It was obvious that Uromi was both the secret and open desire of every spinster in that hall. Though they all sorted his attention, for Oscar that evening, he acted like their was only one woman present in that gathering, that he gave his undivided attention to. And that was the Special Guest of Honor, and the recently crowned most beautiful woman in the world, Miss Jane Margaret Hilda Daniel-Aka.

The high profile guests list was intimidating as they come. Oscar Uromi had spared no costs, he had put in so much to not only impress but to be very convincing of his *open-secret ulterior motives,* that had been well publicized. Even Ambassador Daniel Aka who had his well-informed reservations regarding Oscar Uromi's persona and character, at some point started doubting his own judgment. The chief host also exuded the splendor and charm of one of London's highest hospitality landmarks.Uromi was a paparazzi's delight, and there were quite a handful present that evening whom he was counting on. Uromi, was all over the queen, he was at her beck and call willingly with his trademark boyish smile permanently fixed on his face. He was a picture of a man head over heels in love. He played to the gallery, and the paparazzo's had a field day.

Oscar Uromi, lived up to his billing as the subterranean master of deception. To the utmost envy and dismay of the bevy of willing beautiful ladies, he left no one in doubt that he was in love with the Miss

Cosmos. Most of the guests went home convinced that wedding bells would be ringing in a very short time, since the Miss Cosmos was lapping it all up giggling like a school girl at a moppet show. Even Ambassador Daniel Aka at a point felt really flattered from all the attention his daughter was receiving and the patronizing compliments of colleagues from the diplomatic corps. Oblivious to Uromi, even his whispers on that table was shared with very attentive ears in at the U.S. Embassy a stone's throw away.

Even one of the two waiters waiting on his table was a senior DEA field agent. There were five other experienced agents amongst the troop of waiters engaged to cater to all requests and demands of the other guests. The dinner went well on greased wheels, Uromi held nothing back to impress his guests. They had a three-course gourmet meal accompanied with excellent vintages. The entire exercise, including the whole dinner and the accompanying publicity was to set him back almost a million pounds, but Uromi was not in the least bothered, it was just a pittance of his expected returns.

It was a bill the Claridge's was impressed with, Oscar Uromi was a free spender they were very familiar with, he settled bills with the slightest hesitation, and he was highly respected. As deserts were being served the host stood up to address the gathering, as if on cue a group of waiters wheeled in tables with an impressive array of gift items for the special guest of honor. The impressionable shopping bags and gift wrappers bore distinguishable logos and brands of exclusive fashion shops on New Bond Street, and Knightsbridge. There was also the conspicuous breathtaking 7-piece Louis Vuitton ostrich-skin luggage set. An exclusive creation, specially designed for Jane. The guests as well as the Miss Cosmos were taken aback with the brilliance of another outstanding gift a *Grade F* diamond necklace specifically ordered from the Antwerp head office of Alfred Van Derberst Ltd., the most respected diamond cutting polishing authority in the world.

Oscar Uromi waited for the distracting waiters to leave, and the audience resumed a somber mood, before he started his speech. He was indeed a fine specimen of manhood, he exuded a kind of sex appeal. His rich and golden voice coupled with his good diction made every word he uttered music to his female admirers. It was absolutely difficult for them to conceal the hunger in their starry eyes.

"I am indeed honoured to have such a distinguished gathering honor my humble invitation to bestow honor to whom it is due." He paused and smiled his radiant smile as the audience applauded.

"Tonight distinguished ladies and gentlemen is a celebration of rare natural African beauty. We have all heard of the superlative beauty of the Queen of Sheba that had King Solomon with all his wisdom weak with love. We also heard of the intoxicating beauty of the Egyptian Queen Cleopatra VII that sent the Roman aristocracy falling over each other to have her. Tell me who had not marveled at the bust of another African, the Egyptian, Queen Nefertiti who possessed a remarkable beauty that had refused to die over 3,000 years. Today, we celebrate another beauty whom the whole world and history had already judged. Ladies and gentlemen shall we rise and toast to a superlative beauty that will stand the test of time–Queen Jane Margaret Hilda Aka." The audience erupted with a standing ovation that took time to die down as the host of the evening bent down and kissed the beauty queen on the cheek.

"Distinguished ladies and gentlemen I have to crave your indulgence on my excesses for I am a man in love." Another loud applause again as the audience reeled with laughter.

"Our Queen is an embodiment of all that is good in the continent of both black and white Africa. I am indeed elated to be her compatriot, and as she heads home tomorrow we wish her a successful tenure as Miss Cosmos. The various gift items you find here are just a token of our love. Thank you." Uromi concluded appropriately, as the ovation went loudest. Jane maybe queen but deep down she was still an ordinary girl with normal fantasies related with *the tall, dark, and handsome of the Mills and Boons* saga. There was no doubt about it the young lady was in love already. She had swallowed everything hook, line and sinker. Rakiya seated by her could see through her friend, Jane was getting carried away with all the attention. Jane could not wait for a more private setting where she would surrender herself to Oscar's whims and caprices. She could already feel his strong arms all over her. It was time for the queen to respond to her kind host, as she regrettably disrupted her thoughts.

All her training came to the fore as she began her speech, with a classic touch of stately carriage without revealing any emotion, she thanked their very kind and gentlemanly host for a rare evening well-spent. She also thanked him for the more than queenly gift items he showered on her. The audience applauded her crisply presented speech. She then concluded with a lobsided wink that was calculated to humor.

"On the comparison with Cleopatra and the rest, I am quite flattered and honored to receive such high scores and accolades from an authority and renowned connoisseur of women. I sincerely hope they are not the proverbial Greek gifts from you for a higher reward, because my very loving father is on hand to deal with you." The guests applauded the hilarious side of the beauty queen they were meeting for the very first time. Oscar Uromi did not laugh or find it funny; he was seeing something they were not seeing. For that particular line was loaded with more connotations than all her speech.

"Thank you everyone for coming to honor us. And thank you Mr. Uromi for everything, may God bless you, and thank you once again. May your dreams come true." And the entire Claridge's Ballroom Reception rose to give the queen a well-deserved standing ovation.

As the guests filed out orderly after the guest of honor in high spirits, the DEA field agents did not feel any better for they did not learn anything new. There was a gnawing feeling in their hearts that it was another wild geese chase, where they had once again lost to a *Master*, who had taken them for a ride for the umpteenth time.

Deputy Director Chuck Freeborn was very satisfied with the outcome, his permutations were spot on the nose. He quickly directed his personal assistant to specifically book him on a Club Class seat on the British Airways flight to Lagos the next day. And return on the same flight back to London.

CHAPTER 85

The gleaming charcoal-black massive Rolls Royce Silver Spur with its special registration number OSCAR, surged effortlessly away from the imposing threshold of Claridge's to join the night-time traffic of Brooks Street. It was driven by an all- white clad chauffeur complete with a peaked hat. Settled comfortably behind in its plush maroon Italian first class leather upholsery were two passengers, the current Miss Cosmos and her host for the evening, Oscar Uromi. Following the Rolls was the cream coloured Jaguar courtesy of the Miss Cosmos Pageant, seated in the back was Rakiya. Right behind the Jaguar was a Land Rover Jeep with security officials assigned to accompany the Miss Cosmos in all official outings in London. To complete the convoy was a white Bedford van driven by a staff of *International Links Limited*, a company owned by Oscar Uromi, it was laden with all the gift items.

By the traffic lights, the convoy turned right on to New Bond Street, the monstrous Rolls did not fail to awe the lonely figures of night-time window-shoppers on the now deserted busy street, which is one of the most acclaimed exclusive shopping street on earth. In the clinical spacious interiors of the marvel of British auto- engineering, the sheer captivating music of Harry Connick Jr. filtered noiselessly through the roof with an amazing life-like clarity. Jane was overwhelmed and impressed. She had turned down the offer to ride with her host of the evening, but Oscar had refused to accept no for an answer. And to not create a scene she had accepted in the long run the ride back to the hotel in Oscar's car. They rode in electrifying silence, each engrossed in their individual thoughts, the chauffeur separated by a solid wall of glass partition minded his own business. As they turned into Brutton Street approaching Berkeley Square, as if on cue Oscar without uttering a word took Jane's right hand in his, their eyes met for a brief but significant moment. They both smiled. Jane's disarming, and Oscar's sly and mischievous. The exotic aroma of Oscar's manly cologne was overpowering, almost intoxicating. His palms were warm and soothing, an uncontrollable shiver ran through her veins, and Jane knew she was in love with him. Oscar was simply irresistible as he closed his eyes and sang along with Harry Connick Jr., it was a track titled *A Nightingale Sang In Berkley Square* written by M. Sherwin and E. Maschiwtz;

> *That certain night, the night we met*
> *There was magic abroad in the air*
> *There were angels dining at the Ritz*
> *And a nightingale sang in Berkeley*
> *Square I may be right, I may be wrong*
> *But I'm perfectly willing to swear*
> *That when you turned and smiled at me*
> *A nightingale sang in Berkeley Square ...*

It was Jane who actually made the first move. She stole one look back at the Jaguar and its occupants following sedately behind at a leisurely pace, before her lips engulfed Oscar's in a long hungry fiery kiss. After the kiss Jane knew she was hooked on Oscar like a junkie on heroine. *He was so tempting.*

Unknown to both Jane and Oscar, Rakiya observed vividly the merging of their silhouettes in that brief wild moment of uncontrollable estasy. A bright spotlight in the direction of Berkley Square highlighted their entwined silhouettes. Rakiya was furious. It was a reckless exhibition that was unacceptable in her present celebrity status. If the pageant official observed or noticed the amoral act in the Rolls, he did not show it. She would give Jane a piece of her mind when they get back to the hotel.

"Jane, this is Berkley Square." Oscar said looking into her eyes.

"Yes, I know." Jane answered with a puzzled look.

"What a coincidence? It is the same Berkley Square in the song you just heard a moment ago. That is indeed interesting, Oscar." Jane called the name with a faint hint of sentimental attachment.

Oscar was not surprised he had that addictive effect on the opposite sex. It was one of his greatest assets."It is indeed interesting because for the first time in my life I am in love with a woman." Oscar said with feigned seriousness, trying to meet Jane's eyes who quickly looked out of the window.

Oscar was a convincing actor, for Jane swallowed his lie hook, line and sinker. Jane remained silent. She was dumbfounded. She was shocked by the suddenness of his declaration. She could not believe her ears. She was confused. How she needed somebody like Rakiya to come to her aid. What was she supposed to say? Events were moving too fast for her to keep pace. Then she heard his probing voice deep in her thoughts.

"Why did you call me a connoisseur of women?" Oscar asked accusingly, his handsome face set with pained seriousness.

"I did not mean it, please Oscar, honest I was only trying to crack a joke," Jane's voice sounded sincere. "Are you angry with me?" This time she met his unwavering gaze eyeball for eyeball, and they held, and as if on cue Harry Connick sang *It's Alright With Me* by C. Porter;

... You can't know how happy I am that we met

I'm strangely attracted to you
There's someone I'm trying so hard to forget
Don't you want to forget someone too ....

The words were very distinctly loud and clear, and most of all very apt for the present circumstances. They both burst into hysterical laughter, as their palms clasped involuntarily.

"You do have a friend, in your musical friend. *Who is he anyway?*" Jane tried to change the subject to buy her time to digest events better. Things were happening too fast for her to keep tabs.

"My darling Jane, you are listening to my favourite singer. His name is Harry Connick Jr., the best of the new generation jazz musicians. He sings with a passion, that is absolute. You will soon get used to him sharing me with you. I love his music, but not as much as I love you. For you darling; I will die for." A mischievous smirk crossed Oscar's handsome face, knowing he had Jane where he wanted her.

She was almost blushing, believing every word that came out from his mouth. He knew his ultimate mission was almost accomplished, for at this stage he had Jane tethered and eating from his hand. She would sell her own mother to him for a plate of porridge. As the convoy approached the Hilton through Curzon Street, Oscar hesitatingly let go of Jane's soft and warm hand. Jane could tell from the look of hunger in his eyes that he was really in love with her. For a moment she wanted to hold him to her bosom, and reassure him of her own love, but Oscar's voice then interrupted her thoughts.

"I will leave my driver and the van with you tonight to help convey your stuff to the airport tomorrow morning. I am indeed concerned with the *excess luggage* I have saddled you with." His voice had the right amount of genuine concern.

"Oh, Oscar you are a darling. It is very thoughtful of you. You are a very nice person." And she patted him on the shoulder.

"Come on, Jane" Oscar said carelessly with a wave of his hand, "that is nothing much, what else do you expect. I am a man in love." He paused as they pulled up, and the doorman approached the car with an umbrella. And as the door opened, Oscar said to the hearing of the embarrassed doorman, "Jane I love you to death, and would do anything for you. Please I mean every word of it." He stretched out his hand to hold Jane who moved to get out of the car.

"Thank you Oscar for everything." The Miss Cosmos quickly said, and with a smile tapped him on the shoulder.

"Jane, expect me in Lagos very soon, I will not blink an eye lid until I have you as my wife."

A ruffled Jane could not even utter a word as an answer. She came down from the car amidst more flash lights. She smiled at the cameras and walked with exaggerated aplomb into the lobby, protected by her security personnel from the excited band of pressmen with microphones.

The charcoal-black monstrous Rolls Royce with its now lone passenger in the back, pulled away from the Hilton into the light traffic on Park Lane. As its chauffeur deftly manoeuvred its bulk to join the north-bound traffic, the lone passenger burst into hysterical laughter that shook the sound-proofed cosy interiors of the car. As the cold, leafless trees of Hyde Park rushed past, an oblivious Oscar Uromi continued in his fits of laughter all the way to Marble Arch, until he was interrupted by the calm and calculated voice of his trusted Irish chauffeur of many years.

"Boss, I think we have some *company* right behind us, sir." Oscar was instantly alert. He held himself from looking back, as his mind searched for possible and probable escape routes. He wandered who might be following him.

"Patrick, how long have they been following us?" Oscar asked, his voice sounded calm and under control.

"I first noticed them when we were about Berkeley Square, sir."
"Okay, just drive at a leisurely pace along Edgeware Road, turn right at Marylebone, and turn right again at Baker Street, and drive down to American Burger at Oxford Street by North Audley Street."

Oscar quickly reeled off these instructions, took a cursory glance at his wrist watch and settled comfortably deeper into his seat.

He once again suppressed the burning urge to steal one harmless glance at his hunters. He shut his eyes and felt the surge of the car forward as the green traffic light came on. For the two occupants of the dark coloured Rover car trailing the Rolls, they had no inkling that they were now an open secret. That was why they did not suspect anything any foul play when the Rolls slowly turned into Baker Street, and headed back towards where they were coming from. The Rover maintained a safe distance and followed at what the occupants thought was a surreptitious distance.

When the Rolls finally pulled to a stop outside the popular all-night burger shop, the Rover drove past the shop, and parked in a No Parking Zone. Oscar carefully observed the two white males in the car. He knew without much ado that he had the long arm of the law on his tail. Nobody but the police dare park in a London No Parking Zone. That did not bother him the least, because he knew he was *clean as a whistle* with the law.

Oscar languidly stepped out from the car, and strolled casually into the popular all-night joint. He did not tell his chauffeur anything. The two agents from Scotland Yard, settled back in their seats for what they already considered a long wait, thinking their quarry was going to have a night cap. Oscar in his Nigerian attire looked out of place. The place was parked full with a noisy pack of patrons. There was a lull in their conversations as they noticed him walk in. He ignored them, and as if he had had a change of mind, he proceeded toward the other doors leading onto Oxford Street.

Outside on the street, was quite cold. He could feel the winter cold gradually gnawing at the exposed parts of his anatomy. But he was in luck, he saw the approaching light of a black cab. He hailed it, and it stopped. He gave the driver an exclusive St. John's Wood address and quickly jumped in. He had the heater going full blast in a moment, as he settled down to enjoy the comfort of his new vehicle.

As the cab turned into Portman Street, he had the distant toll of a nearby church bell. It was eleven o'clock, as he confirmed from the luminous dials of his very expensive wrist watch. At that very moment sounded a loud blip that almost startled Oscar. It was the mobile phone in his pocket. He raised it to his right ear and listened without uttering a word. Thereafter, he smiled to himself and replaced the phone back in his pocket. All was going according to plans; no wonder they called him the *Master of Deception*.

The cab driver for once drove in dignified silence, certainly curious about his fare clad in a very strange attire, and his mission to an exclusive highbrow residential area. As the cab zoomed passed the the now deserted London Central Mosque on Park Road. A red dot of light glowed on the small dashboard monitor. To any curious passenger, it would not mean anything, but for the driver it meant serious business. A green glow is from the cab company, while a red glow is a red alert from the Scotland Yard.

It was called a WPWKI-10, *Watch Passenger With Keen Interest*, the number 10 stands for the highest priority, whereby any driver conveying the passenger must contact Scotland Yard unfailingly immediately. With the press of the uppermost black right hand button, the police bulletin, with a complete profile of the passenger would appear on the monitor. The alert was *for a handsome black male in his Thirties. Probably still dressed in a foreign attire. Last sighted around the vicinity of Oxford street within the hour.*

The lower red button on the right, when depressed would immediately tell Scotland Yard of the identity of the driver. The cab driver depressed the red button, he was convinced that he has the man. There was a frenzy of activities at the Scotland Yard, as the cab driver depressed the red button. The giant monitor connected to the computer displated the following information.

The cab driver was Thomas Barley Masters, age 49, and was from the suburb of Croydon. He was married with two teenage children. A well decorated Royal Marine, that is a veteran of the Falklands War. His Special Program Number was WPWKI-D345. Masters was one of the five hundred cab drivers recruited by the Criminal Investigation Department of Britain's London Metropolitan Police to watch passengers with a professional eye to help solve crimes. The cabs were equipped with various sophisticated intelligence gadgets by the department.

They were a block from his actual destination, when Oscar stopped the cab. He paid his fare with a tip. He pretended to be looking for his keys, as the cab drove away. He saw its tail lights turn left into the night, before he walked across the street and proceeded to the secluded beautiful white cottage with very high thick hedge just by the first turn ahead. He knew he was being watched from inside as he pressed the doorbell. He did not see Thomas Masters had melted into the shadows across the street.

"Yes! what do you want?" a dismembered voice queried.

"Mr. Amigo is expecting me", he answered.

He waited for about half-a-minute in the chilly cold before the voice said "You may come in". He swore inwardly to himself, as the front door opened by itself. Though he had visited this house couple of times, yet he could not get over the over-powering ominous silence always in the air. He walked towards the gigantic solid oak door looming ahead, and the spooky sensation of being watched and appraised by unseen diabolical eyes. The impregnable doors, as if by remote control parted inwards as he got to them.

Thomas Masters, a war veteran at his age, was physically well conditioned. The 49 year-old retired Sergeant of the elite Royal Marines Corps, specialized in marine commando combat. He joined the service at 21, and had a well-decorated meritorious service for 22 years. He first saw battle in the Indonesia-Malaysia 1962–1966 Confrontations; then went on to serve in the IRA Border Campaign in 1968-1970; then came the Falklands War in 1982 that he was part of the Royal Marines assault force; then ended service at Lebanon as part of the Multinational Force in 1984.

Though in all the 22 years he spent as a soldier, he was never trained as intelligence personnel, he secretly admired the suave and sanctimonious demeanor of the *secret intelligence boys*. There was always that respect and reserve accorded them by everybody, like the *007 James Bond* character. It was that involuntary awe for somebody who knew so many top secrets that could set nations against nations. That was why he was so excited to be part of the Scotland Yard's Special Branch Program to rely on war veterans. Their orientation was brief and simple; *just use your eyes and ears. No heroics.*

They were trained on simple psychology in assessing and leading on a fare to reveal information without suspicion. There were special numbers to call for assistance, and the special dashboard monitors installed for non-verbal emergency bulletins and contacts; at no point were they instructed to carry out any investigations on their own. Thomas Masters was particularly disappointed regarding this final instruction; they expected more action. Why should men who had seen real action; just listen, talk, and observe, and if need be call in the *real men into action, and to take the glory.*

Masters and his ilk hungered and thirsted for a real piece of the action. He boasted to his friends that he was going to prove all those namby-pamby tacticians at The Yard wrong. This ambition would be his greatest undoing or Achilles' heels.

For four long years he waited patiently for an opportunity like this to come along. He was not going to let it slip; it might even elevate him from the black cab ranks to a cozy respected espionage job. How could he forget the experience of been declared a national or international hero? He could see vividly the glamour and the recognition of the decoration, the anthem, the drum rolls, the camera flashlights, the pictures, and then the newspaper headlines. He would become an instant celebrity.

He had driven-off, leaving the man, whose description fitted the bulletin's profile, fooling himself that he was searching for a non-existent bunch of keys. He took the first turn, and quickly packed the cab and jumped out. He ran back to the street to see his quarry walking briskly towards him. His marine-training and instincts naturally came to the fore as he melted into the shadows. And the man walked by without seeing him. He zipped up his leather jacket as he went after the hurrying dark figure of Oscar Uromi. He did not have far to go as his quarrry turned into the very one-story building surrounded by the high and thick hedge.

He stood and waited in the shadows as Oscar Uromi did the *open sesame*. He took mental note of the address, and was about to move off, when a doubt cropped up in his mind. What he had would not give him even a mention when whatever case, was solved. How he would get all the credits and glory was to single-handedly wrap up the case. So he decided to snoop around, so that he would not end up making a fool of himself by the time he makes his report to Scotland Yard. Yes, that was true he consoled himself, as he started *a journey of no return*.

He stepped quickly into the property that did not show a single lighted window. Except for the light in the porch area, the rest of the outside was in shadows. The wind sang its chilly tone angrily. He quickly blended into the penumbra; becoming one with the shadows of the thick hedge. It brought back long forgotten feelings and memories. He felt that skin tingling feeling when the invisible enemy was about to pull the trigger. It could only be experienced and told by only those who survived raw debilitating fear. Who says fear has no taste? Fear has a sour gritty taste, especially when you do not know the enemy. He felt the piercing eyes of the enemy drilling through him.

It was an immediate transformation. Thomas Masters, an harmless London black cab driver was immediately transformed into the ultimate fighting machine. He eased his body weight over the balls of his feet, his well trained lethal body ready to spring into action. He stood still with his eyes firmly close. He listened. He could pick out the chirping sounds of some nocturnal insects or animal distinctly. When he opened his eyes a flitting moment later, he felt better. He bent low and moved forward to scale the hedge.

Inside the house, Vasco de Zapata, his enemy relaxed and watched with keen interest, the intruder's every move on a 14 inch monitor. They were puzzled first, but it later took shape. Uromi, the man referred to as 'zebra' in the underworld of drugs was indicted. He must have stupidly led the intruder to the house. Everybody was put on alert.

Thomas Masters, within a short while knew the house was impregnable from the ground. the roof he could see was the only weak point. he could easily get on to the roof to find his way into the house. Why was he a commando in the best trained army in the world? He knew he was doing the wrong thing, but he was now like the proverbial stubborn fly that ended up interred with the corpse for refusing to turn back when it was necessary.

He did not even know what he should be looking for, all he knew was that his passenger was a *VIWAL 10*. This was an official term for very important witness at large. The number *10*, stood for the highest priority.

With his acknowledgement, they already knew at the Scotland Yard, that the 'viwal 10' was in cab no. 4537, driven by Thomas Masters, a retired well decorated royal marine sergeant. The rest of Thomas Masters' bio-data they were not interested to read, it was not necessary. On the 8th floor of the New Scotland Yard on Broadway and Victoria Street, the headquarters of the criminal investigation department, some people were getting frantic. The expected telephone call from Thomas Masters was long overdue. They had assured the Americans there was no cause for alarm. It was almost an hour since their man acknowledged their dispatch, something must have gone wrong. The special cabs were fitted with tracers, they could tell where exactly his cab was parked.

At that particular time in the Queen's Suite; the girls were packing for the journey back to Nigeria. The van driver who had told them his name was Esau, had led to the these funny dialogue, when he had personally delivered all the gift items to the suite.

"Yes? Who is knocking?" It was Margaret Hilda answering the door.

"It is Esau, madam." The husky voice answered.

"Which Esau? The brother of Jacob, that sold his birthright for a pot of porridge?" The queen asked with a hint of humor.

"No, madam. This is Esau the driver. The one that makes sure your load is delivered without hitches." The voice too burst into good natured laughter.

"I am only opening the door, since you don't sell birthrights, my friend" as the door opened to admit Esau, who was no more smiling but looking moody.

"It is alright Mr. Esau, I was only joking." Margaret Hilda tried to salvage the situation. If only she knew how prophetic she was with her little piece of joke.

Esau had efficiently done his job, and promised to be back at 7a.m. to convey the items of luggage, with them to the Victoria Station, British Airways Check-in Counter. Rakiya had tipped him with a five pound note, to return his smile.

After Esau had left, the girls had settled down to do a post-mortem of the day. In between were phone calls from Ambassador Daniel Aka, and Don Baldwin, who all promised to be at the Victoria Station check-in, and thereafter follow her by the Gatwick Express to the Airport for the formal farewell ceremony. The queen had expressed her anticipation to hear from Oscar before she sleeps, this comment had finally led to Jane and Rakiya, ever having a real heated quarrel, since they met.

When the Miss Cosmos finally retired for the night, her thoughts were on the delectable Oscar Uromi. She had vehemently refused to join Rakiya for their customary bed-time prayer. She had rebuffed Rakiya's genuine efforts to make peace. She could not understand why Rakiya just did not like her Oscar... *maybe Rakiya was just jealous.* Who, which girl would not want Oscar for herself? The guy was handsome from every angle and stinking rich. Just imagine Rakiya's tongue in cheek warning; *that not all that glitters is gold.* Who is Rakiya to teach her morals? She deserved all that she got... she gave her the acidic and ascorbic side of her tongue. *Nonsense!*

She could not wait for Esau to come in the morning; she was confident that he would bring her some romantic farewell message from Oscar. Maybe something, some borrowed idea from his Harry Connick Jnr., who cares, as long as it speaks for his undying love for her. And she drifted off to sleep...dreaming of her sweet Oscar, who somehow turned into wolf, and started chasing her until she fell into a very deep gorge, that he could not reach her.

CHAPTER 86

for Thomas Masters, his very long night was just beginning. With the commando training acquired over the years climbing up to the roof was going to be a child's play, but if for any reason he is caught, he will be on his own. He decided against the roof, and chose to climb a stout tree growing between the hedge and the wall of the house to see something through the first floor window.

He scaled up the tree easily but could not see through the heavily draped windows. It was on top of the tree his enterprising spirit waned. He had no alternative but to make the expected call to Scotland Yard. At least he tried. He came down the tree sober, but very disillusioned. And that was what affected his strategic survival training; *to pay attention at all time especially to little details, they make difference between a dead, and living marine*. There was a reception party waiting for him when he got down. He was not expecting one, yet he sprang into action out of habit conditioned by training and practical experience. He was like an old samurai; old with age but was still sharp. He was able to dismantle two of his adversaries by dislocating some vital bones, before he was over powered by a cold steel voice who pushed a snub-nosed gun with a silencer on to his back. Vasco de Zapata watched safely from inside on all the monitors with keen interest.

As Masters was led into the house through the porch, the lone figure walking his dog at that time of the night went by without even a glance in their direction. Though the old man muttered something under his breath about the foreigners in his glorious England.

Thomas Masters had steel under his skin. He was a hard nut to crack. He refused to break under intense torture. All he could tell his crude interrogators was his name. Though many years of training hardened him up, but his heart was not getting any younger. Somewhere along the line he passed out, and they could not revive him. Zapata had instructed them to dispose of the body far from the house as possible.

Thomas Masters was a big man, and it was not an easy task for the South Americans of average height to lift his dead weight, so they dragged his body into the garage, and stuffed it into a tiny Ford Escort. The illuminated dashboard clock was showing 1.45, when the Ford Escort with the two live occupants drove through Wellington Road towards the junction with St. John's Wood Road. At the junction they took left and headed into Prince Albert Road, which was deserted by this time of the night. They drove in silence. they did not see any car until they approached the junction with Avenue Road. They turned right onto the Macclesfield bridge to connect the outer circle of Regent's Park.

There was not a soul or head lights of on-coming vehicular traffic in sight. They quickly reversed back to the bridge they had crossed and heaved the naked body of Thomas Masters to the watery grave below. They did not even wait for the body to hit the water, before they hurriedly jumped into their car, and zoomed off turning right into the outer circle. It was by Hanover, near the London Central Mosque that they saw the patrol car parked by the roadside. They drove straight and exited at Baker Street which was almost deserted. They drove all the way to Oxford Street at a leisurely pace, and Edgeware Road back to their base in St. John's Wood.

Oscar Uromi, *Zebra* to the initiates of the international underworld of drugs smuggling, stood still, facing the fearful faceless figure of the man he only knew as *Amigo*. He could not even recognize him in broad daylight because he was always sitting in the shadows. The room was bare, except for the Italian leather settee the man was spread out on. He was known to be shrewd, emotionally cold, and ruthless, from any of the cocaine jungles of Peru, Colombia, and Ecuador. To the consumer streets of London and to Amsterdam his fearsome image was larger-than-life.

To the United States Drug Enforcement Administration officials in Bogota and Medellin, and the rest of the world he was dead and forgotten. He had taken the advantage of his *death*, to perfect a new identity that secured him passage first to Madrid, and then finally to London, just one month after his much touted death, which was of *his double*. The only person on earth who was privy to this information was his longtime friend and aide, Vasco de Zapata. Even Pablo Escobar and the others in the Medellin cartel were in the dark. After the death of all his family, he just felt it was time to call it quits. Unfortunately, for his secret to remain intact, he could not have access to his colossal wealth, without revealing his well kept secret. It was his wealth or his secret new identity securing a new lease of life. Alberto Valdarama, his travelling documents said, he was a native of the olive growing province of Seville, in Spain. He cleared both her majesty's immigration service and customs procedures with ease. On the same flight was the man he could entrust his life to.

The exclusive address in the St. John's Wood was acquired through a Zapata old friend in Madrid. So began their sojourn in London, England; if they had any nostalgia of their old country, none ever voiced it out. In the long run it was the desire to have money for their upkeep that led to re-opening channels into the drug business back in Colombia. It was on this basis that rumors that he was not dead began. Too bad for Enrique Pulido he deserved what he got for his blabber mouth.

Oscar Uromi, stood almost immobile with fear under the unflattering presence of Alberto Valdarama. "How did it go my friend?" the voice was soft, with an underlying authority of somebody who must be obeyed.

"All went well Mr. Amigo, Phase 1 was a resounding success. Everything is in place for Phase 2. By this time tomorrow we would be home and dry." Oscar said, looking forward to reassuring comments from his lone audience.

"Zebra, I need not remind you, of our existing contract terms. Do not forget that in no circumstances would half measures be acceptable. I will keep my eyes glued on you. Do I make myself clear, Zebra?" the big man said with a note of finality.

"Ye..ee..yes, I understand you very well." Oscar could not understand why he was shivering all of a sudden and stammering

"Then good night and goodluck, Zebra."

"Good night to you too." Oscar said and turned towards the huge door which opened by its own accord. He had the dead bolt click behind his back as he proceeded back the way he had come.

CHAPTER 87

Through the morning was typically cold, yet Wilton Travis, 45, a top flight executive with an oil company at Cavendish Square, but lived on Townshend Road, for the past three years, accompanied by his *best friend,* must start their day with a routine of exercises. They would leave the cozy comfort of the home that they share with a Mrs. Joan Travis, run down their street across Prince Albert Road, through the Macclesfield bridge onto the running track by the canal in Regents Park. They would spend an hour burning away fat, both had packed up in their middle ages.

The time spent running was most times in silence. If there was any sensible word uttered it will come from Travis, but this did not in any way affect their friendship. Wilton Travis knew deep down in his heart, that his faithful friend would stake his own life for him. That was why he trusted this friend, than any human alive. Wilton Travis' best friend was an 8 year-old bulldog named Bruno. It had become a tradition for Bruno to take a leak by the foot of the bridge, as his boss and friend would use the opportunity to do 100 push-ups, right on top of the bridge. It was a routine that had never changed.

The trees below the bridge by the canal were bare of leaves at that time of the year. The very philosophical Travis recalled a poem by Chux Onyenyeonwu, titled *Irony of the Extremes*;

> As winter's chilly cold seeps right into the bones
> and man cocoons himself in layers of cotton and wool
> The trees proceed on a naked carnival...
> And in warm sunny summer rays
> when the tree covers up her ugly nakedness

> *Then man begins a conjugal dance of*
> *total submission of pale body and flesh*
> *for the sun to devour in half nakedness ...*

As Travis went down on his knees and hands to commence his usual exercise on the bridge, he noticed in the early morning failing light something out of place in the naked trees below. He was frozen on his hands and knees... spread-eagled on the grey black branches was the half naked body of a white male. It was almost blue. Travis quickly dialed 999 on his Motorola mobile phone. He then dialed his wife who was an assistant news editor with Channel 4 News. She told him to wait right there, that she was coming over.

It took four minutes for the first squad car with siren blaring to screech to the scene. The police officers quickly evaluated the horror in the tree branches first, and immediately cordoned off both ends of the bridge.

Two minutes behind the police car, came Channel 4 News and from the sky. The helicopter hovered overhead beating the police's cordon as they filmed the scene from the sky. Travis could see his wife from the open door of the helicopter waving to him. Then more police cars arrived the scene with an ambulance. The Channel 4 News helicopter was still hovering over the scene recording the scene below with their electronic eyes. Travis could see his wife clearly talking into a microphone, that meant that they were transmitting live on the morning television as *breaking news* item.

At the Scotland Yard, the officers that worked overnight on the *VIWAL 10,* were woken by the ringing telephone in the medium-sized conference room. The highest ranking officer picked up the receiver.

"Richard Pooler here." he answered without any trace of anxiety. The others listened keenly to his side of the conversation with curiosity."All right. What?...Where?... We will be there." he hung up the receiver. He stood up to retrieve his coat from the hanger by the door. Before Richard Pooler, the head of the *VIWAL Special Unit* could tell them what was going on, they were already up and getting their coats too. It was in the lift he told them, that they found, poor Thomas Masters stark naked, and spread out to dry on top of the branches at the canal at Regent's Park. Nobody dared ask for clarifications; for Pooler was angry, this incident was the first threat to his pet project of almost 36 months.

It was on Monday, 18th of December, and the Miss Cosmos was leaving the lobby of the Hilton in a convoy of cars; on their way to the British Airways Check-in at the Victoria Station as scheduled. There were a motley crowd of pressmen and freelance photographers covering her departure from London, with the crown to her native Nigeria. The van from Oscar Uromi, laden with the queen's nine suitcases, was in the middle of the convoy that were escorted by police outriders.

British Airways officials were on standby to formally receive the Miss Cosmos and her entourage, so actual checking-in was with ease, as the Miss Cosmos and chaperon were travelling First Class courtesy of British Airways. The nine pieces of baggage were checked-in without even raising an eyebrow. The tags were put on Rakiya Danbaba's ticket and duly handed over to her. The British Airways manager, a pert British-Indian led the Queen's party to the Gatwick Express waiting below at the Platform Number 2.

The Queen and her entourage, her father and staff of the Nigerian High Commission, as well as the staff of The Miss Cosmos Pageant almost took the better part of a First Class carriage of the train. There were also press-men, and the pack of freelance photographers still hoping for a last minute sensational shot. With the blast of the shrill whistle 7.30am Gatwick Express set off on its 30-minute journey to the Gatwick Airport. They were in good time for the special *Twinkle & Twinkle* sponsored final farewell ceremony, for her 11am scheduled flight for Lagos.

Nestled comfortably in the compartment after the Queen's on the 7.30am Gatwick Express was Chuck Freeborn IV, with two of his DEA officers. They looked relaxed, and spoke in very low tones. He had been briefed all ready about the body of the missing black cab driver. There was no inkling of Oscar Uromi's whereabouts; he had not returned or slept at the *Smooth Sail Cove* for certain. Scotland Yard was still hopeful, they had traced Thomas Masters black cab to a posh street in St. John's Wood, plans were already underway to comb the immediate surrounding vicinity of the vehicle.

In his luxurious suite at the Ritz London, Harry Fenton-Forest clad in a white Ritz London towel housecoat sat engrossed at the breaking news on Channel 4 News. He was shocked to see a sight that would have sounded ordinary in most major cities in America, happening in a very conservative London. He felt like waking up his wife and daughter to witness what he was seeing. That would be going too far, let them be, the waking hours had remained gloomy and miserable since he arrived. She looked to have lost her usual self-confidence prior to the beauty contest. He was going to do everything humanly possible to return that self-confidence.

If only he knew that, what was playing out on television, was connected to the case, his London people were working on, maybe he would have changed his mind. He felt so good that things were actually falling into place by their own accord, without him raising a finger. Even Freeborn would be fooled of why he had been unnaturally cooperative. He was so excited that by Christmas which was in a few days, Sophie Fenton-Forest would be the reigning Miss Cosmos. This he promised himself, he would give his Sophie as a Christmas present. What more could he have done as a loving and protective father. The thought alone was enough to celebrate. He stepped over to the mini-bar and poured himself a stiff brandy, then relaxed to continue the Channel 4 News daring escapades to grab a scoop.

The Scotland Yard team of officers had arrived the scene, there was a crowd gathered already from a safe distance to be part of the live TV coverage. Richard Pooler gave instructions immediately for a man to be lowered by a crane to wrap up the body. Then the body was carefully lifted up to the bridge where a group of special homicide squad got down to preliminary procedures. Wilton Travis and Bruno were for the umpteenth time telling their story to an unending team of police officials. When the police photographer had completed his work, the body was wrapped up and wheeled into the waiting ambulance that hurriedly screeched off in squeal of tyres to god knows where. The next thing on the screen was Wilton Travis and Bruno standing faithfully by his side was relating his story by phone to his wife, and the whole London and the world was hearing.

The flight to Lagos took off as scheduled. It was an uneventful flight. For Chuck who had not slept properly in the last 48 hours, he was able to catch some hours of sleep right after they were served lunch. When he finally woke up, they were about an hour from Lagos. Despite the seriousness of the issue that had brought him to Lagos, he could not help to feel happily excited. It was his ever first trip to Africa. As an African in diaspora, it goes beyond mention, how he felt deep inside. It touched and tickled even the innermost depths of his spiritual being.

Chuck Freeborn IV, in a few minutes was going to tread the same soil his great grandfather, and his ancestors trod. All of a sudden a heaviness pervaded his heart; why would a woman in her most glorious moment get involved in something that would definitely tarnish not only her image, but that of her country and her entire race. He pondered to himself; could it be greed and love. These were the reasons behind various atrocious actions perpetrated by women. Deep down he felt pity for her, but *a man got to do his job.*

He recalled those stories of his great grandfather about life in Africa; how the typical African, and his immediate family would go any length to clear his or her name if wrongly accused. How wives, family members, rival kinsmen or sworn enemies, were made to drink the bath water of a corpse just to prove their innocence. He also recalled the stories of the accused or a close relative who was made to venture into the depths of the forest; and to return with the head of a wild and ferocious animal to prove his innocence or that of the close relative. Many innocent men died in the process, leaving the world to think otherwise.

He remembered the tears that streamed down the old man's face as he recalled the story of how he got sold into slavery and finally landed in America, where he was trying to prove his innocence by clearing his name and his family's. Suppose the queen was innocent? Suppose she was not even aware of the *bombshell* in her baggage? Suppose the lady was just an expendable pawn, in a dangerous game of death? Could she ever prove her innocence to the world? *Baba* was adjudged guilty when he did not re-surface from the belly of the *powerful long oracle*; even when he was innocent of the charge of murder against him and his brother. That he had promised *Baba* to return to his roots and expose the ruse that was an oracle. If only he had time to explore and trace his great grandfathers people. Unfortunately, he was returning back to London immediately he handed the case over to his counterpart in Lagos.

Captain Jack Vanswift, , allowed himself one last luxurious look of the sprawling city below, that was clearly dissected by the lagoon, that gave it its name. Lagos, from the air was awesome in its humongous spread. Captain Vanswift had served well over fifteen years flying for British Airways, and had flown over a hundred times the Lagos Route; but Lagos never ceased to overwhelm him. His experienced eyes roamed through the controls and instrumentation panel on a final check. There were no blinking lights; no cause for alarm. All systems were Go, to commence landing that had been cleared by the Lagos tower.

With a deep breath, he whispered a silent prayer, then smiled and nodded confidently to the younger co-pilot to brace-up for the final approach. He concentrated totally on the important business of landing the jumbo jet safely; first for his life and that of the two hundred and seven passengers and crew on board. He displayed his veteran qualities by the flawless touch-down of the mammoth Boeing 747-400 on runway

01 of the Murtala Mohammed International Airport. It was with the deft touch of a mother gently laying down her sleeping baby.

As the aeroplane taxied to the far end of the runway, the captain heaved a sigh of relief, and handed over control to his co-pilot. He flicked on the public address system, and his relaxed and cheerful voice came out loud and clear to his grateful and satisfied passengers.

"Welcome to Lagos, ladies and gentlemen. It's the way we make you feel that makes us the world's favorite airline." he paused for a brief hearty laughter. "This is your captain on behalf of British Airways saying a big thank you for doing business with us." he paused a little and continued. "It has also been an exciting experience and honor to also have the world's most beautiful woman onboard…the brand new Miss Cosmos. From the entire crew we wish her a very successful tenure, and congratulations Nigeria. Thank you" and he clicked off.

The news of the queen on board was received by the passengers in the other cabins with surprise and excitement. There was an irresistible urge to move forward by the very eager passengers, to catch a glimpse of the first black woman to be crowned Miss Cosmos. When the plane came to a stop. The captain himself, officially ushered the beauty queen over to a team of protocol and security officials waiting by the door.

They now led the queenly train; including her father, through corridors meant for visiting dignitaries. Acknowledging the cheers of excited airport workers and passengers, she was ushered straight to the government's special VIP lounge. An airport reception and press conference was scheduled to hold, as a rousing welcome for the new queen.

After the national anthem, the genial and bohemian Federal Commissioner of Culture, made a big show of welcoming the queen. In his welcome speech, the eloquent minister spoke laudably of the achievement of the new Miss Cosmos, citing the academic laurels her own father won for the whole black race not very long ago. He spoke glowingly of, the honor and glory, not only for Nigeria, but also for the black race, that she brought with her natural endowments.

He carefully chose his words to conclude the speech; "we have once again blazed a new trail for the rest of the black world to follow. Tell me how would a grateful nation honor an illustrious daughter?" he paused and looked around at his attentive audience, then announced the government's largesse, to make her a roving *Goodwill Ambassador*. He also dropped the hint of more goodies from the Head of State.

The queen in her brief response, with tears of joy thanked profusely "the head of state and entire citizenry of Nigeria, for the honor bestowed on her.

"I pledge to uphold Nigeria's honor and glory, during and after my reign. Thank you all for your support. We went, we saw, and we conquered. My victory is for all who believe in the beauty of the blackwoman." It drew a standing ovation from the audience.

As the Federal Commissioner finally made to depart the airport, seeing the tumultuous crowd waiting outside, he formally presented the new Miss Cosmos to the appreciative crowd who sang and waved in excitement.

The Press Conference commenced immediately they got back to the conference centre. Both the chaperon and the ambassador were excused from conference venue to sort out other matters of immediate urgency.

Meanwhile, six floors above the Conference Centre, there was a serious meeting taking place in the office of the airport commandant. The DEA deputy director from London and his Chief of Operations in Lagos were seated on one side of the table, facing the Airport Commandant and heads of National Drug Law Enforcement Agency(NDLEA), Customs, and the Police. The airport commandant had briefed them accordingly, regarding the directive from Alagbon Close on the INTERPOL request; to use the full co-operation and assistance of the United States DEA officials, to apprehend the cocaine courier, a passenger on board British Airways flight BA 095 from London Gatwick.

The Nigerian officials were curious, expecting to hear the facts from the American official from London. The man had decided against anything of that sort since it was principally negative at the long run. He had asked them to proceed to where the incriminating evidence was to see things for themselves. All the man offered was for NDLEA to do a thorough job on the BA 095 that just arrived. They all quickly filed out of the office to the central baggage bay at the basement..

At that very moment, a very high government official working at the airport, in a very highly sensitive section, slipped out of his office. At the car park, he picked up his vehicle and drove off to Hotel Utopia on Airport Road. He booked a call to a mobile number in London. The phone rang only once and was answered immediately.

"Yes?" A male voice rudely questioned.

"The eagle has landed intact." the man spoke calmly into the mouthpiece.

"Good. Its time to activate Step 2. Please be very careful." The man in London spoke with a whisper, and the phone went dead.

The press conference was almost nearing its end. A white journalist expected to ask one of the final two questions was picked from the few fingers that were upraised.

"My name is Mark Thornston, I represent *Hello*, a British Weekly. Once again accept our sincere congratulations. My organization celebrate romantic unions, so it would not surprise you that we put romantic stories in the grapevine in the front burner. Do you by any chance know a Mr. Uromi? If yes, in what nature, or capacity? Say would you consider him a friend?" The man returned the microphone, without betraying any kind of emotion.

"Oscar…yes…I know…yes… I believe I know Mr. Oscar Uromi," the Miss Cosmos stuttered with obvious embarrassment and quickly picked up herself. "Yes, I know Mr Uromi, but purely on em…professional basis. His company is one of the corporate sponsors of the Miss Cosmos contest. And he was kind enough to host us to a most wonderful dinner as a compatriot." She saw that the crowd was with her so she quickly added for effect.

"On the perspective of friendship; since he is not an enemy, I would consider him as a highly respected friend." She smiled with a mischievous wink at the now laughing journalists.

The final question was from a black lady wearing very thick braids who surprisingly spoke English with a foreign enunciation.

"Leticia Blackson for *Ebony Magazine*. Good one sister. Your reign surprisingly came at a time when the world was not expecting a black Miss Cosmos; just like the face of a black pope is not yet imaginable, nor a black face directing affairs and residing at the White House still remains a dream. Your Excellency, do you see your tenure free of controversies to unseat you?" An ominous silence pervaded the entire hall of heads nodding loudly in agreement.

The queen did not answer immediately; it was as if she was weighing every syntax of the question. She looked pensively at her audience, then smiled, with a ray of hope for an obvious mystery solved.

"Do not despair my sister, for this thick black skin," she made a show of pulling up her beautiful skin, "could withstand any demonic conspiracy theory." She went from the calm sage to a fire-spitting battle-ready Amazon.

"You can find solace in the verity that even four hundred years of hard back-breaking slavery could dampen our spirits; talk-less of a few grumbling voices." She paused to dab at her brow dramatically, and proceeded into a soul-searching monologue that held the audience spellbound.

"Though my brow maybe bloodied, I will hold my head high because I stand for every black woman, whose beauty goes beyond the ephemeral to an innate beauty that is insurmountable. Do not ask me what *King Solomon* in all his wisdom saw in the *Queen of Sheba*? And do not ask me too, what the *American Slave masters* were doing in the slave rows in the dead of night, when their *Missus* tossed and turned in their fluffy bed? It was touch and go; the unique beauty of the black woman. They denied it, even when the mulattoes became the burden of proof of their infidelity, and choice of passionate beauty. It was way back then the *conspiracy theory* began against black beauty. My sister, I am a proud descendant of *the sixth finger*, I will survive come what may." She ended on this philosophical note, as the room filled with applause.

On that note the highly relieved compere brought the conference to a resounding close. Both the local and foreign press left with one fact, that Jane Margaret Hilda Daniel-Aka, with her rare intelligence coupled with her sarcastic wit, was going to make one hell of a Miss Cosmos, the world was not going to forget in a hurry. As they filed out of the hall, the Miss Cosmos was led back into the VIP Lounge, their fertile minds were already constructing the most appropriate headlines to report this most educative and informative press conference. If only they knew, what was about to happen to their queen; they would run out of journalistic lingos.

Just one look at them; her chaperon and father, and she knew something terrible had happened or was about to happen. There were five other people in the room with them. Her father tried to take control of the situation which was bad as it was.

"Jane, we think we have a little issue that would need us to iron out, before we leave the airport. This is Group Captain Samson Odeh, the Airport Commandant" he pointed to a robust man in the Nigeria Air Force uniform, who just nodded without any hint of a smile, his penetrating eyes perusing and probing her wordlessly.

"And this is Mr. Danladi of the NDLEA." He was a lanky, dark, and handsome man dressed in a sky-blue kaftan, who tried to avoid meeting her eyes.

Her mind started racing around... *NDLEA* was that not the anti-drug people? What was her business with them? She looked to Rakiya for help, but Rakiya was far gone, crying her eyes out. Then she heard her father's voice.

"These two gentlemen here are American officials in London and Lagos respectively." And he added quickly "pardon me, I just cannot recall the names."

"Chuck, Chuck Freeborn IV", the very familiar looking man answered with a broad confident smile. "I am greatly honoured to meet you maam."

She could only nod her head in reply because her mouth felt dry and stuck. the other American, mumbled some words, and introduced himself as Derrick Gordons. The remaining man, a bulky towering Nigerian with cop written all over him, said something about an Assistant Commissioner of Police or something Margaret Hilda was almost collapsing by then, since the last man looked a bit impatient with all the introductions.

The airport commandant now spoke in impeccable English without any noticeable accent. "I am afraid miss, we have to disrupt your program and schedule for now, to sort out a *little issue*, if am to borrow the words of His Excellency. You have to come with us to personally identify your luggage. This way please." as he led the way out of the VIP lounge.

Out on the passage leading to the Customs Arrival hall were fully armed uniformed soldiers and mobile policemen had already cordoned off all access to the public. It was then the man introduced as an assistant commissioner of police, in a very soft spoken voice politely instructed the Miss Cosmos officials to go back. The queen's father and the chaperon were allowed to go along to the customs arrival hall.

At the now deserted conveyor belt area were scattered more than fifteen suitcases and bags in different shapes and sizes. The commandant asked the queen who was now a ghost of her former confident self to point out her luggage items. With the help of the chaperon and the tags on her passport they were able to gather the nine pieces of the luggage together.

All the while the airport commandant and his counterparts were just observing the baggage identification procedure. When they had gathered items together, the group came closer and the commandant asked her the following questions.

"Are you certain these are all your luggage?" he looked towards her for an answer. which she answered in the affirmative.

"Did you personally pack your bags?" he asked her again, and she nodded.

"Miss Daniel-Aka, it will be highly appreciated if you will restrict yourself to verbal answers in this discussion. I presume you meant "yes" to my last question." he looked inquiringly towards her. "Yes! I personally packed my bags, and they are nine in all." She retorted showing him the tickets and tags.

"Thank you miss. Just one more confirmation. Did anybody or people by any chance give you anything to carry for them."

"No. I did not collect anything from anybody." She answered to the hearing of all those present.

"Very well Miss Daniel-Aka, I hope, then you would not mind if the officials here inspect your luggage." he said giving way to the NDLEA gentleman.

The NDLEA official then signalled to two ladies dressed in the Nigeria Custom uniform, to step forward, before asking the queen to confirm that all the suitcases were intact.

"Yes... they don't seem... to have been... tampered with." the queen hesitatingly said.

"Please, can you unlock them with the keys provided by your chaperon." Each item of luggage to be searched was placed on an elevated platform made of stainless steel. The two ladies wearing latex gloves meticulously went through the items in full view of everybody. They systematically and painstakingly went through every single luggage. This was done to the satisfaction of everybody; even the Americans were impressed with what they saw.

Every item of luggage, when it is to be searched, is first opened with an obstructed view of the probing eyes of the overhead cameras. They were then searched neatly and thoroughly, then all items are replaced. Then the search would proceed to the next item of luggage. The thorough search yielded nothing until they got to the last four suitcases. Which were the largest of the Louis Vuitton 7-piece set given to her by Oscar Uromi.

At this point, even Chuck Freeborn IV felt a little bit uncomfortable. Suppose, there was a mistake back in London? He knew that the embarrassments and the repercussions were better imagined than experienced. He might even be mobbed by even the folks standing there with him. He quickly searched for a means of escape if those bags did not contain that haul that he personally saw on the X-ray machines. As he shifted closer to the elevated platform, he felt he noticed a faint smirk of victory from the Ambassador and his daughter.

All the pairs of eyes in that room were on those last suitcases. The most senior ranking of the two custom ladies pulled the zipper through, and lifted up the lid, everybody in that search area held their breath. Unknown to one another, all the Nigerians in that room were praying for the search to yield nothing again. A thick black solid cardboard curtained off whatever was contained therein. The Custom lady as if on slow motion lifted the thick cardboard aside, to a transparent thick nylon bag fitting snuggly into the suitcase filled to the brim with a white powdery substance. The searcher momentarily froze, while the queen fainted and went crashing down.

Not even the father noticed the collapsed daughter, as they all took a step forward for a better view. The room was silent as a graveyard, as the lady professionally carried on with steady fingers, as if nothing of significance was found. Nothing could be presumed until the forensic unit confirmed the substance. So why get excited over what could be talc powder for all they know.

The custom lady, went on with clinical precision. She pierced the nylon bag carefully with a syringe-like object with a clear liquid solution. Immediately, the solution turned green signifying that, the whitish powdery substance was high grade cocaine. The searcher then looked to her boss, and her homely face could not hide her disgust and disappointment. She felt like screaming. She felt totally betrayed by this beautiful young Nigerian that had her future before, just destroyed like that. The other three suitcases also yielded the same result

The silence was eerie, as the whirling sound of the automatic overhead security cameras and monitors recorded everything as they unfolded. The four suitcases were scaled together, and they weighed One hundred and twenty kilograms. At the going street price in London of about $28,000 per kilogram, the entire haul was valued at about $3,360,000.

The two custom ladies, mission accomplished, filed out like executioners after completing their grisly assignment. It was then the queen regained consciousness.

The Assistant Commissioner of Police signaled to two of his uniformed officers with side arms, who stepped forward as he moved towards the queen who was been attended to by a crying chaperon and the ambassador. It might sound heartless but a man got to do his job.

"Miss Jane Margaret Hilda Daniel-Aka, you are under arrest for possession of a substantial quantity of a substance suspected to be cocaine. This is criminal and punishable under the laws of the Federal Republic of Nigeria...you have a right to remain silent, for whatever you say may be taken up against you as evidence in a competent court of law..."

CHAPTER 88

It was 8pm in London, and Oscar Uromi was seated with the telephone in his lap. He was really looking impatient and nervous. For the umpteenth time, his eyes roamed over to the wall clock again. The second call from Lagos to update him regarding Step 2, was long overdue. That call was absolutely very important; it would make the difference between life and death. The call was to confirm that the consignment was safe at its final destination at an address in Ikoyi, a highbrow residential suburb of Lagos.

He could not concentrate on the television. He channel-surfed through about seventy cable and satellite channels. He could not find any program to catch his interest, or that he could not relax. His mind was on the telephone. He went into the kitchen for nothing particular; he came back with a can of beer. There was the nagging premonition that something would go wrong. He sat down by the telephone once again. When he could not bear it anymore, he just turned off the television. It felt better for some time, as he downed the can of beer in one fell swoop.

And that was when the telephone chose to ring. It startled him, to the extent that he spewed the contents of the beer in his mouth over the marbled floor. He swore aloud as he quickly picked up the receiver.

"Yes!" he answered abruptly betraying his anxiety.

"It is 8.45pm, Zebra. Amigo is expecting you." The gruffly voice answered with a subtle threat, that sent a chill down his spine.

"My friend tell him, I would be on my way soon, I am just making an important call." He tried to bluff the caller who could sense his fear, and decided to turn the knife.

"Listen Zebra, nobody keeps Amigo waiting. You are pushing your luck too far, and its almost running out." He smirked loudly to assert his advantageous position.

"Now *Mister Man Friday,* or whatever you call yourself just pass the message to your boss and stop fooling with me. You are not my mate." And he banged the phone down out of frustration than annoyance. He could not believe what he had just done, but it worked magically for him. For his tormentor got the impression that Oscar still had a bargaining chip.

Oscar Uromi could feel cold sweat break out on his forehead. He could see himself being fished from the River Thames naked. His handsome face a pulpy unrecognizable mess. Why did he ever take up this deal of *no half measures acceptable*? He should have settled off after the Singapore end, he thought to himself.

The impact of the early morning Channel 4 News scoop, was still fresh in his memory. The police had accepted foul play in the afternoon bulletin, and launched a full fledge investigation to the murder of the black cab driver. Though, he did want to concede it because of the distance to where he dropped, something told him that he was not unconnected with the unfortunate end of the man. He could see what Amigo could do, and he was truly petrified. Then the phone rang upsetting him again.

"Look here my friend…" Oscar came firing from all cylinders before realizing that it was not Amigo's man.

He heard the discerning click of international call… a breathless or excited person was on the other end.

"Yes?" Oscar answered with alacrity.

"They got her. She did not make it. The Americans were on her tail." the voice paused waiting to hear from his boss

"You mean they got everything? Not even something for consolation. I am finished." Oscar could not believe what he was hearing.

"Everything sir. Not one dust came out sir." The man in Lagos heard the receiver crash onto the floor in London.

The young operator in the van was busy, just listening to these conversations. He quickly made a transcript of the 35-second telephone conversation, and forwarded it to the embassy.

Oscar Uromi recovered a moment later, and flew up the stairs into his room. His mind was in a panic. He was going to get the hell out of that house now. He opened his wardrobe for a bag he had packed ready for a time like this. In his wall safe he brought out his passport, credit cards and ten thousand dollars in cash. He then quickly pulled on a pair of white Reebok tennis shoes, and a jeans jacket to match his pair of jeans pants. He ran downstairs with his bag. He was just about to leave, when his mobile phone started ringing.

"Yes?" he answered off-handedly though was actually shaking.
"Zebra?" the voice inquired.
"Yes, who is this?" Oscar queried, trying to hide his anxiety.
"Amigo!" The voice was authority personified. "Are you coming or I should come and get you." And the line went dead.

It seemed the chase was on, but he was a step ahead of his chasers. Oscar Uromi took one last look at his beautiful house, and slipped behind the wheel of his cream colored E-type Jaguar, and as he eased the car into the cold London night, he did not hear the shrill ringing telephone upstairs, in the now lonely house. no dice! *Oscar Uromi, was now a man on the run.* He knew the hunter was going to be like a shadow on him. He knew he must outwit, or else he was going to be statistics. Another one in an avalanche of unsolved mysterious murders in London. He was so engrossed in his thoughts that he did not notice, the eyes watching him from the blue Range Rover that drove after him.

British Airways flight BA 074 from Lagos to London Gatwick left on schedule, it was 11.50 pm. Chuck Freeborn IV, was seated in a Club Class window seat, looking down below, regrettably at the sprawling mass of twinkling lights that was Lagos. He was disappointed that he had not had enough time to see Lagos.

After the sorting out of the Miss Cosmos, with her *unholy luggage*, he was rushed to the United States Embassy in Victoria Island, to confer with the US Ambassador. He had told the ambassador in a nutshell what was happening, and why he had personally come. The elderly African American from Savannah, Georgia had listened attentively without even one question. They had later called Washington and London to clarify issues. Freeborn was as planned to proceed back to London on the same plane immediately. While Derrick Gordons would wrap and cleanup the case in Lagos.

Harry Fenton-Forest was also glad to inform him that they had finally located the black cab driven by the ill-fated Masters in the St. John's Wood. He was to wrap up this particular case once and for all, then he could have a vacation at any place of his choice, the administrator had promised him.

It was on the rush back to the airport something totally amazing happened. Freeborn was riding in the backseat of the official embassy car with his colleague, on the wheel was a Nigerian. They were speeding on the 11-kilometre third mainland bridge towards the airport; "Chuks…Chuks take it easy." Derrick Gordons addressed the driver.

"Sorry, I did not get what you said?" Chuck Freeborn retorted.

"Oh! not you, I was talking to the driver."

"But I heard you mention my name." Chuck added adamantly.

"Ok, now I see, his name is Chuks" Gordons pointed to the driver, "Though yours is Chuck." he clarified in good humor.

"My man," Chuck called to the driver, who was now moving at a sedate pace, "Is your name African?"

"It is an African name sir" the driver answered with a wide grin.

"What does it mean, and what language and people speak it?" the DEA Deputy Director asked excitedly, while Derrick Gordon watched with amusement the whole scenario.

"The full name is Chukwuma. Which means God knows. The language is Igbo, and spoken by the Ibo people of South-east Nigeria. The Igbo or the Ibos is one of the three major tribes in Nigeria sir." the driver spoke in good but heavily accentuated English.

"That is very interesting." Freeborn said, without revealing the excitement thumping through his heart.

"That makes both of you namesakes if you both agree to drop the 'c' and 's' respectively." Gordon who was of Irish immigrants said in his usual jovial self.

The rest of the journey to the airport was done in absolute silence, each man engrossed in his own thoughts. Chuck Freeborn IV, the fourth generation descendant of an African slave imported to America, knew he was *onto something phenomenal.*

As the last twinkling lights of Lagos faded below in to a sea of ink-black darkness Chuck thought out aloud; "I shall return!". He noticed a stately lady on the seat next to him smiling. She must have been in her sixties, with her all grey hair stylishly permed.

"I hope you did not forget anything down there." She sounded very educated coupled with her reading glasses that she removed when she started talking.

"No maam. It was because I did not have enough time to explore, what I believe is my great-grandfather's roots." He spoke with some level of confidence.

"I see, that is a very interesting co-incidence." She smiled, as she gave him a complimentary card saying she was a professor of Traditional African History, at the University of Lagos. Professor Ngozi Nzekwu was on her way to Liverpool, to take care of a third grandchild born a few days back, through her second daughter. She had painstakingly explained the tradition that every mother would take up proudly, to nurse and nurture their child and the grandchild down the ages.

Before they fell asleep, Chuck knew that this was not just one of those chance meetings. With her special background she would be very useful in his search for his great-grandfather's roots. Chuck in no time came to like the soft spoken amiable lady, who also had taken to him naturally.

Back at the airport in Lagos, news had filtered out that the new queen was involved in some kind of monkey business, and had been detained. The teeming crowd waiting to welcome their new queen, did not believe what they thought was mere rumor, since there was no formal confirmation of any kind. So both the press and the crowd decided to keep vigil, until they see her. At 4am, only a few of them were awake, as their tired bodies had succumbed to the pangs of sleep. Dotun Maje of Dot Majestic Media was a veteran freelance photographer of note. He was also waiting patiently to make a scoop. He had used his contacts to confirm unofficially the news making the rounds, and had also been told that something would happen at 4am at the secured staff parking at the basement.

In the NDLEA detention cell, the beautiful lone occupant was very angry and weary to the marrow of her bones; yet sleep refused to come to ease her pain. *For somebody had murdered sleep for her, and her loved ones.* The well-armed soldiers watching over her were awake, alert and ready for any eventuality. Suddenly, another set of soldiers led by a Captain burst into the cell, put a black sack over her head and bundled her out. She had two huge soldiers dwarfing her and guiding her footsteps, each on an arm. They went through deserted corridors and flights of steps down to an equally deserted basement car park. They stopped right by the very bright overhead light, and the Captain pulled off the black sack from the queen. He then clamped a leg chain and handcuffs on her. She cut a very miserable comical figure with the tiara very visible on her head. Nobody noticed the huge zooming lens of the freelance photographer hidden safely faraway snapping away hundreds of shots.

The two military Jeeps screeched to a stop, and the queen was bundled into the first one, and the two vehicles were driven away into the night, while her fans and supporters snored away. The camera-man came out of hiding, grinning from ear to ear. He was going to make a kill with this one. He was convinced that he has finally broken into the big league. He got into his car and drove sedately out of the airport as the first light of a new day dawned in Lagos.

Series of cars including the blue range rover took turns in tailing Oscar Uromi's Jaguar around the streets of London. He drove around like a man without cogent plans. His tails should not have bothered about changing cars, because the man was not paying any attention to his behind. To the relief of everyone he finally settled for The Churchill on Gloucester Place, where he took a room.

An hour after checking in, his tails intercepted his calls to various airlines, trying to find out one with the earliest flight out of London to the Caribbean. He finally settled with British Airways flight reservations in New York at that time of the night, for their first flight from London Gatwick to Grand Cayman, departure was 10.10am. For the first time that night, Oscar felt secure. He was not familiar with Grand Cayman but he was told it was in the Caribbean Sea. It was said to be an hour's flight away from the United States, where he could head for in the worst scenario.

That early morning, it was not only the DEA and the Scotland Yard that were into Oscar Uromi's covert travel plans. In the basement of a house in St. John's Wood, a young South American, who was a computer whiz kid was busy stooped over his computer, which was logged into the networks of various airlines. What he was doing was illegal, and criminal, yet he went unperturbed. It took him the better part of an hour to get the desired information, which was printed and sent to Zapata, who in turn took it to the boss, who immediately gave out instructions for Oscar to be truncated without option.

CHAPTER 89

As the typical hustle and bustle of Lagos picks up, Dotun Maje, the freelance photographer, was yet to sleep a wink in his beautiful residence off Allen Avenue, in Ikeja. The Allen Avenue, Ikeja suburb of Lagos was cut-out for the jet-sets who were desperate to venture into anything that yielded fast and easy proceeds that was sometimes aptly called *blood money*.

For a freelance photographer, Dotun Maje lived well. He had conveniently converted the ground floor of his eye-catching residence into a photo studio and also a darkroom. There was obvious moderate affluence and luxury about him. He settled his bills regularly. He was the owner of three well-maintained cars. His three children were in a special private school, at the Opebi suburb that was a status symbol. Over the years he had become used to those curious stares and hush-hush whispers about his wealth. He had peacefully minded his business ignoring them, neither did he publicly deny or refute the stories. He knew that he was not a saint, because of the many skeletons in his cupboard.

As he worked deftly in the dark-room developing the rolls of film he expended on the Miss Cosmos and the soldiers. His ears was also on the transistor radio that was monitoring the Head of State's emergency broadcast. All went until the military Head of State went into a tirade on Nigerian saboteurs, and other economic turncoats, who were working with the so-called foreign powers. Dayo was transfixed at a point as if the head of state was referring to him. He had the raw negatives of the roll of film in his hands but his hands were shaking badly. For the voice from the radio was persistent like a whip flogging in the truth into his stone-cold heart and conscience.

Though he was really touched by the speech, all he could say to himself was *man must wack bo*, this was the Nigerian pidgin English parlance that; *a man must eat*. Dotun was indeed one of those the president was referring to. He had made his wealth selling highly sensitive images almost bordering on national security. He had contacts abroad who normally procure his pictures. All that he cared about was the money they paid well, but it never lasted.

That morning, he was impressed with the negatives, he had put a call through to London his contacts in London were waiting to see him tomorrow morning. That meant he must catch British Airways flight to London later tonight. They had informed him that the world was eager to see and be told, the fate that had befallen the new Miss Cosmos in her own country. The interested groups were looking forward to an exclusive scoop in the days ahead.

In London, it was about 7 o'clock in the morning, and it was cold and chilly as was forecasted. As many Londoners were still embraced in the warmth of their beds, Oscar Uromi, the man on the run, was up and running already. He left the hotel, with his car still parked out in the front to mislead his pursuers. He had hailed a black cab, away from the ones waiting in the front of the hotel to Victoria Station, and caught the 7.30am Gatwick Express. His plan was pickup his ticket, check-in and head straight for the boarding gate, before they even realize that he had left the hotel.

Unknown to Oscar Uromi, there were already two groups of reception parties waiting for him at Gatwick Airport. Each group had its own agenda; very independent and unconnected from the other. The fifteen DEA and the Scotland Yard group, including Chuck Freeborn IV, who had arrived on the Lagos flight at about 6am., quickly held a brief meeting at the North Terminal end of the Gatwick Airport transit train. Their plan was to take him as he made to board the flight.

The Amigo's hit squad was to intercept and liquidate professionally without a single shred of evidence to whom the killer was. The hit squad consisted of just two people, each carrying a blunt-nosed pistol with a screwed on silencer. In addition to that they both had razor-sharp throwing knives secreted within the folds of their top coats. Their own plan was to execute Oscar before he got through to immigration.

As Oscar stepped into the transit train, he did not even give a second glance to the harmless looking man in blue overall mopping the floor. As the transit train pulled away, the government agent spoke into the microphone secreted on his collar, his colleagues at the other end heard him loud and clear. At the north terminal, Oscar tried to blend into the crowd stepping out from the small train, but the DEA and Scotland Yard reception party picked him out a mile away.

Oscar his eyes roaming the faces around saw a tall man speaking into a phone by the pay phone stands, he did not suspect him. Neither did he suspect the stocky man sorting out his coins just by the doors of the north terminal. Oscar passed by a figure who was engrossed in the day's copy of *The Sun*, as he stepped on to the escalator to the departure floor. He went straight to one of the check-in counters, behind a family of three who were being attended to. He stood looking impatiently around him, as the various agents quickly blended into the scenery.

The death squad went into action. It was like a well orchestrated play, as *The Sun* reader came up the escalator, unhurriedly. At the end of the escalator he knew where his partner would be standing, and that also told him where their quest would be. He continued in his unhurried steps into the toilet in front of him. He pushed past the conspicuously displayed yellow sign saying, *sorry, out of use* into the empty toilet. He quickly set to work. He put five pressurized canisters into a waste bin, with the newspaper that he set on fire, and quickly walked out of the toilet casually.

The partner with his top coat draped over his right arm took his cue and went and queued in the line next to Oscar's. By the time, the first explosion and smoke alarm went off distracting everyone, the killer also pulled his trigger at his target. The high velocity bullet tore through its target spelling instant death. In that split moment of confusion, when all eyes were turned towards the supposed bombs and the involuntary action of responding to the fire alarms, the killer naturally blended into the panicky crowd.

By the time people realized that Oscar was down, he was dead, stone cold dead. The special high velocity bullet exploded at impact, blasting away the entire lower back of Oscar Uromi. As the shrill tone of fire alarms mingled with the screams of bystanders, and government agents barking orders to people running helter-skelter, the departure hall was transformed from orderliness into a bedlam of confusion.

All flights out of the Gatwick North Terminal within two hours of the incidence, had a two hour delay. Nobody was seen arrested or fleeing from justice. The perpetrators escaped successfully. It was a perfect execution by true professionals, the crest fallen government agents could not believe how they were bamboozled definitely by a smaller force. They left Gatwick with reels and reels of tapes retrieved from security cameras. Oscar Uromi was dead, and they had lost their only key lead. They had nothing visible left, except for the Thomas Masters' black cab.

The meeting that held later that afternoon at the Scotland Yard was a disaster. It was so embarrassing for everybody as their head scolded all that were part of the *Gatwick Debacle*, as he chose to call it. He ordered them, to sieve through the mass of tapes and to come up with the identity of the culprits, within six hours, or else heads were going to roll. Another group of agents were to study the abandoned black cab and its immediate environment, to see if it has any relationship to the murder of either Masters' and or Uromi's.

London was agape, when the evening papers and the television stations reported the sensational murder of a Nigerian businessman at the Gatwick North terminal, in what authorities suspect to be a reprisal killing for a business deal gone sour. The perpetrators of the dastardly act, the authorities claimed were still at large, and there was a massive manhunt to bring them to justice. Some newspapers had speculated whether the two brazen killings within a space of 24 hours might not be unconnected. Two sensational murders back-to-back was enough to keep the New Scotland Yard awake and on their feet..

Lagos was in the dusty grip of the harmattan season. The Federal Government Guest House on Victoria Island was on very secluded out of the way Close. They had all passed the night there. "Be strong, my daughters you are in safe hands. All hands were on deck to clear your good name. We all believe somehow, somewhere somebody made a grave mistake." Ambassador Daniel Aka tried to console his daughter and her friend. Parting was not easy for father and daughter, but finally the Federal Commissioner of External Affairs, a close friend of Daniel was able to pry them apart, as they departed for the emergency meeting of the Supreme Military Council convened by the Head of State.

The journey from Victoria Island to Dodan Barracks, the seat of government of successive military juntas since the 1960's, took less than seven minutes, as the motorcade with siren blaring cleared the roads of impediments. They gained entry through the Ribadu Road end entrance to the beautiful grounds of Dodan Barracks. They were quickly ushered through the low-roofed walkway and corridors to the council chambers. All the while the Federal Commissioner of External Affairs was consoling his friend to relax, that the Commander-in- Chief had everything under control.

The other Council Members were all present when they arrived. There were only a few heads that nodded in their direction, since many of them were ignorant of the events of the previous evening. There was quiet in the large room, as if it was them that was holding the meeting from commencing. They were still adjusting their seats, when the gap-toothed leader walked in briskly.

He was dressed in *buba and sokoto* made of an African print material. He had a pair of brown leather slippers to match. He assumed his seat at the head of seating formation, and went straight to business.

"Sorry to have disrupted your programs. Unfortunately, we have some form of affront we must nip in the bud before it escalates into a monster. you must have all noticed my outburst during my broadcast this morning." he pulled a flat file marked Top Secret towards him.

"Last night, the current Miss Cosmos came back to the country after our triumph in the global event, with her father the worldly respected Ambassador. At the airport to receive her, was a tumultuous crowd of her fellow compatriots led by the Federal Commissioner of Culture she was indeed given a glorious reception befitting her queenly status." The president turned over the first three pages and stopped.

"Less than an hour later, our goodwill ambassador was cooling her heels in an NDLEA detention cell at the airport." Some of his listeners could not suppress the involuntary exclamations that escaped from their mouths. the president waited for normalcy to return, before he continued.

"One hundred and twenty kilograms of pure high-grade cocaine was found in her baggage." Once again the audience displayed their consternation There was prolonged murmuring as they conferred with one another to the value.

"Till this moment no public statement has been made. Despite my preliminary outburst, we are going to quickly study the situation, and come up with a strategy. So that an official statement could be released tonight. That is why the Ambassador is here with us. The inspector general of police would give us the facts as they are on the ground."

The bulky inspector general of police presented the facts and figures his assistants presented to him. It took the chamber less than 15 minutes to conclude that it was a frame-up by the United States to embarrass out the Nigerian Miss Cosmos so that her first runner-up, who was an American would step into her shoes. Almost all of them agreed that the United States should be held liable in any event.

Before the resolution was taken, the lone dissenting voice begged to be heard. It was the egghead Professor overseeing the Ministry of Science and Technology. He stood up to address the honorable gathering looking pensive.

"Your Excellency, and gentlemen, something just does not add up here in the *dosage*. Why would anybody use a million units, if one single-unit will serve the aim and purpose convincingly?" The brilliant nuclear scientist posited. he looked around at his puzzled audience. he met everyone's gaze unflatteringly.

"Let's follow a simple logic and deductive reasoning. A little pinch of hard drugs found on the Miss Cosmos would embarrass her out of office instantly. At a little below $30,000 for a kilogram of cocaine, why would the United States choose to go through the trouble to use almost $3.6million worth of cocaine, when a gram of $300 would have sorted out the vexing matter. There were uncomfortable movements around the horse-shoe formation.

"My Commander-in-Chief, it is my sincere submission that our obvious patriotic zeal is blinding our good reason. It is my considered opinion sirs, that the *American Conspiracy Theory* is a mere figment of our imagination. The Miss Cosmos as a responsible adult, unfortunately like any other Nigerian must be accountable for her luggage. At least that we know is not contestable." The audience could not meet his gaze this time.

"Your Excellency, I would rather caution that, we tread tactically like a cautious gambler and allow the US to play the ace up their sleeves; that is if ever there was any in the first place. So that we don't end up making a laughing stock of ourselves to the world. I rest my case sir." You could hear a pin drop as the professor sat down heavily. For ten long minutes not one person uttered a word. The Federal Commissioner for Science and Technology was satisfied that the whole room was engrossed in their thoughts.

Then the General cleared his throat loudly to call his team to undivided attention. He leafed through the file in front of him, for want of something to do as he gathered his thoughts together.

"In all fairness, I believe that *the Scientist*," for that was what the president calls him, "had spoken well, but before we make up our minds, I would want our ambassador to tell us his mind regarding the issue on ground." He closed the file, and pushed it to the side, to signify that he was all ears.

Ambassador Daniel Aka stood to his feet, looking a little tardy and unkempt. He was a sorry sight. When he spoke his voice was hoarse and almost incoherent. He declared unconditionally the innocence of his *little baby*, which was quite emotional, though was totally out of place in the present setting. He passionately pleaded and persuaded them not to leave his daughter in the loch. The head of state looked at his watch impatiently, waiting for his most capable ambassador to dispassionately make his point regarding a sound resolution to be adopted by the Federal Republic of Nigeria.

"I am sorry, Mr. Ambassador, I would have to cut you short, because the network news is almost up. We need to issue the public statement in the news. I am sure, all of us as fathers, and your personal friends share in your grief. Even you know that it is Nigeria first, *no matter whose horse is gored.*" The man gradually read the faces gathered around, before declaring the ultimate resolution of the gathering.

"The law is crystal clear that every adult traveler is accountable for his or her luggage. So the law must take its course, or else we will end up sending the wrong signals to our detractors. We would see, how we could all be of help, somehow, somewhere along the line." The military leader pressed a bell, that instantly brought in his very youthful press secretary. He gave him instructions and the press secretary left quickly.

"Mr. Attorney General what next, now that we have chosen the better part of valor." He addressed a totally bald-headed luminary who had a most successful law practice in Nigeria.

"Your Excellency, we must commence legal proceedings, and instead of the usual tribunal, I suggest a normal court of appellate jurisdiction, because of the world's spotlight upon us. We must show that there are no sacred cows in the war against drugs." The man spoke as if he had considered all possible options before the meeting. "Good, Mr. Attorney General. Mr. Ambassador, I want you to know that I believe you, that your daughter is innocent. We are going to get her the best lawyer to fight and get her free in no time; while we shall play along, and continue to talk tough…

CHAPTER 90

Dotun Maje, ace freelance photographer and business-man-*extraordinary*, arrived London Gatwick as scheduled that morning with his *bombshell*. The hurrying passengers from the Lagos flight ran smack into a horde of passengers from the Houston, Atlanta, and Panama City flights who were already in the immigration hall. It took him almost an hour and half to clear Immigrations. His thoughts that he would race through customs, since he had no baggage to claim, to make his 7am appointment was still realistic.

Due to the notoriety of the incoming flight from Lagos, it was always given a special attention; a squad of eagle-eyed Her Majesty's Immigrations, and Customs Services were always posted on duty. They would first peruse the flight manifest for *trouble makers* and those on the *Wanted List*; then pay special attention to the passengers at the immigration queues for first-timers or greenhorns in cross-border criminal activities. They zero in on any sign of misdemeanor or suspicious mien. Most times they gamble and lose, but it worked sometimes. The unsuspecting Maje did not factor this into his calculations that morning.

Unknown to Dotun Maje with his fretting and fidgeting on the immigration queue, he was already a marked man for the customs. His lightweight designer's suit, expensive ostrich skin leather shoes to match, a gold Rolex wrist watch, matching gold rings and bracelet, completed the obvious profile of the drug courier travelling light. And as the animated man came bounding down the escalator to the baggage hall with just his carrier bag, there was indeed a big reception party waiting for him.

Dotun Maje who had not a grain or even a speck of cocaine on or inside his person, was really confident, but was scared silly because of the *bombshell* in the large brown manila envelope. It was not their lucky day, but accepting defeat was never an easy option for the customs, so to save face they had to put him through the works. So, he was physically turned inside out. Every shred of clothing was taken off his body and scanned. Nothing. They, then more-or-less poked and inspected every hole and crevice in his body. They ended up finding out that the man was nuts about a particular Italian designer. Every piece of clothing down to his underwear and handkerchief was of the Italian.

They allowed him put on his clothes back, for fear of the man catching his death from cold, but they were not finished with him yet. The ace photographer, was put through a further verbal grill, after they went through his hand luggage with a toothcomb. It yielded nothing, yet like ferocious bulldogs, they refused to accept defeat, and ease off their fangs. With fixation on hard drugs they did not pay any interest on the envelope of pictures. With not a whiff of cocaine to justify their expended time and energy,they gradually slipped away one-by-one and finally leaving him with the unfortunate expert that must have placed a bet on him. It took another 10 minutes, before the now shame-faced official reluctantly allowed him to walk away. Dotun Maje held himself from shouting with joy for his narrow escape.

It was obvious, that the person from *The Eye* must have left. Their appointment was scheduled for 7.30am. There was no person standing in the lift area with a copy of *The Eye*. He looked at his watch it was almost 8.20am. Just by the left luggage shop, he saw a man seating alone and reading a copy of The Eye. Maje was so impressed with the man's patience, that he resolved to sell his pictures to The Eye. He cautiously approached the man with the agreed secret code; *Is it raining in London today?*

Reuben Ruthers did not work for *The Eye*; but he worked with *The Eye* under circumstances that were not made public. He ran his own public relations outfit that handled clandestine out-of-the- ordinary procedures that normal companies would not touch with a 20-foot pole. Himself and Maje were indeed birds of identical plumage. Ruthers knew when and how to put his cards on the table. By the time they had finished their first cup of coffee, he had perfected his plans to make money from both sides. He had discovered that both parties were so desperate for a result.

The Nigerian was desperate, he wanted money badly, and quickly; while *The Eye* people were desperate to increase circulation that had been on a downward trend. For *The Eye*, the most recent Miss Cosmos Contest imbroglio had not helped matters, and they were desperate to save face at all cost. The Nigerian had asked for $100,000 for the 48 negatives that were in perfect conditions. Ruthers knew he would get them for $50,000 cash right there, and offer them to *The Eye* at his own rate.

Ruthers made another order for coffees, but Dotun Maje would rather go for a double straight shots of whisky, that he hoped would boost his waning spirits from the subtle threats from Reuben Ruthers. All he had on him could not even take him into London to stay the night, he thought to himself. As Ruthers took off to make a couple of calls, Maje took a look at the copy of *The Eye* in front of him. A full-size coronation picture of Jane Margaret Hilda Daniel-Aka was splashed on the front page with the accompanying story the headline;

WHERE IS THE QUEEN

The reigning Miss Cosmos arrived her native country Nigeria, two days ago, to a tumultuous reception by her countrymen and women. At the airport reception, the country's military Head of State, who was represented by his Federal Commissioner for Culture, had conferred and honoured her with the role and status of a Goodwill Ambassador. Right from the airport at Lagos, the queen was never seen again.

Just yesterday, a press release emanating from the office of the press secretary to the head of state, informed the citizens of the discovery of a substance suspected to be cocaine in her luggage. The report was inconclusive, as it said the authorities were still investigating the incident. The world is in the dark...as we echo the minds of every well-meaning people to ask this $billion Question... .

Ruthers had spoken directly to the owner, whom he had convinced the pictures were indeed a bombshell as the man claimed, and to *The Eye,* that they were more than a *goldmine* in scoops. He added to the client that no other pictures of that event in Lagos was captured by any camera. He told him that the man was asking for $500,000, and that he had refused to shift ground, chiefly because the man has appointment to see another London tabloid. The client had told him to call him back in three minutes, so that he could get clearance from higher authority. This angle Ruthers took with a pinch of salt, he did not buy the story one bit.

The client had quickly put a call through to a suite at the Ritz London. The voice at the other end was drowsy from sleep, but was alert to his responsibility. He had agreed to pay the $500,000 outright, if the publication would hit the press by Friday and Saturday, for his own immediate plans to be fulfilled. The client did not hesitate to give him his word. As the client dropped the handset, the phone rang immediately. The client waited for it to ring five times before he could pick up the handset. The Client then picked up the handset. It was Ruthers. The client told Ruthers, that he had received authority not to exceed $250,000; that or no deal. Ruthers grabbed the deal with both hands, but pretended to try his best to convince the Nigerian. He promised to call back soon with an answer.

Maje could not believe his luck, when Ruther offered him the $50,000; with Ruthers' story that it was an all out battle royal between the governments of Nigeria, the UK, and the USA, nobody wants to touch his *bombshell* with even a 20-foot long pole. So the $50,000 offer was indeed on a platter of gold, which he had no choice but to gratefully accept. He knew when not to push his luck, so as not to burn his ten fingers and ten toes. He felt satisfied; $50,000 was a lot of money for one night of work. He would enjoy himself well in London, before heading back to Lagos.

Scotland Yard was a beehive of activities, especially in Richard Pooler's office, some hours later, there was the lucky break they were looking for. There were simultaneous breaks. One came through one of the tape recorded interviews with residents of the street where the black cab was abandoned. An old man claimed to have seen a man loitering around a house front in another street. Then he saw this same man in a black leather jacket being led into the house later by three foreigners.

The other lucky break was through a routine police patrol report filed on the morning of the murder of Thomas Masters. The registration number of a car seen speeding through the outer circle of Regents Park, matched the registration number of car entering the vicinity of the abandoned black cab. The routine precautionary steps required were taken, before the conclusion was made. Then Richard Pooler approved the next step. It was called verification by physical contact (vpc); this was a series of authenticating all leads personally before, physical action was taken to arrest a situation or development.

It was not acceptable within the ambience of the law, but who cares? It was purely a largess from the very understanding head of state, as he promised. Andrew Ezeji, the chauffeur in his late fifties, had known and chauffeured the lady in detention since she was a toddler. He had also cried and wept sadly when he heard the news. He knew where they were going; he had entered Victoria Island through the Falomo Bridge, and was cruising along Akin Adesola Street.

He turned left on to Karimu Kotun Street, and right into Oko Awo Close that led directly to the Kuramo Lodge of the Eko Holiday Inn. Midway through the street, which was called a Close, Andrew pulled up at a black monstrous gate with a 12-foot stone wall for a fence. The residence looked impregnable as the reputation of its owner and occupier. This was the residence of Chief Bode Rhodes, S.A.N., one of Africa's foremost defense attorneys. He was a living legend in the business of legal defense.

An old gateman, who must be an archive on the life history of his renowned employer, came out. he went over to the chauffeur's window to ascertain who the visitor was. He was expecting them, the huge gate swung open, and Andrew drove his employer and his daughter's bosom friend into the heavily protected private world of the colossus of the legal scene. This is the man, Ambassador wanted to retain for his only daughter's defense, he was known to be expensive, but worth every kobo, because he was reputed to deliver the goods… the verdict of *Not Guilty*.

CHAPTER 91

At exactly at 8.53am on Thursday, at the White Cedar Hotel, in Bayswater, a chamber-maid pushed her trolley laden with all the appurtenances of her duty to the door of Room709. She knocked and waited for an answer. There was none, so she opened the door with her master key. She stopped in her tracks; a place that was upside down confronted her. She was totally speechless, because it offended her sensibilities. She was also concerned about the magnitude of work to be done to return that room to status quo, but that was a small matter compared to what was to unfold before her eyes.

Lying naked and dead in the middle of the ruffled bed, was a middle-aged man of the negro race. There was the usual initial shock of confrontation with a corpse, but she got over it immediately. She was cool and calculated. She had once worked as a mortuary attendant for a period of year. Valerie Baker had arrived Britain from the Caribbean four years ago, on a single 6-month entry visa. By the time she discovered that the streets of London were not paved with dollars and pound sterling, it was too late to retrace her steps. She paid through her nose to get her documents regularized through the backdoor. That was before she could procure this job, and two others over London. She had never worked this hard all her life. And the weather and the people were not also friendly. She could not wait to make enough money, and head back to her country, where there was constant sunshine and the people were warmer, more sincere and friendlier.

She was used to seeing human cadavers, she concurred with Shakespeare who said, ...*it is only a child that fears the eyes of a painted devil*. Valerie Baker made sure her latex orking gloves were in place as she approached the wardrobe. She dipped her hands into the hanging coat pocket she fished out his wallet. Inside was a crispy bunch of 50 pounds notes, which she quickly stuffed into her underwear. She replaced the wallet back in the coat pocket. She looked around the room and she saw the Rolex gold wrist watch. She took that too, secreting it away where the money was.

Then a thought crossed her mind; her panties may not be the ideal hiding place if she was searched for any reason. She quickly fished out the money and the wrist watch, knotted them in a small nylon bin bag, and discarded them in the big bin bag containing contents of refuse bins in the rooms. It felt better.

"Thank you mister, from the look of things, you won't need these things over there in hell. I will put them into good use." she said aloud with amusement.

With steady unwavering steps the 37-year old chamber-maid went over to the bedside phone and called her supervisor."Miss Twinkinham! Better come over quickly to Room 709. There is a dead person in there." This she said with the right dose of excitement, to get the 57-year old spinster into action.

That Thursday evening, the massive promotional campaign by *The Eye* towards their special edition on Friday, descended upon the city of London and other British major cities like a blanket of winter fog. The major television channels all had slots for the 30-second advert, while the radio stations were vibrating with the 20-second special jingle. Bus and train stations were also agog with the promotional campaign. *The Eye* was saying categorically that they would provide the solution to the puzzle of the Miss Cosmos that was missing in transit since Monday. The campaign perfectly captivated the minds of Londoners audience, and consequently fired up their curiosities.

The Editorial Board was putting all their eggs in one basket; it was make or mar. It was one big gamble they were confident to stake everything on. The Eye of Friday would have a pullout section in full color with the pictures telling the actual story. They had pushed their printing press to the limits, even going on to recruit other presses to meet the huge sales projection. Their usual daily circulation of 150,000 just paled into insignificance in comparison.

They had also received the feedback from the streets that the people were so curious that had started to book for copies already with their newsagents. They smiled at each other and agreed to up the total circulation next day to 5 milliom copies. This was going to be one dramatic comeback that would go down in history as the most ironic.

On the news bulletin on Channel 4 that evening, was an item of news that came up towards the end. It was the story of a Nigerian male tourist visiting London, that was found dead in his hotel room in Bayswater. The authorities had confirmed that it suspected foul play, and that they were on top of the situation. Even though the statement reassured tourists that there was no cause for alarm, it warned them to stay away from any form of criminal activities and liaisons. The police were making good progress already in the case, they had examined the hotel CCTV tapes and been able to establish that an half-cast lady, was involved. Her profile was already in circulation; she was wanted immediately to assist on-going investigations.

It was like they say; *that the greedy are like diamonds, they are cut by their own dust and greed.* There were going to be no flowers for Dotun Maje's unmarked grave, for even the Nigeria's High Commission was not informed accordingly.

Later that night, as the lights went out in the bedrooms of Londoners, very few people who listened to the various news bulletins recalled or even gave a thought to that news item. It was like good riddance to bad rubbish for the ilk of men like Maje who thrived on blood money...*they lived by the sword, and they die by the sword.* But one thing was on their minds as they drifted off to sleep; *The Eye of tomorrow, they cannot wait to see..*

Finally, Friday dawned over London, England. Bleary eyed production people stayed awake all through the night compiling and distributing five million copies of The Eye. And it lived up to its highest billings. The front-page was the winner; a full length photograph of a barefooted Jane Margaret Hilda, still wearing the tiara, with her hands and feet in shackles, stood aloof and defiant, in between two huge heavily armed black soldiers. And the bold headline declared; *THE QUEEN OF DEVIL'S DUST.*

London and the rest of the world were gripped in horror. The raw and unadulterated image on the front page was enough to weaken the wickedest of men. Though the readers were not disappointed, they were dumb founded. The readers got value for their money.

The inside front page was adorned with the picture of the same Miss Cosmos, with a black bag over her head was embedded between two huge heavily armed soldiers, who almost suspended her feet from touching the ground. The other pictures were spread out in the pages of the pullout. Each picture had a detailed caption.

The Eye, had used a very effective means of communication to tell a very long and complex story with very few words. The images without the black bag gave credence to the front page blow up. Every copy of The Eye newspaper was sold out.

At 10am, an emergency meeting, that recalled all the top management staff from their annual vacation commenced at the headquarters of the Miss Cosmos Beauty Pageant. Don Baldwin sat at the head of the table, with a copy of The Eye that was in every hand around him. There was a kind of pervading silence, as they examined the pictures with all intent and purpose to find anything, or any factor that would discredit their creation or origin.

"Ladies and gentlemen, I once again apologize for spoiling your vacations. We could see here that our corporate wellbeing and existence is under threat from external factors that are beyond our control. We must show a resolve to remain in business. Please study the pictures adequately, to first satisfy our curiosity, and for authentication purposes. If any one has a reservation, please state so." The youthful president looked around for any reactions, but none registered any intention.

"From what we have reliably gathered from The Eye in our hands, I am convinced that the incumbent queen would be indisposed for a while." He paused to see if there was any objection.

"It is our duty to protect the crown, the image and reputation of the pageant. so by the powers conferred on me, subject to your approval, I have no choice but to evoke, Section 27, Sub-section (xiii), Sub-sub-section (f) of our charter. We shall now vote." Baldwin covered and pushed aside the Charter of the Miss Cosmos Beauty Pageant, where he cited the law from.

Charles Wilder, stood up, and spoke to the hearing of his attentive audience. "If you are in support of our resolution to evoke Section 27 of our Charter, please signify by raising up your hand." All hands shot up. Charles Wilder sat down.

Baldwin now said, "Let the records also show that everybody voted in favor of the first runner up, Miss USA, Miss Sophie Fenton- Forest to automatically step in, till a time the incumbent queen is disposed within her tenure. Good." He waited for them to concur.

"Wilder, you are to get the general public and the necessary authorities informed accordingly. And Benny Collins you are to contact and inform Miss Sophie Fenton-Forest accordingly, before any actions on our part. Get her consent recorded, in the event that she chooses to back out..

The Christmas weekend had commenced at The Ritz, you could feel the hint of festivities in the air. Harry Fenton-Forest and his family were having a hearty lunch in their suite, and discussing the very arresting images in The Eye. Harry Fenton-Forest had played along showing a modicum of interest in the publication, while Sophie and her mother were falling over one another in analyzing the fate of possible misfortunes that had befallen the reigning Miss Cosmos. "How could a Miss Cosmos, whether de facto or an ex, soil her dainty fingers with the *devil's dust?*" Mr. Fenton-Forest queried. "What she had done is totally outrageous, and would have far-reaching repercussions." Mrs. Fenton-Forest added.

"Too bad for her…you do the crime; then you do the time." The man burst into laughter.

"I have a strong conviction in my heart that Jane did not do it. I got to know her in close quarters. There must be some kind of mistake somehow and somewhere." Sophie shocked her parents with her contribution.

"Sophie! Do not say what you do not know. What do you know about drugs and these *people*? They can do anything for money." Harry Fenton-Forest admonished his daughter, seeing his daughter's apathy throwing a spanner at the smooth sailing unfolding events.

"Dad! I know what I am saying. The *JMH* I know, with her chaperon would not touch that cocaine with a-mile-long pole." The girl adamantly stood her grounds.

"My dear, if she was such a goody, goody angel, how come her very queenly luggage had enough cocaine to buy a small banana republic?" The mother interjected.

"Mum, that is the *Million-Dollar Question*!" Sophie Fenton-Forest refused to bulge, prompting her father to change tactics and handle her with kid gloves.

"That, I hope the answer is blowing in the wind. My baby, you must not forget that your Daddy is the director of the DEA. My men have tried their best to find the answer to that *Million- Dollar Question*, but no dice." He spoke calmly to gradually prepare her mind to step on to the throne that was almost vacant from all indications.

There was a pervading silence that enveloped that room, as if something ominous was hanging in the air like a sword of Damocles. Then all of sudden the girl burst into tears, and started crying. The dotting parents quickly enveloped her in a warm embrace, while the father went in for the kill.

"Sophie my dear, I know how you feel. I understand very well, it is very unfortunate for your friend. That is why you must not let her down. You must step forward to make her proud *when* the time comes. You remember what Shakespeare said; *...some were born great; some achieved greatness; some have greatness thrust upon them...*" The ringing telephone shattered the order in that room like the deafening sound of thunder.

"Yes?" The mother took the call. "Yes, may I know who is calling?" She listened attentively, and tactically echoed what she heard for the benefit of her husband and daughter.

"Oh, Benny Collins from the Miss Cosmos Pageant, calling to speak with Sophie Fenton-Forest. Good, please hold let me raise her for you.".

Later that afternoon, a press release signed by the president was dispatched to the press. It was straight to the point;

Press Release

Due to recent events still unfolding in Lagos, Nigeria; the home country of the reigning Miss Cosmos, the pageant in a bid to protect the incumbent Miss Cosmos, and in the same vein, to uphold the honor and reputation of the pageant, has evoked the necessary sections of our charter.

Accordingly, the first runner, Miss Sophie Fenton-Forest would take over all duties and responsibilities of the incumbent, until such a time Miss Jane Margaret Hilda Aka is fit to resume her reign.

We still believe in our commitment to serve the whole world. Thanking you in advance for your kindest cooperation, to facilitate a seamless transition.

Don Baldwin,
President.

By 4pm, that evening all television channels featured the press release on their various news slot. By midnight in London, the story of the subtle dethronement of the current Miss Cosmos had gone round the world three times. Though the news was received with mixed feelings everywhere, the Miss Cosmos Pageant had to do what was not only right but appropriate for the situation on ground.

At 12noon on Saturday, 23rd of December, the new queen was crowned, in a very brief but very impressive ceremony at the pageant's King's Square headquarters with the World Press in full attendance. The images and footage of the event was beamed across the world that day for the electronic media. While the newspapers and tabloids of the eve of Christmas was awash with the images of Queen Sophie Fenton-Forest.

CHAPTER 92

The news of the discovery of the huge quantity of substance suspected to be cocaine in the Miss Cosmos' luggage, and the subsequent news of her dethronement was received amidst divided opinions in Nigeria, and the rest of the world. There was the vociferous group that believed in a *conspiracy theory* that was spearheaded by the United States of America, to hoodwink the world to discredit a black woman out of a prestigious office. It was a line of agreement they refused to be faulted, and all they wanted was for the world to take a harder diplomatic stance that would teach America, a bitter lesson not to meddle into affairs where merit was a deciding factor.

On the other hand, was the group who believed strongly, *but- not-loudly*, that Miss Jane Margaret Hilda Aka was guilty. Their stance was that she should not be spared for her greed that led her to be involved in cocaine trafficking. It was their considered opinion, that it was the insatiable desire to have quick and easy wealth, which brought shame to her country and her race, and should therefore be allowed to rot in jail.

Then, came the middle-ground more realistic group, who were not as loud as the speculative two, but whose views tend to have gained more ground and acceptance. All they wanted was justice to be done in a neutral court of law. All they proposed was for the Miss Cosmos to be deemed innocent until proven guilty through non- biased transparent court process in the open.

There was yet another group that was in the majority, but was either silent or totally voiceless. They just sat and watched the events unfold, knowing and believing that what would be, would be. There simple point of view was that the affairs of men were controlled by *the hand or finger of God.* They were convinced that the truth no matter how much we try to hide it must see the light of day. And that the guilty would not go scot free; while the innocent must be exonerated.

From London to Tokyo, from Vancouver to Singapore, from Cape Town to Bogota, there were rave headlines and reviews that had divided the world into the various groups and sub-groups. There were also the outrageous editorials, dangerous hardliners and their almost insane ideas about a new world order. The long existing power balance was being threatened by what would have been considered as non issue at all.

The unfolding situation of the Miss Cosmos Debacle made an instant hero out of Leticia Blackson, the unknown Ebony reporter, who had a positive insight to the present situation. When she point-blank asked the then new queen, in the presence of hundreds of people, whether she could last her tenure, and would not be washed away prematurely by controversies brewed by powerful interest groups.Leticia Blackson was now a household name, as she was a guest in all talk shows in America. Many people, beyond the shores of America were chanced to see Leticia Blackson on *Larry King Live* on CNN. It was interesting to hear her line of argument; which had consistently held on to the Conspiracy Theory angle.

In Lagos, no other official public statement was given, except that, the ex-Miss Cosmos would appear in court as soon as the courts which were on break resume from their traditional annual Christmas break. It was like mum was the word; not a single information leaked out to the local and international journalists. Nobody was talking; both family and government officials were like they were sworn to a sacred oat of secrecy.

In Scotland Yard, there was no dull moment for them. For they were already on hundreds of other cases whose profiling were not related to the Uromi, and Masters' Cases. There was something striking about the case of Dotun Maje, who was found dead in the White Cedar Hotel, at Bayswater. It had been upgraded to culpable homicide, after the post-mortem forensic reports showed death was by drug overdose administered willfully by a suspected third party. They were yet to track down the suspect; the female mulatto, possibly a prostitute who had spent the night with him, had disappeared in the morning.

The interesting angle in the investigations, was the revelation of Dotun Maje's occupation of Freelance Photography over in Lagos. Armed with his itinerary, it seemed as if this mundane low-profile case was gradually picking up a high-profile status. This much Chuck Freeborn IV had gotten from his friends at Scotland Yard, as they met to compare notes on the development on the Masters' Case.

The DEA and the Yard had finally zeroed in on a particular address, but unfortunately the Spanish owners or occupants had all traveled as if on cue. The plan was to pretend to lay off so that they could spring a trap on them when they least expected.

For Chuck Freeborn IV, his presence was urgently needed, in another big case in Amsterdam, Holland, that he did not even think of his vacation again. He thought it was a matter going to be sorted out in a few weeks but it went into months. The DEA Director on his departure back to Washington, had promised an all-expenses paid vacation to reward Freeborn IV, for his selfless service again in Europe. Chuck knew there won't be any vacation until he had finally put the last nail in Bacata's coffin.

CHAPTER 93

It was not until the middle of February that the ex-Miss Cosmos appeared in court for the very first time. She was arraigned before Chief Magistrate Bode Peters, charged with a two-count charge of importation and possession of cocaine. Though, the first day in court was a mere formality, the courthouse in Ikeja, Lagos was full to the brim. Both the defense and prosecuting teams came out in full.

After the usual formal introduction of representations to the court, it got down to business. The charge was read by a thin agile looking court clerk, who looked more than 65 years of age, but since official retirement age was 55, he must have declared a false age. His worsted black suit, that must have seen better days hung on his frail body, like a scarecrow in full regalia. The court clerk surprisingly had a modulated booming voice, and his spoken English was impeccable, with a good diction. The man impressed all present with his knowledge of court procedures as he led the accused through the oat taking.

"...how do you plead?" the court clerk's voice rang out. the court stood still, as they strained to hear the plea of the forlorn figure standing in the dock.

"I am *definitely* not guilty sir." Jane Margaret Hilda Aka declared with her head held high. The words came forth with all the pent up emotions piled up in her.

The crowd sat and waited expectantly. Chief Magistrate Bode Peters sat immobile like the rest of the court. He wished she had pleaded *guilty*; that would have made things much easier for everybody. From his own personal evaluation, there was not enough evidence to defend the accused. He felt pity for this young woman, who he believed was guilty as they come.

The Magistrate motioned the lead counsels to approach him. The lead counsels and one deputy went forward, including the court stenographer with his machine. It took only a moment, and they resumed their seats once again.

"Very well, hearing is fixed for the 23rd of March." His gavel came down.

"As the court pleases!" The court roared.

That would set the ball rolling for a trial the Western press had already tagged *a charade or show trial.* A newspaper in France had forecasted that the world was going to have a case study in the working of a typical *kangaroo court.* Magistrate Bode Peters knew that was the reason this case was not taken before the special tribunals set up to try drug cases. He knew without being told that the world was watching, and his overall performance was going to be put under a microscope. By this case, the entire judicial process of the third world was on trial; he was confident that he was going to hold the fort.

The authorities were leaving no stone unturned in this case to prove to the outside world that, there was justice in its law courts. It was the reason, why the television cameras were allowed permanently in the court. Bode Peters knew this case would go a long way to enhance his own image and resume. He had his eyes on a seat at the international court at the Hague. He was ready to claim his own place in the world history..

The thirty days passed fleetingly. It was 7am on the 23rd day of March, the sprawling city of Lagos was awake already, to a day that was expected to be a normal day. At least, the sun was already rising from the east as usual.

Magistrate Bode Peters, who resided on the mainland of Lagos, was getting dressed for court. His mind was already focused at the hearing that will commence today in the case of the Miss Cosmos; all things being equal, the case would not take more than twenty days, for verdict to be reached. The verdict, the man thought was though a foregone conclusion, that was if there was anything in jurisprudence, as *all things being equal.* He already had a leg in on his trousers, when he flicked on the transistor radio by his bedside for the network news. The radio went into life, as the man raised his other leg to be inserted into the other leg of his trousers.

From the radio came the *distinct sound of martial music*. Martial music at this time. In his confusion, his leg got entangled in the apparel, and he fell over on his bed. To any adult Nigerian, martial music disrupting the usual program on radio meant only one thing. There was a *coup d'etat,* this does not portend well for Nigeria. The free flow of governance was about to be disrupted. The baton of leadership was about to change hands forcefully. *The gun and the uniform playing a decisive role.*

The baffled jurist kicked off his pair of trousers in obvious annoyance. Whether the coup was successful or not, normal life was going to be disrupted. And democracy as seen by the rest of the world, was going to take a blow in Nigeria. The magistrate was splayed out only in his white underwear, when he was shaken awake from his reverie. He rolled over towards the radio. There were loud barking and arguing voices coming from the radio. Then followed an ear-shattering machine gunfire. Then there was a hush that would put a burial ground to shame.

A moment later, a shaky nervous voice came on air, his opening lines were muddled up;*Dear fellow country.. Nigerian men,I am..on behalf..I am Brigadier Alibo Denton Sahudi...there has been a coup this morning. We have overthrown the government of...*there was a loud ear-shattering explosion, and the broadcast was disrupted.

The magistrate thought to himself, that was either a badly done script, or Sahudi needed a drink of water. At that rate, Sahudi will need more than 5 years rehearsal to rule the political entity that was Nigeria.The magistrate forgot he was clad only in his underwear as he ran towards the kitchen, where his wife was making breakfast. There was a coup in progress, what seemed to be putsch, or the about to be toppled government fighting back to gain control and lost grounds. And from experience, this was a most complex situation, that meant Nigerian blood must flow freely, whether it was the army or civilians. Dodan Barracks, the residence and seat of governance was situated in a part of Lagos known as the Island. The Island, true to type was an island only approachable by bridges, from all around, that made escape limited and restricted. What played out that morning took place at the Radio Nigeria station, Obalende, which was only a little away from the huge solid walls of Dodan Barracks.

Lagos Island, was savoring the final minutes of sleep, before they answer to the hustle and bustle of the new day, when they awoke to the unnerving music of shelling and gunfire.They stayed cowered in their beds too scared to make even a move, which was the advisable thing to do at times like that. Nigerians were now used to hearing protracted martial music over the radio, and know that it meant a coup or counter coup. Since the very first military coup in January, 1966, Nigeria had witnessed a series of successful and failed coups. So they were well aware to remain where you were, than run foolishly into the line of fire.

Whether successful or botched coup the economic implications were predictable; all official and commercial activities would grind to a halt, at least for that day. They might as well grab some sleep, and patiently await news through official and unofficial sources.So, while the strong hearted turned around and went back to sleep, the others would rather fret and worry themselves to death or some illness.

It was not until about 4 p.m., later that day, that the *dead* radio station came back to life, with the music of the musical chief commander, who must be obeyed, Chief Commander Ebenezer Obey & His Inter-Reformers Band. There was a steady play of his *oldies*, with no official public statements. As the citizens sat glued to their transistor radios, and waited with bated breath.The extended play of the *Miliki* exponent's music, was even a consolation to many a Nigerian who knew, the coup had not succeeded. All telephone communications across Nigeria were dead; that was always the coupists initial target..

At exactly 4.30 p.m., a voice said to belong to the minister for defence came on air to allay fears that all was well. He had confirmed that there was a military mutiny, which was led by some disgruntled military officers, who had all been arrested. Though he reassured law abiding citizens to go about their normal business, because the insurgence had been put under control. The Head of State of the Federal Republic of Nigeria would address the nation at 7pm, later in the evening.

It was a delight for the various television and camera crews in Lagos to cover the Miss Cosmos case, to have happily taken the coup as a distraction. To the foreign journalist, it was like a carnival of sorts, as they fell over themselves to capture the essence of a military coup that was totally strange in their own climes.

Following the fall out of the coup, was the coverage of its aftermath and bloodletting. The military trials that followed immediately, to the journalists was like manner from heaven, being *at the right place at the break of the news*. The military authorities untraditionally co-operated by keeping its doors wide open, during the court marshal of the 128 coupists.

That was how; once again the Miss Cosmos case suffered another two-month delay. It was not until May ending, after the main coup plotters have been executed by firing squad, and the minor ones been jailed, that the Miss Cosmos case commenced again. The prosecution opened its case, as it called to the witness stand all the officials present on the night of the arrest of the dethroned Miss Cosmos at Murtala Mohammed Airport, back in December.

CHAPTER 94

Monday, 8 July, was a promising sunny summer day, it had almost taken two months of painstaking surveillance to arrive at the decision to go after the mob who had gradually returned, without any suspicion. All was set to finally storm the supposed St. John's Wood address that Thomas Masters was killed. Chuck Freeborn IV had specifically arrived London from Amsterdam to spearhead the operation. The operation was codenamed *Operation Blizzard.*

It was shortly before their rendezvous that they received the news that Pearse Gerrard McAuley and Nessan Quinlivan, two highrisk IRA terror suspects had shoot their way out of the Brixton Prison, London. Freeborn and his Scotland Yard counterpart, Richard Pooler had agreed that there was no going back on their *Zero Hour*; since the massive manhunt to track down the escapees, did not in anyway endanger their own plans. The escaped terrorists were last spotted at Baker Street Station, all tube and rail stations were cordoned off. Though, they were convinced that Operation Blizzard was almost perfect, there was still the slim chance that things might still go wrong.

At exactly 3pm, there was a thunderous explosion heard through the relatively quiet exclusive environment of St. John's Wood, it caused electric lights to blink and go out around the entire Marlborough Place area.Residents waited patiently, hoping for the lights to come back on; they sat waiting by their electronic sets, in their bedrooms, on their computers.

Five minutes later, the light did not come back on. Then an indescribable fear started creeping in.*What was going on?* What was that explosion? Where did it happen? Was it fatal? How long in this modern world can we survive without electricity?When was the light going to come back?Not one resident had an answer except a few people at the New Scotland Yard. The residents were getting frantic. *Somebody please call the electricity company...*

That very moment, the electricity company van sped to the front of a beautiful cottage. Three workmen dressed in blue overalls climbed out. They were each carrying a red metal tool case. On their back was emblazoned in reflective yellow the legend; *NorthWest Electricity.* They walked briskly to the porch and rapt loudly on the front door. The front door was opened immediately by a young man with handsome Spanish features. Before the workmen could say anything, an older man with a frowning face joined the younger man first man.They pointed to the identification tags pinned to their chest, but it was not necessary, it was obvious they that were welcomed. The third workman worked back to the van for the remaining equipment, as the older man led the workmen to the basement with the aid of a flashlight.While the younger man waited behind holding open the door for the third workman who lumbered up with a heavy canvas bag, which he dropped by the doorsteps, and as if on cue, the lights came up, his gun was already in his right hand.

The young man at the door gasped with fright as he found himself staring into the gruesome single eye of a snub-nosed pistol. He could not believe his eyes. Where did they come from? The whole place was swarming with heavily armed police assault squad rushing into their own fortress.He was quickly led away towards the van. More armed people kept appearing from all around the house. The young man knew the party was over.

It was a different story for Vasco de Zapata; when the lights came on, they were in the basement already on a narrow stretch leading to the electric mains. When he discovered that Richard Pooler had a gun jammed on to his spinal cord. He then reacted on impulse. It was an expensive gamble, because it cost him dearly. Without ascertaining the distance or the armed status of the third party, the stocky big man swung into action. Surprise was the name of the game here. He threw a surprise power-packed right, that connected on Richard Pooler's forehead squarely. To say, it threw poor Pooler off balance, would be an understatement. Pooler was knocked out cold. His gun flew out of his hand, propelled backward by his sudden jerking movement. It dropped at the feet of Chuck Freeborn who stepped back at the narrow passage entrance. The man was fast. before Pooler's semi- conscious body could slumped to the cold concrete floor, he sprang over the falling body. He was a human canon ball in motion, zooming towards his target. That was how he miscalculated, for his target was too far away with his own gun out in his hands.Chuck Freeborn saw his British counterpart collect the blow, and the bundle of muscle flying through the fifteen feet separating them. Chuck was still, his aim steady on his assailant.

Either the assailant did not see the gun pointing in his general direction, or he was bent on *committing hara-kiri*. There was grim determination on his contorted face showing inverted surprise, as he pulled the trigger as he stepped aside from the path of the human projectile. It was a point blank impact. The momentum carried the dead man in a few ghostly steps into the solid brick wall in front of him. By the time the stocky fellow crumpled to the floor he was stone dead; for the bullet blew apart his forehead.

The sound of the gunfire was muffled within the confined space of the basement. Chuck scrambled over to Pooler who was just coming back to reality. He sat him up propping his back against the wall. Pooler felt groggy. Apart from the slight swelling the size of an egg on his forehead, he was alright.The muffled sounds of rapid gunfire seeped through from above. They carefully made their way up to the floor above.

Lying on the floor in a pool of blood, was the man who shot Oscar Uromi dead at Gatwick Airport. He too was dead, and the policeman he shot at was also dead. There was dead silence in the room. The dead police officer was only a 22 year-old rookie that was only recruited barely a year ago.The dead silence was broken by an excited call by some officers in the labyrinths of the house.

They ran, through the maze of corridors with their arms at the ready.They ran through a solid oak door into a living room almost bare of furniture. The dim lights did not help matters as the figure tend to blend into the shadows. The figure seemed to be shell- shocked, as Chuck Freeborn stepped forward to examine closely the sphinx-like image of one of the most dreaded human beings that ever walked this earth.

"I thought I had seen the last of your face in Yarumal." Chuck Freeborn reverted to the Spanish that was spoken in Bogota.

There was a flicker of recognition or acknowledgement, without any utterance. This was no doubt the man that Chuck had been to hell and back. It was him; it was the drug lord.

"You may not know nor remember me, but I know you, for all that you have put me through. It was my family that you decimated in the Miami Vice Squad way back in the 1977. I have lived for this day, Ramirez" Chuck could not help but chuckle.

All of a sudden the sphinx-like figure bust into nerve-racking laughter, that set his audience on an edge, as he skillfully pulled out a revolver from the folds of his skin. And five smoking guns spewed instant death from their nuzzles, for a devil's incarnate, that only Chuck Freeborn IV knew his secret. For *Alberto Valdarama* lay dead; nobody but Chuck Freeborn knew the truth, that *Ramirez Castro Bacata finally lay dead for good..*

In Lagos, the proceedings of the Miss Cosmos case was crawling at a snail's pace. Though its progress was frustrating, but the delays through adjournments were within the ambience of the law. The defense attorney was adopting every possible and legal avenue for delays. He only finished his cross examination with the prosecution's final witness the previous day. The defense was expected to have opened its case yesterday, but an adjournment was asked, and granted on the basis of fatigue.

Chief Bode Rhodes was in his office cum conference room. The ebony panelled walls, were covered with endless volumes of books, covering all subjects. He was seated at the head of the table, in conference with his *war cabinet*. The *war cabinet* was a group of fifteen young law graduates who were his assistants; they all have one distinguishing factor, that they were at one point or the other the most outstanding student in the Nigerian Law School. *Madam Kikelomo Abike Rhodes Memorial Prize* at the law school, was instituted to honor his dead mother who never attended school but taught herself how to read and write.

The MKARM Prize as it was popularly called was for the most outstanding graduate. With the monetary prize of $1,000, was also attached an immediate job offer by the legal luminary in his Rhodendron Chambers. The *war cabinet* was led by Bode Rhodes Jr., 30, his first son who was fondly called B-Jay by everyone. Their exercise for the umpteenth time was to attack with their entire mental arsenals his own strategies and legal arguments. It was a mentally exerting exercise considering the superior caliber of intellect possessed by his young assistants.

For instance, his chosen line of argument for the Miss Cosmos Case, was torn to shreds, by these young and mobile sets of brains. It was based on their suggestion he had accepted the brief from Ambassador Aka, *pro bono*…free of charge. His team had after exhaustive salvos and counter salvos in legal gimmicks, posited that the former Miss Cosmos must cool her heels in prison. There was no escape route for her, he also had agreed with them. That was why he had chosen the better of patriotism to defend her free of any charge, to garner some nationalistic goodwill.

All that he could do now was to stall proceedings tactfully for that lucky break that would make the difference. The defense team was still doing their *mock battles,* to find a means no matter how remote, through the maze of overpowering evidence..

As the month of July came to an uneventful close, the Miss Cosmos Pageant had convened a World Press conference to publicize their annual contest that would hold in the second week of November. Miss Sophie Fenton-Forest had matured overnight and comported herself very well as the reigning Miss Cosmos. Don Baldwin had asked the pressmen behind camera to soft pedal on questions regarding the scandal-embroiled and dethroned queen. Though Mr. Baldwin had spoken highly of Miss Jane Margaret Hilda Aka, whom the pageant was doing everything in its power to see justice done.

Oscar Uromi was not missed too, since another corporate sponsor had taken over the *Twinkle & Twinkle* slot. All questions were managed very well, as not to ruffle feathers or embarrass the pageant. From every indication it was a very good outing for the pageant, and the world could not but look forward to another wonderful outing.

CHAPTER 95

It was late September in London, and Hyde Park was a sea of gold, glowing in the evening sun. The black nondescript US Embassy car sped up Park Lane, and turned into Brook Gate, and with the traffic light on green, immediately crossed into Upper Brook Street. Chuck Freeborn IV was seated in the back, on his way to work. It was his last day at work for the year, for he was proceeding on his three months of accumulated leave. Even his director, who was a difficult man to impress, commended Freeborn on his overall success.

Everybody agreed, that it had been a very busy year for the DEA deputy director, in Europe. Chuck Freeborn IV had had a very marvelous score card. He was also credited with the permanent dismantling of Oscar Uromi, a mole and catalyst in the European drug trade for many years. Everyone agreed he deserved a long rest; and as promised by the director, the DEA was picking up the tab for his choice of vacation; an all expenses paid trip.

He had chosen to spend his vacation visiting West Africa to the utter amazement of his staff, friends, and family alike..

Derrick Gordons had arranged Chuks, the American Embassy driver, to be at the Murtala Mohammed International Airport to meet Chuck Freeborn on arrival in Lagos. He was driven straight to the Sheraton Lagos Hotel and Towers, in Ikeja, where a reservation had been made prior to his arrival. The first telephone call he made from his room was to Professor Ngozi Nzekwu, the elderly lady he met on the flight to London on his first visit. The phone was answered on the third ring.

"Good evening, this is the Nzekwu's residence." A female voice answered.

"Good evening maam, please may I speak to Professor Ngozi Nze...qui...I am very sorry, I can't get the name right." Chuck's obvious effort to pronounce the last name ending in an almost disaster. "This is Professor Ngozi Nzekwu speaking. Who is this murdering my name?" The voice said with a hint of humor.

"Good to hear your voice again, Ngozi. This is Chuck Freeborn, that promised you on that BA flight that *I shall return*. Remember me?" There was a note of desperation in his voice.

"*I shall return*? Oh! Of course, I do. What a pleasant surprise? Where are you? When did you arrive?" There was pure excitement in the elderly woman's voice.

Their pleasantries lasted for another few minutes, before Chuck told the pleasant woman, he was in Africa to trace his roots, as he told her then. They had fixed a dinner date at his hotel for seven p.m. the next day. He had thereafter showered, then taken his dinner, and retired for the night. And for the first time in years, he had slept peacefully like a baby.

At exactly five minutes to 7p.m. the next day, Chuck was already in the hotel lobby. He had to wait another fifteen minutes, before his guest dressed appealingly in ankara, strolled in. He had forgotten that this was Lagos, not London where people were fussy about appointment and time.Poor Freeborn, who had worried himself sick was so relieved to see the erudite scholar of African History. She smiled her lovely smile, and in the din of her excited greetings, forgot totally to apologize for coming late.

Chuck Freeborn led her over to the Pili-pili Restaurant for dinner. They had a good meal, by all standards. Sheraton Lagos has a reputation to protect. It was unarguably, the best hotel in Lagos.After the meal, Chuck ordered a bottle of red wine and they moved to the poolside under the full moon.

"So Chuck you are here to trace your roots." the elderly women laughed.

"Something tells me I am at the right place." He said defiantly.

"What makes you think you are at the right place."

"Ngozi, I am very positive, that I am in the right place."

"For all we know your roots, may be any of the countries bordering the Atlantic coastline. You will need something to work on, or else you will be wasting your time and resources."

"I have my name and my great grandfather's stories." Freeborn replied on a serious note.

The older woman could not control the laughter that burst from her. Chuck did not find it funny.

"Chuck Freeborn, that is your name? Right?"

"Yes!" it was an unwavering answer.

"Do you mind telling me, what is African about your name?" the professor spoke with all seriousness.

"Ngozi, I am going to tell you, but it is a long story. Let me order one more bottle of wine, because we will need it, to get through the story of the old man, my great grandfather."

The old woman made herself comfortable, wrapping her shawl over her neck area, she got out a notepad and pen. She began to take notes, as the African American told the story as he had heard it told by his great grandfather who was born in Africa. She would sometime stop him to make clarifications, and make him say something over and over again, until she could grasp the meaning.

It was a little before midnight, when Chuck Freeborn finally finished his narrative. Professor Ngozi Nzekwu dabbed at the tears streaming down her cheeks, she was speechless as this great grandson of an African was on a noble journey to cleanse his great grandfather's name. She quickly ran her eyes through the pages of analytical notes she had made. Crossing out some, highlighting others, underlining some. The moon was full, and in its full glory, as she handed the notes to him as they said their goodnights. As the elderly lady drove carefully into the Lagos night, Chuck could not wait to see what verdicts the professor would arrive at.

He quickly took the lift to his room, and literally tore of his shirt, and settled comfortably on his bed to read the professor's very neat and orderly handwriting. It was professionally done, and was of an academic excellence. The names of places and things were juxtaposed with facts. A comparative study of issues and characteristics were viewed in the logical and reasonable light. He read on, with himself getting up from time to make his own notes.

Chuckma: very possibly Americanized. Stands for name– meaning God knows.The Ibo or Igbo, call God the creator Chukwu or Chuku. To say God knows will be Chukwuma or Chukuma.

Arrow of God Oracle: Convinced of Americanization. Could be the Arochukwu oracle, the long juju of Arochuku, was known far and wide, were litigants traveled from distant places to seek its wisdom. Guilty parties were believed to have been devoured, but hidden away and later sold into slavery. Later destroyed by a British Field expedition in 1903 when the truth was known. Today, it is a tourist attraction.

Matrilineal Society: Practice is very rare in Iboland, Ohafia is one of the very rare cases. The saying still exist there,...*that a man's best friend is his matrikin.*

Warfare & Head-hunting: Ohafia people were known for their head-hunting campaigns... they were mercenaries to their neighbors like the commercial minded Aros.

Greeting: Typical greeting in ohafia is *'udo di kwa'*, and this translated from Igbo; *Is peace there.*

<u>*Geographical location:*</u> Ohafia is surrounded. It is also positioned north of Arochuku, which was not, and is still not a part of Ohafia. *Age of living in separate hutthe practice of living*: Separate hut for young men from their mothers is between 16 and 18 years of age. It was still practiced to date.

Ohafia is not a town. Ohafia is still a collection of inter-related villages. Shedding of an Ohafian blood by another Ohafian is still forbidden.

My verdict: Your great grandfather was from Ohafia. I am convinced. I have for your benefit written out the above logical deductions to make us conclude without any doubt that Ohafia is your roots.

By the time he finished all the notes; his hands were shaking and he began to cry. He had been led by the *finger of God* to his great-grandfather's roots, right on the very first try. It was indeed miraculous. He knew sleep would not come today; because he was really excited. He thought against calling his family in London. It was 3am in Lagos already.

For want of something to do, he just switched on the television, and surfed his way through the sea of channels to CNN. It was the Headline News, which a male and female where anchoring. An image of the former queen receiving her crown, and another of her in handcuffs appeared, Chuck Freeborn sat up immediately, his total attention focused on the screen.

Tomorrow might be judgment day for the ex-Miss Cosmos, Jane Margaret Hilda Aka who was apprehended in late December last year with a haul of substance suspected to be cocaine. Our correspondent Freddy Tijani was at the court premises today in Lagos and spoke to the father Ambassador Daniel Aka, who is Nigeria's High Commissioner to the United Kingdom.

The face of the ambassador appeared on the television screen. The ambassador in an emotion laden voice was making an appeal to all and sundry who might have any information that would be helpful to his daughter or else she was bound for jail. The man then broke down in tears.It was very emotional. Chuck was furious. The fury was from deep within. How thoughtless of him. He was so angry with himself; that he turned off the television set.

He rang Derrick Gordons number first, it rang and rang, but was not answered. It was then he put a call through to his boss in Washington DC. It was only about 9pm in the evening, in Washington DC. He immediately came on the line.

"Yeah, Chuck my old buddy, how is the vacation making out?"Chuck was not ready for his antics.

"Harry, I just called to let you know that *your game is up*. In case you are still wondering, that I am going to appear as a defense witness in the ex-Miss Cosmos trial tomorrow."The man in Washington was speechless; but it took him only a moment to recover.

"Listen Chuck, you are not going to do any such thing. You will embarrass the United States government. Do not be silly. The ex-Miss Cosmos is history." Harry Fenton-Forest declared with some element of bravado.

"Sir, do you think it is proper then for the young lady to go to jail?"

"Freeborn, you listen to me!" there was authority in his voice, "It is not my place to make morale justification for any casualty. There is a war going out there. It was a question of one becoming a cannon fodder."

"At least we could save her from jail. So, I am not going to seat here and see you destroy a human being. I am going to be in that court, and nobody is going to stop me. *Goodbye sir.*" he banged the receiver down.

The man in Washington DC winced, and dropped the receiver thoughtfully. He took some time to do some serious thinking. If he allows Freeborn to appear in that court, it would mean serious collateral damage to his Sophie's reign. Then he said aloud to himself: *"I am fed up with this bloody nigger stuff. I am going to teach him the bitterest lesson, his black nigger ass had ever seen."* The man was raving mad. He put a call through to somebody in Harlingen, Texas, then another to Seattle, Washington..

Chuck Freeborn IV, took his unpacked bag and went down to the lobby to check out. He took an hotel taxi to a smaller hotel in downtown

Lagos. The hotel was about three minutes walk from the courthouse that the Miss Cosmos case was taking place. He now got himself ready for court the next day. He finally fell asleep thinking about Booker T. Washington of blessed memory.

Al Houston, Apache Oil boss in Nigeria, had had a great time at the club, it was time to go home. He left the posh night club driving the Pathfinder at a leisure pace, with a security escort following him. Security escorts was the exclusive preserve of the expatriates with a privileged class. He got to his Ikoyi residence at about 4am in the morning. He was at the front door when the phone started ringing. He quickly picked up the receiver in the sitting room. It was a call from his own boss in Washington DC. It was a special K-Project for an African American that must be stopped from appearing in a particular courtroom in Lagos. The target's motive was to embarrass the United States of America.

"No problems sir, I will see that we stop him accordingly. Consider it done. Good night."

He looked through his desk telephone directory and put a call through to one of his pilots, named Lionel Osmond, who was sleeping over at Warri. He gave the pilot very explicit instructions. Then he put a final call to an offshore oil rig in the Bight of Benin, Fabrice Deleon was to arrive in Lagos for K-Project. Al Houston was a consummate professional, he did not go to bed until he was certain that Deleon and his deadly squad were on the way.

CHAPTER 96

Papa Alfa Os..car abort landing. Ab...Abort landing. Repeat, abort lan...landing." The alarmed stammering voice drummed into the pilot's ears.

"It is an emergency. Repeat, it is an emergency." The pilot said in a calm and calculated voice.

"Visi...visibility is almost z...z...zero. You will endanger lives. I beg yo..you abort lan...landing."

Captain Lionel Osmond, 50, the *American* pilot totally ignored the cackling panicky voice of the air-traffic controller, as he concentrated on the manipulation of the elevators to reduce attack for the plane to descend.

His eyes burning with sweat strayed to the altimeter. Satisfied, the Jetstream 31, with two Garrett TPE 331-12 engines, was obeying orders, he settled down to the impossible task of landing the aircraft safely in the exceptionally severe tropical harmattan haze. Though it was broad daylight, the furthest he could make out outside the cockpit was the nose of the aircraft burrowing through a giant cocoon of fluffy brilliant cotton wool. It was an exceptional severe case of harmattan haze in November, which was quite odd, but not impossible.

"Gentlemen, fasten your seat-belts, and brace yourselves for landing. It might get a bit rough." Captain Osmond addressed his five passengers in a tone underestimating the situation.

As the engines went from their usual drone to a blood chilling whine, the dial of the altimeter went tottering from 1000 feet, ...950, ...800, ...700 ...600 ...450 feet. His excited heart pounding out a staccato rhythm, the pilot wiped his brow for the umpteenth time. Only a desperate and demented person would dare what he was doing, he thought to himself. He peered, and peered into the haze, expecting at this altitude to make out the lights of the runway, but all he could see was the nose of his aircraft tearing through the foggy *fluffy cotton wool*.

The cockpit air was chill, yet he was perspiring profusely. The tension was raw and was arresting, he could even taste the bile in his mouth. His hands were clammy on the control stick. The whining sound of the engines, as he throttled back to reduce speed was unsettling. It sounded like the shrill cry of a witch beckoning initiates to share in a bloody concoction of human cadaver diced with snake's gall. It also sounded like a death knell to him, yet he was bent on touching down. Captain Lionel Osmond was a man that was loyal to order and command, but this time, he had indeed gone beyond the call of duty.

"Papa Alfa Oscar! Please, please abort landing. It is not possible. I beg you in the name of God." A more authoritative voice, but equally desperate came through his earphones from the control tower.

This plea did not budge Captain Lionel Osmond. His mind was made up; he was going to land that plane through thick and thin. He was one of those rare and exceptional homo sapiens who go out of their way to court danger…*thrill-Seekers,* they are called. Osmond, now adamantly maintained a one-way radio silence, his sweaty thick lips curled back in a demonic grin to reveal nicotine- blackened dentition. He knew they would throw the book at him, even if he lands this plane safely in one piece. But who cares, after all his time is up as a soldier of fortune in peacetime Nigeria. It was high time he moved on to places were his kind of service was in great demand; Liberia, Iraq, Bosnia …

The steady red glow of red light rudely intruded his thoughts. It was now or never Osmond decided. The altimeter read 300 feet, yet not a single rooftop, shiny or rusty could be sighted in the vibrant city sprawling below. Captain Lionel Osmond was not a weakling; but he knew when to concede defeat. A cold shiver shot through his body as he realized his foolery. *A dead mercenary was of no use to anybody.*

"Papa Alfa Oscar to Control." Osmond pushed the right button to break his radio silence.

"Loud and clear Papa Alfa Oscar. Go on." There was genuine anxiety in the voice down below.

"Landing aborted. Repeat, landing aborted. Problem sorted out. I am climbing back. Confirm altitude."

"Affirmative! Papa Alfa Oscar," It was a very relieved Traffic Controller, "take 3,000 now and to 8,000 gradually, and set course for general north, on NGX-36 Degrees. Ibadan is reporting better visibility. Confirm."

"Lift to 8k, on north NGX-36." Captain Osmond replied calmly.

"Good, Papa Alfa Oscar. Bon voyage, and break a leg. We will keep you company all the way." The relieved tower control officer signed off on a happy note, glad to have the *crazy* American off his neck. The strange antics of Lionel Osmond were well known at the control tower. No wonder they call him *The Crazy Yankee..*

The small aircraft owned by the American conglomerate– Apache Oils Worldwide, with Osmond in control had indeed hovered over Lagos for over thirty minutes. It had onboard just five rugged looking passengers. The passenger manifest identified all of them as oil rig engineers from the company's off-shore oil rig in the Atlantic coastline. Even Captain Lionel Osmond did not know the true identities of his passengers, yet he recognized that look that distinguished soldiers of fortunes from normal people. He had never bothered himself about the identities of his passengers. It was a working policy that he had successfully adopted over the seventeen years of his employment with Apache Oils.

The young Osmond, was not an American when he arrived Nigeria during the Civil War with the Soviets Fighter Jets as a pilot. He was born in Cuba in 1941 as Julio Leonceto, who through the Soviets underhand deal with Cuba against the US, arrived Moscow to be trained as young pilots. He was flying the MIG Jets, until he was shot down and captured over Biafra under very bizarre circumstances.

Under even stranger events, he had remained as guest of the embattled War General on the Biafran side, hoping against hope for the arrival of the war machines that would have changed the tide of the war. He went everywhere with General Chukwuemeka Odumegwu Ojukwu. He saw, and felt first-hand the carnage of the Nigerian Civil War. Till this day, he could not erase the sights of the orphans of war afflicted with *kwashiorkor*, flown out to Gabon, Equatorial Guinea and the Ivory Coast, by the help of the humanitarian missions. Julio Leoncito, with his very daring escapades, the rebel general fondly gave him the pet name of *Agu Ukwu;* the grand lion.

He was part of those who had hoped against hope, that Biafra would win the war, with legends likes of Okokon Ndem and the Sam Nwaneris to keep the propaganda machine talking through the invincible *Radio Biafra Enugu,* that was actually broadcasting from Obodo Ukwu in the final days of the war. It was not until that fateful dawn in early January, 1970, when the crestfallen leader, in his characteristic eloquence had broken the news to them all, *that it was all over.* The charismatic leader first spoke of his disappointment and the betrayal of the British

Government and other powers who tactfully withdrew their pledges and supports. He declared to his emotionally unmoved audience that the war was over for them all. The ferocious leader with the mien of a lion, was actually bleary-eyed as he admitted that the sun had set for his Biafra, *The Land of The Rising Sun.*

Couple of days later, in the wee hours of a moonless night, the disillusioned Igbo rebel leader, with a select few surreptitiously climbed aboard a small aircraft, and slipped into the night sky; and into self-exile. *Agwu Ukwu*, though disappointed that he did not get a place on that flight, and the other soldiers of fortunes were left to fend for themselves. It was a case of everyman to himself, and God for us all, *Agwu Ukwu* conveniently adopted a new identity with *Lionel Osmond; a Cuban American from the state of Florida.* In a last minute diplomatic maneuver, after the surrender of Major General Phillip Effiong, Osmond, the only assumed American on the Biafran side of the divide was rescued by the Americans.

Al Houston was the man that handled the negotiation with great dexterity. He had told him along the line that he knew he was not an American, but a Cuban. That was how he got himself entrapped in the covert services section of Apache Oils Worldwide. For his rescue, he had indeed signed an unwritten pact with Al Houston, his benefactor to work for him as a pilot. That was about 20 years ago; twenty long years he had been serving his benefactor loyally and faithfully. It was about time, he moved on.

As Captain Osmond deftly operated the hinged flaps in the rear to gain pitch, he once again recalled the 3 a.m., telephone call that set him on this assignment. It was from his boss, Al Houston the Vice President overseeing all operations of Apache Oils on the African continent. Al Houston was a man of few words;

"...Captain Osmond, it is very important you get those engineers to Lagos, through thick and thin and against all odds. *I repeat through thick and thin."*

Captain Osmond stole a quick glance at his wrist watch, it was 8.50 a.m. He was already running behind schedule. His passengers were due at an important meeting twenty minutes ago. With this new detour, which he had desperately tried to avoid, his boss Al Houston was going to have a fit. As he leveled out at the required altitude he put a call through to the Apache Oils communications facility in Lagos, on the short wave radio. It was marked priority, and for Al Houston; it regards the detour, and arrangements by road to be made to convey the engineers to Lagos from Ibadan. Captain Jeff Osmond then clicked on the public address system to address his passengers. He cleared his throat twice to draw their attention.

"Gentlemen, I regret to inform you that, it had not been possible for us to land in Lagos as a result of the evidently atrocious weather. I tried my possible best, but we could not make it. We have been diverted to Ibadan where visibility is better. Plans are underway to get you to Lagos immediately we touch down." He spoke in a calm and relaxed voice.

"Ibadan…" for want of anything to say to comfort his passengers, the pilot changed into an enthusiastic tone, "…the ancient city scattered and sprawling over seven hills is about an hour's fast driving on the dual carriage way to Lagos. The city, regarded to be the heart of Yoruba land and culture, with its hilly topography, is regarded to be the largest city in black Africa. It has a unique scenic contrasts of the ancient and modern merging in a staccato rhythms of colors, could be seen from the seven prominent hilltops that abound, but even better from your seats." Captain Osmond sounded as if he was discovering an innate quality.

"Ibadan's unique scenery was aptly described by J.P. Clark, a Nigerian poet, and literary critic in this few lines;
Ibadan
Like Broken China In The Sun."
Osmond said these lines with so much gusto that he could not help but laugh out loud cheerfully.

"Gentlemen, our flight time to Ibadan will be 25 minutes, please relax and enjoy the trip. Thank you."

"Que habrian de creer que un analisis de sangre verdadera y carne de Leonceto se retiranian de la batalla con el rabo entre las piernas" he had not switched off the overhead speakers, so the Spanish was loud and clear; *Who would believe that a true flesh and blood of Leonceto would retreat from battle with his tail between his legs.*

There was a tinge of sadness in the words, *"El leon se esta ponieda Viejo…"* the final were muttered and was not audible enough; *the lion is getting old.* The overhead speakers went out with an audible click.

Fabrice DeLeon sat up erect when he had those familiar words. This is going to be one interesting adventure he thought. The others sat with disinterested faces looking out of the windows. Who cares about Ibadan? There were more serious things in their minds; matters of life and death. In their kind of business there was no room and time for emotional display, it is where the killer instinct is for real. *You either kill or be killed.* They were trained to kill with the least squeamish; a bunch of lethal human killing machine, equipped and oiled by the most powerful government on earth, the United States of America.

This group of five virile looking black males, was an arm of a global network maintained by their government for hush-hush covert missions to troubled spots in the African continent and the West Indies. They were known in official quarters as The X-Squad. Only a very privileged few in the corridors of power in Washington knew of their existence, and only a proportion of these few knew their modus operandi.

During the Nixon administration, just before the Watergate can of worms, a Senate Committee Hearing condemned and banned the activities of this elite killer squad. It was confirmed that the services of the squad was been abused, and had been used to settle personal scores and vendetta by the privileged bureaucrats. Though in the White House, the X-Squad was non-existent officially, the powers that be had found a way to keep the squad alive for obvious reasons. The X-Squad, ably led by Fabrice Deleon, used the various Apache Oils offshore rigs as bases to operate. They were moved around intermittently to avoid suspicions. And under the disguise of oil rig engineers, they had perpetrated their nefarious activities like a smooth operator. An helicopter is on standby to take them to Warri, the oil refinery city, were they are flown to Lagos with the Apache Oils jet. The X-Squad had indeed lived up to expectation in dealing summarily with all difficult *friends* of the United States.

It was the X-Squad that assassinated the Prime Minister of *Lakarandi* two years ago, in what looked like a typical air crash. The Prime Minister spelt his death when he became too vociferous about America's imperialist tendencies. He was gradually gaining international respect as the *Messiah* of the Third World. His views were well respected. He was on his way to Addis Ababa, Ethiopia, to address the conference of African leaders to boycott the forth coming Olympic games in the U.S.A., when his American-made aircraft was shot out of the sky. At the end of the day, the crash was carefully orchestrated and attributed to engine failure based on human error, by the manufacturer's team of assessors.

It was also the handiwork of the X-Squad, when *Ataba Obombo*, the main opposition voice in the oil-rich Republic of *Thichaka*, was killed, in what looked like a rival tribal killing, that set the little peaceful African nation at civil war. Ataba's death knell sounded, when he solidly opposed moves to give all mining concessions to United States owned oil companies.

It was another tale of woe, in the rich, and upcoming Independent State of Jalango, when the X-Squad adopted strategic killings always pointing to the government to destabilize a once tranquil nation. *What was their crime?* That Jalango, took sides with Cuba to vote against the United States on the floor of the United Nations.

Over the years, the X-Squad had successfully left their indelible call card from Gadaffi's Libya in the north of Africa, to Mobutu's Zaire, and the Apartheid enclave of South Africa. The X-Squad had been the catalyst that started the insurgence in Haiti, and the palaver that engulfed the West African state of *Kimbalu*, that had pulverized the once bubbling French colony.

As the Jetstream streamed toward Ibadan, Fabrice Deleon looked down at the sea of vegetation slipping below him with nostalgia. The virgin land below reminded him of his native Cuba, where he had grown up in the Sierra Maestra region, at the foot of the Turquino, Cuba's highest peak. His father, Batiste Leonceto was a negro peasant farmer, who was the son of Calvin, the older of the only two sons of *Leonceto* (the little lion) that arrived Cuban soil as a slave straight from Africa. Batiste and his only brother Ernesto minded their business working the sugar cane and tobacco fields that provided them a means of livelihood.

For Fabrice, the younger of the Batiste boys, he was restless and outgoing, never satisfied with life. It was not surprising then, when Fabrice had left home for Havana, when Fidel Castro after two foiled attempts, successfully overthrew the 19-year old dictatorship government of Fulgencio Batista. Fabrice, had joined the swelling ranks of other Cubans who had thankfully welcomed the sweeping social and industrial reforms of Premier Castro.

It was not long before Castro's ideologies, became a flash in the pan for the young Cuban firebrands. Fabrice Leonceto, and a lot more of his cadre would not subscribe fully for their Cuba, to adopt the Marxist-Leninist economic and social policies. Fabrice was in the forefront of the unrests that finally culminated to pockets of trouble here-and-there that created insecurity amongst the citizenry.

The mode and manner Fabrice and his cohorts went about the call for a change, did not go down well with the Castro government, and the government turned the heat on them. It became a deadly game of hide and seek, as Castro a veteran in guerrilla warfare pulled the rug from under them. Castro had launched the biggest manhunt in Cuban history for Fabrice Leonceto and his patriotic friends. They were 17 in all; 11 males and 6 females. They became fugitives in their own country, traveling by night, and hiding by day.

It took the better part of three months for them to move from Havana through Camaguey, to Santiago de Cuba from where with a raft, made of banana trunks they crossed into Haiti. By then there were only three of them left. Fabrice actually lost some good friends during that flight. This one experience, tested his survival instincts and human endurance to the full, a preparation of sort for the things to come.

It was from Port-au-Prince, with the help of the Americans they fled to the United States of America. Fabrice and his friends weather-beaten, but determined to unseat Castro arrived Miami, Florida, the haven of Cuban refugees. By then, Castro had gone ahead to nationalized all American companies in Cuba. The United States government was not ready to lick its wounds from the Castro's nationalization policy, it was going to fight back indirectly.

It recruited all willing Cuban exiles into an assault force that it trained and armed. They were going to have Castro's pound of flesh, to level out the scores. The blueprint of the entire invasion to unseat the difficult friend of American was initiated by the Eisenhower administration. Though it finally culminated into the fiasco that was the invasion of the Bay of Pigs in the Kennedy administration.

Fabrice Leonceto, was one of the leaders of that assault team, and he would remember that fateful day, April 17, 1961 at the *Bahia de Cochinos,* as it was called in Spanish, for the rest of his life. His 1,500 United States-sponsored Cuban exiles had slicked silently in assault boats into that inlet about 90 miles south west of Havana that cold dawn, with the sole mission to overthrow Castro. All signs were go, for what they thought was a surprise attack on Castro. But they were *totally wrong, wrong, and wrong!*

Fidel Castro had a *red carpet reception party* ready and waiting for the insurgents, the only things missing were garlands and the fattest Havana cigars, though in their place was plenty of the cold deadly comfort of Russian-made carbines. Only a fool, and the innocent ever argues with a gun. Till this moment, the Americans had not been able to explain to him satisfactorily, how all intelligence reports collated long before the invasion, failed to reveal Castro's offensive. *The bungling nincompoops;* it almost cost him his life. That single mistake, or oversight cost him the battle, 1,173 of his men were taken prisoners. It was only Fabrice, and the dead that escaped the comforts of Fidel Castro's dungeons of hell, that fateful day.

Fabrice survived the day, because he knew, *he who fights and run away, lives to fight another day.* Fabrice Leonceto had a tenacity for survival; it was what he inherited from his great-grandfather, Leonceto. It was that uncanny habit, and his resolve to fight Castro not Cuba, to the end, that kept him alive to this moment. His second flight out of

Cuba was even more desperate and dangerous than the first one. It was the ultimate test in human endurance and survival.

After wading through a swampy terrain, booming with blood thirsty insects, and blood cuddling reptiles, he had swum halfway across the shark-infested Straits of Florida with the aid of plantain tree raft as taught him by his grandfather, who had it passed down from his father Leonceto. Fabrice was timely rescued by the U.S. Coastguards, who took him to the Naval Base at Fort Lauderdale for debriefing, and recuperation.

At Fort Lauderdale, he was handed over to his friends at the Pentagon. His mentors still smarting over from the unrelenting acidic American tongues over the failed invasion, readily offered him a place into the elite X-Squad. He was the sole survivor of the original gang.

Yes, Fabrice Leonceto had all the qualities they were looking for, he was the ultimate human survival machine. And over the years, Fabrice Leonceto who metamophorsized to Fabrice Deleon for obvious security reasons, had not for once acted out of character to disappoint his friends in the C.I.A. He had come to be regarded as one of the most reliable agents, and he had continually adopted his trademark tenacity in carrying out his official duties. And to reward him accordingly, he had risen from the ranks to his current position in a relatively very short time.

And as a top member of the X-Squad he had had cause to travel all over the globe not incognito, but as a citizen of the most powerful political entity on earth. But today, sitting alone in the front row of the Jetstream heading yet to another special assignment, his mind was greatly troubled.

He was worried sick. For the first time ever in his blooming career with the CIA, he had doubts about the motive of his assignment. He actually doubted his orders,... *to exterminate Chuck Freeborn IV*. Not even to demobilize or deactivate; his current orders connoted a note of definite finality without any option to life; *it meant to Kill, Destroy, Dissipate, Demolish the target or subject.* This was indeed one mission Fabrice was worried and squeamish about. For the very first time since he joined forces with the United States, his target was an American citizen.

The other highly disturbing fact was that, Chuck Freeborn IV, was more than a close friend, they were very close in the real sense of it. There had even been remote cases when they had been mistaken as indeed blood brothers. They had first met back in the 60's, when Chuck Freeborn IV, as an officer of the U.S. Coast Guard personally pulled him out of the Strait of Florida, denying both sharks and the bloodthirsty Castro, a cause for relish. Very few men forget people who saved their lives, Fabrice in that vein, had kept touch with his savior over the years,.

Fate had brought them together again in the 80's, in the cocaine jungles of Colombia, South America, when the heat was fully turned on against the plundering Drug Lords, by the Ronald Regan administration. Then Chuck White was a senior field agent with the Drug Enforcement Administration (DEA), and Fabrice had climbed up the rungs of the X-Squad. They were all part of the American team, though in different ways. The X-Squad was there to de-mystify the myth surrounding the drug lords and barons who had taken over Colombia. They had remained in Colombia under different veils, which never fooled any of them.

Back in the States, and over the years Chuck had told, and retold to the fascination of his bosom friend, of the exploits of his direct ancestors, his own great grandfather, and his brother, who arrived America as the last batch of slave cargo from Africa. And how his name Chuck, was an African name passed down over the generations to keep the spirit alive by his great grandfather who only passed away in the 50's. Fabrice remembered vividly, the spark in his friend's eyes as he boasted that one day, he was going to go back to his roots in Africa to redeem his ancestor's image, who was sold into slavery for the wrong reasons.

Chuck had left Colombia not long after the 'death' of Ramirez Bacata, the man with a larger-than-life image, as the Guru of all the drug lords. After the well publicized demise of Bacata, the rest of the other drug lords went down to the stifling vicious claws of the X-Squad. Fabrice was part of those left behind in Colombia to clean up the mess. While Chuck on his heroic pioneering roles got to be decorated by the President of the United States for his input to the fall of the drug lords. Chuck Freeborn IV, became an American hero overnight, and went up the ladder of the DEA, with a lot of promise.

The friends met last the previous year, when he was enroute to his current West Coast of Africa posting. They had watched the crowning of the first black African Miss Cosmos together in his office at the US Embassy in London. Chuck had spoken candidly of the factors militating against his further elevation in the DEA. He blamed the American social order, as well as his color. Fabrice had sympathized, and told him to keep doing what he thought was right, that someday, somebody, somewhere, would accord him his due respect and recognition.

They had parted on that note, but Chuck had called him back to remind him: "Fabrice keep an eye and ear open for my ancestors over there in Africa, I wish I were in your place."

"Don't worry Chuck, I will give you an elephant trumpet wail when I find your *Kinta Kunte.*" They burst into laughter as they shook hands once again, each conscious of the protuberance at the base of their index fingers. The feature that had indeed puzzled them, in the subject of their identical looks. Was it a mere co-incidence? Now, Chuck Freeborn IV, was an enemy of the United States of America? How could that be? *Something was very wrong!* We should see how it pans out, with all these delays and diversions, the odds were already in his friend's favor...

The Jetstream went into a turbulence, as the pilot prompted his passengers to fasten their seat-belts. Fabrice Deleon's deep reminiscence was distracted for a moment. He took time to look back at his boys who were all engaged in looking out of their windows down below at the panoramic scenery.

He went back to his thoughts. Fabrice as a consummate professional had kept his thoughts and premonitions to himself, not a word to his boys. With this diversion, Fabrice was indeed happy, because it will definitely give Chuck a break, and himself. His orders were explicit:...*the subject must be exterminated. Must not step into the premises of the court house.* Period. So what if the subject is in the court house already. His orders were silent on that. It was a loophole he was going to use to his advantage, more so were he doubts the motive of his orders to kill an American citizen, whom he had sworn to defend with his own life.

The Captain's announcement to prepare for landing distracted Fabrice Deleon's thoughts. He looked out of his window, and his breath froze. Ibadan, was one gargantuan artistic canvas spread across hills, and valleys with frenzied splashes of a cacophony of rusty browns. It was endless, it spread as far as the eye could go. Now the next puzzle for Deleon to solve was; *who was Captain Lionel Osmond?* How in the world was he related to the *Little Lion.*

CHAPTER 97

Ibadan Airport, was more like an abandoned airstrip for emergency purposes like the one they had. There was not any kind of action. The security guards looked as if their flight was one that they were recording for sometime. There was a white Land Rover of the United States Information Service (USIS), on ground waiting for them. The driver had given them the message from Al Houston that; *No need to come by road, emergency overtaken by events. Head back to Lagos when visibility improves.*

Captain Osmond had contacted Lagos Control Tower, who confirmed that visibility was still poor but would improve as the day matures. He had informed his passengers that they would spend about an hour on ground, before takeoff. The men just sat down patiently, as men who were used to waiting and bidding their time. As they sat waiting inside the plane, they were abnormally quiet, as some started reading magazines and books. Fabrice Deleon waited for the right moment to approach the captain.

He got his chance, when the pilot stepped down to stretch his legs. He followed him immediately. When they were out of hearing by others, Fabrice took his shot in fluent Spanish.

"I can't believe I am meeting my long lost brother; a descendant of Leonceto." The words stopped the captain as if he walked into a brick wall.

"There cannot be two Leonceto; you cannot be anything less than my brother." Osmond replied in fluent Spanish too, and embracing his supposed blood brother.

"I am Fabrice, second son of Baptiste, who was also the second of Carlos Manuel, the first born of Leonceto. Who are you?" He asked excitedly.

"I was born as Julio, Miguel's second son, who was the only son of Maximo, Carlos Manuel's younger brother." He paused and showed him his hands saying. "Here, see my *sixth finger*." And they both burst into tears and laughter.

"Tell me your story, this is incredible!" Fabrice exclaimed.

After the slave ship left Cuba with his younger brother to an unknown destination, their great grandfather, *Obele-Agu* was acquired by the very rich Sugar Mill owner, Carlos Manuel de Cespedes. The young man and the other slaves that were purchased were taken to *La Demajagua*, Cespedes' estate and sugar mill in Bayamo. Just few days on arrival, their progenitor endeared himself to his new owner, as he battled to save the lives of many slaves that came down with dengue fever. Everyone knew that dengue fever had no cure and it could be fatal. It was the relatively new slave who resorted to his knowledge of herbal medicine, to use the extract of raw papaya leaves on all the patients and had them safe within twenty-four hours.

When Cespedes asked for his name; the older slaves who were Ibos had translated it verbatim in Spanish; *Leonceto*. Coupled with his boldness and bravery, Leonceto became a steady feature by his owner's side, as Cuba interestingly turned into a theatre of wars. In all the wars that led to Cuba's independence from Spanish colonization and revolutions lasting over 100 years; Leonceto and his offspring fought back to back.

It all began in the early morning of October 10, 1868, when Cespedes declared the cry of independence in what came to be the *10th of October Manifesto*, he started with the declaration of freedom for all his slaves in *La Demajagua*, and requested them to take up arms to join him in the struggle against Spanish rule. As the mixed- grill Cuban Force took its first tottering steps, it was Leonceto who assisted Maximo Gomez, a former calavary officer in the Spanish Army that was stationed in the Dominican Republic to train them. Leonceto had introduced the specialty of the Ohafia warriors; the *machete charge*. Coupled with the firearms, the machete charge became their most deadly maneuver.

On the twelfth day of April, 1869, Carlos Manuel de Cespedes, with Leonceto standing by his side was elected as the Cuban Republic In Arms first president. A year later, when Federico Fernandez Cavada, a veteran and a colonel in the American Union Army assumed the position of the Commander-in-Chief of the Cuban Forces, he never toyed with Leonceto who had become a cult-figure hero in Cuba. That was why when Carlos Manuel de Cespedes was killed by the Spanish soldiers in 1874 in the absence of Leonceto, he was inconsolable.

When Calixto Garcia in 1878, supported by the likes of Jose Maceo, Guillermo Moncada, Emilio Nunez issued another manifesto opposed to Spanish rule in Cuba, Leonceto was standing by him. When the Garcia led war began in 1879, Leonceto knew the battle-weary population coupled with non support from the outside world, would lead to their defeat. And true to type, the war lasted only a year, as they suffered a most humiliating defeat.

Within the next fifteen years of relative peace in Cuba, Leonceto settled down to start a family. In 1880, his first son was born, whom he aptly named Carlos Manuel after his idol. Three years later, his second son was born, and whom named Maximo after his good friend and colleague in the early Cuban forces. Leonceto was not surprised that both boys were born with the *trademark sixth finger*. Some times he would wonder what happened to his brother, *Chukwuma*. With the abolition of slavery in Cuba in 1886, there was a kind of improved status for former slaves to move up the social ladder.

Leonceto remained a relevant factor in Cuba, even as the likes of Jose Marti repositioned to the United States and began organizing Cuban exiles into a veritable political machine to be reckoned with, that led to the birth of *El Partido Revolucionario Cubano* (The Cuban Revolutionary Party) in 1892. During the famous Proclamation of Montecristi 1894 by Jose Marti that set out the policies for consequent Cuban's war of independence, Leonceto was standing together with his old friend Maximo Gomez and Antonio Maceo.

Leonceto was fighting by the side of Jose Marti on May 19, 1895 when he was killed at Dos Rios. He had continued fighting with the duo of Gomez and Maceo, until Maceo too was killed on December 7, 1896. When the American battleship *USS Maine* in Havana harbor was rocked by a mysterious massive explosion that decimated 258 crewmen on February 15, 1898, this incident finally led the US to declare war on Spain in April, which favored the rebels with their effective sea blockade of many Cuban ports.

On Deember 10, 1898, Spain capitulated to sign the Treaty of Paris, granted and recognized Cuban Independence. Ironically, Cuba itself was prevented from both the Paris Peace Talks and the treaty signing. Even at the surrender ceremonies in Santiago de Cuba, American

General William R. Shafter refused Calito Garcia and his troops to partake in the event. That led to the US brazen occupation of Cuba. And even with the sacrifice of 82,000 Afro-Cuban lives as compared to 26,000 whites, in the Cuban War of Independence, the Americans refused to treat them well. For some time there were race issues that shook Cuba to its *bone marrow*.

Finally, in 1902, Tomas Estrada Palma became Cuba's very first elected president, who served the first four long years and was re-elected for a second term that was truncated before its end. It was only in 1908 Jose Miguel Gomez became president and ending US intervention. By 1910, Leonceto had become a proud grandfather three times over. Maximo, who was still living with his father in 1907, gave birth to a son who was named Miguel. While the more adventurous Carlos Manuel, whom had moved on to find new frontiers, gave birth to Ernesto in 1908, and Baptiste in 1910. These three grandsons were also born with the incontrovertible *sixth finger*. Leonceto never got tired telling them about his African origin, and how he ended up in Cuba through the ignoble slave trade.

Cuba was reputed to have one of the most volatile political landscapes and climates in the world. Between 1902 to 1959, when Fidel Castro became leader, more than 27 leaders held control at different times some for only a few days or weeks, or months. Two events happened in Cuba in 1933 to give the about 88year-old Leonceto great joy. The first was the birth of his first great grandson, Stephan, through Ernesto, Carlos Manuel's second son. The second was the installation of Carlos Manuel de Cespedes, as president to replace Gerardo Machado who was chased into exile. Carlos Manuel de Cespedes was his slave owner's son, that he brought up.

Unfortunately, President Carlos Manuel de Cespedes reign only lasted for twenty-three days. Leonceto died the day, President Carlos Manuel de Cespedes was overthrown in a coup led by Sergeants, with a colored Fulgencio Batista spearheading.

In 1938, two great grandsons were born, Jose came through Baptiste, while Emilio came through Miguel. Both grandfathers Carlos Manuel and Maximo made sure they past down the stories and things they learnt from their father Leonceto. Then Fabrice was born 1940 to Baptiste, while Julio was born in 1941, all of them possessing the evident *sixth finger* at birth.

Between 1957 and 1958 alone certain events almost wiped out the descendants of Leonceto. The good news was that the very intelligent Julio gained a Soviet Government scholarship to go and study aeronautics engineering in Moscow. The bad news was that Ernesto and his son Stephan were killed by President Fulgencio's secret police. As if that was not enough, both Jose and his cousin Emilio were killed that they were non-communist insurgents. These sad events finally led Fabrice to join the July 26 Movement of Fidel Castro who was gaining everyday on President Batista.

On New Year's Eve of 1958, President Batista packed his bags with over $300million of ill-gotten Cuban wealth and escaped into exile, paving the way for Castro and his main man Che Guevara to take over Cuba, to the chagrin of the *Cuba for Cubans.*

In the years of the War Against the Bandits, which was an organized rebellion against Fidel Castro's communist government, the remainder of the Leonceto offspring within Cuba were totally exterminated. The only survivors of Leonceto alive were Fabrice and Julio, or so they thought.

That morning back in Lagos, Chuck Freeborn had cleverly made it into the heavily guarded courtroom in the midst of some foreign journalists. Covering the short distance of less than a quarter of a kilometer, from his hotel to courthouse took almost the better part of an hour. He had cautiously detoured every possible vantage point of a sniper. He had double-checked every bend and corner on his route. By the time he finally made it to the gates of the courthouse, his shirt was drenched with sweat under his jacket, not necessarily because of the humid heat, but partly due to fear. He had all the while felt that tingling feeling of a silent bullet thudding into his back.

Mother luck was on his side, he was still wondering how to get beyond the gates, when the group of foreign journalists arrived. He did not have to identify himself; his foreign accent was enough to convince the soldiers on guard.

In the courtroom, he had waited patiently for the defense team to show up, but they barely made it to the courtroom just before proceedings began, that left Chuck no time for him to brief them of his mission. Chuck just sat and watched despairingly as all his troubles and effort just went up in a whiff of smoke, as the courtroom rose to acknowledge the entrance of the magistrate. Chuck almost burst into tears, for his heart was broken, *but destiny had something in stock for him.*

The courtroom was jammed, and the air was stale and almost choking. It was evident that even the trial magistrate perched on his elevated dais was not comfortable. He assessed the situation with his owlish eyes and stopped proceedings immediately to decongest the courtroom that was almost bursting from the seams. It was a timely decision to avert possible danger of suffocation.

Except for the press gallery, the entire courtroom was evacuated. Chuck could not believe his luck. It was *now or never,* he decided, he left the confines of the press gallery, and quickly approached Chief Bode Rhodes, whom he saw on television the previous night. He was a man-mountain of a man, that was larger-than-life. In din of on-going activities, Chuck almost had to shout for the embattled lead defense attorney to hear him.

"Sir, I am interested to give evidence to save the queen." He said emphatically.

That was enough to galvanize the mountainous bulk of a man into action as he detailed one of his lawyers to lead Chuck over to the witness room. Chuck waited for a minute that seemed almost like an hour. What was keeping them he thought, almost fit to walk up the blank walls surrounding him. Chuck's thoughts were disrupted by the hurried entrance of a well-groomed young man, fitted in pin stripped black suit and the added appurtenances of a lawyer's wig and gown. He sat before Chuck, and put a gold fountain pen and legal yellow pad. Chuck could discern a whiff of his enchanting cologne. The fingers he place on the desk before him were neatly manicured, he was clean shaven, with a crop of black woolen hair, that looked as if he had just stepped out of his barber's. Chuck knew a silver-spoon fed kid when he met one.

"My name is Bode Rhodes Junior, you can just call me B-Jay, everyone call me that to separate me from my father." He was soothing and calming.

"My name is Chuck Freeborn IV, I am really excited to make your acquaintance."

"I was told that you have something for us." He sounded nervous all of a sudden.

By the time Chuck finished a brief summary of his evidence, the young man almost jumped on him with excitement. He quickly scribbled Chuck's name on the legal pad and rushed out to brief his father with these words; "Please wait here sir, I better let the old man know that indeed a Daniel has come to judgment."

Chuck smiled to himself, and felt safe and relaxed for the first time since he left his room at the Sheraton Lagos the previous night. And a sense of fulfillment to improve mankind held him spellbound.

Decongesting the over crowded courtroom lasted for about ten minutes. The displaced audience was to make do with the public address system of Public Information Department van. The van was strategically positioned in the center of the spacious grounds of the courthouse to cater to milling multitude outside, most clustered under the shady trees.

Inside the courtroom, it felt a lot better, with the audience really settling down with relief written all over their faces. The press gallery had both local and foreign journalist. Recognizable amongst them were *CNN, BBC, NTA, SABC, C-SPAN* etc; there were audible beeps emanating from their busy laptops. There were cameras placed on pedestals with an uninterrupted view of the entire courtroom, and manned by a white crew. Their brilliant klieg lights *digested* every spot of shadow within the courtroom.

B-Jay with eyes flashing with excitement burst into courtroom, as television cameras followed him across the room to his father on the defense stand. He bent down to whisper into his father's ears. The father's startled giant head shot up like a rubber ball. As the entire press gallery sat forward, curious to know what transpired between father and son.

Just then came the three loud knocks, to usher in the magistrate. A television camera panned over to the Magistrate, to do a close profile of him. The entire courtroom rose in obeisance to the eminent jurist clad in his full black regalia of office. The man walked briskly over the short distance to his dais. The courtroom remained standing in dignified silence until he sat down.

There was palpable excitement in the defense camp, that even the old jurist could sense it. He thought over what must have entered their possession to give them the renewed confidence. The client sitting beside the massive frame of the lead defense attorney, was certainly the most beautiful woman in that room, she had a beauty that shone through her very dejected and degrading circumstances. The magistrate noted with a hint of sadness that her beautiful face was an intricate work of a skilled craftsman. *What a shame and waste* he thought to himself.

The silence in the courtroom was intimidating after the audience took their seats. The squeaking sound of a particular ceiling fan was almost maddening. The magistrate scribbled for like two minutes, before he cleared his throat loudly, to call his court to pay attention. The sudden amplified sound startled most of the audience. The accused too was rudely awakened from her reverie. Her heart was hammering out a panicky rhythm; it felt like it was going to implode at any moment. She felt a pervading feeling of doom, that she was bound for prison. They had said, *it would only take a miracle for her to escape a long prison sentence.* God where are you?

The mere thought of Kirikiri Maximum Prison gave Jane Margaret Hilda Aka goose pimples. She clasped her palms together between her laps, and involuntarily applied pressure on the hitching points on the bases of her little fingers. *I am an Akachukwu...finger of God save me. The words in the 59th Chapter of Prophet Isaiah, rang loud and true to her.* She almost felt a calming effect.

Magistrate Bode Peters, with his spectacles perched low on the bridge of his broad nose, pulled the single microphone closer to him, as his eyes roved over to the old archaic wall clock. It was exactly 10.30am. He cleared his throat loudly...

"The court sincerely regret all the accumulated delay so far, and humbly tender its unreserved apologies to all parties concerned. I thank you all for your dignified patience and utmost understanding." The jurist paused to adjust his pince-nez, and to allow his words to sink in.

"If the defense has no more witnesses to call, then the court would listen to the final summations. If time permits, I would give my judgment today. It has been a very long trial, much longer than was expected." He heaved a deep sigh of relief, and looked toward the defense table for its response. *It was now or never; time to see what the old fox had up his sleeves.*

Chief Olabode Rhodes (SAN), the veteran lead attorney, rose like an elephant from the seat he had been ensconced. By Jove! The man was intimidating like Field Marshall Idi Amin of Uganda, without the uniform, the magistrate's thoughts were echoed by many in that courtroom. He had his son's yellow legal pad clasped in his bear-like paws. He looked around the courtroom as if searching for somebody; he was afraid was non-existent. The man was convincing in his theatrics. His booming voice shattered the silence.

"If the court pleases, the defense would crave the indulgence of my opposite learned friend for the people, before I call my last and final witness..." The awe-struck audience immediately murmured its displeasure and impatience, that swallowed his final words.

There was no mistaking the repeated sound of the gavel banging against its base. The veteran defense attorney pretended to be shocked into disbelief by the reaction of the audience whom he knew were trodding on thin ice with the magistrate, and decided to rub it in to stay on the same side with him. And Chief Magistrate Peters swallowed it, hook, line, and sinker.

"I would not sit here, and have you disrupt proceeding with impunity. One more disrespectful outburst from you, and I would not hesitate to empty the courtroom. Behave yourselves." The man was livid with rage, which pleased the lead defense counsel, as the audience quickly withdrew into their shell.

"Thank you, your honor for your deeper understanding and wisdom." No harm in oiling the magistrate's ego, the great lawyer thought to himself.

"Thank you counsel, you may continue, I am all ears." The magistrate urged him on trying very unsuccessfully to hide his impatience.

"Yes your honor. The defense is like a drowning man that would reach to grab even a straw out of sheer desperation to make sure an innocent person does not pay the price for a crime she did not commit. I believe, I share those sentiments with my learned colleague." If only looks could kill Chief Olabode Rhodes would have been dead, but fortunately for him looks do not kill or have any lethal power, so he smiled, bowed, and sat down heavily to give the prosecutor his fair response. For the students of law in that room; this was a virtuoso at his best. He did everything to the letter disarming all and sundry. "This is indeed a discomforting surprise, defense counsel" the magistrate did not hide his displeasure and disappointment, but had to tread carefully, "you are right that even though the symbol of justice is blindfolded, she is definitely not deaf, and must hear you out for justice to prevail, but do not forget that there is a limit to everything. Prosecution counsel?" The magistrate looked inquiringly towards Professor Okiki, expecting the obvious objection from all intents and purposes.

Professor Ereko Okiki (SAN), 54, was the Attorney General leading seven other prosecutors in this battle of wits and legal pyrotechnics against what he too admitted without bias, was an intimidating judicial prowess in Africa. In as much as it was his duty to get a conviction against the accused, he too was a patriotic

Nigerian who was not happy about the fate that had befallen the ever-first black Miss Cosmos. Howbeit, he must sincerely perform his duties of a prosecutor appropriately. He buttoned his expensive suit that sat very well on him like a model, as he got up from his chair to address the court. The former president of the Nigerian Bar Association, came firing from all four cylinders.

"Your honor, my respected learned colleague knows what he is doing. Their action is a flagrant sandbagging bordering on brazen subterfuge. It has become their stock-in-trade to lately hold the court to ransom. Your worship, unfortunately the people will surprise them; we would not object, let them call their *witness from Atlantis or from Mars, or wherever*. The people are tired. The court is tired. Even the defendant is tired. We just want to get this judgment over with, for it is *done and dusted.* Your worship, let the defense know that justice delayed, legally or otherwise is indeed justice denied." Professor Okiki took his seat amidst nodding heads that agreed with him totally.

"Very well counsel. You may call your witness, defense counsel." The magistrate made himself very comfortable for another possible very long day.

"Thank you, your honor, and the Defense also acknowledges the very warm compliments of the People. Yes, though our brows are bloody, but we are still standing. The defense calls Mr. Chuck Freeborn IV." His booming voice carried through the air.

It was like the entire courtroom watched and waited with bated breath. The court stenographer cocked his head to one side as a court official proceeded to the witness room to usher in the mystery Mr. Chuck Freeborn IV.

The oat was taken in English language without much ado, with all eyes and camera lenses focused on the pensive looking witness. The veteran lead attorney gathered himself together to approach the witness, while actually giving all and sundry time to size up the witness and evaluate his credibility. For himself, he was impressed with what he saw. There were no prepared questions, *for a divine miracle was about to play out.*

"Good morning sir," the legal luminary greeted with a reassuring smile to calm down the stranger, "It was kind of you to come." The lawyer placed his hands on the edge of the witness stand, his eyes almost appealing.

"Could you sir, please state your name and address. Then your employment or vocation if any, and your state of origin for the purpose of the court's records." The tone was firm, calm and reassuring.

"My name is Chuck Freeborn IV," the witness took time to spell out the names in his American intonation, "my address is the US Embassy, Grosvenor Square, London. I am the current Deputy Director (Europe and Asia) of the Drug Enforcement Administration (DEA). I was born in Birmingham, Alabama." The man marshaled out authoritatively.

The audience was almost at the edge of their seats straining to pick out his every word. This was getting interesting the magistrate thought. The Press Gallery, the lawyer noted was equally straining to hold themselves back from firing the questions themselves. The prosecution team was totally taken aback by the caliber of witness that was appearing at the last minute.

"Mr. Freeborn IV, do you have any form of acceptable identification to substantiate your claims?" Chief Rhodes asked lightly to negate any negative outcome.

"Yes sir, I have my international passport, my work id., and my driver's license." He dipped his right hand into his coat pocket and handed over the items to the huge man.

Chief Rhodes inspected them painstakingly, and in turn passed them over to the court clerk for onward transfer to the magistrate.

"If the court pleases, may these be examined and copies made to be admitted and marked as exhibits."

The magistrate took the items from the clerk and examined them personally before asking them to be passed to the prosecution team. The witness watched with keen interest the unfolding events.

"Mr. Freeborn are you here on your own volition or under duress." The question was dropped carelessly.

"I came here purely on my own volition, to state the facts of the case." He answered calmly, as if he had nerves of steel.

"Mr. Freeborn, so what? *To state the facts of the case;* so what?" He was interrupted by Professor Okiki's voice

"Objection my Lord" the magistrate looked surprised, "counsel is harassingly being speculative." The lead prosecutor sprang up like a jack-in-the-box.

"Over-ruled" the magistrate said, and nodded at the defense counsel to continue.

"To state the facts of the case; to tell the truth, and not hold back the facts for any gain." The witness sounded convincing.

"Mr. Freeborn, that is sure a strange name for an African American..." Chief Rhodes stopped in his stride, as if an impulsive child was constituting a nuisance.

"Your Honor, totally irrelevant and diversionary line of questioning." The lead prosecutor stepped forward.

"Objection, over-ruled counsel." He growled like a bulldog.

"Thank you, your honor. Tell the court Mr. Freeborn, did you come forward to give evidence today, because you are a black...? Chief Bode Rhodes was unruly interrupted again by his opponent.

"Objection...Objection...Objection my Lord. My learned friend is not only intimidating, but also misleading his witness." The professor could not hide his frustration; and that means he was stepping on the magistrate's toes.

"Over-ruled…Over-ruled…Over-ruled." And the magistrate retorted for crying out loud, "Will the witness answer the question." The magistrate was unperturbed.

The prosecution counsel noting that the atmosphere was explosively charged, decided to choose the better part of valor, to back down, than incur more wrath and brimstones of the magistrate. And the veteran defense attorney grabbed to his advantage, this moment of brief respite from the prosecution to rub in.

"Mr. Freeborn, did you come here to tell the truth because you are black?" Chief Rhodes' voice went an octave higher in feigned anger, as he braced his intimidating bulk in front of the witness, his glaring eyes drilling into his unshaken witness.

You could hear a pin drop, as Chuck Freeborn IV, not just decided to play along with the unfolding drama, but to grab his own glorious moment of history in the making. He took a deep breath and exhaled as the very sensitive microphones amplified the sound of his breath. He took his time until…

"Mr. Freeborn answer the question." It was a plea that was an order from the eminent jurist.

"I stand here today, not just as a black man; I came here to tell the truth, to set free the innocent. May I borrow the words and thoughts of Booker T. Washington; *that there is something in human nature which always makes an individual recognize and reward merit, no matter under what color of skin merit is found.*" Chuck Freeborn picked and dropped each word as if he was counseling some juveniles.

The defense attorney threw a dramatic glance across at his opposing number, who pathetically looked totally deflated, Professor Ereko Okiki and his team had suddenly developed a certain case of frigid pedal extremities. Everyone in that courtroom saw the handwriting on the wall; *that a Messiah has come to the rescue.*

"Could you please tell the court what your duties are as Deputy Director of the DEA, in London." He walked back to his table as if to get something.

The room was dead silent, as if the audience was even scared to breath. All eyes were trained on the mystery witness.

"As the deputy director of the DEA, I co-ordinate the war against international drugs smuggling activities in all of Europe. The case of the consignment of cocaine that was found in the queen's luggage, was planted by a Nigerian drug kingpin named Oscar Uromi, without her knowledge. I was in-charge of that case, sir." He acted as if he did not know that he had just dropped the bombshell, to change the course of history.

An unsettling hush enveloped the entire courtroom and premises. The ticking wall clock could be heard loud and clear. The squeaking ceiling fan was now almost deafening, then came the deafening crash of broken furniture as the accused slumped to the dusty ground *lifeless*. The resultant uproar and confusion that engulfed the sanctimonious proceedings was beyond Magistrate Bode Peters gavel to control, as the court went into a forced recess to rush the accused to a medical facility. *She must not die...Jane Margaret Hilda Aka must not die.*

It was exactly 6.30 am in Washington DC, the lone figure of President Charles Sharpshooter, 60, a known early riser was already seated in the Oval Office at 1600 Pennsylvania Avenue, which was more popularly known as the White House. The White House had served as both office and residence of the presidents of the United States since 1800, when second President John Adams and his wife Abigal moved in after it took all of eight years to build.

The president had as usual arrived the Oval Office ahead of time, because of his busy schedule for the day. He had a bulky file boldly marked *NIGERIA* in front of him; the meeting with the Nigerian Ambassador was scheduled for 10am. The file had remained unopened since his eyes were glued to the television screen, where the CNN live coverage of the case of the Queen of Devil's Dust was showing.

President Sharpshooter sat on the edge of his chair too, as the courtroom went haywire with the dramatic turn of events made possible by an American witness. *What was his name again?*

As the beautiful and elegant Alice Ward, CNN's correspondent in Lagos appeared on the screen, the president sat forward hypnotized. The camera zoomed in for a perfect profile, that showed her to be flushed and excited. It was evident that she too was infected by the euphoria of the moment, as she could not tamper down the obvious excitement in her voice.

Yes, consider it a miracle if you believe in miracles. If you don't believe in miracles, then consider it as the finger of God in action, saving the Biblical Daniel from the den of lions. You might say SAVED BY THE AMERICAN. What we have just witnessed this morning is what the great author Jeffrey Archer would aptly call; A Twist In The Tale.

The last minute mysterious defense witness, who co-incidentally is a top ranking government official and an American citizen, named Chuck Freeborn IV, with his timely appearance had thrown a life line to the embattled and dethroned Miss Cosmos who was certainly bound for a long time in the notorious Kirikiri Maximum Prisons here in Lagos.

The advent of Chuck Freeborn IV, for the defence had not only thrown the spanner at the air-tight case of the prosecution, but had sent the most vocal legal pundits and bookmakers running for cover. This is definitely going to be the watershed in a case that seemed doomed for the defense from the onset.

There is an irony here, we cannot overlook. The United States, you may recall had been bashed from all quarters conceivable for being indicted in the whole case. Yet today, it looks like salvation had come through the testimony of the supposed enemy.

If this trial continues at all, after the break, we are certain of one thing; its doomed course is definitely going to change. We have also received cheery news that the dethroned Miss Cosmos, that physically collapsed a moment ago has regained consciousness fully and certified medically fit.

The million dollar Question now viewers is; would the State, or the People, or the Prosecution throw in the towel? We would find out after the commercials with the trio of our legal pundits in Lagos, London, and Atlanta.

This is Alice Ward reporting from Lagos, Nigeria, for CNN.

President Charles Sharpshooter turned off the volume entirely as Alice Ward's pretty face melted into a bank commercial. He shook his head in disbelief. He noticed that his hands were shaking. He stood up and walked over to the huge fireplace where a warm fire was burning. His mind was busy considering varied options as he stood over the fireplace. He smiled to himself as a thought crossed his mind. He later went over to his desk and punched a button on the grey-colored telephone.

"Yes, Mr. President, a good morning to you sir." A very cheerful masculine voice answered.

"How are you doing William? Please get me the Nigerian president or whatever he calls himself." The American president ordered his personal assistant, who answered in the affirmative. He knew that it was done; these were the trimmings of the office.

A little moment later, he saw a red light on one of the five phones blinking. The Head of State of Nigeria, was on the phone. The two presidents were on the phone for exactly seven minutes, and ended their discussions in a friendly banter and genuine hearty laughter, as could be testified by unseen listeners that had enhanced electronic ears criss-crossing above the Earth in space.

"Your Excellency, I sincerely hope, I did not interrupt any official stately business or your lunch? I hope all is well *with?*" The US president fired-off as a parting shot.

"Mr. President, all is well, though I have adopted the wise counsel of our elders to *choose a very long spoon if I must dine with the devil."* The 5-Star Army General burst into genuine laughter.

"No wonder, they call you the Nigerian Maradona." Mr. President also choked with laughter. "Well, congratulations once again on the outcome of the Miss *World* case in Lagos. *Did you notice the Twist in the Tale?*

"Oh, yes I did. Nice work by you. I was so touched. And the *guy you sent to do the job; so full of wisdom.* Mr. President you are a good man. Not as badly colored by our mutual friend in *Tripoli*." The Nigerian leader spoke frankly.

The President held his breath. He thought fast. *Damn it,* there was no harm in claiming the glory, *after all the buck ends on his table.* "I am really flattered, after all I was only doing my job." Mr. President dramatically intoned humbly.

"On a final note, good luck to you Mr. President, you are the politician, you will need it to sort out your diverse voters' interests. I am a soldier, so I don't need it; *after all nobody but a fool argues with a gun."* And the men all burst into genuine laughter in signing off.

The President was very happy with the way things were playing out. And he was so happy with this DEA man. It was on that happy note he asked for a call to be put through to Harry Fenton-Forest the DEA boss. As he waited, one of the most powerful men in the world, walked over to the huge window with the elaborate scallop- style decorations in the lofty arches. He pulled apart the drapes, to see that the lawn was a sea of green. Then the light was blinking on the telephone again. It was the Harry Fenton-Forest call.

The desperate man who had finally dozed off on his desk as he waited so late, expecting news from Al Houston in Lagos. A bucket of ice-cold water splashed over Fenton-Forest would not have done better in waking him up than the voice that told him that; *the president was on the line.* In his confusion he could not find the pen that had dropped over the desk.

"Harry, too bad I had to wake you up," came the boisterous booming voice of the president with excitement "tell me how you got that *raw dynamite* Freeborn over to Lagos?"

Harry still drowsy from sleep, was confused, and shocked. Something must have gone wrong in Lagos. His first reaction was for self-survival and to absolve himself from blame, and so he fumbled big time

"Em…em Mr. President, that lousy man is on his own, and totally against my orders. Not to worry sir, I have sent out a reception party to silence him. I am certain he must be wherever black people go when they die." Harry Fenton-Forest declared gleefully, and almost had cardiac arrest with the response of the President of the United States of America.

"What! What have you done? You stupid-dumb-no good two-bit die hard KKK clone, and sonofabitch racist bigot. You have a minute to rescind that execution order, and get Freeborn to me alive and in one piece, or I will have your slave-driver pink fried ass tossed from coast to coast." And with this livid rage the president banged the handset down.

CHAPTER 98

The British Airways Boeing 747-400, touched down safely on the runway of Gatwiick North Terminal right on schedule. it was exactly 5.25 a.m. on Friday. As the aircraft taxied to its embarkation point, the familiar voice of the captain came over the public address system once again;

"This is your captain, on behalf of the world's favorite airline saying thank you once again, for flying with us. We appreciate your patronage. We are also honoured as always to fly the Miss Cosmos, Miss Jane Margaret Hilda Aka. We share with you in your victory yesterday in the courts." There was a resounding applause through the cabins.

"Our very dear passengers, do not forget, it's the way we make you feel that makes us the world's favorite airline. Welcome to London and do have a wonderful Merry Christmas." The passengers applauded the cheerful pilot once again.

In the first class cabin, a smiling Queen Jane Margaret Hilda Aka, nodded her appreciation to the passengers. She raised her hands and waved across at Chuck Freeborn IV, seated on 4j, who was enroute to Washington DC to meet with the president. There were various rumors and speculations flying around, that the president wanted to honor and elevate him. She was very happy for him.

Seated on 4a, was the proudest parent and patriarch in the universe, Ambassador Daniel Aka. From the very misfortune that threatened his daughter's freedom, he had *rediscovered a family that was almost at the brink of extinction.* He smiled at the duo of Fabrice Deleon, and Captain Lionel Osmond, who used to be Julio Leonceto, applauding their niece. While Rakiya Danbaba chaperoning her cousin protectively was the only remnant of his cousin Uzoka, whose only male offspring, paid dearly for choosing the path of perdition. The Danbaba's were also applauding the Miss Cosmos, who had replaced the adoptive daughter they lost earlier on. God had effectively used them to preserve and protect *an arm* of his extended family. It would have all sounded unbelievable if not for the ever- present invincible *finger of God*, over all these years.

At the arrival hall, Don Baldwin, President, Miss Cosmos Pageant, and a retinue of his staff arrived the airport since 5 a.m., to receive the reinstated Miss Cosmos. She was billed to crown her successor, the next day, in the grand finale of the 1991 Miss Cosmos contest in London. Don Baldwin, the man with an uncanny knack for planning and organizational ability, took a glance at the newspapers an aide handed him a moment ago. He smiled with satisfaction as he examined the front page of the *Daily Mail* complemented with a full portrait of Jane Margaret Hilda Aka, of her coronation with the bold headline; Miss Cosmos Regains Her Throne, and lower down on the front page too, was a related story;

White House Rewards Merit

Chuck Freeborn IV, the present DEA Deputy Director, who co-ordinates DEA activities in Europe and Asia had received presidential accolades for his brave and uncompromising stance in the trial of the embattled current Miss Cosmos for possession of a huge amount of cocaine, planted in her luggage. Freeborn's meritorious service in the renewed war against drugs was duly recognized in a White House press release yesterday. He is billed to be decorated today, with the US Medal of Merit by President Charles Sharpshooter at a special dinner at the White House.

In the same press release, the former DEA Director was officially relieved of his position for engaging in anti-state activities, that the president felt was not in tandem with his administration's policies. It is widely speculated that Chuck Freeborn IV, all things being equal may become the natural choice to replace Harry Fenton-Forest in the recent developments. Fenton-Forest's disgrace out of the privileged Washington Groups, is believed to be not unconnected in his involvement in various clandestine activities bordering on racist hate groups.

It is worthy of mention that Harry Fenton-Forest, is a great-grandson of Fenton Forest a plantation owner, and a very prominent member of the Ku Klux Klan in Alabama. Fenton Forest was beheaded under very mysterious circumstances in 1908, with a burning cross, (the inglorious call card of the KKK) by his neatly decapitated body.

EPILOGUE

George, Washington DC
December 24, 1991

The past thirty days were totally unbelievable, they all felt as if they were dreaming and would be woken soon. Chuck Freeborn IV had resumed work immediately as DEA Director in Washington DC, at the same time Fabrice Deleon had been recalled to the Pentagon for a more befitting desk job. Captain Lionel Osmond and his Nigerian wife and three sons had also relocated to the US; the DEA had promptly offered him a job to fly reconnaissance flights into trouble spots, that he knew best to do.

It was also confirmed at the gathering that Rakiya Danbaba had ended up as Oscar Uromi's only living proven relative to inherit his vast estate, through a Scotland Yard official source. The United Nations had rewarded the former Miss Cosmos, Jane Margaret Hilda Aka, with a job as its roving ambassador for one year. Ambassador Daniel Aka as the oldest of them all, had assumed the role of a patriarch naturally; he had told them all that *Akachukwu* even on his death bed had maintained to all that cared to listen that his lost sons would come home back to their *Roots*. It was his joy and happiness that it was fulfilled in his lifetime and tenure as patriarch; that most of them felt the old man went mad due to the tragedies that besieged his homestead.

It was Amos Alexander, Chuck's friend and mentor, who had asked him to convene and sponsor a reunion of the *Akachukwu Family Home*

& Abroad, in his spacious new residence in Georgetown. The writer in Amos Alexander was curious about piecing this saga of an African family encompassing over two hundred years together creditably. He had had his doubts and would want to *dot the i's and cross the t's with the conventional DNA tests.* The DNA tests, was adopting reliable technology to prove or disprove what God had used *the sixth finger* faithfully to accomplish in over 200 years of history. Mr. Alex had also invited his younger lawyer brother, Randy Alexander in Washington DC, to be part of the Aka's celebrations

It was a full house; as all the younger offspring were all there. The Danbaba's also came with their *daughter*, Rakiya to open their secret of almost 30 long years. The entire gathering held its breath as Dr. Danbaba went all the way back to 1960 to commence his tale, that had *an impossible twist at the tail.*

It was that moment of the day when twilight set in to make seeing somehow tricky. Danbaba's car had hit the young man at an angle, that threw him on to the bonnet of the car, and kept him splayed and plastered on the windshield without falling off. It was when he braked, and brought the car to a halt, that the body tumbled over to the ground. He thought, he had killed him. Strangely, there were no witnesses on the lonely street that led away from the church, as he lifted the lifeless body and carried it on to the back sit, and sped to the nearby General Hospital on Dipcharima Road. That was how *Uzoka Aka,* came into the young Danbaba's seven-year-old marriage and household.

The young man recovered fully, with Danbaba bearing all the costs, and finally ended up as their unofficial houseboy. He had confided in Danbaba that he was actually homeless, since he arrived in Zaria a few days back, and could not trace the family he came looking for. It was about a year later he told Danbaba the truth that he was actually on the run after making a girl pregnant back in Lagos. *That his brother who was a soldier would kill him; that was if Deacon Uromi, the father of the girl did not kill him first.*

It was later he was encouraged to learn driving, and was fully employed as driver and gardener by the Danbaba's who remained unfortunately childless. They had acted as his sponsors, when Uzoka married another Ibo girl whom he had gotten pregnant along the way. In August, 1965 the girl gave birth to a set of twins, all girls. with a sixth finger on each hand that were stringed off a few days after birth. Mrs Danbaba, from their birth actively took up the traditional role of *African grandmothers.*

Sometime before the first riots in the north, in May 1966, Ngozi was pregnant again, and that meant Mrs Danbaba always had the twins with her. Both Uzoka and Ngozi who could speak Hausa fluently, had survived the ghastly pogrom with the help of the Danbaba's. So many Ibos who had fled to their homelands in the East, were guranteed safety to return back to the north again. Uzoka and Ngozi who had made up their minds to head east fell for that *safety guarantee* by the Head of State, General Aguiyi-Ironsi, who was co-incidentally also an Ibo. There was an uneasy calm in the land as the Ibos tried to pick up the broken pieces of their lives together again.

Then came the July, 1966 coup that was staged by officers of northern extraction, that led to the killing of General Ironsi and mostly Ibo officers.

On its heels in September 1966, was the second round of riots that were more ghastly, that led to the massacre of Uzoka and tens of thousands of Ibos. Uzoka, went into war mode and fought like a lion to protect his wife and unborn child.

Danbaba related how Uzoka with his machete went berserk and slew as many as 15 members of the blood thirsty mob armed with every kind of weapon. He went down fighting like a lion; he had poisoned arrows protruding from every part of his body yet he fought on. When he finally went down, the mob literally tore him apart limb from limb. The mob had then descended on his pregnant wife with an unimaginable venom. With such a bitter vengeance they crudely eviscerated the unborn foetus from the helpless Ngozi, as if it was a coveted prize.

Fortunately, the twins were with Mrs Danbaba on that fateful day. It was immediately after the pogroms that they had relocated to Kaduna, with the twins conveniently becoming *Rakiya and Zainab Danbaba* without any suspicion. The Ibos were daily singled out, and mob justice was meted out to them. The nature of the mob justice that started off as civil disturbances gradually escalated into a pogrom of the Ibos in the northern region of Nigeria. The world watched helplessly as mayhem and death was unleashed on the industrious and enterprising tribe that was present in even the remotest crannies of the northern region. The central government of the country lost control to the mobs, it could no longer guarantee lives and properties of the Ibos of the south.

Finally, the governor of the Eastern Region, himself an Ibo declared the Republic of Biafra. The central government did not find this idea of *Biafra funny*, consequently a war was declared by the federal government to keep Nigeria a united polity. The Nigerian Civil War lasted the better part of three years; as the world shuddered at the images of *kwashiorkor* ridden and dying children on the Biafran enclave, which went against all odds to withstand the fury and might of the rest of the Nigerian state.

The girls grew up with the Danbabas without knowing anything about their biological roots. And not even the closest of their relatives in Kaduna had an inkling of their well-kept secrets. Zainab later died in a motor accident, a vacuum Margaret Hilda readily filled when she appeared into their lives; and certainly *reconnected the lost river of Uzoka back to its source.*

And it was indeed rivers of tears in that room, as there was not a single dry eye. Lionel Osmond had chosen that brief sober moment to complete his own side of the saga too. He cleared his throat loudly three times to catch their attention, as they did and still do in their native Ohafia.

Beginning life in a Moscow in the height of a severe winter, while coming from Havana's tropical sun, was better imagined than experienced. The very first hurdle was the one-year language training course at Novosibirsk, Russia's third largest city with a population of under a million people was four hours by air from Moscow. He had felt then that Novosibirsk was to discourage any idea to run out of Russia. It was 3328 kilometers by road, and 2811 kilometers by air from Moscow, and with a 3-hour time difference. He had never felt that lonely in his life; he never saw his colleagues from Cuba again. It was a policy not to keep students from the same country together, for whatever reason best known to them.

After completing his course in Military Aviation, came the practical field study that took him to Nigeria, and finally to Biafra. Forty Russian technicians had arrived in Kano ahead of them to fit out 15 Soviets MIG bombers. Biafra was only recognized by about five nations, so many did not give it a chance in this very unequal battle to last over a couple of weeks. It made all the military experts liars; *for the war lasted the better part of three years.*

As the war raged on in the Eastern part of Nigeria, the rest of Nigeria was in relative peace. Julio and his Russian pilots were then joined by real mercenaries from Egypt to operate an air power that was very lethal compared to Biafran Air Force laughable improvised aeroplanes that were kept afloat by *Jean Zumbach,* a veteran mercenary who chose to fight on the Biafran side on principles rather than money.

Julio felt pity for Biafra, that there was no way they could withstand the onslaught of Nigeria's six Ilyushin jet bombers, and various MIG fighters. Then when Nigeria blockaded Biafra from land, air, and sea to cut Biafra from all aids and supplies his heart melted, as *Caritas*, an International charity institution continued its supplies through a corridor, until one of their aeroplanes was shot down.

The first day he saw the Kwashiorkor ridden children of Biafra he cried himself secretly to sleep. He had known way back in Cuba that he had originated from an Ibo slave, that he was actually fighting his own people. He had actually planned to defect to Biafra with his MIG-17 fighter, when the Biafrans shot him down over Biafra. He was about to be executed when a Biafran officer he had spared his life, did the most impressionable thing he had ever seen. The Biafran officer jumped in front of the bullets meant for him.

This was how, he was finally given a hero's welcome by the Biafran leader and his people. Even as they waited for the jet fighters that never came as promised by some world powers; Julio had carried out some very daring raids that impressed everyone that he was indeed a *Lion*. Julio who was now given his official Ibo name, *Agu- Ukwu*, by the Biafran leader. He had remained a loyalist to General Ojukwu; and felt so depressed when he did not find a place in that aircraft that flew Ojukwu into exile on the eve of 13 January, 1970, when Biafra officially surrendered.

He had informed them how he became *Lionel Osmond* with the involvement of Al Houston, who negotiated his release and gave him the American identity, at the end of hostilities. He had immediately after the war traced his savior *Colonel Adam Aka to Ohafia.* Where he had been told that Akachukwu's Homestead was bare, *but for one son who was far away in England.*

He had later married an Ohafia woman, from Elu; who later gave birth to his three sons, with the indelible sixth finger. He had aptly named them based on the stories he was told in Ohafia. The first he named Obele-Agu; the second he named Chuma, and the third he named Chuka, who were all present in that room.

Ambassador Daniel Aka, was not crying this time, he was smiling a fulfilled smile. *"Every loose end had been taken care of; everyone of us has been accounted for."* He unrolled a white scroll-like cardboard, and handed it to Amos Alexander and his brother, who took time to examine the document. It was the *Akachukwu Family Tree*. The room went totally quiet, as if a courtroom was in for a make or mar verdict.

Finally Mr. Amos Alexander, took off his glasses, which Chuck Freeborn observed, that he had never seen before, since he knew him as a toddler. He rubbed his weary eyes together and uttered these words thoughtfully to the whole gathering.

"This is incredible. *Akachukwu* finally leading home its brood of chickens to roost. Even the wives of the second and third generations back inTuskegee were from the Cuban Connection. Akachukwu is indeed awesome. Randy, we must help them to tell their story to the world. If I am not there, you must go out of your way to help them to tell their story." He was interrupted by his brother.

"What do you mean by, that you won't be there?"

"Randy, read my lips, you know me well. There is something uncanny about *Akachukwu*; it is God in the affairs of men. Just make sure we help them to tell the story, we must let the world hear this saga down 250 years in five continents. I may not be here then; which is always the case with a forerunner. Where is our daddy that started this relationship with the Aka family? I am tired, I don't feel too well..." He sounded truly tired, as if it sapped all of his energy to bring the past up to date with the presence, then it took all his inner spiritual being to prophesy the immediate future that he would not outlive the forthcoming year.

Just as if on cue, Matthew Alexander dressed in a black light-weight suit and white shirt came bustling into the hall, all excited. He walked briskly over to his eldest brother and whispered something to him. Amos Alexander's face lit up with whatever news he received from his brother, as he smiled proudly at his expectant audience. He cleared his throat loudly to create more suspense.

"Very well, ladies and gentlemen, let us start telling your amazing story to the world through *Oprah* now. Matthew has just informed me that they are here... the entire crew lock, stock, and barrel, to do a Special Edition with our Miss Cosmos." Though the hall was totally silent, Amos Alexandar raised his voice to get to everyone in that hall, "Matt, what did she they *titled* it?

"To Hell & Back For A Crown", Matthew Alexander called out in a very deafening voice, as the relative silence was shattered by the resounding boisterous applause of the lost but found relatives.

Then there was the distinct cacophony of noise, as the front door burst open, and the *unarguably* queen of Talk Shows breezed in surrounded by every paraphernalia of her thriving business; cameras, lights, and microphones etc. It was indeed a grand and intimidating *entry* for Oprah Winfrey, who was so excited to tackle one of the *biggest scoops* in her Talk Show career. The queen of Talk Shows came face-to-face with the beauty queen with the most inglorious reign in history... the two women sized-up themselves like *predator and prey,* before embracing in a bear hug. Meanwhile, their immediate audience silently waited with bated breaths for the no-holds-barred interview to begin, as the two ladies went over to where the makeup people have already setup a makeshift stand complete with mirrors.

Deft professional hands in a jiffy transformed the room into a set, rigging up klieg lights beaming from the ceiling, over an ebony coffee table, with two satin armchairs facing each other. It was a beehive of coordinated activities, as the studio hands put things in place, as the sound engineers perfected the microphones. The director, sitting on a collapsible canvas chair boldly marked 'DIRECTOR", had a final brief chat with the three cameramen, who quickly sauntered over to their positions, as the lights went out in the rest of the room, save the spotlighted coffee table area. A red light flashed by the engineers, as the director whispered into his mouthpiece. The makeshift studio was now dead silent, as a flashing green pinpoint of light replaced the earlier red, as the two ladies took their seats, while makeup people dusted and patted into place, every loose end. Miss Cosmos was resplendent in a flowing black Senegalese boubou with gold embroidery, that accentuated her light complexion. Her richly glowing hair in cornrow braids, highlighted her stricking facial features. A sound engineer carefully put a huge glass vase of freshly cut flowers on the center of the coffee table, and signaled his team to checkout the high definition microphones hidden within the flowers. Then the cameras noiselessly swung into action on cue; and in another brief moment the rest of the *world was present inside that room.*

Oprah was not called the queen of Talk Shows for nothing. Her professionalism was amazing. She oozed her usual *mother-hen ambience,* to ultimately relax her guest, as she went on a diatribe of the events back in London to Lagos. A montage of the earth-shaking events were interspaced, as the interview progressed. Oprah knew when to drop the bombshell, it was now or never.

"Miss Cosmos, you spent almost a year, in the famous Kiri- kiri Prison, waiting and hoping, for a dramatic turn of events," She paused to let the message sink in, then continued, "did you ever think of *him?*" Oprah's gaze was intense, eyeball to eyeball, and the Miss Cosmos held her ground not blinking.

"I was positive that he was going to get me out...*his hand is not shortened...*" She paused to rummage through her handbag.

"*Who?* The same Oscar Uromi, that put you through this agony." Oprah cuts in.

"Hell no, Miss Oprah." She burst into a good natured laughter, as she pulled out a small leather-bound book from the handbag. Oprah was curious, and waited to see what the book contained.

"Miss Oprah, I held on to his promise…", she paused to flip through the pages to where she wanted, and read aloud, "Chapter 59, from verse 1 of the Book of Prophet Isaiah…*Behold, the LORD's hand is not shortened, that it cannot save, neither his ear that it cannot hear. But your iniquities have separated between you and your God, and your sins have hid his face from you, that he will not hear. For your hands are defiled with blood…*" She made to close the Bible, but Oprah urged her on.

"Miss Oprah, at Kiri-kiri Prison, I became closer to God, and held on to his promises. I knew that it was only a matter of time, that he would come to rescue me. And he did, I knew who I am…a progenitor of *Akachukwu, the Finger of God*…" She handed over the Bible to Oprah, who was shedding tears already.

****

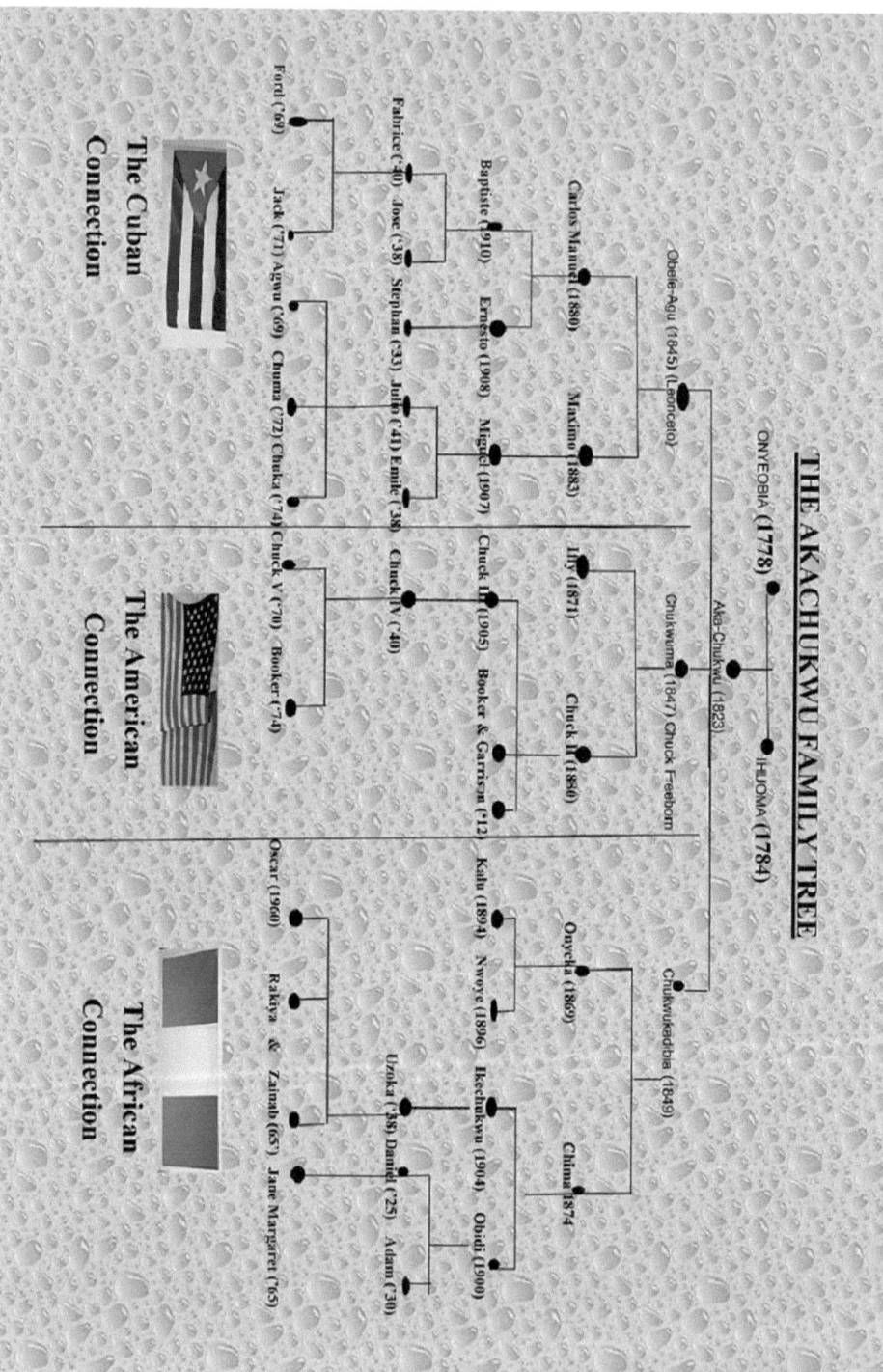

Printed by Libri Plureos GmbH in Hamburg, Germany